I0601968

RECKONING IN AN UNDEAD AGE

A.M. GEEVER

ZBZ-1 PRESS

In memory of George Floyd

I had a 20/20 vision of the last of the wrongs undone. No more hate, no division, no one is free until the war is won.

—ANTI-FLAG

1

DOUG FROWNED as he stepped through the doorway into the yacht's fore cabin. Mario lay on the berth, limp as a rag doll. He coughed, a deep, wet hacking that went on for half a minute, before he spit into the bucket on the floor.

"How are you feeling?"

Mario fell back against the mattress. He looked spent from the coughing fit. His breath wheezed in and out for a few seconds before he answered.

"Worse."

Doug stepped closer and put the back of his free hand against Mario's forehead. It burned hot against his skin. He held up the mug he carried, a wisp of steam curling from it.

"More pepper-honey tea."

"I'll drink it later."

"No," Doug said. "Now. You have to stay on schedule."

Mario pushed to sit up, but seemed to struggle with the effort. Doug set the mug down and slipped his hands under Mario's arms to give him a boost.

"How's Tessa?" Mario croaked.

"Pretty much the same."

Tessa actually seemed a little worse than yesterday, even though her cough was not as bad as Mario's, but Doug didn't want him worrying about that. Had Doug not already been concerned, the fact that Mario just accepted his help to sit up instead of shooing him away would've set alarm bells ringing.

"We're going to find somewhere to put in tonight, find a dry building where we can stop for a few days," Doug said as Mario sipped his tea. "I'll check in on you later."

"Okay," Mario said. "Thank you."

Doug plastered a smile on his face. "Anytime."

He stepped into the parlor, catching sight of the breakfast dishes in the galley's sink that still needed to be washed. He reached the ladder and climbed up into the yacht's cockpit, squinting his eyes despite the overhead canopy that shielded him from the bright sunshine. He twitched his fine, sandy-colored hair out of his eyes.

Everywhere Doug looked, he saw beauty: calm blue ocean, golden sunshine, and a dark, craggy coastline edged with green forest. He zipped up his windbreaker against the chill. The sunshine that seemed to promise warmth might as well be a siren calling sailors toward sharp rocks on which to founder. Oceanside temperatures this far north along the Pacific coast, even now in late August, rarely ventured beyond the seventies. Though less than a mile from the shore, topside temperatures on the yacht hovered another ten degrees cooler due to the ever-present breeze.

Skye looked up at him. "How are they?"

Doug dropped into the seat beside her. "Worse."

"Watch the helm," Skye said, reaching out to steady the mid-sized, wagon-like wheel that Doug had jostled. "So we shoot for Eureka, and we'll see what we see?"

"Yeah," Doug said, frowning. "Mario didn't protest at all

when I helped him sit up to drink his tea. He sounded like he was coughing up a lung. He would've just gone back to sleep if I hadn't told him he had to drink it right away. Tessa's cough isn't as bad as Mario's, but it's getting there."

Skye took Doug's hand in hers. He looked at her, his breath catching in his throat. Those blue eyes got him every time.

"They'll be okay," she said, giving his hand a squeeze. "We'll hole up somewhere dry and keep them on the antibiotics. They'll be right as rain in a few days."

"If it's bacterial pneumonia, and if the antibiotics we have are the right ones," Doug said, worry creeping into his voice. "Or maybe it's viral, and then we've wasted antibiotics we might need later."

"I know," Skye said. "But we are where we are, with what we've got."

Doug shook his head and scowled. She was right, of course, but— But what? Skye was right. He was already doing all he could, even though it felt inadequate.

"What if he dies?" Doug whispered. "I'll have to tell Miranda, and then she really will... God, I hate this."

"Hey," Skye said softly. When Doug looked at her, she said, "Do you remember Avi Lehr?"

"The Rabbi rock climber?" Doug said. "Yeah, of course."

"It will have to be sufficient. He said that all the time."

The corner of Doug's mouth quirked up in a wry smile. Now she was using the Torah to reassure him. "That's not exactly how it translates, but close enough." The smile faded as quickly as it had appeared. "It's so loud when they cough. Sometimes I think we should just stay on the yacht in case it attracts zombies, but this damp can't be good for them."

"We're talking about sheltering in a city that wasn't even thirty thousand people before, in a part of California that didn't have a lot of people to begin with. There's no way every zombie stuck around." Skye narrowed her eyes. "What's going on? You're usually more optimistic than this."

Doug squeezed her hand, sure that it would sound as stupid out loud as it did in his head.

"He's in the same cabin as Connor, when he..." His voice petered out. "I know it's stupid, but it kind of freaks me out."

Skye grimaced. "That would freak me out, too."

Buoyed by Skye's answer, Doug gave himself a mental shake. "So," he said, forcing a cheerfulness that he didn't feel into his voice. "Eureka it is. We'll hole up somewhere dry, get some rest, and they'll both be right as rain in no time."

Skye leaned over and kissed him lightly. Her lips were soft and warm.

"That's the spirit," she said. "This is just a quick detour. We'll be back on track soon."

"WE'LL BE FINE. JUST GO—"

Tessa's attempt at reassurance was interrupted by a coughing fit. Doug frowned, concern for her deepening. Normally, she reminded Doug of a pixie with her slight build, short blond hair, blue eyes, and pointy chin. Now she looked like a waif from a Dickens novel on the verge of dying from consumption. She seemed to have shrunk, and she wasn't tall to begin with, though Doug knew it was only her hunched shoulders. He remembered how she had wriggled into the tiny crawl spaces at the Institute, never once complaining about the cobwebs and rat turds sticking to her clothes while she helped get the electricity. She'd seemed to relish the opportunity to use her skills as an electrician on a grander scale than her regular duties at LO afforded. She'd even been a good sport when she learned how Mario had given her the slip so he could get food to Jeremiah that first time they'd gone to P-Land. It seemed a lifetime ago, and Doug found himself wishing that she'd stayed at LO instead of coming with them. She'd be healthy there, and safe, instead of hacking up a lung and getting sicker by the minute.

Tessa finally quit coughing and spit over the rail. "We'll be okay, Doug. Quit dicking around and find somewhere we can crash."

The anxious, vertical line appeared between Skye's eyebrows as she studied Tessa's pale face. Doug felt his lips turn down, a reflection of what Skye's lips were doing. Tessa was bundled in sweaters and jackets, a knit cap pulled over her head so low that her eyebrows were hidden. Her cheeks were scarlet, which combined with the many layers of outerwear made her look like a kid coming in from playing in the snow. Even her blue eyes looked washed out. She shivered, but the chill that caused her to bundle up had nothing to do with the weather.

"If you need us for any reason, send up a flare," Doug said.

"I will." When she tipped her head toward the dock, her pointy chin popped out from under her scarf. "Now go, so I can sit back down. We'll be fine."

Skye turned to Doug. "Ready?"

Doug nodded, then stepped off the yacht onto the dock. He hated being forced to leave two sick people on their own.

Skye shaded her eyes with her hand as she walked. "It looks pretty clear. With any luck, it'll stay that way." She grinned and added, "And if not, I'll protect you."

"You repelling zombies does come in handy," Doug said.

The marina where they'd moored, on the south side of Woodley Island near the confluence of the Humboldt and Arcata Bays, looked shabby, years of neglect taking their toll. Remarkably, several boats along this dock—one a small sailboat, the others cabin cruisers—were still intact, though in need of serious maintenance. Far more had sunk. The tips of masts poked through the water's surface, all of them at crazy angles along the empty slips, the shadowy outlines of the submerged vessels visible up close. Another dock, parallel to where they were moored, had twisted along its length before spiraling into the water. Their hollow footsteps clunked against the planks, the sound jarring in the silence, but this dock seemed sound enough.

"D'ya think this has been maintained, given that the other dock sunk?" Skye asked.

"Maybe...or the other dock suffered damage this one didn't."

They reached land, where a low building faced them, its fenced, outdoor patio a jumble of knocked-over tables and broken umbrellas. A faded sign, Cafe Marina & Woodley's Bar, hung askew from the eave above the patio.

"Must have been nice back in the day," Doug said, picturing a bustling marina in the world before zombies. The tall rigging of pleasure craft would have been silhouetted by the sunset. Tables of tourists getting pleasantly buzzed on the bar's patio could have enjoyed the view. "Would have been a perfect place to take you on a date."

Skye grinned at him. She refastened her hair, tucking the silvery-blond ponytail into her jacket collar.

"Maybe we can have a drink before we go."

After a cursory inspection of Woodley Island, he and Skye had decided to venture into Eureka proper. The island had the restaurant, a lighthouse, a National Weather Service station, and not much else. It had meant a mile-long trek into the town, but they'd managed to find a place to stay that was directly across from the marina at the end of Eureka's I Street. After scrounging up a rowboat, they could make the trip across the water to the yacht in two minutes.

So far, it was the only good thing he could say for their stay in Eureka.

He hovered with Skye in the bathroom's open door. Its walls and floor were padded with mattresses, from this house and the one next door. It made the sick room cramped, but it was worth it to muffle the worst of Mario's and Tessa's coughing. Mario lay closer to the door, alongside the tub, limp with fever. Tessa was farther into the room, by the sink and toilet. She woke for short periods, but in her fevered state everything she'd said was gibberish. They both had thick, wet coughs, and hacked up gobs of phlegm so chunky that Doug and Skye were taking turns watching them, just to make sure they didn't choke. In addition to the antibiotics, they pumped them as full of found cold and flu medicine as they could, and home remedies, too, but they only seemed to worsen.

They kept a campfire going just outside the kitchen door so they could fill the tub with heated water from the bay. Sheets were draped from the wall over the tub, tucked through towel and shower curtain rods, and around the mattress edges. It looked like a kid's pillow fort run amok, but it helped confine the steam in a smaller space. Without the sheets, it dissipated almost as quickly as they poured the heated water in the tub. Doug wasn't sure if the steamy air helped them breathe more easily, or if he and Skye were just running themselves ragged.

He stepped into the hall, and Skye followed him to where it opened into the living room. Only then did they pull down the found N-95 masks they hoped would prevent them from falling ill.

"I don't know what else to do," Skye said. "They're just getting worse."

She mumbled with fatigue, her voice bleak. Dark circles wreathed her eyes, more prominent because she'd become so pale that Doug worried she was getting sick, too.

"I'm going to check out the hospital," he said.

Skye's mouth compressed to a hard line. "No," she said firmly. "Hospitals are always death traps."

"What we're doing isn't working," he countered. "I can't believe they've gotten so much sicker in just two days. Maybe I can get different antibiotics there."

"No," she said. "It's not—"

She looked past him, out the windows that overlooked the bay, then said, "A sailboat."

Doug turned, and a moment later he saw it: a sleek hull sitting low in the water, with graceful rigging sprouting high above. It looked a lot like their yacht, fifty feet long if it was an inch. Its sharp prow sliced through the water, heading toward the marina.

"They must have seen the yacht," Doug said softly. "We should have moved it somewhere less visible."

Any boat or ship that entered the bay and turned north would be able to pick out the yacht without too much investigation. It was the only seaworthy watercraft at the marina, which meant it probably had good stuff on board.

"I've got to get over there," Doug said, already reaching for his leather jacket. He buckled his holster around his hips. The weight of his Glock felt reassuring, and a distracted part of his brain recognized that this made him utterly American.

"I'll climb onto the roof and cover you from here with the rifle," Skye said. She rested her hands on the lapels of his jacket. Her beautiful blue-gold eyes were filled with worry. "Be careful. I love you."

"I love you, too."

Two minutes later he was tying the rowboat to the dock. The other boat, which was indeed a yacht similar to theirs, was a hundred yards from the marina. Doug scurried aboard, stationing himself aft on the starboard side, and waited.

As it neared, the yacht slowed to a crawl. Doug saw two people—one in the cockpit, another dropping the main sail. Task completed, the figure who'd dropped the sail walked back toward the cockpit. When the yacht was thirty feet away it was almost dead in the water. Doug rested his hand on the butt of his Glock, tension thrumming in every cell. This could be good, bad, or a wash, but the encounter had to play out before he'd know.

"I wish we hadn't stopped here," he muttered, second-guessing his decision. He'd have preferred to run into no one; it lessened their chances of having an altercation. Most people he'd met while traveling were okay, but the ones who weren't were always high on the dirtbag scale.

A man made his way to the prow of the other yacht. All Doug could tell was that he was dark-haired, with a slender build. A woman joined him, her body language tense. She mirrored Doug's stance, her hand resting on the gun on her hip.

"Hello," the man said, waving his arm over his head. "We come in peace."

Despite his anxiety, the corners of Doug's mouth quirked up. The only people he'd ever heard say that were some old Dead Heads he'd met at a concert when he was in college. They'd asked Doug and his friends if they minded them squeezing into the too small spot beside them. Doug and his friends hadn't minded and made some room. The Dead Heads shared their magic mushrooms, which left Doug tripping for two days. He aced a physics pop quiz he didn't remember taking, but decided against hallucinogenics as a strategy for academic success.

"Hello," Doug replied. "How many of you are there?"

The two exchanged a glance, then the man said, "Three. I'm Hussein. I'm traveling with my daughter and mother. And you?"

"Four," Doug said.

"Is it safe enough to stay here for a few days?"

Doug shrugged. He really didn't like where this was heading. "As safe as anywhere."

The woman spoke, his daughter presumably, since she wasn't old enough to be the man's mother. "Do you mind if we stop? *Nene's* seasick. We'd like to give her a break and see if we can find something for her. We still have a ways to go."

The olfactory memory of Miranda puking her guts out almost the entire way to Seattle filled Doug's nose. If they really were traveling with an old woman and not a strike force of assassins, they were all likely miserable to some degree. He wasn't getting bad vibes, and they'd asked if he minded. As a rule, brigands didn't ask. If he sent a seasick old lady packing, he'd feel bad about it, but he needed a better read on these people. With Mario and Tessa so ill, they were stuck here.

"Where are you headed?"

"San Jose," the woman answered. "They have a vaccine for the zombie virus there."

Doug chuffed a surprised laugh. "You better stay, then. You don't want to go to San Jose. You want to go to Portland."

HUSSEIN TURNED OUT NOT TO BE A BRIGAND, BUT A middle-aged man with a swarthy brown complexion, milk chocolate-brown eyes, and dark but graying hair. His mother's name was Fatima. She resembled her son, just twenty-odd years older, and with an accent so rich it was as if she'd never left her native Turkey. She still looked a little green around the gills, and intensely grateful to be on land. They'd moved to the sidewalk by the restaurant to accommodate her, where she sat on a backpack. Fatima kept fussing with the tie on her headscarf, and Doug wondered if it was a nervous tick. Susie, Hussein's daughter, seemed to be in her early thirties, with blue eyes, and was as American as her dad. She was wary, but not unfriendly.

"How do you know all this?" Hussein asked Doug, after he'd heard what Doug had to say.

"I'm from San Jose. We're headed back there from Portland. They won't give you the vaccine in San Jose. The people in charge are very serious about keeping it for themselves. It's how they stay in charge. That's why we went to Portland, to try and make it there. It won't matter what they do in San Jose once word gets out about Portland."

"God, people suck," Susie said. "And the people in Portland... They'll really share it?"

Doug nodded. "I'm one of those people. We've only just started manufacturing it, but if they've got enough, you can get vaccinated. You might have to wait a bit, but it'll happen."

Fatima called to her son. "Hussein, I'm tired."

"Yes, *anne*," he said. Then to Susie, "We should find a place for the night."

"You can stay with us," Doug said. "There's nothing here on this island, except this restaurant, and it's pretty rough inside. We're just across the bay. I've got a rowboat so we don't have to walk around. The thing is, two of my friends are sick. Pneumonia, we think, but we don't know if it's viral or bacterial."

"How long have they been sick?" Hussein asked.

"About four days now."

"Are they getting better or worse?"

"Worse," Doug said. "Scaring me, actually. We've got some antibiotics, but—"

"I'm a doctor, Doug," Hussein said, interrupting him. "Let us get our things, and I'll take a look at them."

"Really?" Doug couldn't hide his surprise, nor the relief in his voice. "That would be great... That would be really great."

Hussein nodded and hurried to their yacht to get his things.

"Thank you," Doug said aloud, his prayer of thanksgiving heartfelt. "Thank you, thank you, thank you, Lord."

"I'M JUST GLAD WE GOT HERE WHEN WE DID," HUSSEIN said to Doug.

Doug stood on the dock with Hussein, Fatima, and Susie. They were taking their leave after a week of Hussein tending to Mario and Tessa, but now were bound for Portland. Skye had said her farewells at the safe house. Mario and Tessa were still weak, forget fighting off zombies.

Hussein said, "I know you're all anxious to get back on the road, but it takes months for the lungs to fully recover. It will be another month before they really feel well. Give it a week at least before you set out again. Whatever that bug was, it was a nasty one. It was just luck that I had something stronger than you were using. Another few days and Mario, certainly, might have died."

Doug shook off the shiver that slithered down his spine. "I don't know if you believe in anything, but I've been thanking God for you coming here."

Hussein pressed his hands together in front of his heart and dipped his head. "Sometimes the mountain comes to Mohammed," he said, his eyes sparkling.

"If you count the blessings of Allah, never will you be able to count them," Fatima said, laying her hand on Doug's arm. "But that medicine to keep me from getting seasick is one of them."

"It's nothing," Doug said. "Especially compared to what you did for us. Avoid assassin squads if you can," he added, and Fatima, in particular, laughed. "I'm sure you're formidable when you need to be, Fatima, but I'm glad you weren't looking for an opportunity to kill us."

She looked at Doug with a fondness he reciprocated. He'd enjoyed Fatima's company, especially her sense of humor. Once it was clear Mario and Tessa were on the mend, he'd been able to enjoy getting to know all of the Sadik family.

Susie gave Doug a hug. "We'll give your message to Miranda. Take care."

"You too."

A few minutes later, they cast off. Doug watched their yacht until it rounded the bend and slipped out of sight. Loneliness stole through him like a chilly breeze, now that they'd gone. He wasn't worried that Mario and Tessa would get worse. Hussein said they'd get better and Doug had no reason to doubt him, especially after how quickly they'd improved under his care. It was just that good people were hard to come by, and more important than ever. Even as he said a silent prayer for their safe journey, to a place where he knew more good people would welcome them, he hated to see them go.

EIGHT DAYS AFTER THE DEPARTURE OF THE SADIK FAMILY, Mario and Tessa had improved to the point that Mario had begun a campaign to leave as soon as possible. Doug empathized with Mario's frustration at the delay; they'd been in Eureka over two weeks already, but neither he nor Tessa were yet fit to travel.

Doug stretched his arms high over his head, groaning a little as he twisted onto his side inside his sleeping bag, and pulled at the zipper. The air in this bedroom of the little beach house was chilly—cool, but not enough to raise goosebumps. He smoothed his hair back as he disentangled his long legs and reached for his boots. Skye's crumpled sleeping bag lay on the floor beside him. Doug hadn't realized how accustomed he'd become to sleeping with Skye beside him until they'd needed to split nurse duty and night watches between them.

He found Skye, Mario, and Tessa sitting at the kitchen table when he entered. The kitchen faced the bay, with lots of windows that gave it a nice view. Skye's feet were propped on the lone empty chair. She looked up from the book she was reading.

"Hey you," she said, smiling.

Mario and Tessa looked up from their game of cards. Both were much improved, though still pale and coughing. Tessa seemed to be rebounding more quickly than Mario, but Mario was far more annoying about wanting to leave.

"Good morning, beautiful," Doug said, pecking Skye on the cheek. To Mario and Tessa, he added, "How are you two feeling?"

"Good," they said in unison. Then Tessa added, "We could leave today, I think."

"Nope," Doug said, shaking his head. He rooted in the small bag of food on the bare kitchen counter, chose an apple, then nudged Skye's feet from the empty chair to sit beside her. "Hussein said a week *at least*. Skye and I are going to see if we can find more meds today. Then we can talk about when to leave." He bit into the apple, breaking its skin with a crisp snap.

"We have plenty of meds," Tessa said.

"We can always use more," Doug said cheerfully. Mario stayed silent. Doug hadn't missed that Mario left it to Tessa to argue for their departure. He squinted at Skye. "What are you reading?"

She looked up from a faded fat paperback that had either been well-loved in the days before zombies, or had not fared well since.

"*Little House on the Prairie*. It's as good as I remember from when I read it as a kid. And a lot more racist."

"They had different standards for what was considered broad-minded when those were written," Doug said.

Skye snorted, then resumed reading.

"Think you can manage while Skye and I take a look around for a few hours?" he said to Mario and Tessa.

Tessa nodded, while Mario mumbled something that almost sounded like an affirmative. They were all anxious to get underway, but there was an urgency to Mario's impatience that was different from the rest of them. The pinched expression, the tightness around his eyes and in his jaw, could not be put down to his illness. He rarely mentioned his brother Dominic, who had tried to kill not just Mario, but Miranda and Doug as well. Dominic's plan had succeeded in killing other people—good people, who'd given them the benefit of the doubt when they had no reason to and who'd helped them achieve their goal of developing a new vaccine for the zombie virus. People who'd become friends after giving them shelter and aid. Mario never mentioned his brother and the destruction he'd rained down on people Mario held dear, including the woman he loved, but Doug caught glimpses of the fury and heartache that his brother's plan had wrought. Combined with the rawness of his and Miranda's breakup, Mario was not in a good place. Doug found himself worried for his friend, and helpless to ease his suffering.

Doug pushed his worry aside and nudged Skye's foot. She nudged his foot back, a grin tugging at the corner of her mouth, her eyes never leaving the page in front of her.

"Leave once I've brushed my teeth?" he said.

"Let me finish this chapter. Mister Edwards is visiting. He always tells the best stories."

"IT NEVER STOPS BEING EERIE."

Doug nodded. He knew exactly what Skye meant, for Eureka was a ghost town.

There were lots of human skeletons, falling down buildings, and disintegrating roads in varied stages of reabsorption by the natural world, but so far, very few zombies. They'd seen foxes, bald eagles, a pack of wolves that had melted back into the trees, and even a fleeting glimpse of a mountain lion. Doug half expected to cross paths with a grizzly bear. Before the zombie apocalypse, grizzlies had been extinct in California for over a hundred years, their existence acknowledged only by their inclusion on California's State Seal. Doug knew that grizzlies had reclaimed their place in California, even though they were not the same subspecies. He'd never seen one himself. This far north, he reckoned his chances were higher. He also hoped that if it happened, it would be at a distance.

"Should we keep going or call it quits?"

"I don't know," Skye said, squinting up at the clear sky, then back to him. "We've been gone a good three hours, and we lucked out at the hospital."

"Yeah," Doug said. "It was weird there were hardly any zombies, and all those meds."

Skye's eyes held a warning. "Don't look a gift horse and all that. You're lucky I agreed to check out the hospital in the first place." She paused, then said, "The animals we've seen haven't seemed spooked by anything but us. Let's go a little farther."

"Maybe we shouldn't press our luck."

She smiled at him, the make-his-heart-flutter-in-his-chest smile. "You love pressing your luck."

Doug shrugged, unable to refute it, but also knowing that this truth didn't fit him quite as well as when they'd met. He had loved to push the envelope, to balance on the edge of what was prudent and what was foolhardy, even dangerous, for as long as he could remember. He still did. But he didn't enjoy it with the same abandon as before, when it had just been him. Skye could handle herself. No one survived this long who couldn't. They were good together beyond the protective walls that sheltered what was left of the human race. Not like he and Miranda, who were almost one organism after the years they'd spent partnering on missions and patrols, but that would come in time. He could tell already. They anticipated one another's moves, noticed what the other overlooked, instinctively understood when the risk was worth it and when it wasn't.

But the idea of returning to the world before Skye, to a life that had felt so full until—abruptly—it hadn't, that had become gray and flat until she breathed life into it with her laugh and resilience and the way she moved, tempered the thrill. He didn't know how to tell her this, didn't have the language to parse this feeling of temperance, to distinguish it from hovering or lack of confidence in her capabilities. Maybe one day he would, but not today. Today he had to live with the emotional dissonance and trust in them both. He had to take that leap of faith.

"You know me too well," he said. "Let's give it another hour and head back."

They continued south, continually scanning the wide, flat street, buildings, and parking lots. After a few minutes, Skye stopped in front of what had once been a charming, green cottage turned dentist's office but now was a ruin.

"Maybe we should go back," she said. "It's just going to be more of the same, and you're right. We've already found a lo—"

Doug's mind raced as he tried to identify the threat that had caused her to stop speaking mid-word. His heart jumped into this throat for a moment when he didn't see her, before he realized she'd crouched down. It looked like she was pretending to tie her bootlace.

"What is it?" he said, keeping his voice low.

Never raising her eyes, she said, "Don't look or I think he'll bolt."

"What? Who will bolt?"

"The kid on that balcony."

Doug felt his eyes go wide but stayed still. "Where?"

"The building on the corner behind you, same side as this one." She pointed to the green cottage, the movement of her arm casual, then looked up at him. "Gray, with blue gutters. Looks like apartments on the second floor."

Irrationally, Doug felt eyes on the back of his neck when the moment before he hadn't. "What the hell is a kid doing out here?"

Skye shifted onto her other knee and raised her foot that had been tucked behind her. She began to fiddle with its shoelace, too. "Doesn't look well cared for."

"Feral?"

"Only one way to find out."

Doug held his hand out to her. "Kiss me. We'll hold hands and keep walking so he won't figure out that we've seen him."

Skye took his hand, a grin splitting her face as he helped her up and pulled her to him. He could feel her distraction while they kissed in the tilt of her head, the angle not quite right since she was trying to peek over his shoulder. When they parted, she kept hold of his hand.

He kept his gaze straight as they continued down the road, but held his head a little higher. The building Skye had described was so near that they reached it in seconds. Darkness framed by the jagged edges of broken plate glass windows lined the building's lower story. Rusting cars were parked, bumpers touching, parallel to the building's edifice to reinforce the entrance. In the periphery of his vision Doug saw the balcony, which ran the length of the long building. Tucked in the corner at the near end, the top of the boy's head peeked over the solid wall of the balcony. His tight, curly hair looked matted and ratty, and his face was covered in dirt. Even though he only caught a glimpse, Doug thought the kid looked too thin.

"What about that blue building down there?" Skye said, her voice raised. She pointed to a building farther down the road. "That pharmacy."

"Okay," Doug said.

It really was a pharmacy, but half burned down. Between the pharmacy and the building where the boy was hiding sat a large parking lot.

Dropping his voice again, he said to Skye, "The balcony stairs are on the end, by the parking lot. Dash over when we reach them?"

"Yeah."

A few moments later, a door slammed. They looked at one another, then dashed for the stairs. Skye pulled ahead, both of them knowing by unspoken agreement that a woman might be perceived as less threatening. Doug took the steps three at a time. He turned onto the balcony a few seconds behind Skye. She was already halfway to the other end.

"Wait for me, Skye!"

"We don't have time. We spooked him."

A muffled whimper stopped Doug in his tracks. Skye whirled around to face him.

"Did you hear that?" she asked, only mouthing the words.

Another whimper, louder and more distressed than the last. They crept along the balcony toward the end, where they'd seen the boy. At the second to last apartment, a loud groan was followed by a body slamming against the closed door; definitely a zombie there. They reached the last apartment, the zombie next door moaning and snarling as it thrashed and pounded. Underneath the noise made by the zombie, Doug could hear whimpers.

Skye looked over to him, her eyes excited. He nodded and she turned the knob.

The door didn't open. From its other side came an anguished cry.

"Bun Bun!"

Doug kicked the door open. Two voices, one crying, were coming from one of the bedrooms. They raced to the back of the apartment. Doug reached a bedroom door just as two small, dark hands let go of the windowsill.

"Wait!" Skye cried.

A lower roof extended from the back of the building about eight feet below the window. Two small figures ran across it, the larger of the two pulling a smaller, howling figure along.

"I've got this," Skye said, already halfway out the window. "Go around!"

Before Doug could answer, Skye disappeared. Racing from the apartment, he sprinted down the balcony. He leaped down the staircase in three soaring strides that left him stumbling on the uneven concrete walk, but the tactical soles of his boots found purchase. He sprinted alongside the building's short end, skidding around the corner. A burst of adrenalized energy propelled him forward to Skye's calming voice that was competing with high-pitched screams.

"It's okay, it's all right," Skye said.

Another voice, with a child's high pitch, shouted, "Let her go!"

Doug saw the boy ahead, down on the ground. He was looking up at Skye, who was still on the roof. She was trying to hold on to a struggling tangle of arms and legs—and lungs. They had to achieve two outcomes at odds with one another as quickly as possible: get the kids to trust them and shut the howler up.

The boy tensed, his brown eyes filling with fear when he finally saw Doug approaching. Dirt was smudged over a nose broad across the nostrils that hugged close against his face. His dark-brown skin was dirty, hair matted and tangled, his frame on the scrawny side. He backed up a few steps, as if to run, then stopped, unwilling to leave the screaming, squirming girl Skye was wrangling on the roof.

"I want Bun Bun!" the girl shrieked.

Doug slowed and held his hands out, palms up, about twenty feet from the boy.

"Hey," he said, trying to keep his voice low, but needing to be heard over the other child's shrieks. "It's okay. We won't hurt you."

"Let her go," the boy demanded, fear and fury swirling over his pinched face. "Let her go!"

"Where are your parents?" Doug asked.

At Doug's question, the boy's lower lip began to quiver. So, no parents.

"Let her go," he cried again, but now he sounded on the verge of tears.

Skye seemed to have a secure grip on the now sobbing girl, whose occasional hiccups sounded like *b-b-bun-bun*.

"What's bun bun?" Doug asked the boy.

Tears suddenly filled the boy's eyes. "Violet's rabbit. You were coming and we had to leave him."

"A rabbit?" he said, taken aback, feeling pretty sure that the apocalypse had finally thrown every weird thing it could at him. Aloud, he said, "Is Bun Bun back in the room?"

"Mister Bun Bun," the boy said, his voice quivering.

He looked small and frail, and so vulnerable that Doug's heart ached. The boy's chest began to hitch hard as tears trailed down his dirty face. Doug walked closer, waiting for him to spook and run. When he was five feet away, Doug dropped down to his knees.

"How about we go get him? Will you let us help you get Mister Bun Bun?"

The boy began to cry in earnest. Doug could see his relief that maybe this adult was someone who could be in charge. Someone who could take responsibility for him and the still distraught girl from his too small shoulders.

He nodded, wiping at his face, smearing the tears and dirt together into a muddy smudge.

"Skye," Doug called, partially turning his head so that his voice would carry, but not wanting to take his eyes off the boy. "We're going to get Mister Bun Bun. Okay?"

"We're going to get Mister Bun Bun?" Skye echoed, clearly bewildered. Immediately, the little girl's crying began to subside. "Okay," she continued, her voice becoming a soothing singsong. "We're going to get Mister Bun Bun."

Doug returned his full attention to the little boy.

"What's your name?"

The boy looked at him, wary, but the doubt and fear lurking in his eyes was quickly giving way to exhaustion. He looked like a scared kitten, the kind that startles and runs from a leaf blowing on a breeze. Doug would not have been surprised if the kid said his name was Kitty.

"Silas."

Doug smiled and held out his hand. Slowly, Silas extended his own. Doug took hold of his grimy fingers.

"It's nice to meet you, Silas. I'm Doug."

2

"I DON'T KNOW why I thought things couldn't get worse," Rocco said.

The stems of withered and discolored leaves he'd been holding fluttered to the ground. Crouched beside another plant, Miranda chewed on her lower lip. Curled, discolored leaves covered the potato plant. Some had turned yellow; others were still green but had dark splotches. Every plant in the field was in a similar state, except for the ones that were completely dead. She was so familiar with the mildewy smell wafting from the plants that at this point, it almost didn't register. She dusted her hands and stood up.

"I thought maybe we'd caught it in time."

"You didn't think, you hoped," Rocco said. "By the time you discover it, it's too late."

Miranda sighed, then said softly, "This is bad."

Rocco snorted. "Understatement of the century."

They walked between the mounded rows in silence to the field's edge. It was a hell of a way to begin September, knowing that nursing and babying of their crops all summer hadn't been enough. Rocco scrubbed his face with his hands, which only exaggerated the worry lines around his pursed lips and the bags under his dark-brown eyes. Even his eyebrows, one of the more prominent features of his blunt face, looked diminished. He leaned against the side of the pickup truck's bed. Miranda joined him, even though the metal was hot from sitting in the sun.

"We're gonna have to start sending people out to look for food," Rocco said.

"How far will they have to go?"

"Everything inside the sound defense perimeter is cleaned out, and everything beyond it for ten miles, probably."

She felt her mouth fall open. "That far?"

He nodded.

"Fucking Dominic," she muttered, but without the venom that had been present at the beginning of the summer. It was an automatic response, like how you wished someone a good day, or said someone's kid was cute. Even the venomous hatred for San Jose's City Council President had been beaten into submission by one disaster after another. "Can we please kill Victor now?"

Rocco chuffed out a laugh. "You're relentless, you know that? We're not executing the guy, Tucci."

He held his hand up to silence her when she opened her mouth. She thought he was going to say more, but he didn't, so she said, "He's the reason we're in this situation in the first place."

"I know, but killing him isn't gonna fix this."

"It'd make me feel better. He's sitting on his ass in the stockade, eating our food during a food shortage that he caused when he led the attack that almost got us overrun by zombies. And killed your predecessor."

Rocco shook his head, then said, "So what do we have?"

"What?"

Rocco scratched his forehead. "For staples, we have the two potato fields that border P-Land's fields, and the corn."

Victor conversation over, she thought. Aloud, she said, "And the barley, too." At his baleful side-eye, she held up her hands to concede the point. "I know we lost most of it, but we have some."

"A month's worth, at best," Rocco grumbled. "The two big southern vegetable fields, so cabbages, green beans, broccoli..." He gave her a questioning look.

"Eggplant, tomatoes, carrots, garlic, onions...squash?"

Rocco shook his head. "Squash was planted in the east field —trampled."

They were both quiet for a few moments, then Miranda said, "So between zombies trampling the fields when LO was surrounded, the wire worms infestation in the barley, and now this blight, we've lost what? Fifty percent?"

"Try seventy-five." When Miranda winced, he said, "That doesn't even include P-Land's losses. Last time she was here, I think Zoe said thirty percent."

"They can absorb that."

Rocco nodded, but by the distant look in his eyes, Miranda knew his attention was focused inward. "Can't help us out much, though," he said absently, then seemed to rouse himself. "If P-Land wasn't giving us feed for the livestock, we'd have to slaughter it. We'll have milk and dairy, and eggs until the weather turns cold."

"You know some genius is going to want to eat them, right? If things get tight enough, we'll need to post guards."

"Tucci, I know things are shitty where you come from, but that won't be a problem here."

Miranda laughed. His naivety was refreshing. She'd never

realized Rocco could be naive. "When people get hungry, they get stupid. And things can always get worse."

"You're just a little ray of sunshine today," Rocco said, elbowing her, but he smiled.

"How much food is in the emergency stores?"

"Two months' worth. Jesus, Mary, and Joseph...I don't know what we were thinking," he said softly. Then he said, his voice firm, "Actually, that's not true. We never had a loss like this. Even the first two or three years, and believe me, the most experienced people were backyard gardeners. We had no idea what the hell we were doing. But there weren't that many of us, and we hadn't told people to come find us."

The last part, telling people to come to Law & Order, the nickname for their community that most people just called LO, was the icing on the worry cake they'd been eating for the last two months. When they'd sent teams of people out to gather the raw materials to manufacture the vaccine, and before they realized the scope of the crop failures, they'd told anyone they met that there was a vaccine in Portland. They told them to come, and to spread the word. It wasn't like the old days; word didn't spread fast, but it was spreading. Over the summer they'd had at least a person or two arrive every week. In the last two weeks the number of people arriving to get the vaccine had noticeably picked up. If the trend held, they were going to have two hundred people or more by Christmas, and seventy-five percent less food to feed them.

They weren't publicly rationing food yet, though they were behind the scenes with how much food was prepared for communal meals, and the size of the portions. Miranda had no difficulty conjuring the terrible scenario most likely to play out: the community breaking into factions of those who wanted to keep LO what it had always been—welcoming—and another that would want to keep their meager resources for themselves.

But seeing as how that hadn't happened yet, nor the commencement of scavenging parties to look for food, she decided not to dwell on it. As Father Walter would say, why borrow trouble?

"This sucks; don't get me wrong," she said. "But at least people at LO are committed to the community thriving, to each other. A lot of places aren't like that. You just have to lay it out there and kick ass when needed." A thought suddenly occurred to her. "People have their own little vegetable gardens, too."

Rocco groaned. "Like that'll be enough."

"Well, no shit," she said. "But let them keep some of it, take the rest for the community. Some people will be assholes, but most people will be okay with it. Especially when you frame it as a way to keep everyone fed, and ask them one-on-one. Make them feel special."

"So we're taking it no matter what, but we're asking all nice?"

"Yep." She pushed off the truck. "We should get back. The meeting tonight is gonna suck. I might need to pre-game it."

Rocco barked out a laugh, which made her happy. He was carrying the weight of the world, or their small slice of it, on his shoulders. If she could lighten it, even by something as small as a joke, she would.

Rocco caught her arm in his paw of a hand. "Hold on a sec. I need to talk to you about something."

"Okay," she said.

"I need you to come to Portlandia with me tomorrow."

She couldn't suppress a groan. "You want me to come to P-Land? Whatever I did, I'm sorry. I'll talk at the meeting tonight and you can let people be pissed at me instead of you."

"Sorry," he said, shrugging. "I know they drive you crazy there, and you're already on the hook for the regular meeting next month, but River can't come. What's her name...Veronica?"

"The one on bed rest?"

"Yeah," Rocco said. "The one having twins. She went into labor right before we left. River expects it to take at least twelve hours, but it's high risk. She has to be here."

Twins, she thought, disliking the pang of envy it caused, but not able to completely tamp it down. Veronica's group had arrived two months ago. She'd known she was pregnant, obviously; she'd already been as big as a house. She and her boyfriend hadn't known it was twins until River did an ultrasound. Before getting pregnant herself, before the excitement and hope, people having babies had filled Miranda with incredulity and poorly masked scorn. Why would anyone bring a kid into this? she'd always wondered. She got it now, even though things hadn't worked out as she'd hoped. That Veronica got good news from her ultrasound wasn't something Miranda would ever begrudge her.

"Okay," she said, resigning herself. "Why are you making a special trip to P-Land anyway? What else is there to discuss apart from new arrivals and no food?"

"I don't know," Rocco said. "They were real squirrelly about it. And you never know with them...could be practical, could be about someone's aura." He blew out a heavy breath, his cheeks puffing up. "The food situation is bad, Tucci. I'm worried. I'd be lying if I said I wasn't. It's gonna put us to the test."

"If there's any place that can get through this, it's LO."

She wasn't just blowing smoke up his ass; she meant it. She'd always been impressed with how cohesive the community was, but transitions were tricky. Rocco was still new in the role... This was a test of his leadership. A tough one, at that, and right out of the gate. "I know you're worried." She gave his shoulder a squeeze. "We'll figure it out."

"We're back to scavenging for food... Christ, that's depressing."

"At least there's the vaccine."

Rocco's laugh was bitter. "That we can't make a priority." Miranda opened her mouth to object. "We'll still do what we can. Don't get your panties all in a bunch. It just won't be what we thought."

"Kind of par for the course right now," she said.

Rocco said, "When I have time to think about the vaccine, all I see are problems there, too. People are gonna be uptight about the food and needing to go out and look for more. We'll have new people thinking they can get the vaccine and being told they have to wait. Oh, and by the way, new people, we have no food," he added sarcastically. "If people get restless, or some ass gets impatient and stirs people up, things could get bad fast."

Miranda pushed off the truck. It was getting hot in the sun, and talking about it more wasn't going to change anything. Not today, anyway. She squinted, looking over the blighted field, and called for Delilah. The pit bull was in there somewhere. Belatedly, Miranda realized she might eat some of the blighted potato plants. Would that make her sick?

Miranda turned to Rocco, who squinted at her because of the sunshine. "Whatever we end up managing with vaccinating people, maybe we should start a pool for the new arrivals. Pick at least one new person every time we do a round. It'd show them we're serious about them getting the vaccine, too."

"That's not a bad idea," Rocco said. "And the P-Land crowd will eat it up with a spoon. It'll be more inclusive."

Miranda chuckled. She turned around when she heard

Delilah behind her. The pit bull trotted up, two inches of pink tongue hanging from her mouth.

"Hey, baby girl," Miranda said, reaching down to pat her. "I was an idiot and didn't bring any water. You'll have to wait till we get home."

"There's something else, Tucci."

Miranda cocked her head his way. Wariness prickled under her skin at the change of tone in his voice. Whatever he was going to say next wasn't good.

"We found Courtney's journal."

She took a step backward, like she'd been given a good, hard shove to the chest. The birdsong receded, washed out by the blood roaring in her ears. She felt dizzy, but it wasn't from not drinking enough water while they'd been out in the sun. She leaned over and put her hands on her knees.

"You okay?" Rocco asked, gravel crunching under his feet. She felt the weight of his hand while he patted her back. He performed the gesture so awkwardly that Miranda wasn't sure his hand was attached to his body.

She'd thought about Courtney's journal, dreamt about it. Like a family needs a body to bury, she needed to know it had been Courtney who'd told Jeremiah things he shouldn't have known, because what if it had been someone else? Someone still living at LO, who she said hello to every day? What if it was someone she considered a friend, or who laughed at her jokes? What if it was someone who fussed over Delilah, and gave her belly rubs and treats? What if it was someone who, if not a friend, she at least hadn't known was an enemy?

Hands still on her knees, she looked up at him. "Was it her?"

"Yeah. She told Jeremiah about you being pregnant, and what you called the baby."

A weight sloughed off her shoulders. "Just her?"

Rocco's voice was gentle. "As far as we can tell."

"What else?" Miranda asked, straightening up.

"She sabotaged the sound defenses at Station Eight, the day you went to investigate. It wasn't clear how she ended up in the trench with the zombies."

"Did she kill the others there? And the dogs?"

Rocco shrugged. "Didn't say. Just that she'd sabotaged it and was saved by you guys, but yeah. Probably."

"Phineas almost died because of her," she said, a furious anger flaring inside her. She took a deep breath. "Can I see it?"

"If you want," he said, brow furrowing over his lowering eyebrows. "Are you sure you want to?"

"Yes," she said. How could Rocco think she wouldn't want to see it?

"Okay, Tucci," he said, putting his hands up as if to ward her off. "You wanna see it, you can see it. But... What exactly do you think reading it is gonna to do for you?"

Rocco's question brought her up short. She'd thought about finding proof, a journal or diary, notes on napkins, she hadn't cared what, just as long it told her how Jeremiah had known about her pregnancy, and that they'd call the baby Tadpole. She'd lost him because that monster had bitten her, the virus in his veins poisoning her just long enough to doom her child. Now the proof had been found. What did she think reading it would do for her? Did she really need to experience what Courtney saw and thought and felt as she was pulled into the web of lies and delusion that Jeremiah had spun around her?

"I don't know," she said. "But I want to see it."

"Okay," Rocco said. He took her hand and gave it a squeeze. "Just remember that if you change your mind, that's okay."

"I know."

Rocco rolled his eyes and shook his head. "No, Tucci, you don't. You'll make it into a test."

She stared at him, flummoxed. She had no idea what he was talking about. "A test of what?"

"Of whether or not you're tough enough to take it."

She opened her mouth to deny it, then stopped. If she was honest with herself, it sounded like something she would do. She closed her eyes for a moment, trying to figure out exactly what she was feeling, but that would require opening a box she'd sealed shut. She opened her eyes and looked at Rocco.

"I want to see it."

"I already said yes," he said, the expression on his face suggesting that he'd somehow failed her. "Just take a little time to figure out how much energy you want to put into this before you look."

"Since when are you Mister Feelings?" she countered, deflecting his concern.

Rocco shook his head, but he smiled. "You're killing me, Tucci. You know that?" He nudged her with his elbow. "C'mon."

They climbed into the truck, Rocco driving, with Delilah between them. Dust kicked up from the dry, parched road, but cleared as the truck sped forward. They lapsed into a companionable silence, which she needed—at first. Her brain whirred, the sound getting louder and louder until she could barely hear. She'd thought she would feel differently if she knew for a fact that it had been Courtney. She'd thought she'd feel...calmer? Better? More sure of herself and her ability to judge threats? But she didn't feel any of those things. Her body felt heavy and light at the same time, like it might collapse in on itself or fly apart, broken into atomic particles. Her heart twisted and her stomach churned, like a boiling pit of tar, so much that it hurt.

"That bitch," she hissed, the heat behind her words so hot they almost burned her mouth. "That fucking bitch."

She seethed, anger roiling inside her. She was so goddamn furious you could probably see it from space. Her fingers itched. She wished Courtney was still alive so she could strangle the life out of her, get medieval on her ass, and murder her. And then bring her back to life so she could do it again.

The truck eased to a halt, followed by a soft clunk from the gearshift being put into park. A faint whirring chirped over the low rumble of the engine.

"You okay?" Rocco asked.

Miranda opened her mouth, but nothing came out. It was so clear in her mind, but when she tried to put it into words they got muddled and snagged on her tongue.

"You're pissed at her, aren't you?"

"Yeah." She looked at Rocco in wonder. How had he known?

"Kinda wishing she was still alive so you could kill her yourself?"

"Yeah," she said again. She groped for words that felt slippery when her mouth tried to form them. Astonished betrayal cascaded through her body, making the tips of her fingers and toes tingle. "I— I fucking warned her. I told her how dangerous he was, how manipulative, and that she had to keep her guard up. I told her how violent he was, that he was a rapist, for God's sake. I tried to keep her safe and she told him...everything."

"She did."

Tears filled Miranda's eyes, which just pissed her off more. She wanted—needed—to stay angry as she struggled to make sense of it, because she could feel her defenses faltering. She could feel the weight of her heartache pushing against the door she'd slammed shut on losing the baby, and Mario, and everything connected to it. If she didn't stay angry, it would get out.

Delilah nudged Miranda's shoulder with her snout. On autopilot, Miranda began to scratch the pit bull's chest. She dashed away the tears with her free hand.

"I... I want to kill her. I want to fucking kill her." Rocco nodded. When he didn't say more, she said, "Why would she do that to me?"

Rocco's sympathy poured across the space between them. "Because he was all the things you warned her about."

The truth of his words resonated in her chest like the deep buzz of an amplifier, but it didn't help.

"I read the journal," he said. "Her family were really strict fundamentalists."

"So?"

"She wrote about it. Men are the head of household kind of thing, supposed to lead the family, don't let the little woman usurp your authority. They thought women were... What was the expression she used?" He thought for a moment, then snapped his fingers. "Inferior vessels. All straight from the guy upstairs. It wasn't there before she started guarding him. It only cropped up after. I think it made her susceptible to him. If we'd known about her background, she'd never have been put on that guard duty."

"But that's so stupid! Who thinks that way?"

Rocco snorted. "A lot of people did. When there used to be a lot of people."

Miranda pushed her fingers against her temples so hard it hurt. Her head had begun to pound. "I warned her, and she stabbed me in the back."

"She did," he said. Then, under his breath, she heard him mutter, "Better than getting stabbed in the neck."

Through a strangled half laugh, half sob, she said, "You're such an asshole."

She felt stupid, like she'd been played for a sucker. Hurt.

Discouraged. She'd tried to help Courtney, because she'd been young and pretty, which made her a target. Because she'd been a human being, and Jeremiah a monster. All she'd accomplished, in the end, was to give Jeremiah a way to hurt her and Tadpole, and Mar—

She shoved it away. She couldn't think about him right now, she couldn't. She took a few shallow breaths. Her limbs felt like lead; the question she wanted to ask felt like dust filling her mouth, but she had to know.

"Are you sure there was no one else?"

She felt her face screw up. She couldn't stop the tears, nor the soft sobs that followed. Rocco turned the truck off. Even more bewildering, he got out. When he reached her door, he opened it.

"C'mere," he said, giving her arm a tug.

Her feet barely touched the ground before Rocco's strong arms encircled and pulled her close. If Courtney had an accomplice they might still be here, which made LO feel unsafe. Made it feel like a minefield. One wrong word, one wrong decision...she'd never know what hit her.

"It doesn't look like there was anyone else involved," Rocco said softly. She could feel the vibration in his chest when he spoke. "And if there is, I'll find them. I promise."

He rested a hand on the back of her head, stroking her hair with his thumb, rocking her like she was a baby. She felt like a child in the shelter of his arms, small and vulnerable in a world that was big and frightening. Before she realized she was doing it, she said, "I don't want to read the journal."

She hadn't thought it through—at all—but once it was out, she knew it was the truth. She didn't need a ringside seat to Jeremiah's manipulations and lies. Didn't need to watch him victimize Courtney, like he had so many others. Didn't need to watch the series of events unfold that led to her baby having a heart that wouldn't work outside her womb, and arms and legs that would have doomed him eventually. She didn't need one more depressing thing in her life, one more thing to feel bad about when she couldn't ignore it or drink it away. She already had more than enough. She shrugged out of Rocco's arms, swiped at her face, and took a deep breath.

"For what it's worth, you're making the right call," he said.

She sighed, then said, almost to herself, "It won't change anything that matters."

MIRANDA SAT WITH RIVER AT A TABLE NEAR THE FRONT OF the dining hall. Rocco lingered near where people lined up when meals were served, at the front of the room, shifting his weight from one foot to the other. He glared at latecomers as they passed by him.

"He looks nervous," River said.

Miranda nodded. "You should have seen the fields," she said, lowering her voice. "They were a mess."

"Is this seat taken?"

Miranda and River looked up. A tall guy stood next to the empty chair beside Miranda. He was big. Tall, with a rangy frame. He had long, kind of unkempt red hair, fair skin with freckles, and pale-blue eyes. He could be on a postcard that said, "Kiss me, I'm Irish." Or possibly, "Run for your life, I'm a Viking."

"All yours," Miranda said. She held out her hand. "I'm not sure we've met. I'm Miranda."

"Sean," he said, giving her hand a short but firm shake. "Sean Malley."

"Oh, you're the mechanic," River said.

Sean nodded as he sat down, giving them both a smile. It

was a nice one that made him look approachable. Miranda was surprised she hadn't seen him before. With the red hair and the height, he'd be easy to pick out.

"Guilty as charged," Sean said. "I arrived a couple weeks ago."

"Always need a good mechanic," Miranda said. "You are good, right?"

A pink flush crept up from Sean's neck. "Good enough."

He introduced himself to River. She said, "Ignore her. She's like a barky dog that gets all waggy when you're up close."

"I am not," Miranda objected.

River considered for a moment, an appraising look in her eye. "That's actually true," she said to Sean. "She's not that nice waggy dog. She's the standoffish, cranky one."

Rocco's voice boomed across the dining hall. "Okay, folks... Let's get started. If you can quiet down..." Rocco's voice trailed away as the room quieted. "So, thanks for getting here on such short notice, everyone. I appreciate it."

He paused, scrubbing the back of his neck with his hand.

"As you know, we lost some crops when the sound defenses failed during the attack a few months back. We've also had a bad year with pests and a blight on the potatoes. Between all of it, right now I estimate we've got a seventy-five percent crop failure."

Gasps echoed from one side of the room to another, and a low murmur began.

"Did you say seventy-five percent failure?" a voice called from the back.

Rocco patted at the air in front of him, trying to quiet the murmur, which was getting louder. When it subsided, he said, "Yes. Seventy-five percent failure, which means we're looking at a food shortage."

Questions started coming from all directions.

"What about P-Land?"

"How much do we have in our stores?"

"What are you going to do?"

"Hold on, everybody," Rocco said, raising his voice again. "I can't answer your questions when you're all talking over each other."

Again, the crowd quieted—kind of.

"P-Land has already said they'll help us. They lost about thirty percent of their crops, too. I've got a commitment that includes feed for all the livestock through next spring. You all know how things work here," he said, his gaze sweeping to take in everyone. "We may get hungry, but P-Land won't let us starve. They know we'd do the same if the situation were reversed."

He let the words hang for a few beats, just to drive the point home. "That said," he continued. "We've got two months' worth of food in storage if we don't change anything. We're going to have to cut back on how much we eat at meals. And," he said, patting at the air again and raising his voice. "We're gonna have to start sending out scouting parties to look for food."

That caused a stir and more shouted questions. Rocco did his best, acknowledging that the scouting would be dangerous because of how far they'd need to travel to find anything, and that yes, a lot of what they found would be expired.

River muttered under her breath, "Who worries about that? Canned food lasts for decades."

Miranda shrugged. She didn't get it either.

"What about the new people?" someone called out.

"What about them?" Rocco said.

People were craning their necks, trying to see who had asked the question. Miranda felt the eyes of the people around her table shifting and sliding to Sean, then away. A man stood up in the back. Miranda only knew him to see him.

"People are coming for the vaccine, Rocco, and now you're telling us there's not enough food for those of us who already live here. What are you planning to do about new people?"

"I'm glad you asked," Rocco said, not looking glad at all. "We're going to do what we've always done here at LO. We're going to welcome them, and work it out."

Miranda could feel an undercurrent of fear zip through the room as people began to shout more questions. If Rocco didn't get this back on track fast, the community was going to end up more fearful than the situation warranted. Things were unnerving, even scary, but there was no reason to panic yet.

"Look," Rocco said. "It's been a rough couple months, and the hits just keep coming. I get it." He paused, then said, "If Commander Smith was still alive, what would she be telling you right now?"

Heads began to nod, and the last bit of worried murmuring faded away.

"That right," Rocco said. "She'd be telling you exactly what I'm telling you. This is serious; I'm not trying to say it's not. But we have a way of doing things here, and it's not to tell people to come, and then send them away to fend for themselves because circumstances have changed. That's not who we are. When new people get here for the vaccine, this is what I'm gonna tell them."

As he spoke, he ticked his points off on his fingers. "A, that the vaccine is being produced, but it's getting back-burnered to an extent, because B, we've got a food shortage. And C, we want them to stay, which includes helping scout for food to the extent they're able. That doesn't mean everyone in every group of newcomers will become the scouts. We're not shifting this onto the new people so we don't have to do it. It means volunteers, a small number of them. Just like the volunteers among all of us...just enough people to make this work."

"He pulled that out of his ass," Miranda said softly. "I was a little worried."

River nodded.

"I know you still have a lot of questions, and I want to hear them. I might not always have an answer," he said to a sprinkling of chuckles. "But I know we can do this. We just have to stay calm and remember that we're only as strong as our commitment to one another."

Rocco wrapped the meeting up and was immediately mobbed. Sean had wrapped his arms around himself, and his mouth was turned down in a worried frown.

"It's shitty, I know," she said to him. "But we'll work it out."

Sean nodded, forcing a smile. "Sounds like it. It's just..."

"You're new here."

"Yeah," he said.

River said, "I've been at LO almost from the beginning, Sean. You have nothing to worry about. We've had ups and downs before. Not quite like this, but we've stayed the same when it comes to what this community cares about. You might run across a jerk here or there, but we do want newcomers here. We always have. Please don't worry about that. And if there's a problem, tell Rocco, or one of us. He'll want to know."

"Thanks," Sean said, giving her a smile. He stood and said, "Nice meeting you both. I'm sure I'll see you around."

"Where'd they put you?" Miranda asked. "The apartments?" When he nodded, she said, "We're both in the housing plan, by the Big Woods. We'll see you around."

As Sean disappeared into the crowd, River said, "I've got to go check on Veronica."

"Is it going okay?"

River nodded and stood, then pushed in her chair. "As well

as a first pregnancy with twins can. I only came over because I knew this wouldn't be a long meeting."

"Tell her good luck, okay?"

"Will do."

Miranda threaded her way through the people still milling around the dining hall. The level of agitation was a lot lower than she'd expected, though she had a feeling Rocco might be detained for questioning for the rest of the month. It had been smart to bring up Commander Smith. She wasn't just a former commander whom people had trusted and respected. She was as close to a martyr as LO would ever have.

Miranda took a deep breath as she exited the building, the evening cool. Rocco was right about one thing; this crisis would put LO to the test. She looked back at everyone still gathered in the dining hall, the glowing windows making them look cozy and friendly, instead of scared.

I hope we're up to this, she thought.

3

SHE WAS SO TIRED. She could barely keep her eyes open. Miranda looked around the dim room, the only light coming from the small solar-powered lamp by the crib. She decided to try one more time to crawl into bed, but as soon as she did, the baby began to cry again.

"Omigod, kiddo..."

She dragged herself off the bed, almost stumbling as she took the few steps to the crib. By the time she reached him, his little face was screwed up tight, red, and angry. She reached down and checked his diaper, but it was dry.

"Are you hungry again?"

He hadn't eaten well earlier; maybe that was it. She picked him up, holding his tiny body to hers, his soft baby smell filling her nostrils. She settled into the gliding rocker beside the crib, putting her feet on the matching footrest. Whoever had designed these things had been a genius.

She held the baby in the crook of her arm as she unbuttoned the top of her nightgown. She hadn't worn a nightgown since she was a girl, but tee shirts weren't easy to nurse in, and nursing while nude felt weird. Already, she could see milk leaking from her nipples. She nestled him against her breast, smiling at how he was already turning his head toward it. He latched on immediately and sucked hard, grunting like a piglet.

She sighed, smiling at the noises he made, a familiar feeling of contentment spreading through her body. All she had to do now was switch breasts before he got too full and sleepy. She leaned her head back, had just closed her eyes for a moment, when his sharp teeth nipped her.

"Ow!" Her eyes snapped open. "Careful, you," she said, looking down. "That h—"

Another sharp bite sent a spike of pain through her breast, but Miranda could only stare, horror rushing through her. A dark stain spread on her breast and nightgown, warm and sticky. Blood smeared the baby's face, but...

"No," she gasped, as sharp teeth bit her again.

She wasn't holding a baby to her breast... She was holding a zombie. It grunted as it gnawed on her, tiny, perfect fingers opening and closing. Perfect, except they were blackened at the tips, the skin split and cracked. Its squirming body felt cold in her arms. The curve of his cheek was marbled with delicate black streaks just under the skin and smeared with her blood. She recoiled, pushing it away, but the zombie she had thought was her baby bit her harder, gnawing on her mangled breast. Blood flowed over her body, drenching the nightgown. She felt the scream clawing its way out, opened her mouth—

Miranda jerked awake, a strangled cry stuck in her throat. She bolted upright, gasping. Her body felt sticky from the sweat that covered her. She clasped her breast in her hand, her other arm crossing over her chest to protect herself. Heart thundering against her sternum, she looked across the room.

There was no gliding rocking chair and footrest, no crib, just the chaise lounge next to a small table littered with books, and the little solar-powered lamp. She lifted her hands to her face, covering her nose and mouth.

"Oh fuck," she whispered.

She rocked back and forth as the shock and fear subsided. Delilah wriggled closer, whimpering and licking her hands. Miranda buried her face in the pit bull's neck, holding on tighter than she knew dogs liked.

"Oh fuck, Liley," she gasped. "Jesus."

She let Delilah go, though her trusty canine friend stayed glued to her side. She'd had a particularly bad run of nightmares lately. This was the tenth night in row. Sometimes, the baby was a zombie. Sometimes, Mario handed her their child, his face aglow with love and happiness, before he told her it was her fault that it was going to die. All were variations on a theme, like the director's cut of a horror film with endless, alternate endings.

She squinted at her watch, then crawled out of bed. Five hours until she had to get up to go to P-Land with Rocco. She wouldn't be going back to sleep. If she tried, she'd just lay there, staring at the ceiling or the insides of her eyelids, while the instant replay rattled from one side of her skull to the other.

She retrieved an over-sized tee shirt from the floor, tugging it on as she padded down the stairs in the dark. She smacked her lips, tongue tacky against the roof of her mouth from thirst. The kitchen's linoleum floor felt smooth against her feet as she tugged on the handle of the fridge. She looked inside. Her lungs expelled a sigh that her body sagged into. There were still six bottles of hard cider in the empty, half-sized appliance. She'd had a few before bed, but hadn't been sure there were more. She picked up three bottles in one hand, letting the fridge door swing shut as she pried the magnetic bottle opener from it. She opened the bottles, left two on the counter, and lifted the third to her mouth. The cold cider bubbled on her tongue and fizzed against the inside of her mouth, crisp and tangy. She swallowed, enjoying the chill as the cider made its way to her stomach. She leaned against the fridge, trying not to think about the dream. Trying to ignore the jumble of feelings it stirred inside her.

"At least he wasn't in it," she whispered to herself, because the dreams with Mario were always worse than those with just the baby.

She took another pull on the bottle, then another, and tried not to think.

"I THINK WE CAN ALL AGREE ON THAT," ZOE SAID.

Miranda closed her eyes against the sunlight pouring in through the windows, almost whimpering with relief. Her head had started to pound about the time they arrived, one of those stealth hangovers that lulled you into thinking you were okay, until you weren't.

Zoe, one of P-Land's three governing council members, was a plump, middle-aged woman. Her long straight hair was always parted in the center, and mostly salt and pepper, but there was still some brown that hadn't thrown in the towel. Miranda could never decide if Zoe was turn-into-a-Dasher plump, because she dressed in flowing smock dresses made of fabric so loud that looking at them hurt. Today was no exception. Her favored scents seemed to be a mix of weed and patchouli. She even had some of those hippy beaded necklaces and round wire-rimmed glasses.

Miranda liked hippies. They were usually good-hearted folks trying to put some positivity out into the world, and God knew the world needed positivity in a big way. Zoe was doing her damndest to give hippies a bad name, not in terms of her intentions, but execution. She kept saying things like 'honoring the process' and 'I invite you all to think deeply about this' and 'it's important that we be intentional.' The woman was a marvel, really, but with the way her head was pounding, Miranda couldn't appreciate the absurdity of it. If Zoe invited her to think deeply and intentionally while honoring the process about one more no-brainer decision, her brain was going to leak from her ears.

Rocco leaned over to whisper in Miranda's ear. "If this goes more than another ten minutes, pretend you have the runs."

She snorted. When Rocco's eyes bugged out at her, she realized he was serious.

"We'll have to take it to the working groups, of course, but I think once everyone has had a chance to discuss and process your proposal, they'll agree it's the most inclusive solution."

For the mother fucking love of God, Miranda thought, lowering her forehead into her hand.

"Are you okay, Miranda?"

Miranda snapped her head up and smiled—she hoped sweetly. The last thing she needed was for Zoe to get on a tear about medicinal herbs. "I'm fine, Zoe. Just a little tired."

Rocco gave Zoe a pained smile, as if the exchange between the two women hadn't happened. "I think that would be great, Zoe. I can't wait to hear what your working groups think."

"I'm so happy we can have such a productive dialogue, Rocco. I know you're not as much of a process person as we are here."

All three of the P-Land council members chuckled good-naturedly. Rocco looked like he had a bad case of gas. Miranda could see it was taking everything he had to not scream, because it was taking everything that she had to not scream.

They'd just spent an hour discussing her idea to include newer arrivals in the vaccination schedule. She and Rocco had agreed it was the way to go in ten seconds, making their decision-making process point-insert-a-shit-ton-of-zeros-before-a-one times faster. They still hadn't gotten to the point of this meeting, either. Everything discussed so far could have waited.

"Why are we here?" Rocco said brusquely.

Miranda looked at him sidelong. His brow furrowed so deep that his eyebrows had practically knitted together. His mouth had become a hard, straight line, which was usually a precursor to—

Oh, there's the scowl, she thought.

The council members quit chuckling and cast one another furtive glances. Zoe shifted in her seat, eyes downcast, shuffling the one piece of paper in front of her.

"We could have productively dialogued at our regular meeting," Rocco said, impatience finally cracking his admittedly thin veneer of politeness. "Quit beating around the bush and tell us whatever it is you're tap-dancing around."

The council members weren't used to Rocco being this blunt, even though Miranda knew he was holding back.

"Uh, yeah, well... There is one more thing."

Heads swiveled to Toby. Toby was on the high end of middle-aged, with light-brown hair, thin eyebrows, and a small, tight smile. Every time Miranda had seen him, he wore hiking pants, Keen hiking boots, long-sleeved button-down shirts that were light blue or tan, and the kind of vests once sold in over-priced camping stores. Before zombies, he'd probably driven a Subaru with a kayak on the roof, with both the 'Darwin' little fish with feet and a planet Earth 'Respect Your Mother' bumperstickers, kept chickens, and subscribed to an organic food farm share. He'd been an outdoorsy, science-loving, organic and local food-eating Portlander before it had become the punchline for a joke. Toby might drive Miranda a little nuts with the hemming and hawing, but he was on the right side of things. He also wasn't very talk-y.

Toby pushed his wire-rimmed glasses up his hooked nose. What's with these people and wire-rimmed glasses, Miranda thought.

"Uh, yeah, well," Toby said. "We have a little bit of a situation."

Silence, during which the three P-Landers traded furtive glances. Rocco had a shoot-me-now look in his eyes that seemed likely to veer into going postal.

"It might be helpful if you tell us what it is," Miranda said.

"Right, right," Toby said. "Uh, yeah, well... We've got a group that's gone missing."

"Missing?" Miranda said.

"Uh, yeah," Toby started, but then Zoe cut him off.

"They're two weeks overdue. A scavenging party, six people."

"And you're only just telling us now, after we've been sitting here over an hour?" Rocco said, his annoyance plain.

The corners of Zoe's mouth turned down in an anxious, caught out frown.

"The thing is," said Daphne, the last member of P-Land's council, who hadn't spoken until now. "They were looking for something important."

Daphne bit her lip. She was the youngest member of the council, in her early thirties, with brown eyes, light-brown hair, and a freckled face that looked wholesome enough to have been plucked from an L.L. Bean catalogue. Miranda put her hand on Rocco's arm as his mouth opened. With the way his jaw had tightened, and the scowl on his face deepened, she could tell he was about to lose it.

Miranda said, "Where were they going, and what were they looking for?"

"Uh, yeah, well," Toby said. He cleared his throat. "We have a newer community member, Alec. He's been with us a few months." He gave a small, tight smile again, as if it was all he could manage for fear of offending them. "Uh...Alec had some information that we thought warranted following up on. On his way here, he met a man who told him about a cache of weapons at Nanitch Lodge—"

Rocco's bark of laughter cut him off. "Are you fucking kidding me?" he said, incredulous. "Did he tell you the Easter Bunny is real, too? People've been talking about that place for years. If anything was ever there, it's long gone by now."

"We thought it couldn't hurt to look," Daphne said, her face flushing pink. Her clipped voice implied she didn't appreciate Rocco's mockery.

"Fucking sent people to Nanitch Lodge," Rocco muttered, sounding incredulous.

"What's Nanitch Lodge?" Miranda asked. Whatever it was, this was the first she had heard of it.

"It was a Boy Scout camp on Mount Hood," Rocco said, his voice dripping with derision. "People have been talking about the hidden weapons up there for years, but you have to go through or around Portland to get there. Even if there aren't zombies at Nanitch Lodge, getting there will kill you."

"We don't know that," Daphne objected, her voice rising. "It—"

Miranda found herself grateful not to be on the receiving end of the filthy glare Rocco silenced Daphne with. He said, voice flat, "I suppose you want me to send Tucci and Rich up there to see if they're still alive."

Zoe's hands flapped the air in front of her. "Let's not

argue," she said. "In retrospect, maybe it wasn't such a good decision, but..."

"I resent that," Daphne snapped. "We took it to the community for a vote!"

"That probably took a year," Rocco snorted.

Daphne glared at Rocco. "That's the kind of attitude that gives LO a—"

"Okay, okay," Zoe said, raising her voice and cutting Daphne off. "None of this is helpful. Let's just take a moment to center ourselves, okay?" She gave Rocco a feeble smile. Good luck trying to placate him with that, Miranda thought.

"In retrospect," Zoe continued, "I think that maybe it wasn't such a good decision." Daphne opened her mouth, but Zoe kept talking. "We would like Miranda and Rich to go look for them." She took a deep breath. "It's a big ask, we know, but they're the only ones who can do it without being in danger themselves."

"No way," Rocco said, at the same time Miranda said, "Yes."

Rocco side-eyed her. "No! No way."

"Oh, stop it!" Her headache had decided to ramp things up, robbing her of patience for Rocco's temper tantrum. "You're annoyed they didn't start with this, but you don't mean that."

Rocco glowered at her. "If Tucci and Rich are willing to go, fine," he said. "But you shouldn't beat around the bush. And you sure as shit shouldn't be sending your people out like Ponce de Leon looking for the goddamned Fountain of Youth."

An uncomfortable silence filled the room. Finally, Toby said, directing his words to Miranda, "Um, yeah, well... We really appreciate you even considering it, Mi—"

"Do the people they're going after know they repel zombies?" Rocco said, interrupting him.

Toby froze, the bobbing of his Adam's apple making him look like a startled turkey.

"Great, fucking great," Rocco said. "Are they people who can keep their mouths shut at least? What about this new guy?"

"Keep their mouths shut? I think so," Zoe said, sounding apologetic.

"So no," Rocco said.

"It's going to get out sooner or later," Miranda said to him.

"That's not the point," he snapped. Rocco rose to his feet, advancing to the table to loom over the P-Landers. "If they find any of your people alive, they're coming to live at LO. If they're even thinking of flapping their jaws, I want them where I can remind them not to."

He didn't wait for an answer, but stomped from the room, cursing under his breath. Miranda stood, brushing her hair back from her face.

Zoe sighed, a defeated sound that bordered on a whimper. "That could have gone better."

"It could have gone a lot worse," Miranda said.

Toby said, "We didn't think he'd get so angry..."

Miranda looked at Toby, surprised. She'd never heard him say anything that wasn't prefaced with at least an 'Um,' if not the entire 'Um, yeah, well.'

"He wouldn't have, normally," Miranda said. "We have people showing up because they've heard about the vaccine, and you know our food situation. Vaccine production and rollout has to slow down, like we discussed, since eating is a higher priority." Her stomach plunged when she realized she'd mentioned the vaccine situation; Zoe might want to talk about it more. She added hastily, "Rocco told the whole community where things are last night, and that we need scouting parties to go out and look for food."

Zoe nodded, brow wrinkling, a worried frown tugging at

her mouth. "After ten years, everything nearby has been picked clean."

"That's not our problem," Daphne muttered.

"What?" Toby said, almost yelping in surprise.

"Daphne," Zoe scolded, scandalized. "You don't mean that. They do things differently at LO than us, but we always help each other out."

Daphne scowled at Zoe, before scowling at Miranda for good measure. "We lost some of our fields, too, when the sound defenses failed. We'd never have sent anyone up there for weapons if it wasn't for them bringing their trouble up from San Jose." She jutted her chin at Miranda. "If anyone should be solving LO's food shortage, it's her, not us."

"You should be ashamed of yourself," Zoe snapped, two spots of pink coloring her cheeks.

"If it's all about food for LO, they're not going to hold up their end to get supplies to make the vaccine, are they?" Daphne said, her face flushing a deep red. "I guess that'll all be on us now."

She stood abruptly, pushing her chair back so hard that it teetered on its back two legs before bumping back down. She stormed to the exit like a thundercloud.

With a touch of iron in her voice that Miranda had never heard before, Zoe said, "We'll manage because we help each other, Daphne. We always have."

Daphne whirled around, turning on Zoe like a caged animal. "Maybe that's something we should revisit at some point."

Miranda raised her eyebrows. She'd never seen Zoe snap at anyone; she hadn't thought her capable of it. Usually, when someone went after Miranda like Daphne had, she at least knew them enough to have pissed them off. She'd exchanged pleasantries with Daphne maybe twice.

Zoe watched the younger woman leave, her face a study of pure astonishment. "Wow," she said. "Well, I never."

"Um, yeah," Toby said, rising to his feet. His tone was apologetic. "Sorry about that, Miranda. She's got a few friends in the group that's overdue."

Miranda waved his apology away. "It's not like Rocco was a model of decorum."

Toby grinned at that. "He's got an Italian temper, all right."

"Toby, don't stereotype," Zoe said absently.

"He *does* have an Italian temper," Miranda said. "Rocco will settle down, and I don't mind doing this for you. I know Rich won't mind, either."

Zoe's watery smile seemed hastily pasted over her troubled expression. "Thank you, Miranda," she said. "We really appreciate it."

"You hear that?"

Miranda cocked her head and listened. If Rich hadn't said something, she'd have thought it was the wind in the trees.

"There's a buzz," said Phineas, stopping as he pulled abreast between her and Rich.

"Yeah, I hear it. Haven't seen any animals for a good fifteen minutes," she said, taking a quick look around.

"Just once," Rich said. "I'd like to go hunting for lost people and not find them surrounded by zombies."

"Or worse," Phineas said.

"How close are we?" Miranda asked Rich.

Rich had slung his rifle over his shoulder and had a map in one hand. He squinted at it, then consulted the compass in his other hand.

"Half a mile, maybe? And it only took us what...five days to travel seventy miles?" He pulled his sunglasses down from the top of his head, even though the day wasn't particularly sunny. They were polarized, and he said they helped with the glare. He folded the map in half. It took three tries to stick it back inside the breast pocket of his jacket. "Good Lord," he muttered. "It's a good thing I repel zombies or I'd be in trouble."

"Ready?" Miranda asked, nickering to get Delilah's attention. She latched the leather leash to the pit bull's collar. When the guys nodded, she said, "Let's go see. Stick close, Phineas."

Phineas grinned, the freckles scattered over his nose almost black against his cocoa-brown skin. "Like I need an invitation."

"To Rich," she answered dryly. "Stick close to Rich."

"Aw, Miranda, don't be like that," Phineas chided, not sounding the least bit put out.

Rich said, sounding amused, "How 'bout we keep our minds on the job?"

It was nice to know they'd soon reach their goal. Rich had said the elevation was about three thousand five hundred feet, and Miranda could feel it. She was just happy this fool's errand hadn't taken them to Timberline Lodge, which was another two thousand feet up Mount Hood. They'd left Highway 26 about an hour ago for the narrow, windy path that led to the old Boy Scout camp. It had probably been a two-lane road once, but now was no more than a game trail. The forest had encroached, the conifer trees sprouting straight and tall to the sky. The dried, rotting leaves that covered the road in drifts crunched under their feet. Delilah strained against the leash, not appreciating her freedom of movement being curtailed. Miranda gave a few tugs, until she quit pulling so hard.

As the buzz turned into faint moans and hisses, she said, "Sounds like the world's most miserable garden party."

Ahead, Miranda could see slivers of a building through gaps between the trees. A low growl rumbled in Delilah's chest.

"It's all right, Liley," Miranda said softly.

They rounded the last bend. A swaying mass of zombies, twenty bodies deep, milled along the length of a large building that looked like an old three-story barn. In the center on the ground level was an entry sheltered by a gable. Miranda could just see the top of a door below the gable. Zombies wriggled and swayed, milling in place as they groaned and hissed. There was a row of windows on the second story that ran half the building's length. On the right-side end from where Miranda stood was a two-story timber porch to the second story, but the staircase that led up to it was missing.

"They're here," Rich said. "Or they were. I can't think of another reason for there to be that many zombies this far up the mountain, all in one place."

Miranda judged the width of Nanitch Lodge at approximately sixty to eighty feet. She stood on tiptoe, straining to see over the horde. "That's a fuck ton of zombies."

"There don't seem to be any windows on the ground floor," Phineas said.

"That we can see," Miranda murmured. She dropped her heels to the ground, lips pursing as she surveyed the horde. "There must be two hundred of them on this side."

"I haven't heard of groups of zombies this large out here normally," Rich said. "There just aren't enough people to draw them out. How the hell did they attract so many?" He sighed, then looked to Miranda and Phineas. "You should walk with me, Phineas. Miranda will have her hands full with Delilah."

"Why don't you just let her off the leash?" Phineas said. "The zombies won't eat her."

"We have to open the door again if she doesn't come in with us," Miranda said, surprised it wasn't obvious.

"Oh, right...of course," Phineas said, looking embarrassed.

They set off, Phineas tucked against Rich. Rich put his arm

around the younger man's shoulders. Miranda walked alongside Phineas' exposed side, taking no chances. Delilah's growls became more menacing. When she barked, almost as one the horde turned. It surged toward them in a slow, stumbling sort of way.

Phineas wrinkled his nose. "My God, they stink."

Miranda braced herself as the horde hit. It didn't matter that they wouldn't attack her. The wrongness of them, their existence despite—in defiance of—the natural order, never changed. They flowed around her, snapping teeth and grasping arms reaching, then shying away. They jostled her and Delilah, who barked and strained against her leash. Miranda pulled the pit bull in close, arms trembling with the effort of restraining her. Another reason she wanted to keep Delilah close was she didn't want her leading more zombies to them.

Rotting faces with sores and bite marks, open maws and snapping teeth, exposed bone peeking through rotting scalps, noise from all sides, assaulted her. The horde churned around them, the zombies farther away from the human epicenter pushing against those that were shying away. It felt like being in a mob one punch short of a riot.

Phineas' forehead was dotted with beads of sweat as the horde jostled around them. So was hers, and her upper lip, too, as the zombies shoved and recoiled on all sides.

"Phineas on the door?" Miranda said, raising her voice.

"Yeah," said Rich.

"Goddammit, Delilah," Miranda muttered.

Delilah hadn't stopped barking. She wasn't lunging in a way that would yank Miranda into the horde, but that didn't mean she wasn't being a complete pain in the ass. Miranda knew the pit bull would settle down once they were out of the horde. If there aren't too many zombies inside, she amended silently. It was still better to have her along. She'd find any zombies they missed, and when she wasn't being obnoxious, like now, Delilah was better company than most people.

Phineas stepped to the door. Miranda and Rich stayed behind him, sheltering him from the unruly zombie mob. He gave the doors a tug, but as expected, they didn't budge. He squatted down, examining the crack between the doors.

"It's dead bolted," he said, straightening up.

"If there's anybody in there, they won't think us banging on the door is anything but zombies. We could try climbing that porch," Rich said. "Did we bring anything we could use as a grappling hook?" At their blank faces, he said, undeterred, "Let's check it—"

"Hello?"

Miranda cocked a brow at Rich.

"Hello?" called a voice, louder than before.

"Is someone in there?" Phineas said, facing the door again.

"Aye," the voice said, a man's voice, with the faint trace of an accent. "How're you out there?"

"Never mind that," Rich shouted, because the zombies had gotten louder. "We were sent by P-Land to look for you. Can you open the door?"

No answer, then, "Are ye out of your mind?"

"We can get in without letting them in," Rich said.

"You need to find another—" the person began, but Miranda cut him off.

"I'm standing out here with a dog that's trying to dislocate my shoulder and a horde of goddamn zombies at my back. Open the fucking door. We'll keep them out." To Rich and Phineas she added, "Idiot."

"I canna open the door. You can climb the porch there, at the side of the building."

"We haul our asses all the way up here and we're supposed to climb to a second-story porch," she said to Rich.

"Well, we can," Phineas said, shrugging.

"I'm not— Fuck it," she said, shaking her head.

She knew her irritation was getting the better of her because she was tired. Whoever was on the other side of the door didn't know they could repel zombies. At the same time, they were standing outside the door and they weren't being eaten. Anyone with half a brain should be able to puzzle out that they were doing something right.

"Okay," she said. "I guess we—"

Delilah barked, louder than before, and lunged, pulling Miranda off-balance. Miranda's free arm flailed, waving in the air as if she might find something to grab on to. Instead, she hit the ground hard on her hip and elbow. The leash cut into her wrist. Delilah strained against it, barking to raise the dead—or the undead, depending.

"Goddammit, Delilah," Miranda groaned.

She pushed up to her knees and yanked on the leash as hard as she could. Delilah yipped, and started toward her, a look of reproach in her eyes. She wasn't used to being yanked on and didn't like it. Miranda knew how she felt. She put one foot on the ground to stand up, turning to Rich and Phineas as she did.

"Phineas, no!"

Phineas reached to give her a hand up, but he moved a step too far from Rich. A gaunt, weathered woman, with long patches of stringy hair that hung lank from a rotting scalp, cloudy eyes both ravenous and vacant, snagged him. Her filthy, almost taloned fingers, dug into his shoulder. He yelped, eyes rounding with fright. Miranda vaulted up, slamming into Phineas' solid frame just as Rich tackled him from behind. Starbursts flashed across her corneas when Phineas' chin connected with her forehead. His breath huffed out in an *oof* as her momentum was arrested by Rich's tackle from the other side.

They trio twisted as they fell to the ground in a heap, both Phineas and Rich more than less on top of her.

"Are you okay?" Rich said urgently.

Phineas sucked in a breath. "I think so."

Miranda lay still as they climbed to their feet, blinking hard to clear her vision. She'd lost hold of Delilah's leash. She searched for the pit bull as she sat up, but it was impossible to see anything but the zombies surrounding them. The noise had hit a crescendo, the struggle riling the horde to a fever pitch. Miranda stood, now furious with the idiot on the other side of that door. She helped Rich check Phineas, who had been squished but nothing more. Then she pounded on the door.

"You're obviously okay here and don't need our help. We're leaving. See you never, asshole."

"Wait! No," the voice cried.

Rich looked at her askance. "You don't really think that's going to work, do you?"

"I don't care if it works! Phineas almost died. As soon as I find Delilah, we should leave. They asked us to find them. They never said anything about bringing them back."

"Okay, okay!" the muffled voice said. "I'm opening the door."

The hideous squeak of the door hinges grated against Miranda's ear. It sounded like an animal in its death throes. She'd have to look for Delilah later. If they didn't go inside now, they might miss their chance. She stepped back behind Rich and Phineas. She'd let Rich take the lead, because she was so aggravated she was liable to punch whoever met them.

The door opened a crack, then a little more, before Rich grasped the handle and pulled it just wide enough for Phineas to slip through. Miranda sidled up beside Rich and followed him inside. They slammed the door shut and turned the deadbolt. It was so dark that Miranda couldn't see her hand in front of her face, though there was some weak light ahead of them.

"This way," said the disembodied voice of the person who'd let them in.

He kept talking, and they followed him through the dark to a set of stairs. The light improved as they climbed the stairs, until they stood in what used to euphemistically be called a great room. The windows she'd seen outside, which hadn't looked that big, ran the length of the room, almost floor to ceiling. A huge stone fireplace was against the opposite wall, with firewood stacked high beside it. Comfortable couches and chairs were arranged around the fireplace. The room was open to the third story, and managed to be both grand and homey, probably because of the furniture's plaid upholstery. The areas beyond the room's edges faded into a murky darkness.

"You can put your things here," the stranger said, gesturing around him at nothing in particular.

"Where are you from?" Phineas asked.

"Scotland," he said. "I'm Alec, by the way. Alec Campbell."

Miranda dropped her pack by the fireplace. After introductions were made, and Alec's connection with P-Land confirmed, Phineas and Rich sunk onto couches along with Alec.

"You're the only one left?" Miranda asked. She didn't sit, since she had to go back outside to find Delilah.

Alec nodded, his eyes an arresting shade of hazel that looked haunted. He told them a story they'd heard before, of something that didn't seem important at the time, which led to something else, and ended in disaster. He was the only survivor, and the fabled weapons store was just that.

"How were you able to get to the door?" Alec asked when he'd finished his story. "You had zombies all around."

You sounded like yew when he said it. The burr of his *R*s

stretched them out, as if his tongue snagged the consonants a few seconds too long as it left his mouth. He had a heavy but not overpowering brow above his hazel eyes. His short black hair was grimy and swept back from his face. His bone structure was beautiful...high cheekbones, the kind of chin people liked to call rugged, and a jaw that was just square enough. His nose fit his face, which was to say it was beautiful, too.

"It's a side effect some people get from the vaccine LO developed," Rich said.

"What?" Alec blurted. "We haven't heard about that."

"Your council knows," Rich said. "But out from that, it's need to know."

"Aye," he said absently, nodding his head as he absorbed the information. "That might make you a target to the wrong kind of people." He looked from person to person. "All three of you have it?"

"No," Miranda said. "Just me and Rich. You have to stay close to us to be protected. That's why Phineas almost got killed while you refused to open the door."

Alec's mouth fell open. "I'm sorry," he said to Phineas, sounding horrified. "I didn't know. Obviously. And I didn't see how you could get through the door without..." His voice trailed. "I am truly sorry."

"Yeah, whatever," said Miranda, dismissing him. "I've got to find Delilah, Rich. Will you help me with the door?" She looked pointedly at Alec. "So no zombies get in?"

Alec winced. "Who's Delilah?"

"My dog," Miranda said. "Don't worry, she'll like you. She has terrible taste in men."

DELILAH SPRAWLED AT ALEC'S FEET, BLISSED OUT WHILE he rubbed her tummy.

"You're a good wee doggie," he crooned to her.

Oh Delilah, Miranda thought, able to appreciate the irony even if she was still annoyed with this Alec Campbell. It turned out that there had been a weapons cache here once. Alec showed them the storeroom full of empty crates and ammo boxes that he and his companions had found, before someone got a bright idea that ended up with only Alec and a guy named Chris making it back. Chris had been bitten, so he ate a bullet, and now lay rotting a hundred yards into the forest. Miranda had known Chris a little, and killing himself rather than waiting to turn fit. Still, she'd searched for and found him, just to make sure the details of his bite and their flight back to the building matched Alec's story. It was easy enough to find their route. They hadn't been trying to cover their tracks, and that played with running for their lives. Even so, she didn't know Alec from Adam. The P-Land Council trusted him, but seeing as how they had agreed to the fool's errand that started all this, she wasn't putting a lot of store by their judgment.

Delilah left Alec behind to settle in front of the hearth. The fire in the huge fireplace crackled and spit, firelight dancing in the windows of the rear lounge. Distorted, flickering shadows danced across the high ceiling. The building had cooled down noticeably once the sun set, even though it was still early fall. None of the windows in the building had been opened in a while, making the air stale, but the woodsmoke smell of the fire masked it.

Rich stretched his arms overhead with a groan. "Well, I'm just glad you're okay, Alec. It's a damn shame about everyone else, though."

The noises of the fire, coupled with the musical drawl of the American South and the lilt of the Scottish Highlands, had mellowed Miranda's annoyance. Phineas had sacked out a while ago, uncharacteristically subdued, but brushes with death sometimes did that. Miranda lay on the couch opposite Rich and Alec. She closed her eyes, but could tell she wasn't going to sleep well, even though she was exhausted. If only I had these two to talk me to sleep every night, she thought. She cracked an eye, giving Rich the once-over. If he wasn't already taken, she might consider seducing him just so he could talk her to sleep at night. She was pretty sure his voice would keep the nightmares away, too.

"You might have to move to LO, Alec, unless Rocco has settled down," Rich said.

Alec said, "Come again?"

"Rocco, LO's new commander, was pissed about this," Miranda said. "Not coming to look for people." She paused, remembering his initial refusal, and added, "Not that much. But the whole Nanitch Lodge weapons cache thing. He was pissed that your council sent people to look for it."

At Alec's puzzled face, Rich added, "People have talked about the weapons sitting here ripe for the taking for years."

"I still don't see why that means I have to move to LO."

Miranda chuckled. "Rocco doesn't trust P-Landers to not yap about us repelling zombies."

"I was a reporter," Alec said, sounding affronted. "I have loads of experience protecting my sources."

"Rocco won't care," Miranda said, pulling herself upright. "He thinks everyone at P-Land are flakes until proven other-wise. He values the relationship, but he's not a process person."

Rich laughed. "That's one way to put it."

"I haven't been at P-Land that long...two or three months," Alec said. He paused, then a slow, sly smile spread across his face. "They are a bit airy fairy."

That smile—slow and sly—transformed Alec from gorgeous

to stunning. It was the kind of smile that made you feel like you were the only person in the room worth being with. The kind of smile that had women tripping into his bed as easily as her dog had sprawled at his feet, tummy exposed for a good rub.

"Well, get ready for LO," Rich said. "When Rocco gets a bee in his bonnet, it's practically impossible to change his mind."

"It'll be one less mouth for them to feed," Miranda said. "That ought to make Daphne a little happier."

"Daphne?" Alec asked. "You know her?"

"No," Miranda said, shaking her head. "I went to the meeting with the P-Land Council, to keep Rocco from being a bigger ass than he was. She was pissed when he gave them a hard time about sending us here...brought up the crops P-Land lost when the sound defenses failed. She was not understanding about needing to eat being our priority. We never said we were completely halting our part of getting vaccine supplies, or leaving it totally in P-Land's lap, but she acted like we were. She was really bitchy about it."

Alec's brow wrinkled, and his lips pursed in a frown. "That's hardly fair of her, from what you and Rich have told me. Daphne can be a little...black and white."

"Friend of yours?" Rich said.

He hesitated, then said, "You could say that."

Ah, Miranda thought, the Scotsman was a player. It fit, with that smile of his. Aloud, she said, "Girlfriend?"

Alec's eyes met hers, sizing her up. "No," he finally said. "We've had some fun together, but nothing like that."

Miranda laughed. "I have a feeling she has a different answer to that question."

Alec looked at her for a moment, then shrugged, unwilling to commit himself.

"Besides having the best wife in the world, that right there is why I'm glad I'm married," Rich said. He stretched his arms over his head with a groan. "You want me to take first watch, Miranda?"

She shook her head. "I can't sleep yet. You guys go to bed. I'll wake you up in a couple hours."

She wondered, idly, if Alec was going to say he'd stay up a bit longer. That slow, sly smile, and the way his eyes twinkled with an easy confidence, made her think he might. Which would be flattering if she were interested, but she was done with men who said one thing and did another. She'd never let anyone hurt her like Mario had, and she'd never let herself want anything like she'd wanted their baby. She was done with that—permanently.

"I'll get some kip as well," Alec said, surprising her. "And my apologies again for being an arse when you arrived."

4

"SOMEONE'S WITH THEM."

Tessa didn't sound alarmed, but Mario could hear the undercurrent of tension in her voice. He hurried to the porch, suppressing a cough and pretending his lungs didn't hurt when in point of fact they hurt like a bitch. He stepped through the door, squinting as he raised his hand to shade his eyes. Doug and Skye were several blocks away along I Street. Tessa was right; they weren't alone.

Between she and Doug, Skye held the hand of a small child with a halo of dark hair. Doug carried some kind of square container in his right hand. His left clasped the hand of another child, bigger than the first, with shorter dark hair cut closer to his head. Both children were black. Even from this distance, Mario could see that they were dirty and tired. The one holding Doug's hand stumbled every few steps.

"This complicates things," Mario said.

Tessa said, "How do you figure that?"

"I take it you've never traveled with small children."

"No," she answered. "Their parents might be nearby."

When Doug and Skye and their charges reached the far end of the block, they walked out to meet them. The box Doug carried was a pet carrier. A pet... This just gets better and better, Mario thought.

"Hey guys," Skye said when they were close enough to greet Mario and Tessa without needing to raise their voices.

"See you found something there," Mario answered.

Doug smiled. "Sure did." When he, Skye, and the children stopped in front of them, he said, "Meet Silas and his sister Violet." He lifted the carrier in his hand a little. "And Mister Bun Bun." He directed his next comment to the children. "These are the friends we told you about, Mario and Tessa."

"Violet is six, and Silas is eight," Skye said.

"Eight and a half," Silas corrected.

Mario smiled. Half years were important at that age. It was something he'd forgotten until he became a parent. Silas leaned into Doug. His big brown eyes regarded Mario and Tessa warily, as if he expected them to bite. His hair was filthy. The dirt both lighter and darker than his mahogany skin made his face resemble desert camo print fatigues. Violet was much smaller than her brother. She might be six if what the children had told Doug and Skye was accurate, but she looked younger. Silas was also small for his age, so perhaps it was a family trait. Violet smiled, a wide, happy grin that lit up her face. Her features were birdlike, her nose straight and narrow where her brother's was broad, lips thin where Silas' were generous.

Tessa crouched in front of Violet. The girl let go of Skye's hand and threw her arms around Tessa's neck.

"Oh," Tessa said, surprise in her voice.

Silas darted over and yanked his sister away. "She's a stranger, Violet," he scolded, putting himself between Violet and Tessa. "Strangers are dangerous."

Violet pulled away from her brother and scampered over to the pet carrier. "Mister Bun Bun is my bunny," she said.

"You can show him to me later," Tessa said, straightening up.

"It's okay, Silas," Doug said, touching the boy's shoulder. "Mario and Tessa are friends. They'll help and protect you, just like me and Skye."

Silas looked up at Doug, eyes still wary, but with a sliver of wanting to believe him.

"Let's get them fed and cleaned up," Skye said to Doug. She motioned to Silas. "He's dead on his feet."

"Where are we going?" Silas asked, his voice pinched with anxiety.

"To that house right there," Doug said, pointing. "It's the one I told you about."

"Is it safe?"

"Yes," Doug said firmly. "It's safe."

Silas' whole body sagged. It had obviously been a long time since the boy had felt safe. Mario followed Tessa, lagging behind Skye and Doug and their small charges. If their parents were gone, of course they'd take these children with them. The duty was so obvious that the decision made itself. Having them along would complicate the rest of the trip. The nagging impatience over their detour and delay blossomed into a deep reluctance that rippled through Mario's body. It settled in his heart like a heavy stone that pulled him down, tethering him to an obligation he wanted no part of.

———

THREE TUBS WORTH OF HEATED WATER LATER, HEADS shaved due to lice because they had no medicines to treat it, infested clothing and hair burned, small bodies scrubbed clean, and bellies—human and rabbit—filled to brimming with food, Silas, Violet, and Mister Bun Bun were out cold on a mattress pulled into the living room. Silas had been unwilling to be away from Skye or Doug, and since the adults needed to eat and confer, moving the mattress was the best option. Doug and Skye had the foresight to get more clothes for the children on the way back. Otherwise, they'd be stark naked or in adult-sized shirts. Their shoes had been salvageable and were good enough for now.

Getting Silas and Violet settled in and fed took a good three hours. They considered taking them to the yacht, since it had hot running water, but Silas' trepidation when Doug tried to coax him into the rowboat had quickly escalated to an almost full-blown panic attack. Mario looked around the table where he and the others were finishing up the same dinner that he'd made for the kids. Yawns rippled around the table, and he realized the children were not the only ones tuckered out by the day's events.

"Thank you for cooking dinner, Mario," Skye said, her voice low.

"Thank you for doing bath and barber duty," Mario replied. "You too, Doug. It's a big job when it's just everyday dirt, never mind how dirty those two were."

"Yeah," Doug said, looking over to the small, sleeping forms. "I feel bad about shaving their heads. They look even more vulnerable now."

Mario said, "It's the rabbit that clinches it."

Tessa pushed her plate aside. "Remember the good old days, when you just went to the pharmacy and picked up the lice-killing shampoo?" When everyone looked at her, her face began to pinken. "Oh. Well... Head lice is actually very common among small kids." Looking somewhat desperate to change the subject, she said to Doug, "What were you able to find out about them?"

Doug yawned, which set off another chain reaction around the table. "It seems their settlement was overrun a few weeks ago at least. Silas couldn't tell us where it was or how long ago. They've been on their own a while. You saw how scrawny they are."

Mario nodded. The possibility that the children might be slight of frame had proved false as soon as their clothes were removed for their baths. He winced at the memory of their too skinny arms and prominent ribs.

"Were they alone the whole time?" he asked.

Skye shook her head. "No. There were zombies at the apartments. Silas hasn't mentioned any adults, but Violet said the one in the apartment next to where they were staying was their mother. She locked herself in the apartment next door to the one we found them in. She told them to get far away, but they stayed."

Mario shook his head, imagining Silas and Violet huddled in the apartment next to the one occupied by their undead mother.

"Jesus," Tessa muttered. "Have they seen many zombies in the area?"

"Not too many since they got farther away from their settlement," Doug answered. "But Silas did mention there were more from 'down the street.' We think he meant south. We ran into...what, three or four on the streets?" he said, looking to Skye for confirmation. "We were able to avoid them. There were a few at the hospital, but nothing we couldn't handle."

"You two shouldn't have gone to a hospital alone," Mario said.

Doug shrugged off his warning. "It paid off. I can't believe how much medicine was still there. Besides," he said, grinning mischievously at Skye. "Skye is such a badass when she's killing zombies."

Skye rolled her eyes. Doug moved his chair closer to hers and pecked her on the cheek. She was good for Doug, and not just because they were so crazy about one another. She wasn't fazed by Doug's adrenaline junkie ways. Skye had been one of the top women rock climbers in the world. Judging risk was something she had more experience with than the average person when the world changed. Doug wasn't an idiot. He rarely did anything outright stupid, but if he thought something could work, he pushed the edge when others wouldn't. But he'd become more cautious since they'd gotten together. People who didn't know him might not be able to tell, but Mario could.

All that aside, there was something special about Skye that worked with Doug. Their dynamic was different from the girl-friends that Mario had seen him with back in the day. They didn't need to tell the other to rein it in. There hadn't been too many opportunities for Mario to witness this, but Skye didn't have the air of fretful anxiety that had enveloped his previous girlfriends, especially if he shared a story about his latest forays beyond the walls. Mario wasn't throwing stones; that same fretful anxiety had surrounded him like a shroud in the early days of his and Miranda's relationship. With Doug and Skye, if anyone worried it was Doug, but so far he was doing all right.

Misery welled up in his chest at the thought of Miranda. He worked so hard to not think about her. It was more difficult to do now. Before they'd departed, he'd stuck to the Institute as much as he could, avoiding LO entirely, and kept himself busy. Sixteen-hour-days-falling-on-his-face busy. But once they left Portland—

He still didn't understand how everything had fallen apart so quickly. Why she'd shut him out like she had, nor why she'd been so angry with him. Losing the baby hadn't been his fault but she'd acted like it was. If she'd given him the slightest hint, the barest sliver, of what was eating her up inside, then maybe he wouldn't feel so baffled, but she never did. She just got more angry and remote, less *there*, until he lashed out at her as angrily as she lashed out at him.

Part of him was certain that if she'd just given him something, some reason or explanation, he could have figured it out. That was what he did; he figured shit out. He banged on problems until he found solutions. The problem-solver in him refused to believe he couldn't have fixed things with Miranda if she'd only cared enough to give him a hint.

What a fucking mess, he thought, trying to push it aside. He forced himself to pay attention to the conversation around him, to claw his way out of the mire of pain and longing that was always waiting for the opportunity to suck him under.

"I don't think so," Skye was saying. Doug had leaned back in his chair. His arm was draped loosely around her shoulders. "Neither of them mentioned a dad. If there was anyone else, they're not around anymore."

They all fell silent, and Mario could feel sleep's strong pull on everyone. Tessa slid her arm along the table and rested her head on the triangle of her bent elbow. Her eyelids drooped, shaping the blue irises of her eyes to half discs. Skye's eyes were drooping, too. One of them had to stay up for the first watch, and it was looking to Mario like he would be doing the honors.

"I guess this sets us back a few days," he said.

Doug yawned again. "Another two days, I think. Maybe we stretch it to four, to let them rest and see if we can find anyone they might know."

"Has anyone considered they might be bait for a trap?"

Mario's question was met with crumpled brows and disbelieving eyes.

"You haven't seen how deserted it is out there," Doug

scoffed. "You need to quit reading the thrillers on the yacht. Maybe try a romance."

Mario saw the flinch as Doug realized what he'd said. He waved it away, giving Doug an indulgent shake of his head.

Doug said, "Looks like we're all aunties and uncles for the foreseeable future. At least we've got a pro right here."

Mario made himself smile, but it felt like a lie on his lips. He'd done his best to be a good father, better than his own dad, anyway, which hadn't been hard. That bar was so low he could have stumbled over it blackout drunk. He hadn't known what he was doing half the time, had winged it as he went, but Emily said she felt the same way and she was a natural. They hadn't been the best husband and wife to one another, and Mario knew that a lot—most—of that was on him, but he and Emily had parented well together. They'd played to each other's strengths, balanced out the weaknesses. Even with the... Mario didn't know what to call it, had always resisted giving it a name. The episode? The mistake? Or as Doug had suggested, the manipulation? Even with that, Emily was a wonderful mother. Her confidence that he was a good father had given him the confidence to believe it, too.

But that was before he left his children behind. Before Tadpole. Before he knew that there were still new ways for his heart to break. Mario didn't want anyone looking to him as an expert. He didn't want the responsibility, because he didn't want to be the culpable party when it all fell apart.

"You're all falling on your faces," Mario said. "I'll take first watch."

"See," Doug said. "He's already staying up all night with the kiddos. We're gonna be fine."

5

MIRANDA'S STOMACH GROWLED, so loud that Rich's head cocked.

"You or me?" he asked.

"Definitely me," she said. "I'm so freaking hungry."

Rich nodded. "Just knowing how tight we are on food makes me hungry. I know the scavenging parties have already started but..."

His voice trailed away, and Miranda understood why. There was lots of food in the world that was still good, expiration dates notwithstanding, but it wasn't nearby. Miranda and her friends planned to pick up what they could on their way back but they were only four people, and on foot, until they reached the bridge. The scouting they'd do for future trips would be their most beneficial contribution to the food effort this time.

Despite all this, their spirits were high. They'd spent another three very quiet days at Nanitch Lodge. Miranda and Rich led parts of the horde on a merry chase farther up the mountain before giving them the slip and sneaking back to the lodge. They could have just walked through the horde the day after they arrived and pulled ahead of them, but then they'd have an entourage. Even if it was miles behind them, there was no telling what attention a parade of zombies might attract. About a third of the original horde was still around when they left, and they'd outpaced them quickly.

Phineas sidled up to Miranda and slung his arm around her shoulders. He grinned at her, his teeth flashing bright against his dark skin. "Just say the word, Miranda. I'll be happy to take your mind off being hungry for food."

Miranda laughed and nudged into him. "You're incorrigible."

"We both know the truth, babe," Phineas replied, his grin widening. He gave her shoulder a squeeze, then released her. "I don't know why you keep fighting it."

"He's gonna wear you down one day," Rich said.

"Don't encourage him," Miranda said, giving Rich a good-natured glare. She said to Alec, "I saved his life once, and he's been a lovesick puppy ever since."

"He doesn't look like a puppy to me. I'd say Phineas is more of a strapping young lad looking to prove his worth."

"I like this guy," Phineas said.

Miranda said, "Forget it, kid." Then to Alec, though she was grinning, "Don't encourage his delusions."

The good cheer and high spirits continued, as did the teasing for a few more minutes. Even though the weapons cache had been a bust and most of the P-Land group was dead, Miranda was enjoying herself. They had a survivor, which was more than she'd expected, and another bolt-hole to add to the list. It was remote, so they'd probably never use it, but that was beside the point. It was beautiful on the mountain, green and lush, with huge pines and firs towering overhead, filled with birdsong and the scurry and chitter of animals. Most had lost their fear of humans, with only the older generation of longer-lived species being especially wary. None of the animals stuck around to investigate, but the curious stares were longer. One of the few good things about zombies was that they didn't eat animals. Humans were the only food source—and infection vector—that interested them. Miranda knew there were still threats to the environment and wildlife—nuclear power plants that had melted down, and toxic chemical dumps without humans to maintain them—but on the whole, the nature had been the post-apocalyptic world's only winner. She was glad there was at least one.

They set a brisk pace, following the remnants of the road at first. It petered out after two miles, a washed-out section the initial chink in civilization's foray into the wilderness. More sections had washed out and eroded, accelerating the cycle, until it was almost impossible to tell where the road had been. The semi-solitude of the hike was a double-edged sword. It was nice to not have many conversational demands; they didn't talk much, mostly out of habit. Right now, though, Miranda didn't like the space it gave her mind to wander to things she'd rather not think about—mostly Tadpole. How different things would be if she hadn't lost him, and—

Delilah barked, then crashed off into the underbrush.

"Delilah!" Miranda shouted, quiet forgotten as she watched the pit bull shoot off like a rocket. "Leave it!"

Delilah didn't look back, nor break her stride, still barking like a maniac.

"Goddammit. I'll be right back, guys," Miranda said, not bothering to wait for an answer.

A second later, Phineas caught up with her. They picked up the pace. It wasn't smart to go off on her own, even if she could repel zombies, though concern that Phineas' recently healed broken leg might not be up to this steeplechase niggled at her. Within a minute, all thoughts but watching her footing were driven from her mind as she darted through the trees, jumped over fallen logs, and ducked under branches.

"Good thing there are hardly any zombies up here," Phineas grunted.

"Tell me about it," she said, a little breathless.

They pressed on, following Delilah's barking. Miranda looked ahead and thought she saw Delilah stop. The pit bull's growls and agitated barking continued.

"She's just ahead," Phineas panted. "I see her."

Delilah's barking set birds in the trees above them into the air. Then a high-pitched, terror-filled squeal cut through the forest.

"Delilah!" Miranda cried, anxiety skyrocketing.

A burst of energy propelled her forward. She leaped over a downed log, then lurched to a halt in a small clearing. Delilah crashed through the underbrush, squealing and yipping. She zoomed by, in the direction they had just come, a caramel-brown blur of motion.

Phineas caught up to her. "What the fuck was that? Where is she going?"

Miranda scanned the clearing. "I don't know—"

Her words dried up, crumbling inside her mouth like dry autumn leaves. Fear flooded her body, and a cold sweat that had nothing to do with her sprint slicked her skin. A rumbling growl, followed by an agitated snarl, filled the clearing. Miranda's feet rooted themselves to the ground.

Phineas said, "Holy shit."

Miranda had seen her share of exotic animals, released from zoos by well-meaning zookeepers, when it became apparent that humanity was getting its ass handed to them. The cat roared from a boulder above them on the other side of the clearing, hackles raised along the orange and black fur of its spine. Its pink nose crinkled over peeled-back lips, revealing inches of long, sharp incisors. Its rounded ears were almost lost, flattened back against the massive head. The menace and death in the golden eyes wasn't a threat, but a promise. Miranda felt as mesmerized as Mowgli, the boy from *The Jungle Book* raised by wolves. Only this time, the hypnotist wasn't a snake using psychedelic eyes, but slashes of black covering the white and orange face of a tiger.

A strangled gasp of terror scraped out of her mouth. The tiger's proportions were massive: seven feet long from shoulder to haunch, paws like dinner plates, and easily three feet tall at its front shoulder. A long tail stretched behind it, twitching in agitation. Raised above them on the boulder, it looked like it could leap the twenty-foot clearing in a single bound.

Miranda could hear the rasp of Phineas' ragged breath alongside her own. The tiger roared again, the sound echoing through the forest and reverberating in the marrow of Miranda's bones. Should she try to shoot it? She wasn't sure she could draw fast enough, despite the distance between them. Tigers were fast; she knew that much from stories she'd heard. Her heart twinged at the idea of killing such a magnificent beast because her stupid-ass dog—who was going on a leash for the rest of her life—had been idiot enough to chase a predator that could eat her in one bite. But she didn't want to be eaten today, and if it came down to her or the tiger, she wasn't going down without a fight.

"Do y-you...know...what...t-t-t-to do?" Phineas stuttered.

Miranda shook her head infinitesimally, afraid the movement might increase the tiger's ire. Then a tiny, fuzzy orange and black head popped up from behind the boulder near the tiger's hind paws. A moment later, it was followed by another, and another, and still one more, until four little cubs blinked at them from the shadow of their mother's deadly protection.

"Fuck," Miranda breathed.

The tiger had cubs. Delilah had probably chased one of them until she ran afoul of mama tiger. Now, mama tiger was doing what any mother—no matter the species—does: protecting her babies. A rush of empathy for the mama tiger welled inside Miranda's breast. She knew how it felt when your child was threatened. She knew how primal it was, how deep the instinct to protect, to sacrifice, felt. How you'd do anything —cut off a limb, leave your home, sell your soul—to keep your baby safe. She'd failed to protect her baby, been powerless to save him. But she knew how it felt to be ready to take on the world, even if it meant your death, if it would keep your child safe.

"Shit," Phineas whimpered.

They had to do something to save themselves, but shooting that tiger and orphaning her cubs was out of the question—for Miranda, at least.

She kept her voice low. "We're gonna back up, okay? Real slow."

"What?" Phineas squeaked.

"She doesn't want us. She just wants her babies safe. We can't outrun her, and if we turn tail, she'll probably attack."

At least, that's what Miranda thought the tiger would do. Dogs chased if you ran, and you weren't supposed to run from mountain lions, but back away, fight if you had to. But this was no mountain lion. Resistance—apart from a firearm—would be futile.

Miranda said, "Ready?"

She saw Phineas' tiny nod from the corner of her eye.

"We're going real slow, no sudden movements." She took a shallow breath, her pounding heart roaring in her ears. She flinched when the tiger roared again. "Take your time to find your footing. Slow and easy. One, two, three."

She raised her foot, slowly, like thick honey on a cold morning. She put her foot behind her, touching it lightly on the ground before placing it down, toe to heel. Then her other foot, touch down lightly, toe to heel. Her eyes were riveted to the tiger. She kept track of Phineas in her peripheral vision. Even though its mouth was still contorted into a snarl, the tiger's ears raised from its head. It snarled again, a menacing rumble in its throat, but it didn't roar. One of the cubs climbed up on the boulder and walked under its mother. It roared at them, a tiny squeak, as if to say, 'Don't mess with my mom!' It was so charming that despite her terror, the corners of Miranda's mouth quirked in a smile.

They continued backward at a snail's pace. Now twenty feet from the clearing, Miranda could still see the tiger. Mama tiger still watched them retreat, but her body language had relaxed. She even licked the head of one of her cubs. After another ten feet of crawling retreat, Miranda heard the tiger chuff low in its throat. She lowered her massive head, gently butting it against the most playful of the cubs, then turned away. She stepped off the boulder onto higher ground, waiting only long enough to make sure her babies were following.

"Holy shit," Phineas said. "Holy shit, holy shit, holy shit."

The tiger, followed by her tumbling, rassling cubs, tail now moving languidly behind, disappeared into the forest.

"Holy shit," Miranda said, echoing Phineas.

"We're still alive, right? I'm not dreaming this?"

Miranda's laugh was high and sounded a little unhinged. "No thanks to my fucking dog."

She looked over to Phineas. If his eyes got any wider, they'd take up his entire face.

"Let's get the fuck out of here," he said.

As one, they turned, and crashed through the forest.

"Is this the right way?" Miranda asked after a few minutes. "It doesn't look right."

"It's away from the tiger. That's all I care about!"

Miranda reached out and grabbed Phineas' arm. "Wait," she said, her chest heaving. She pulled him to a stop. "This isn't the way we came."

Phineas stopped, though he looked like he didn't want to. He turned in a circle, taking in their surroundings.

"We got a little turned around," he said. "As long as it's away from the tiger..." His voice trailed, then he said, "What's that?"

He didn't sound panic-stricken, so at least whatever he saw wasn't another tiger. She followed the line of his pointing hand. Miranda squinted, then took a step forward. The hillside in front of them sloped up toward Mount Hood, which told her they had indeed gotten very turned around. A hundred feet to their right, the ground lowered, making a bowl-shaped depression. On the bowl's far side, a boulder jutted out from the hillside, forming an overhang covering what looked like a cave, but the lines were all wrong. The boulder had lichen and moss growing on it, and some fallen branches and years of pine needles lay in drifts on it, but it was too straight.

Phineas said, "Is that a door?"

"Let's check it out," she said, unease prickling over the back of her neck.

They walked closer, scanning their surroundings as they progressed toward the boulder. The closer they got, the more Miranda realized it wasn't a boulder. It wasn't even natural. On either side below it, slanting inward just a few degrees, were cast concrete supports that connected with the underside. It looked like a lintel.

"That's a door," Phineas said, his voice low and a little awestruck.

"Oh my God," Miranda murmured.

Phineas was right. Recessed fifteen feet into what Miranda had first mistaken for a cave, stood a blast door painted with splotches of green, brown, and gray. It was wide enough for a large vehicle, maybe even a truck, to drive through, and about twelve feet high. She heard a high-pitched buzz. Above the door, a tiny red light blinked, affixed to the top of a security camera. The camera swept left to right and then back again, the buzz only pausing at the apex of each sweep of direction. Had she not been looking at an unmarked door built into the side of a mountain, she'd have thought it was a mosquito.

Phineas turned to her, thunderstruck, and said, "It's a bunker."

***

AN HOUR LATER, EVERYONE WAS BACK AT THE BLAST door. Miranda and Phineas blazed their route once they established where east was, which had been easy because Mount Hood was east of Portland. They eventually stumbled onto a section of road they'd already traveled, so finding Rich and Alec had been pretty straightforward. Delilah had been with them, with a long cut, not quite a gash, on her left hind leg from her run-in with the tigers. It wasn't very deep, and she was still alive, so it must have been one of the cubs she'd tangled with. Rich had already given her first aid and tied a length of paracord to her collar, so they'd been ready to go once the tiger adventure, and subsequent discovery, had been recounted.

"I don't think we'll be able to hack this keypad," Rich said. "Someone might be able to, but I don't have the skills."

"Who built this?" Phineas wondered. "And why is it out here?"

Alec said, "It doesn't look military. Was there anything of strategic importance in Portland?"

"Not that I know of," Miranda said. "They didn't usually put secret bases near metropolitan areas."

"That you know of," Rich said.

She looked up at the camera again. "Hello? Anyone there?"

The camera continued its lazy sweep, left to right, right to left, every thirty minutes. Clearly, it was automated.

"Maybe it was one of those prepper people," Alec said. "You know, who stored supplies to ride out nuclear wars and such?"

Miranda shrugged. If this was a prepper bunker, it was someone with a lot of money. How they'd built anything like this so close to Portland, and on Mount Hood, would have required serious connections, maybe even payoffs and bribes.

Rich said, his voice thoughtful, "There were a lot of hate groups, white supremacists, and separatists in the northwest. Could one of those groups have built it?"

Miranda said, "They'd have needed to be well-funded. This land wasn't cheap." She bit her lip, brow furrowing, as she looked around the forest. "It doesn't seem like a very good location to bug out to, though. There's a water source with the stream, but there's nowhere to grow food out here without clearing the land."

"Wouldn't the area have been crawling with zombies early on, being so close to the city?" Alec asked.

Phineas nodded. "Getting here wouldn't have been a sure thing. There are so many bridges in Portland. They all ended up being choke points."

"Unless you were rich enough to have a personal helicopter," Miranda said.

Rich said, "True. So, what do y'all want to do? There might

be people in there, but if there are, they don't seem in a hurry to answer the door. And it might be empty."

"We should—" Phineas began, but Miranda cut him off.

"Let's talk over there," she said, motioning away from the blast door.

"Why?" Phineas asked.

But she was already walking away, followed by Alec and Rich. Delilah limped along beside her. When they clustered together again, she said to Phineas, "There are microphones and speakers over there. If there's anyone there, we don't want them knowing what we're thinking, or to give away anything about LO."

"That is a whole new level of paranoia, Miranda," Phineas said. "Even for you."

"With what happened recently, it's not," Rich countered.

Phineas scowled at them for a moment, but didn't argue further. "We should go home and tell Rocco," he said. "Let him decide what to do. There are tigers out here."

"Aren't you the least bit curious about what's inside?" Alec asked the younger man. His face lit up as he speculated. "If it was someone's bolt-hole, it might have food, especially if whoever built it isn't here. Though that still leaves us needing to get inside."

"I was thinking about food, too. There could be a lot in a place like this," Miranda said, looking to Rich. "We can't ignore this, and I'm dying to know what's inside. How about we camp out?"

Phineas said, "There are tigers."

Miranda waved his protest away. "She was just defending her cubs. She's not interested in us, and we're not going to chase after her like *some dogs*," she said, staring at Delilah for a moment. "If we stretch, we have a week's worth of rations. We're far enough from the Nanitch Lodge that those zombies won't get here right away, if they even make it this far. Rich and I can keep you two safe. Let's stay a night or two... We'll leave if we need to. Maybe if we camp out on their doorstep, they'll let us in."

"I'm game," Rich said. "There's an overhang if it rains, and enough of us to have a good watch rotation."

"That's the spirit," Alec said, grinning.

"But there are *tigers*," Phineas moaned, almost whining.

"Just a night or two," Rich said to him, amusement suffusing his voice. "I won't let any tigers eat ya. Zombies neither."

Phineas' shoulders slumped in defeat. He turned and trudged back to the blast door, Rich following.

"You don't really think this will work, do you?" Alec asked Miranda. Despite his query, he looked excited, like they were now on a bona fide adventure.

She shrugged, then grinned at him, his excitement infectious. "No idea. But a secret bunker is super cool."

"I do feel a wee bit guilty making poor Phineas stay. The tiger really shook him up."

Miranda snorted. "It was fucking terrifying. I knew they were big, but dude... It was massively big. Like jump the clearing in a single bound big. The cubs were super cute, but the mama was terrifying. I don't even want to think about how much bigger the males are." A shiver ran down her spine. Male tigers had to be as big as baby elephants. "Don't worry about Phineas. He'll be back to wooing me by morning."

"How do you think he'd react if you ever said yes?"

Miranda blinked, surprised at the question. She'd never thought about it, because it didn't mean anything. It was just her and Phineas' thing.

"I don't know," she said. "He's a smart kid, though. He'd probably run with it."

THEY DISCOVERED THE GENTLY GRADED RAMP SOON AFTER setting up camp. After ten years of forest debris falling on it, it had been easy to miss it. They'd thought it was the ground that sloped, given that the entrance was built into the high side of a bowl-shaped depression, and it was a shallow angle, perhaps five degrees. Rich and Phineas had found what they thought might be remnants of the path leading to it, based on trees that were smaller, with sparser undergrowth. It was all conjecture, of course, but it passed the time.

They set up around a small campfire, passing the time by playing cards and shooting the shit. Every so often Miranda would walk over to the door and ask if anyone was there, and announce their intention to stay for as long as it took. By early evening, she was so tired that she said she'd take a later watch. She'd barely slept the night before, her dreams full of deformed zombie infants.

She slept a good few hours into the evening, if the level of grogginess upon waking was any indication. She always felt groggy after a good snooze when she came into it with a sleep deficit. Delilah had wriggled close alongside Miranda's front, since she slept on her side. The pit bull's soft breath sighed in and out, and the fire crackled.

Alec and Rich sat at the fire, their backs to her, speaking softly. It was nice to just lie there, listening to the sound of their voices and the rain and Delilah's even breathing. The soft lilt of Alec's Scots accent—still new to her ear—sounded musical.

"—think we had maybe ten doses at the time," Rich said. "They used six of them on me. I got the first two within half an hour of being bitten, and the rest soon after. Then I almost died anyway, but the Lord was watching out for me."

Miranda listened to Rich telling Alec how he'd become a

zombie repeller, shocked that he was giving away the secret, even though Alec had seen their ability with his own eyes. Despite knowing him for only a short time, Miranda believed Alec would keep his mouth shut. He'd told them about his work as a reporter. Assuming he wasn't blowing smoke up their asses, he'd been part of a team that broke a huge government scandal in Britain that caught the rest of the British press flat-footed. A person couldn't pull off a story like that without keeping secrets.

Miranda could hear the astonishment in Alec's voice. "Your vaccine does that? It works after the fact?"

"Well, that's the thing. We don't know. It worked on me within thirty minutes of being bitten. I'm the only one, so." Miranda saw Rich's shoulders rise and fall. "One person is not a representative sample. The only way it can be studied is if it happens again, since control groups with placebos won't fly. The repelling we do understand. AB negative blood type and a strong—usually life-threatening—reaction to the vaccine seems to do it."

"AB negative? That's one of less common ones."

"Less than one percent of the population."

"And you've two people with it?" Alec said.

Rich chuckled. "Three, actually, but the third person isn't at LO anymore."

"Wow."

Wonder filled Alec's voice, and Miranda realized how miraculous it must seem to someone looking in from the outside. She was so used to it now she never thought about it.

After a good ten minutes, Alec said, "You said you were the only one to get the vaccine after being bitten, but Miranda repels them, too. I saw the scar on her hand."

Her pulse skyrocketed. She didn't think Rich would tell Alec what had happened, but if she 'woke up' right now, they might realize that she'd been listening. She held her breath, indecision battling with the desire to keep her private life private.

"That's not my story to tell," Rich said. His voice softened. "Miranda's good people, and she's been through a lot. If you get to hear her story, it'll be because she decides to share it with you."

If she hadn't already been lying down, the relief that she felt would have sent her slithering to the floor to collect in a puddle. Miranda felt her heart begin to slow, and the muscles she hadn't realized had tightened relaxed.

"You're right. I'm sorry, Rich. I'm certainly not trying to pry into her private affairs. It's the reporter in me."

She could practically see the shrug of Rich's shoulders when he said, "I should have taken more care choosing my words when the person I'm talking to is intelligent enough to parse them so well."

Alec chuckled. "My granny used to say my curiosity would be the death of me. It's why I became a reporter. Best job in the world. Getting paid to ask uncomfortable questions to lying prats. There's nothing like it, especially when you catch them in a lie."

Rich laughed softly. His voice still sounded amused, but there was an undertone of warning when he said, "Questions are fine, so long as you know you won't always get an answer."

A rush of affection for her friend hit Miranda all at once. Hearing Rich's protective tone felt like a salve. Even if he wasn't talking about her just now, she knew his protectiveness included her. It was the kind of thing Doug might have said, before their argument. Maybe even still—she had no way of knowing. And Mario—

She squelched the thought, and the irritation that came with it. She didn't want to deal with the anger that flared when she let herself think about him. She could feel it hot on the irritation's heels, and she didn't need that right now. Didn't need it at all. When he'd left with Doug, Skye, and Tessa, she'd felt nothing. If she hadn't experienced it herself, she wouldn't have believed it. But after they left, the anger returned. Whatever had numbed her out in the six weeks leading up to their departure evaporated almost as soon as they left.

She wondered if the detachment had been fallout from killing Jeremiah that she'd mistaken for emotionally uncoupling from Mario. She'd talked to River about killing Jeremiah a bit, but only because she knew people expected her to. She felt justified, even though killing a person was different from killing a zombie, even a person as depraved as Jeremiah had been. Everything he represented—greed, insanity, depravity, predation—were not subjects she wanted to dwell on. Whatever the cause, it turned out that her anger with Mario hadn't faded after all. It had only gotten worse.

She thought again about getting up, but she didn't have to pee, and Delilah was warm and snuggly. She closed her eyes and let the soft, lazy drawl of the American South and the lilting burr of the Scottish Highlands weave together as the two men talked quietly. Without even meaning to, she drifted off.

"I THINK WE NEED TO CALL IT."

She knew Rich was right. As frustrating as it was to admit defeat, her on-the-fly plan had produced zero results.

"I know," she said. "It was stupid to think it would work. There's probably nobody in there." She turned around and looked into the camera. She and Phineas had been sitting outside the blast door, as if their presence would suddenly make the door open. "But just in case, just so you know, we're coming back. If anyone's in there, we'd really like to talk to you."

The camera's light blinked at her. Oh well, she thought. It had been fun to spend so much time with Phineas. He was funny and irreverent and the running joke that he would one day get a date with her was so ridiculous that it always made her laugh. She'd enjoyed getting to know Alec, too. He was smart and had a sly sense of humor. So sly that sometimes it took her a second or two to catch up. And he didn't ask stupid questions. She had no evidence to support the feeling, other than these limited interactions, but he seemed like a good guy. Time would tell.

"It's about time we get out of here," Phineas grumbled. "Freaking tigers and God knows what else in these woods... elephants and polar bears. I want to get behind the palisade."

"You're thinking about it all wrong, laddie," Alec said as Miranda joined him and Rich at the bottom of the ramp. He raised his voice so that Phineas, still by the blast door fifteen feet away, could hear. "If you spin it right, just think of the stories you can tell some pretty lass... How you faced down the fierce She-Tiger before realizing she was only defending her cubs. That's danger, bravery, and kindness to baby animals all in one. They'll be throwing their knickers at you."

Miranda snorted, and Rich laughed out loud. Phineas shrugged into his pack and stepped out from under the lintel.

"I never thought of that," he said, his face contemplative, then he jutted his chin at Miranda. "But she'll probably ruin it for me by telling what really happened. I'll look like an idiot."

"Phineas," Miranda said, amused but dead serious. "If making the story into what Alec just said will get you laid, I promise— Move, Phineas! Now!"

She had no idea how it was there and none of them had seen it, except that the zombie wasn't upright. Everything about it was a color found in the litter of twigs, stones, leaves, and branches on the forest floor. The skin was the same grayish-brown as the stones and boulders. The wisps of filthy, matted hair still attached to patches of its scalp the dull yellow of dead leaves. The scraps of drab brown shirt were so ragged and dirty that it was impossible to tell what color it had been before.

The zombie's ragged stumps of fingers curled around the lintel's edge, directly above Phineas. It pulled itself forward, enough to peer down. One more pull and it would topple down on him. Phineas looked at her, puzzled. The zombie moaned. Miranda sprinted to him as he looked up, eyes widening in slow motion. The zombie tugged itself forward and tumbled over the edge. Miranda barreled forward, colliding with Phineas just as the zombie hit him.

Miranda's momentum slammed all of them against the blast door. The zombie's moans mixed with Phineas' bark of surprise and Delilah's growls. Miranda found herself in a tangle of arms and legs as Phineas tried to wriggle free. She grabbed the zombie, its cold flesh yielding like putty under her fingertips. She shoved it away, out from under the lintel. It found its footing and lurched toward her, then abruptly pulled back. She took a step forward and it stumbled backward.

"That's right, fucker! Run!"

The zombie staggered away from her. She pulled her knife and followed. It turned back, and lacking the brain power to realize it had just run away from her, lurched forward to make a second pass. It jerked away again. Miranda rammed her knife into the zombie's eye. It went slack, and she tugged the knife free. Black goo leaked from the gash, dripping from the knife's point.

"It's clear up here," Rich said, slightly breathless. He stood above the entrance to the blast door, his cheeks flushed from exertion. Alec gave Phineas a hand up. He stepped out from under the lintel and into the brighter light. He shook, teeth chattering. His eyes were so wide and afraid that he looked much younger than his twenty years.

When Miranda hugged him, he added, "The shit I do to get your attention."

"Let's go, before something else happens," Rich said. "We've had enough misadventures—"

A squawk of static interrupted him. Miranda looked at Rich, confused.

"Excuse me," a tinny voice said.

She turned to the camera, which was bobbing up and down, as if nodding at them—to get their attention?

A voice said, "Excuse me. Uh, hello."

Miranda looked at Alec. Rich had come down from above the entrance to stand beside them. Both were looking at the camera. So was Phineas, whose mouth had fallen open.

Slowly, Miranda said, "Hello?"

"Um... Do you want to come inside?"

They all looked at one another, uncertain. They'd been out here for two nights with no response, but now they were being invited in?

"You've been watching us the whole time?" Rich said.

"Yes," said the voice.

"Why now?" Miranda asked. The timing made her spidey sense tingle.

"You want to come in, right?" the voice said.

"What do you think?" Miranda said to Rich, voice so low only he could hear. Or so she hoped...who knew how good the microphones on the camera were.

"I think we should check it out," Rich said, but he sounded uncertain.

"First tigers, now this," Phineas muttered.

Ideally, they should all agree. Alec nudged her with his

elbow and whispered, "Where's your sense of adventure?" He looked up at the camera and said, "Aye, we want to come in."

"Okay," the voice said.

A deep clunk reverberated under Miranda's feet, followed by a low pneumatic hiss. And then, slowly—centimeter by centimeter—the door began to swing open.

6

THE WIDE, rectangular door swung open. Miranda said to Rich, "Should we all go?"

"I'm going," Phineas said. "I'm not staying outside with tigers roaming around."

Rich said, "I don't think splitting up is a good idea."

"Nor do I," Alec said.

As a group, they stepped over the threshold. Track lighting was built into the gray concrete walls near the ceiling. Ahead, Miranda saw another blast door. The space between the two doors was large enough for the second door to open while a truck was between them.

"Please move inside so I can shut the outer door," the voice said.

They complied. When the door thudded shut behind them, Miranda felt a sharp stab of dread. Whoever that voice belonged to might be a psycho, or a group of psychos.

"Or they might just be regular people," she muttered to herself.

"What's that?" Alec asked.

"Nothing," she said, flashing him a nervous smile. "Just talking myself off the ledge."

―――――

THERE WAS ANOTHER DEEP *THUNK*, THEN A PNEUMATIC hiss from the door in front of them, and it, too, began to swing open. Delilah whimpered. When Miranda looked down, she could see that the pit bull's hackles were raised, and her tail curled between her legs to her tummy. Miranda dropped down beside her, and petted Delilah from her shoulders to her rump.

"It's okay, Liley," she said, making a mental note to calm down. "I'm here with you. It's okay."

While Delilah would always have her own assessment and reactions to a new environment, she also took cues from Miranda. Right now, Miranda was really anxious. Kind of scared, honestly, but excited, too. After Delilah relaxed some, untucking her tail a bit, Miranda stood up. Alec, Rich, and Phineas were all ahead of her. Once they were over the second threshold, the door swung shut behind them with a smooth, hydraulic hiss. They all glanced at one another, then started down the long corridor.

Rich said, "Can any of you see the end?" When a chorus of 'No' answered him, he added, "How long do you think this is?"

"Doors ahead," Miranda said, pointing to two doors set into the walls, across from one another.

The doors looked like they belonged in a bank vault. One was solid, the word MECHANICAL stenciled on the gray steel. The door across from it was almost identical, but had an inset window. SECURITY was stenciled below the window, but the room was dark. Rows of small lights—red, yellow, green, and white—were lit up along the wall.

"Do you think security being unattended means there aren't many people here?" Alec asked softly.

No one answered, since they didn't know. One by one, they stepped away from the window and continued down the corridor. From this point on, it began to slope down.

"What do you think the angle is on this?" Phineas asked. "Ten degrees?"

"Not even close," Miranda said. She stopped and looked at the angle of her foot. "It's hardly anything...two or three degrees, maybe."

She looked up when Rich said, "There's a wall ahead. The ramp must switchback."

They continued, the silence thickening until it seemed to have stuffed the wide corridor around them with foam. At the wide landing, the corridor did indeed switchback one hundred eighty degrees. The angle of the slope remained the same. They walked the same distance by Miranda's step count before rounding a second, and then a third switchback.

"How deep are we?" Phineas asked.

He sounded anxious. Miranda glanced his way. His eyes were as big as dinner plates, but he looked excited, too.

"If we assume a three-degree slope over five hundred feet three times," she said, doing the math. "About forty-five feet. But if it's two degrees, then it's around thirty."

Rich whistled. "Whoever this is, they are not playing around."

Alec said, "There's a door ahead."

Miranda saw that he was right. This door was different. It looked like an airlock from a sci-fi spaceship, with an inset window. The light above it went from red to green. They went through into an airlock, Delilah requiring only a little coaxing. The door on the other side of the airlock also had an inset window. They crowded around it. Miranda stood on tiptoe, craning her neck to see over Phineas' head. An open hallway was straight across from the door, but the central opening narrowed, offering only a six-foot-wide field of vision. She saw two pieces of furniture—the end of a couch and the corner of an upholstered chair. The floors were wood, and the plants looked real.

"A living room?" Rich asked.

"It's open to another chamber on the far side, but I can't get a good look," Miranda said. She tried to see what was on either side of the opening to the left and right. A corridor similar to the ones they had just traveled, but half as wide, curved out of sight.

"I think it's round," Alec said, just as Miranda was about to say the same. "Are there converted missile silos in the area?"

"Those silos were out in the middle of nowhere," Rich said softly.

The voice crackled over the speakers again, making everyone jump. "I don't suppose you're willing to leave your guns there?"

It was an odd choice of words. Miranda traded a glance with Rich. He looked around for the camera and spoke to it.

"I'm afraid not," he said.

His voice oozed a friendliness that he made sound genuine. It just might be, Miranda thought, because Rich was that kind of guy.

He continued. "I know we're on your patch, but that puts us at a disadvantage, and there are only four of us. I'd sure feel better if you'd let us bring all our gear with us. I'm Rich," he added. "This is Miranda, Alec, and Phineas, and the dog is Delilah. If that's not acceptable to you, we'll leave."

There was a long pause, then the voice said, "What settlement are you from?"

Wary glances were traded among the group. From the look on Rich's face, Miranda knew he would play it straight.

"We're out toward Beaverton."

"Oh," the voice said, sounding warmer than before. "You're in the park?"

Miranda said, under her breath, "Who the hell is this guy?"

Rich shrugged almost imperceptibly, then said, "Yes."

Miranda had never heard Rich sound unnerved, until now.

After a long pause, the voice said, "Is the dog trained?"

This is getting fucking weird, Miranda thought. Aloud, she said, "She's basically a couch potato who thinks she's a lap dog. She's very friendly." As an afterthought, she added, "I'll clean up after her, of course."

Another long pause. Then the voice said, "Okay. You can keep your weapons. We're armed, too, just so there are no surprises. The second door won't open until the airlock is closed. Please walk straight through to the central dining area."

The sound from the speaker clicked off.

"Dining area," Alec said, his low voice faux-impressed. "He said it like it's something fancy. D'ya think it has a Michelin star?"

They closed the airlock door behind them. Almost immediately, a loud click came from the other door, and a whirring sound. The light switched from red to green. They all looked at one another. Miranda reached for the lever, turning it ninety degrees. She gave the door a push, then stepped through. She found herself in a finished concrete corridor similar to the ones they had just traveled but half as wide; it curved out of sight in both directions. The ceiling overhead was much higher than in the airlock or entry corridor. Indirect lighting glowed above them. The ceiling arched up and away from the wall.

Eye- and foot-level track lighting was built into the corridor wall. The corridor curved out of sight in both directions, the concrete walls stained a light tan. Indirect, overhead lighting made the space feel airy. To their left along the inner wall of the corridor were doors, with signs: Bedroom 1 and Bedroom 2, presumably with more beyond the curve.

They walked straight ahead, into a room shaped like a piece of pie. Shelves lined the walls, with games, books, and other knickknacks—the kinds of items found in any home. The furniture looked expensive but comfortable. There were a lot of plants, some suspended from the ceiling, others in planters that jutted out from the wall. The room reminded Miranda of a hotel lounge.

"Wow," Rich said softly.

They kept walking into a huge circular room. A round disc of light hovered at the ceiling's central apex twenty feet above them. Suspended around the disc's edge were chandeliers—tangles of small white lights that looked like a collection bird nests. Curved dining tables of gray wood, with matching chairs lining both sides, faced one another in the center of the room. They resembled halves of a circle, arranged with a gap that formed a pathway through the center of the room.

"It's a dome," Alec said, wonder in his voice. "This room must be fifty feet wide."

Miranda trailed her hand along the smooth wood of one of the tables. Directly across from the pie-shaped room they'd walked through was another room just like it. There were four in all, like the arms and post of a cross. The narrower ends were adjacent to this center room, and the wider ends were along the curved hallway.

This central room had activity rooms along its edge, between the openings to the pie-shaped lounges. All had curved glass walls with sliding glass doors.

"That curved glass must have cost bank," Miranda said softly.

The glass was opaque, a smokey brownish-gray that should have been an ugly color but wasn't. Each door had an acid-etched name on it. Classroom and Gym were next to one another, flanked on either end by one of the lounges, likewise for Theater and Library. A double-sized, pie-shaped room housed the kitchen, which was a gleaming oasis of industrial stainless steel left open to the dining area. The last of these activity rooms, the same size as the kitchen, was labeled Medical/Surgical.

Rich turned to Miranda. "Where are they?"

She shrugged, but Rich was right. The voice had said we, but no one was here. The security room they'd passed was operational, if the blinking lights were any indication, but it wasn't manned. That was weird. Whoever had gone to the trouble to build this place didn't strike her as the type who would neglect security, so where were the people? Weren't they as curious about newcomers from the world they had shut themselves away from as Miranda and her friends were about them?

Footsteps from the outer corridor caught everyone's attention. They sounded like they were coming from the dome's far side. Everyone tensed.

"Don't be threatening," Rich said. "Keep your hands away from your guns."

They waited; an electric fizz of excitement filled Miranda's chest. She wanted to know who was here and who had built this place. A man walked through the lounge on the far side, stopping well short of them. He held a pistol in one hand. Miranda could tell immediately that he wasn't comfortable with it. He stood, looking at them but saying nothing.

Finally, Rich said, "Hello."

"Hi."

Miranda studied the man. There was nothing remarkable

about him, apart from the fact that he was here. He stood about five foot ten and looked to be maybe in his early forties. His light-brown hair was combed back from his face, and he wore a slightly scruffy beard of the same color, but with a slight tint of red. His eyes were brown, and he looked nervous as hell.

Rich said, "Thanks for letting us in. This place is something."

The man nodded, glancing around the room. "Sure."

"I'm Rich," Rich said, stepping forward with his hand extended.

The man started, surprised, and Rich stopped. Then he collected himself and came close enough to offer his hand.

"I'm Kendall," he said.

His voice was surprisingly deep, though Miranda wasn't sure why it seemed so to her. Phineas and Alec introduced themselves to Kendall, who reminded her of an old-fashioned doll with stiff, articulated limbs. Miranda still held Delilah by her leash. Delilah strained against it, tail wagging.

"Do you want to meet Delilah? One of the guys can hold her."

For the first time, a relaxed display of emotion crossed Kendall's face. "I like dogs," he said, fishing in his pocket. He pulled out a dog biscuit—the kind that used to be sold in stores. Miranda stared for a moment. They had dog biscuits here?

Delilah's tail wagged hard enough to whip up a tornado. Kendall offered the biscuit, which she took from his hand. After she finished munching, he petted her, starting with her chin. The pittie scooted closer and sat on his foot, head upturned to beg for more. Kendall laughed, the sound scratchy, like his vocal cords were rusty from disuse. Then he straightened up.

Miranda held out her hand. "I'm—"

"Miranda," he finished for her. "I remember." She must

have looked confused because he said, "You introduced yourselves on the speaker."

"Right, of course."

Kendall's hand was cool, but his shake was firm. His eye
contact, not so much. His eyes kept sliding away from
whomever he was talking to.

"Can I let her off the leash?" Miranda asked. "She'll take
off to explore."

"Uh..." Kendall hesitated. Miranda was about to retract the
question when he said, "Yes. That would be okay."

Miranda unclipped Delilah's leash, and as predicted, she
shot away to begin checking the place out.

Rich said, "Is it okay with you if we set our stuff down? I'd
like to get this rifle off my shoulder."

Immediately, Kendall's body language relaxed. Miranda
smiled to herself. Rich was good at the people stuff.

"Sure," Kendall said, nodding.

They set everything down, Rich and Phineas removing
their holsters, which forced Miranda to do the same. The
feeling of lightness surrounding her hips instead of the weight
of the holster made her feel exposed. Kendall holstered his
pistol, snapping it in place like he was unaccustomed with the
procedure.

"Where's everyone else?" Alec said.

"Well..." Kendall said slowly. "Actually, it's just me."

"Just you?" Alec said, at the same time Phineas barked,
"No way."

Kendall's eyes widened, as if startled by their reaction.
Beads of sweat popped out on his forehead.

"Um, yeah," he stammered, beginning to look anxious, and
Miranda began to wonder how long he had been down here.
"There were others."

Rich opened his mouth to say something, but Miranda

interrupted him. Kendall seemed to be getting overwhelmed fast.

"Guys," she said. "I could use a bite to eat. You know how I am when I get low blood sugar. What do you have in your packs?"

Rich, Alec, and Phineas all looked at her as if she had lost her mind. They'd only eaten breakfast an hour ago. Admittedly, it hadn't been much, but enough for more than an hour. Her request must have clued them in that something was going on, even if they didn't know what it was.

"Sure," Rich said. "Good idea."

"I have food," Kendall offered. He pointed to his right. "In the kitchen. Help yourself."

Her mind raced at the offer of food. How much food did he have? Would he be this willing to share some with LO? Trying not to sound excited, she said, "Are you sure?"

"It's probably better than camping food," said Kendall.

She smiled. "Thanks. I could use a drink of water."

"There are bowls, for the dog," Kendall offered.

She nodded. Then she looked at the guys, tipping her head toward the kitchen. A curved counter, with openings on either end, demarcated where the dining area ended and the pie-shaped kitchen began. Along the back wall, on the wide end of the room, were two industrial refrigerators and a separate freezer.

"Dishes are under the counter," Kendall said.

"Phineas," Miranda said. "Will you get some plates, and a bowl of water for Liley?"

He nodded. Miranda walked into the kitchen to see where everything was. Lights overhead blinked on automatically. On the right were stainless-steel tables for food prep, rather than counters. Their lower shelves were stacked with pots and pans of almost every variety, but only a handful showed signs of regular use.

Alec whistled. "You've got everything you need here, Kendall."

At the end of the counters, and before the refrigeration units, sat a six-burner gas cooktop with what had been—and still was—a state-of-the-art ventilation hood that fed into the heavy-duty ductwork overhead. Beside it sat a vertical three-unit industrial oven that was almost as tall as Miranda. In the center of the room was a stainless-steel island with an integrated double sink, a wine fridge that had bottles of white wine in it, and one industrial and two residential dishwashers. The other longer wall opposite the stoves and tables had floor-to-ceiling cupboards.

Rich opened a cupboard, while Miranda and Alec headed for the fridge.

"Woah," Rich said.

She swiveled around, eyes widening at the amount of foodstuffs inside the cupboard. If they were all that full of food... She reached the fridge, unsure of what she would find inside. She pulled the door, cold air making her arms prickle with goosebumps. Over her shoulder, she heard Alec's sharp inhale.

"Christ on a bike," she said softly.

The contents of the fridge were...impossible, and plentiful. The produce crisper, which spanned the width of the fridge under a shelf of glass, was full of leafy greens and root vegetables—carrots and radishes and beets—as well as red bell peppers, some tomatoes, even what looked like fresh herbs. There were apples and peaches and plums. Three pint cartons of milk were inside, one opened, the others not. Miranda wasn't familiar with the design, but they had to be shelf-stable. Similar cartons were labeled cottage cheese, sour cream, and yogurt. There were various jars of condiments, a few of jam, and butter. It wasn't a lot of food given the size of the fridge. At the same time, it was so much food. Those cupboards alone would feed a few households at LO at regular portions for a month.

"Doesn't shelf-stable milk have a shelf-life of six months?" asked Alec, who now stood beside her.

"As far as I know."

"Is there anything there we can use to make pasta?" Rich asked them. "It'll be the easiest thing. There's a basket of onions in here, and a jar of minced garlic."

"Fresh onion and garlic, and all this?" Miranda asked softly, shooting Alec a sideways glance. "There's a garden somewhere."

Alec looked in the crisper and pulled out a bunch of a dark leafy greens with red stalks. He said to Rich, "Pasta will work. I can do something with this."

Alec looked again at the fridge Miranda still stood in front of. "You're letting all the cold air out, lassie. And if you don't shut your mouth soon, you'll draw flies."

Miranda shut the fridge, then said to Alec, "Who the hell is this guy?"

Alec gave her a sly grin. "Between you and me? I think he's Kendall Grant."

AN HOUR LATER, EVERYONE—EVEN KENDALL—HAD EATEN, and despite the early hour, two bottles of really excellent wine had been drunk. Kendall said he hadn't had any wine in a long time, and had suggested it in a tone so hopeful that no one had the heart to say no. And a good thing, as it turned out, because after a glass, Kendall loosened up. Rich had suggested before they sat down, quietly, that they keep the conversation light and not bombard Kendall with questions. He too had noticed that Kendall seemed to get easily overwhelmed.

They were gathered around the end of one of the long dining tables, Kendall on the end, with Miranda and Phineas on one side, and Alec and Rich on the other. Phineas' tale of the tiger had finally gotten a laugh out of Kendall.

"There are several I've seen through the security cameras," he said. "I think they're Amur tigers."

Miranda said, "Amur tigers? I've never heard of them."

"Siberian and Amur are the same subspecies," Kendall said. Then he snapped his mouth shut, a look on his face as if he'd said something rude.

"I don't care what kind it is. I never want to see another tiger that close again," Phineas said. "I almost peed my pants."

The conversation lulled, and Miranda was just about to ask who had built the place when Kendall stood abruptly.

"I need to attend to something. Are you planning to stay a while?"

Miranda and Rich traded a glance. "A night or two, if that's okay with you, but not more. Our people will worry about us if we're overdue," Rich said. "It would be nice to hear your story and learn more about your place."

Kendall nodded, as if this was both acceptable and terrifying.

"There are residence domes off the outer corridor, and single bedrooms, too, on the inner side. Everything's marked. Use any of them you like." He started to walk away, then stopped and turned back. "I should...help with the dishes?"

"We've got it, Kendall," Rich said, pouring on the easygoing charm. "It's the least we can do."

Kendall nodded. "Okay."

He walked from the room, but the haste in his step made it

seem like a retreat. No one spoke for a full minute until Phineas said, "What the actual fuck?"

"Yeah," Miranda said, nodding.

"When was this thing built?" Phineas whispered. "And how does nobody know about it?"

"That's kind of the point of a secret bunker," said Alec.

"I think we should do the dishes and pick out our beds," Rich said. Then he lowered his voice so only they could hear him. "We'll talk later, on our own, okay?"

Heads nodded, and plates were collected. Miranda carried glasses to the kitchen and set them on the counter. She tried to smother a yawn and grinned when Alec caught her.

"Wine in the morning catching up with you?" he said. His hazel eyes fairly sparked with mischief.

"Maybe a little." Then she murmured, "Have you told Rich who you think he is?"

"I will when we talk later." His expression became speculative. "Are you always such a lightweight, Miranda?"

She barked a laugh. If he only knew.

"Hardly. I'm no stranger to day drinking, but morning's a little early, even for me.

7

SHE COULD HEAR the baby crying, and Mario's low, singsong voice as he tried to soothe him, but the baby continued to squall. She pushed the door to the bedroom open. Mario walked back and forth across the room, the baby in his arms. When he saw her, he shrugged.

"I don't know what's wrong with him."

"Let me try."

Mario held the baby out to her. She reached for him, then froze, plunged into a pool of frigid shock. He wasn't holding a baby. It looked like a baby, had once been a baby, but its skin was gray, and the arms that reached out from the blanket around it were thin and shrunken—deformed. It didn't have any hands. Black veins traced under its skin. Its shrieks reverberated off the bedroom walls from a tiny black-lipped mouth. Then they turned into moans.

"Miri, take him."

She looked into Mario's face. He looked fine. Calm. Like what he was holding was totally normal.

"That's not," she said, stumbling over the words. "That's not our baby."

Mario's brow furrowed. "Of course he's our baby. Here, take him."

"No," she said, taking a step back.

"Miranda," Mario said, but his voice was taking on an edge of annoyance. "Take him."

She looked at the baby in his arms. "Where's our baby?" she gasped.

"This is our baby," Mario said. He took a step toward her. "Here, take him!"

Miranda looked at the thing in Mario's arms. It wasn't their baby. But if that wasn't their baby, what had happened to him?

"Where is he?" she asked, desperation growing.

"He's right here," Mario said, his face twisting with anger.

He started to push it into her arms, to force her to take it. She recoiled, stumbled backward, almost falling when she tripped. Her throat closed, as if it was caught in a vise.

"What did you do to our baby?"

Mario's eyes blazed with sudden anger. His mouth twisted in a sneer. "You did this. It's your fault he's like this. Now take the goddamned baby, Miranda! He's like this because of you and—"

HER ARMS THRASHED AND LEGS KICKED, TRYING TO PUSH Mario away, but she was twisted in the sheets. She felt damp, slicked in sweat, heart pounding in her chest. She looked around, eyes wild, expecting to hear more crying, but the room was silent. It wasn't a familiar room, though. Was she awake or still dreaming?

Miranda sat up, then took a deep breath. One glance reminded her where she was: Kendall's bunker.

They'd settled in one of the apartment domes that stuck out from the central dome like petals on a flower. There were six residence domes and two garden domes. An oval that seemed a little bigger than two of the round domes put together was marked STORAGE and included a wine cellar. Kendall's apartment was an oval, too, and Phineas had joked he now lived in a doublewide. Rounding out the setup was a swimming pool.

Miranda got out of bed and padded to the attached bathroom to pee. This dome had four bedrooms, two master suites with their own baths, two doubles with a shared bath between them, and single bedroom. She had turned down one of the master suites, which she now regretted. A warm bath might be just the trick, but she didn't want to wake Alec, whose room also used this bathroom.

She left the bathroom and switched on the bedside light. The bunker had a massive supply of clothes, so she helped herself to a soft, stretchy pair of yoga pants, the kind with a wide cut leg, and a few V-neck tee shirts. The shirts had cap sleeves, and the cut hugged her body more than the traditional square tee shirt shape. Even the clothes in this apocalypse bunker were stylish. She searched the dresser for an elastic band before finding it draped over the top of an empty wine bottle. She didn't remember putting it there.

She plucked it off the bottle and pulled her hair back. That bottle she'd drunk on her own, a dry Pinot Grigio that had transported her back to parties at her parents' house when they entertained the political movers and shakers so important to her father's career. She'd been sure the combination of swimming and the wine would knock her out enough that she wouldn't dream. Or at least, that she'd be so tired that even a shitty dream like that wouldn't wake her up, but it hadn't worked.

The baby in the dream danced behind her eyelids...shriveled and gray and deformed, the perfect encapsulation of what had happened to Tadpole in one efficient package. Mario's confused, then angry, face, insisting she hold it, insisting the baby was that way because of her.

If he hadn't left, she thought, anger flaring. If he hadn't left them behind, none of this would have happened and—

"Fuck this," she said.

She looked at herself in the mirror over the dresser. She hadn't been sleeping well since losing the baby and sending Mario packing. The cumulative effects showed. She had bags under eyes. Mornings were hard since she was chronically sleep deprived. She didn't have the dreams every night, but enough that she dreaded them. Enough that she drank if she could, to smooth out the ride. If she could get her hands on some Percocet, or something like it, that and a glass of wine always did the trick. She'd drink herself into oblivion every night if that was possible, but there wasn't always enough alcohol available to do that. She wished, for the millionth time, that she could smoke pot. It grew all over the place, but it just made her paranoid. It had been nice to drink a bottle of Kendall's good wine. He never came back out, even though he'd left for his room at close to ten in the morning. He'd told them to explore, take a look around, so she might as well.

Phineas picked the dome they were in when they'd settled in earlier.

"It has a baby grand piano," he had said.

"You play?" Miranda asked.

"No," he answered. "But it's a piano. We're staying here."

After choosing rooms and stowing their gear, they regrouped in the kitchen. The whole place was an open floor plan, probably to counter claustrophobia.

"You think he's Kendall Grant?" Rich said, repeating what Alec had just told him.

"I don't think it," Alec said. "I know it. It's him. One of my mates worked at Grendall Industries and stuck a picture of Kendall's face on his dartboard. He said it made him feel better about selling his soul. It's the right part of the States; his name is Kendall, and who else would have the money to build a place like this?"

Rich said, "I can think of five off the top of my head. You do know what companies were based out of Portland and Seattle, right? There was—"

"Who's Kendall Grant?" Phineas asked. At the quizzical looks, he added, "I'm twenty, guys. I wasn't paying attention to business tycoons."

Miranda laughed. "I forget what a kid you are."

"Don't start with trying to pretend I'm too young for you, Miranda. We all know you want a piece of this." Phineas pointed at himself like he was gameshow hostess showing off a prize.

"Kendall Grant," Alec began. "Founded Grendall Industries. It started out as a tech company, but by the time zombies came around, it had its fingers in everything from cloud computing to military weapons systems. It's him. I'd bet my life on it."

"What is he doing here alone?" Miranda asked. "This place is clearly meant to hold more people."

"I saw an occupancy plaque on the wall by the storeroom," said Phineas. "This place can hold a hundred people, with supplies for five years."

Miranda's head swam at the idea of so much food. That would be more than enough to get LO through to their next harvest. They wouldn't have to risk people going out to scrounge food. If Kendall would share with them, they could set up a corridor from here to LO, something that would decrease the danger of traveling through Portland.

Rich said, "Maybe no one else made it, and that's why it's just him."

Even in a place like this, with all the luxe comforts of excessive pre-apocalpytic wealth, Miranda couldn't imagine a decade of isolation. Just thinking about it gave her a nasty shiver.

"Where are his weapons?" she said. The attack had depleted LO's ammunition stores. It wouldn't hurt to get more if they could.

Rich nodded. "I've been wondering about that. There are the lockers in the main corridor, but a place like this with just three firearms lockers? No way."

"What about the security office?" Phineas suggested.

"There might be something there," Rich allowed. "But there's got to be more. If you spend the money to build a place like this, you're gonna have serious weapons. Three lockers is not that. And there's got to be food storage somewhere."

"And you want it," Alec said to Rich. A statement of fact, not a question.

"Not enough to steal from him. Yet," Rich said. "But we're facing a serious food shortage. P-Land is helping but they lost crops, too. We don't have enough to get through the winter, never mind till next fall's harvest. And we're taking in people coming for the vaccine."

"You could stop taking them in," Alec said.

Rich shook his head. "That's not how we do things. Besides, they're coming because we sent people out before the blight put us over a barrel. We can hardly tell them to come and then tell them to fend for themselves."

"But if we could get some food from him," Miranda said. "That'd be huge."

No one spoke for a minute, each lost in their own thoughts.

"We have to get to know him better," Rich said. "If we ask too soon and he says no, it'll get real awkward real fast."

Then Miranda had said, "Maybe he'll want to come to LO with us. It would only make sense to bring supplies if he did."

They had ended the conversation without a firm plan.

Delilah, still snuggled on the bed, opened an eye when Miranda opened the bedroom door.

"Wanna come, Liley?" Miranda asked.

Delilah didn't budge; that settled that.

Miranda left her room and walked across the quiet living area. The furnishings alone for this whole complex had probably run a million bucks; how much had it cost to build this place—twenty million? More? She debated putting on her boots for a millisecond, then decided to stick with bare feet. She doubted she had to worry about zombies in this fortress. She left their dome, thinking she'd get a book from the library.

The overhead lights in the corridor were off, but the floor level track lighting was enough to see by. She'd only given the library a cursory glance earlier. She'd find something to read, and hopefully fall asleep doing it. Anxiety began to gnaw at her stomach at the idea of having another dream like this last one. There was always another bottle of wine if she needed it.

She was about to turn into the nearest lounge that led through to the dining area, where she could then get to the library, when she saw a light farther down the corridor. Curious, she decided to investigate, and realized the light spilled out from the larger of the garden domes.

The moisture in the air when she opened the door felt like a balm on her skin. She hadn't noticed that the bunker was especially dry, but compared to the humidity here, it was. Seconds later, she was surrounded by a riot of green. She'd checked the gardens out earlier. The fresh fruit mystery had been solved then. The smaller circular garden dome was planted with dwarf apple, peach, pear, and plum trees. This dome housed both hydroponics and raised beds. There was probably fertilizer in the storage dome to replenish the soil, and there had to be a composter somewhere.

A pang of loneliness welled up. Memories of the farm at home in California, and the people who worked there, tugged at her. She wondered how they were doing. If Timmy, whom Allan had tried to fire after he'd been bitten by a zombie, was doing okay. Was Harold still working there? She hoped so. She wanted to know where she could find him if she ever went home so she could wring his neck for selling them out, his ability to find good lingerie be damned. Maybe we can stop at that house on the way back, she thought, recalling the stash she had found on their way to OHSU's main campus. The look of surprise, followed by hungry desire, on Mario's face when she'd worn the lingerie bubbled to the surface. For a moment, before she could shut it down, longing made her body hum, but a burst of anger followed it. She concentrated on the smell of the plants and soil, the warmth that caressed her skin. Longing banished, she could almost hear Father Walter's voice playing devil's advocate when she'd pitched the idea of the vertical farms to him and Father Gilbert. Mario and Emily had been with her for moral support.

"Jesus," she muttered.

Mario was popping up in more than her dreams tonight. She resolved again to get him out of her head. She'd just been a kid, Phineas' age, when she proposed they try building a vertical farm. She chuckled to herself... No wonder he thought he was old enough for her. At twenty, after surviving those first few horrible months, she'd thought she was old enough for anything.

She heard the murmur of a low voice and followed the sound. Kendall tended to small plants at a nearby raised bed.

They were more than seedlings, but still too small for her to tell what they might be. She approached, clearing her throat before speaking.

"Hi," she said. "Mind if I join you?"

Kendall started. His eyes flicked to hers, then slid away. "Okay."

Miranda closed the distance and stood on the opposite side of the raised bed. There was another to her left. Unlike the one they stood at, it was low to the floor. Three circular containers with soil in them jutted up from the floor, with six inches of shaggy green leaves poked up from the soil. They weren't containers, on closer look, more like expandable tubes about two feet wide. They could be pulled up, she realized, changing the height. They reminded her of the round tunnels that could be made longer or shorter, and were flexible enough to curve, that she and her brothers had crawled through when they were kids.

"Potatoes?"

Kendall looked up, then to the next garden bed.

"Yes," he said. "How did you know?"

"It's what I do at home. I'm a farmer. It's smart to grow them up rather than down. Then the bed doesn't need to be as deep."

Kendall nodded, then looked back to the plants in front of him.

"Can't sleep either?" Miranda asked.

"I've always been a night owl."

"I guess time's different down here," she said.

Kendall nodded. It was like talking to a three-year-old on the phone, the adult needing to offer all the conversation prompts.

"How long have you been here?"

Kendall stopped thinning out the plants. "Since the beginning."

"You've been by yourself the whole time?" She couldn't keep the astonishment out of her voice. It would account for his somewhat limited conversational skills.

"Just the last seven."

"What happened to the others?"

He glanced up at her before answering. "Van, my— Well, he got me here, then went back out to see who else he could pick up and never came back. The security team was here when I arrived. After a while they wanted to go outside."

"No one else made it?"

Kendall looked at her with a furrowed brow, then nodded.

"That's a long time," Miranda said, softly.

"I've always been an introvert."

Another silence. She said, "Can I help? You're thinning them all?"

"Yes." He paused, then added, "That would be nice."

She began thinning the row of tiny plants in the row in front of her, carrots she now saw, enjoying the feel of the soft, dark earth on her fingers. Seven years... It explained his absence for the rest of the day after their meal. Four people after years of isolation had to be overwhelming.

"Are you a night owl?"

She looked at Kendall, surprised that he had initiated some conversation.

"Not sleeping very well."

They lapsed back into silence. Miranda moved away from Kendall as she worked her way down the row. She hadn't done it intentionally, but maybe it would make him more comfortable. She couldn't wrap her head around being alone for so long. She'd never thought about it, to be honest, but was pretty sure she'd be jumping for joy at the idea of people to talk to after so long. But she wasn't Kendall.

She was about to start thinning the next row and work her way back toward the center of the bed, when he said, "How do you do it?"

She looked at him. He was studying her intently.

"Do what?"

"Chase them off. I saw them move away... When you helped your friend."

Now it made sense, why he'd let them in after ignoring them for two days. He wanted to know how she repelled zombies. They hadn't known how much, if any, of the scuffle he'd seen. When he hadn't asked, she thought maybe he hadn't seen it. Then he disappeared after they ate, and they'd seen neither hide nor hair of him since. It was weird he hadn't asked immediately. Then again, he hadn't interacted with real, live human beings in quite some time.

"The zombies, you mean?"

Kendall nodded.

"It's a side effect of the vaccine if—"

Kendall's voice was a shocked whisper. "There's a vaccine?"

"Yeah," she said, beginning to fully comprehend just how isolated he'd been. "There's been one for about five years. The first one—" She stopped when she saw Kendall's mouth fall open, and his eyes go wider. "You really don't know anything about this?"

Kendall shook his head.

"Oh."

She took a moment to think about what and how much to say. This guy was so isolated, it probably didn't matter what she told him. She hadn't asked, but was starting to think he hadn't been outside since getting here.

"There are two kinds of vaccines. The first is an inoculation, so you can't become infected by the virus. The other is post-bite. If you get it within twelve hours of being bitten, it'll save you, but you have to take it every day."

Kendall looked dazed. Miranda continued.

"They were developed in California. There were a couple different groups working together, and...well, long story short, one group kept the vaccines and have been using them to stay in power ever since."

"And the other groups?"

"There was a treaty eventually, called the Agreement. The other group gets a small amount from the City... It's kind of complicated. The important part is they've reverse-engineered the post-bite, and were working on the other, but in secret."

Kendall's brow furrowed. "How do you know all this?"

"Because I'm from that other group. We stole the preventative vaccine serum to try and break the monopoly, but..." She sighed, remembering the disastrous journey to Santa Cruz: New Jerusalem, everyone who had died, nearly losing Jeremiah to the people in Santa Cruz who they'd helped. Connor. "That didn't go as planned. But we found another guy who was immune, and one of the virologists who worked on the first set of vaccines was with us, so we came here to try again."

"Because of the vaccine institute," Kendall said.

Miranda nodded.

"And it makes people repel zombies?"

"Not everyone." She paused, trying to think what to call Jeremiah. "It was a different subject's antibodies this time, and what turned out to be a different strain of the virus. He repelled them, which we'd never seen before. But with the vaccine, repelling them is a side effect of having AB negative blood, which is the same as his was. It doesn't happen with other blood types."

Kendall stood with his hands in the dirt, his task forgotten.

"We're working on ramping up production and getting the vaccine out to people. And letting people know we've got it. They're already starting to come. Then San Jose, and the people there who control that vaccine, will become irrelevant."

Kendall stared at her. He seemed to realize his mouth was hanging open and shut it. "You were out here looking for people to tell?"

"No," Miranda said, shaking her head. "We were— It doesn't matter. I make it easier to move around. If you stick right next to me, they'll stay away."

"That's...incredible," Kendall said softly. "I've seen things by flying drones, but—"

"You have drones?"

Kendall shrugged. "Some small ones. I saw it happen...how fast it spread. Almost every place people tried to keep safe was overrun, eventually. So many were terrible to each other, the people, I mean. I stayed here."

What would it have been like to watch it happen from a safe place? she wondered. Not in a place you thought was safe, or was safe for the time being, but truly safe. It must have been terrifying, though not as much as being in it.

"Not all people are bad." She remembered something he'd said through the speakers before they entered the bunker. "You knew where we're from. You're the one who brought up the park. You've seen it from your drones, haven't you?"

Kendall suddenly looked trapped, like he'd been caught out in a lie.

"It's fine," she said quickly. She didn't want him clamming up. "It's not like you've tried to mess with us. It's great here, compared to home. Everybody gets along, and they work together. They aren't trying to screw each other for a buck."

Kendall didn't respond, and Miranda wasn't sure what else

to say. Had she said too much? Had she freaked him out? It was a lot to dump on a person all at once. She went back to thinning the plants. When she and Kendall were in the same spot again, he started to talk.

"My family said I was crazy for building this place."

"So it is yours."

Kendall nodded.

"Must have cost a fortune," she said.

Kendall almost smiled; it looked like a grimace. "It was expensive." His voice dropped to a whisper. "I just wish the others had made it." He paused, then added, "It surprises me, though."

He didn't say more. Having to ask a follow-up question for almost every one of his statements was starting to make her tired. "What does?"

"That more people weren't prepared."

Miranda barked a laugh. "For the zombie apocalypse? I don't think anyone saw that coming."

Kendall shook his head. "No. I mean for an emergency. It's not that hard to pull together supplies and a plan, and have a place to go. Property wasn't that expensive in more remote areas. You wouldn't need a place like this...just something."

She narrowed her eyes and had to work at not frowning, for his statement rankled. He sounded smug, like he'd been so much smarter than everyone else, instead of realizing that he had the ability, the resources, to do something most people on the planet could only dream about. He was right about property being cheaper in the middle of nowhere, but most people hadn't had that kind of money. Some people never owned a home, and it wasn't for lack of wanting to or working hard.

An intense dislike for Kendall bloomed in her chest. Maybe seven years alone wasn't enough for someone so arrogant to learn much of anything.

Aloud, she said, "Not everybody's Kendall Grant, with more money than they could ever spend."

His eyes widened. He was Kendall Grant, just as Alec had said.

"That's not what I meant," he said, defensive. He also looked alarmed, as if it had only just occurred to him that they knew where he was and what he had, and what that might mean.

Miranda sized him up for a moment, pretty damn sure that was exactly what he'd meant.

"Don't worry. None of that matters anymore, and we don't care who you used to be. My family was rich. San Francisco Gold Rush money, and it didn't do diddly squat to save my mom and dad and brothers. I'm only here because San Jose managed to scrape through somehow, and I was in the right place at the right time. This kind of stuff—" She waved her hand around to indicate the bunker. "Was nice to have, obviously. Still is. But I like where we live, out there, and the work we're doing."

Kendall blinked at her, which made him resemble an owl, and pushed up his glasses. He swallowed so hard his Adam's apple bobbed up and down. She dusted off her hands.

"I'm going to bed. See if I can get back to sleep." She gestured to the infant plants between them. "Thanks for letting me help. And don't worry that we'll tell anybody about your layout here. We have no reason to." She chuckled as she said, "And nobody's getting in that door of yours."

Kendall nodded. After a moment he said, "I...enjoyed talking. With you."

A corner of her mouth curved up. "You must be a glutton for punishment, Kendall. My friends are always telling me what a pain in the ass I am."

He grinned, just a little, as if he was unused to doing so. He started to blink like an owl again. She supposed he was rusty, after so many years alone. She could feel his eyes on her until she was through the door. She detoured to the kitchen for another bottle of wine before heading to her room, feeling justified in liberating a tiny bit more of Kendall's excess wealth.

She looked at the label: Harlan Estate. She recognized it; her mother had liked this winery, and their wine had cost several hundred dollars a bottle. More than some people had made in a day. More than some made in a month, or more. Not because they were stupid or lazy, but because of what country they were born in, or what school district their parents could afford to live in. Not buy a house in, but live in, period.

Kendall Grant had started out in life so far ahead of so many people, just like Miranda had. His family hadn't been wealthy like hers, but he'd mentioned attending Stanford or Harvard, a place like that. He probably thought he was a self-made man, but there was no such thing. That was one thing her parents had drummed into her head at least, when it came to money or success. He'd been able to take advantage of opportunities that most people could only dream of, and got a lot of help to do it. Mentors and connections from college, business loans when he started his company, and later, favorable legislation he'd had the money to make a reality, yet he thought surviving the zombie apocalypse had been about having the foresight to plan for the unimaginable? An emergency, sure, but a full-on global disaster that had been impossible to get ahead of anywhere? Most people hadn't lived their lives that way, and the people who had tended to be completely fucking paranoid.

There'd probably been a hundred people on the planet with the money to build a place like this. Her family had been loaded, but she wasn't sure they could have built this. A smaller, less snazzy one maybe, but who the hell did so in the old world except for people like Kendall? And after all this time he was smug because he'd had billions, and spent half of one percent of it building a bunker? It made him smarter that he flew drones around to see what was happening while people were getting eaten by zombies, but did nothing to help anyone?

She shook her head, disgusted. Kendall was a hoarder, nothing more. He'd hoarded wealth in the old world, keeping far more than he'd ever need at the expense of everyone else. Just like her family, for that matter, even if they soothed their conscience with charity work and foundations that were well-intentioned, but a drop in the bucket compared to what was in their bank account. They'd had so much when so many had so little, and she'd never questioned why that was until she got to college. Until her horizons were broadened, and she met people with backgrounds different from her own. It didn't seem that Kendall had ever made that connection. He was still hoarder of wealth; only the currency had changed.

Apart from the sleazeballs on San Jose's City Council, people didn't think that way so much anymore. Survival was too immediate, and the margins too thin. Yet here, in this tomb to the old world's excess, the 'Me, me, me, I did it on my own and fuck everyone else' mentality seemed to be alive and well.

"What an asshole," she muttered.

As far as she was concerned, they couldn't get back to LO fast enough.

8

MIRANDA LOOKED UP WHEN DELILAH, who lay on the floor beside the couch she lay on, began to thump her tail. Alec had entered their domed apartment. She set her glass of wine on the coffee table and resumed reading the Irish police procedural she'd taken from the library. The writing was excellent and story really creepy. It made her wish there was still such a thing as international travel as it once had been: easy and fast.

Alec rubbed Delilah's tummy, then sat down sideways near Miranda's feet so he was facing her. He folded his right leg under him, his other foot touching the floor, and lay his arm along the couch's back.

"What's with the sourpuss?"

"I didn't know I had one," she said.

That slow, sly smile started at the right corner of his mouth and worked its way left. It hadn't escaped Miranda's attention that Alec was handsome, with those hazel eyes and strong jaw and black hair. And there was the accent. But it was when he smiled, as if he knew how good he looked and liked what he saw of you, that he transformed into the bad boy your mother warned you about. The one you just couldn't stay away from, even though you knew it would end in heartbreak. He had charmed his way into many a girl's bed with that smile, of that she was a thousand percent sure.

"When you haven't ignored our host the last two days, you've been a wee bit snippy. Hurt his feelings at breakfast, I think."

Miranda rolled her eyes.

Undeterred, Alec said, "Then you got a book and a bottle of wine, and you've been hiding here ever since." He glanced at the three-quarters empty bottle, then added, "You're ripping through that at a fair rate, lass, and it's not even lunchtime."

She returned to her book. "I like to read. And drink. This is good wine."

Alec caught her toes and wiggled her foot.

"What?" she said, not looking up from her book.

"So why've you gone off our lad Kendall? Rich told me you had a midnight chat with him. What did he say?"

"Trying to read here, Alec."

She wasn't reading, of course, since he was distracting her. He started to tickle her foot. She snatched it away.

"Stop!" She glared at him. She should probably slow down on the wine. "Go be charmingly annoying somewhere else."

"I'm charming, am I?" he said, laughing. "Seriously, though. What's with the attitude? He's a lot looser when you're around."

Miranda dropped the book to the floor and scooted up so that the small of her back was propped against the arm of the couch, and her feet were out of Alec's reach.

"It's stupid... He was saying how it surprised him that more people hadn't prepared some place to go to if there was a disaster like zombies, because, you know, everyone saw it coming."

"Ah," Alec said.

"He talked as if everyone had the money to do it," she continued. "He was saying how land was cheap east of Portland, and they didn't have to build this kind of place but could have done something. He's right that land was cheaper, but most people didn't have the money to buy land that was hours away, much less build on it. He was so...smug about it, like he was so much smarter than everyone else. Meanwhile he's hiding here, all by himself, for years on end. It annoyed me."

"I can tell."

Miranda scowled. "He's telling me how he flew drones around, and saw it happening, but he didn't try to help anyone. He just watched and hid."

Alec shrugged. "If I'd had a place to stay that was safe and stocked like this, I don't know that I'd have gone out."

Miranda snorted dismissively. "You're not a chickenshit, Alec."

"And you were always this tough, I suppose?" he asked, eyebrows raised, that charming smile daring her to contradict him.

"Hardly," she answered. "I was twenty years old and scared shitless. My best friend even told me she wasn't dying for me if I froze or did one more stupid thing. But you know how it was —you decided if you were going to live or not. A lot of people are stumbling around out there trying to eat the rest of us because they decided not to."

He nodded. "It's easy to get unlucky when you decide living is too hard."

"Exactly. I got in touch with my anger and channeled it."

Alec's bark of laughter was so loud that it startled Delilah, who began to bark.

"Oh, I'm sorry, doggie," he said, reaching to pet the startled pit bull. "I don't want to see you angry then, lass," he said. Then his expression sobered. "We could use your help. He's more relaxed with you. Probably finds you less threatening."

"He doesn't know me very well," she muttered. A silence filled the room. Had Rich told him how she couldn't outlast a long silence? It was time she figured out how to do it. Just be a little uncomfortable, she told herself; it won't kill you.

She lasted thirty seconds.

"Fine. I'll come back out and play nice. He just reminded me so much of the jerks I went to school with... Bunch of over-entitled assholes."

Alec cocked his head to the side. "Are you telling me you were a woman of means?"

She shrugged. "You might say that."

The grin reappeared. "How rich were you?"

"It really doesn't matter anymore, Alec," she said, but she was grinning, too. She took another sip of her wine.

"Oh, I see," he said. "You were from one of those modest, old-money families. The kind that didn't like to flaunt their fortune, in case the peasants like me decided to round up the pitchforks."

Miranda laughed. Alec's eyes flashed. He was enjoying himself. She was, too.

She swung her legs around as she sat up. "If you must know," she said, then stopped, as if she were weighing whether or not to continue.

"Oh, I must," he said.

She stood up. "Before my great-great-great-grandmother married outside the tribe, which apparently her parents never forgave her for because she let him raise the kids Catholic, my family sold blue jeans."

Alec's eyes narrowed, then he burst into laughter. "Levi's?

Are you telling me your...what? Four or five times great-grand-father was Levi Strauss?"

"I didn't tell you anything of the sort," she said primly.

She headed for her room, thinking that she was walking just fine, even though her ability to walk was something she never thought about normally. *I drank more wine than I thought,* she realized.

"I'll be out in half an hour. I'm going to take a shower first."

"I'll make you some coffee," Alec said, chuckling. "Your grasp on your balance doesn't look that firm, lassie."

She flipped him off over her shoulder, his laughter ringing in her ears. She shut the bedroom door behind her, still smiling. Alec really did have a nice laugh, even if he was a rogue.

She slowed her steps as she approached the lounge nearest to the bunker entrance, listening from around the corner.

"What are you using for your solar grid?" Kendall asked.

"I don't know," Rich said. "It's not one of the things I do. Is there an advantage to the different systems?"

Christ, he's good, Miranda thought. She could hear the butter in his voice. She plowed ahead and turned the corner just as Kendall began to speak. His face lit up like a firefly.

"Oh. Miranda."

"Hi, Kendall," she said.

Kendall and Rich sat in easy chairs among the furniture arranged for conversation in the lounge, their backs to the dining area behind them. Rich looked relaxed, but Kendall fidgeted. Phineas lay sprawled on a couch across from them, taking up all the cushions. The scent of coffee, which smelled as good as the crushing disappointment of how bad it tasted, wafted from the kitchen.

Phineas grinned at her. "My sleeping beauty graces us with her presence."

Miranda flopped onto the other end of the couch, pushing Phineas' feet out of the way. She said, "Is there any caffeine for your sleeping beauty, or just flowery words?"

"Alec made some coffee," Kendall said. He stood up abruptly. "I'll get you some."

"That would be great, but I don't—"

Kendall was already out of the room and turning into the kitchen.

"Like coffee."

She hadn't told Alec that she didn't like coffee earlier. There didn't seem to be any point in telling eager beaver Kendall now.

"Nice to see you, Miranda."

Miranda nodded at Rich in acknowledgment. "How's the solar system doing?"

"Writ large, I have no idea," he said. "But at LO, seems there might be some improvements to be made."

"Too bad you don't know what you're talking about," Phineas snorted.

"I am establishing a rapport," Rich said, voice low. "Do you need to look that one up?"

"That's hurtful, Rich. Seriously," Phineas said, not sounding hurt in the least.

Kendall returned, carrying a tray with a mug, a carafe of coffee, a small pitcher of creamer, a pot of honey, and what looked like a sugar bowl full of sugar, and a few squares of dark chocolate. She hadn't seen chocolate in years that wasn't spoiled. Kendall set the tray down on the coffee table in front of Miranda, then blinked at her like an owl.

"I forgot to ask how you like it, so...I brought everything."

"Thanks." She leaned forward to add sugar and milk. God, I hate coffee, she thought, but she needed to sober up, and beggars can't be choosers.

Kendall glowed under her praise, like a child who had pleased his favorite teacher. He was so attention-starved, and clearly suffering from extended solitude. Solitary confinement, really, despite the luxe trappings. She had a sneaking suspicion that he hadn't been super skilled with people at the best of times, never mind expressing himself well to strangers after an extended period of time alone. Perhaps she'd been a little too hard on him last night. She should give him the benefit of the doubt, especially now that sugar and chocolate had been thrown into the mix.

Alec joined them, sauntering in from the dining area.

"That's an incredible library you've got there, Kendall," he said. "Have you read it all?"

Again, Kendall blinked like an owl. "All the print books, yes, but not the e-books. There are over ten thousand of them. I'm still working my way through."

"I'm impressed," Alec said, taking what had been Kendall's seat without realizing it. He looked at Rich. "There's a lot of non-fiction there. Some of those history and philosophy books are not easy reading."

Kendall stood by the couch, looking awkward and out of place.

"Sit with us, Kendall," Miranda said, gesturing to the cushion between her and Phineas. "He can move his feet."

Kendall started to blush. Phineas jumped to the center spot, next to Miranda.

"Take mine, Kendall," he said. His voice became teasing as he leaned against her. "I wanna sit next to my best girl."

Miranda shook her head and jabbed him with her elbow,

nudging him away to create a more reasonable space between them. She put a square of the chocolate in her mouth, letting it melt on her tongue, the silky feeling warming her like a long-lost friend. Oh my God, she thought. She'd forgotten how buttery it tasted, even with the slightly bitter undertaste because this was the fancy seventy percent cacao stuff. She waited until the taste faded into a memory before taking a sip of the coffee, knowing she needed to keep the grimace off her face. To her surprise, the coffee was good. Really good. She'd put in a lot of milk and sugar, but even so, that usually wasn't enough. Kendall sat at the other end of the couch, his blush beginning to fade.

"Don't mind Phineas," Rich said. "He's annoying, but he's harmless."

Miranda said, "This is really good. I don't usually like coffee, but I like this."

Kendall looked at her, stricken. "You don't like coffee? I would have made tea."

"Honestly, this is—"

"You don't have to drink coffee. If you don't want."

"This is very good," she assured him. "I'm glad I kept my mouth shut. I wouldn't have tried it otherwise."

"I can still make tea," Kendall said weakly.

Oh boy, she thought. She glanced to Alec, who shrugged.

"Kendall," she said. She waited until he looked at her. Glanced at her, really, before looking back to his feet. "Thank you."

He said nothing, just blinked like an owl.

An awkward silence descended before Rich said, "What were you reading in the library, Alec?"

"I browsed, mostly."

The conversation turned to the books in the library. Once the topic of conversation changed from being about him,

Kendall relaxed. Miranda slurped down her coffee and fixed another. She really needed to not be buzzed for this.

"You know who tells good stories?" Phineas said. He patted Miranda's knee. "This lovely lady. In fact, there are a few really good ones about the two of us." His voice was suggestive, and the merriment that danced in his eyes made Miranda laugh so hard she almost spit out her coffee.

"Are you talking about the time I left you with a broken leg and told you we'd go on a date not in your lifetime, or the time I told you that you are, in fact, way too young for me?"

Everyone laughed, even Kendall, though his was tentative. His eyes darted from person to person anxiously, like he wasn't sure he was participating in the conversation at an acceptable level.

"I'm gonna wear you down one day," Phineas said, undeterred.

"Dream on."

She glanced at Kendall and was surprised to see that his eyes had narrowed. He looked at Phineas, the vibe distinctly unfriendly.

"Do you ever think about going outside?" Alec asked.

"Me?" Kendall squeaked, looking at Alec as if he'd just suggested he cut off his head. "No, it's dangerous. And I'm...not much of a fighter." His voice trailed, embarrassment filling his face. "That's why I built this place," he continued, a touch of smugness creeping into his voice. It made him sound more like the asshole Miranda had spoken with last night, the one who thought he'd been smarter than everyone else.

"I can teach you that stuff," Alec said, as if it was the best idea he'd ever had. "I was a reporter. If I can learn, you can, too."

Kendall didn't say anything. He stole glances at Alec, surreptitiously appraising his body as if he were checking him out as a romantic prospect. He might be, Miranda realized, except Kendall's reaction to her suggested otherwise.

"Would you like to come back with us?" Rich asked. "You must miss people. We don't have to tell anyone where you came from."

Kendall picked at the seam of his jeans. "I'm not sure…"

His voice was high and sounded not panicked, but definitely uncomfortable, and high on the discomfort scale at that. They'd make the same offers of assistance and friendship no matter what. Even though the guys were only asking questions and making offers that were low stakes to them, Miranda could see that they were frightening for Kendall to contemplate. She frowned at Rich and Alec, giving her head a subtle shake.

"I haven't seen a movie, like in a theater, in years. I wouldn't mind watching one," she said to Kendall. "If you're up for it."

Kendall nodded. "Sure, I'll turn the system on." He practically jumped up and ran from the lounge.

"I'm going to go to the bathroom and grab a snack first. I'll be right there," Miranda called after him.

"He is one weird dude," Phineas said when Kendall was out of earshot.

"He's not weird," Miranda said. "He's just not used to people."

Rich sighed. "I guess we overwhelmed him. That wasn't my intention."

"Thinking about learning to fight and go outside was probably too much at the same time," Alec said. He looked at Miranda, a twinkle in his eye. "He seems to have taken a shine to you."

She stood, picking up the tray that held the accoutrements for her coffee. "Try not to be fourteen, Alec."

"I keep telling her what a babe she is, but she doesn't

believe me," Phineas said to Alec. "My girl doesn't realize she's a stone-cold fox."

"I am not your girl," Miranda said, walking to the kitchen.

Their teasing made her uncomfortable. She didn't want some needy, reclusive, tech gazillionaire mooning after her, and she didn't need them encouraging him. She stopped in her tracks and turned around. "You guys are coming to watch the movie, right?"

"I'll come," Rich said.

"Are you sure, Rich? Three's a crowd," Alec asked. That sly smile played at the corners of his mouth. He looked at Miranda and winked, then looked back to Rich. "You don't want to be cramping your man's style."

"Yes, he does," Miranda said.

"Ah, well." Alec sighed. "Your romantic assignation will have to wait, Ms. Levi."

He shot her such a devilish grin, his *R*s rolling so much he sounded like he was purring. She felt her cheeks flame with heat. Of all the times to blush... Now he'd never stop.

"Her last name is Tucci," Phineas said to Alec.

"Oh, is it?" he said, all innocence. "My mistake."

She turned on her heel, heading for the kitchen. He is trouble, she thought, wondering exactly what kind of trouble Alec might be.

"Take him."

Her annoyance bubbled over into anger.

"No."

Mario glared at her. "Take the baby, Miranda. You have to. He's yours."

But she didn't want to take the baby. She wanted Mario to

keep the wriggling bundle wrapped in the blanket that he held out to her. Chubby pink arms waved from within the blankets, and tiny dimpled fingers flexed, catching nothing but air.

"You never wanted him," she spat, so angry she could barely speak. "You never wanted him, and now you're giving him to me?"

Mario sighed. He had that impatient look on his face, the one that set her teeth on edge.

"Look, Miranda," he said, his tone reasonable. "This is your baby, and you have to take him. That's all there is to it."

He thrust the baby against her, her arms instinctively catching him as Mario dumped him against her.

"You never loved him! You never cared! You never wanted him," she shouted, so angry she felt like a bomb about to explode.

Mario didn't answer. He just stood there, looking at her impassively. The baby wriggled against her, mewling. She pushed the blanket away from his face and gasped. The world around her warped and stretched, because it wasn't her baby. It wasn't even a baby, like Mario had insisted, but a zombie. Black veins spider-webbed its gray, translucent skin. Clouded eyes roamed in directions they shouldn't in the little eye sockets. It mewed and gurgled, clutching at her with emaciated, rotten fingers.

She flung it away, recoiling, and stumbled back against a dresser. She hit the corner, causing her hip to flare with pain. The zombie baby writhed on the floor.

"What are you doing?" Mario cried. "You killed him!"

She turned her head, catching sight of herself in the mirror, and froze. The reflection wasn't her. But it was, she realized, just not the her she was used to, because of the blackened, split lips, and the gray skin sagging away from the bones of her skull, the hollows under her cheeks and eyes, exaggerated to the point of gauntness. Spidery lines of black streaked her neck and face. Her eyes were cloudy, but she could still see. She was looking at a zombie, but she still felt like herself.

Mario crouched on the floor, moaning as he rocked the small bundled figure.

"Miranda, you killed him." He looked up, his anguished eyes meeting hers. "You killed our baby. Look at yourself! This is all your fault."

She looked at herself in the mirror, then touched her hands to her face. Her skin felt spongy. She pressed her finger against her cheek and it poked right through, like it was a piece of cotton candy. The hard enamel of her teeth clicked against her fingernail.

"I'm a zombie," she whispered, terror sucking her breath from her lungs.

"Why did you do this?" Mario said. "Why did you kill the baby?"

She looked at him, stunned that he hadn't seemed to notice that she was a zombie. On the outside, anyway, because she still felt like herself on the inside. Is this what they were? Was the person still inside, watching helplessly as the zombie it had become devoured the living? She looked down at the tiny figure bundled in the blankets at Mario's feet. It was moving, and it wasn't a zombie. She could see the chubby pink arms, the dark-brown eyes, the rounded cheeks and toothless smile. Mario hadn't noticed that the baby he kept insisting she'd killed was alive.

She opened her mouth to tell him, but all she could manage was a moan. Low and deep and like no sound she'd ever made before. It sighed out of her mouth. She never stopped to take a breath between one moan and the next. He still didn't understand, still didn't see that the baby was alive. She raised her arm to point, but her stomach felt so hollow that she couldn't remember why she'd raised her arm in the first place. Hunger gnawed her insides, strong and sharp and so painful—too painful to bear. She couldn't remember when she'd last eaten. All she knew was that she was ravenous.

Mario still shouted at her, but she could barely hear him. The baby was still on the floor and had kicked itself out of the blanket. Her hunger intensified a millionfold. It felt like it would swallow her whole. And the baby was beautiful...so pink and plump. It smelled like ambrosia. How had she never noticed before? She stumbled to Mario and the baby, falling to her knees.

"All of this is your fault," Mario said.

She leaned closer, the smell of her baby sweet, like a soft summer day when the sun is warm. She leaned closer, her lips brushing his warm, butter-soft cheek, and opened her mouth.

SHE WOKE CHOKING AND GAGGING ON HER TERROR. SHE didn't know what was wrong, what was so frightening, only that she was so afraid she didn't dare open her eyes. Tears leaked from beneath her closed eyelids, making cold tracks down her temples. Her heart pounded like a bass drum, the vibrations of every thump rumbling through her body. She hocked like something was caught in her throat, until finally, whatever it was that had been clogging her windpipe suddenly wasn't. Blood roared in her ears, drowning out everything but the rumbling beat of her heart.

She jerked and cried out when something touched her hand, before realizing it was only Delilah snuffling and licking, whining as if to comfort her. If Delilah's here, it must be okay, she thought, beginning to cry harder. I must be okay, I must be okay, I must be okay, she repeated, trying to work up the nerve to open her eyes, for terror still lingered at the edges of her consciousness, reluctant to release its hold.

When she finally cracked her eyes open a full minute later, by just the barest of slits, her lungs had almost quit shuddering when she drew in a breath. The thump of her heart had faded enough that the blood it pumped wasn't the only thing she could hear and feel.

The curved concrete ceiling was above her. The indirect lighting glowed along the base of the wall like a nightlight. She was still in the bunker. She sat up, pulling her knees to her chest, as the dream rushed back. She gagged, as if to spit out the chunk of the baby she had torn off with her teeth. Her chest swelled with heartache, the pain so sharp and deep that she could feel it turning to pulp. Her head felt like it could split as easily as an overripe melon falling to the ground. She pressed her forehead into her knees, holding them tight, and rocked in place.

It had been so vivid, so real, almost more than the waking world. She'd only had a glass of wine with dinner, since they were leaving in the morning. She'd had a hard time getting to sleep, and now, the dream. The nightmare, she thought, wondering why she always thought of them as dreams. Dreams were supposed to be good. They sustained you through the hard times with the promise of better things to come. Nothing about these were what dreams were supposed to be, but still, that's always how she thought of them.

She took a deep breath, then lifted her head and scrubbed her face. She squinted at her watch: 4:13 a.m. Almost four hours of sleep, which wasn't good, but wasn't horrible, either. They were leaving in a few hours and she couldn't sleep now. Wouldn't even try, for fear of what might be waiting for her.

She climbed out of the bed and pulled on one of the nice bunker tee shirts and a pair of yoga pants. She like how the soft, stretchy fabric of the yoga pants hugged her curves, and the V-neck of the shirts showed off the swell of her breasts. She spent practically her entire waking life—and sometimes her sleeping one—dressing for utility and safety because of zombies. It was nice to dress for something else. It was nice to show off her curves and remind herself that she was still desirable enough to catch the eye of most anyone, despite everything that had happened in the past year. Not that there had been anyone since she and Mario split up, but there could be, if she wanted.

She took Delilah to the small garden dome, where Kendall had said it would be okay for her do her business. She went to the kitchen to grab a snack—milk chocolate. She'd been eating the chocolate—dark and milk—nonstop, along with drinking the wine. Like a junkie on a bender, she gobbled it down until it almost made her sick. How Kendall's hadn't spoiled, she didn't know and didn't care.

Chocolate melting on her tongue, she headed for the large garden dome. She hoped Kendall wasn't there. She could creep away if he was, she supposed, and go back to the small one, but she liked the big one better. It felt less subterranean, which was probably why Kendall favored it, too. She just wanted to sit where it was green and try not to think about the dream. Sometimes, she was so angry at Mario when she woke up that it took all day to let it go. The anger she'd felt after losing the baby, her fury at Mario that she still didn't entirely understand, would be there, resurrected as if it hadn't begun to take any time off. Other times, like now, she was just massively freaked out. Dreams like the doozy she'd just had, the ones where she woke scared out of her mind, stuck around—sometimes for days—like the worst hangover ever. They unnerved her, leaving her jumpy as a cat.

She took a deep breath as the air turned moist in the garden dome. Earth and green and moisture—the best smell there was.

She could tell immediately that Kendall was present. He had a habit of talking to himself, and she could hear his voice. She already talked to herself, just not as loud as Kendall did, so no weirdness points there.

A recording began to play. She signaled Delilah to stay. Kendall stood at the potting table working on another set of small plants. The recording wasn't instrumental, just voices. She couldn't pick out the words; it was another language, Latin maybe? He sang along, his voice, a rich, bright tenor, and surprisingly expressive. Despite the fact that it didn't look like anything had been done to improve the acoustics, the music filled the dome without echoing. The voices soared—soprano, tenor, alto, and bass—intertwining like intricate lace. The melodies and harmonies rose and fell, their counterpoint to one another perfectly balanced as they moved together before separating, only to join and coil around one another once more, like lovers.

Miranda stood, transfixed, listening to angels, because this was how they sounded—just like this. They had to sound like this, because she couldn't imagine anything more beautiful than what she was hearing right now. She closed her eyes, listening to Kendall's voice rise and fall along with the others, with a grace so light, so tender, so transcendent, her heart ached. She didn't know when she began to weep, unable and unwilling to move or wipe away the tears, or anything else that might break the spell of this magic she had stumbled upon.

The melodies and harmonies converged in a way that filled her body, a longing that stretched toward a beauty that would always be just beyond her fingertips. The final note, crystalline, hummed in the silence that followed its end. Still, she didn't move, but listened to the hum suspended in its wake. When she opened her eyes, tears still slipping down her face, Kendall was looking at her. A mixture of surprise and embarrassment filled his brown eyes. She hadn't noticed what a beautiful shade of light brown they were before.

"That was beautiful," she whispered. He looked down at the floor, a flush of color filling his face. "I'm sorry," she said, swiping at her face. "I wasn't trying to intrude. It just...stopped me in my tracks."

She saw a tiny smile twitch at the corner of Kendall's mouth. He looked up at her again, embarrassed but pleased. "It's Palestrina. 'Sicut Cervus.'"

She moved closer, coming to a stop a few feet shy of him. "Latin?"

He nodded. "It's the same. Throughout the whole song, I mean." He stopped and looked at the ceiling, shifting from one foot to the other. His Adam's apple bobbed up and down. "The lyrics repeat until the end... *Sicut cervus desiderat ad fontes aquarum, ita desiderat anima mea ad te, Deus.*" He dragged his eyes down from the ceiling and did the blinking owl thing. "Like as the hart desireth the waterbrooks—"

"E'vn so, longeth my soul after Thee, oh God," Miranda finished. "The forty-second Psalm."

"Yes," Kendall said, the owl blink becoming more rapid. "How did you know?"

"Seriously Catholic nana. And my best friend is a priest." Then she shrugged her shoulders and added, "Was a priest. He fell in love."

Kendall nodded, but didn't say more. She looked at the bench, littered with empty pots, soil still clinging to their insides. Larger pots, with plants in earth still loose around them, were arranged at the table's end in neat rows.

"What are you doing with these guys—repotting?"

Kendall nodded again.

She walked the last few feet to the table. "Pardon my

reach," she said, leaning past him to pick up a larger clay pot from those stacked neatly beside him.

She picked up a plant and got to work. Kendall pushed the empty pots and the container of soil over, so that both were within easy reach. He tapped on a remote on the shelf behind him, and the music started again. This time, he didn't sing along. She hated to think that she was the reason he no longer sang, but of course she was. Kendall was as at ease when he sang as he was awkward while conversing. She wanted to listen to him sing some more, and even opened her mouth to say so, until she thought better of it. He was unused to having other people near, never mind singing for them. It was clearly something special to him. If she hadn't stumbled upon it, she'd have never heard him. She would never have known.

Never stop a child singing... Her nana had said that more times than Miranda could count. She'd always understood it in terms of what not to do: don't stop a child being joyful; don't squash their capacity for joy and wonder. But she realized now it was more than that. It wasn't only about avoiding harm, but nurturing the spirit. Kendall stood just two feet away, humming the melody, when before he had sung. She felt the diminishment that her presence, however inadvertent, had caused. She had stopped a child singing, even though he was a grown man.

She focused on the plants in front of her, letting the music carry her on its rise and fall. A feeling of calm that she hadn't felt in what seemed like years, but was only since she lost Tadpole, enveloped her. Kendall didn't need the food. He grew these plants so he had something to do, so he didn't go crazy. He sang along to this music, the addition of his voice making it even more beautiful, to be a part of something. To nurture the need that all people have to be connected to one another.

She glanced at him sidelong. He noticed and cautiously returned her smile. She would befriend him if she could. She would try to back-burner her expectations of what he might be able to give LO, even though they desperately needed the food he must have. He was awkward, possibly smug. He might be a bit of a prick, maybe a complete one; she just didn't know.

What she knew about Kendall would fit in a thimble, but she'd learned something about him tonight. She knew that he sang like an angel. It was as good a place as any to start.

THREE HOURS LATER, THEY WERE GETTING READY TO HEAD out. Miranda paced in the central dining area, growing more impatient by the second. She wanted to leave instead of farting around while Phineas took one last look to make sure they hadn't forgotten anything. The whole point of a doomsday bunker was to be self-contained, but despite its luxury and abundance, she was starting to feel constrained by its purpose.

"Anxious to hit the road?" Rich asked.

"Shows, huh?"

He smiled. "Just a little."

Kendall had disappeared half an hour ago, despite knowing that they were soon departing. If he didn't show soon, they were going to need to knock on the door of his dome to say goodbye. Not to mention get out; they didn't know the codes to unlock the doors.

"Where'd Kendall go?" Rich asked.

Miranda shrugged. "No idea."

"Did you get any sleep? You look terrible."

"A little," she said. "I may have drunk a little too much the last few days."

"More sleep and less booze is always a good combination. Might wanna try it, darlin'."

Miranda looked at Rich sidelong. "You are one of the few

people who never lecture me, Rich, but you keep this up and you'll break your streak."

"Fair enough," he said.

Phineas returned, his restless energy hitting Miranda like a wave—the kind that knocks you down and beats the shit out of you. He confirmed they hadn't forgotten anything.

"Where is everybody?" he asked.

"I'm here," Alec said, walking in from one of the lounges. He pointed over his shoulder to his thumb. "I grabbed a few toothbrushes from the bathroom. I think there must have been a dentist coming here. There's loads of them in every one."

"Where's Kendall? He's knows we're leaving, right?" Phineas said.

"Yeah, he knows. He'll be out soon," she said. Then added, "I think."

"I'm grabbing a snack," Phineas said, leaving for the kitchen.

Miranda rubbed her eyes, wishing she'd been able to get more sleep, but also glad that she'd spent time with Kendall. The music still echoed in her head, the melody haunting but beautiful.

Kendall appeared, entering from the lounge beside the movie theater. He looked freshly showered and wore faded black jeans and a tan tee shirt that made his eyes stand out. For the first time, she wondered how old he was. He was one of those people who could be anything from twenty-five to forty. He pushed up his glasses. The prescription had to be years out of date.

"Hey, Kendall," Rich said, "We're ready to head out."

Kendall nodded. "Yes. Of course."

"Thank you for your hospitality. We really appreciate it," Rich added.

"We do," Alec said. "It was very gracious of you to let us stay."

Kendall nodded. He looked flustered, unused to such praise.

Phineas beelined over from the kitchen, wiping his mouth. "Thanks, Kendall," he said, thrusting out his hand.

Kendall looked at Phineas' hand like he was being offered a pile of dog shit. Maybe it was because Phineas had just used it to wipe his face, or maybe another reason. Slowly, he took Phineas' hand for a millisecond, then let go like it scalded.

The guys put on their packs and followed Kendall to the interior door of the airlock. Miranda held one of the straps of her pack in one hand, and Delilah's leash in the other. She lingered behind to take a last look around. The central dining area was as beautiful as ever, with the gleaming wood tables and bright chandelier. Through the open doors of the various rooms—library and theater—and the lounges and kitchen that were open to it, she saw all the comforts and luxuries of home as it had once been. And the necessities, too, in the Medical-Surgical and Classroom suites. She couldn't see the swimming pool and gardens, nor the gym, but knew they were there. Hours of visual and reading entertainment, so much food—and the ability to prepare it deliciously—and more wine and liquor than a person could drink. Unless they went on a yearslong, first-class bender, which would be understandable.

She turned away, walking toward the voices down the hall, Delilah's nails clicking on the finished concrete. A leaden feeling settled on her chest. This whole place depressed her, and they were leaving Kendall here alone.

She heard Rich ask, "We'll be back in a few weeks, maybe sooner, if that's still okay with you?"

Kendall nodded, and Rich stepped through the airlock door. Delilah trotted up to Kendall, tail wagging. He reached down to pet her and gave the pit bull a dog biscuit, as well as one of the few easy smiles that Miranda had seen. He straightened up when Miranda reached him.

"Thank you so much, Kendall," she said. "Thanks for letting us come in."

He nodded, his head bobbing as if it were on a tight hinge that restricted his range of motion. He pushed up his glasses, and she could see that his eyes were...frightened? He opened the compressed, thin line of his mouth, then didn't say anything. Miranda waited, resisting the urge to prompt him. When he finally did speak, his voice was thick with anxiety.

"You are coming back, right?"

She tried to keep her voice cheerful. "Yes. We said we would."

He nodded again, looking unconvinced. "I mean...it would be understandable if you didn't. I—" He gulped, then muttered, his eyes sliding to the floor, "People have never been something I was...good at."

His fear they wouldn't come back was palpable. She reached out and took his hand in hers. His head snapped up.

"We'll come back, Kendall."

He attempted a weak smile but wasn't able to pull it off. She let go of her pack. As it thumped to the floor, she stepped close and wrapped her arms around him. He almost jumped, clearly not expecting the hug. He was thinner than she expected. His clothes fit but made him look like he had more meat on his bones. He had that fresh smell from basic soap. No scent, which surprised her. She'd assumed that he'd use something fancier. For a few seconds he just stood there, tense, his arms at his sides like a kid being forced to hug an unfamiliar relative. Then he relaxed. His arms came up to rest lightly—if awkwardly—on her shoulder blades.

"I want to hear you sing again," she whispered.

She felt his head nod. She gave a little squeeze, then released him. He stepped back, looking surprised, and doing the owl blink. He smiled, tentatively, but unlike his other attempt, this one reached his eyes.

"I'd... Like that."

She gave his shoulder a squeeze, then picked up and shrugged into her pack. Delilah followed her into the airlock. It closed behind her with a thud that reverberated through her body. The outer airlock door unlocked, and they stepped through, single file.

The walk to the outer blast door was mostly silent, apart from Phineas hoping they wouldn't run afoul of another tiger. They'd discussed whether the bunker had listening devices, so were saving real discussion for when they were outside.

When they got to the blast door, it slowly opened. When the cool, moist air filled Miranda's lungs, she felt her spirits rise. She paused on the stoop of the bunker, exhaling the last of the bunker's recycled air and replacing it with a deep inhale of air from Earth's atmosphere, all the way to the very bottom of her lungs. The scents of the forest filled her nose, the fresh smell of water from a recent rain shower, the pungent earthy smell of decomposing humus that blanketed the forest floor, all the more pleasantly fragrant for being damp. A light breeze caressed her cheek as she blinked, needing a moment to transition from the indoor light to the watery sunshine, even though they'd only been underground for a few days. She wondered what it would be like for Kendall to come outside, into the sun, after being underground so long. He'd probably need special sun protection for his eyes.

Delilah strained at the leash, nose twitching, eager to explore and move now that they were somewhere with so many scents and room to run. Miranda wished she could let her run off-leash, but she didn't want to run into another tiger any more than Phineas did. They watched the blast door close, the slight hiss of the hydraulics that controlled the door's movement no match for the birdsong. When the door thudded shut, they stood for a moment. Miranda raised her hand at the camera and waved. When Alec saw her, he waved, too.

No one spoke until they were a good hundred feet away, picking their way through the trees. Miranda let the guys do the heavy lifting conversationally, mostly answering questions and giving her opinion when they asked. Her mind was still back at the bunker. It would be worse for Kendall, now that they were gone. Like when you realized you were ravenous after a bite of food, when the moment before eating had been the furthest thing from your mind. He'd probably been getting along okay, but they'd interrupted the homeostasis of his existence. Despite his awkwardness, he was desperately hungry for human connection. No matter how fabulous the trimmings might be, the bunker was still just a place.

"If you had to get stuck somewhere, you could do a lot worse," Alec said, the burr of his accent catching Miranda's ear and pulling her from her thoughts.

"Indeed," Rich said, his soft Southern drawl a gentler counterpoint to Alec's. "It's ironic, in a way. He had more than he could ever use before, and he still does."

Phineas sighed. "I should have watched more movies."

Miranda smiled a little at that. Despite what he thought, he was such a kid.

"You're quiet, Miranda," Rich said. "What did you think of it all?"

Miranda thought for a moment, then said, "I think he's incredibly lonely. And that place? It's a prison."

9

MARIO COULD HEAR Skye's voice in the main room as he gathered up the few belongings he'd brought over from the yacht.

"Laura didn't like it. But Pa was on the wagon seat and Jack was under the wagon; she knew that nothing could hurt her while Pa and Jack were there. At last the—"

"Does Jack kill zombies?" Silas asked.

"No," Skye said. "Jack is just a regular dog, and there are no z—"

"Brindle," said Violet. "Jack's a brindle bulldog."

"That's right," Skye said.

"What's brindle again?" asked Silas.

"Brindle's the color and pattern of Jack's fur. You know how some dogs are more than one color?" There was a pause, for nodding heads, Mario guessed. "Brindle is a few colors all mixed up: black and brown and orange, and it's usually kind of stripey."

Silas said, "Is it just brindle dogs that don't kill zombies?"

"No," Skye said, chuckling.

As Mario walked into the room, Silas said, sounding grave, "It doesn't seem like a good idea to have a dog like that, even if Jack's nice."

Skye sat on the couch between Silas and Violet, the battered copy of *Little House on the Prairie* in her lap.

"What doesn't seem like a good idea, Silas?" said Skye.

"A dog that doesn't kill zombies."

Skye sighed, looking exasperated.

"You're fighting a losing battle," Mario said. "My kids had a terrible time understanding a world without zombies when they were really small."

"Oh," Skye said.

The front door opened and Doug's head popped through it. "Everyone ready to go?"

"Morning," Mario said.

"How'd you sleep last night?" Doug asked, his eyes bright.

"Well enough," Mario replied, lying through his teeth.

He'd barely slept at all. He'd had dreams about Miranda. They seemed to come in batches, usually as variations on a theme. Last night it was a Miranda who didn't know him, or didn't remember him, or who couldn't see him. He gave up on sleeping entirely around four in the morning.

"How about you?"

Doug grinned. "Like a baby. It was nice hearing all the familiar creaks the yacht makes."

"I'll bet you slept like a baby," Mario said. "Creaks my ass."

Doug smirked, but said nothing more. He and Skye had slept on the yacht the last two nights, since some presence on the yacht seemed prudent. From the improvement in both of their moods, the alone time didn't hurt, either. Since they'd found the children, if you saw Doug or Skye, you also saw Silas or Violet—or both. They had to wait until the kids were asleep, then sneaked out like a pair of teenagers with promises to be back before they woke up.

"Okay you two," Skye said. "Time to go. We'll read more later."

"You're coming with us, right?"

Silas' voice was anxious, his face pinched with worry from one blink of the eye to the next. He looked so much like Anthony, with his grave expression and dark eyes, that Mario's breath caught in his abruptly tight throat.

"We're all going together," Skye said. "If you still don't want to try the rowboat, then me and Doug and Mario are going to walk with you and Violet, and Tessa will take the rowboat to the yacht."

"Okay," Silas said, but he sounded uneasy.

"That rowboat is easy-peasy," Doug said. "It'll be over almost as soon as it starts." He crossed the room and picked up Violet. "If we walk, I call Violet to ride on my back."

Violet squealed, her delight as Doug swooped her up and down shining in her face.

"Don't get them riled up," Mario cautioned.

"You know how to play Who Can Be The Quietest, don't you, Violet?" Doug said.

Violet giggled, then said proudly, "Better than Silas."

"Do not," Silas protested.

"Do too," said Violet.

As he and Violet passed by Mario, Doug murmured, "If he won't try the rowboat, this is going to be a long walk."

Mario smiled despite himself and went to get his pack. It was three weeks to the day since they'd arrived in Eureka. He was happy to be getting underway again.

THEY SAW TESSA OFF AT THE SHORT DOCK BESIDE A GRAY warehouse with a faded blue and white sign that read Caito Fisheries, Inc. To his credit, Silas had almost gotten into the rowboat and spared them this walk, but he lost his nerve at the end. Doug and Skye had found liquid Benadryl at the hospital. They'd dose Silas up if need be to get him on the yacht, but if they were going to resort to drugging the children, they'd save it for when it really mattered. Mario hoped Silas would feel more comfortable on a larger vessel.

Violet wouldn't leave her brother, so the five of them set out on foot. Doug had suggested Mario go with Tessa, but it made Mario uneasy to have just one adult per child. As they walked back to the remnants of the road, Silas ran his fingers over the square, wire fishing traps stacked taller than his head. Mario thought they were lobster traps, which conjured memories of weekends on Cape Cod with his girlfriend when he'd been a doctoral student at M.I.T. They'd stayed in the working-class fishing hamlets near the more upscale, picturesque villages where they'd spent their days, since they couldn't afford the refined bed and breakfasts. Their nighttime retreat to cheap motels hadn't bothered Mario. He'd been far more interested in the girl next to him in the bed than the bed itself.

The breeze blowing in from the bay riffled the tall grasses. Mario looked down when a small hand slipped into his own. Violet looked up at him and smiled. He put his fingers to his lips to remind her of their game. She nodded, then looked ahead, seemingly content. Silas walked ahead of them with Skye and Doug. Doug held Mister Bun Bun's carrier. Sending Mister Bun Bun with Tessa on the rowboat had threatened a full-scale tantrum—and the noise that went with it—from Violet, so that had been that.

Kids are such a pain in the ass sometimes, he thought, but

the warmth of the small hand in his reminded him that they were also—

Stop it, he said to himself. He still tired easily, so he was prone to wandering thoughts. And the children distracted him, which was dangerous. He needed to stay focused. Doug looked back, and Mario gave him a thumbs-up, even though his lungs ached. They were only walking, but it was the most activity he'd had since they'd been waylaid in Eureka. He'd had pneumonia once before. It had taken a few weeks before the coughing and achy feeling subsided.

Silas pointed at an old railroad crossing signpost, and Skye nodded her head. The water lapped softly, now a few hundred feet on their left as the road followed a more direct path toward the low bridge to the island. Seagulls swooped overhead, their harsh cries filling the air.

Mario held his machete loosely in his free hand. On his right the land rose, a gentle slope that turned into a short but steep hillside to the backyards of a row of houses. Mario pulled Violet along with him as he closed the small gap between them and the others. He pointed to the houses at the top of the hill, which would put them on the same level as the road that led to the bridge. A section of fence at the back of a large yellow house had fallen down, leaving a gap.

Mario said, "We can cut up to that gap in the fence."

"Looks like a good spot," Doug said. He stopped, set down Mister Bun Bun's carrier, and crouched low. "C'mon, Violet. Time to ride piggyback."

A smile lit her face, and she scrambled up on Doug's back, quietly, Mario noticed.

"I'll take point," Skye said. "Silas, walk between Doug and Mario, okay?"

"Okay," Silas said. "Should I carry Mister Bun Bun?"

"I'll take him," Skye said.

"Let me," Mario said.

"But you've got Silas, too," she said.

"You repel zombies. Don't you think you should keep your hands free so you can kill some of them?"

Skye conceded the point, and they veered off the road into the tall grass. The gulls still screeched above them, their caws high and thin. Mario felt himself lulled by the swishing grass, the lapping water, even the noise of the gulls. Together it was almost like a hum—

He stopped, really paying attention now, then said, "Doug...hear that?"

Doug slowed, then said, "Shit."

"What's wrong?" Silas asked, his small voice high and reedy.

"Shh," Mario said, putting his hand on the boy's bony shoulder.

Skye had heard it, too. Mario turned his head, the dull drone filling his ears. He couldn't smell the rot of dead bodies, but with the wind blowing in off the bay, that didn't surprise him.

"It's that way," he said. "On the other side of the bridge overpass."

Doug and Skye nodded, agreeing with his fix on the direction the zombies lay.

"When we start up the last part of the slope, where it's steeper, they might see us," Skye said. "We have to make it fast."

Mario motioned for Silas to take his hand, but he had to set down Mister Bun Bun to do it, since he held the machete in the other. Silas obeyed, but he picked up the carrier first. It was oversized and awkward next to the boy. He looked up, eyes huge in his face. Mario leaned in close to Silas' ear.

"It'll be okay. We won't let anything happen to you. If we need to run, you drop that carrier."

Silas' head whipped toward him so fast that he almost hit Mario's nose. "No."

"We can come back for him," Mario said.

Silas whispered, "You're lying."

Goddammit, Mario thought, because Silas had caught him out. If they had to run from a horde of zombies and didn't have Mister Bun Bun, the chances that they would come back were next to none. Mario needed a hand to hold on to Silas and a hand to hold a weapon. Silas wouldn't be able to keep up if he was holding the carrier. If Mario carried Silas piggyback, Silas definitely wouldn't be able to hold the carrier. And carrier or not, having a child on his back would hamper Mario's ability to fight. He couldn't prioritize a rabbit over a child, but he didn't like how Silas was looking at him, like he was nothing but a disappointment the boy had expected all along. He didn't know why it was important to him that this boy he barely knew believed him, but it was.

"I promise that I'll try," Mario said, incredulous that he was even making this bargain. "If I can save Mister Bun Bun, I will. Okay?"

Silas' steady gaze never wavered. The silence stretched for a moment, then he said, "Okay."

Doug asked, "Everyone ready?"

They sped through the tall grass, ducking low. When they reached the foot of the hillside, they paused. Behind them, the sound of the zombies grew louder. Maybe they'd seen the movement in the grass and were already pursuing them. Mario sheathed his machete. If they had to run, he had to carry Silas.

"Hop up on my back. I'll carry Mister Bun Bun," he said, crouching down. Silas didn't move, just looked at Mario, his brown eyes wary. "I will not set him down. I promise."

Silas looked at him for another long moment before scrambling onto Mario's back. Mario stood, cursing himself for being such a goddamned idiot. He grasped Silas' left leg and hooked it over his elbow. Silas clasped his hands around Mario's neck, then Mario picked up the pet carrier with his other hand.

"Ready?" Doug asked Mario and Skye. When they both nodded, he said, "Go."

They sprinted up the hillside, and the moans and hisses swelled. Mario felt a tightness in his lungs from the extra effort immediately, his upward momentum slowing as he compensated to keep his balance. With Silas on his back he was top-heavy, and with the carrier he couldn't use his hand to push off the hillside. By the time they reached the fence, he was coughing. Zombies were swarming into the high grass in pursuit—a lot of them—and the hill wouldn't slow them down enough. The horde extended beyond the other side of the raised roadway of the bridge. He followed the others through the broken fence. They crept to the front yard. The decayed street, with grassy patches and saplings growing through the asphalt, looked clear. They turned west, walking single file.

Mario's head was on a continuous swivel as they walked through a residential neighborhood of simple bungalows and low-rise apartment blocks. Now that they were up on the same level as the rest of the town, they couldn't see beyond what was in front of them. Skye led them south, then west through a narrow alleyway. It had originally been wide enough for cars, maybe even wide enough for them to park and not block traffic, but now they threaded their way through shrubbery, listening for moans or the scuffling of zombies.

They paused at the divided thoroughfare at the alley's end. To the left, the road inclined gradually, turning into the overpass to the island. Mario breathed a sigh of relief. Fog was rolling in, but their route was clear. A loud, hollow pop like a champagne cork was followed by a high trailing whine. A bright-red flare streaked into the sky, cutting through the fog, from the direction of the marina. A column of black smoke snaking skyward, getting blacker and thicker by the second.

"Holy shit," Doug said. "Is that the yacht or something else?"

"Guys," Mario said softly. "We need to go."

Ahead of them, rounding the gentle curve of the overpass, a few zombies straggled into view. Silas' body trembled against Mario's back, and Violet whimpered. Doug and Skye moved closer, flanking him. From the corner of his eye, Mario saw zombies at the far end of the alley they'd just traversed.

He started forward, knowing that Skye and Doug would follow. The fog was thicker on the bridge, cutting visibility. They jogged up the gentle incline, not wanting to go too fast in case there was a mass of zombies ahead they couldn't see. Mario suppressed a cough.

Skye darted forward and slashed at the first few zombies, which all shied away from her. If there weren't too many, she could clear a path for him and Doug, since they were carrying the children. They cleared the buildings obstructing their view of the marina. What Mario saw sucked the air from his burning lungs.

Bright-yellow and orange flames engulfed the yacht. It listed to the side, flames licking up the mast. The edges of the sails flickered red and orange. Mario could see Tessa, backlit by the fire, throwing supplies to the dock. Then he saw a horde of zombies ahead of them that had already reached the island. They tripped and shuffled toward the fiery beacon of the burning yacht. Silas began to cry, and Violet's whimpers grew louder.

Skye said, "We've got to fall back. Tessa will have to hole up and we'll get to her later. I don't know if I can protect all of us," she said. She dropped her voice as they retreated. "Even if I can, I don't know that the kids can handle being surrounded by a horde."

Smoke from the fire reached them, the taste of charred wood and melting plastic filling Mario's nose and coating his throat. Violet, too, began to cry. Her sobs reminded Mario of a frightened animal.

Voice low and not unkind, Doug said, "Silas, Violet, you've got to stop crying. The zombies can hear it. We need to be quiet to get away."

It didn't make a difference. Both children continued to sob. Mario could feel the hiccuping shudders of Silas' small frame against his back. He wanted to comfort the boy, and shake him. His reaction to the situation was normal, but they couldn't afford it. A thousand feet ahead of them, shadows in the fog stumbled out of the alleyway onto the thoroughfare. They ran toward the zombies, veering to the left of the curb-height traffic islands dividing the road. It wasn't much, but anything that would slow the zombies down was an advantage they desperately needed. The stench of death and sewage and rot wafted along with the zombies funneling out from the alleyway.

Skye ran ahead, scouting around the corner. She waved them forward, onto a street of both residential and industrial buildings. Mario coughed, phlegm filling his mouth. He spat, his lungs burning, unable to stop coughing. Zombies stumbled out from yards and parking lots. Skye tried the first two bungalows, to no avail. She sped past a one-story, flat-roofed warehouse to another bungalow. Mario saw her stumble and overbalance when she shoved against the bungalow's door with her shoulder. The door must have given way easily. Then she disappeared inside to clear the house.

Mario and Doug ran alongside the warehouse. Mario caught a blur from above, then was on the ground. He fell onto his side, Silas' limbs coming free from around him. The hard plastic of the pet carrier skittered away. He heard the snap of teeth at his ear over Silas' scream. The stench of the zombie writhing on top of him hit him like a punch. He struck out instinctively, his elbow connecting with the zombie's jaw. He rolled over, the rotting corpse now below him. A zombie dropped from the sky. It landed beside him with a sickening thud. He looked up, heart seizing. Zombies were falling from the warehouse roof, spilling over its edge like a waterfall.

"Silas," he croaked. "Run!"

Mario lurched to his feet, slashing at the zombie attacking him. He ducked away from another, feeling the scrape of its fingers grazing his elbow. Doug wrestled with what had once been a short woman, but now looked more like a horror movie scarecrow. Its eyes were sunken, and a broken jaw bone jutted through leathery skin. At least thirty zombies struggled to their feet in the hundred feet between Mario and Doug. They listed side to side, their gaits awkward from smashed feet and ankles. Skye ran from the porch of the bungalow and scooped up Violet. A violent flash of Doug's knife sent the zombie attacking him slumping to the ground.

The only person Mario didn't see was Silas. Another zombie lunged at him, wisps of filthy hair hanging lank over its face to expose a rotted bald spot. Mario kicked out the zombie's knee and turned back the way they'd come. Silas was running to get the pet carrier.

He sprinted after Silas, toward the approaching horde following them. His lungs were on fire. His legs felt like they were moving through molasses. Harsh breaths rasped painfully in and out of his throat. The approaching zombies were just steps from Mister Bun Bun's carrier. So were the zombies from the warehouse's roof. He scooped up Silas and pivoted toward the bungalow.

"You promised!" Silas screeched, struggling against Mario's grip. "You promised!"

One glance told Mario they weren't going to reach the bungalow. There were too many zombies, and Skye wasn't going to reach them in time to help.

He might as well get the fucking rabbit.

He shoved his machete into its sheath and kicked at a zombie pouncing on the carrier, his boot connecting squarely with its face. He stooped, grasped the carrier's handle, and ran. Silas quit squirming, though his breath still came in raw, hiccuping gasps. There was one gap in the ragged line of zombies beside a squat brown brick building across the street. Mario had no idea if the zombies coming over the bridge would be on the other side.

He ran for the gap, racking coughs robbing him of air. He ducked low when a zombie at the vanguard of the rooftop zombies took a swipe at him. The broken asphalt crunched under his feet. He slowed at the corner of the building, where its driveway dumped them into an alleyway. Half a block to Mario's left, zombies flowed from the bridge, unaware of them. Mario loosened his grip on Silas enough that the boy could slide alongside his body to the ground. He took Silas' small hand in his own and pulled him down the alley parallel to the road where Doug, Skye, and Violet were hiding.

At the next corner, a house that faced the other side of the block had a low wooden fence. Mario looked over it, biting his lower lip to suppress his coughing, so hard that he tasted blood. He picked up Silas and set him down into the weedy yard. He handed Mr. Bun Bun's carrier into Silas' shaking hands, then hopped the fence. He crouched down on his knees, trying to catch his breath. His chest felt pinched in a vise, his throat filled with razors. When he finally quit coughing, he saw that Silas peered inside the carrier, his face pinched with anxiety.

"How is he?"

Talking turned out to be a mistake, because it immediately triggered another coughing fit.

"Okay, I think," Silas said when Mario's hacking subsided. "He's scared."

Mario nodded. He took a careful, shallow breath without coughing. He took another with the same result. Voice shallow so he didn't use much air, he said, "So am I, kiddo. Stay here while I check that house, quiet like a mouse."

Silas nodded, his eyes huge in his face.

He wanted to tell Silas it would be okay, that he'd be right back, but could feel the cough rising in his throat. Instead, he tousled Silas' bare head and left him with the rabbit.

TEN MINUTES LATER, THEY SCUTTLED UP THE STAIRS TO the second floor of the small house. Mario shepherded Silas into a bedroom that overlooked the tangled grass and weeds of the backyard. He set down the pet carrier and closed the bedroom door, then sat on the edge of the bed. He dug in his pocket for the inhaler that Hussein had given him. He shook it gently and opened his mouth. Holding the inhaler an inch from his parted lips, he pressed the cylinder down. A medicinal mist puffed into the air and he breathed it in. He repeated the puff-inhale five more times. The original dose had been two puffs, but it was so old that Hussein had said to use five or six, then see how he felt.

The viselike tightness in his chest eased. After a minute, he felt like he could breathe without coughing and gagging. Thank you, Hussein, he thought; I'd be totally fucked right now without you.

Silas was crouched in front of the pet carrier, talking to the rabbit. "It's okay, Mister Bun Bun. It's okay to come out." Silas' tear-streaked face was forlorn. A few seconds later he looked up at Mario and said, "He's scared."

Mario crouched down beside Silas and looked inside the carrier. The brown rabbit was crammed against the far end of the carrier, eyes shut tight and shaking like a leaf. The poor thing was probably in shock. Mario peeled off his leather jacket and rifled through the pockets of the vest he wore. In the breast pocket he found the crumbled crackers he'd put there an hour ago. An hour ago...it felt like a year. Slowly, so as not to startle the rabbit even more, he slid half of a cracker inside the carrier. Silas started to look inside again but Mario's hand on Silas' shoulder stayed him.

"Just give him a few minutes."

After a while, Mario heard a few tentative crunches, soon followed by more. He slipped more of the crushed crackers into the carrier, this time a little closer to the entrance. Ten minutes later, Mister Bun Bun's nose poked out of the open door. Mario could feel Silas' body tense with excitement, but he didn't reach for the rabbit. After a few more minutes, the rabbit took a tentative hop out.

Silas looked up to Mario, eyes bright. Mario thought Silas would burst when the bunny hopped into his lap. Gently, Silas began to stroke the rabbit.

"It's okay, Mister Bun Bun," he said softly. "It's okay. I knew Mario would get you 'cause he promised."

A surge of tenderness swelled inside Mario's chest. Silas had needed to insist—to shriek and struggle—to hold Mario to his promise. He wasn't sure if the boy truly believed what he'd said or not. Even so, his words filled Mario's eyes with tears. The trust of a child, the simple sweetness of their belief, made him want to sob. He didn't want this. He didn't want to feel the fierce protectiveness that swept through his chest like a wildfire. He didn't want to feel like he couldn't let this child down. He didn't want Silas' trust. What if he broke it?

What he wanted didn't matter—it had already happened. Silas and Violet needed him. He couldn't turn away.

Silas' head began to droop, then snapped up.

"Come on, Silas," he said, patting the boy's head. "Let's lie down and rest."

Silas nodded, his face filled with fatigue. "Mister Bun Bun, too."

Mario smiled. "Mister Bun Bun, too."

He took the rabbit from Silas' lap. It had stopped shaking and nestled itself into the crook of his arm. Its fur was soft against his hand, and the wiggling nose and whiskers, the brightness of its black eyes, soothed his frazzled nerves. He'd been an asshole to think of leaving the rabbit. It needed his protection as much as Silas and Violet did.

Silas crawled onto the bed. Mario lay beside him. The mattress smelled faintly of mildew and strongly of dust. He set the rabbit on Silas' tummy. Silas petted Mister Bun Bun for a few minutes, then turned on his side, cradling the rabbit to him.

"I knew you'd save us," Silas whispered, his voice heavy with sleep.

Silas' breathing grew deep and regular, despite the moans and hisses of the zombies filling the streets outside. Mario turned to nestle Silas against him, his arm draped over the boy's slender body, the rabbit's fur a soft caress against his hand. This boy, who had lost his father somewhere along the line, snuggled close. And he, who loved but had abandoned his children, and lost another son before he was born, cradled him.

He'd loved Tadpole, but hadn't been able to grieve for him, not properly. Not the way he'd wanted to, with his mother. Softly, Mario wept, until exhaustion pulled him under, too.

10

"YOU'RE SHITTING ME," Rocco said.

"Not one little bit," Rich answered.

"Huh," he said, sitting back in his chair.

Miranda tried, and failed, to smother a yawn. Rocco had set up his office as LO's commander in the back of the Boy's Home dining hall, where there was a hallway of offices and storerooms. His office was the same one where Victor, the mercenary from San Jose, had told them who had ordered the failed attack on LO that he'd been part of. She thought it was strange that Rocco chose this one, until she remembered he hadn't been there for that gem of a conversation—

Not thinking about that, she told herself. Not my problem.

"Kendall Grant, huh?" Rocco looked thoughtful. "Just how weird is the guy, after spending all that time on his own?"

"Kinda?" Miranda said. "I don't think interpersonal skills were ever his strong suit. But considering how long he's been there, it could be a lot worse."

"Agreed," Alec said, nodding his head. "Too many people for too long stresses him out. He runs off and hides."

"Sounds about right," Rocco said. "You didn't see where the food is stored, or an armory?"

Rich shook his head. "No, but it's got to be there. Capacity for a hundred people for five years, I think. There might be another level below the one we were on."

Alec said, "If he's going to show it to anyone, it'll be Miranda."

Miranda rolled her eyes, noticing Alec's grin. "Don't start," she warned him.

"He's got a crush on Tucci?" Rocco said, brightening. "We could use that."

"Let's back up right now," Miranda said. "I am not a hooker. I think he'd have found any woman attractive after so long. Assuming he's straight."

"He did take a shine to you," Rich said, his tone matter-of-fact. "He was more relaxed around you, easier to talk to. Just less jittery overall."

"Even so," Miranda said. "I am not whoring myself out to 'work' that angle. No way."

"Tucci," Rocco said. "No one is suggesting that you do anything like that. Just... Show a little interest, you know?"

"Maybe I should smile more?" she said.

Rocco looked at her, pained. "How likely do you all think it is that he'll trade for or give us anything?"

"No idea," Rich said. "He's been there a long time. He has to get used to being around people first. He's jumpier than a cat in room full of rockers."

Miranda thought about what they were proposing, not liking the taste of it in her mouth.

"You're all thinking about this backwards. This can't be about what Kendall can do for us, but what can we do for him. He's been locked in a prison—a swank one, but still—for a decade. I know we need the food, but how do you think he'll react if we sidle up to him just to get his shit? I'm sure he got enough of that in the old days."

"So what do you think we should do, assuming we don't starve in the meantime?" Rocco asked her.

"I think we should hold off talking to him about our food situation. We should hold off telling him anything. He needs people to show a genuine interest in him, as a human being. If we do that, the rest will fall in line on its own. He's a person, not a goldmine."

"He's a bit of a goldmine," Alec said.

Miranda ignored him. "I saw a man who's dying of loneliness."

Confusion in his voice, Rocco said, "I thought you didn't even like him."

Miranda shrugged. "I'm not sure I do, but I saw these glimmers of..." She cast around for a word. "Humanity, I guess."

Miranda thought of the time she'd spent with Kendall in the garden in the middle of the night. Even when they hadn't talked, he'd seemed starved for companionship. She closed her eyes for a moment, the beauty of his singing a faint echo she could still hear. It had been so beautiful, but now, being back in LO, it also seemed pathetically sad.

They lapsed into silence. Rocco pursed his lips, looking pissed off. Then he said, "You're right, Tucci. Of course you're right. I don't know what I was thinking."

"You were thinking we need food now. And that more weapons wouldn't hurt, and he probably has both."

"Well, I feel like a jerk," said Rich.

Alec nodded. "Me too."

"And that," Miranda said. "Is why women should run everything."

That cracked some smiles on their faces, which was fine, but she was completely serious.

"If there's nothing else, Rocco, I'd like to go see my wife and kids," said Rich.

"Yeah, of course." Rocco looked at Alec. "So. You need to move here."

"I heard that might be the case," Alec said.

"Not might," Rocco said, suddenly looking fierce, like he had a kid to protect. "You are. I told your council that was the deal. You don't like it, I don't care."

Miranda smiled, noting the surprise on Alec's face. She and Rich had told him, but apparently he hadn't quite believed them.

"Well, if you feel that strongly," he said.

"I'm glad we understand each other," Rocco said. "You wanna get your stuff now, or get something to eat first?"

"Now would be fine," said Alec uncertainly. He clearly hadn't expected this to happen so fast.

"Okay, good." Rocco narrowed his eyes. "Where the hell is Phineas? He should be here, too."

"He said he'll come see you, but he had something to do," Miranda said. "I told him he was taking his life into hands."

"That fucking kid," Rocco muttered. "Good thing he's all right, or I'd wanna smack him." He looked back to Alec. "I'll find someone to take you to get your stuff. And don't get any ideas that once you get there, you can change your mind."

Alec held up his hands. "Wouldn't dream of it. I just need to speak to some people so they don't think I've disappeared."

"Some people?" Miranda smirked. Alec got a little pink, which surprised her.

Rocco said, "Okay, just sayin'." Almost to himself, he said, "I don't know how anyone stands it over there."

Alec smiled, but didn't contradict him.

When they stood to leave, Rocco said, "I need to talk to you, Tucci."

She smothered another yawn, said goodbye to Rich while Alec excused himself to the hallway, and sat back down, sliding low to slouch in her chair. Delilah resettled herself on the floor with a groan when she realized that they weren't yet leaving.

"What's up?" she asked when they were alone.

Rocco leaned back in his seat and looked at her from across his desk. Unlike Commander Smith's piles of books and papers that had been prone to avalanching, Rocco's desk was neat as a pin.

"You look like shit, Tucci," he said. "You feeling okay?"

"Rich was a lot more polite when he asked."

"Yeah, well, I'm not Rich."

Miranda rubbed at her eyes, which were starting to itch, and yawned. This time, she didn't bother trying to hide it.

"I'm tired," she admitted. It made her uncomfortable when people asked how she was doing. It usually led to wanting to talk to her about everything that had happened. The less she thought about it—never mind talked—the better.

"Still not sleeping so well?"

She shrugged. "Sometimes better than others. You know how it is."

Rocco gave her a long, appraising look that said he wasn't buying it. She didn't know what else to tell him. It was the truth.

"You should try that valerian root tea that River makes. It works pretty good."

"Okay, I will."

After a pause, Rocco asked, "You having bad dreams?"

She blinked at him, feeling caught out. It wasn't that she thought Rocco was totally clueless, but she'd also never thought of him as overly perceptive when it came to reading people emotionally.

"Sometimes," she admitted, not looking him in the eye. She

didn't like this line of questioning, but Rocco was a bull in a china shop. Well-meaning, but still a bull, with a streak of dog with a bone. It was easier to just cop to it—to a degree.

Rocco nodded. "You've had a lot happen the past few months."

Also true, and also nothing to be done about it, so she said nothing.

"So..." he said. "Kendall. You seem to have a pretty good read on him."

"Not any better than Rich."

"You got us back on track about how to deal with the guy, so I'm thinking you do."

She thought for a moment, then said, "I spent a little time with him in the gardens. It was the middle of the night; I couldn't sleep." Fuck, she thought. She didn't need to give Rocco more ammunition. "Kendall just happened to be there. I thought he was an asshole after our first conversation, to be honest. Then I decided I might be jumping to conclusions and should get to know him better. Maybe he is, maybe he isn't... He's been so isolated for so long. I might be a bit rusty on the social graces, too, if I were in his shoes."

Rocco snorted. "You might be? Tucci, you already are."

She chuckled. "Anyway...that's just the sense I got. That he's starved for human contact, and that it'll be worse now that we've been there."

"Plan to stay longer when you head back."

"But the food scouting...you need me and Rich. We can make it a little safer."

"I know," Rocco said. "But this could make them unnecessary. I think you're better utilized getting to know this guy. I'd like to send River with you to check him out, but I don't think introducing another person to the mix is a good idea."

"He gets overwhelmed one-on-one."

Rocco raised an eyebrow. "Even with you?"

"The guys say he's more relaxed around me. Easier to talk to. If it's true, it isn't saying much." She added, almost as an afterthought, "He wasn't so keen on Phineas."

Rocco's brow furrowed. "Everybody likes Phineas. Even I like Phineas. He's a good kid."

"Alec was teasing me about Kendall liking me. You know, like liking." She shrugged. "And you know Phineas..."

"The eternal campaign to get into Miranda's pants."

"The not-so-serious campaign..."

"It's more serious than you think," Rocco said. "Should we not send Phineas back?"

"Fuck no," she said, sitting up straighter. "If he's got a crush or whatever, I'm not changing who my friends are and how we are with each other." Then she amended, "Unless we're actually starving. I know he's been alone for ten years, but he'll just have to deal. *If* he likes me that way."

She stood up. "I'll do my best to be the guy's friend, see if I can get him to trust me, but that's it."

"Fair enough," Rocco said. "But if you think he's sweet on you, don't rule out playing along. Okay?"

"Rocco..."

"You know how much trouble we're in. Just think about it. You're gonna have your hands full getting to be his friend, so it probably doesn't matter."

"What does that mean?" she asked. "I can be his friend."

"Getting him to trust you," Rocco said. "You're not very good at it. Makes it kinda hard to teach."

"I trust people," she said. It came out more defensive than she meant it to. "I'm going to sack out for a few hours. I'll see you later."

Rocco stood and walked around his desk. He put his arm

around her shoulders as they walked to the door. "You do that, Tucci. Good to have you back."

"Good to be back. C'mon, Liley."

They left the office. Rocco said to Alec, "Okay. Let's get you a driver."

Miranda waved goodbye and started down the hallway. Rocco called after her.

"Get that tea from River. I'm serious, Tucci...you look like hell."

"Thanks for the pep talk," she said, giving him the one-finger salute over her shoulder.

She sighed as she walked away. She'd have to get the tea now; he'd check. Underneath his gruff exterior, Rocco was just a big softie. She'd never give him away, but right now, with this, it made him a bit of a pain in the ass because he cared. She didn't have to drink the tea, though, just get some.

If only tea could provide a solution. She was suffering from insomnia, both getting to sleep and, when she finally did, staying that way. But it wasn't sleeping that was the biggest problem. It was dreaming.

***

Miranda's eyelids cracked open to a squint. She squeezed them shut again and groaned.

Sun streamed through the window. She'd forgotten to pull the curtains last night. Obviously. She crawled out of bed and yanked the curtains shut. The bright sunlight was replaced by a soothing gray gloom that didn't send lightning bolts shooting through her brain. She checked her watch: 6:35 a.m.

Three hours, fuck me, she thought. She'd been home a week, but her quest to get enough sleep was coming up short. She took one step toward her bed, then her foot shot out from under her. Her butt slammed against the floor, followed by the hard smack of her head against the windowsill.

"Ow," she said, leaning forward, the room swimming through the tears filling her eyes. Gingerly, she touched the back of her head. She could tell already that she was going to get a goose egg of a bump. She searched the room to see what had pulled her feet out from under her.

"What the— Oh."

An empty cider bottle lay several feet away. She had a vague recollection of ending up by the window last night when she hadn't been able to get back to sleep. She must have set the bottle on the floor when she finished, or dropped it. Either way, the result was the same.

She didn't have any ice, but she might be able to get some from Noelle. She didn't want to go to River. She'd get the third degree about how she'd smacked her head, and then she'd have to lie. But she had to get the thumping—from this bump as well as what was shaping up to be a monster hangover—down to something tolerable if she was going to do her morning run. She'd made a rule for herself when she decided to stay here rather than go back to San Jose; if she didn't run, she couldn't drink.

She shook her head to clear it, despite the pain and pounding the motion produced. She padded down to the kitchen in bare feet and pulled the fridge open. There was still a cider inside.

"Thank you, Jesus," she whispered, popping the top and taking a healthy swig. A little hair of the dog would help the hangover. She finished the cider before she noticed that Delilah hadn't joined her.

"Liley," she called.

Nothing.

She walked halfway down the hall. The front door was open an inch. Gemma—Noelle's three-year-old daughter, must have come in and collected the dog. She did it every time Miranda forgot to lock the door, and LO wasn't the kind of place where you needed to lock your door. She'd been making a concerted effort to lock it though, because Noelle didn't like Gemma wandering off. Before she'd been pregnant, Miranda had thought Noelle was a little over the top with the hypervigilance. She got it now.

She ran upstairs, hopping into a pair of jeans and tucking in her sleeping shirt. Her hair was long enough to pull into a nubbin of a ponytail or two pigtails. She grabbed two elastics and smoothed it into pigtails. Maybe pushing thirty-one was too old for pigtails, but Miranda liked them. And Phineas had said they were cute.

She stepped onto the shared porch of the duplex, the concrete cool under her bare feet. Just as she raised her hand to knock, the door flew open. Noelle started, her china-blue eyes going wide. Her black hair was unkempt, and her eyes were puffy with sleep. She looked paler than usual, her skin an almost chalky white. She reminded Miranda of Snow White, but Snow White had never been surrounded by the aura of perpetual anxiety that pinched Noelle's eyes at the corners and pressed her mouth into a tight line. She looked thinner, too, and she'd never needed to lose weight. Was the rationing so severe already? The more Miranda got to know her, the more sympathy she had for Noelle. Raising a child on one's own had always been hard. Doing so now must feel next to impossible. She got it, now, why a person might choose to have a child despite how dangerous the world had become, but she pushed the thought away.

"They're not with you?" Noelle asked.

"No," Miranda said. "I thought they were here."

"She gotten good at unlocking the door," Noelle said, sounding on the verge of tears.

"It's not a big deal," Miranda said. She placed her hands on Noelle's shoulders. "They can't have gotten far, and everyone will steer them home. How about I take the Big Woods and you take the housing plan?"

"Okay," Noelle said, taking a deep breath. She gave Miranda a tremulous smile. "Thanks, Miranda."

"You should be yelling at me for not locking my door," Miranda replied. "Meet you at River's in fifteen minutes?"

Noelle turned away, not bothering to close the door. Miranda pulled it shut and trotted down the walk.

Goddammit, she thought. She would either have to remember to lock the door or start shutting the bedroom door so Delilah didn't have the run of the house. Being awake was bad enough, and hitting her head had been worse. Dragging her hungover ass outside in search of her dog and a three-year-old, while ice picks of sunlight stabbed her eyes, was a whole new level of suck.

She'd also forgotten to put on her shoes.

She jogged under the high canopy of the Big Woods, the sun's overcast glare cut by fifty percent and replaced with a suffused green glow. She turned right off Big Fir Trail, one of two main trails, onto the Ash Loop. She went this way on her morning run, so the probability that Delilah had turned this direction was high, but she didn't find them.

She turned right onto the Trillium Loop. Nothing. She continued toward the Nature Center...or where it used to be. She squinted up Owl Path, but decided to keep going. If she didn't find them by the time she reached the south end of Ponderosa Loop, which at half a mile was one of the longer loops, she'd double back on it, then backtrack again to the Nature Center.

She'd just turned onto Ponderosa when she heard Delilah bark, followed by a high, piping voice. Relief flooded through her as she trotted toward Gemma's voice. Delilah barked again. It was her playful bark, and Miranda heard the low buzz of a man's voice. Someone had found Gemma and Delilah and was bringing them home, just as she'd predicted. She rounded the bend and stopped in her tracks. Gemma and two men—one in front of the other—walked down the path. The larger of the two, with close-cropped blond hair and a strong, chiseled jaw, held Gemma's hand. He looked down at her as she explained something—Gemma loved to explain things—a smile curving his lips. His brown tee shirt strained to contain his muscled frame, as did the work pants he wore. It was Phineas who followed them. He faced the opposite direction, and Miranda saw a stick fly through the air. Delilah took off after it like a rocket.

The big man looked up and froze, just for a second. Miranda stared at him in openmouthed shock. Victor, the mercenary who had led the attack on LO only a few months ago, held Gemma's hand, while Phineas threw a stick to her dog. What the ever-loving fuck was going on? Her stomach filled with lead. Sudden, overwhelming fear of Gemma being harmed felt like a blow. She dashed over and snatched Gemma away.

"Are you okay, Gemma?" she said, her arms trembling with the need to keep the girl safe.

Gemma squirmed in Miranda's arms. "Manda," she whined. "Let go!"

Miranda's grip didn't loosen. She hadn't bothered to put on her holster, with her handgun, knife, and machete, and really wished she had.

"What's going on?" she demanded. She glared up at Victor as Phineas came abreast of him. "What is he doing out?"

"It's okay, Miranda," Phineas said quickly. "I'm escorting Victor to breakfast."

"We met Gemma and Delilah, so we're walking them home on the way," Victor said.

"Shut up," Miranda snapped at him.

"Ow," Gemma whined, wriggling harder, and Miranda realized her grip on the child was too tight.

"He's supposed to be in the stockade," Miranda said to Phineas.

"Rocco told me to bring him to the dining hall, that he'd meet us there," Phineas said, sounding apologetic.

"What?" she fairly barked, because there was no way she had heard him right.

"I want the nice man," Gemma said, the whine in her tone much more pronounced. She reached her pudgy arms for Victor, who watched Miranda and Phineas' exchange. A wary amusement danced in his brown eyes.

"You don't even have a weapon, Phineas," Miranda said, both dumbfounded and furious, which intensified the pounding in her head.

"I'm not going to hurt him," Victor said mildly. "Besides, where am I going to go?"

"Not talking to you," Miranda said at precisely the moment Gemma began to wail.

The high-pitched shriek felt like a jack hammer against Miranda's temples. Gemma's thrash became a whole-body endeavor. Delilah had returned and began to bark, distressed by the girl's distress, but unsure what her role was in keeping Gemma safe since Miranda was holding her.

"I want the nice man," Gemma wailed, sounding like someone was murdering her soul.

Victor looked at Miranda. "Just let her walk with me."

Gemma thrashed, her wails getting worse by the second.

Miranda didn't know what the hell was going on, or why this murderer was out and about with access to children. But she also knew she wasn't making the situation better. Despite the desire to hold Gemma tight and flee, she relented. Get a grip, she told herself, unsure what was driving this feeling of fear. Maybe it wasn't fear. Maybe it was pain, because if she had to keep listening to this shrieking, she was pretty sure her head would split open.

"Fine," she said.

Despite every instinct in her body telling her not to, she set Gemma down. The wails ceased immediately, replaced by hiccups and few pathetic whimpers. She ran to Victor and wrapped her arms around his massive leg. Delilah wriggled close and licked at Gemma's face.

"Nice man," Gemma said.

Victor pulled a bandana from his pocket, old and threadbare, and bent to wipe Gemma's tear-streaked face. The muscles of his torso rippled, and his biceps flexed. Miranda watched, horrified. All she could think was how he could pop Gemma's head off her body as easily as flicking a dandelion from its stem with his thumb, and she'd be too slow to stop him.

Victor wiped Gemma's face and smiled at her. "Better?"

She nodded, rewarding him with a sunny grin. She took his hand and resumed her childish prattle as if the last two minutes hadn't happened.

"I'll follow," Miranda growled, gesturing him past her.

Victor nodded and resumed his way down the path, even skipping with Gemma for a few steps. Phineas fell in step beside Miranda, looking at her like she was a bomb.

"You weren't even watching them," Miranda whisper-yelled at Phineas. "I don't know what the hell Rocco is thinking. You were playing with the goddamned dog instead of watching him." She fixed him with a withering stare. "You don't even have a weapon."

Phineas gulped audibly.

"Why aren't you walking her? What the fuck, Phineas?"

"She ran right up to us, and Delilah was with her," he stammered. "She just took his hand."

Phineas's lame explanations set her teeth on edge. Normally, he was sensible, but this...

"I didn't—" he started.

"Don't talk," she snapped. "Just. Don't."

Phineas shrank away despite still walking alongside her. Birdsong, the scuff of Delilah's trotting paws, and Gemma's high, babyish voice, punctuated by Victor's deep, basso answers or comments, were the only accompaniment for their journey. Miranda studied Victor, noticing that his arms and neck, and now that she thought about it, his face, were tanned, as if he'd been spending time outdoors. He walked with an easy, relaxed stride, even though it was shortened by Gemma's short legs, and did not seem distressed in the least by being a prisoner. But if this was how Rocco thought murderers should be treated, no wonder he looked that way.

As they emerged from the Big Woods into the housing plan, Miranda had mostly regained control of her temper. She saw Noelle at the corner, pacing in front of River's house where she was waiting for Miranda. She looked up, and when she saw them, her petite frame sagged with relief. She hurried over to meet them.

When they were twenty feet apart, Noelle called, "Gemma!"

Gemma looked up, then let go of Victor's hand and ran to her mother. Noelle swooped Gemma into her arms and held her close.

"You scared Mama," she said. "You can't leave like that."

Gemma pointed to Victor. "The nice man!" She glowed with happiness, like she had found a buried treasure.

Victor halted, and Miranda sidled up so she almost stood between them. Noelle smiled, relieved, then looked up to Victor. He towered over Noelle, as big and brawny as she was tiny and petite.

"Thank you so much," she said, relief filling her voice. "I hope she wasn't a bother. I almost had a heart attack when I realized she was gone."

"It was my pleasure, ma'am," Victor said.

Miranda snorted. My pleasure? Ma'am? Who did he think he was kidding?

"And she had that pittie looking after her," Victor added.

"Yes," Miranda said, her voice hard. "She did."

"I can't thank you enough..." Noelle trailed off, a question in her voice.

"Victor," Victor said.

"Noelle," Noelle answered, shifting Gemma to her hip before shaking Victor's hand.

"It really was my pleasure," Victor assured her. "Gemma told me all about the woods."

He smiled, and goddamn if the man wasn't charming. Miranda glared at Victor, then Phineas, who was trying hard to blend into the background. "Don't you have somewhere to be?" she asked pointedly.

"Yeah," Phineas said, leaping into action to escape Miranda's wrath.

Victor said, "Bye, Gemma."

Gemma buried her face in her mother's shoulder, playing shy. If only she'd done that when she met them on the path and ended up with Phineas in charge of her.

"The nice man," Gemma said, peeking out at him.

"Let's go, Victor," Phineas said, a note of desperation in his voice.

"Miranda," Victor said, with a small incline of his head.

Miranda said nothing, working hard to not throw up in her mouth at Victor's performance. Phineas and Victor walked away, down the street toward the thin spit of trees that separated the housing plan from the ground of the Boys Home, where the dining hall was located.

Delilah leaned against Miranda's leg. Miranda could tell Delilah's tail wagged by the way her body vibrated. Gemma worked her way around her mother's waist like a monkey until they faced one another. Noelle held Gemma under her arms, the child's legs wrapped around her waist, and held her a little bit away. She looked at her daughter severely.

"You cannot do that, Gemma. You have to wait for me, or wake me up, if you want to play with Delilah. And you cannot wander off. You scared Mama."

Gemma's lower lip, pink as the blush on an apple blossom, jutted out in a pout. She looked down and studied her belly button through her nightgown.

"I'm not mad at you," Noelle said, her voice less severe. "But you can't do that again."

Gemma nodded, then wrapped her arms around her mother's neck and stuck to her like a sea urchin.

Noelle said, "Thank you so much, Miranda."

"I'll lock my door, I promise. Hopefully she'll just go back inside if she opens your door again."

"Thank God they came across her before she fell in the pond or something..." Her voice trailed away, then she said, turning to Miranda, "That Victor must be one of the new arrivals coming to get the vaccine. I've never seen him before. He seemed nice."

Miranda hated to be the one to crush the hopeful look in

Noelle's eyes that the return of her baby had sparked, but talk about getting it wrong.

"He's one of the men who attacked us," Miranda said.

Noelle's eyes widened. Her mouth formed a perfect cartoon princess O of surprise.

"I don't know why he's not in the stockade," she continued. "But I'm going to see Rocco about it. He's a—"

She'd been about to say murderer, but caught herself in time. Gemma was always asking questions, wanting to know what things were and how things worked. She'd asked Miranda why birds didn't land on leaves. When she'd explained they couldn't bear the weight, Gemma told her that wasn't it, so she'd said they were slippery. The last thing Noelle needed was to have her asking what a murderer was. She was already stressed out.

"He's not what he seems, Noelle," she said instead. "You should steer clear of him."

"Yeah," Noelle said softly, her arms tightening around Gemma. "I will."

11

ROCCO WASN'T at their usual table by the window. Phineas and River were, but Rocco must have finished eating. When she caught Phineas' eye, he quickly looked away. Miranda scanned the rest of the dining hall, but she didn't see him. She threaded her way through the tables, nodding in acknowledgment to greetings as she veered toward the door at the far end of the room.

She saw Rich approaching from her peripheral vision. He fell in step beside her. "Have a tough night?"

Miranda realized her hasty pigtails were probably untidy, and she hadn't even brushed her teeth after she walked Noelle and Gemma home. She had put on shoes, then come straight here to talk to Rocco.

"Something like that," Miranda answered. Mathilde and their children sat a few tables away in the direction they were walking. She caught sight of Rich's plate. The portions were measly.

"Is that your whole meal?"

He shrugged. "They offered me a little more, but not much.

We're going to the bunker soon, and I'll have plenty to eat there."

"Okay," she said.

When they arrived at his table, she said hello to Mathilde and the kids, and goodbye to Rich.

The amount of food on Rich's plate wasn't quite half of normal. So they must be at about two-thirds rations. The pressure of needing to get to the bunker, to do something to get food for everyone, settled on her like sandbags.

She entered the hallway of offices at the back of the building, pushing stray wisps of hair behind her ears. She had her hand raised to knock on the door to Rocco's office when she heard the low murmur of voices. She fell back and leaned against the wall. Her temples throbbed. She smacked her papery-dry tongue against the roof of her mouth, but there was no moisture to speak of, even after the cider she'd drunk before. Now that she thought about it, though, her hangover had eased a little.

After what seemed an age, but was probably ten minutes, she heard the rustle of movement from Rocco's office.

"—talk again later this week," Rocco said as the door opened.

"Sure thing."

Victor filled the doorway, more than even Rocco's broad frame did. He nodded to Miranda and made his way down the hall back to the dining room. Miranda pulled her stare away from his retreating form.

"You look like a truck hit you, Tucci."

Miranda marched into Rocco's office. "Why is he out? Why is he walking around with an 'escort'?" She made air quotes with her fingers. "And why is the escort unarmed?"

"I can see what side of the bed you woke up on." Miranda narrowed her eyes at Rocco and scowled. He added, "I've been meeting with Victor a couple times a week the last few weeks. To get a read on him, and—"

"Why aren't you doing it in the stockade?"

"And," Rocco continued, emphasizing the word to make sure she understood he was annoyed at being interrupted. "I've decided to give him something to do."

"Since when?" Miranda asked.

"Since you left on the P-Land errand."

"Really?" They'd stumbled across Kendall's bunker two weeks ago. "He's Navy, Rocco, which means he's scum. He led the attack on us just a few months ago. He's a killer."

Rocco settled back into his chair, arms crossed. "So are you."

Miranda crossed her arms, mirroring his posture. "That was different. I know I owe you for smoothing the way after I killed Jeremiah, but bringing him up all the time is bullshit."

"Look," Rocco said, his tone more conciliatory. "I'm sorry for saying it that way. I was just trying to draw a parallel, not imply you still owe me, 'cause you don't. Okay?"

Miranda nodded, partly mollified.

Rocco said, "Locked up, he's a drain on our resources, but if we put him to work, we're at least getting something out of him being here. He says he wants to make amends and start over here."

"Oh for fuck's sake."

"He's a hard worker," Rocco said. "He showed me how they sabotaged the sound defenses. We were able to upgrade them so that's not possible anymore. And he dug out and built those new outhouses at the apartment complex. Now the people over there don't have to hike all the way to the dining hall."

"He built the whole thing?" she said, surprised.

Rocco nodded.

She'd seen the latrines when they got back from Kendall's

bunker, ten of them, which was a shit ton of digging, never mind building the outhouse structure and the brickwork and venting. She'd assumed there'd been a work detail for the job... He couldn't have done it all by himself in that timeframe.

"One person couldn't do all that."

"Calling me a liar now?" Rocco said.

"I didn't know about improving the sound defenses, but that doesn't square things. Give him a participation award. Don't let him roam around."

Rocco sighed. "He's not roaming around. He's always got an escort."

"Who was throwing a stick for my dog and letting him walk with a child."

Rocco rubbed his forehead with the heel of his hand. "Jesus, Mary, and Joseph, Tucci...you're killing me here." His hand dropped to the desk. "I'll talk to Phineas. And if you want, you can pick out the escorts. Not you...you're too much of a hothead."

"I don't trust him."

"I don't trust him, either," said Rocco. "But I like to think I'm a good judge of people. He's done some horrible stuff, but he's not motivated by inflicting pain. He's been a mercenary, not a psychopath."

"And you're qualified to make that diagnosis how, exactly?"

"I really think he wants to start over," he said, ignoring her question. "I'm going to give him a chance to do that. We gave Mario the benefit of the doubt when you arrived here."

"It's not the same thing," she said irritably. She didn't want to think about Mario, much less have him trotted out as an example.

"With the reputation he had when you got here, yeah, it was. We've always tried to give people the benefit of the doubt. It's what Anna would've wanted."

Miranda threw her hands up in exasperation. LO's previous commander was dead because of the attack that Victor had led.

"I know, I know," Rocco said, his voice softer than before. "I do. I knew her a lot longer than you. Trust me... I know what he did. He's not going back to San Jose; he's said as much. Even if we send him packing, we can't make him leave the area without devoting a lot of resources to it. Resources that we don't have right now, quite frankly. I'm keeping a very close eye on him, and I've got others doing it, too. ,I had River assess him and she agrees that he's not a sociopath or anything like that."

"Just a scumbag."

"If he really does want to change," Rocco said, ignoring her comment, "doesn't it make sense to get him invested in this place? He's got some valuable skills. He does the shit jobs I'm giving him without bitching, and he does them right the first time. Wouldn't you rather have him fighting with us than against us?"

A shiver raced through Miranda's body. "Now I feel like I need a shower."

Rocco snorted. "You look like it, too," he said. Then he said, sounding like he was bracing for an attack, "As long as you're freaking out, I've got Victor working on getting a ham radio working."

It felt like the floor giving way below her feet, the sensation of falling was so strong. She gaped at Rocco, so stunned she literally couldn't speak. "I can't have heard you right."

"You did."

She pressed the heels of her hands against her temples, elbows sticking out at the sides, and paced in a tight circle.

"Oh my God," she said. "Oh my God, oh my God, oh my God..."

"Settle down, Tucci. My thinking is—"

"Oh my fucking God. What the—" She stopped circling and stared at Rocco, her eyes wide. "Have you lost your goddamn mind?"

Rocco had gotten to his feet. When he put his hands on her hands still clutching her head, she jerked away.

"Look," he said. "I've got a handle on it. I've got a plan."

There were words coming out of his mouth, but it was like he was speaking Japanese. They didn't compute.

In a calm, even voice, Rocco said, "We need to get word out about the vaccine by more than word of mouth when we're ready to scale up."

"But—"

"After we've hit a critical mass locally," he said. "After we've got a couple labs set up that are isolated and hidden. We're gonna need to do this on a bigger scale."

"But you're inviting an attack," she said, incredulous. "Isn't that the reason LO decided to not use long-distance radios? Isn't that what you told me?"

Rocco sighed, running his hands through his hair. His brown eyes betrayed apprehension. "Yeah... But that— It was a long time ago, when we were smaller and weaker and didn't know what we were doing. We got our asses handed to us. That's when we put away the long-distance radios. But we fought them off last time. We lost people, and it's fucked us for food, but we're still here."

"We got lucky, Rocco," she countered. "There were zombies inside the palisade."

"I know," he said. "I know that. And because people know what to do, nobody got bit besides Anna."

"But why Victor?"

Rocco sighed. His broad shoulders sagged, but his hands started waving in the air as he talked. "Because he knows what he's doing," he said, frustration bubbling in his voice like a pot about to boil over. "We've got old radios that've been sitting for years. They don't work! The guys who knew how to use them aren't here anymore, and forget about the flakes at P-Land... We don't have anybody who knows how to do it, never mind fix one."

"Get a fucking manual!"

"You're killing me, Tucci," Rocco muttered, shaking his head. "We have 'em, but he knows what he's doing. He can do it faster and better." He put his big hands on her shoulders. This time, she didn't shrug him off. "Believe me, I don't trust the guy. Do I think he can be rehabilitated? Maybe, but I don't trust him." He sounded wounded when he added, "I'm not an idiot."

"I never said that."

She felt the fight draining away, leaving tired resignation in its wake. Rocco wasn't going to keep Victor locked up unless he had to, no matter how much she disliked it, and he was set on this ridiculous idea of letting him near a radio. She knew they needed to focus on getting enough food and providing housing for the people who were arriving to get the vaccine. Ramping up vaccine production had taken a distant second in the community's priorities, because leaving people to fend for themselves wasn't how things were done here, even if it meant they were scrambling.

She knew they'd have to scale up getting word out to people if—when—they got to that point, but h

er entire life had been turned upside down. Her friendship with Doug was careful and strained. Mario was gone, but tormented her in her dreams. Father Walter might be able to help her sort things out, maybe even fix it, but he might as well be on the moon. Karen wouldn't know what to do, except take her shopping and bring her soup from Chef Chu's, but it would help because it would be motivated by love.

And Tadpole... She almost whimpered out loud as the familiar feeling of desolation swamped her, sharp and bright as it rubbed like rough leather against the blister of her loneliness. She was so lonely she ached. She had friends here, but they weren't the right ones, somehow. They weren't the people who knew her best. That Mario was one of those people who did made her feel so crazy she choked on it, but so lonely she wanted to cry, and now this.

"Just give it a chance, okay? He'll be under guard the whole time—not Phineas," he said quickly, when she opened her mouth to object. "Larry, for one, because he gets the technical shit. And a couple bruisers who can't be manipulated. Who hate his guts. I promise."

"Jesus, Rocco..."

"And if it turns out you're right and I'm wrong, we'll lock him up again. He helped Gemma get home today. Seems encouraging to me."

Rocco's pinched face and beseeching eyes implored her to understand. He's scared...desperate, she realized. That wasn't a good mental state for making sound decisions. This whole thing scraped against every instinct for self-preservation she had, but his mind was made up; she could see it. Not only that, he needed her to believe in him. Now that her temper had been checked, she could see just how much.

"Fine," she grumbled. "We'll do it your way."

For a second, she thought about telling him how terrified she'd been when she first saw Victor with Gemma. How the instinct to protect the toddler had hit her so hard that it might as well have been her own child. She couldn't stand the idea of another baby lost to a monster.

"You okay, Tucci?"

Miranda blinked, surprised by the tears beginning to pool in her eyes. Her exhaustion wasn't just making this morning's developments hard to take in; it was loosening her grip on her emotions.

"Yeah, I'm fine. I didn't expect this much drama before breakfast."

Rocco's eyes narrowed. "You still having trouble sleeping? Are you drinking that tea?"

"A little, sometimes," she said, deflecting his concern. "I woke up with a headache."

Rocco didn't look like he was buying it. "Have you been drinking this morning?"

"What?" she said. "No!"

"You smell like booze."

"I had a few ciders last night and spilled one. I grabbed the first thing I laid hands on so I could go look for Gemma. I'm not drinking my fucking breakfast." She plastered a smirk on her face and said, "If you don't like me objecting to your cockamamie schemes, come up with something better than that to harass me with." The hair of the dog, he didn't need to know about. She wasn't getting into the falling on her ass part, either.

"I still don't like this."

"You wouldn't be you if you did."

Miranda crinkled her nose and pursed her lips. "That was weirdly complimentary. You aren't going to hug me or anything?"

He snort-laughed. "Hardly. You still leaving for the bunker tomorrow?" She nodded. "Go get that shower and bother someone else, okay? I've got work to do."

Rocco was still adjusting to being LO's new commander. He needed people who believed in him, not people who stormed into the office to yell at him. It wasn't that the two were mutually exclusive, because she already believed that Rocco was good at his new job. Once he got more comfortable with it, he'd be great. This nonsense aside, she ought to let him know that she had faith in him, even if she disagreed with him sometimes.

"I hope I'm wrong about Victor," she said.

Rocco gave her a wan smile. "You and me both."

PORTLAND MADE MIRANDA'S NECK ITCH, AND NOT THE kind relieved by scratching.

It wasn't like their world was predictable, not in the way that the old one had been, but the zombies in Portland were weird. You could walk for hours without encountering them, then turn a corner and bam! You'd find yourself in the middle of a horde. In the ruins of other cities, large areas with no zombies weren't as common; they were pretty much everywhere even if density varied. In Portland this wasn't the case, and there didn't seem to be any rhyme or reason for why sometimes you'd find zombies in an area, but the next time you wouldn't.

Rhyme and reason with zombies, she thought to herself. I'm more tired than I thought.

Maybe it was because, coming from the West, Portland felt like a tease. Most of what was in the city's limits—not that that meant much these days—was east of the Willamette River. The idea that reaching the Willamette was the same thing as being through Portland wasn't true, but somehow, the notion that it was had become embedded in Miranda's brain. From the crossing at Ross Island Bridge, it was fifty miles to Kendall's bunker, give or take. They would drive beyond the bridge until the roads got so bad that they had to set out on foot, which still left at least two day's walking.

She hated the Ross Island bridge. It was a reminder of when she'd arrived here. When she'd still been with Mario, and they'd been happy. When there hadn't been the emotional distance she now felt between herself and Doug, and none of them had any idea what the next six months would hold or how badly everything would go off the rails. She tried not to think about it when she made the crossing, but she always did.

The bridge was a waypoint, and something caught her eye as they approached the barricade. There was one at both ends, made of welded steel slabs that had been used in road work to cover holes in the road. Rectangular inset windows about a foot long and covered by bars were at eye level every few feet, so the integrity of the fortifications could be checked before entering. They stopped the truck and Miranda and Rich got out. She shaded her eyes as she peered through.

"It's the food scouting party Rocco took out yesterday," she said softly, a jolt of surprise running through her at the sight of a white box truck.

"Didn't they have two trucks?" Rich said, turning to her.

"They did," she said.

A few minutes later they were through the gate and pulling up to the scouting party truck. Rocco was near it, and recognized as they drew near. Sean, the red-headed mechanic Miranda had met at the meeting about the food shortage, was with him. Sean's right arm was in a sling, and he winced with every step.

"Why's Rocco doing this?" Alec asked. "Surely he's too valuable to lose, since he's running things."

"That's why he went," Rich said. "To set a good example."

"Good to see you guys," Rocco said when they were in earshot. He looked like he'd aged since Miranda had seeen him yesterday. His mouth was set in a grim line, and his broad shoulders slumped.

"What happened?" Miranda said.

"Nothing good. We got to the grocery distribution center,

like we planned. It was farther away, but there was more food there than I expected...canned stuff. Peaches mostly, but better than nothing. We got both trucks loaded up and were on our way back when the other truck got a flat."

Rocco shook his head and closed his eyes. Miranda could tell he was blaming himself.

"Rocco's truck was already around the corner when we got the flat," said Sean.

Rocco said, "We backed up into the intersection so we could turn around to go back. We'd already decided to leave the truck in place and come back for it, and then there were zombies everywhere, from one minute to the next. Bill and the others weren't even twenty feet from the truck when they had to run back to it."

"Did anyone make it besides Sean?" Rich said.

"Yeah," Rocco said. "Victor was in the cab with me, and—"

"Victor's with you?" Miranda said. The idea that Rocco would take the mercenary out to cover anyone's back beggared belief.

"Victor's the only reason we got anyone out of the truck Sean was in," Rocco said tiredly. "Gloria and Phil—they're newcomers—were in the back of our truck with the food, so I wasn't worried about them. We drove into the horde."

He paused at the collective intake of breath. Driving into a horde was never a good idea. Bodies got tangled in axles, windows broken. A box truck sat high enough that zombies would have a harder time swarming the cab, but they'd all seen it happen.

"We got our cab about three feet from theirs, on the passenger side. Victor climbed to the roof of our cab, to make room. Bill was—" Rocco stopped.

Sean said, "Bill had been driving, but he couldn't shut the door after he got back inside. They were trying to get over him, drag him out. I was firing at them." His voice got tight, and Miranda saw tears well in Sean's eyes. "He was trying to hold on to them while they were attacking, so they wouldn't fall back out. So they couldn't get to the rest of us. It was one of the bravest things I've ever seen."

Rocco sighed, scrubbing his face. "Victor shot enough of them between the trucks that they could open the door. We got Alicia through no problem, but—"

Phineas barked, "Alicia's with you? What the hell is she doing with you?"

Alicia was the virologist who'd worked with Mario to create a new vaccine for the zombie virus. From the appalled looks on everyone's faces, Miranda and Phineas weren't the only ones shocked that she was participating in the food scouting.

"I didn't want her to come, but she and Bill have been dating..." Rocco grimaced. "I figured if I let her come this time, she'd get it out of her system and that'd be that. I fucked up. Obviously."

"But she's okay?" Rich asked.

Rocco nodded.

"What happened to your shoulder?" Alec said to Sean.

"One of them caught my foot when I was jumping over. Victor caught my arm and pulled me up, but it got wrenched pretty bad. He thought we should immobilize it till the doctor can look at it."

"Good Lord, Rocco," Rich said. He put his hand on Rocco's shoulder. "Is there anyone in the back of the other truck?"

Rocco's laugh was bitter. "Of course there are people in the back... We'll try to get them tomorrow or the next day, once things settle down. They've got water and food."

After a moment's silence, Rocco turned and walked toward the truck. Everyone followed. The back roller door was up. The truck was crammed to the ceiling with boxes of canned goods.

The ones Miranda could see had PEACHES IN SYRUP written on the sides. Not a lot of caloric value, but like Rocco had said, better than nothing. The stacks of boxes looked like a lot, but she knew this wouldn't last a week at LO. And they needed more than peaches.

A man and woman Miranda didn't know, the newcomers Rocco had mentioned, looked rattled. They were sharing a rollie cigarette. Alicia sat on the tailgate. Her dark, curly hair was braided close to her head, the ends pinned in place at the base of her skull. Her blood-streaked face was upturned to Victor, who was applying a butterfly bandage to a cut above her eye.

"That'll be good enough until River can check you out," he said.

Alicia nodded. When she saw Miranda and the others, she offered a weak smile. Victor stepped away after a glance at Miranda, which she returned with a frosty stare, and joined the other newcomers sharing the cigarette.

"Alicia, I'm so sorry," Miranda said.

"Yeah, me too," Alicia said. "No more scouting for me, I guess. I don't need another reminder I'm more valuable at the Institute, even if things aren't moving along like we'd hoped."

"You went north today, right?" Miranda heard Rich say to Rocco.

"Yeah. You're going south; you should be okay, but I wouldn't stick around."

Miranda squeezed Alicia's shoulder. "Let me know if you want to hang out, okay? We should be back in a couple weeks. I'll check in with you then."

Alicia nodded, and Miranda rejoined the others. They said their farewells and walked back to their truck.

Rich said, "Sounds like it was a good thing Victor was with them."

"Yeah," Phineas agreed.

Miranda said. "I still don't trust the guy as far as I can throw him."

"Why's that?" Alec asked.

"Long story," Rich said. "Tell you later."

Alec nodded, and let the matter drop. Miranda was grateful to Rich for saving her from explaining it. The attack on LO was enmeshed with other things she'd rather not think about, and deep down she felt guilty for bringing the problems of San Jose here. The last thing she needed right now was getting distracted by Victor's 'good deeds.' They needed to stay vigilant to get to the bunker alive, even with two people who repelled zombies in their group. The fate of Rocco's scouting party had reminded them of that fact.

RICH AND ALEC WALKED TEN PACES AHEAD OF MIRANDA and Phineas. Delilah brought up the rear for most of the past hour since they'd left the truck behind, but in the last ten minutes ventured ahead. She stayed in sight, but something had caught her interest. The mood of the group had lightened somewhat since leaving the food scouting party behind. What they were doing required vigilance, but letting it amp up into rattled paranoia rarely led to performance improvement. You learned to shake even the most horrible things off when you needed to. Your brain could spring it on you later for processing, assuming you were still alive for that to happen.

Rich looked back to Miranda over his shoulder. "You all right back there?"

"Yep," she said. "Just bored."

"Now you've done it, lassie. Jinxed us for sure," Alec said over his shoulder.

"Don't be talking smack on my girl," Phineas said.

Miranda shook her head, a smile tugging at the corners of her mouth. The journey might feel endless, but Phineas could be counted on to defend her honor.

Alec looked back at them, grinning. "It's not smack if it's true."

"Hold up, Alec," Rich said. They stopped, waiting for Miranda and Phineas to catch up. Rich pushed his sunglasses up on his head. "I think we should look for a place to stop. I know it's a little early... I don't know about y'all, but I'm tired."

"Another mile?" Miranda said. "That'll get us to Gresham. There are a few good places there."

"Sounds good," Rich said with a nod of his head.

Over his shoulder, Miranda saw Delilah stop at the end of the block. Her body tensed, then she turned and ran back to them. "I think you're right about me jinxing us, Alec."

They all looked to see Delilah's approach. A moment later, staggering figures rounded the corner into the intersection.

"Oh, Lordy," Rich said, sounding resigned. "Let's see how many there are. We might be able to go through."

"Time to get cozy," Miranda said to Phineas.

He raised his eyebrows as if she had just propositioned him, then did as told and sidled up close. They passed the first group of zombies that had already turned the corner. About fifty zombies were shambling up the block. Too many for most people, but nothing they couldn't handle. Alec walked behind Rich, keeping a hand on his shoulder. Phineas did the same with Miranda.

"You can get closer," Miranda said.

"I don't want to step on your feet."

"I'd rather that than the alternative."

"I will if I need to," Phineas promised.

Even though she knew the zombies would shy away and

not harm her, the feeling of walking through groups of them was so unnatural that Miranda wanted to jump out of her skin. Her breathing grew shallow, rasping in and out of her lungs too quickly.

The zombies turned toward them, shuffling closer on unsteady feet. Even though the breeze was blowing away from the horde, the overpowering stench of rotting meat was so strong Miranda's eyes began to water.

"These ones really stink," Phineas said in a tone of voice that gave her a mental image of his crinkled nose.

"Yeah," she said, breathing through her mouth.

The hisses and groans grew so loud they became grating white noise. Rich and Alec walked five steps ahead of them, which mitigated the pinball effect when the zombies withdrew from pursuing them and turned toward her and Phineas. We must look like ducks paddling up a stream with zombies instead of water rippling in our wake, she thought.

Phineas yelped. His hand jerked off her shoulder. Miranda whirled around. A zombie had latched on to Phineas' pack and held him in place. The other zombies had noticed his lack of protection and turned to him. In two steps, Miranda threw her arms around his neck, body pressed tight against his.

"Jesus, Phineas!" she said, the rush of adrenaline flooding her body enough to give her the shakes. "You can't drift back!"

"I didn't," he protested.

"You must have."

She wanted to shake him—hard. Shake some sense into his not fully developed twenty-year-old brain. The temptation to become complacent when Miranda or Rich were around was real; she'd seen it happen before. She'd also seen it in some of the small cohort who had received the vaccine, despite lacking the repelling effect. A vaccine couldn't save anyone from being ripped limb from limb.

"Are you two all right?" Alec asked, concern making the burr of his accent stronger.

"Yeah, we're fine," Miranda called over her shoulder.

Around them, the zombies retreated, though they were more agitated than before.

"Really, Miranda," Phineas said, his voice low as he spoke into her ear. "I was right behind you."

His breath felt like a puff of warm breeze against her skin, and now that the jolt of adrenaline was beginning to recede, she noticed how nice being pressed up against Phineas felt. He was a little shorter than her. The warmth of his chest against hers felt solid and strong. The stubs of his newly styled dreadlocks were soft on her skin.

Fucking hell, she thought. Phineas was a sweet kid. She enjoyed their harmless flirting and banter because that's what it was: harmless. It was flattering to be admired, but it was never going anywhere. Even if her body wasn't quite on the same page, she wanted Phineas to get his emotional baggage from someone else. She practically drank herself to sleep most nights trying to avoid nightmares... Nobody needed that.

"You weren't close enough," she said, putting a few inches between them, but still keeping her hands clasped around his neck. "I don't care if you're halfway up my ass. Stay as close as you can."

A rakish grin split his face. "If that's where you want me, babe."

"Oh, for Pete's sake."

They joined Rich and Alec. Phineas was a lot closer to her this time. Close enough to be annoying in any other circumstance, but it was welcome now.

Alec said to her, "At least we're through this pack. We'll get a nice distance on them in no time."

They turned at the next corner and Rich said, "We need to find somewhere to spend the night now."

The smell hit her like a brick. A few blocks away, the street was crammed, block upon block, almost as far as she could see. It hadn't been the zombies they'd just encountered that stunk so bad, but this horde. It was so thick it would take ages to get through. Miranda was glad that Rocco and the others were on the other side of the Willamette.

"Do you know any buildings here?" she said.

"No," said Rich. "We'll have to pick one."

They walked over several blocks to get some distance from the horde.

A minute later, Alec said, "What about that one? The liquor store?"

The building he pointed to was of newer construction with a stucco exterior. There were bars on the windows and door, and all of the glass was intact.

"Let's go around back and see," said Rich.

———

THEY SET UP IN THE BACK OF THE LIQUOR STORE, AND THE intervening hours passed uneventfully. Miranda could sometimes hear the nearby horde. The swells of sound probably due to the direction of the wind. At least, she hoped so. She couldn't sleep, so had volunteered for first watch. Rich and Phineas were out cold. Alec had wandered off half an hour ago to check out the surprisingly plentiful stores of booze. It seemed like no one had hit this store—ever. It had more alcohol in one place than Miranda could recall seeing in quite some time, apart from Kendall's bunker. She heard the soft scuff of shoes, then Alec's shadowy outline appeared in the light of her covered headlamp that sat on the floor beside her.

"So you're all moved in at LO now," she said as Alec sat on the floor. He set a bottle-sized box down beside him.

He nodded. "Building six in the apartments."

"You didn't waste time getting out of P-Land."

Alec chuffed a soft laugh that conveyed a healthy dose of trepidation. "Rocco made it pretty clear he expected me to move immediately. I don't want to get off on the wrong foot with him."

"Rocco's okay," she said. "He's kinda scary when he's pissed, but he's fair. He'll like that you didn't drag your feet." She paused, then said, "I hope they got home okay."

"I'm sure they did," Alec said. "They don't have far to go until they reach the sound defenses."

Miranda nodded, but didn't comment. Wanting to distract herself, she said, "How'd Daphne take your move?"

Alec averted his gaze. "Not especially well."

Miranda snorted. She'd had a feeling the P-Land Council member might not be thrilled by this development. "That's what you get for leading her on."

Alec arched an eyebrow at her. "I did not lead her on. She just didn't want to believe me when I said I wasn't getting serious with anyone." Then he muttered under his breath, "Women are like that."

"Oh my God," Miranda said, laughing. "You didn't just say that, did you? I thought you might not be one of those men who are asses, but I guess I was wrong."

"One thing I will say for Rocco," Alec said, ignoring her comment, but with that sly smile she'd seen before. "He makes a decision and that's that. They're a wee bit over the top in the other direction at P-Land."

"They're good people," Miranda said. "But I wouldn't last a week. I am not a process person. Assess a situation, make a decision, get it done. Talking things to death makes me want to scream. And my way of doing things makes them want to scream."

Alec's laugh was a low rumble. "I'm not as bad as you—"

"No one's as bad as me."

Alec picked up the box and set it on the floor between them. "Guess what I found?"

"Booze?"

"Pah," he said dismissively. He lay the box down longwise and began to tease the lid away. He pulled the bottle out, but gently, as if he were cradling a baby. It flared like a slightly opened fan from a narrow, tapered bottom. "Scotch. The Macallan Reflexion."

Miranda's mouth began to water. She was partial to bourbon, but Scotch was good, too. "I like Scotch," she said. "Fancy bottle."

Alec pursed his lips and, even in the very low light, fixed her with what she could tell was a pained expression.

"This isn't just Scotch, lassie," he said, holding it out so she could get a better look. "This is the good stuff. A bottle of this used to go for over a thousand Euro."

"Pass it over, then," she said, hand outstretched.

Alec snatched it to his chest. "You're a right savage, Miranda. You don't drink this from the bottle. You sip it, ideally from crystal, or at least a real glass, but we'll have to make do. Get your cup out of your pack."

"C'mon," she said, beckoning him to hand over the bottle with her wiggling fingers. When she realized he was serious, she suppressed a laugh. "For Pete's sake," she said softly, rolling her eyes.

Alec was already digging in his own pack. Miranda did as he asked and got her cup; she wouldn't get a drink if she didn't.

The spicy, rich scent that wafted from the bottle almost as

soon as the stopper was removed filled Miranda's nose. "That's the antidote to zombie stink," she said.

"It's the antidote to a lot of things," he said, pouring some in her cup.

She waited while he poured his own, re-stoppered the bottle, and scooted over to sit beside her. She held up her metal camping cup, then took a sip. The taste of almost burnt caramel flooded her mouth as she leaned against the wall, accompanied by the faintest undertaste of smoke. She rolled the liquid over her tongue, hints of cinnamon and something she couldn't quite identify lingering as she swallowed. The heat was pleasant, smooth as butter with no burn.

Alec had been right. It would be a crime to drink this out of a bottle. She was pretty sure it was a crime to drink it out of her metal cup, but needs must. She took another small sip, let it settle on her tongue, savoring the taste for close to a minute before she swallowed.

"Oh. My. God," she said slowly.

"I am a right savage for wanting to take a slug like it was cheap rotgut."

"You are," Alec agreed. "But you're learning."

"Where did you find this? I didn't see it on the shelves when I looked earlier."

"There's a locked storeroom. That's where the good stuff is."

She took another sip, savoring the smooth warmth with not a hint of peat. "How much is in there?"

"Six full cases, and a couple cases of Cristal and Veuve Clicquot champagne, but I quit searching when I found this. We're stopping on the way back."

"Damn right."

They sipped their Scotch, the quiet companionable. After a time, Alec refreshed their drinks before putting the bottle back in the box and carefully replacing the lid. Sitting around and not talking, especially with someone she didn't know well, usually made Miranda want to talk to fill the silence. When she did that, she ended up babbling. Maybe it was because she had something to do, even if it was just sipping her drink, or maybe Alec was one of those people.

"You're easy to be with, Alec," she said. "And this is really good Scotch."

A corner of his mouth quirked up. "It is." He paused, then said, "I figured you for someone who's at ease with pretty much anyone."

She shook her head. "Nope. No time for whiners, and quiet people can set me babbling to fill the silence. Kendall's tough."

"I didn't find him that hard to talk to. He's awkward, sure, but he's not hopeless."

"I didn't say he was hopeless."

"He's rusty," Alec conceded. "It doesn't help that you're a woman."

"I'm the first he's seen in years. If he's into me, that's why. I'm not so vain that I think it's because I'm all that."

Alec took another sip, then said, "He does seem to have taken a wee shine to you."

"Men are annoying," she said. Alec looked at her askance. "Present company excepted." She gathered her thoughts for a few seconds. "Women spend a lot of energy trying not to hurt the feelings of guys we don't like. It wasn't so bad when—"

She snapped her mouth shut. She'd been about to say she hadn't dealt with it as much when she'd been with Mario, since most people knew they were together. Alec knew her as Miranda—just Miranda. Not Miranda who'd broken up with Mario, or Miranda who'd been bitten by and then killed Jeremiah, or Miranda who'd lost her baby. She wanted to keep it that way for a while.

"Do me a favor when we get there," she said. "Pick up some of the slack."

Alec smiled. "I will. It'll be easier for me, seeing as he doesn't want to get into my knickers."

"Your what?" Miranda asked, confused.

"You know, your knickers," he said, gesturing at her hips.

"Oh," she said, getting his meaning. "My panties."

Alec snickered. "Panties sound like something my granny would wear."

"Do you miss home much?" she asked, the question slipping out before she had time to consider whether or not she should ask.

A lot of people didn't like to talk about their lives before, herself included a lot of the time. But like she'd said before, he was easy to talk to, and the warm glow of the Scotch had taken hold.

"Scotland? Yes, I do," he said. "Glasgow and Edinburgh were brilliant cities. Different, mind, but brilliant. The countryside was always a bit wild, kind of like us Scots." He was quiet for a moment, then said, "I've missed good Scotch, but not the wee village where I grew up. People were too set in their ways." He took another sip, then continued. "But I don't know... I could have ended up in a worse place than I did. Could have still been on the plane when people started turning."

"You were flying?" she said. She didn't know many people who'd been flying when it started.

"I didn't see the first zombie until the baggage claim, and we thought the fella was crazy. That was on the Sunday. By Friday...well."

She remembered that Friday. The day Sam had coaxed her out of her dorm room, and Karen had told her she wasn't dying for her. The day she'd decided she was going to live.

"I've seen a lot of America over the years, just not how I thought I would." Alec shrugged. "In a way, this world suits me."

"It suits you?" she said, coughing, because she'd gulped her Scotch in surprise.

He looked abashed. "Of course I'd rather have it the way it was. I just didn't have deep roots anywhere. My parents and grandparents were dead. No brothers or sisters, or other family to speak of. My job kept me moving all the time, from one war zone to the next."

"You were a war correspondent?" she said, surprised. "I thought you did government stories."

"Same thing, different form. Seeing all those conflicts is what saved me. When you see the latest savior turn into the next dictator, see the slaughter that goes along with it enough times, you get good at spotting the next storm."

Coming from a large, extended family, where Sunday dinners at her nana's house with her aunts and uncles and cousins had been the default throughout her childhood, she had a hard time fathoming what he was describing.

"There must have been some people you were close to."

"I'm not saying it verra well," Alec said. "Of course I had my mates. I just... I never wanted to settle down. It never made sense to me. People leave in the end, want different things. Want different people. I thought it was better to be the one doing the leaving. And now, well... It's even easier to get yourself killed. It doesn't pay to get too tangled up." He looked at her sidelong, a mischievous gleam in his eye. "Enjoy the moment, don't get too serious. It's easier. And more fun, in my experience."

His smile set butterflies fluttering in her stomach, and a warmth that had nothing to do with the Scotch made her cheeks hot. Alec was flirting with her, in his low-key way, and she liked it.

"In mine, too," she said.

She took a long, slow breath. This wasn't the same as Phineas' flirting, which was just in fun. Alec was flirting with intent. And with the way she'd just agreed with him, so was she. It might be the Scotch clouding her perceptions, but as she studied him, all she saw was an easygoing, good-looking man who didn't want anything demanding, and wouldn't demand much in return. After how things had ended with Mario, with his desperate needing that had felt like it was sucking her dry, an undemanding lover, only interested in the here and now like Alec seemed to be, was appealing.

Warmth filled her belly, then sunk even lower. A low-grade tingling seemed to skate across her skin. Alec's lips, which she hadn't paid attention to until now, when they were only eighteen inches from her own, looked just right. And the way he carried himself, brimming with relaxed confidence, all but guaranteed he rocked in bed.

"Thanks for sharing the Scotch," she said.

"Anytime," he said, covering his mouth when he failed to suppress a yawn. "I think I'll turn in." He climbed to his feet, then added, as if it were an afterthought, "I'm not sure what Kendall thinks, but it wouldn't be you being vain."

He gave her another one of those smiles, sly and easy. She couldn't see his eyes, just the low light reflected in them, but there was almost an invitation in his voice.

She said, "Dream sweet."

The burr of his accent buzzed gently against her ear when he said, "That won't be a problem."

12

DOUG SCRUNCHED HIS EYES SHUT, tight as he could, then opened them and blinked rapidly. He shoved the sextant, pencil, and the small, tatty notebook filled with his tight handwriting into his pocket.

"I think this is it..." His voice trailed as he shrugged his shoulders. "I don't know why I feel so unsure about this. Math is math."

Speaking up to be heard over the wind, Skye said, "Even if you're wrong, it'll be nice to stretch our legs."

A light spray of salty water misted Doug's face as she leaned close, snuggling into his side. Mario sat near the small sailboat's rudder, guiding them to shore. Silas sat in the well of the seat, next to Mario's knees, his peach-fuzzed head the only part of him visible. He looked miserably cold, but had insisted that he wanted to be topside. After all his carrying-on about the rowboat, he hadn't batted an eyelash about following Mario onto the sailboat.

Kids, Doug thought, go figure.

The stretch of deserted beach looked like a scar of tan

against the dark rocks. Mario had agreed with him that this was the right place, but all the beaches looked the same. Despite the fact that he and Mario had three math-intensive Ph.D.s between them, the sameness made Doug second-guess his measurements with the sextant.

The high, craggy cliffs were heavily forested right to the water's edge, punctuated by beaches, strips of sand both wide and shallow, or rocky jumbles of gray, brown, and black. Rocky or sandy, they were similar...bleached driftwood scattered like bones, long ribbons of kelp at high tide marks, and sometimes dark tumbles of rockfall where sections of the cliffs above had collapsed.

Doug could hear Violet's piping voice from the cramped lower deck of the sailboat, along with Tessa's low murmur. It was funny, thinking of this twenty-footer as small, but compared to the yacht, it was tiny. Where the yacht had been luxe and, in retrospect, spacious, this sailboat was cramped and utilitarian. No honey-colored wood paneling, gourmet galley, real beds, or being able to stand fully upright in the cabin below, at least for him. And definitely no hot showers.

Doug sighed. It had been nice while it lasted, but the hot showers had screwed them. Tessa had been planning to repair the electrical system that heated the water before they left Eureka, but her illness had pushed it to the back burner. She thought the delayed repair—and ensuing smoldering connection on the heating element when the battery was turned on—was what started the fire. By the time he, Skye, and Violet met up with the others two days later, the yacht had long since burned to the waterline and sunk. That Tessa had saved as much of their supplies as she had was a minor miracle.

That day had been the high point of the rest of their stay in Eureka. To Doug, it was a blur: fortifying the little restaurant on the island after their safe house on I Street was also overrun, and cannibalizing what was left of other watercraft, to get this sailboat—pronounced by Mario as 'a piece of shit when it was new'—seaworthy, and killing zombies. So many freaking zombies; Doug's arms still ached.

They lucked out, too. The mostly intact Road Atlas and National Parks guide, circa 2021, in the restaurant's office had helped them decide where to make landfall. Mario had warned that there were too many people for the size of the boat, and that he didn't think it would be seaworthy for a three-hour tour, forget about a voyage as far as San Jose. He'd been right. But at least the atlas had given them a few possibilities for where to make landfall. They managed to make it almost as far as the best-case scenario: Black Sand Beach in Mendocino County.

It wasn't that far from Eureka—maybe two hours by car back in the day—but the coastline farther south was too wild a place to begin a journey on foot. The forest of the King's Range had been remote in the old world, never mind this one. Doug would have preferred Shelter Cove, which was the next place worth trying to land, but it was too far. Another zombie-free forty miles of coastline couldn't be enjoyed if they drowned. They'd traveled almost fifty miles today; it was good enough.

Thanks, Big Guy, he thought, looking to the sky. He wasn't a priest anymore—in his heart if not by official channels—but he still believed.

"How close do you think you can get us to shore?" Doug asked Mario.

"We're not taking this hunk of junk anywhere else. The beach looks sandy and shallow. Once we know it's safe, we're running aground."

"I thought you said that was bad," Silas said, his upturned face puzzled.

"Well, usually it is," Mario said. "But this isn't a good sailboat, and we don't have a dock."

Under his breath, Doug heard Mario mutter something about a hunk of junk and better than it deserved.

"It's been better than walking, even if it is too cramped for more than a day," Skye said to Doug.

Doug pulled Skye close and kissed the side of her head. "That was the idea. I'm counting this as a win."

"I'm tired," Violet whined.

Doug swatted at the mosquito buzzing around his head and turned back, wilting in the sun along with everyone else. Violet's brown skin had an undertone of pink that made her look red-faced. Her lower lip jutted out, along with a budding look of mutiny.

The first three miles of the sixty-mile hike to Garberville— the first place they could catch Highway 101—had been okay. Violet and Silas had run along the beach, and even frolicked at the water's edge with an adult supervising. The last hour, however, had convinced Doug that the only thing more hellish than traveling on foot in unknown terrain with no idea how many zombies might be in the area, was doing so with small children.

Assuming no complications, an adult could make the hike in three or four days. Doug had no idea how long it would take now, and had revised the day's goal. They were aiming to reach a retreat center, south of Petrolia, a don't-blink-or-you'll-miss-it town. The National Parks part of the road atlas must have assumed a general interest in camping, because indicators of natural points of interest and campgrounds not in the parks system were plentiful.

As soon as they left the beach for the path made by remnants of the old road, the whining began. Doug appreciated that someone had trained them about the importance of being quiet, but it was still whining. The slow, sustained incline of the past hour had only intensified Silas' and Violet's protests. There was only so much ignoring a person could do before Doug found himself thinking maybe they just needed a good smack. Since being smacked by adults was not how Doug had been raised, it occurred to him that Silas and Violet weren't the only ones who were tired.

Frequent stops were required for Mister Bun Bun. Despite the emergency blanket attached to the top of the carrier to reflect the bright sunshine away from the rabbit, Silas fretted that Mister Bun Bun was overheating. Mario had taken the lead in dealing with Mister Bun Bun, and Silas seemed to think that Mario knew how to care for rabbits. Or maybe he was just young enough that he still thought adults knew everything. Mario had told Doug how he'd rescued the rabbit, despite how stupid it had been with zombies closing in on them. No good deed goes unpunished, he thought, smiling. Silas seemed to trust Mario implicitly now. What Silas couldn't see was how much his trust freaked Mario out. Perhaps following her brother's lead, Violet gravitated to Mario as well.

"Mawree," Violet said, the desperation in her voice a notch higher than the last whine a few minutes ago.

"Take over for Mister Bun Bun?" Mario said to no one in particular.

"I'll do it," Tessa said, reaching for the carrier.

Mario turned to Violet. "C'mon, kiddo. I'll carry you."

"Give me your—" Doug began, but Skye had already stepped in to take Mario's pack. "You want me to carry that?" Doug asked her.

She shook her head. Violet crawled onto Mario's back, wrapped her hands around his neck, and lay her head to the side. She'd be out cold in two minutes.

Gravely, as if he were conducting a job interview, Silas said to Tessa, "Do you know about rabbits?"

Doug saw Tessa look quickly to Mario, who smothered a grin.

"I know enough to carry him safely until we get somewhere for the night," Tessa said.

"Okay," Silas said. "The carrier is heavy, and we've been walking a long time."

"There's an 'Are we there yet?' coming," Skye murmured softly.

They continued, and soon everyone was silent. When they were near the halfway mark to Petrolia, Doug looked back to Mario, Tessa, and the children. Tessa smiled and raised her free hand. Doug could tell that Mario saw him, and he acknowledged Doug's check-in, but without really doing much beyond meeting Doug's eyes. Between Tessa and Mario, Silas trudged, looking almost asleep on his feet. Doug shrugged off his backpack. For the first time since they'd left Eureka, he didn't feel the sting of the supplies they'd lost. He unbuckled his belt and threaded it through the loops of the small backpack.

"Doug, what are you doing?"

Doug looked at Skye, raising an eyebrow. "Get your mind out of the gutter. I'm going to give Silas a piggyback ride. You already have two packs, and Tessa has Mister Bun Bun."

Doug dropped back to walk beside Mario, collecting Silas as he went. Violet slept against Mario's back. Doug fished in his pocket for a bandana, which he tucked around the girl's head, since he wasn't sure if she'd get a sunburn. Which makes me the whitest person in the world, he thought. He made Silas shade his head and face, too, just in case. Within minutes, he could tell that Silas was out.

"I knew Humboldt County was sparsely populated," Doug said to Mario. "I didn't really get it, though."

He looked at the forest that edged the road behind them. It had spent the intervening years encroaching over the fields that people had cleared. Every step they took away from the beach seemed to increase the temperature. Doug knew the forest helped with the heat—while you were in it—which they were not. Approaching the summit of the hill, Doug wouldn't have been surprised to find it was over eighty degrees.

"You doing okay?" he asked Mario.

"Yeah," Mario answered. "Why wouldn't I be?"

"Silas and Violet have taken a shine to you."

"This is not my first rodeo."

Doug said, "You were just kind of...aloof with them, before we left Eureka."

Mario took so long to speak that by the time he did, Doug had decided he wasn't going to answer.

"It's not like we could walk away," Mario said. "It's a complication I didn't see coming, but we'll manage. Right now isn't the time to talk."

"Okay," Doug said. He was sure the kids were asleep, but Mario was right. "I'm all ears if you want."

"I'll let you know."

Mario was right that now wasn't the time to talk about it. Still, his reluctance made Doug uneasy. Mario's refusal to talk about where he was at, what kind of emotional toll this might be taking on him, felt too much like Miranda after she lost the baby. *I don't think either of them knows how alike they are sometimes,* he thought.

Silas stirred against Doug's back, then resettled with a sigh.

"You don't think we'll get stuck carrying them all the way to Garberville, do you?" Doug asked.

Mario grinned, a real one. "Only when they're tired, but they'll definitely try."

"IT SHOULD BE RIGHT AROUND HERE," TESSA SAID. SHE squinted at the atlas again, then nodded as if it was settled.

The winding mountain road turned east, continuing across a river by a bridge that had seen better days. Doug wasn't sure it would hold a heavy vehicle, but it was safe enough on foot. He'd looked at the atlas earlier. Their destination was clearly marked on the west end of the bridge. He searched their surroundings, looking into the tall redwoods and pines. He didn't see anything resembling a camp.

"It's probably up a drive or dirt road that's overgrown," Tessa said.

"I see it," said Skye. She waded into the brush. "Here's the sign."

She pushed back the branches and brambles to reveal a dark wooden sign. Letters that had once been painted bright white or yellow, but were now the same color as the sign's face, were carved into the wood. In its current state, it was almost unreadable.

"How the hell did you see that?" Doug said.

Skye took a few steps beyond the sign, peering into the trees. "We need to take this..." She hesitated, then said, "Non-road."

Doug looked in the direction she pointed. The road leading the Mattole Camp and Retreat Center must have been narrow and unpaved. They would need to cut a path through the trees and undergrowth. In a lot of places, the bushwhacking wouldn't be worth it because of the noise, but they hadn't seen any zombies. And there was nothing out here. There were surely abandoned houses and barns in the area, but unlike this campground, they didn't know where they were. They might stumble on a house if they left the main road, or they might miss it by fifty feet and never know.

Doug jiggled Silas' knees. He felt the boy stir against his back.

"Time to wake up, small fry."

Silas' soft groan sounded like the sigh of a sleeping puppy. Doug crouched down until he could let go of Silas' legs. Silas looked up at him, rubbing his eyes.

"Are we there?" he said. "Where's Violet?"

Doug shook his head. "It's still a little ways, but we need our hands free. Violet's right there."

Silas turned around, then left to join his sister. Doug saw him make a visual sweep of the group and detour to collect Mister Bun Bun from Tessa. Doug arched his back, stretching his arms high overhead. The kid wasn't that big, but sixty pounds of dead weight on your back for ten miles was no joke.

Violet announced, "I have to pee."

"Me too," Silas chimed in.

Tessa held out her hands. "Come on, you two. I'll take you."

Silas looked at Tessa askance. "Together?"

Doug smothered a laugh. He saw a flicker of exasperation pass over Mario's face.

"C'mon, Silas," Mario said, any annoyance deftly mastered. "Let's go."

The kids and their respective escorts walked in opposite directions, staying so well in sight that the sudden modesty was a moot point. Doug joined Skye to study the atlas. Unfortunately, the camp was just a dot and a name without an indication of the size of the property or location of the buildings.

"There's got to be some sort of caretaker residence, or at least a check-in gate, before we get too far along," Skye said.

"Here's hoping."

As he leaned into Skye for a kiss, he heard the first moan.

Low and guttural, it sounded so full of hunger that the hair on Doug's neck stood on end. It was quickly followed by another. Doug whirled around, trying to locate which direction it came from.

Skye stepped closer, head cocked. "I think it's coming from the other side of the bridge."

"Mario, Tessa, let's go," Doug said, pitching his voice to carry without raising it. "We've got company."

Not for the first time, Doug wished that just one more of them repelled zombies. If they had two people who were repellers, they could hold hands around the rest of the group. It would be tight, and moving through zombies that way would mean setting a glacial pace, but it would be safe. Skye could move through zombies easily enough, and run interference with a small group of them, but not much more when they were confronted with a larger horde. The moans skipped from one location to the next, like embers of a wildfire blowing across the treetops to ignite the whole forest.

"Is it monsters?" Violet whimpered.

"It's okay," Tessa said, hoisting the girl to her hip.

Doug looked farther down the road on the far side of the bridge just in time to see a cadaverous figure stumble into view. Several more followed, lurching awkwardly, only five hundred feet away. Flies buzzed around the zombies like electrons around the nucleus of an atom.

Silas stuck close to Mario, his eyes as big as saucers. He clutched the handle of Mister Bun Bun's carrier in his tight fists.

"Give me that, Silas," Doug said, reaching for the carrier.

Silas shrank behind Mario, pulling the carrier closer to his body.

"Give it to Doug," Mario said. "I need to carry you. He'll keep Mister Bun Bun safe. I promise."

Silas looked at Doug, then released the handle of the carrier and scrambled up onto Mario's back. Doug gripped the carrier in one hand, the familiar heft of his machete in the other.

"Skye, take point. I'll bring up the rear, with Mario, Tessa, and the kids between us."

Hisses came from the direction they'd just traveled. What started as a single faint moan was now like noisy ocean surf. Skye plunged into the overgrowth of the road, shoving her way through. She hacked only what couldn't be pushed aside. Tessa and Mario flinched away from branches that flexed back at them like whips.

Doug looked over his shoulder. He could see figures struggling into the woods behind them. A yelp from Silas snapped his head forward in time to be slapped across the face by a whipping branch. A bright, shiny sting tingled across his cheek. Silas held a hand to his face, a smothered sob caught in the boy's throat. He buried his face against Mario's neck, his thin shoulders shaking.

A flicker of movement flashed in Doug's peripheral vision. To his left a few zombies stumbled down the hillside, banging into trees like pinballs or falling to the ground like actors in a slapstick routine. If not for the heavy forest slowing the zombies down, they'd be screwed. He cast another glance over his shoulder, felt his foot stick, then crashed to the ground. Mister Bun Bun's carrier twisted to the side, causing his arm to bend awkwardly. The rabbit squealed, a piteous shriek of fear that grated on Doug's ear.

"Doug! Are you okay?"

He looked up to see Mario starting to come his way.

"I'm fine," he said. He pulled the carrier to him, checked quickly to make sure its door was still secure, then lurched to his feet. His ankle throbbed a little with the first step. He suppressed a wince. "Keep going."

"I see something," Skye cried.

Doug kept his focus on his footing, on the whipping branches knocking against the hard plastic pet carrier with hollow thuds, on the ache in his wrist. The thicker trees gave way to a small clearing of high grass and spindly saplings deprived of sunlight by the redwood canopy overhead. A long, low building—caretaker's cottage of bricks and stucco with sturdy wooden shutters covering its windows—was a hundred feet away. They picked up speed as the terrain cleared, racing toward the house.

The door cracked as Skye kicked it open. She barged inside, then pinwheeled backwards, knocking into Tessa. Zombies poured through the open door, one after another. Skye slipped, then crashed backwards onto her ass. Doug heard the breath rush from her lungs and Tessa's cry of surprise, followed by a thin high-pitched scream.

Violet still clung to Tessa's back, her shrieks of terror almost as unearthly as the zombies moaning around them. Zombies poured through the open door to lunge at Skye, only to recoil. Some pulled away upright; others fell on the ground, leaving Skye in the middle of putrid melee. The unexpected obstacle she presented caused a bottleneck at the door.

Mario shook Silas from his back, pointing at the far corner of the house. The boy obeyed instantly, running where Mario had indicated. Mario darted forward, attacking the zombies staggering in their direction. Skye got to her feet.

"Take her," Tessa shouted at Doug.

Doug shoved his machete blade between the top of the carrier and his knuckles clutching the handle. He snaked his now free arm between Violet and Tessa, yanking the screaming child free. Tessa ran, her machete already in hand, to skewer a zombie through its open mouth. Doug retreated to where Silas stood rigid, quaking with fear. Silas pointed to the woods they had just emerged from. Four zombies were breaking free of the tree line.

"We'll be inside before they get here," Doug said, not sure if Silas could hear him over Violet's screams.

"Violet, it's okay, we'll be inside in a minute. You have to be quiet!"

Violet kept screaming, either unable to hear him or too hysterical for his words to register. Silas huddled close to Doug, as silent as his sister was loud.

"Doug, let's go!"

Skye beckoned him from the doorway. At least a dozen zombies lay outside the door of the house, their heads hacked or stabbed. Before he could say anything to Silas, the boy pulled the carrier from his hand.

"Careful," Doug cried, catching the machete falling from the handle.

Silas ran to Skye, lopsided from lugging the pet carrier. Doug dropped the screaming and wriggling Violet as the door thudded shut behind him. Violet barreled across the room, running into Mario with such force that he almost lost his balance.

"Woah... Hey, hey, it's okay," Mario said, crouching in front of the sobbing girl. "You're okay, it's okay."

Violet kept screaming.

"Violet, look at me; look at me."

Mario snapped his fingers in front of her face, repeating the command. She finally looked at him, no longer screaming, but blubbering loudly. Mario held up his hand, fingers splayed, and pulled hers to it. Then he moved her finger along his index finger, tracing its outline.

"Watch your finger," he said. "Breathe in on the way up, and out on the way down. Like this." Mario inhaled deeply, while her finger moved up the side of his middle finger, and then out through his mouth as it traced down. "You try, c'mon... Big breath in. Now out. Breath in...keep going."

Silas, who clutched Tessa's hand and worriedly watched his sister, relaxed. Mario kept inhaling and exhaling along with Violet, moving her finger along and whispering encouragement. By the time she worked her way back to his middle finger, she'd quit crying. When she reached his thumb, she was tracing his fingers on her own. They went back and forth again, beginning and finishing at Mario's thumb.

"Good job," he said and hugged her close. "Feel better?"

Violet nodded into his shoulder, her face tear-streaked, but calmer.

"The house is secure. Just a crawl space above," Skye said, putting her hand on Doug's arm. Her blue-gold eyes were filled with concern. "Are you okay?"

"Yeah, I'm fine," Doug said, nodding. "You?"

"Aside from falling on my ass?"

"That's one way to bottleneck them at the door."

Skye shook her head, chagrined. She hooked her thumb to a long table beside the door. "Help me move this?"

By the time they had shifted the table against the door, Mario held Violet in his arms. He shifted his weight from foot to foot, like he was rocking a baby. Tessa sat with Silas, who lay on his stomach beside her. He had opened the door of Mister Bun Bun's carrier, arm stuck inside to his elbow, his gaze intent on the rabbit.

Silas lifted his head and said to Tessa, "Mister Bun Bun's okay. He's not shaking as much since I'm petting him."

Tessa murmured something in reply. Doug leaned against the wall, then slid down. The adrenaline draining from his system made every tweaked joint ache. The welt on his face itched. Skye sat down beside him as the first zombie banged against the door. Everyone startled. The door didn't budge, even as more zombies gathered outside, banging on the shutters and walls.

"How many do you think are out there?" Doug said to Skye.

She shrugged. "Don't worry. We'll sit tight, let them settle, and then come up with a plan for me to herd them away so we can get back on the road."

Doug sighed. "We need two of you. It would make this a lot easier."

They lapsed into silence. Doug pulled off his gloves and took Skye's hand in his before holding it to his lips. Her skin was soft, and even though it smelled of sweat and wood and very faintly of zombie, it smelled alive. With few trees directly overhead, the hot, stuffy air of the house was infused with the sharp stench of rot and the rancid reek of decaying flesh. It permeated everything—the carpeting, the furniture, probably the stuccoed walls. Opening anything to air their refuge out was out of the question.

"This place smells like a charnel house."

Skye's nose wrinkled. "It's better than being eaten." She paused for a moment, then said, "How did he do that?"

"What?"

"Mario," she said. "How did he settle her down so quickly?"

"Anthony, his son, used to have panic attacks. He and Emily did that with him."

Doug looked over to Mario. He sat on a moldering couch. Violet was curled in his lap, fast asleep. Silas had left Tessa's side to sit next to Mario, too. He held Mister Bun Bun in his thin arms, the rabbit's rump in his lap, the rest of it nestled against his torso. Its ears lay back against its body as Silas slowly stroked its fur. Doug couldn't catch what Silas was murmuring to the bunny, but the cadence was reassuring. Mario looked tired, as if they'd spent all day dodging zombies, not just the last fifteen minutes. But he looked peaceful, too.

Doug said, "I think they've decided he's their person."

Softly, so only he could hear, Skye whispered, "It's such a shame about him and Miranda. They were so happy. They would've been great parents. He looks so content with Silas and Violet."

Doug didn't say anything, because it wasn't required. And because Skye didn't have it quite right. Miranda and Mario had been happy, the happiest Doug had ever seen them. He knew that letting herself want the baby had been an emotional risk for her in a way it just wasn't for other people. It had devastated her to lose Tadpole after admitting, after allowing herself, to want him in the first place. If she hadn't been so intent on driving them all away and doing anything but feel how much it hurt, Doug knew they could have gotten through it together, maybe even had another child. To have seen them so happy, and to see how miserable both of them were now, broke Doug's heart. Mario and Miranda would have been great parents—the best. In that at least, Skye was right.

But Mario and these kids...content was not the word Doug would have chosen. Conflicted was more like it. Doug could see the push and pull Mario seemed to be caught in since they'd found Silas and Violet. It seemed to Doug that Mario didn't want to get close to them. But when it came down to caring for them, protecting them, his heart trumped his head. Mario did what he'd do with his own kids, without thinking. But after he'd quieted the hysterical child, or saved the rabbit, or kissed the scraped knee, he became uneasy. It was only after he was already cradling Violet, or with Silas snuggled against him holding the combo rabbit/security blanket, that Mario seemed to realize that they were right there. It was when they got up close and personal that he was caught out by how much he cared about them, despite his attempts to protect himself by being aloof.

It didn't matter that it had only been... Doug had to think about it. Today was September twenty-eighth or twenty-ninth, so they'd only had Silas and Violet with them for four weeks. Just four weeks... That can't be right, he thought, but when he did the math again, he realized it was. It didn't matter that it had been so short a time—they all cared. Doug even cared about Mister Bun Bun, for crying out loud. He could see the fear in his friend's eyes. Fear of letting these kids down, letting them die, letting himself enjoy being with them when he felt so guilty about leaving his own kids behind in San Jose. Or maybe it was something else, something that Doug couldn't see and didn't understand. Whatever it was, Doug could see the conflicted feelings that Mario didn't want to talk about roiling beneath the steady facade that he presented to the rest of them.

Content wasn't the word Doug would choose to describe Mario, not by a long shot.

He closed his eyes for a moment. They needed to eat something, all of them, and set up a watch so everyone could rest. They needed to survive this journey. There were so many things Doug had to make happen to get his friends safely to San Jose, and he did them gladly, but he didn't know what Mario needed, or how to help him. He was worried for Mario... worried that he might slip away, just like Miranda had.

13

VIOLET LOOKED UP AT MARIO, only a slit of brown iris visible from her squinted eyes. Her face was a collection of smudges and smears from the fine, dry dust that puffed up from the path. It stuck to the sheen of sweat on her upturned face.

"Mawree," she said. "When are we getting bicycles?"

Mario groaned, cursing himself for the millionth time. If he'd just kept his mouth shut, but no. That would have been too easy.

"As soon as we find some."

"But when?" she persisted.

A few steps behind him and Violet, Mario heard Doug snort. Not an impatient snort, but the amused kind that didn't quite succeed in smothering the laugh that banged against the inside of the snorter's teeth.

"We just gotta keep looking."

"But we've looked everywhere," Silas chimed in.

Silas skipped past Mario and tagged Tessa, who walked at the front of the group. Then he turned back, skipping past Mario again. He was heading to Skye, at the rear. He played this game from time to time, tagging between the first and last member of their small party as they walked.

Violet made a soft sound in her throat, the kind that conveyed that Mario's answer was unsatisfactory. "I liked the canoes better. This is boring."

"I liked the canoes better, too."

The day after they fled to the cottage at the campground, Skye had scouted the site. She'd come back grinning, with news of canoes. She'd paddled two to the bank of the Mattole River just a few hundred feet from their refuge. After huddling around the road atlas, they figured they could probably take the river as far as Ettersburg before they would need to start walking again. Thirty miles in a canoe beat thirty miles on foot. They left early the following morning, paddling against the current, but the river was placid and rarely deeper than ten feet. The nice thing about California weather was its predictability. It was the end of September, so now that they were inland it was dry—cool in the shade of the forest and blazing in the sun. The dome of sky above them was a deep blue with the occasional scrap of wispy white clouds.

Twice they'd needed to portage around rapids that looked a little too dicey to try in a canoe. Doug would have gone for it if he'd been on his own; Mario was sure of that. It was just the kind of slightly dangerous, bordering on foolish, challenge that he liked, but they had two kids and a rabbit. Even if they hadn't, Mario was burned out on adventure for adventure's sake.

When they'd left the canoes for the road again, the journey proved uneventful. The hamlet of Ettersburg was devoid of people and zombies, and that's when Mario mentioned bicycles. Everyone agreed bicycles would be great, even if some of the inclines were punishing, but so far they had not found any. It was almost as if they'd entered a parallel world where bicycles were never invented, or the entire town had evacuated on them. They'd found a few tricycles, but no bicycles that they could use. So on they trudged. Or in Silas' case, sometimes skipped. And Violet and Silas asked when they were going to find bicycles—repeatedly. Mario's mother had been fond of saying that people make their own hell. He'd done it with the bicycles.

An hour ago they turned north onto twisty, two-lane Briceland Road, which hugged the ascending ridge. The morning's stated goal—the town of Redway—had been revised to whatever suitable structure they could find for the night.

"There's a building ahead, around the bend," Tessa said, turning back to the rest of the group. "I can see it through the trees. It's on the right, one-story, I think."

"I see it," said Doug, just as Mario saw it, too.

By unspoken agreement, everyone picked up the pace. They passed a dusty track on the left that wound up the hillside, then the building came into full view. It was long and low, set about a hundred fifty feet from the road. The weedy overgrowth between the building and the road was dead, burnt yellow and brown from the combination of full sun and no rain.

"Will there be bikes?" Violet asked, looking up at Mario.

Mario shared a weary smile with Tessa over the girl's head. "Maybe."

Excitement shone in Silas' eyes, despite his obvious fatigue. He peeked inside Mister Bun Bun's carrier. "I think we should stop here," he said, squinting up at Tessa, then Mario. "Mister Bun Bun is tired."

"Me too," Tessa said, a knowing smile crinkling the corners of her eyes.

The building was white with red trim and a red metal roof that sloped toward the road. Briceland Volunteer Fire Dept. was painted across three closed garage doors that were bays for the fire trucks.

"Not much more than a garage," Mario said. "But if it's secure..."

"Hey, guys," Tessa said. "There's a house up there on the hill, up that little track we passed."

Everyone turned around. Sure enough, Tessa was right.

"High ground is always better," Skye added.

"Let's do it," Tessa said.

Silas looked back at the drive they had passed and then said to Violet, "I bet there are bikes! I call dibs!"

He bolted away.

"No!" Violet cried, and took off after him.

It took Mario's brain a second to register that the kids were running away.

"Silas, Violet, stop!"

His heart rocketed out of his chest, lodging in his throat. Everyone sprinted after the children. The kids paid him no attention. Skye reached Violet first and snatched her up, her small legs kicking in the air as her feet left the ground. Mario pushed on, blood thundering in his ears. Silas was just twenty feet ahead of him. He glanced over his shoulder at Mario, grinning. It was a game now. Dust from the road rose in puffs around his small feet.

"Silas!"

Silas tripped. He tumbled to the ground with an *oof*, dust swirling all around him. Mario grabbed him roughly by the shoulders, pulled him to his feet, and whirled him around.

"Never do that again!" he shouted, fear for the children's safety quickly giving way to anger. Silas' eyes grew wide as Mario shook him by his shoulders. "You don't know what's ahead of us! There could be zombies, traps, anything!"

Silas stared at Mario, fear in his eyes. He had wiped out partially on his face. Half of it was covered in dun-colored dust that stuck to his sweaty skin like kabuki-style makeup. His lower lip began to wobble. Regret for scaring him quickly beat back the blind panic, the deja vu replay of a small boy being led into danger right in front of Mario's eyes.

"Oh Silas, I'm sorry," he said, dropping to his knees. Voice softer, he said, "I didn't mean to scare you, but you can't run off like that. There could be anything out here. You have to let the adults check first and make sure it's safe. Unless we're somewhere we know is safe, you always have to be with an adult. Always. That's the rule."

"Okay," Silas managed, his voice small and unsteady.

A tear streaked down his dusty cheek, exposing a shining line of his mahogany-colored skin, followed by another. Silas looked down at the ground. More tears dropped to the dusty earth, making tiny calderas. Mario could hear the rest of the group approaching. He tipped Silas' face up with a finger under his chin.

"I'm not mad at you, Silas. I got scared that I might not be able to keep you safe."

Mutely, Silas nodded. Mario pulled him into a hug, felt the small, stiff body relax against his shoulder. Silas couldn't understand how small and slight he felt in Mario's arms, how especially vulnerable he was in a world hell-bent on killing them all.

"I just wanted to see if there's any bikes," Silas whispered.

"I know," he answered, patting Silas' back.

Mario felt a hand on his shoulder. He squinted up into the sunshine to see Doug standing over him.

"Everything okay here?" Doug asked.

"Yeah," Mario answered.

He released Silas, who looked at him with a wisp of caution. Mario pulled a handkerchief from his pocket and brushed away most of the dust clinging to Silas' face.

"We'll find you a bike. Don't worry. You keep this hanky in case you need it later."

Silas nodded, crumpling the smudged hanky in his hand. Mario stood, then held out his hand. Silas took it. They fell into step beside Doug to walk up the twisty drive.

"I hollered at Mister Bun Bun once, when he was bad," Silas said.

Mario smothered a laugh. "I'll try not to holler anymore, Silas."

"Okay."

Mario looked at Doug over Silas' head—chagrined—but Doug's usually mischievous face was a study of knowing concern.

"You okay?" Doug asked.

Six years had passed, but the fear had welled up as thick and suffocating as it had then. As it had only two months ago when they learned what had happened to Tadpole, and he'd floundered, powerless and alone and unable to do anything, while Miranda pushed him away.

"I'm okay," Mario answered. Then he added, his voice light, "But I have to find bikes."

***

THE DUSTY TRACK ENDED IN A WIDE WEED PATCH. TO THE left sat the one-level house, a sprawling structure of redwood, glass and steel. To the right was a three-car garage.

"Sweet setup," Doug said, turning in place for a three-hundred-sixty-degree view.

Mario nodded. "We should check out the garage first."

"Because that's where the bikes will be?" Silas asked.

"Well, maybe," he said, not bothering to explain that he was hoping there might be a vehicle they could use, despite how slim those odds were.

Tessa said, "There are solar panels on the garage. There might be a charging station inside."

"An electric car?" Skye said.

"Don't get too excited," Tessa cautioned, but she sounded excited.

The presence of an operational charging station had been confirmed. There were two Tesla SUVs in the garage. If the batteries would still take a charge, they might have some wheels.

All of the windows in the house, whether floor to ceiling to take advantage of the view, or the smaller, higher frosted panes of bathrooms, were grimed over by years of dust. Mario had waited outside with the kids while Skye, Doug, and Tessa cleared the house of three zombies. They'd been mummified because the closed-up house had been broiling inside. They must have been there for years, but were chomping for a human snack.

They opened what windows they could to air out the house. The interior had been broiling—instantaneously drenching them all with sweat. Now, the living area end of the house was very warm but bearable. The breezeway between the living and sleeping areas, shaded by a massive Live Oak tree, was downright pleasant. The walls of the breezeway were made of retractable floor-to-ceiling glass panels. Having both of them opened halfway required a watch, but it was worth it. And if they needed to fall back quickly, the doors into the house at either end of the breezeway were sturdy and undamaged.

Silas and Violet were out cold on a mattress that Mario had dragged into the breezeway. The lack of bicycles in the garage had triggered a cranky-fest that lunch had not allayed. Despite protestations of not being tired, both of them had fallen asleep in minutes. Mister Bun Bun was in a playpen they found in a closet, with a dish of water and some chicken feed from the garage.

Mario climbed to his feet and stretched. Waves of sleepiness had his eyes threatening to droop, along with near constant yawns. With Doug, Skye, and Tessa still in the garage, he couldn't afford to fall asleep unless he shut the breezeway doors, which he didn't want to do.

Even through the grime, the view from the hilltop was beautiful. The dark green of conifers and deciduous trees were interspersed with small patches of brown and gold. The thin ribbon of the road they had traveled threaded its way through the mountains. Even though tall, brittle grasses now covered the hillside between the house and the road, rows of grapevines looked healthy and thriving, as had the small vineyard behind the house. Mario made a mental note to look for homemade wine later this evening. He had lived in California long enough to know that wine made in someone's basement or garage could be just as good as what commercial vineyards produced.

A few minutes later, he heard the voices of the others. Doug, Skye, and Tessa turned the corner into the breezeway. Doug stopped abruptly when he saw the sleeping children but Mario waved him on.

"As long as we keep our voices low, they're not waking up," Mario said when the others reached him. When he sat down, his body ached with the need to rest. "How's it looking?"

Tessa finished a pull on her water bottle. "I think I can get it running," she said. "One of the SUVs is taking a charge. Might take a few days, but with two of them, I can cannibalize the other for parts."

"It would be nice to have a day or two to rest," Skye said. "Especially for Silas and Violet. And poor Mister Bun Bun. He needs a break from that carrier."

Doug smiled at that. He tugged on Skye's shoulder and she

leaned back against him. "There's a ton of water in the mudroom off the kitchen. I used to think those water coolers were ridiculous, but I'm so glad now that people used them."

"Yeah," Mario said, then yawned so wide his jaw popped. "As long as zombies don't show up, this seems like a good place to stop."

"Ever the optimist," Doug said. He glanced over at the sleeping children. "If there were bikes, everyone would be happy."

"I'm too," Mario yawned again, "tired to be optimistic. I'm glad there are no bikes. They'd have wanted to ride them, and that'd be too nerve—" He yawned again. "Racking."

"Take a nap, Mario," Skye said. "You too, Tessa. Doug and I can keep watch. We'll wake you up in a couple hours."

Mario didn't want to say anything other than yes, but he asked anyway. "You sure?"

"Let's skip the ritual three denials," Doug said. "Next you'll start saying you aren't tired, like the kids."

"Not a chance in hell of that," Mario said.

DOUG'S EYES NARROWED AS MARIO STALKED FROM THE garage to the house, his posture rigid. His mood worsened every day they spent here, even though he knew that after sitting ten years, Tessa couldn't predict when the repairs on the Tesla would be finished. She and Skye were doing their best; it would take as long as it took. If they got it working, it would be well worth it. They could cover more miles in day in a vehicle than they could in a week on foot, especially with the small fry in tow. Mario had been okay the first few days, but after that...not so much. Doug was getting sick of Mario's shitty attitude.

"I don't like those," Violet said, her mouth downturned.

"You're missing out," Doug said. "See?" He pulled a purpled grape from the vine and popped it into his mouth. The bright, sweet taste flooded over his tongue. The seeds crunched, but he didn't spit them out. "I bet Silas will try one."

Silas took the bait, then broke into a grin. "They're good!"

"I told you."

A moment later he said, "What are the hard things?"

"The seeds," Doug answered, popping another few grapes into his mouth. "You can eat them, or you can spit them out."

Silas looked up at Doug, squinting in the bright sunshine. "Avery told me if I ate seeds, the plants might grow out of my ears."

Doug laughed. "I'm pretty sure he was teasing you. That won't happen."

Silas crammed more grapes into his mouth.

"Who's Avery?"

"She used to live with us, before," Silas said. His voice was soft, but he said it with a finality that let Doug know he wouldn't talk about Avery more.

Silas pointed at the bunches of grapes. "What are these called again?"

"Grapes."

Silas nodded. Doug glanced at Violet from the corner of his eye. She was eyeing the grapes and looking like she regretted her earlier pronouncement.

She said, "Maybe I like these..."

"Go on then," Doug said.

She pulled a grape from a bunch, hopping back in surprise when it pulled a few free that fell to the ground. Then she put it in her mouth, looking hesitant. Her eyes widened.

"I do like these!"

Doug chuckled softly, and they all stuffed themselves with grapes. Everyone was bored, but the kids were really bored.

There was only so much *Little House* they were prepared to listen to, and Skye didn't want to burn through the book too fast.

"I bet I can beat you to the end of the row," Doug said as the grapefest wound down.

He looked at the kids a beat, then started jogging away. Silas and Violet tore past him, and he gave chase. They played race and tag until everyone was hot and sweaty. Then they ate more grapes, and picked a few bunches to take to the house.

They tromped into the kitchen. Mario leaned against the counter by the sink, his back to the window overlooking the vineyard where Doug and the kids had just played. Silas ran up to Mario, holding a bunch of grapes up to him.

"They're called grapes! Eat one."

"I don't want one now, Silas," Mario said. He sounded irritated.

"But they're really good! See?" Silas popped a grape in his mouth. "You can eat the seeds or spit them out. I eat them, like Doug. Try one."

"I don't want one. Maybe later."

"But—"

"I don't want a goddamn grape, Silas," Mario snapped angrily. He didn't yell, but his tone was sharp, almost mean.

Silas took a step back, startled. His eyes filled with tears. Doug handed Violet the cup of water he'd just poured from the water cooler. He walked to Silas.

"C'mere, Silas," he said. "I have a cup of water for you." He took Silas' hand. Over his head, he mouthed at Mario, "What the fuck?" Mario glared at him, then stormed away.

Doug said to the kids, "Let's go to the garage and see what Skye and Tessa are doing. Maybe we can help them."

He took the grapes from Silas and set them on the counter. Silas was trying to blink back tears, but one slipped down his face. He looked confused and hurt. Doug wiped the tear from his face.

"Don't pay any attention to him. He's having a bad day."

He took the children back outside, fuming. If Mario wanted to be in a bad mood, that was one thing. But snapping at Silas, who practically worshipped the ground Mario walked on? That was out of line. He left them in the garage, Skye reading his look at a glance before she invited the kids to help them. He stomped back through the rooms of the house, finding Mario in the breezeway. His arms were crossed. He glowered at the vista below, which Doug was pretty sure he wasn't seeing. And if he was, it offended him.

"What the hell is wrong with you today?"

Mario didn't look at him. "Nothing," he said, sounding sullen.

"Tell that to Silas. You're being an asshole, and you're being mean."

Still, he didn't look at him, but Doug could wait. Mario's scowl deepened, his eyes almost slits, impatience and anger coming off him in waves. He looked at the ground, sucking on his teeth.

"We've been here a week already," he said, shrugging, like it was an annoyance to explain himself. "I just want to get on the road again. Tessa keeps saying just one more day, but then it's another. The longer we're together, the more attached they get, and I can't— It's almost mid-*October*, Doug, and Silas and Violet need—"

Finally, he looked at Doug. His mouth twisted in a miserable frown, pain flashing in his eyes, but he quickly looked away again.

Doug said, "It's October sixth, Mario."

"You know what I mean," he said irritably.

Doug smothered the flare of annoyance at Mario's childish rebuttal. "What is it that you think Silas and Violet need?"

"They need something stable. Permanent. They need to be behind walls where it's safe, with people who are going to be there for them."

"Someone not you, you mean."

That raised his head. His expression became impatient, the lines around the thin slash of his compressed lips deepening. "You make it sound like I don't care. I just— I don't want them getting attached to me."

Doug started to laugh. "It's a little late for that."

"I didn't ask for any of this," Mario said. "I don't want them getting attached. I don't want to be responsible for them when I can't protect them. I can't even keep my own kids safe. I couldn't do a damn thing to protect Tadpole, or Miranda. I don't know what's happening in San Jose. If Emily and the kids..." His voice trailed off, but not before becoming a frustrated, impotent growl. "Silas and Violet are looking at me like I'm the person they can depend on, and I don't know that I am."

Doug frowned. Not because he was angry with Mario anymore, but because it hurt. It hurt to see him so frightened. It hurt to watch him build walls to protect himself from the purest thing in the world: the love and trust of a child.

"You better figure it out pretty fucking quick, Mar, because they've already picked you. It doesn't matter that you didn't ask for it; you've got it all the same." He softened his tone. "This isn't just about what Silas and Violet need. You need them just as much as they need you, but after everything that's happened the last six months, it's got to be scary."

Mario took a deep breath. "I left my kids behind, Doug. I feel like I need to step in and be Silas and Violet's...not their dad, but someone. How long will it be before I abandon them, too?"

For the first time, Mario really looked Doug in the eye. He looked like he was drowning, waves sucking him under. Worse, he looked like he wanted to let them. Doug stepped in closer and put his hand on Mario's shoulder.

"I know you feel like you failed with yours and Miri's baby, but there was nothing you could do...nothing either of you could have done. It wasn't your fault, and it wasn't hers. It was horrible, and unfair, and there wasn't any cosmic plan, anything redeeming about it. It was just a bad thing that happened to two good people who didn't deserve it."

"But my kids—"

"You weren't safe in San Jose, Mar. You still aren't, but you're going back anyway. Not just to finish this, but because of your kids." Doug sighed, unsure that any of what he was saying was getting through to Mario. "I know you feel like you abandoned Michael and Anthony and Maureen, but you didn't. You just couldn't stay."

Doug gave Mario's shoulder a squeeze, then turned away. He didn't want to keep beating him over the head about Silas and Violet, and he wanted him to think about what he'd said. Mario was already in it, was already where he didn't want to be: responsible and attached, despite how much it scared him that he would fail.

"They need more than I've got, Doug."

Surprise stopped Doug in his tracks, and a cold shiver raced down his spine. He'd heard this before, almost word for word. He turned back.

"She said the same thing about you." At Mario's look of incomprehension, he added, "Miri. She said the same thing about you."

"What?"

"She said you needed more than she had to give when she lost the baby."

The effect of his words wasn't what Doug had intended. He thought maybe it would nudge Mario to not want to do the same thing that Miranda had done to him. Instead, he looked like a stake had just been driven though his heart.

"I pushed too hard, didn't I? You can't push Miranda, but I did. I needed her and...the more she withdrew, the harder I pushed."

"You were—you are—hurting," Doug said. "I don't know if it was true. I don't know if you needed her too much. She was in so much pain, and she pushed you away because she felt like she was drowning in it. If she didn't think she could stay afloat, maybe she was afraid she'd drag you under with her."

Mario looked at Doug like he'd just thrown him some sort of lifeline, an answer to a question that he hadn't even known he should be asking. But he also looked inconsolable, as if he'd gotten the answer he sought too late.

Softly, Doug said, "They're little kids, Mario. Don't do the same thing to Silas and Violet. They don't deserve it... Neither did you."

14

KENDALL'S glowing face filled the airlock window. As they stepped through, he said, "You came back."

"Good to see you, Kendall," Rich answered.

"Hi, Kendall," Miranda said, giving him a grin.

She hoped she'd kept the pang of pity swelling behind her sternum off her face and out of her voice. Kendall's excitement had a palpable undercurrent of astonishment. He'd been afraid they weren't coming back.

This time, Kendall gave her a hug that, while still awkward, lacked hesitation. He actually gave her shoulders a quick squeeze that held her snugly, rather than stiff back pats like before. Within minutes, they were gathered in the kitchen. Kendall pulled dish after dish of food out of the freezer.

"I wasn't sure what time of day you might arrive, or if you'd be hungry when you got here," he said, closing the freezer and moving to the fridge. He grabbed several containers of vegetables that he set haphazardly on the stainless-steel prep table behind him, then reached back inside for a head of lettuce. "There's a lasagna Bolognese, and a vegetarian one, too. Or I can make you something else, if you want?"

"Lasagna sounds brilliant," Alec said.

"And salad?" Kendall said, a note of hesitance creeping into his voice.

Miranda looked at the food with greedy eyes. Two frozen lasagnas, and another covered dish Kendall hadn't identified, sat together, a fine sheen of condensation beginning to form on the silver wrapping. Carrots, lettuce, green onions, apples, red bell peppers... She hadn't seen this much food in one place for so few people since before they discovered the first blighted vegetable patch.

"I'd love a salad," Phineas said. "I'll set the table."

Kendall's eyes narrowed a little when Phineas spoke. When she glanced at Alec, it was obvious he'd seen it, too.

"Salad sounds great," Rich said. "I'll help you chop."

KENDALL LINGERED OVER THE MEAL WITH THEM LONGER this time, until halfway through doing the dishes. He even suggested perhaps watching a movie later, before announcing he needed to see to some things in his domed apartment. Miranda had been pretty sure those 'things' was time for him to process their return.

Freshly clean, her hair still wet from her shower, she shrugged into the charcoal-gray, long-sleeved cashmere cardigan sweater that had been neatly folded on the bed she'd used last time. A gift from Kendall. It swung loosely around her hips, since it was the kind designed without buttons, meant to drape softly rather than ensconce. The downy-soft fibers of the yarn caressed her bare arms beyond the cap sleeves of the black tee shirt she wore, and the soft black yoga pants were as comfy as she remembered. She idly wondered if there were any cash-mere lounging trousers knocking around the storeroom Kendall had gotten the sweater from.

She looked at her bed with a mixture longing and dread. She wanted to crawl into it and sleep, especially after the heat of the shower and the fullness of her stomach after their meal. And she wanted to avoid it, because she might have another nightmare. Anymore, her sleep was fitful. Once every couple of days she'd get in a night or nap when she slept deep, without nightmares. Sometimes she could tell how it would go, but not right now.

Besides, the group needed to talk.

She joined the others, who were lolling on couches and chairs in their dome's living room area, in varying degrees of food comas. Phineas had actually sacked out on the floor, a throw pillow under his head. Throw pillows... This place is like a freaking time capsule, she thought.

"Why is Phineas on the floor?" she asked, plucking a small blanket from the back of a chair to lay over him.

She sat on the couch opposite the one Rich lay on and put her feet on the coffee table. She could hear her mother's admonishing voice in her head as she did so. She knew at a glance that the coffee table had cost as much as most people used to spend on a car.

"He said he was going to stretch, but conked out," Rich said, not opening his eyes.

Alec had chosen the recliner chair near the foot of both couches. It bore no resemblance to the recliner chairs Miranda remembered from her grandparents' house. It had sleek lines and rose to a sitting position in a smooth, unhurried movement. Alec fixed the gaze of his half-open eyes on her.

"Don't you look a picture," he said, a sly grin quirking a corner of his mouth.

An electric tingle tickled over her skin. She was suddenly aware of how the yoga pants hugged her hips, and the snug fit of the tee shirt. She had dispensed with a bra, since the underwire had been driving her crazy all day; because of the sweater, it wasn't that obvious. She pulled the cardigan a little closer around herself, self-conscious. She glanced away, hoping the heat in her face didn't mean she was blushing.

"I haven't eaten that much in one sitting since the last time we were here," she said, yawning.

"Tell me about it," Rich agreed. His voice had a dreamy quality. "Lasagna, with meat in the sauce."

"It was really good," Alec agreed.

"It was the noodles," said Miranda. "He made them yesterday or today."

"How d'ya know that?" Alec asked.

"Fresh homemade noodles melt in your mouth."

They lapsed into silence for a minute, the sleep vibe getting stronger by the second. If she didn't do something, she was going to fall asleep whether she wanted to or not. "So what's the game plan, guys?"

Rich sat up with a groan. "I feel kinda guilty, having eaten so well."

"Me, too," she answered. "It would be worse to waste it."

"I know... So. You gonna do a little gardening tonight?"

She nodded. "Probably. Just check in, see how he's doing."

"We need to help him with being stuck in here," Alec said, adjusting his chair to fully upright.

"Yeah," Rich said. "Us being here before made it worse for him. He was so happy to see us... It was kind of pathetic." He looked at Miranda. "You think we could maybe coax him outside?"

She shrugged. "We can try. Then he'd at least have some options about what to do with himself."

"And his food," Alec added. "D'ya think he might be agoraphobic after all this time?"

Miranda's brow furrowed. She'd never considered it. "Only one way to find out. I'll talk to him about going outside."

"Great," Rich said, resuming his horizontal position on the couch. "Good talk, team. I'm taking a snooze. All those carbs are like quaaludes."

Her 'Okay' devolved into a yawn. Alec got to his feet, the throw blanket over the back of his chair in hand. He walked to her and snapped it open, like a flag catching the breeze.

"Lie down and take a nap, lass," he said.

She looked at him, wanting so badly to do it. Rich was right about the carbs; she was getting sleepier by the second.

Alec's eyes twinkled, but softly. The flirtatious liveliness she was used to seeing in them was almost absent.

"You barely slept last night. I noticed," he added, cutting her off when she opened her mouth to deny it. "You'll not have bad dreams out here, with all of us snoozing together."

She looked at him, surprised. How did he know that? He must have heard her crying out in her sleep through the connecting bathroom when they'd been here before, though he'd never mentioned it. As for last night... She'd been dragging her ass the whole way here; she was so tired. He'd put two and two together. It wasn't exactly rocket science.

"Go on, Miranda. We're all right here," he said, gesturing to the others. "If you're not well rested, you might not be able to fend off Kendall's advances."

The idea of Kendall making advances of any kind was too awkward to contemplate, and amusing, which tamped down her anxiety.

"Okay," she said, stretching out on the cushions. "Don't let me sleep all day."

Alec grinned at her, but the slyness wasn't there, just

friendly solicitude. The blanket fluttered onto her, and he tucked it in at her shoulders.

"I'll make no promise on that. I might sleep all day myself." He straightened up, then added, "I'm not sure it matters. I think time's a little different in this bunker."

———

Kendall's panicked brown eyes met hers.

"I don't think I can do it," he said.

The owl blink was in overdrive, like windshield wipers on high that sloshed a torrential downpour away, but only for a second before the glass sheeted over again.

Miranda took a deep breath. When Kendall had agreed to try going outside, she'd known it would take some time. Even so, the nervous wreck of a man she'd met in the kitchen shocked her. They stood in front of the hatch to the airlock. Sweat beaded on Kendall's forehead, and his Adam's apple bobbed convulsively. The owl blink never stopped, and if he shifted his weight much more, she was pretty sure he was going to bolt down the corridor. She had to readjust her approach.

"Okay," she said. "If you can't, you can't."

Kendall relaxed, but it was more like a slump. "You're disappointed."

"No," she said, though she was. She paused, then said, "I am disappointed, but not with you. I'm asking you to do too much, too fast."

Kendall looked at the floor to hide the pink of embarrassment coloring his cheeks. She had to salvage this before he felt too defeated to try.

"I've got an idea," she said. "How about we just open the door and sit here?"

Kendall raised his head, the color draining from his face.

What had she been thinking, suggesting they go outside? Until they'd arrived a few weeks ago, he hadn't opened that airlock in years. Kendall took a deep breath, gathering his resolve, and nodded.

Miranda smiled, then reached out and squeezed his hand. "You can do this, Kendall. I know you can." She turned to the airlock, then realized she didn't know the code to the lock. "Want to unlock it?"

Kendall took the three steps to the keypad like an automaton. Stiffly, he raised a shaking hand. He took another deep breath, then shielded the keypad as he punched in the code. A moment later, the locking mechanism clicked.

"Good job," she said, trying to keep her voice encouraging without becoming patronizing. "Sit down. I'll get it."

Kendall stared at her, his face blank, then leaned against the wall. Miranda pushed the door's lever-handle ninety degrees, then pulled it open about a foot. She sat beside Kendall on the floor again.

"That's not so bad," she said.

Kendall muttered, his eyes downcast. His voice was so low she couldn't hear him. She asked him to speak up, and he said, his voice just above a whisper, "This is embarrassing."

"Why?" she asked.

"It's just a door," he said.

"That you haven't set a foot through in ten years, with monsters outside."

Kendall sniffed.

"No, I'm serious," she said. "It's dangerous out there. If you weren't scared, there'd be something wrong with you. But you're still trying, which is brave in my book."

"You were probably brave from the start," said Kendall.

Besides being untrue, she didn't like the tone in his voice. It suggested not just that he was lacking now, but that he would always would be.

"All I wanted to do at the start was hide. If it wasn't for my boyfriend, I'd have starved in my dorm. I was too afraid, even to save myself."

Kendall digested this information, frowning. "You aren't afraid now."

"I do get scared," she said truthfully. "Zombies are scary as fuck. I've just gotten better at hiding it. Getting angry helps."

She turned her head when voices drifted down the corridor from the direction of their dome. Alec and Phineas appeared a moment later They stopped at the entrance to the lounge that opened to the center of the main dome.

"What are you up to?" Alec said.

"Just shooting the shit," she said mildly.

Alec nodded. The polite interest in his hazel eyes and slight smile seemed to suggest that sitting on the floor across from an opened airlock hatch was a natural place to have a conversation.

"Not going—" Phineas began.

Miranda glared at him. Kendall was already embarrassed at his perceived weakness. The last thing they needed was a wise-crack that would embarrass him more.

Haltingly, Phineas finished with, "To get lunch?"

Kendall glanced at his watch, then muttered under his breath, "It's only ten thirty."

No one spoke for a moment, then Alec said, "I'm off to the library to find a book." He nodded, then disappeared into the lounge.

"I'm gonna get something to eat," Phineas said lamely. And then, because Phineas couldn't help but be Phineas, he added, "Don't be stealing my girl, Kendall."

He winked and was gone. Fucking Phineas, she groaned to

herself. Maybe bringing him back hadn't been a good idea. She needed to have a talk with him later. Delilah appeared in Alec and Phineas' wake, her nails clicking on the polished concrete. She said hello to Miranda, then snuggled between her and Kendall. The pit bull's presence—waggly-tailed and solicitous —calmed him. She made a mental note to make sure Delilah was on hand for their outside sessions going forward.

Kendall said, "Phineas eats all the time."

"He's twenty. Of course he does."

"I guess so," he said.

His tone was so even that she wasn't sure if it was just a comment, or a criticism. Phineas did eat a lot; they all had since getting here... There was so much food. A sudden thought occurred to her. What if the abundance of food in the bunker was an illusion?

"You have enough food here, right? Because if you don't, we can..."

We can what—bring it from home? Scavenge more on the way here? Everything nearby was thoroughly picked over apart from the liquor store. Goddamn City Council, she thought bitterly. If they'd never attacked LO, they'd have enough food for everyone and more.

"There's enough," he said, sounding perplexed by her question. "More than enough."

"Good," she said, feeling relieved—and guilty—because the relief held a hefty dose of self-interest. "We just didn't think about it, with it being just you here. We lost mo—"

She snapped her mouth shut. She'd just been about to say they'd lost most of their harvest. She shrugged, unease making the movement feel false. "It just occurred to me that maybe some of your food spoiled or something," she finished lamely.

Kendall looked at her—stared—and she wondered if he'd

figured out what she hadn't said. Kendall was a lot of things, but stupid wasn't one of them.

Casting about for a change of subject, she said, "Is the open door okay?"

"As long I'm not thinking about it."

"Maybe we'll open it the whole way tomorrow, and just hang out again."

Kendall's mouth formed a hard line. He looked at his knees, eyes screwed into a tight squint. Even Delilah noticed the change, for she raised her head and nudged Kendall's hand with her snout, then began licking it.

"Or not," she added, again worried she was still pushing him too hard, too fast.

"I feel like a coward," he muttered.

She reached out and touched his knee. He looked up, a scowl twisting his narrow features.

"You aren't a coward, Kendall. You've just been down here a long time. If I were in your shoes, I'd be freaked out too. There are zombies out there. Hell, there are tigers!" She chuckled, remembering running into the tiger. "You should have seen Phineas when we ran across that tiger. He almost peed his pants."

Kendall frowned. "He's sure of himself, though."

"He doesn't have the sense to know what he doesn't know."

Kendall's frown deepened.

"What?" she said.

"It's nothing," he said, looking down at Delilah while he scratched her head.

She let it go, and they lapsed back into an excruciating silence...for Miranda, at least. Then Kendall said, "Are you?"

"Am I what?"

"His girl."

For a moment, she had no idea what he was talking about. Then she laughed, so abruptly it sounded like a bark.

"Phineas? God, no. He's just a good friend. The teasing and flirting are...just our thing."

Kendall nodded.

"The day Phineas and I are an item is the day we really have problems."

"Okay." Kendall seemed to digest this information, then said, "What happened to your boyfriend?"

For a split second, she thought he was talking about Mario. A cold stab of pain pierced her chest, taking her by surprise, before she realized she'd mentioned being in her dorm at the beginning. He meant Sam.

"He was killed, about six months into it." She took a deep breath, the stab of loss replaced by a familiar sorrow that had been softened by time. "It was my fault. I tried to hold a line when I should have run. He came back for me when he should have kept going."

"I'm sorry."

She shrugged. It was a long time ago, and there was nothing to be done about it, except keep living. It was what Sam had wanted for her.

"What about you? Was there anyone special?" Kendall shifted, looking more uncomfortable than he usually did, and she added, "You don't have to answer. It's none of my business. I don't usually talk about before much."

Kendall smiled nervously, the owl blink returning. "I had girlfriends in college and grad school, but after that I worked all the time, getting the company off the ground." He stopped, his face crinkling like he had tasted something bitter. "After the company started doing well, people always wanted things from me. It was hard to tell if it was me, or what they wanted from me, that interested them most."

Her stomach hollowed out as she realized she'd fucked this up. Kendall already suspected they wanted something from him. Because of her slip before about the food, he seemed to have pulled together a hypothesis about their motives. His comment felt like a shot across the bow.

Then he said, "But maybe things are different now."

They wanted something from Kendall. The conundrum of his old life hadn't fallen away, as he wished—as most everything else had. Miranda told herself they would befriend Kendall even if he had nothing, and that was true. She'd decided to befriend him after the night she'd stopped him singing, for reasons that had nothing to do with the things that LO needed. But after going back to LO to dissect and discuss what their discovery might mean, would they have made the effort to come back out here again so soon if all he had was dried squirrel, and odds and ends he'd scavenged? She knew the answer, even if she tried to tell herself otherwise.

But they offered Kendall something, too. They offered connection—community. They had the ability to give him the sense of belonging that every human being hungers for. And as much as she hated it, they had her, or rather, Kendall's interest in her. She'd resisted the idea, brushed off the teasing from Alec and the others as fanciful nonsense, but she could see it in Kendall's eyes, in the nervous flutter of his lips when he smiled. She'd seen it in the relief on his face when she'd grinned at him through the windows in the airlock door. She couldn't predict if it would wax or wane, but right now, Kendall wanted her.

The idea of stringing him along rubbed every molecule in her body the wrong way. It made her psyche shoot sparks the way static electricity crackles inside a tangled blanket. But there were five hundred odd people at LO who needed to eat, and more were arriving every week. There was a vaccine they needed to get out into the world, but the urgency of the food shortage had pushed it aside when it should be their number one priority. Kendall, and what he had, might be the difference between usurping the San Jose vaccine in six months or in a year. Or—she realized with a start, with a cold unease that trickled down her spine—at all. The Council had already attacked them once. If they found out their raid had failed, they would try again. Given a second chance, they might even succeed.

The wave of nausea rising in her throat made her feel a little dizzy, thinking about what that would mean. Nothing would change. Everything that had happened—coming here, losing Tadpole, killing Jeremiah, her estrangement from Doug, even how things had imploded with Mario—all of it would be for nothing.

She forced a smile and gave Kendall's knee a squeeze. His eyes widened in surprise, and a blush began to flush his face.

"I think that's the only thing I like about the way the world is now," she said, giving the self-loathing rising in her chest a hard shove to send it back where it came from. "Who you were and what you had before isn't important. It's who you are, what you do now, that matters."

THREE DAYS LATER, SHE WAS FIRED. SHE'D JUST FINISHED her breakfast when Alec entered the main dome. He sauntered over to where she sat at the end of one of the long, curved dining tables.

"Good morning," he said, plopping into the chair to her left, around the table's corner.

She rushed the last gulp of her drink, then said, "Good morning, yourself."

Alec looked down at her plate. "You've got a healthy appetite."

She considered her place setting. Faint orange streaks from the powdered eggs with cheese and tomato were sprinkled with crumbs from her toast. Toast that had been buttered, which set her mouth watering even though she wasn't hungry anymore. An empty bowl with the filmy residue from oatmeal with raisins held the browning cores of two apples. Next to it was an empty glass ringed at the bottom with a few drops of milk.

"When in Rome."

Alec said, "Things have been going well with Kendall the last few days."

She nodded. "Yeah. Better than I expected. We're going to hang out in the airlock today."

His lips pursed to the side. An apology filled his eyes. "No, you're not."

"What are you talking about? That's the plan we made yesterday."

"Kendall's still going into the airlock today, but you're not. He asked me to do it."

"He did?" she said. "Why would he do that?"

Alec cast a quick glance around the dome, then said, "He didn't come out and say it, but I think he doesn't want to look bad in front of you."

"But he's doing gr—" She stopped abruptly, then sighed. "Is this the feeling like a coward thing? I told him that's not true."

Alec's half smile was sympathetic. "He fancies you, Miranda. I know that makes you uncomfortable, but he does. There's not a man on earth who wants to seem weak in front of the woman he fancies. Even me, and I'm fantastic."

She snorted, then sat back in her chair.

"You need to make yourself scarce, lassie. We're starting soon."

"Men really are stupid," she muttered, collecting her dishes and taking them to the sink. She wasn't sure why she was so miffed. What did she care if Kendall didn't want her around? If she was getting in the way of his progress, then she was the wrong person to do it.

"Do I have time to do these dishes?" she asked.

Alec had followed her as far as the counter that separated the main dome from the kitchen area. "I'll get them," he said.

"Guess I'll beat it."

As she walked past him, Alec reached for her arm. "Don't get your nose out of joint, Miranda."

She stopped. "It's not." Alec raised his eyebrow at her. "He could have told me, is all."

Alec gave her arm a squeeze before letting go. That smile of his, sly and roguish, lit up his face and arced to his eyes. Since their nightcap at the liquor store, she enjoyed it more than she was completely comfortable with. She wasn't sure she was ready for anything like whatever this was. But she wasn't sure she wasn't, either.

"Don't you worry after that," he said. "I have a feeling you don't lack for company when you want it."

The butterflies filled her stomach again. "Good luck," she said, sounding cooler than she felt.

She walked across the dome, past the dining tables, and through the lounge opposite the kitchen, feeling Alec's eyes on her until she turned into the corridor.

A FEW NIGHTS LATER, SHE WENT TO THE GARDEN. SHE knew Kendall was inside—she could hear him singing.

She padded into the garden dome in bare feet, the moisture in the air caressing her nasal passages. She wasn't familiar with the music—classical, with Latin lyrics. Kendall seemed to like singing in Latin.

It took a few moments to find him, since he wasn't at the potting table, but watering plants.

"Hey," she said.

Kendall stood at the far end of a row of bush beans. He looked up, then smiled. His smile was and wasn't the same as when they'd arrived. It still had the slightly apologetic edge, but there was also more confidence since he'd ventured outside the airlock and into the corridor leading to the surface. Everything about him had more confidence. He walked with purpose. His posture had straightened. The way he participated in conversation over their meals had improved. Miranda wouldn't exactly call him talkative, but his voice had lost that edge of learned helplessness that had trapped more than his body. He still hadn't made it outside, but he was no longer trapped in the same mental prison as when they first met him.

She smiled in return, then fingered the leaves of one of the bean plants. The blossoms had withered, and tiny bean pods were forming within them.

"They look good," she said. Kendall nodded. Without looking at him, she said, "I heard you might open the blast door soon." When Kendall didn't respond, she looked at him. "Unless Alec and Rich are pulling my leg."

"They're not," he said, and the owl blink started, along with shifting his weight from one foot to the other.

"I'm really proud of you, Kendall, if you don't mind me saying that." When he didn't say anything, she glanced over. He stared at her, his face filled with astonishment. "Don't look so surprised. It'd be easier to stay here, keep doing what you're doing. It takes guts to do something different, especially when it can be dangerous."

A blush crept up his neck. Eventually, he said, "I'm tired of being inside."

"I honestly don't know how you've done it."

Kendall shrugged. "I decided my apartment, this place, was all I needed, so long as I was alive. But I want more now."

"You know what?" she said, seeing an opportunity. "I've never seen your apartment."

"Do you want to?"

"Yeah. I do."

She hadn't expected him to ask her that. Kendall was so reserved, so guarded... She'd expected it to take weeks to get to this point. He did the owl blink a few times, his brown eyes seeming to grow wider with every flutter of his eyelids. He set down the watering wand.

"Come on."

She followed him out to the main corridor. They walked in silence, chlorine scenting the air outside the dome that contained the swimming pool. When they reached the door to the short hallway to his apartment, Kendall glanced at her uncomfortably, his hand hovering over the keypad. She averted her gaze, counted eight beeps, then followed him through the door.

She wasn't sure what she'd expected, because it looked very much like the other residence domes, except it was oblong like the garden dome. Along its length a wall had been built, creating a space to hang paintings. Miranda walked over to them, admiring the range from modern to classical.

"I like this," she said, stopping in front of a portrait of a young girl whose shoulders were lost in the shawl wrapped around them. She looked over her shoulder, wide eyes, her pale, heart-shaped face seeming almost disembodied against the dark background. The painting was old, and the girl had the kind of face that could blossom into great beauty, or fade to plainness.

"It reminds me of that one with the earring... Where her head is wrapped in a scarf," Miranda said, gesturing at her head while her mind's eye conjured the painting from an Art History class she had taken.

Kendall nodded. *"Girl with a Pearl Earring,"* he said. "This is by the same artist."

Miranda looked at Kendall, then said slowly, "But wasn't that by one of the Dutch Masters?"

"Vermeer," Kendall said, nodding.

She saw a flash of pride on his face that almost bordered on smug. Kendall had been a billionaire several times over, certainly rich enough to buy a painting by a Dutch Master, or any other kind. The expression on his face—proud and possessive—reminded her of the things she disliked about him. Or maybe he was proud to have preserved a painting of such significance. She looked at the rest. A few she knew, more she didn't. She felt awed by the collection, looking at painting after painting after painting. Even though money was irrelevant now, this wall had hundreds of millions of dollars' worth of art hanging on it. Just hanging here, underground, outside of Portland. It struck her as a little absurd.

"Do you want something to drink?" Kendall asked.

"Sure," she said. "Thanks."

She turned away from the art collection to look at the rest of his apartment. She'd expected different furnishings, a higher level of restrained opulence, but that wasn't the case. There was a nook with several electric guitars and an amp, and a bunch of brown cardboard boxes. Couches and chairs, bookshelves, and a dining area with a crystal chandelier. The kitchen was in the center of the room, small and cramped, like it had been an afterthought. The kitchen in the dome she and her friends were in was much nicer.

She heard a hollow pop—he was opening a bottle of wine.

She kept strolling, pausing to read the spines of books, trailing her hand alongside tables as she wandered through the expansive apartment. She stopped at the dining table, counting fourteen chairs. Almost the entire table was covered by picnic tablecloths, the waterproof kind with a felted back. Dozens of tiny bowls were at one end, all with an inch of water at the bottom. Labels were on the side, all with small block lettering. Miranda looked closer and realized there were seeds in the water. She knew what Kendall was doing; he was harvesting the seeds.

Most, if not all, seeds from fruits and vegetable had a slimy, outer coating. If left on the seed it hardened, protecting it over the winter when it fell to the ground or was pooped out by an animal. When seeds were stored to be cultivated, it was best to remove that slime before it hardened. Cultivated seeds didn't need protection from the elements that broke down that outer coating in time for the growing season, but sitting in water for several days achieved the same thing. The seeds would still germinate despite the hardened outer coating, but it took longer, sometimes so much that you missed the best growing window. Late harvests often meant failed harvests when the weather turned. When you depended on subsistence farming for your survival, you had to maximize your chances of success.

Farther down the table was a large piece of cloth over the tablecloth—a bedsheet, she realized. Seeds were spread on it in small groups, with little pieces of masking tape next to them. She knew what this was, too. These were the seeds set out to dry. Once they dried, they could be scraped off the cloth and stored. She looked at the labels: Tomato—Hawaiian Pineapple; Bean—Rattlesnake Snap; Tomato—Black Krim; Tomato—Brandywine; Pepper—Anaheim Mild; Carrot—Dragon; Garlic—German Extra Hardy, and so on. There were seeds from pumpkins, zucchini, corn, broccoli, radishes, cabbage, and more. A stack of envelopes and a few pencils were scattered just beyond the sheet in front of a chair not fully pushed into place. That must be where Kendall sat while he put the seeds into envelopes. The few sealed envelopes on the table were dated by year. Beside the chair were two cardboard book boxes, like she'd bought from a moving company when she first left home for college. She peeked inside one and saw that it was crammed full of small envelopes of seeds.

Kendall rejoined her and gave her a glass. She sniffed the light-gold liquid, the scent of oak and citrus filling her nose. The crisp coolness of the wine lit up her taste buds.

"This wine is lovely," she said. Kendall nodded, looking pleased. She motioned to the table. "Saving seeds, I see."

"Yes," he said, nodding. "They're heirlooms, of course, so the seeds can be grown the next year. Hybrids don't work well for that. And heirlooms grow true to type."

"I know. I've done a fair bit of gardening," she said. She took a closer look at the book box full of seeds by the table, then looked back to the boxes by the guitars. They were also book boxes. "Are those boxes of seeds, too, by the guitars?"

Kendall nodded. Miranda blinked, surprised. She counted; there were fifteen boxes over there. Book boxes were about twelve inches on all sides, a little bigger, actually. She knew he'd been here ten years, but still... Kendall had enough seeds to supply fifteen farms. Not just dinky farms, either, but farms with some serious acreage.

Without thinking, she said, "Can I have some? You must have seeds for varietals I've never even heard of."

Kendall just looked at her for a moment, then the owl blink started up. "I, uh— They're my seeds."

"Yeah, I know," she said, beginning to grin. "You've got more than you can ever use."

Kendall just stared at her, the owl blink getting worse by

the second. He opened and closed his mouth, Adam's apple bobbing, then said, "No. I'd rather not. I might...need them myself."

Woah, she thought, so shocked she had no idea how to respond. He was right, of course; they were his seeds. The fact that he wouldn't give her any practically had her jaw on the floor. There was no way he'd ever use them all, or even half, not if he lived to be ninety.

Recovering herself, she tipped her head to the end of the apartment beyond the kitchen. "Bedroom's that way?" When Kendall looked at her blankly, she added wryly, "I'm not suggesting we go there."

"No, I— Of course not," he stumbled, blushing furiously. Then he muttered, "Bathroom is there, too."

She took another sip of wine as she made a slow three-hundred-sixty-degree turn. She didn't want to add to his embarrassment by watching him blush, and she wasn't entirely sure she was covering her shock at his refusal of the seeds. She examined the walls and floor, looking for somewhere a door might be hidden by furnishing or plants. As her eyes skated along the art collection, she looked more closely at the wall, wondering about the space behind it, where the dome sloped up from the floor. It would be easy to hide a door behind that. Or it might be a closet, she thought, not wanting to get ahead of herself.

"It's a nice place," she said, giving him a quick smile.

He looked at her like she was a prize, but also a trap. It had been a mistake to ask for the seeds. She hadn't even meant to; it just came out. For someone who had a hidden luxury bunker, she couldn't think of anything less consequential than a few envelopes of seeds he'd never use. She'd met people with far less who had been more generous. She felt the pressure of time, knowing it wasn't on LO's side. Part of her had wanted to just ask him for help, play things straight and not beat around the bush, but she abandoned that idea once and for all. If this was how Kendall felt about sharing seeds, she didn't see how he'd ever share something as valuable as ready-to-consume food. They'd only known Kendall for six weeks, but it was already mid-October. If the scouting parties didn't find something more than peaches soon, they could be out of food by late January, and January would be here before they knew it.

Kendall looked at her as if her true motives couldn't possibly be altruistic, while at the same time hoping it might be true. Hoping they liked him for him, not for what he had. She felt desperate after being refused the seeds, and disgusted by how easily it let her rationalize her dishonesty.

Kendall said, "Would you like some more?"

It took her a moment to realize she'd drained her wineglass. She nodded. "Please. It's very good."

She examined the room while Kendall refilled her glass, trying to ignore the hollow feeling that gnawed at her stomach. She *was* interested in helping Kendall, but keeping the people of LO from starving and getting the vaccine rollout back on track trumped everything. Just once, she wanted doing the right thing—the ethical thing—to be clear-cut, but it never was. Kendall was a person and shouldn't be treated as a means to an end, but there was no history, no relationship, to draw upon. He wouldn't even give her a few lousy envelopes of seeds. They couldn't depend on him to help them because it would be the right thing to do, not with the scarcity mentality he'd just displayed.

When it came down to it, if he had the surplus of food they suspected and their people were starving, they'd come visit one day and take it. She'd always known this, but it was easier to rationalize in the abstract. It was easier when it was a nameless hoarder who didn't need it all, not a person with a name. A person who blinked like an owl when he got nervous and gardened to stay sane, and sang with a tenderness that belied his awkward exterior. A person she could see was beginning to have feelings for her in a way she would never have for him.

Stop this, she said to herself.

She took a deep breath, steeling herself against the hesitant, hopeful glimmer in Kendall's eyes. She couldn't think about what was right or wrong, kind or cruel. She couldn't indulge her ambivalence, or think about how this secret agenda cheapened her genuine interest in helping Kendall get out of this prison of a bunker. She had to think about what was, which was very simple: LO didn't have enough food; the vaccine rollout was stalled because of it, and the delay threatened their chance to make San Jose irrelevant by breaking their monopoly.

Kendall might hold the key to fix those problems, and she had to get it. How she did was beside the point.

15

THEIR TEMPORARY REFUGE was quiet now, the darkness like an embrace. Doug was almost used to the gentle creaks the house made, and the sound of the wind as it sighed through the trees and grasses. Cool night air trickled down from the open window, one of the high ones used for ventilation that a zombie couldn't reach. Even he couldn't reach it and needed to use a chair, which was not an experience Doug was used to having. Mario had gone to bed early, as had Tessa. She'd been up since dawn, working on the Tesla, and had practically fallen asleep while they ate their evening meal.

He heard Skye's light footsteps a few moments before her shadowy form appeared in the kitchen, which was open to the living room. She sat next to him on the couch.

"Bad dreams crisis averted?" he asked.

Skye's gentle laugh felt like a caress. "Nothing *Little House* couldn't fix. Violet sacked out after a page, and I don't think Silas ever really woke up."

"Good."

He took Skye's hand in his, then brought it to his lips. Her skin was warm and smooth, and the moonlight shining through the kitchen windows was just bright enough that he could see the outline of her face, and the swell of her cheek. They didn't use lights while on watch because it messed with their ability to see outside. The dim light partially obscured her features but not her beauty. A rush of desire washed over him. He wished he could lose himself in her, feel her hands in his hair and her legs around his hips, feel her moving beneath him, her mouth on his, breath soft and ragged, her hungry lips scorching his skin, instead of keeping watch and brooding about things he couldn't fix.

"Are you okay?"

"I'm fine," he said.

She was quiet for a moment. "But Mario's not."

"No, he's not," he agreed quietly. "And I don't know how to help him." He almost changed the subject, not sure that he wanted to spend this time with Skye trying to puzzle out something he couldn't really do anything to solve, then said, "Did Silas or Violet say anything to you this afternoon?"

"About Mario going off on them? No, but Silas was upset. Tessa let him help her by handing her the tools. He gave her the wrong one a couple times and got upset that he'd made a mistake. Like it was a big deal, and Tessa would be angry. It took him a while to settle down."

"I'm worried about him. Mario, I mean," Doug said.

"He's having a hard time," Skye agreed. "It's weird, because he's so good with Silas and Violet. They make up little games, and he's so good at seeing when they need a hug or a nudge, and when to pull out Mister Bun Bun to settle them down. And how he settled Violet down at that campground. I couldn't have done that. I can see how much he cares for them. And then it's like he gets freaked out and pulls away. They don't understand it doesn't have anything to do with them, especially Silas. He really takes it to heart."

Doug chewed on his lip a moment, then said, "He's beating himself up about his kids, and the baby...like he could somehow have done something to change it. And leaving San Jose like we did. He's acting like he left his kids behind on a whim, because he didn't want the responsibility anymore, which is ridiculous. The Council knew he'd betrayed them. They'd already tried to apprehend him and would've killed him, no question about it. He had to leave."

Doug felt rather than saw Skye's shrug. She said, "Even if it was necessary, I can see how he'd feel like he was letting them down."

Doug sighed. "Well, I don't know what to do to help him, besides telling him he can't act like he did today. It's not fair to Silas and Violet, or him. It's like he realizes that he's enjoying being a dad, and he shouldn't because they're not the right kids. I haven't seen him like this since Emily—"

Doug snapped his mouth shut. He hadn't meant to say that. He wasn't used to keeping things from Skye, so wasn't very good at monitoring himself when they talked.

"Since Emily what?"

"It's a long story."

Skye's soft chuff of laughter felt like a balm on his frazzled nerves. "It's not like we're going anywhere. Maybe if I know what's going on I can make a suggestion, or at least stop you from being an idiot and telling Mario off when it's not called for because I don't have the backstory."

Doug nudged her with his elbow, then said, his tone teasing, "You're supposed to build me up, not call me names."

"You know what I mean." When he didn't say anything, she said, "Are you going to tell me or not?"

Doug hesitated. He wasn't sure it was his story to tell. His part was, of course, but it was inextricably entwined... Fuck it, he thought. Skye was smart and caring and discreet. Maybe if she knew the whole story, she'd at least understand why he was so concerned.

"It was about six months before the preventative vaccine was developed in San Jose and all hell broke loose," he said.

It had been so hot that day, so hot that it hadn't cooled off much overnight. It was already seventy-five degrees going on six a.m., which meant today was going to be a scorcher, too. Right now, hardly anyone was out and about.

He'd barely slept the night before, outside of SCU's walls. It took longer than anticipated to clear out the block of houses near Fremont Park so they could keep expanding the SCU settlement. And they'd made too much noise. They'd been forced to use guns, so attracted every zombie around in the process. They'd only been several blocks from a secure part of the campus settlements, but close didn't mean jack where zombies were concerned. They'd spent the night in one of the houses, almost every window closed, which made the already uncomfortably warm house sweltering. When morning rolled around, help arrived to shift the remaining zombies east, so they could get home.

Doug's back foot was still on the curb of Franklin Street near the Jesuit Residence when he saw a flicker of movement in the corner of his eye.

"What the hell?" he said softly, his feet already moving him toward the Lafayette Street gate at the other end of the long block.

People were shouting and pointing at something on the other side of the wall, and someone was running along the catwalk with a rifle. Another person, a man, was shouting for the gate to be opened. Not shouting—screaming—like he'd completely lost his shit. There must be a person approaching the gate who'd been caught by zombies. They wouldn't use a rifle otherwise, not this close to the main settlement. He was halfway to the gate when he realized that the screaming man, now joined by five others, was Mario. Doug sprinted, drawing on the last of his depleted reserves. One door of the gate swung in, just enough for Mario and two others to get through.

"Clear a path," Doug shouted at the men who'd stayed behind to guard the door. They scrambled out of the way as he shot through the opening at a flat-out run, machete already in his hand.

He expected to see at least a small clutch of zombies, but there weren't any. Mario and the other men sprinted north on Lafayette—then Doug saw why. A thousand feet beyond Mario, a tall, willowy woman walked in the road. The morning sun set fire to her golden hair. In one arm she held a toddler, and her other hand held the arm of a little boy, still almost a toddler himself. The boy was crying, struggling, but could not break the grip of the woman's hand. The toddler in her arms was crying, too. And beyond them, so far in the distance that Doug could barely make it out, a lone zombie staggered in the road. Only one, rather than the usual churn, because the work crew that Doug had been on yesterday had pulled them away.

It was Emily. She was walking away outside the walls, taking Anthony and Michael with her.

Doug felt his stomach heave. What the hell had happened? He approached the next intersection, scanning the area to see if zombies were coming from farther west. When he looked ahead again, Mario was yanking Anthony from Emily's arms and into the waiting hands of a companion. The other man had picked up Michael. Mario pulled Emily with him and she followed, unresisting. Doug stopped, waiting and keeping watch at the intersection until they reached him.

The boys were crying but otherwise looked okay. Anthony

recognized Doug and practically leaped from the arms of the man carrying him. Doug had to drop his machete to catch the crying toddler safely. Emily radiated a beatific serenity. She looked like a Renaissance painting of a saint, she was so calm, while her husband was glassy-eyed, his face a rictus of terror.

Anthony's sobs grew louder as they reached the gate. Inside, Father Gilbert, surrounded by a phalanx of his brother-priests, hovered, his anxiety palpable. Doug felt the deep thud of the gate closing behind them as if it were penetrating his bones, its purpose—protection—resonating more viscerally than it ever had before. Doc Owen crossed Franklin Street ahead of them, his hair the wild nimbus of one just roused from their bed, his black doctor's bag in his hand. Someone wrapped a blanket around Emily as everyone was hustled into the Jesuit Residence, even the people guarding the gate. Priests were taking over for them, their faces pinched and serious. Several of them were too old for gate duty.

After handing Anthony off to Mario, he waited in the kitchen along with those who had been on the gate. Mugs of tea and coffee were passed out, the room buzzing with hushed conversations. After a while, Father Walter, who was for all practical purposes Father Gilbert's first officer, appeared and motioned for him.

"Mario wants to see you," he said.

Doug nodded. "Does anyone know what happened?"

"Emily's with Doc right now. We'll know more later."

Doug followed Walter to Father Gilbert's office. Walter turned to him before opening the door.

"He's in a terrible state, as you can imagine." Walter's hazel eyes might have been granite when he said, "We're keeping this quiet, if we can. I don't know the details yet, but—" He hesitated. "He doesn't want Miranda to know."

Doug nodded. After what had just happened, he was unable to muster surprise that Father Walter was acknowledging Mario and Miranda's relationship. Miranda was like a daughter to the priest. It wasn't that he didn't know they were together—obviously, he did—but he disapproved. Strongly. You didn't have to be a genius to figure out that while Father Walter liked Mario, he placed the lion's share of blame for the relationship with Miranda at Mario's feet. Mario was married, and older, and he'd made promises to another that Miranda had not.

Doug nodded, then stepped inside. Mario sat in one of the two chairs by the window, off to the side of the desk. He clutched a glass with an inch of amber liquid. Doug saw the bottle of Irish whiskey on the desk. Mario looked up as Doug sat in the other chair. His eyes were red-rimmed, his skin ashen. He looked like he'd aged ten years.

"How are you doing?"

Mario looked at Doug, shell-shocked. He raised the glass to his mouth and gulped the whiskey down. His hands shook, though an hour had passed.

"I can't believe this," Mario whispered. "I can't... Oh my God..."

"Do you know what happened? Is Em cracking up again?"

"I—" Mario started, then stopped. When he spoke again, his voice was barely more than a whisper. "I... We had a fight last night. Me and Emily. I told her I was leaving, that I was tired of living a lie. Tired of...making what was left of our marriage a joke. I told her I'd always be there for her and the boys, but I wanted to be with Miranda."

"Oh," Doug said, the import of Mario's confession hitting him like a massive wave that clobbers you into the sand. "Oh. Wow."

"She said I'd regret it but I never thought..." He looked at

Doug, imploring his friend to believe him. "Doug, you have to believe me, I never thought—"

"Of course you didn't," Doug said, interrupting him.

"She's been so much better this past year, you know? She really seemed to not...need me like that. To function. I knew it would be hard, but I thought it would be okay. I never thought she'd do something like this." Mario stopped and swallowed hard. "This is my fault, Doug. It's all my fault."

Mario searched Doug's face as if it were a lifeline, as if he was seeking absolution from a priest. Which would be funny if this wasn't so serious, since Mario was talking to him. Then a thought occurred to him—a terrible one. One he wanted to reject outright, but he couldn't.

"What were you doing at the gate?" Mario looked confused; Doug persisted. "You don't work the gate, Mario. What were you doing there so early?"

"I was supposed to meet Dominic. What does it matter why I was there?" he said uncertainly.

"Humor me," Doug said.

Mario's eyes squinted shut, like thinking was an effort. "Dominic stopped by last night, right after Em and I argued. Dominic was staying the night with the guy he's seeing, Will. Will was working the gate this morning at seven. Dominic wanted to introduce us, get breakfast before his shift. He was insisting it be in the morning... I don't know why. I said I'd meet them there."

"And you didn't see Emily and the kids leaving?"

Mario shook his head. "After Dom left, Emily told me to get out. I went to Miranda's."

"But she's in Livermore."

"I have a key. I knew you weren't back, or I'd have gone to your place. They announced at dinner that your work party was sheltering in place because so many zombies had been drawn north to you."

Doug turned it over in his mind, chewed on the idea forming in his brain, the conviction that none of this was a whim, or an accident, or the desperate act of an unhinged mind solidifying in his own. The terrible thought was true. He couldn't explain how, which went against everything the scientist in him believed, but Doug knew he was right. He knew it in his bones.

"She wanted you to see," he said.

"Miranda? She's not even here."

"No," Doug said. "Emily. She wanted you to see. She said you'd regret it, and she knew you were going to be at the gate this morning."

"I don't understand what you're saying," Mario said, sounding downright befuddled.

"She did it on purpose, Mario, because you told her you were leaving her. If it was announced yesterday that we'd drawn zombies north of campus, she would have known the chance of there being many of them here this morning was really low. She's not cracking up. She's scaring you into staying."

"No," Mario said. "No. She wouldn't do that."

"Emily is not as fragile as you think."

"She wouldn't do that, Doug," Mario said, anger in his voice now. "She wouldn't put the boys in danger unless she wasn't right." He stood up, swaying. "I need to get back to the boys and see if Doc has finished examining Em."

Doug stood, too. "I'm not wrong, Mario. I know I'm not."

Mario glared at him, a fierce protectiveness flaring in his eyes. "I don't want to hear this! This is my fault, not Emily's. Don't ever say that about her again."

Doug shook his head. If Mario didn't want to hear it, he didn't want to hear it. He should let it go, but couldn't seem to help himself.

"Are you going to break up with Miranda?"

The fierceness drained away, leaving nothing but a swirl of guilt and Mario's ever-present fear of losing Miranda on her next expedition in its wake. Doug wished he'd kept his mouth shut.

"No," Mario said softly, looking both surprised, and like he hated himself for how quickly he answered Doug's question. He looked at Doug for a moment more, fear and pain and most of all guilt hovering in the air between them. "I have to go."

Doug watched Mario leave, more convinced with every passing second that he was right, that this had been a methodical, intentional move on Emily's part, not a desperate cry for help. In the heat of the moment, even Doug had forgotten that the chance of there being zombies outside the Lafayette Gate this morning were almost nil. He'd been part of the reason why they'd moved off in the first place, yet it was instinct that had kicked in, not his intellect. When Mario had seen his family out there, instinct would have been the only thing to kick in.

The whole situation was dreadful, Doug got that. Could Emily regress in the face of such a stressor? Doug had to concede it was possible but...it didn't play. The look on her face as Mario pulled her along with him to get back inside had been almost serene. Doug thought about it more... Not serene, he realized, but triumphant. She hadn't looked zoned out or unaware or in shock. She'd looked like a woman who was getting exactly what she wanted.

Doug had seen Emily take on things that would have made her crumple before. And he'd seen her scheme to make things go the way she wanted. Not in a bad way, never at the expense of anyone else, but it signified a resourcefulness that Mario clearly wasn't aware of, or just couldn't see. Maybe she still thought she needed him to function, but Doug hadn't thought so for a while now. It was clear she wasn't in love with Mario. They got along well enough, and she cared about him, but that was as far as it went. Emily had decided she could live with her husband being in love, being with, Miranda, so long as he didn't leave, but Mario had threatened to upend everything. While Doug could sympathize, it pissed him off to think she'd do something so foolhardy—so cruel—and use innocent children to do it.

The tangled, enmeshed relationships, and the wildly diverging wants and needs behind them, all of it was totally fucked up and corrosive. Life after zombies seemed to have more than its fair share of fuck up-ed-ness. Miranda and Mario made it even more so by feeling responsible for Emily's grip on reality. Emily had desperately needed Mario in order to cope once; maybe believed she still did, but Doug did not buy that she would kill her children. Even if he was wrong about the rest, she'd never hurt her children. She wasn't psychotic. She wasn't postpartum. She wasn't even especially unhinged by today's standards. And Mario hadn't told Miranda he was planning to leave Emily because Miranda would have flipped. Mario staying with Emily was the only big thing that he'd ever seen them fight about.

Doug watched Mario go, incredulous that Mario couldn't see it, even though he understood why.

"You're not leaving Miranda," he had said softly to the empty room. "But you're not leaving Emily, either."

SKYE SAID, "HOLY SHIT. DID SHE REALLY PLAN IT TO manipulate him? Like, did she tell you later in confession or something?"

"No!" Doug said, shocked, and much louder than he meant to. He lowered his voice. "Of course not! I'd never reveal anything a person confessed. Jesus, Skye. I can't believe you even suggested it."

Skye snickered, then started to giggle. "Are you kidding me?"

"What?" Doug demanded, still utterly scandalized.

"Technically, you're still a priest and that hasn't stopped you from sleeping with me—a lot."

"That's not the same thing, Skye. At all."

Doug could feel her body shaking with suppressed laughter.

"I mean, it's frowned upon. Obviously," he said, beginning to feel ridiculous that he was even arguing this, but Skye wasn't Catholic. Confession wasn't something she was familiar with. "Confession is a whole other thing. You just don't, no matter how much you fall down in other areas."

Skye's giggling took a while to subside, and it took all of Doug's willpower not to kiss her. She was so outrageously cute while she laughed at him. Even in this minuscule bit of light he could see, or imagined that he could, the sparkle in her eyes, the pucker of her lips. The way her body shook with barely suppressed laughter as she tried and failed to pull herself together had him almost panting, thinking of how her body quaked when she came, and how much he wanted to go down on her right now and make that happen. But if he kissed her, he wouldn't want to stop.

Just like betraying the seal of confession, screwing on watch was something you just didn't do.

"So," Skye finally said, the giggles almost gone. "If she's never told you, how are you so sure?"

"It came up once, when it was just the two of us, right after Maureen was born. I'd told her I was happy she was still here because we'd have missed out on this gorgeous little baby, and she said, 'I'm not stupid, Doug. I knew we'd be okay.'"

Skye whistled. "Damn. That's cold."

"When she realized what she'd said, she backtracked immediately, but I could see it in her eyes. She'd never felt in danger, even though it could have gone terribly wrong. She looked like she felt bad about it, but—" He shrugged. "It was almost two years later. Mario had already pretended to side with the Council so we could try to get the vaccine back. Miranda wanted nothing to do with him, and had finally quit doing her damndest to drink herself stupid twenty-four seven."

"And they stayed married?"

"They're *still* married. I mean, what were they going to do? It was what Emily wanted, and Mario was more convinced than ever that if he left her, she'd take the Express Bus to Cuckooville." Doug's voice trailed as he thought, because he'd never put it into words before. He wanted to get it right. "When he decided to stay in his marriage, it was never a question of choosing Emily over Miri. You've seen them; he was so in love with Miranda... He wasn't going to give her up. But he stopped letting himself want the kind of life he wanted with her. He was going to do right by Emily as far as he could, but things between them changed. His expectations shifted—priorities, too. It's not that it became an arrangement between them, but it felt that way for quite a while."

"But they had another child."

"Yeah, well, six months later we had the vaccine and then everything blew up. When he 'defected,' Mario and Emily had to leave SCU. They went to Palo Alto, where the real power players on the Council lived. They were on their own. When it came down to who they could really trust, they only had each other. It's not surprising they grew closer again. They actually care about one another, and they've got the kids. If you didn't know all the history, you'd never know looking in from the outside that their marriage is as screwy as it is."

After a moment, Skye said, "I can totally see Rocco doing something like that. Staying, I mean. It's that old-school Italian thing."

Doug nodded. She had summarized Mario's motivations better than he'd ever been able to. "But you can't count on getting a second chance. Would he let the one he loved slip past him?"

"Like me, you mean?" Skye teased.

Doug's heart swelled with love for her until it ached. "Definitely like you," he said softly.

He reached for her, and this time he did kiss her. The head rush of desire hit him like a train. Their kiss deepened, heat exploding between them. His hands slipped inside her shirt. He shoved her bra up, cupping her soft, yielding breasts. Her nipples were already hard and she gasped into his mouth as he caressed them.

Skye broke the kiss, her breathing fast and shallow. Even though all they had was moonlight, he could see the blush of color in her cheeks.

"You know we can't," she said, breathless.

Doug groaned, his forehead resting on hers. "I know."

She whimpered, for his thumbs continued to caress her erect nipples. They were so stiff...he would swear to God they beat in time with her pulse. And the way she was whimpering... Christ Almighty, he wanted to fuck her so bad. He forced himself to stop, though he wanted to keep moving his hands on her body, listen to her whimper and gasp and groan, dive into her like she was cool water on a sweltering day.

"I'd have been a fool to let you get away, but being on this fucking watch is killing me."

"Me too," she said, still a little breathless. "But—"

"I know," Doug grumbled. "I know...fucking zombies."

Skye grinned as she rearranged herself back into her bra. Doug stood up to adjust his pants around the raging hard-on he now had.

Skye said, "Mario really doesn't suspect? Is he afraid she might lose it?"

"I don't think he's afraid she'll hurt the kids. More that she won't be able to cope. And now... He can't seem to reconcile that he let Emily down in a way he never thought he would, by leaving them all behind, I mean. It feeds into this..." He cast about for the right word. "Misconception he has about her still being fragile and helpless. It's a blind spot. He just can't see it."

"And Miranda really doesn't know?"

Doug smiled at the skepticism in Skye's voice. "You'd be amazed how well priests can scheme. And part of it was luck. That kind of thing could have caused division in the community that we couldn't afford. Everyone on watch that morning understood that."

He raised his arms above his head and stretched, trying to dispel some of the nervous energy the all-too-brief make-out session had generated. It didn't help much.

"The people who knew didn't want to tar Emily with that brush," he continued. "She and Mario might have had a failing, fucked-up marriage, but if it got out, she would always be the crazy lady who took her kids outside the walls. She didn't deserve that, no matter what she may have done. She really is a lovely person. She's just damaged, like everyone else."

Skye held out a hand and pulled him back beside her. She snuggled close and lay her head on his shoulder. He was relieved to have told her. He'd never shared the story with anyone, and had never realized how heavy it was.

"He was afraid Miranda would break it off. That's why he didn't want her to know?"

Doug sighed as he stroked Skye's silky hair. "I'm sure that's part of it, but honestly? I think it's because she's the mother of his children, and he's still protecting her."

16

THE PLUME OF DUST BELOW, followed by the crunch of the Tesla's tires in the driveway, lifted Mario's head. A moment later, Tessa and Doug drove into view, the smiles on their faces triumphant. The Tesla had passed the test drive. Mario felt a grin spread across his face. Finally, they were ready to go. He walked over to greet them as the SUV came to a halt.

"Wanna ride?" Tessa asked through the open driver's side window.

"Definitely," Mario answered.

Doug rounded the SUV as Tessa's door opened. "She's an electrical genius, and Skye's a mechanical one."

"You've got about ten years to stop with the praise," Tessa said, her voice dripping with pleasure. She squinted in the bright sunshine as she looked around. "Where are Skye and the kids?"

"In the breezeway, I think," said Mario. "I'll go get them."

He walked around the front of the house. Mario could feel the soft breeze from the open breezeway before he started up the steps. Skye sat with one of the children on either side of her, reading from the battered copy of *Little House on the Prairie*. Violet had Mister Bun Bun, who looked asleep, in her lap. Absently, she stroked his soft fur. Silas looked at him warily as he approached.

"They're back," Mario said.

"Yeah?" Skye asked, a grin splitting her face.

"Tessa says we're ready to go."

Violet squealed as she picked up Mister Bun Bun and jumped to her feet. "I wanna see!"

"Wait for me, Violet," Skye said. "Mister Bun Bun needs to go into his playpen."

Violet complied reluctantly. Silas stood, looking solemn while he waited. Mario's heart felt like it was sinking into his shoes. Skye barely had time to snag Violet's hand once Mister Bun Bun was in the playpen.

"Come on, Silas," said Violet.

"Actually, I was hoping I could talk to Silas for a minute," Mario said. He looked to Silas. "If that's okay with you."

Silas shrugged. Skye gave Mario an encouraging smile, then left with Violet, whose high-pitched voice squealed with excitement as they walked around the corner of the house. Mario walked the remaining two steps up to the breezeway and sat down in the open section next to where Silas stood.

"Sit down?" Mario asked him, patting the spot beside him.

Silas looked at him a moment, his dark eyes peeking out from below his downcast, furrowed brow, and shrugged again.

"That's okay, you don't have to," Mario said. "I owe you an apology, Silas. I was a real jerk yesterday, and it had nothing to do with you. I am so sorry that I hurt your feelings, or if I scared you."

Silas mumbled something Mario couldn't quite catch.

"What's that?"

"Doesn't matter," Silas muttered. "You're not my dad."

The metaphorical knife plunged into Mario's heart and twisted. Painfully.

"I'm not your dad, but I like taking care of you. And I really like being with you."

"Then why are you so mean sometimes?" Silas said angrily. "You shouldn't be mean. Especially to Violet."

"Or to you." Mario took a moment to gather his thoughts. "You know how sometimes things are really hard? So hard you just want to fight and yell and kick things?"

Silas gave him a grudging nod, which was more than Mario had expected.

"Things have been really hard for me lately, and I haven't been dealing with it very well. I've been acting like a jerk sometimes and that's because of me. It's nothing you did."

"Doug said it's because you're sad."

Mario nodded. "Yeah. I've been sad about things that happened before I met you."

Silas' body language loosened and relaxed. The furrowed brow smoothed. He sat down next to Mario.

"What's making you sad?"

Mario almost laughed, because if he was better at dealing with his feelings about everything that had happened, then he wouldn't have an earnest eight-year-old inquiring about the state of his interior life. He took a deep breath.

"My girlfriend and I were going to have a baby, but...sometimes it doesn't work out, and we lost him."

"Did she have the baby too soon? Mama had a baby too soon, and she was never even alive."

Mario nodded, a dull ache making his throat feel tight. Partly because of Miranda and Tadpole, and partly because Silas' first mention of his mother since they'd found him and Violet involved death and loss.

"Something like that. It makes me really sad, because I really wanted to be his dad."

"Where's your girlfriend?"

"She didn't come with us. She got really sad, too, and broke up with me."

"Oh." Silas seemed to digest this information for a moment, then said, "Mama used to get sad after...after Devon died."

"Was Devon your brother?"

Silas shook his head. "Her boyfriend. He was nice."

"I'm sorry, Silas. It sounds like you liked him. Having nice people with you is really important."

"Yeah," Silas whispered, the expression on his face faraway, as if he was seeing something he didn't like. Then his face cleared and he looked up to Mario. "I think you're nice, when you're not—"

He stopped speaking abruptly, and his eyes went wide. He looked at Mario guiltily.

"When I'm not being a jerk?" Mario said, smiling.

A grin tugged on the corner of Silas' mouth. "Yeah," he said, beginning to laugh.

"I think you're nice, Silas," Mario said, blinking back the tears that had sprung to his eyes. "Violet, too. I'll try not to be a jerk. And if you think I'm heading that direction, you can tell me. Or you can tell someone else and they can tell me. Deal?"

He held out his hand, but Silas didn't take it. Instead, he wrapped his thin arms around Mario's neck. Mario pulled Silas to him and gave him a squeeze.

"Deal," Silas said.

His hold on Mario's neck loosened after a few moments, so Mario reluctantly broke the embrace. He wanted to hold Silas tight, this quirky, little person whose need for protection—for love—had made him feel like a father again. A good one, instead of the guy who kept doing the wrong thing.

"I want to see the Tesla, Mario. And I want to sit by the window."

Mario smiled. "Then let's go see it."

Silas skipped down the steps, waiting for Mario close up the breezeway. When he reached Silas, Mario held out his hand. Silas took it.

"And I want to find a bike," Silas said. "There must be one somewhere."

"There are definitely bikes somewhere," Mario said as they walked around the corner of the house. "We'll get you one. I promise."

———

MARIO RUBBED, BUT IT ONLY MADE THE ITCH BEHIND HIS eyelids worse. It felt like sand had adhered to their underside to scratch and scrape. He shoved his hands in his pockets to avoid the unsatisfying temptation to keep rubbing.

Highway 20 East was not the type of road that anyone wanted to take. It was in terrible condition, remote, and wound its way through sometimes rugged terrain. But it was still there, which was more than they could say for Highway 101. They'd driven south on 101 until Lake Mendocino, where they discovered that miles of the highway and the access roads that ran alongside it were simply not there. Their best guess was that at some point, someone had the bright idea to destroy the road. Maybe they'd only destroyed sections, but the intervening decade took care of anything that might have been left behind.

They wasted several hours while Doug and Mario hiked south, hoping that the destruction wasn't for a long distance, to no avail. After a mile and half, with the ruined highway stretching to the horizon, it was clear they had to go another way. Even if the road picked up again, and at some point it would, the Tesla wasn't an all-terrain vehicle. They couldn't risk losing it, especially since Highway 20, despite being in poor condition and taking them on a more circuitous route, seemed to be a better option.

Four hours after detouring onto Highway 20, what had once been an hour drive was nearing its end. The kids were still asleep. Miraculously, only a few lone zombies had appeared in the road—one standing in it but easy to get around and one arriving at the berm just as they passed.

Tessa said, "What's the name of the town we talked about? I just saw a sign for North Lakeport in ten miles."

"That's it," Skye murmured.

Skye reached around the back of the seat and shook Doug's shoulder gently. "Sweetie, wake up."

Doug shifted in his seat, then jerked awake and lunged forward. A dull *thwack* coincided with his head hitting the windshield.

"Easy, babe," Skye said, belatedly cautioning him.

"Jesus," said Tessa, who'd taken over driving. "You nearly gave me a heart attack."

Doug sat back, rubbing his head. "It's a little late for easy," he grumbled. "Sorry, Tessa."

They were all on edge. Mario just wanted to find somewhere to hole up for a while and sleep, though he doubted he'd be able. He felt simultaneously strung out and exhausted, as if he'd drunk too much coffee that kept his weary mind and body unable to rest.

Tessa slowed the vehicle. Without the ambient light from cities and towns, it was hard to pick out buildings. Instead, they looked for driveways.

"There's... Oh, forget it," Skye said. "Trailer park."

Mario suppressed a shudder, remembering the time he'd been stranded in a trailer so long that he'd started to consider drinking his own urine. Trailer parks were too densely packed and out of the question after dark.

"There's one ahead," Doug said, pointing.

Tessa slowed and nosed the Tesla into the end of the drive. It wound away, no house in sight.

"I think it's worth checking out," she said, pressing on the accelerator.

The few buildings they'd seen so far were right up against the road; perhaps this was an old farm. As they rounded another gentle bend, they saw a collapsing farmhouse. And beyond it, a barn.

"Maybe the barn isn't falling down," Doug said softly.

That would be too much to ask for, but they had to check it out. Tessa pulled up close to the barn. Closed doors faced them, the barn's siding bleached and weathered by the sun, a washed-out gray in the headlights.

"You game, Mario?" Doug asked.

"Do we have any sort of light?"

"Matches," Doug said. "Because matches and barns...what could go wrong?"

"Just let me put Mister Bun Bun in his carrier before you open the doors," Skye said.

A minute later, the two men climbed out. Even though the day had been hot, goosebumps prickled Mario's arms when the cool night air brushed against them. On his shadow in the head-lights, any motion looked exaggerated. He headed to the person-sized door to the right of the big barn doors, then he and Doug banged on it and waited.

When nothing happened after a minute, Doug opened the door and poked his head inside. He lit a match and held it in front of him. "Here, zombie, zombie, zombie."

Mario chuckled. Even after as crappy a turn as today had taken, Doug could still crack a joke. The snick of a match being struck was followed by a hissing flare of ignition and a tiny flicker of flame that was swallowed by the dark almost immediately.

"Come on," Doug said softly.

Mario stepped into the barn.

Doug held the match before him, his voice raised in an inviting singsong. "Come on, you undead fuckers."

Nothing.

Mario felt his shoulders drop away from his ears a little. A large tractor was parked on the left-hand side of the barn, and more equipment he couldn't identify in the dark was on the right. He wouldn't have fancied poking around it if there had been moans. They made their way through the barn, stopping every few steps so that Doug could light another match. The spent ones he held in his hand. The dark was so complete that Mario could not see the roof.

"I think we're in the clear," Doug said eventually. "I'll just check the loft."

Doug scampered up the ladder before Mario could object to being left in the pitch-black, or Doug investigating on his own. He continued to call for zombies, and the dim glow of lighting matches flared and guttered, one after the other.

"Looks good," Doug said, his voice raised but not loud. "I'm coming down. Let's get everyone inside."

"The Tesla, too, if we can get the big doors open," Mario added.

As they exited the barn, Mario saw Tessa and Skye looking their way. The interior of the car was the only light in the dark nightscape.

From the open window, Tessa asked, "Are we good?"

"Yeah," Mario answered.

He opened the back door. Violet and Silas were awake, blinking like owls beneath the dome lights.

"Mawree?" Violet asked, turning to the open door. Her voice was tight and anxious.

"It's okay," he said, ducking inside to pick her up. "Come on, Violittle. Let's get some sleep."

"My name is Violet," she said, still sleepy.

"I know," Mario said. He kissed her forehead. She smelled of little kid sweat and mown grass. "But you're little, too."

"Is it safe?" Silas asked.

Silas' voice, so full of worry and seeking reassurance, made Mario's throat tighten. His mouth flooded with a bitter taste. He hated this world sometimes. Miranda had said the same thing to him, after they knew what had happened to Tadpole. After they knew that it had been too good to be true.

He shook the memory off. He didn't have time for that right now. It wouldn't make a difference for Tadpole, nor for he and Miranda. The stupid, thoughtless, hurtful things they'd said to one another made sure of that. Her refusal to be present had cut him to the quick, but he was starting to see that he'd been part of the problem. He'd needed her so much that he'd assumed what she needed was the same. When he realized his mistake, he all but said what happened to Tadpole had been her fault. He'd hurled the vicious accusation to absolve himself, because she was right about one thing: he *had* left her that night. He'd pitched in and helped out, did the thing that needed doing; what happened after hadn't been his fault. But he couldn't shake the feeling that she might have stayed safely indoors if he'd been there. He wished she'd been more cautious but when it came down to it, Miranda had done exactly what he'd done: pitched in to get things done. What happened next hadn't been her fault, either.

Nothing would make enough of a difference for he and Miranda, for Tadpole, but he could make a difference for Silas and Violet. He had to make the world better—make it safer—for them.

"Is it safe?" Silas repeated.

Mario would have run his hand over the tightly curled fuzz growing in on Silas' head were Violet not in his arms.

"It's safe enough for now."

———

THEY WOKE EARLY, ATE SIMPLY, AND WERE HEADING TO the lake for which North Lakeport was named within an hour of sunrise. Doug had scrounged up two water containers tucked in a corner of the barn.

They filled them at the lake without incident and got back on the road in minutes. They would filter it later; right now, they just wanted to make up some time. Silas and Violet's soft chatter in the back seat when they asked Skye a question was soothing. She was reading *Little House* again; they were almost finished with the book. How she read in a moving vehicle was beyond Mario. If he did that, he'd get queasy. Tessa rounded out the back seat contingent. She had Mister Bun Bun's carrier on her lap, and last time Mario had looked back, she had been petting him through the grill of the door.

"You've had time to look, navigator," Doug said. He glanced over to Mario. "Does Highway 29 still look like the best route?"

Mario felt a dissatisfied rumble building in his throat. None of the routes were particularly good. Taking Highway 20 East had taken them far from the 101 Interstate. Their best bet at this point was to go through the Napa Valley by the circuitous Highway 29.

"Yeah, I guess so. Highway 175 would get us to 101 at Hopland, eventually, but it's through the mountains." He lowered his voice so the kids wouldn't hear. "This thing's charge might not get us the whole way anymore, no matter which way we go."

"One thing at a time," Doug said. "At least the view of the lake is nice."

Ahead, Mario could see the sharp westward bend in the road that would change their direction by ninety degrees. He consulted the atlas again and told Doug the best route.

As they moved through the turn, they slowed, then stopped. A small group of people congregated in the road just before where they needed to turn left. They were armed, and outside what Mario assumed was a settlement that began at the corner. The wall—some sections made of metal sheeting, others of wood or concrete slabs, stretched from the corner to at least the end of that block. It also continued along the road they needed to turn onto, but for how far Mario couldn't see.

"Oh," Skye said softly from the back seat.

"I guess we need to at least say hello," Doug said, not sounding happy about it. He guided the Tesla forward, stopping about forty feet away from the people, who had of course noticed them. They looked relaxed, but Mario noticed that two of them had set their hands on their holstered firearms.

Doug pulled the parking brake and put the vehicle in park but didn't turn off the engine. "You mind getting behind the wheel, Tessa?"

"Sure," she said, repositioning Mister Bun Bun's carrier after she climbed out.

"Are they bad people?" Silas asked, his voice anxious.

By the time Mario turned in his seat to reassure him, both Silas and Violet had hunkered down on the floor between the front and back seats. Silas was between Skye's feet with Violet huddled next to him. Their heads almost touched as they looked at Mario through the gap between the front seats with huge, frightened eyes.

"It's okay," Mario said. "It's going to be fine."

He turned back, then opened the glove compartment and retrieved another magazine for his Sig, which he stuck in his jeans' back pocket. Behind him, he heard Skye's door open. Doug opened his door and got out, too.

"But you're getting more bullets," Silas said.

"I was gonna get them anyway," Mario said, smiling at them over his shoulder. Neither Silas nor Violet looked like they believed his bullshit explanation. "You can stay there on the floor if it makes you feel better. I'm just gonna go with Doug and Skye to say hello."

He traded a quick glance with Tessa as she slid behind the wheel, one that said, What the fuck ever happened to nodding hello before ignoring each other at the gas station? Then he joined Doug and Skye.

A woman and two men walked over to meet them. The woman wore a leather jacket and pants, which had to be sweltering in the heat, but signified someone who took the realities of their world seriously. Her brown hair was cut short and pushed off to the side behind an ear. She looked in her thirties or forties, but she had one of those faces that made it hard to tell. The man on her left was middle-aged, powerfully muscled, but with a bit of a pot belly. He wore black leather pants and a faded 82nd Airborne Division tee shirt. Another man, quite younger than the first, looked like he spent all of his free time at a gym. Unlike his companions, he wore camo cargo pants and a long-sleeved plaid shirt over a dark tee shirt. He squinted at them, as if his eyesight was poor.

"Hello," the woman said, stopping well short of them.

"Hello," Doug said.

"I'm Elise," she said. "That's Carl." The big man inclined his head. "And that's Albert. What brings you this way?"

Mario rested his hand lightly on his Sig. He wasn't trying to threaten, just let these strangers know that he wasn't afraid to use it. Skye mirrored his posture, though Doug left his hands at his side.

"Just passing through," Doug said, not offering introductions.

Elise looked past Mario, Doug, and Skye to peer at the Tesla.

"How many of you are there?"

"Just us, our friend in the car, two kids."

"We don't get a lot of people coming through," Elise said. "You're welcome to stop for a while, grab a meal, before you go on your way."

"I'm not sure that we have the time to stop," Doug said. "We've still got a ways to go."

"I don't see the kids," Elise said.

"They're afraid," Mario answered. "They're hiding in the back seat."

The older man, Carl, shook his head, his mouth twisting down in rueful frown. He scratched at his collarbone.

"This world," he said. "When I was a kid, we rode our bikes in the neighborhood all summer long. My biggest worry was pissing off my old man by being late for dinner. He said it was disrespectful to my mother."

"Things have changed," Doug agreed. From his tone, Mario could tell that Doug seemed to have made a decision. He held his hand out to Elise and closed the distance between them. "I'm Doug, by the way. This is Skye and Mario."

Hands were shaken and introductions made for real. The feeling of nervous tension in the air lessened markedly.

Albert, the younger man, said, "Where are you coming from, if you don't mind my asking."

"The Northwest," Doug said.

Carl whistled. Elise's mouth made a perfect O of surprise. Albert just looked at Doug for a moment, like his words did not compute.

"Really?" he said. "What's it like out there? I haven't been more than a hundred miles from home in years."

"It depends," Doug said, shrugging. "Really deserted in some places, lots of zombies in others. Sometimes the deserted places, too, if you're unlucky."

"April, that's my wife, we always wanted to go to eastern Washington State. Even talked about moving to Idaho, but we never got the chance."

"Too bad," Skye said. "Idaho's beautiful."

"Even if you aren't going to stop, which way are you headed?" Carl asked. "We can at least let you know which roads are in good shape."

Doug, Skye, and Mario all traded a glance. While that would be helpful to know, sharing their route wasn't really something any of them wanted to do with strangers.

"We're planning to take 175 West, but not as far as Hopland," Doug said. "Knew a guy who had a place up there. Things...didn't work out where we were. Thought we'd give it a try."

"That road's in bad shape," Elise said, shaking her head. "Not a lot of zees up there, but it's pretty remote."

"That's the idea," Mario said.

Elise said, "I know everyone's paranoid these days, but people would love to hear whatever news you have of the outside world. Let us feed your kids at least, and then we'll send you on your way. We can stay outside the gate, if it makes you feel more comfortable. We patrol heavily, so it's pretty safe near the settlement, especially if we're just outside."

Doug looked over to Mario and Skye, his eyebrows raised in question. Mario looked Elise, Carl, and Albert over again. He wasn't picking up any creepy vibes. They weren't being insistent about them stopping, just nice. And after the offer to stay outside their settlement, he felt pretty sure that if they declined, they'd go on their way and that would be the end of it.

"It's okay with me if it's okay with you two," Skye said, her voice low, so only Doug and Mario could hear her.

Mario nodded, and Doug said, "Sure. We can stop for an hour."

"I'll get Tessa and the kids," Mario said.

"I'll help, if that's okay," Albert said. "April and I lost our... well." His smile became tight, and pain flashed in his eyes. "It'd be nice to see some small fry."

"Sure," Mario said, sympathy for Albert making his heart twinge.

As they neared the Tesla, Tessa slid out from behind the wheel. "We're all good?" she asked.

"Yeah," Mario said, nodding. "Silas! Violet! Come on. We're going to stop for just a little bit."

While Tessa and Albert said hello, Mario went to collect Silas and Violet. Both children regarded him warily.

"They're nice people," he said. "It's okay. Come on."

Silas gave him a tentative smile, then crawled up from the floor. He stuck close to the Tesla, like he was suction-cupped to it.

"What about Mister Bun Bun?"

"We'll leave him for now, but we can bring him some water. Maybe they have lettuce or carrots."

"I want you to carry me," Violet said, her big brown eyes still uneasy.

"Come on then, Violittle."

Mario held out his arms and hoisted Violet onto his hip, then pushed the door shut. Silas took his hand, still looking nervous. As they came around the front of the vehicle, Tessa and Albert turned to them. Albert squinted in the morning sunshine, but the look of anticipation that had made him seem young and naive withered. Hostility pulsed off him in waves. He took an involuntary step back, which seemed to make him angrier. His upper lip peeled back, twisting into a nasty sneer, and his eyes, which had been mild and curious just moments ago, filled with the purest distillation of contemptuous hatred that Mario had ever seen.

"You never said they were—"

Mario couldn't prove what stopped Albert from finishing his sentence. Had he been a betting man, the odds on favorite was probably the fury that caused his face to grow hot, because h

e knew what Albert had been about to say—knew it for Gospel truth. He just couldn't believe it.

"What were you going to call them?"

"You never said... We keep our Aryan blood pure."

The disgust on Albert's face intensified when he pulled his shirt aside to reveal the tattoo on his shoulder: a swastika.

Mario didn't remember setting Violet down, but he must have, because he was in Albert's face and his hands were free.

"Shut the fuck up about my kids."

"Doug, Skye," Tessa called, her voice tense. From the corner of his eye, Mario saw her waving her arms over her head, her jerky movements frantic.

A look of revulsion filled Albert's face. "You mean you fucked—"

Mario didn't hear the rest, just felt the *thwack* of his fist hitting Albert's face. Rage—wrath—surged through his body.

How *dare* this racist piece of shit... Albert staggered back a few steps while Mario advanced. Albert lunged but telegraphed his punch. He deflected Albert's punch with his raised forearm, sending the blow glancing up the side of his face.

Then Doug was between him and Albert, pushing on Mario's chest. Carl was pulling Albert away. Albert's hatred was a palpable, growing presence. Elise was just a step behind Carl, alarm and surprise filling her face.

"What's going on?" she asked, bewildered.

"They're race traitors," Albert spat.

Elise and Carl both looked around, uncertain, before their eyes settled on the cowering forms of the children. They shrank away, clinging and hiding behind Skye, who had gone to them. Violet began to cry.

"They're fucking Nazis," Mario said to Doug, spitting out the words through his gritted teeth.

Doug's face filled with confusion. "What?"

"Neo-Nazis," Mario growled. "White supremacists."

Comprehension, quickly followed by trepidation, flashed in Doug's eyes. "Fuck," he said under his breath.

Doug turned back to the others, keeping himself in Mario's path. Elise looked to Skye, and the children clinging to her. When she looked back to Mario and Doug, her eyes were hard.

"Their kind isn't welcome."

"Their kind?" Doug said, incredulity filling his voice. And anger, too. Mario could tell he was working hard to keep it in check.

Behind their erstwhile hosts, Mario saw people coming out of the settlement—people with guns.

Elise didn't say more, but Carl picked up for her.

"We keep ourselves apart from..." A look of distaste filled his eyes. He wrinkled his nose, like he had smelled a fart but didn't want to cause a fuss in polite company by mentioning it. "Lesser races."

Doug's voice was flat. Lethal. "You've got to be fucking kidding me."

"It's our history, our heritage," Albert said hotly. "All of this was a chance to start again."

"Zombies weren't enough for you?" Mario demanded. "You had to make it worse?"

The group coming from the settlement were drawing near. A few men had rifles to their shoulders. When Carl took a step forward, Doug, Mario, and Tessa all raised their guns at Carl. He lurched to a halt and held his hands up.

"Woah... Let's just take a minute."

He looked to Elise and tipped his head toward the reinforcements. She turned to them and motioned they should stop and lower their weapons. Incredibly, they did, but the anger in their eyes showed that could turn on a dime.

A hard, cold calculus entered Carl's eyes, a shrewd menace that Mario hadn't seen before stirring in their depths.

"All of you can go on your way," he said. His eyes darted to Silas and Violet. "But we're keeping them."

Mario's contemptuous bark of laughter sounded like a snarl. "Over my dead body."

"Skye, get the kids in the car," Doug said. To Carl, he said, "We're leaving. We won't be back."

Carl said, "All of you can go, but—"

"If you wanna do this the hard way, you'll win. No question," Doug said, cutting him off. "But I will kill you first. Guaranteed."

"Let them go, Carl," Elise said, her mouth a hard line. "It isn't worth it this time."

This time, Mario thought, reeling from the implication of her words. What the fuck were these people doing out here?

Carl looked at them another moment, coldly assessing, then tried to approximate a smile.

"Sure," he said. "You folks go on along. We're all still Americans, after all."

The pressure inside Mario's head sent a cold spike of pain through his temples. Had the white supremacist neo-Nazi in the 82nd Airborne tee shirt really said that?

"We're all still *Americans?*" he spat, parroting Carl, so enraged he could barely speak. He released his Sig with one hand and pointed at the faded insignia on Carl's shirt. "You're either with the guys who fought the Nazis, or a fucking Nazi. You don't get to be both!"

Doug nudged Mario with his elbow. "Shut up and get in the car before you get us all killed," he hissed.

Mario felt his cheek begin to tremble from the snarl twisting his lips. When he caught Albert's venomous glare, his fingers twitched. He'd gone from friendly to calling Silas and Violet... That fucker had called his kids—

His field of vision narrowed, everything around him fading away while Albert came into focus with crystal clarity. He adjusted his aim, the sight lined up perfectly. The look on Albert's face was everything—was beautiful—his fear a work of art. It showed in the sweat that popped out on his brow and the tremble of his body, that fucking swastika twitching on his shoulder like a venomous spider. The trigger felt smooth under Mario's finger, soft as silk and just as inviting. It would be so easy. Just a little squeeze, and Albert's head would explode in a rain of blood and bone and brain. It would splatter the 82nd Airborne insignia Carl dishonored. But if he gave Albert what he deserved, then Silas and Violet would fall into the hands of these people, and God only knew what horrors would be inflicted upon them.

He shook himself with an effort, blinked rapidly as his

peripheral vision returned. He took a step backward, the dull crunch of the gravel under his feet sounding far away. Another backward step, followed by another, until he reached the Tesla. He kept walking backward, past Skye standing behind the open front passenger door, her gun trained on their adversaries. Tessa was already behind the wheel. Doug backed up along the other side of the vehicle. When Doug reached the back door on the driver's side, he, Mario, and Skye all ducked inside.

Silas and Violet huddled on the floor, silently crying, both clutching Mister Bun Bun's carrier. The Tesla accelerated with a squeal of tires, the centrifugal force pushing Mario against the door as they raced away. The SUV lurched when Tessa took the turn too fast. Silas and Violet both cried out.

"Holy shit, holy shit, holy shit," Tessa said. "Holy shit."

"Are you okay?" Mario said to the children.

Skye pulled Violet to her in the front seat. Silas scurried into Mario's lap, attaching himself leech-tight around Mario's torso. He shook so hard his teeth chattered.

"Where the hell am I going?" Tessa asked.

"Umm...stay on this road till it ends," Mario said, trying to remember. "You turn left, and then when you have to turn again, right."

"They're following us," Doug said. "Give me that atlas, Skye."

"The atlas?" she said. "What do you—"

"Just give it to me," Doug snapped. "We need to look like we're taking 175 West, like I told them. I don't know how to go to make it look like we're taking 175 but still get to 29. If we get stuck going west and they follow us, we're screwed."

Skye retrieved the atlas after a moment's scuffling. She barely turned toward the back seat when Doug snatched it out of her fingers.

Mario looked out the back window.

Elise had said they had patrols. How far did they go? If they had radios, they could be driving straight into a trap.

"You said they were nice," Silas whimpered.

"Oh, Silas," Mario said.

How was he supposed to explain this to a little boy? How did you explain that there were people twisted enough, vile enough, to still care about this evil legacy from the old world?

He held Silas' dark, little face in his hands, never more acutely aware of what mattered and what didn't. "I'm so sorry. I was wrong. But I'll do anything to keep you safe—anything."

Silas began to sob. Mario crooned in his ear, trying to soothe him. But what he really wanted to do was go back and kill every last one of those Nazi fucks so they would never hurt Silas and Violet, never hurt anyone, again.

"Where am I going, Doug?" Tessa said, sounding desperate. "Highway 175 is just up ahead."

Mario turned to look back. The van and motorcycle still followed them.

"Take it west, and when we hit the straight part, floor it. There's a bend after, and we want to take 405, it'll be a left-hand turn. If we miss it..." Doug's voice trailed, then he said, "We can't miss it."

They streaked down the uneven road, past rusted cars and collapsed buildings, past the green blur of low fields with vivid glimpses of yellow and orange. The Tesla rocked and jerked. They zoomed through an intersection, the Tesla going airborne before thumping down hard. The countryside opened up to wide-open spaces of pastures and farms still clear from the lack of water that kept the vegetation in check, interspersed with stands of Live Oaks and other old trees not dependent on the rain for survival.

"They're still behind us," Doug said. "You need to punch it!"

The landscape blurred. They hadn't made any turns, so this must be the straightaway. Mario had heard straight and thought flat, which of course wasn't true. There were no hills, just undulations of the road.

"I don't see them in the mirror anymore!" Tessa said.

Doug said, "Keep going."

"Here's the bend!"

Tessa wasn't slowing down. Mario held Silas tight, shut his eyes, and prayed. Then the vehicle slowed, so suddenly it felt like they were attached to the end of a rope that had hit its limit. Mario and Silas jerked violently to the left, banging into Doug and the hard plastic of the pet carrier. We're going to flip, he thought, steeling himself as he clutched Silas tighter.

Miraculously, they kept moving forward.

"Ahead! That's the turn!" Doug shouted.

Mario opened his eyes again. Tessa was plastered into her seat, knuckles white on the steering wheel. She yanked it left in a squeal of tires, sending them all tumbling. Then the Tesla thumped and churned over an uneven, crumbling road. Mario twisted in his seat but couldn't see around the bend.

"I think we lost them," he said.

Tessa took the next turn, the next bend, and the one after at speed.

"I'm not taking any chances," Tessa said, and gunned the engine.

17

KENDALL LOOKED at Miranda in astonishment. "Why didn't you just tell me from the start?"

Miranda cast about for an explanation that wouldn't sound self-serving, that wouldn't be insulting. The girl from the Vermeer painting peeked over his shoulder.

"I couldn't... I didn't— Shit," she muttered. She looked at him, feeling stupid. How had she thought she could keep this hidden? "I thought it would make you feel differently about me."

Kendall shook his head, disappointment pursing his lips. The rapid owl blink of his eyes made them look like a stutter-stop animation.

"Why would I care that you have a child?"

She glanced at the bassinet behind her. Her breasts were uncomfortably heavy, needing to be relieved of their burden. "I was just about to nurse. Do you want to see him?"

Kendall nodded, and she motioned him over. As he leaned over the bassinet, she said, "His name is—"

"He looks like you," Kendall said softly.

Tadpole did have her coloring, with a tuft of auburn hair on the crown of his head and her pale complexion. But his dark eyes were all Mario.

From behind her, another voice said, "Too bad he's dead."

She whirled around and realized they were in the atrium at the Institute. Mario stood at the hallway to the BSL-3 lab.

"No, he's not," she said. "He's right—"

The words died in her throat. There was no bassinet. Kendall wasn't leaning over it. She turned back around to find Kendall standing next to Mario. He held a tiny, limp form, its dark eyes open but seeing nothing. The edges of the baby's lips and the tips of his fingers were blue. He looked emaciated—starved. She could see every rib, every bone, but her breasts were so heavy they hurt. Her nipples leaked milk, wetting her nightgown. Then she felt Mario's arm around her shoulders as all the air in the room vanished, making her light-headed. She stared at the dead baby, her baby, that lay motionless in Kendall's arms.

Kendall said, his voice pained, "You lied about everything."

"Don't worry, Miri," Mario said, his voice gentle and kind and full of concern. "We can have another baby, and you'll make sure that one dies, too."

She stiffened, unable to shrink away from the arm around her shoulders. She turned her head to look at Mario. His countenance was serene.

"What?" she whispered hoarsely.

He kissed her forehead, his lips soft and warm. His dark eyes overflowed with compassion. "We'll have another baby. If you don't want it to be a zombie, choose another way. You could beat it or smother it with a pillow. Whatever you want to do... I'm flexible. But first you have to sleep with Kendall."

"I don't... I didn't..."

"Of course you did," Mario said, not unkindly. "Of course you—"

AFTER SHE JERKED AWAKE, SHE LAY IN HER BED, CHEST rising and falling in time with her pounding heart. She couldn't seem to get any air. She sat up, looking around the room slowly, fearfully, as if Mario and Kendall and the dead baby might be hidden in the shadows.

She looked at the clock on the bedside table. It was the middle of the night, and tomorrow was a big day. She didn't need this. She didn't need her brain torturing her. The sharp ache of her heart for Tadpole... She already felt so empty and miserable when she let herself think about him. So she tried not to. And then, when she realized she'd managed it, she felt worse.

And Kendall... She already felt sleazy enough without dreaming about him. She hated the mire of self-interest that their discovery of him and the bunker, and the food shortage at LO, had sucked her into. All she wanted was a little peace, some respite. She was starting to think it would never happen.

I wish I could go outside to clear my head, she thought. The idea of danger—of doing something reckless—filled her with longing. She didn't want to get killed. She wanted the clarity of purpose that danger demanded. She wanted the serenity of life or death, not the teetering, knife's edge of ambivalence that she balanced on. She wanted the instinctive drive to live that took over and made the hard choices clear-cut. The thrill of cheating death that would follow was as intense as great sex, and when the second followed the first...

"I need a drink," she muttered.

She crept through the living area to the small kitchenette but found nothing. She wrapped the cashmere cardigan tighter around her body, the concrete floor cool on her feet as she walked down the hallway, then through the nearest lounge.

She opened the small wine cabinet near the silverware drawer in the kitchen, where some reds were kept, and chose a 1974 Chateau Margaux Cabernet Franc/Petit Verdot blend. It sounded expensive. She hoped it was as good. She had the cork halfway out when Alec said, "What're you doing up?"

She yelped and jumped, her heart in her throat. "Jesus!" she said. "Don't do that!"

"I'm sorry," he said, holding his hands up in front of him, as if to ward her off and soothe at the same time.

He was glistening, she realized, and short of breath. Sweaty, upon closer examination, with rosy cheeks and a damp spot on the front of his tee shirt. She'd never seen his legs before, well formed and muscular, but they were on display now between the bottom of the black shorts and athletic shoes.

"Did you have the gym door shut?" she asked.

"Aye," Alec said, wiping his forehead with the back of his hand. "I was on the treadmill, but I saw the movement through the glass."

"It has good soundproofing," she said. "I didn't even hear you."

Alec jutted his chin at the wine bottle she held. "Having a wee nightcap?"

She nodded. "Want to join me?"

"Why not?"

Butterflies careened inside her from head to toe when the smile appeared. His gaze was steady, almost as if he were asking her a question with it. She felt like he was undressing her with those hazel eyes, could see the goosebumps that were rippling over her skin. She looked down at the half-pulled cork still skewered by the corkscrew to hide the hot blush she felt creeping over her cheeks. She had a long tee shirt on beneath the cardigan, which was long-sleeved and fell almost to her knees, but she felt exposed, especially after the unsettling dream.

She finished opening the bottle, got two glasses, and joined him at the end of the curved dining tables.

Alec raised his glass after she filled it. "To tomorrow?"

"Tomorrow," she said, gently clinking her glass against his.

They both took a sip. Miranda closed her eyes, the fullness of the wine exploding across her tongue.

Alec gave an appreciative sigh. "How much do you reckon this cost?"

Miranda grinned. "I have no idea, and whatever I guess, it's probably too low."

"Kendall does have good grog," he said, grinning.

She sat on the table, the wine bottle beside her, and tucked the cardigan around her thighs. The table was just high enough that she could swing her feet. Alec pulled out a chair, turning it so he sat parallel to the edge of the table and could rest his elbow on it.

"Big day tomorrow," he said.

She nodded. They were opening the exterior blast door tomorrow for Kendall. Unlike the past week, while Kendall had worked his way out of the airlock and then up the switch-backing ramps with Alec or Rich, Miranda would be there, too. The LO crew had wanted everyone on hand, in order to make it as safe for Kendall as possible. Kendall hadn't liked the idea of leaving the bunker empty, even though he was the only one who knew the lock codes for the doors. He insisted that someone stay behind. When the choice came down to Miranda, who he didn't want to embarrass himself in front of, or Phineas, who he didn't like, dislike proved less palatable than embarrassment.

She said, "Do you think he can do it?"

Immediately, Alec nodded. "Absolutely. He's a trooper, our Kendall. I think he'll be fine. Having you there will help."

She arched an eyebrow. "I thought he was afraid of embarrassing himself in front of me."

"And that's why he won't lose his nerve."

She took another sip of her wine, feeling the anxiety her dream had triggered recede.

"Fresh air for the first time in a decade," Alec said softly. "Can you imagine?"

She shook her head. "I was thinking of this place as a prison, but when you put it like that, it feels more like a tomb." She shook the morose thought off. "Why are you working out in the middle of the night?"

"Can't sleep, same as you."

She finished her glass of wine and refilled it. Alec shook his head no when she held the bottle out to him.

"I wouldn't mind seeing Kendall's art collection," Alec said. "Maybe when he's flush with victory after going outside, he'll say yes."

"Have you asked him?"

Alec shook his head, the sharp edge of a smile squaring his jaw. "Maybe you could ask him for me."

"Don't," she said, imploring. "Just don't."

Alec sat up straighter. "I'm only teasing, Miranda."

She looked in the direction of Kendall's apartment. She hopped off the table, pulled out a chair, and sat down, leaning toward Alec.

"I know," she said, her voice low. "I just feel...shitty. He likes me, and I'm not exactly leading him on, but I'm not discouraging him, either."

Alec cocked his head to the side. "D'ya think he'd help us if we just asked?"

Miranda shrugged. "No," she said, thinking of the seeds.

"Not soon enough to make a difference back home, anyway. It's like Rich said, if we ask and he says no..."

"Things get awkward fast," Alec finished for her.

"We'd help him even if he had nothing. Especially if he had nothing. It'd be the right thing to do, and it's how they do things at LO, which is why I like it so much. But knowing that doesn't change the rest." She looked at the floor, then back at Alec. "It taints everything. I see the way he looks at me, how hopeful his eyes are behind that owl blink, and..."

At her characterization, Alec smiled. Despite how shitty she felt—from the dream, from not checking Kendall's interest—the butterflies started up again.

"We should have a party."

She'd just told him how crappy she felt for leading Kendall on, and he was suggesting they throw a party. "A party?"

"To celebrate, after Kendall goes outside." His voice softened, and his eyes filled with a gentleness she hadn't seen before. "And to cheer you up."

The corners of her eyes prickled, the rush of emotion surprising her. Alec barely knew her, but could see she needed...something. Rocco knew it, River and Rich and Phineas, too, but she always deflected their questions, their concern, their attempts to help. How was this man she hardly knew managing to wriggle past the barriers her friends couldn't? And why did it have her on the verge of tears?

"We'll make party hats," she said, plastering a smile on her face, trying to get her emotions under control. "And a banner."

Alec's grin widened. "We'll break out the good Macallan for a proper toast. But right now, we both need to get some sleep."

He stood and held out a hand. She took it, letting him give her a hand up that she didn't need.

"You're a good scout, Miranda," he said. "Your intentions are good. It's the situation that twists them about."

"You know what they say about good intentions."

Alec laughed softly. "I do, lass. I do. My own road to Hell is smoothly paved."

Rich said, his voice gently encouraging, "You ready, Kendall?"

They stood near the top of the ramp, just beyond clearance of the outer blast door's inward swing. Kendall stared at the keypad, the digital readout above it a bright line of zeroes. He blinked almost nonstop, and Miranda could see sweat on his upper lip. He looked again at the security monitor, which again showed nothing outside in the immediate area, just forest.

Kendall nodded, but his hand—hovering in front of the keypad—didn't move. Rich looked at Miranda, his eyes bugging out at her under raised eyebrows that were in danger of reaching his hairline. Beside him, Alec made a circular 'hurry up' motion with his hand. She set her hand on Kendall's shoulder. He startled and gulped, then looked at her as if he wanted to crawl under a rock and die of embarrassment.

"This is the worst part, before you do it," she said. "Fuck zombies."

Dismay filled Rich's face. Whatever he'd been expecting her to say, it hadn't been that. But she had a feeling that tender encouragement from her wouldn't be helpful. She thought it might even fuel Kendall's fear that she'd think he was a coward. Kendall gulped, his Adam's apple bobbing. Then she saw it— determination filled his eyes and set his jaw. He looked back to the keypad and punched in the numbers. Rich smiled, looking impressed.

The pneumatic hiss of the door lock signaled disengagement. Alec held out sunglasses to Kendall.

"Don't forget these."

Kendall took the sunglasses with shaking hands, only getting them over his ears on his second attempt. A crack of light appeared as the door swung toward them.

"You've got this," Miranda whispered to him.

She didn't think Kendall heard her. Alec stepped forward, taking point as they had agreed. When the door swung open enough that a person could get through, he hit the red button on the wall, arresting the door's movement. He paused, then stepped out. Fifteen seconds later, he called, "C'mon out."

Miranda walked to the open door, watery afternoon sunshine illuminating the concrete at her feet. She turned back to Kendall, and to Rich, who stood behind him.

"Coming?" she asked.

She couldn't see the terror in Kendall's eyes through the dark lenses of the sunglasses, but she could feel it rolling off him in waves, despite the heavy boots, and the kevlar pants, jacket, and gloves he wore. And then, after a halting first step, he followed her.

"To Kendall!" Rich crowed, glass upraised.

Whoops and shouts—from her friends and her own—filled Miranda's ears. She laughed as their glasses clinked together, the enthusiasm with which they were wielded bordering on dangerous.

"Watch it," Alec cried, some of his Scotch slopping out of his glass.

Miranda could only give herself over to the laughter that bubbled up and out of her. Beside her, Kendall glowed like a firefly under their praise. He took another sip of his Scotch, then screwed up his face.

"Somebody get this man a drink he likes, for goodness' sake," Rich said. His party hat—hastily constructed of stiff paper—sat askew on his head.

"Already on it," Phineas said, jumping to his feet. He scurried out of sight, then reappeared a moment later with a bottle of white wine and some glasses. He set it on the coffee table in the center of the couches and chairs in the lounge they occupied and fished around for a corkscrew. A moment later he handed Kendall an overly generous glassful, murmuring, "I don't know how they drink that crap."

"It's supposed to be very good," Kendall said, his dislike of Phineas forgotten in the merriment. "Must be an acquired taste."

"I'll just acquire yours, then," Alec said. He reached over Miranda, bumping her into Kendall.

Kendall's party hat fell off when he turned his head to follow the path of his stolen glass of Scotch. It tumbled over the back of the couch, and set off another round of uproarious, drunken laughter. Miranda turned in her seat, hung over the back of the couch, and fished it from the floor. She set the hat on Kendall's head, fiddling with the string so it would stay behind his ear and hold it in place.

"I think it's a lost cause," he said.

Miranda tried a moment more, then said, "I think you're right."

Kendall shrugged, then grinned and knocked the hat off his head. Miranda watched it tumble over the back of the couch again. She got up and went over to the stereo to choose a new song. The music was too loud, causing them all to speak a bit too loudly—or maybe it was the alcohol. Dirty dishes and empty bottles littered the table. She switched the music to a better song and turned it down a little. The volume of her friends didn't lessen—drunken high spirits for the win.

Kendall and Alec sat on either end of the couch, laughing at the story Rich was telling. Kendall looked exhausted, but happy. He'd done it—he'd gone outside. He'd stood outside the bunker door for half an hour. More astonishingly, he'd then walked a short distance into the forest with Miranda and Rich while Alec minded the open blast door. Kendall had been terrified out of his mind, but he'd done it. Thankfully, they'd encountered no zombies. They'd gone back inside to celebrate, surprising Kendall with party hats and a banner and snacks.

Rich stood near the chair he'd abandoned, waving his arms as he regaled them with a story. He stumbled, losing his balance. She hurried over and caught him.

"Careful," she said.

He grinned, then said ruefully, "I think I better go to bed."

"Aw, c'mon, man," Phineas whined. "This party is just getting started."

"No, no, I'm done," Rich said, resolute. He turned to Kendall. "My hat is..." He reached up, pulled it from his head, then said, "Off to you."

Kendall smiled unreservedly, nothing shy or uncertain about it. Happiness burbled inside her, to see him this way, to see his confidence boosted.

"I'll walk you," Alec said, getting to his feet.

Rich tried to wave Alec away, but Alec insisted. Miranda sat back down on the couch next to Kendall. Phineas left for the kitchen to get more snacks.

"So...was this a good day?" she asked Kendall.

His smile grew broader. "Yes." He paused, then said, "I feel free."

Miranda took his hand in hers and gave it a squeeze. "I'm so proud of you," she said, meaning it.

She went to pull her hand from his, but Kendall held on. His brown eyes had a warm, hopeful look that she didn't like at all. Fuck, she thought. She let it go a few more seconds. When she pulled away this time, he gave her hand a final squeeze and let go.

"Yo, Kendall!" Phineas called. "You want some pizza or... What is this?"

"You better go rescue him. If he's too drunk to figure out the food, I don't trust him to put it in the oven."

Kendall laughed. The confidence going outside had given him—at least now, while he was loaded—was amazing.

"You were right," he said, standing. "Phineas isn't that bad."

He lurched to the kitchen. Miranda reached for her Scotch, the spicy, earthy scent filling her nose as the amber liquid lit up her taste buds. That had been uncomfortable, but thank God for Phineas. He'd saved her from things getting really awkward. She drank the rest of her Scotch, the music filling her ears as she lay her head against the back of the couch and closed her eyes.

WHEN SHE WOKE, SHE WAS STILL IN THE LOUNGE, AND still a bit buzzed. A blanket had been draped over her. The lights were dimmed, except for the thin track of safety lights that ran along the floor. She stretched as she sat up, groaning when her spine crackled. She squinted at her watch—past midnight. She went to the nearest bathroom, where she relieved her poor bladder and brushed her teeth. Thank God for the mystery dentist who hadn't made it here. The toothbrushes, toothpaste, and floss in every bathroom was coming in mighty handy just now. The Scotch had been wonderful, but after a couple hours asleep, her mouth wasn't.

She walked under the dark chandelier and around the dining tables in the center of the dome, on her way to the kitchen to get a glass of water before she headed to bed. Flickering light through frosted glass of one of the activity rooms caught her eye; someone was watching a movie. She got her glass of water, gulped it down and refilled it, then went to the theater. The door was open to the central dining area, and the closing credits of a film were scrolling up the screen.

"How was it?" she asked. She couldn't see who was watching since the room was dark.

Alec's low voice said, "Pretty terrible."

She found the switch inside the door. Bright light filled the room before she hastily turned it down to the lowest setting.

"Trying to blind me?" Alec said.

He looked over the back of his seat and squinted at her like a mole surprised by bright sunlight. There were six rows of an assortment of single and love seat-width reclining theater seats. In all, the room could comfortably fit forty people, more at a squeeze.

"Sorry," she said.

Alec grinned, and she heard the low whirr of his seat being brought upright. He held aloft another bottle of the fancy Scotch that was almost full.

"You broke out another?"

The sly grin appeared. "D'ya want one? There are glasses on the bar there."

She grabbed a glass from the small bar against the shared wall with the library next door. When she turned back and saw Alec still looking at her, she felt a crackle of attraction arc between them. A frisson of electricity flared inside her, and the butterflies in her stomach began to run riot. She sat beside him on the wide love seat. He turned toward her as he boosted himself up onto the armrest separating this love seat from the next. He poured her a drink, a generous two fingers.

"To Kendall," he said, the intent stare of his heathered hazel eyes pinning her in place.

"To Kendall," she echoed.

Instead of the smooth, lightly burnt caramel taste she'd come to expect, the Scotch tasted bitter. She coughed, then gagged, remembering that she'd just brushed her teeth. She took another bigger gulp and swished the Scotch in her mouth, trying to get it into every nook and cranny.

"What the hell are you doing, lass?" Alec said, his brow crinkled with surprise.

She swallowed, grimacing, then said, "I just brushed my teeth."

He stared at her a moment, his mouth falling open. "I take what I said before back. You," he said, poking her just under her collarbone, his accent making you sound like a stretched out yeeeew. "Are a right savage, treating fine Scotch like mouthwash. If I'd known, I'd never have offered."

She shrugged, arching an eyebrow at him. "The damage is already done." She smiled over the rim of her glass as she took another sip. This time, it tasted better.

"The party was a good idea."

Alec nodded. "Having him open the door was the hardest part."

"Isn't it always?"

She caught the sharp edge of his grin. "I reckon so." He paused, then said, "You seem cheered up."

She considered this a moment. "I am."

His eyes lingered on her face as they drank. The air around them fizzed with an electric hum, ionized like the air before a thunderstorm. She felt goosebumps ripple to attention on her arms, attraction and hunger buzzing beneath her skin as she finished her drink.

"Another?" he said.

She should go, before something happened that she might regret. Deciding who to screw while drinking rarely stood up to the harsh light of day. She would only regret it. Or, a small voice whispered, maybe she wouldn't.

"I should go to bed," she said.

Life felt complicated enough; she didn't need more, but she didn't want to go. Didn't want to lie in bed, thinking about Kendall holding on to her hand and how she'd let him. Didn't want to wonder what she was passing up with Alec. Didn't want to slide into nightmares of zombie babies and the insomnia that would follow. She wanted to stay. She wanted to find out if she was imagining the hum in the air, the attraction that seemed to swirl thickly around them.

Alec slid off the love seat's arm and touched his hand lightly on her neck. His thumb stroked down, his fingers tracing forward to meet it. Her breath caught in her throat, her skin tingling where his fingers skated over the pulse pounding in her neck. His hazel eyes were hooded, burning bright with a desire that he didn't bother to hide.

"I wish you wouldn't."

She took a breath, fast and shallow. He leaned in, lips meeting hers, and she fell into the kiss. She twisted her hands in his shirt, pulling him to her, the hum and hunger detonating like a bomb.

Alec's hands slipped into her hair, the deepening kiss requiring no adjustment, no effort, only her desire and tongue and lips. She ran her hands down his body, the muscles of his chest hard underneath the softness of his skin. He broke the kiss, the sharp, inward hiss of his breath as her hands slipped beneath the thin cotton of his shirt and skittered over his muscled abdomen. She pulled the shirt over his head, then kissed and nipped his chest, the tremble in his body making her hotter. She wanted to tease and touch and taste all of him at once.

A glass hit the floor, the dull thud sounding like a gunshot in the quiet. They both jumped, and Miranda was on her feet before she knew it, looking around to see what the hell was going on. But it was only a glass, not a threat, and the absurdity of being so startled hit her hard. For a second, they looked at one another, then she covered her mouth, trying not to laugh. Alec doubled over, elbows on his knees, snorts of suppressed laughter squeaking into the room.

He stood, his eyes flashing, still shaking with mirth, and pulled her to him. His lips found hers, laughter still welling up between them. He pushed her shirt up, the friction of the tee shirt against her hardened nipples causing her to shiver. He pulled the shirt free of her head, and for a moment, he simply looked at her, devouring her body with his eyes. Then he dipped his head, his lips caressing the swell of her breasts before his tongue flicked over her nipples. She moaned low in her throat, her body quaking, the feel of his lips and tongue and hands drenching her touch-starved body like a storm after a long, dusty drought.

She undid his belt, the crack of the leather snapping out of the buckle fairly making her swoon. He kicked his pants free. She closed her hand around his cock, his groan in her ear setting every nerve in her body alight. She released him to push her stretchy yoga pants down to puddle around her ankles. His hand reached for the love seat behind him, fumbling for a moment before he found the recline button. She pressed against him, her bare skin against his, the heat of his erection pulsing between them. Then the rising footrest nudged their ankles, and they tumbled down.

Miranda grinned up at him, running her hands and lips and tongue over his body, his musky scent filling her nose. She climbed astride him, pushing him back, wanting to feel him inside her now—no more foreplay, no more delays. She took him in her hand and guided him inside, impaling her soft wetness on him. He groaned, squeezing the orbs of her breasts in his hands. He pulled her down to claim her mouth as they moved together, the upward scoop of his hips meeting the downward grind of hers.

She reared up, arching her back, rocking against him and curling her neck as he levered up to kiss it. She caught a flash of movement through the open door. Her eyes snapped over the row of upright seats behind them, raking over the darkened dining area, but it was only the flicker of the nighttime track lighting in the far lounge.

It could have been Kendall, a distant part of her brain thought as her body moved with Alec's, the heat and urgent need enveloping them getting thicker, stronger, swirling between and around them like soft, sticky taffy. If Kendall saw them fucking, if he saw her—white-hot from Alec's touch, hunger consuming her, pleasure that magnified every passing second rippling through her body—it would be a disaster.

She lowered her eyes to Alec's face, to his rakish smile and eyes that flashed with his desire, and couldn't stop. She needed this. She wanted this. She wanted Alec. She wanted to sate this hunger, even though she already knew that wasn't what would happen. It would only sharpen, gnawing in her belly until she satisfied it again. She wanted that, too. Wanted to be consumed by desire for someone else—someone who didn't know her past, who wasn't part of the loss and anger that still plagued her. She wanted to fuck Alec and know it would be without demands or baggage or expectations.

She didn't want Kendall—she never would. Even if she was

in a position to do the right thing, even if she discouraged him, she couldn't control his romantic desires any more than she could control the zombies and blight that had wiped out their food. The only thing she could control was herself, and her actions. If wanting Alec was more than Kendall could deal with, she would deal with that reckoning when it came. The consequences of being discovered now were lost in a haze of lust that she couldn't, and didn't want, to control.

Alec's hands gripped her waist as he moved beneath her, his fingers digging into the thin layer of flesh that cushioned her hip bones. They moved up to her breasts. His hands kneaded them gently, thumbs circling her pebbled nipples and triggering a shiver that started at the base of her skull. It zipped down her spine, each vertebra rippling in its wake until her hips rocked side to side. The wave-like motion rippled back up through her body, twisting through her shoulders and ending in a languid forward roll of her head.

His laugh was low and smooth, like the Scotch they'd been drinking. "You're so hot and bothered you're smoking."

He drew her closer, like a moth to a flame. Heat filled her body where he touched her and where he didn't. She could feel it pulsing out from her center, flushing her face and chest, casting a dewy sheen on her skin. He pushed up on an elbow, reaching for her. Her hand clasped his, their fingers interlacing. She pulled them into her mouth. But instead of just letting her suck, he surprised her by exploring her mouth. She relaxed her jaw, the erotic thrill of his fingers moving over her tongue before sliding beneath it surprising her. His thumb glided along her teeth, catching and dragging her lower lip inside out, before he trailed it over her chin and down her neck.

He took her hand again, guiding it down between them to where their bodies were joined. Gently, he manipulated her fingers over her clit, then said, "Let me watch you."

She was yanked out of the moment, away from the heat and the feel of Alec's body against hers, the hardness of his cock, and the cascade of pleasure where he moved inside and against her. No one had ever done anything like that except Mario. And suddenly, he was here, between them while they fucked on the reclined love seat. She closed her eyes to banish him as she moved her fingers over her swollen clit, groaning as the lush heat burned higher and hotter. But Mario was here, too, wrapping her in a fog of sweet intimacy as they melted into one another on the edge of the bed at the Institute, her arm and wrist cradled around the gentle swell of their baby between them while she stroked herself until she came, falling into the deep of his dark, knowing eyes.

No, she thought, snapping her eyes open. He wasn't here. She wouldn't let him pull her away from what she was doing, and from the man beneath her she was doing it with. She wanted to be here. She wanted to look into Alec's eyes, into the same heathered hazel color of Scottish moors. She wanted the low burr of the Highlands to caress her ears, to feel the slick leather of the sofa beneath her knees and shins. She pulled herself up straighter, spread her knees wider, so that Alec could better see her slippery fingers. So he could see how she fed the roaring fire he had kindled. She looked into those hazel depths, bright with hunger and lust and anticipation, but without expectation, completely in the here and now.

"There's my bonny lass," he said, satisfaction filling his voice, curling around her like a caress.

His eyes lowered to watch her fingers. A laugh chuffed in his throat when she couldn't hold back the whimpers escaping her lips while she touched herself, while she masturbated for him as he moved inside her. Mario hadn't watched, not like this. He hadn't watched how she carried out the work of pleasuring herself, but Alec did.

"You're beautiful," he whispered.

For the first time in what felt like forever, she felt in control. She felt like she could stop herself from careening off the cliff's edge that her life had become. She had balanced on it for such a long time. But now, with their bodies connected while he moved inside her, with her, exploring the swells and hollows of her body with his, while she touched herself to please them both, she could feel herself stepping back. She could feel herself choosing to leave it behind, to find safer ground, to live in this moment, rather than miring herself in the past.

She tangled the fingers of her other hand in the dark line of hair that began beneath his belly button, his flexing abs grounding her, tethering her to his body, to here and now and this. She kept her hazed eyes open, locking them with his when he wasn't watching her, wanting to understand the fascination that filled his face when he watched her do as he'd bid, her arousal growing and blooming under his watchful study of her. She locked her eyes with his, hoping to catch a glimpse of what he saw when he smiled at her with that sly, roguish grin that made her insides fizz.

When she felt herself tipping and falling, hurtling into the orgasm consuming her shuddering body, her eyes never strayed from Alec's. When he followed soon after, his dry fingers interlaced with her damp ones, the lilt of the Highlands stronger than before as he laughed softly, telling her again what a bonny lass she was, Mario wasn't even an echo of a memory. He'd been gone for a long, long time.

18

"ALEC KNOWS I want to talk about when to head home, or did I imagine that conversation?"

Rich's voice brimmed with annoyance. They were going outside with Kendall in half an hour.

"Maybe he went to get some breakfast," Phineas said. "I'll go see."

"No," said Rich. "Then we'll be looking for both of you."

Miranda didn't say anything, just sipped her tea and put her feet up on the coffee table. Alec was either already on his way here, or still in the nearby residence dome where they'd slept the last four nights. If she had to, she'd go get him, but she preferred to wait and see. They'd been alternating who returned to the shared dome first, and she'd done her part by waking him when she got up to get ready for their outing today. She smiled faintly, thinking about how Alec had done his part in delaying her departure, which put him behind schedule, too. Being this late was sloppy, but damn...it had been worth it.

Maybe he'd fallen back asleep, because thinking of it as where they'd slept was probably overstating things. As she'd suspected, Alec *rocked* in the sack. Actual sleeping the past few nights had come in a very distant second. But when she had slept, it was better than in months, since before—

She pushed the thought away, not wanting an intrusion on her endorphin-drenched state, but a glimmer of anger managed to wisp through her brain anyway. She couldn't even fuck how angry she was with Mario into submission. Maybe she should talk to River, or maybe even Rocco. When he wasn't busting her balls, Rocco was a surprisingly good listener. He had a way of looking at things from different perspectives that she'd never have considered on her own. Most of the time they were even helpful.

Delilah woofed, and a moment later the door opened. The man of the hour stepped through, a cup of coffee in his hand, looking decidedly rumpled.

"Sorry I'm late, Rich," he said, flashing an apologetic smile. "I fell asleep in the library."

Christ, that's a terrible lie, she thought.

"I didn't see you in the library this morning," Phineas said.

Alec shrugged. "I can't account for your eyesight, lad."

At least he knew enough not dig himself into a deeper hole, but they had to come up with a better way of doing this.

"We're all here now," Rich said, waving Alec and Phineas over to the sitting area.

Rich's ability to let go and move on was one of the many things Miranda liked about him. Over the last couple months, she often wished she could do the same—just let it all go. Rich was easygoing until he wasn't, and she'd never seen him put his foot down when it wasn't warranted. He wasn't petty or a control freak, either. She couldn't always say the same for herself on that second count...and sometimes the first. He'd told her once, 'After the dust settled when all this started, I decided

I'd rather be happy than right if I lived long enough. Unless it involved some fool trying to get me killed.'

"It's Halloween in eleven days, and I told my kids I'd be back to go trick-or-treating with them. So I'm thinking we should fix to head back in a week. It'll be almost a month we've been here by then." Rich's shoulders twitched, like he was suppressing a shiver. "I don't know about you all, but this place makes me claustrophobic."

"Me too," Phineas said.

"We need to tell him right away. As soon as we get back from today's outing," she said. "Give him time to mentally prepare and think about coming with us."

"You think?" Phineas asked her. "He's done okay so far, but being outside near the bunker isn't the same as really being out there."

Miranda shrugged as she sipped her tea, then said, "We've all had to deal with the fear, especially when all this started. He's got the advantage of having us."

"I think Miranda's right," Rich said. "You're staying behind today, right, Phineas?"

"Yeah," he said, still grinning. "I'll see you guys at the airlock. I want to grab a snack before you go out."

"Mercy, that kid can eat," Rich said as Phineas disappeared from their dome. "And there's not an ounce of fat on him. I wish I still had a metabolism like that."

"I'll be kitted up in five minutes," Alec said, rising.

Rich said, "Yeah... About that."

Oh no, Miranda thought, seeing the uncomfortable but resolved look on Rich's face that made her stomach sink. She and Alec traded a glance.

Rich continued, the discomfort morphing to the beginnings of a shit-eating grin. "I don't care what you two are doing, but do it here, okay? You've got connecting rooms, for Christ's sake.

What if Kendall were to see you skulking around like teenagers sneaking home at night?"

Her face was on fire, she was blushing so hard. Alec looked genuinely surprised that they'd been caught out. The teenager analogy was apt; this felt exactly the same as when she'd been busted by her parents. Rich hardly ever swore and had just dropped a 'for Christ's sake.' It didn't matter that she was almost thirty-one; the floor couldn't open up and swallow Miranda fast enough.

"Rich, I... We were trying to be—"

Rich interrupted her, saving her from making an even bigger fool of herself. "Everyone's shy when things are new. I get it," he said. A wicked, teasing gleam filled his eyes. "I trust you two can keep it down enough that you don't wake the rest of us?"

"She can be pretty loud," Alec muttered.

Miranda rounded on him, incredulous, then snapped, "Go get dressed!"

"Sorry, lass," he said quickly. "I didn't..."

He wilted under her withering stare. Looking chastened, he beat a hasty retreat to his room.

Miranda looked at the floor a second, sucking on her teeth. Rich was right, *of course* he was right. Using another place had seemed like a good idea, until now. Kendall's hours were erratic, and he never entered their dome without knocking. Spending the night together anywhere else was just foolish, even though they'd been careful.

"Well," she finally said. "This is pretty mortifying."

Rich chuckled and motioned for her to walk with him to the door. "Like I said, Miranda... I don't care. Y'all are adults. Just don't be stupid about it, seeing as how Kendall's nursing a crush."

She stopped, then said, "I'm not doing it anymore, Rich."

She hadn't been aware of deciding anything, but as she spoke, she realized she had. When Rich's eyebrows knitted together in a surprise, she said, "Not Alec—Kendall. I'm not going to ignore or encourage his crush. It's wrong, and it makes me feel like a complete dirtbag. He either helps us because we ask him, or we take what we need. If we end up stealing his shit, I'd like to do it in the least sleazy way possible."

"I don't think it's possible to just take his extra food without being sleazy, but I understand. However you want to do it is fine, Miranda. If he won't help us and you have one less crappy feeling about all this, that's a win. Sort of."

Across the dome, the door to Alec's room opened.

"I'll visit his apartment again after dinner, like we discussed," she said. "If one of you guys can pull him away and I can wait for him in his place, I could search for a door to another storeroom."

"We'll try that in the next day or two," Rich agreed. He opened the door and stepped into the main corridor.

Miranda held the door, waiting for Alec to reach her. "Loud?"

Alec looked abashed. "I didn't mean to say that out loud, Miranda. I really am sorry." He stopped, then said, "How long will I be on the shit list?"

She motioned him through the door. "I don't know," she said mildly. "It probably depends on how loud you can make me."

THIS TIME, BEFORE THEY LEFT, KENDALL PROGRAMMED temporary security codes for the bunker and shared them. He trusted them enough to make a temporary change... This was a huge step in the right direction. The codes were only good for two hours, but baby steps. Kendall being Kendall, the blast doors, and the inner and outer hatches of the airlock, each had a unique code. They were only going out for ninety minutes at the most, so they had plenty of time to get back. Miranda had pulled out a pen and written the codes on the inside of her forearm. Phineas could open any of the doors from inside. They had prevailed upon Kendall to enable that functionality so that whoever had stayed behind wouldn't be trapped if, God forbid, they failed to return.

As they walked they'd pointed out what was special about the topography, and talked through scenario after scenario with Kendall, choosing where the zombie was, how many, what weapons he had, and what he could or should do. Ever a dutiful student, Kendall always gave the first three default answers in order—don't panic, listen to see if you can hear more of them, avoid if you can—before carefully but quickly weighing his options. He was doing pretty well theoretically and had only once made what would be a one hundred percent fatal error, in Miranda's opinion. How he'd do in real life was anyone's guess.

Miranda wiped her knife on the leafy litter of the forest floor next to the zombie she'd just killed, then slipped it into its sheath. She'd been able to dispatch it with minimal moaning, which was the only reason they even bothered. It had been a bit of a pain in the ass to kill. Twice it had actually bumped into her before shying away. Coupled with the uneven ground, it threw off her timing. Then it had lunged again.

"Yo-yo zombie," she said under her breath. "Now I've seen everything."

Kendall had been pretty freaked out when they first saw the zombie, but he kept it together with both Rich and Alec reassuring him. Even without the zombie's appearance, they were almost at time anyway. She was glad that they'd decided to kill rather than leave it, because she'd seen a few more farther up the mountainside. Those zombies would never catch up, but if they started moaning...

When she was twenty yards from the others, she saw movement to her right—to the north of Rich, Alec, and Kendall. She stopped, shading her eyes.

"Shit," she said softly.

A small clutch of zombies, about ten, were fifteen yards from the guys and getting closer. She scanned the area quickly, frowning. The wind ruffled the strands of hair that had pulled free of her nubbin of ponytail. That's why they hadn't heard them; the southerly wind carried any noise the clutch was making away from them. With zombies above and now these, there might be a lot more. They'd been planning to turn back, but now it was urgent, driven by need rather than time.

Even so, she was only concerned, not alarmed. There was plenty of time to give them the slip. Rather than whistle, she waved her arms over her head. When she had their attention, she whirled her hand in a circle—turn around—then pointed. They turned around. Now ten yards from the zombies, she saw the posture of each become more alert, like an electric current had been applied to their bodies.

Then Kendall bolted.

"Kendall," Rich cried, while Alec shouted, "Stop!"

"Goddammit," she hissed, taking off after him.

Kendall hadn't just panicked and taken off—he was going the wrong way, angling down the slope of Mount Hood northwest. Away from them, and the bunker.

"Kendall! Stop!" Rich shouted.

Miranda's feet pounded the ground, sticks hidden by leaves and moss breaking and rolling under her feet. She raised her arm to shield her face from whips of underbrush that lashed her. Blood rushed in her ears, her heavy breath pounding in and out in a steady rhythm.

Kendall had caught them unprepared, so his head start was sizable. But Miranda could see Rich was gaining on him.

Alec's shout boomed like a thunderclap. "Stop! Now!"

Kendall screamed.

"No," Miranda gasped, still pelting to her friends, for she'd seen what Alec had.

Zombies were staggering up the mountain toward Kendall. They were so brown and gray that they blended in perfectly, only their movement giving them away. He'd either been too panicked, or had seen them too late, but he'd almost run right into them. He jerked to a halt too quickly, lost his balance, and fell on his ass. He scrabbled backward like a crab. Rich poured on the speed, leaping over downed logs and rocks. He just had to reach Kendall, and then he'd be safe.

Alec had stopped, which was the only thing he could do. Unlike she and Rich, he didn't repel zombies. Rich dove, tackling Kendall as he tried to get up. There were zombies everywhere and they needed to leave, but now Rich's repellant effect would keep them both safe. Miranda reached Alec and stopped, so she could protect him. They were close enough now that she could hear Kendall's panicked jabbering. Hisses and moans that the breeze wasn't strong enough to blow away filled the air. Rich hauled Kendall to his feet by his jacket collar. Kendall screamed as the nearest zombie closed in, just three feet away. Rich turned Kendall around, giving him a sharp shove between his shoulder blades, then smacked at the closest zombie to move it out of the way.

The zombie didn't stop.

The gasp of horror sounded distant, but she felt the inhalation fill her lungs. Miranda watched for a moment, disbelief rooting her feet. The zombie grabbed Rich's hand and pulled instead of moving away from him. Rich reared back, trying to yank away, his startled yelp carried away by the breeze.

"Get Kendall," she shouted to Alec, already running to Rich. She crashed through brambles, branches and uneven footing, darting around trees and tripping over rocks. Rich had pulled his knife as he teetered, his footing unsteady. Rotting corpses floundered toward him. The sharp steel flashed, disappearing into the zombie's eye. It collapsed. Rich tripped back a few steps, over a log, landing awkwardly on his arm and shoulder.

Miranda reached him and grabbed his collar, caught a flash of blue when he snapped his head back to the new threat.

"It's me," she said.

The sharp, harsh scent of his adrenaline-drenched sweat filled her sinuses. The lead zombie was so close she could see into the triangular hole of exposed bone, no longer hidden by a nose. It was the only part of its face not hidden under filthy, matted hair.

Rich grunted, scrabbling his feet against the ground. She felt the lift from his legs pushing up as she dragged him to his feet. A blow from behind shoved her into Rich. She fell to the ground, and Rich slipped from her hands. Whatever had hit her pushed off her back with two hands. Had Alec come over? The rank stench of rot filled her nose. She saw the zombie when it stepped over her. It wasn't attacking, like the ones after Rich, but it wasn't staying away from her, either.

She lurched to her feet, Rich only steps away. She just had to reach him, throw herself over him; she could still save him. She charged the zombie and caught it by the shoulder when Rich screamed. She pushed the zombie aside. His anguished cry rolled up the mountainside. Liquid and terrible, a gush of red caught her eye. Another grunt from behind her—a zombie. A surge of energy fueled by panic made her nerve endings convulse. The last zombie had crawled over her, but what if this one didn't?

A hand clamped on her shoulder. An arm snaked around her waist. Miranda thrashed, punching over her shoulder at the zombie that clutched her. It yanked her back so hard that she lost her balance. Her heels scraped in the dirt as she screamed. Her knife was gone, jarred from her hand. More zombies closed in, would reach her any moment. I'm going to die, she thought wildly, knowing it was true, yet unable to comprehend that this was really happening.

"It's me! Quit fighting," Alec said, his breath hot against her ear.

"What?"

"Now, lass!"

He paused, just long enough to help her right herself. Rich was on the ground, still screaming, still bleeding, still trying to fight. Zombies swarmed him like flies, biting and clawing, ripping his protective clothes from his body. The reanimated corpses shoved between and squirmed over those in their way.

"No!"

Then a sylph-like form, a small woman or child once, slipped past two others wresting to get closer and bit into Rich's throat. His screams morphed into strangled gurgles. Blood gushed from his neck, streaking his skin. Pink foam bubbled at his mouth.

"Miranda," Alec yelled at her, dragging her along. "There's nay ya can do for him!"

He turned her around and shoved her in front of him, away from Rich. She felt disengaged from her body. Her feet and legs did the work of their own accord—jumping over rocks, steering her around trees, trying to choose the surest footing they could.

"Are ya right?"

Alec's voice, low and urgent but controlled, snagged her

attention, sharp as a metal hook. She concentrated on it, felt her senses sharpen.

She looked over to him, saw the danger they were in reflected in his hazel eyes. "Yeah," she said. "They aren't staying away."

"Kendall's just there," he said, pointing. "They're all over the fucking place."

A slumped form leaned against a tree. They skidded to a halt next to Kendall's lanky, limp frame. His head lolled back and forth, and his brown eyes were unfocused.

Miranda said, "What happened?"

"I punched him." Alec caught Kendall under one arm, then looked to Miranda. "Help me."

She looked at Alec, trying to pull Kendall to his feet. Kendall had panicked, not listened. If he'd only listened they'd be on their way to the bunker—all of them. Instead, Rich lay dead, the flash of his blue eyes branded on Miranda's brain.

Her mouth curled in a sneer. "Leave him."

The grunts of the zombies feasting on Rich were so loud. She shook her head, but they filled her ears. From every direction, the moans and grunts and hisses filled the air. Zombies tripped and stumbled and tottered closer, and Miranda felt the thin veneer of her lost protection sloughing from her body. When they reached her, they wouldn't shy away. They'd yo-yo like the one she'd killed only minutes ago, or brush past her. Then again, maybe they wouldn't. Her repellant ability was in its death throes. It probably had been for a while. She just hadn't known it.

Alec's eyes drilled into her, demanding that she understand. "What if we don't make it back in time to use our codes? What if Phineas can't open the doors? D'ya remember Kendall saying Phineas would still be able to after two hours, because I don't. We need him."

She wanted to leave him, to flee in a way she hadn't in months, knowing she might be unable to protect the people with her, but Alec was right. Who knew what happened at the end of two hours that Kendall hadn't bothered to tell them? She'd been shocked that he'd made it possible for them to get back inside on their own. He was so fearful of the outside world, terrified that he might lose the abundance he had. He'd spent his life amassing incomprehensible wealth, using it to insulate and protect himself—even from a threat that no one could have predicted—but all it had done was fill his mind with scarcity and want.

That leaving him to die would be a mortal sin, almost murder, was a concept too abstract to make sense, but Alec's words got through to her. They might need Kendall to get inside the bunker.

Miranda took him by the other arm, and together with Alec, hauled the babbling Kendall to his feet. She pulled his arm over her shoulders, taking some of his weight.

"We've got to go, Kendall," Alec said, tugging him along. "There's a good lad. That's it."

Kendall mumbled unintelligible as they pulled his staggering form with them.

"They're ahead of us," Alec said, pointing east with the tip of his knife.

Ten zombies, maybe more, tripped and swayed, moving in and out of sight between the tall trees. After all this time outdoors, if they had any clothes they hung in tatters. Most of the clothing was a washed-out gray or tan, some colorless; still others were naked, but they all blended into the browns and grays and greens of the forest. It was the movement that caught her eye more than the forms. The zombies pitched over, then got up—bumping off trees, each other, but always toward them. The horde behind them was more agitated, the grunts and snarls as they fought over Rich's body rising and falling.

Kendall was almost no help, barely lifting his feet, which caught on rocks and sticks. A flicker in the corner of her eye turned her head. The zombies that had been farther up the mountainside when she'd gone to kill that first one were now within fifty yards. She jerked to a halt when Kendall's boot tangled on a rock.

"How hard did you punch him?"

"Three times. He wasn't stopping." Alec looked behind them and almost tripped. "We can't go on like this. Help me get him over my shoulder."

Alec handed her his knife. He crouched down, and Miranda maneuvered Kendall onto his shoulder for a fireman carry. He grunted as he stood, wincing, even with the hand up she gave him.

"You okay?" she asked, giving him her machete. With Kendall over his shoulder, he needed a weapon with a longer reach.

He nodded. She flipped the snap on her holster and pulled her sidearm. Its weight in her hand felt reassuring, a measure of power restored after the abrupt loss of her invisible shield. Every zombie in a square mile knew they were here. Silence was no longer a priority. She wasn't even sure if they were going true east, but they didn't have time to check a compass. The boulder ahead she recognized, offering some reassurance.

"To the right," she said, as they closed in on two zombies ahead. A form lurched out from a tree as Alec passed. She darted around him, barreling into the zombie's back with her shoulder. Its rib cage depressed under the force of her shove. The damn thing didn't even fall down, but swayed on rubber-like legs. She shoved it aside, felling it this time, and leaped away.

"More ahead," Alec said, sounding breathless. Then he added, warning in his voice, "Mind your step!"

She swerved around him, and the earth fell away, a four-foot drop interrupting the path, hidden until she was almost on top of it. She was going too fast to stop, or to get back to Alec's other side, where the path was wide enough. She jumped over the gap, the jolt as she stumbled onto the earth in front of Alec ricocheting through her joints. Alec slammed into her, he and Kendall falling in a tumble. She wriggled away while Alec pulled himself free of her. When he stood, he gasped. Doubling over, his hand went to his back.

"What is it?" she cried, for he was clearly hurt.

"Nothing. Help me lift him," he said, crouching to pick up Kendall.

Of the zombies behind, two staggered along the path, only feet away. Three zombies blocked the way, and the trees were too thick to go around. She grabbed Kendall by the hips, lifting him when Alec nodded. He gasped as he stood, pain flashing across his face.

She whirled around. The first zombie ahead of them was just feet away. Maybe it had been a lithe man once, but half of its face had been gnawed to the bone. Its scalp looked like a mango with the peel pulled back, but leached of vibrant color. Thin strips of flesh that looked like leather flapped when it turned its head. Teeth without lips snapped as it lunged, the reek hitting her like a kick to the face. She barely got her hand up in time to catch its shoulder. She stabbed into the shadow of its empty eye socket, then pushed it backward, into the one behind it. She landed a forward kick in the last upright zombie's stomach, sending it over the drop-off she'd just jumped over.

Alec barely made it past the downed zombies. Whatever injury he'd suffered, it was serious. She caught up with him, her breath coming hard but steady. The only thing louder was the zombies pursuing them, but she recognized their surroundings. They were almost to the bunker.

"Do you know where we are?" Alec asked, his voice harsh from exertion. "I'm turned about."

"It's just up there," she said, catching sight of the bowl-shaped depression and the lintel over the bunker's blast door. Relief energized her. She could run all day now that she'd seen that door. Zombies still closed in, but they would make it. She checked her watch: ten minutes to spare. Their codes would still work.

She flashed Alec a grin of relief, underpinned by the kind of fear she hadn't felt in a while. His eyes narrowed, pain pinching their corners, his face drained of color. The hard line of his mouth looked like a scar.

"Are you okay?"

He didn't answer.

Kendall was awake but still looked dazed. They raced down the slope of the bowl in the hillside, screeching to a halt under the linteled stoop. Alec dumped him like a sack of potatoes, grimacing while he reached for his gun.

"Get the door. I'll cover," Alec panted.

Miranda jammed her gun in its holster. She unzipped the to-the-elbow zipper on the sleeve of her leather jacket, then pushed both the jacket and shirt sleeve up. The codes were a little smeared, but legible.

"What happened?" she heard Kendall mumble.

She punched the keypad, the amber numbers lighting up the squares of the display.

"What the hell, guys?" Phineas' voice squawked over the speakers. "What the fuck is going on?"

Miranda entered the last number. Nothing happened. She

compared the numbers to what was on her arm. They matched. She checked her watch—seven minutes.

Alec backed up beside her, still looking out to the forest. "What's wrong?"

"It's not working!"

She jabbed at the keypad again, trying not to panic. The groans and hisses of the zombies grew louder.

"Phineas," Alec shouted. "Open the door."

She didn't stop entering the code. Again, it didn't work.

Phineas sounded frantic through the speakers. "I'm trying! It says my code isn't valid!"

"Let me try," Alec said.

She pulled her handgun and looked to the forest. The closest zombies were forty feet away. She crossed to where Kendall still sat, bleary-eyed and out of it, in five steps.

She crouched in front of him. "Kendall! You need to open the door."

"What?" he said, confused.

"Mine's not working either," said Alec.

"Kendall," Miranda said again, but his eyes looked unfocused. She slapped him—hard. "You need to open the door right now."

"The door?" he said, looking at her with more 'there' in his eyes.

She flinched at the sharp report of Alec's gun. The zombies were thirty feet and closing. And behind them, from all sides, up and down the slope of the mountain, more staggered through the trees, their moans a haunting soundtrack.

"The bunker door, Kendall!" She hauled him to his feet, shoving him to the keypad. "You need to get us in the bunker right now or we're going to die!"

Alec fired again and again. He was taking longer shots than she would, but then she saw a zombie trip over the one he'd just shot. It fell flat on its face, lay still for a second, then slowly pushed up to hands and knees. He was trying to slow them down with more obstacles, even if just for a moment.

Phineas' voice shouted through the speakers. Miranda grabbed Kendall by his jacket and shook him.

"Open the fucking door, Kendall! Open it now!"

Kendall's brown eyes focused. Finally, the peril they were in clicked. He stooped, tapping the keypad so quickly she could barely follow his fingers. This time, when the last number was pressed, it was followed by a deep, pneumatic hiss. The door finally opened, and they scrambled inside.

19

PHINEAS WAS frantic when he met them at the airlock.

"It wouldn't open," he said, talking so fast it was almost gibberish. "I don't know what happened." He looked from person to person, then said, "Where's Rich?"

"He's..." Miranda said, choking, unable to get the words out. She turned on Kendall. "This is your fault."

"But—"

Miranda shoved Kendall in the chest, grief and fury—but most of all, fear—flooding her body. His eyes grew wide, shocked.

"You didn't listen! You fucking panicked and now Rich is dead. All you had to do was listen, but you ran toward them. We could have gotten back, all of us, but you—"

She broke off, the pain so overwhelming she couldn't finish. Instead, a strangled sob slipped out. Alec's hand settled lightly on her shoulder.

"Miranda, back off. It's not—"

She jerked away, shaking his hand off, and rounded on him. "Don't tell me to back off."

Alec raised his hands, as if surrendering. "I'm sorry, lass. We're all—"

Kendall said, "You were supposed to repel them."

Oh my God, she thought, the weight of what had happened suddenly sapping her strength. She felt crushed, like the Wicked Witch of the West must have felt when the house from Kansas landed on her. She slumped against the wall, stunned.

"We did," she whispered, her anger falling a notch. "We did, but... Jesus Christ."

"You don't repel them anymore?" Phineas barked, his eyes as wide as wagon wheels.

Alec nodded. "They attacked Rich. He went to help Kendall, thinking they'd react like before, and then... They don't seem interested in Miranda, but they aren't staying away from her."

"But... I thought once you repelled them, you repelled them," Phineas said.

Miranda shook her head. "River mentioned it might not last. That we just didn't know." Her voice became hard when she looked at Kendall. "But it shouldn't have mattered. If you hadn't run away, we'd all have made it back, whether we repelled them or not, but we had to crash through the forest after you, and pull in every zombie in earshot."

Kendall looked at her like he was a puppy she'd just kicked. "I didn't want any of this... I like Rich..."

His voice faded away. He looked forlorn. Lost. Her fingers twitched, balling into fists before unfurling and doing it again. She felt enervated, her body so depleted that sliding down the wall to sit on the floor felt impossible. Alec took her hand, dipping his chin to catch her eye. His own were exhausted but brimmed with concern.

She wanted to scream... To lash out and rage against the unfairness, against the way the world just seemed to take and take and never stop. Rich was a good man. Thoughtful, and charming in his self-deprecating way. Always mindful of the manners he gave his mother credit for. Incredibly smart but not flashy about it. The guy she wanted next to her when the chips were down because he was—

He used to be, she thought, he used to be those things.

Through the stunned haze, something tugged at her. Something Phineas had said. "Did you say the doors wouldn't open?" she said to him.

Phineas nodded, the movements of his head jerky and off-time. "I don't know what happened. I tried them again after you left, just the airlock like Kendall suggested, and they worked just fine. But after an hour, it said they were invalid."

"Mine didn't work either," Alec said.

Neither had hers. She shook her head. It didn't make sense. Kendall had given them the codes. Why hadn't they worked? She rubbed at her eyes. They felt filled with sand. Her last glimpse of Rich's face had been the terrified, cerulean blue of his eyes. She instinctively knew she'd see it her nightmares.

"Oh my God," she said, the pieces falling into place like complicated clockwork. She stared at Kendall in horror. "You gave us codes that didn't work."

Silence filled the corridor. It pushed against her with an oppressive ruthlessness. Alec's gaze was turned inward, while he thought. Phineas' face had gone slack. Kendall's eyes shifted from person to person under the owl blink, like a pin ball dragged around by a magnet.

Phineas' stunned voice broke the silence. "You were going to leave me here with no way to get out?"

Kendall shook his head. Phineas catapulted into Kendall, grabbing him by the shoulders. The loud smack of Kendall's body against the wall echoed in the confined space of the corridor.

"You were going to trap me here?" Phineas shouted, spittle flying from his teeth. Even though he was shorter than Kendall by half a foot, he seemed to tower over him. "Leave the others with no way to get inside?"

"No," Kendall said, gasping, shaking his head. "No... They worked! Just not—"

"Just not what?" Phineas shouted, rattling Kendall's lanky frame.

Alec wrenched Phineas away, barely able to pry the two men apart. Delilah barked and growled, running between the scrabbling men and Miranda. Once freed, Kendall retreated, staggering back.

Miranda never moved. Her feet felt cemented in place.

"Just not what?" she asked.

Kendall's eyes blinked so rapidly that they looked like the flicker of windows of one train speeding by another, but she could see the trapped look in their brown depths. When he didn't answer, Alec said, "We almost died, Kendall, because none of our codes worked."

Kendall closed his eyes, visibly steeling himself, maybe from an expected attack, or maybe from the truth. "I— They did work, just..." His voice dropped to a whisper. "Not as long as I told you."

"What?" Alec said.

"They...they worked for an hour," Kendall said, his voice so low Miranda could barely hear him.

Shock hit her like a blow, sent her stumbling back against the wall. "Why would you do that?"

But she already knew the answer. It was this place, and what he had. It was his fear that he'd lose it. It was the scarcity mentality that had probably predated his lonely exile into this tomb, when he'd had more money than God. What she didn't understand was why. Why the ruse, the pretense of trust?

Kendall's chin trembled. His face screwed up, tears pooling in his eyes.

"Don't you dare cry. Don't expect us to pity you," she spat. "You cared more about keeping this place than our lives... You'd rather have died on your goddamned doorstep than risk losing this shit! Why do it at all?"

He stood there, frozen, his mouth open. When a tear slipped through his eyelashes, bile rose in her throat.

"You fucker... Stay the fuck away from me," Phineas said, shoving Kendall hard against the wall before stalking away.

Alec took Miranda's hand. "C'mon. Let's wash up."

She followed him as if in a trance. It was only when he winced while opening the outer door to their dome that she remembered he was injured.

"You're hurt," she said. Like a gusting wind, concern dispersed the fog of shocked anger. "Where? Are you okay?"

"It's my back," Alec said. "A slipped disc from years ago. I'll be fine."

"We need to get out of here."

"I know," Alec said. He looked tired, the pain in his eyes draining them of their brilliance. "But we can't get through the zombies outside right now."

"I'll get you some ice, and see if there are any painkillers," she said.

Alec caught her arm, a warning in his eyes. "Steer clear of Kendall. Don't do anything stupid."

"I won't." When he gave her a hard look, she said, "I promise."

"ARE YOU SURE YOU'RE UP FOR THIS?"

Alec held her gaze, looking at her across the bed while they hastily crammed their belongings into their packs. Both his question and concern for her were in his eyes. She nodded. The small motion set off a chain reaction of agony, starting with the cleaver that split open the top of her head, followed by ice picks stabbing behind her eyes.

He said, "If you stay sober, we can wait until tomorrow when you're not hung over."

It didn't matter how hungover she was, they needed to get out of here, but Alec might be another story. "Are you okay? Will you be able to handle your pack with your back?"

"I'll be fine," he assured her. "It's sore, but I can manage. I got more painkillers from the med bay."

She sighed, unsure if she believed him. The care in Alec's eyes hurt almost as much as her head. The rake—with the sly smile and the rogue's twinkle in his eye—had been MIA since they got back yesterday.

Her surroundings felt fuzzy at the edges. She'd barely slept last night, kept up by dreams of babies that were really zombies, blue eyes filled with terror, and Mario's gentle voice insisting she love something, or kill something, or accept the blame—take your pick. She'd walked rings in the living area, trying to calm down, and began to feel guilty about what she'd said to Kendall. She'd been upset, but blaming him for Rich's death? That had been low, no matter what he'd done. What he'd done wasn't the point, horrible as his charade was. Blaming him was just like Mario accusing her of leaving the baby behind, and goddamn him for it. Half the bottle of Scotch turned down the psychic noise enough that she'd been able to crawl back into bed beside Alec, the warmth of his body reassuring enough that she'd drifted asleep.

The enormity of Rich's death was beginning to hit her. She'd lost a good friend and been helpless to do anything other than watch—and then flee. She had to tell Mathilde that her husband was dead, that their children were fatherless. Zombies didn't notice her—for now—but she no longer repelled them. She'd only gained the ability what...six months ago? She'd come to rely on it more than she realized. Never mind that she'd never asked for it, never wanted it, never known what its price would be.

And Kendall...

She gave her head a sharp shake, pain slicing through her skull. She couldn't even think about Kendall right now. She cursed herself for drinking so much last night, because dying would be preferable to this hangover, but staying in the bunker for another night felt too dangerous.

"We need to get out of here," she said.

He regarded her with a level, appraising gaze for what felt like years. "What about LO and the food?"

She'd expected this, because she'd racked her brain about it last night. "He told us we could get back in here on our own, but that was a lie."

"He lied about how long our codes would work," Alec countered.

"Did he?"

Alec narrowed his eyes. "Phineas unlocked the doors after we left, so he'd be familiar with how it worked. He was able to open them, so our codes must have worked, too, for a time."

"Really? We never tested them." Her head pounded when she spoke, and when she didn't. She really needed to get something for it. "Phineas checked his right after we closed the blast door, just like Kendall told him to. He didn't try again until we got back, when they didn't work. We don't know how long Phineas was able to open them, or if our codes ever worked. We know nothing but what Kendall told us."

Alec's brow furrowed. His lips wrinkled into a frown. "But

it makes no sense! We went out before with only him able to open the doors. Why put on this elaborate show?"

Miranda shrugged. "I don't know. But if he was willing to leave us out there to die if he did, and trap Phineas inside, he'll never share his food willingly. We have to go home and come back with enough people to take it."

Alec's troubled face smoothed into tired lines of resignation. "Maybe they've found some while we've been here. Maybe we won't need Kendall's."

"Maybe. But I doubt it."

"We should still stay another night," Alec said. "You don't have to see him. You don't have to leave our dome. You're in no fit state to be going outside, lass. You've a massive head on you."

She was pretty sure he meant she was hungover, not that her body was out of proportion. "We're still depending on Kendall to let us out. We need to leave, Alec. The sooner, the better, while he's still feeling guilty."

"Christ...I didn't think he might not let us out."

"You're an optimist. I'm not."

"There are still a lot of zombies around," Alec said. His eyes went out of focus while he thought for a moment. "You're thinking to use the emergency exit tunnel. The one off the pool?"

"If the diagrams he showed us of this place are real, it should put us half a mile down the mountain."

"I'll find the emergency exit camera... There's got be one with all the others. If it looks all right outside that door, we'll go."

"Fine by me."

Thirty minutes later, Delilah raced ahead of them, disappearing into the door of the swimming pool dome. The bright squiggles of light reflected from the motion of the water set off a new cascade of pain. She stopped for a moment, clamping down on her gag reflex when the smell of chlorine hit her. Delilah woofed, the sound echoing.

"Fuck me," she muttered under her breath, then followed Alec around the pool to the far end of the dome where Phineas waited by the open door. The tunnel on the other side of it was gray concrete, and as utilitarian as the rest of the bunker was opulent. Kendall hovered just inside its open door, his face almost panicked.

Phineas' brow wrinkled when he saw her. "You sure you're up for this, Miranda?"

"Absolutely," she said.

She did her best to ignore everything while Alec and Phineas entered the tunnel. She steeled herself before stepping through the hatch, unable to slip by Kendall as quickly as she'd have liked on account of her pack.

"Miranda. Please," Kendall said when she didn't stop, sounding desperate.

She saw the guys, now ten paces ahead of her, stop and turn back around.

"In private?" Kendall added, his voice hopeful, and raised just enough that Alec and Phineas could hear him.

Alec's face was impassive. Phineas was another matter. The anger on his face looked unnatural, like an ill-fitting garment. She waved them on. Kendall's brown eyes were filled with anxiety. He looked pale, and like he'd barely slept, bags that almost looked like bruises under his eyes. His restless energy couldn't be contained as he rocked from foot to foot. He fidgeted, gnawing on the fingernail of his pinky finger, before rubbing the back of his neck, then jamming his hands in his pockets. The owl blink was doing double-time.

"Please...don't leave like this."

Keeping her voice even, she said, "I have to tell Rich's wife he's dead."

Kendall blanched. "I know— I didn't mean..." He took an audible breath. "I care about—"

"Please stop talking," she said, not unkindly, but cutting him off.

She'd promised herself that she wouldn't lose her temper. The shame she'd felt last night about some of the things she'd said to Kendall prickled her conscience. It wasn't his fault that he'd panicked. He was new to it all: going outside, dealing with zombies, keeping the fear in check. It was impossible to predict how people would react when confronted with that reality for the first time. She'd seen people jumpier than Kendall turn out to be rock solid, and big, tough guys turn into gibbering idiots. It had been wrong of her to blame him for Rich's death. She knew that, even if she hadn't said it.

But he'd lied about the codes. The whole thing was so stupid, but even if she could sympathize with why Kendall had done it—and she couldn't—it wouldn't change anything. If Kendall had died yesterday instead of Rich, or in addition to Rich, she and Alec would probably be dead. Phineas would be trapped here. Miranda had lied to Kendall by omission. She'd flat-out lied, too. But her lies had never put him in danger.

"Don't tell me you care," she said. Her voice was soft, and she couldn't keep her anger out of it. "Not when you let us go out there thinking— If you'd died, too, we'd have run back here thinking we could get inside, and we'd be dead." Her head ached. Figuring out what she was trying to say made it worse. "I don't understand what giving us fake codes was about. And I don't want to, so save it."

He stared at her, frozen. He opened and closed his mouth several times, but nothing came out.

When she realized he wasn't going to say anything, she said, "I'm sorry for saying it was your fault Rich died." She swallowed, her mouth and throat once again dry. "It wasn't your fault, and I shouldn't have said that. Rich knew the risks when it comes to zombies and people who've never dealt with them. We all did."

"I'm sorry," he said quickly, his eyes filling with tears. "I care about you."

Anger flooded her body, hard and sudden and hot. She wanted to punch him. She wanted to slap those needy tears out of his eyes, slap him so hard that if he ever caught up with himself, it would be next year. She might as well be looking at Mario, because that's what it felt like—the needing, the wanting, the sucking her dry. Kendall's neediness slithered into the space between them, coiled her in its sticky tentacles, squeezed her in its greedy grip.

"Don't tell me you care, Kendall," she hissed. "What you care about is this place, and your stuff. You know what's more important than weapons or hiding places or anything when you're out there? People you trust. Maybe I haven't been honest with you all the time, but it was never about anything that would get you killed."

Kendall shrank into himself. He swiped at his face, dashing the tears away. "You're wrong," he whispered, almost gasped. "I do care."

A sneer curled Miranda's lip. "You didn't care if we died out there. Just like you didn't care about the people you watched die when all this started, flying your goddamned drones around to watch the biggest disaster movie ever. You might want to fuck me, but don't care about me, and you don't care if everyone *I* care about starves."

A mirthless laugh chuffed in her throat, jagged and sharp like broken glass. She turned on her heel and stalked away.

Kendall's quavering voice echoed down the tunnel. "Are you coming back?"

She stopped, turning around to face him. "Are you even going to open the door, or is this just more street theater?"

Kendall's face crumpled. His whole body slumped. New tears made his eyes glitter.

"Yes," he whispered.

She snorted in disgust, then walked away.

20

THEY DROVE.

After an hour on the road they discussed, briefly, finding a place to hole up awhile. Mario wasn't even sure why they'd bothered, because all anyone wanted was to get as far away as they could from the community of white supremacists. After studying the atlas, they decided to leave Highway 29 and take a secondary route which still took them south, but would not be as obvious a choice.

There was a reason for this, of course, and Mario had been ready to put Bottle Rock Road in the rearview mirror forever. The road, which followed a mountain ridge with at least ten thousand feet of elevation, was well and truly trashed. All the things that had made such roads in Northern California idyllic before zombies—twisty, forested, remote—made it a nerve-racking nightmare now. All he could think was if they broke down out here, they were screwed. If they'd never needed to take Highway 20 and instead stayed on 101, they might—theoretically—be in Marin County by now.

They rounded a bend. The T intersection with Highway

175 East, which also signified the merciful end of Bottle Rock Road, lay ahead.

"I need a break from driving," Tessa said. "This looks like an okay place to stop."

"Agreed," Doug said, straightening himself up.

Across the intersection was an old gas station, the kind of small, mom and pop operation that had been common in rural areas. And because it was a gas station, the paved area around it was concrete, which was more durable than asphalt, so it kept the area relatively clear. Tessa stopped the Tesla in the middle of the large lot, to the right of the canopy that had jutted out from the front of the building and was now half-collapsed over the station's two pumps. Beyond the lot was an open meadow with a small ramshackle barn. The ground dipped away past the barn, but from here Mario couldn't tell how big the hill was. Tessa turned off the Tesla. For a moment, nobody moved.

"We should eat," Mario said. He looked to Silas and Violet, in the seat between him and Skye. "You two hungry?"

Silas shrugged. Violet nodded her head absently. They had been on the road for three and a half hours and traveled about twenty miles. The events of the morning seemed both long ago and immediate. One look at the subdued affect of the children reflected just how traumatic it had been.

Skye and Doug did a quick check on their surroundings before Mario, Tessa, and the kids got out of the vehicle. And Mister Bun Bun, too, at Silas' prompting. After a bathroom break and a few minutes to stretch their legs, Mario, Skye, and the children ate, sitting on the ground with their backs against the Tesla. Doug was looking at the atlas, spread out on the Tesla's hood. Tessa was on the other side, keeping watch in that direction while eating her meal.

Mario handed out lunch—crackers and apples, along with a jar of peanut butter that somehow had not gone rancid. Despite their noncommittal interest when lunch had been mentioned, Silas and Violet wolfed down their first helpings and asked for more. When they were finished, Violet crawled into Skye's lap. Silas leaned into Mario, his breathing steady. The weight of his head on Mario's chest fastened him to this moment, and to how much he loved these two little people who had become his own.

"I was scared," Silas said, his voice soft.

"Me too," Mario said.

"Why did they get so mean?"

Mario looked over to Skye, feeling flummoxed, knowing he had to give Silas an answer. Have *The Talk*. It should have died, along with everything else, and freed those who survived from having to be told that there were people so hateful, so scared, so rotten, that they didn't think the lives of these sweet children mattered. He couldn't even give them an idea who to be careful of; it used to be the police—how to talk, how to move —but now? Mario opened his mouth, to say what he didn't even know.

"Some people want to feel special and important," Skye said. "But they can only feel that way if they're taking something away from someone else. When you do that long enough, when you cling to believing things that are lies, that aren't right or kind, it makes you mean. And when what you believe is as bad as those people, it makes you want to hurt others."

"But... Don't they know it's wrong to hurt people?" Silas asked. He turned toward Skye but stayed nestled against Mario.

"I think they do know it's wrong," Skye said. "But they tell themselves that what they're doing is okay, that it's for the good of everyone, even the person they're hurting. They believe in their lies so they can act like they want to act. I don't know why they choose to act that way, Silas. I really don't."

She smiled at him gently. "We choose how we are in the

world, Silas. We choose how we treat other people. Sometimes people will say they can't help how they act, but that's not true. It's an excuse."

"Why would they want to stay mean?" Silas sounded genuinely puzzled. He twisted around and looked at Mario, his brow furrowed. He looked like Skye had strained his brain.

"Because it's hard to change, Silas," Mario said. "It doesn't mean you can't change, but it's hard. And sometimes it's scary."

Silas considered what Mario said, frowning, like he thought what they were saying was ridiculous. He turned back to Skye.

"I'm going to be nice," he said. "It's not that hard."

Skye laughed. She had a silvery, tinkling laugh that seemed to Mario the answer to why Doug had fallen in love with her as completely as he had.

"You already are nice, Silas," Skye answered.

Silas looked at Mario again. "When I was little, Mama and Devon had a fight about a man. I don't remember it all." He tipped his face up to Mario, looking guilty. "I was sneaking. They didn't know I was there. He used a bad word... Not like cursing, but Devon was real mad and wanted to fight him, and Mama didn't want to." Silas' brow furrowed, then he said, sounding unsure, "She told him it wasn't worth it, and to offer it up?"

Mario smiled at Silas, amused that he thought he was no longer 'little,' but pained that racism clearly wasn't new to him, even if he didn't completely understand it. He said, "I think your mama was a churchgoing woman, if that was her advice."

How the fuck had anyone done this with all of their children, Mario wondered. How did you live with the fear for their safety, for your own, without going crazy? It was only an accident of birth that he'd never had to deal with this himself.

"I think that man your mama and Devon fought about was like those people back there," he said. "They think they're better because of the color of their skin. And they think anyone whose skin color is different and darker, whether they're black or brown or whatever, isn't as good as them. I think the word he used is a very, very bad word that they call people who are black, like you and Violet."

Mario stopped, taking a moment to gather his thoughts.

"In the old world, and even now, people with lighter skin like mine were called white, and people with darker skin like yours and Violet's were called black. A very long time ago, way before I was born, white people used to own black people. They called them slaves. Thinking it's okay to own another person is wrong, but people did because they thought having white skin like mine made them better than people with dark skin like yours. Those people back there still believe it."

Silas' brow was creased. "That's what Mama and Devon were fighting about?"

"I think so."

Silas' forehead crinkled together, and his mouth drew into a pout. "That's stupid."

Mario smothered a laugh, because it wasn't funny, but the look of incomprehension on Silas' face was priceless.

"It doesn't make any sense, Silas. A lot of things about the old world didn't make sense. Hating someone because their skin is a different color is one of the stupidest, meanest things. Setting up how people live so they can't have as good a life because of the color of their skin happened in the old world, too, and it was wrong. Sometimes people were killed for no reason at all, except that they were black."

He sighed, angry that he had to explain the evils of a world that didn't exist anymore to a child. But racism was still alive and well for reasons he couldn't wrap his head around. They lived in a world with people, and monsters that eat people. Nothing about that equation was confusing, but Mario knew he'd be putting the children in danger by not helping them understand racism, all because of dirtbags who needed to notch up the misery factor.

"I like to think that now, more people realize that no one kind of person is better than another, Silas," he continued. "But I know that's not always true. The people back there are the kind who believe it the most. They're very dangerous. They'll try to hurt you and Violet."

"But why?" Silas asked, still confused, his eyes wide.

"Because they're fucking assholes. I know those are bad words," he said. Silas' eyes had widened in surprise that he'd cursed while talking to him. "They're really dangerous assholes, Silas. I don't have a better answer for you. But I'll protect you and Violet from them if it's the last thing I ever do. I won't let them hurt you."

Silas leaned against Mario. Mario looked over Silas' head to Skye, who gave him a discreet thumbs-up. He mouthed a silent thank you. She grinned and winked, like helping him explain something as complicated as racism and fascism was no big deal. Violet had fallen asleep in her lap.

"Look," Silas said softly. He leaned forward, pointing at the edge of the lot that bordered the meadow behind the gas station. "There's a bunny."

Mario followed Silas' pointing finger. Sure enough, a small brown rabbit nibbled the grass.

"I see him," Mario said.

"Do you think he and Mister Bun Bun can be friends? Can we take him with us?"

"No, that's a wild rabbit. It wouldn't like being with people. It needs to be free."

Silas looked up at Mario, his face filled with anxiety. "Does Mister Bun Bun need to be free?" he said, sounding alarmed. "Is he a slave?"

"No, no," Mario said, chuckling as he reassured him. "It's not the same thing. He's your pet, and you take care of him because you love him, and you're good to him. Besides, he doesn't know how to be a wild rabbit. It would be cruel to put him outside to fend for himself. He doesn't know how to live out there."

"I'm going to put Violet in the car," Skye said.

Gently, she shook Violet awake and stood her up, then stood and picked up the still half-asleep girl.

"You too," Mario said to Silas. "We're going to leave soon."

"I don't want to get back in the car," Silas whined. "I want to watch the wild bunny."

"You can watch that bunny from the car and tell Mister Bun Bun all about it."

"Okay," Silas said, a grumble in his voice.

They climbed to their feet, and Silas said, "I was scared before. But I knew you'd take care of us."

Mario's heart softened and warmed, like butter in a hot pan melting into a golden puddle. Silas reminded him so much of Anthony, whether he was serious, like now, or when his dark eyes glinted with mischief. He could see them together, growing up as brothers, because that was what he wanted. He'd called Silas and Violet 'my kids' when they'd been threatened, without even realizing it, because they were.

He helped Silas up into the back seat, blinking back tears, and gave his head a rub.

"I love you, Silas."

Silas smiled, and said simply, "I love you."

He looked at Silas for a moment, and Violet sleeping beside him. He'd do anything to keep them safe, pay any price. He just needed to get them somewhere he might be able to do it.

"I'm going to talk to the others." Mario shut the door, then said through the half-open window, "Be right back."

Silas nodded, then began to tell Mister Bun Bun about the wild rabbit.

Mario took a few deep breaths, trying to get the wave of emotion that had hit him under control. Skye was snuggled into Doug, her back to his front. Doug held her around the waist and scowled over her shoulder at the atlas. Tessa was still eating peanut butter and crackers. Mario took a quick look around, but their surroundings were still blessedly clear of zombies.

"If you're not careful, your face will freeze like that," Mario said to Doug.

Doug looked at him sidelong. "Never heard that before."

Tessa said, "We got away from Nazis and lived to tell the tale. It's been a shit day but I'm calling this a win."

"There are just no good routes home," Doug said, frowning. "We'll have to go through Napa at this point."

Skye gasped. "Oh no! There could be wine."

"You're a brat," Doug said, then kissed her on the neck.

Mario squinted at the atlas. Doug was right. They were wildly off track from what they'd planned.

Doug sighed. "I guess we'll just take the least crappy route we can, hopefully without a repeat of racist assholes. Jesus... I still can't believe that even happened."

Mario picked up the atlas, but froze when he pivoted toward the Tesla's doors, because one was open—the door Silas had been sitting at.

"Silas?"

In two steps he could see that Silas wasn't inside. Violet was still sacked out on the back seat. Mister Bun Bun was in his carrier, eyes bright, his velvety nose twitching.

"What's wrong?" Tessa said, catching up to him. "Where's Silas?"

Everyone spun in place, searching the parking lot.

"I think he's behind the station," Skye said, already on the move.

"The rabbit," Mario hissed, furious with himself for not paying more attention. He'd seen how taken with the animal Silas had been. He should have kept a closer eye on him.

Doug started after Skye, but Mario said, "Stay here with Tessa and Violet."

Mario was halfway to the meadow when Silas screamed. He bolted, saw Silas, and the world spun. Silas had wandered past the old barn and down the hill. The barn that zombies now spilled out from...thirty at least, with more still emerging. Scalp-pricking moans carried across the still air.

"Silas!"

Skye was already running for him, lithe and swift as a gazelle. Mario raced to catch up, shouting for Silas to run wide, to go around, where Skye could meet him. Skye darted past the first zombie. It lunged and caught her ponytail. She was yanked back hard, like a little dog on a leash.

Mario gaped at what was playing out in front of him. The zombie was *attacking* Skye. She struggled to keep her footing as more zombies turned her way. Mario charged, ramming the zombie that had Skye's hair from behind, his shoulder down like linebacker. The zombie lost its footing and stumbled forward, yanking Skye down with it.

His machete slashed through Skye's hair, dispersing it like a gossamer web. He dragged Skye to her feet and pushed her toward the station, toward Doug, who was running to them.

He ran for Silas. He'd understood what Mario had told him, to run wide, but now Skye wasn't there to meet him. The zombies hadn't melted away from her, hadn't parted like the Red Sea, like they had so many times before.

"Mario!" Silas screamed.

Silas' sobs were wild with fear. Zombies staggered down

the hillside. And if he wasn't so small, it wouldn't matter. But the zombies were coming down the hill, gravity assisting them even when they fell, and Silas was only a little boy.

Doug fell in step beside him, charging down the hill beside Mario, firing his Glock. Mario pulled the Sig and started firing, too. Trying to clear a path, trying to make just enough room, trying to—

A zombie caught Silas' arm. He screamed like a trapped animal, making that horrible sound that Mister Bun Bun had made when they ran and jostled him inside his carrier. Silas shrieked with terror, struggling and fighting. Mario stopped and sighted, remembered to breathe because he couldn't miss, and squeezed the trigger.

The Sig clicked.

He was out of bullets.

"No!"

Doug continued firing, but Silas' next shriek rent the air. The blood arced high, spurting from his fragile throat. The zombie ripped into his soft flesh, ripping his mahogany skin that smelled so sweet: sweat and earth, salt and sunshine. Silas' screams became mangled as another zombie, and another, fell upon his small, thrashing form.

Mario screamed, charging toward the zombies that had turned away from Silas and now trudged toward him, attracted by the gunshots. He'd promised to keep Silas safe. He'd promised—

He was knocked to the ground, thrashing against a zombie he hadn't seen. It grabbed him by the arm, then dragged him to his feet.

"We have to go!"

Mario tried to push it off, confused that it was talking, but it wasn't a zombie. It was Doug.

"We have to get Silas!" he said, trying to pull away, trying to look back, to not leave his sweet, small boy with those monsters.

"We have to go," Doug said, his face ashen, but with a grip on Mario's shoulders that felt like iron. His blue eyes were haunted by what he'd never be able to unsee. "We can't help him anymore. He's gone."

"No!"

Doug looked over Mario's shoulder, at the zombies coming closer. If they stayed much longer, he'd be past helping, too. Past fighting and trying and dying. Past failing and losing the people he loved, like his sweet, innocent son who was right here but out of reach. What was the point? It was going to happen someday. Why not today?

"Violet needs you."

A chasm opened at Mario's feet. Another child, sweet and innocent like her brother, who needed him. Who demanded he keep trying, keep living, no matter how heartsick and weary he was. No matter how many more people he lost.

A silent scream tore Mario's throat. He had to protect Violet. He had to leave Silas. Leave him, perhaps, to wander the earth...undead and ravenous and damned.

Doug pulled him, pushed, almost carried Mario to the crest of the hill. When they reached it, he tried to turn back but Doug dragged him away.

"Don't," Doug said. "You don't want to see."

21

WHEN THE TESLA'S batteries finally crapped out about five minutes after they passed a sign for something called Worship Central, Doug wanted to put his head down on the steering wheel and cry. It was too much. Fucking neo-Nazis, who had altered their route and sent them straight to disaster. *Was it really just yesterday we left the house with the breezeway?* he thought. It felt like months ago. He puzzled at it, at how skewed his perception of time had become, knowing it was a coping mechanism. If he kept his mind occupied with why time seemed so distorted, he wouldn't have to think about the rest.

Highway 175 had been as bad as they'd feared, forcing a lengthy detour because of a massive landslide. They'd backtracked, following a circuitous route that got them back on the highway a mile past the landslide, but it had taken close to two hours. Doug had been incandescent with rage. He knew his inability to roll with it wasn't the detour, but he still seethed. He managed to settle down finally, which was a good thing, because not long after the Tesla gave up the ghost.

Mario had barely spoken since they drove away, since they

lost poor Silas, except to murmur words of comfort in Violet's ear. He sat glassy-eyed in the back seat, Violet on his lap, clutching the catatonic child to him. She clutched Mister Bun Bun to herself in exactly the same way.

Nobody spoke, and the silence was oppressive, but what were they going to talk about? Silas being eaten by zombies? Skye no longer repelling zombies? Mario hating himself for taking those three seconds to save Skye, which might have made the difference to save Silas? And then feeling guilty about feeling that way? Maybe they could dissect Doug's bed-wetting panic when the zombie had grabbed Skye's hair instead of recoiling, as they had for months now.

Tortuous images had plagued Doug since. Broken, dirty teeth biting into her soft, pale skin. Her screams, the blood, needing to kill her so she wouldn't turn. Or worse yet, not being able to, and knowing that what was left of her—once so beautiful and vibrant—roamed the Earth as a hungry, mindless, corpse.

Nobody spoke all right, because the oppressive silence was as good as it was going to get.

"We should get what we can carry and get moving," Skye said. "It'll be dark in four or five hours. We need to get settled in for the night."

She pushed her door open and shut it quickly, perhaps relieved to escape the oppressive silence.

"Let's put Mister Bun Bun in his carrier," Tessa said.

Immediately, Violet began to sob. "No," she cried, so piteously that Doug's heart, which he'd thought was already smashed into a million pieces, broke a little more.

Doug turned in his seat. Violet held the rabbit too tight. Mister Bun Bun began to struggle, ready to bolt at the first opportunity.

"Give Mister Bun Bun to Tessa, sweetheart," Mario said, his voice low.

Violet's sobs increased in volume. She shook her head, gripping the rabbit tighter. Skye appeared in the window, her brow furrowed. Tessa looked at Doug, sending him a beseeching look to do something.

Mario kept murmuring to no avail. Finally, he said to Tessa, "Get hold of him."

She did, and he pried Violet's arms from around the rabbit. It bolted out of Tessa's hands for the safety of the open carrier. Thank God none of the doors were open. Losing Mister Bun Bun would have been the crowning turd on this shitstorm of a day. Violet began to thrash, kicking and screaming. The empty seat in front of her vibrated every time her foot connected with it.

"Pack up, I'll deal with her," Mario said as he slid his arm around Violet's thrashing body and got out of the SUV.

Doug joined Skye and Tessa at the rear hatch. They began to sort through the gear. Skye filled water bottles, Tessa split the meagre supply of food between their packs, while Doug rooted through their dwindling medical supplies. Violet screeched and howled over the low murmur of Mario's voice.

After a few minutes of this, Doug looked around them. If there were any zombies nearby, Violet's cries would attract them. He knew it, Mario knew it, they all did.

"What are we going to do with her?" Skye said, looking anxious.

"Goddammit, Violet," Mario's strangled voice shouted. "Shut the fuck up!"

Doug heard the sharp smack of a hard hand on soft flesh. The screams ceased. Doug looked at Skye for a split second, then he, Skye, and Tessa dashed around the Tesla.

Violet was backed up against the vehicle, holding her cheek. She looked up at Mario, her dark eyes wide with shock. Tears still leaked from them, and her lips trembled, but she was silent. Mario recoiled from her, his face a mirror of the shock on Violet's, but mixed with a horror so profound he might as well have been looking at a monster, not a little girl. His mouth opened and closed but no sound came out. He backed away, reeling on unsteady feet. He fell to his knees in the road, mouth contorted by a silent scream. His whole body convulsed, as if it were trying to vomit out the pain.

Doug followed and crouched beside him. Mario's sobs were raw and wild and utterly devastated, as if the entire world around him had collapsed in on itself. Doug put his hand on Mario's shoulder. It heaved like a ship buffeted by a storm, wave after wave of grief threatening to swamp him, when Violet appeared. Her furrowed forehead, wide, dark eyes, and almost pouty frown made her look like a miniature Black Madonna. She walked to Mario's other shoulder and began to pat it with her small dimpled hand.

Doug started crying, too. She was six years old, yet somehow she knew that what Mario had done a few moments ago wasn't who he was as a man, or a father. Mario turned to Violet, remorse and grief carved into his bones. He looked ancient—vanquished—as he pulled her into his lap and held her tight.

"I'm sorry," Doug heard him whisper through his sobs. "I'm so, so sorry, Violet. I'm sorry..."

Doug stood and stepped back, wiping his eyes. He cast a quick glance around, to make sure no zombies were in sight. He walked back to the Tesla, where Skye and Tessa stood crying, too. Without a word, he went back to the open rear hatch and picked up where he'd left off.

THEY WERE BACK ON HIGHWAY 29, WALKING THIS TIME. IT had only been about an hour, but it already felt endless. Their boots striking the pavement, the occasional rattle of the wire mesh door of Mister Bun Bun's carrier, and the crinkle of the pages when they consulted the atlas, were the only sounds from the party of five. Or six, if you counted Mister Bun Bun, and Doug did.

Tessa walked up alongside him. "We need stop soon," she said. "Mario looks like he's going to pass out, and he won't let us carry Violet."

"There's a group of buildings up ahead. Let's check them out. Tell Skye to stay with Mario and Violet."

Tessa nodded and fell back to do as he asked. He hadn't talked to Skye, not really, since they'd started walking. Every time he looked at her, panic welled up and fogged his brain. He couldn't afford to be panicked right now.

Tessa rejoined him, and together they walked over the brittle brown grass to the access road that ran parallel to the highway. A ribbon of Live Oak trees edged most of the property they were going to, and more shaded the cluster of buildings.

They walked up the dusty drive, machetes at the ready. A small, one-story building painted a cheery yellow announced itself as the Otter Bay Winery tasting room.

"That's out," Doug said, seeing immediately that the small building, with floor-to-ceiling windows on one side, would be impossible to secure.

"Let's check out the house."

He looked beyond the tasting room to a house, an old one. It was two stories and made of red brick, which was unusual in California. It looked like the kind of Colonial style houses back east—the real ones—that whether made of brick or wood had the same spare lines. The window shutters on both stories were closed and nailed shut. When they found the front and back doors locked, Doug began to feel optimistic. He banged on the door. When nothing moaned or shuffled inside, he banged again. After another minute of silence, he said, "Check it out?"

"Yes," Tessa said. "And if this and the other buildings are okay, let's find the wine. I need a drink."

AN HOUR LATER, THEY'D CONFIRMED THERE WERE NO zombies in any of the adjacent buildings, so they closed them back up to keep it that way. The house was hot but not stifling once they opened the upstairs windows. They found the wine —a lot of it—and brought a case of Cabernet into the house. The label said it was organic and biodynamic, whatever that meant. Doug was pretty sure Mad Dog would've been deemed acceptable, but they hadn't sunk that low—yet. He'd had a sip from Tessa's glass and the little Cab wasn't half bad.

Mario and Violet were sacked out in one of the second-story bedrooms at the front of the house. Doug had looked in on them, saw that they were dead to the world, and crept away. The first-floor windows were already boarded up from the inside, and they'd blocked the front and back doors with large pieces of furniture.

Tessa lounged on the couch in the living room when Doug got downstairs. Beside the couch, Mister Bun Bun was in a puppy pen they'd found in one of the outbuildings. He drank water from a dish, his little nose always twitching. Several half-eaten crackers that Skye had given him littered his pen. She knelt down beside him, wiggling her fingers through the mesh.

She looked up when he entered. "This poor thing is going to be a junk food junkie if we don't get him some veggies soon."

Doug wasn't sure what Skye had said. It was like when it took a moment for his brain to catch up with what his ear had heard, but this time, the catch-up part never happened. He was distracted by how pink her lips were. Her dirty face. How her hacked-off hair, though still long enough to pull into short pigtails, hit at about her shoulders, and was shorter on the right than on the left. Now that they were in as safe a place as they'd been in what felt like years, all he wanted was to be alone with her. He needed to hold her close, to know she was really here.

She must have seen it, for she said to Tessa, "You mind keeping an eye on things for now? We'll do the next watch."

To her credit, Tessa kept the smirk out of her voice. She held out the open bottle of wine and a glass, passing them off to Skye. She picked up another and started ripping off the foil with the corkscrew they'd found.

"I'm too wired to sleep. Knock yourselves out."

Doug followed Skye into the bedroom farthest from the one occupied by Mario and Violet. He crossed to the windows and opened the top sashes another foot, hoping to get a cross breeze. He turned back to Skye. She'd pulled the door shut behind them but hadn't come farther into the room. She leaned against the door, looking at him. She'd kept her cool today, kept it together in a way most people, in Doug's experience, didn't. But now that they were alone, he could see the fear in her eyes. The sadness and loss. The hunger.

"You okay?" he asked.

She shook her head no, then took a swig of wine straight from the bottle as she pushed off the door. She stooped to set it on the floor next to the empty glass. Doug felt hypnotized, watching her as she walked around the bed, drinking in the grace of how her body moved as she came to him.

"Are you?"

"No," he said.

She touched his hand. He pulled her to him, harder than he meant to. An inferno raged through him, fanned into being from one second to the next. His lips found hers, and the desperation fueling his desire, born of a fear more complete than any he'd known before, demanded that he touch her, taste her, fuck her—artlessly, without restraint.

She moaned into his mouth, her body pressing into his. She tugged his jacket off his shoulders. He pushed her shirt above her head, inhaling the heady mixture of her scent mingled with dust and sweat. They stumbled in a semi-circle as she kicked off her boots and he yanked away her bra to squeeze her milky, yielding breasts. She pulled on his belt, the snap of the leather flipping out of the buckle cracking like a whip that electrified every nerve ending in his body. He pushed her fumbling hands away, but his own were so clumsy in his haste that it probably wouldn't have made a difference if he'd let her finish the task.

She shoved her pants and panties down, kicking a leg free. He gripped her naked ass, his fingertips boring into her flesh as he lifted her against the wall. Her eyes, so impossibly blue, held his like a magnet. The hacked edges of her hair clung to her sweaty neck, a jarring reminder of how differently this day could have ended, fanning Doug's ache to possess her body with his. Her long legs wrapped around his hips, her arms wrapped around his neck. He groaned into their kiss as her silky body enveloped him, his lips rough against hers. Doug hurtled into her, the heat between them fanned by his longing, her lust, their need to connect.

Her breath grew sharp, as harsh as his own. The desperation, the speed, his raw need for her and hers for him, sent them rocketing toward consummation like a runaway train. He could tell she was almost there, almost gone. And he wanted to fall with her into that euphoric release while she writhed and pushed against him, her hard nipples pressing against him through his shirt.

In her eyes he saw the forlorn ache, the senseless loss, the urgent need to know they were alive.

"Doug," she gasped.

She smacked her head hard against the wall, her body bucking against his, quaking as she came. He followed, groaning, falling into her shuddering body. He pinned her to the wall, panting against her neck, her hair sticking to his face. They froze in place, gasping, caught in the voluptuous fog of their frantic coupling. Her legs still held him tightly to her, hands tangled in his hair. He gripped the flesh of her thighs in his hands with bruising force.

Then her legs slackened, and his hands fell away. Skye nestled into his embrace as her feet hit the floor, her strong arms encircling him. The first sob took him by surprise. He clung to her as if he were drowning, sobs racking his wiry frame. His terror prowled around them like a hungry ghost, searching for a chink so it could spirit her away.

When his fear receded, and his tears subsided, Doug held her face in his hands. Her eyes shone with love and relief and still more hunger, promising that they would soon repeat this rite of the living, of lovers who had cheated death.

"I thought you were dead," he whispered. "I thought... Oh Skye. I thought I'd lost you."

Tears glittered in her eyes before trickling down her flushed, dirt-smudged faced. He'd seen her cleaner, but never more beautiful than she was in this moment.

"You didn't," she said, pushing the hair that had fallen into his eyes out of the way. She wiped his cheek with a cloud-soft touch, then slid her arms around him once more. "We're here, together. That's all that matters."

LATER, THEY WERE GENTLER, MORE TENDER THAN BEFORE. Doug explored Skye's contours—the swells and hollows, the pliable and firm—with languid intention. The parts that tickled under his touch. The parts that reduced her to a puddle while he kissed and caressed and stroked and teased. The parts that set him ablaze, which was every inch of the wonderland of her body. When he kissed her to release, the musk of her sex filling his nose and making him hard, her body shaking and shuddering, her usual throaty cries were almost noiseless, like the fluttering of wings. When they moved together, while whispered promises flew fast and thick between them, the constant refrain of *Thank God, Thank God,* buzzed in the back of Doug's brain like a ward, or a charm, an unconscious benediction of how much he loved her, needed her, wanted her with him—always. When he finally came, long after having coaxed the same from her obliging and eager body, nothing could penetrate the pleasurable oblivion of his offering to the goddess beneath him.

They lay together, limbs entangled, ensconced in a haze of drowsy contentment. "I can't lose you," he murmured into her hair. "When we get home, I'm done with this shit. I want to stay where it's safe, get married, have babies. I don't want to do this anymore."

For a split second, he cringed. He meant it—all of it—but hadn't meant to say it like that. Against his chest, he felt her cheek lift in a smile.

"That's the fear talking. Not you," she said through a yawn. "It's sweet, and I love you for it, but you'd be climbing the walls." She raised her head, her chin resting on his chest, and arched an eyebrow. "Besides, what about what I want?"

Doug looked down at her, scowling.

"You know I'm right," she said, her voice a teasing singsong.

"I don't have to like it," he grumbled.

Skye's burst of laughter was contagious, because it sounded like tinkling bells and sunshine and fairy dust. The kind of thing Miranda would razz him about without mercy if he ever admitted to it, but it was true. She reached over him and picked up the bottle of wine from the floor, half hanging off the bed, giving him a view of her ass so magnificent that he reached out to hold it. She took a swig, once again straight from the bottle, swishing the wine in her mouth before swallowing.

"My God, that's good."

She twisted toward him, the swivel of her lithe body sending a ripple of desire through him that he was too exhausted to act on. She held the bottle up in question, but he shook his head. She crawled up him to kiss. When her tongue met his, he thought that this was a much better way to taste the wine. She looked at him so tenderly when the kiss ended, stroking the side of his face with her hand, then lay back down, snuggling her head to his shoulder. The weight of her breasts against the side of his body, her head on his shoulder, her leg twined around his, were sticky in the too warm room, but Doug didn't mind.

"Why don't we play it by ear?" she said.

Doug sighed. He didn't want to play it by ear. After this dreadful day, he wanted a plan, and assurances of safety, even though he knew there was no such thing.

"That's the best I'm going to get, isn't it?"

"Pretty much."

He fell silent, stroking her back, enjoying the feel of her dewey skin, so smooth and soft under his fingertips. The drowsy pull of sleep began to tug on him like the horizon tugs the setting sun.

"I meant the rest," he said, voice hushed. "Getting married, having babies."

If he hadn't been so utterly exhausted it would have made him nervous, saying it intentionally instead of spontaneously, as he had before. It wasn't like they had talked about long-term anything, but he wanted her—needed for her—to know. He wanted a life with Skye, not just a lover and a partner in crime. He wanted to be her husband and be able to call her his wife. He wanted there to be a them, their union witnessed by their friends and sanctified by faith.

"I know," she said, a deep, sleepy fondness filling her voice.

"So... If I ask, you'll say yes?"

Her breathing deepened, smoothed out. Doug wasn't sure if she'd heard him or drifted off.

"I just did, my love," she murmured. "Go to sleep."

22

THE SCRAPE of teeth against leather sent a bolt of fear through Miranda's brain. She tumbled down, the zombie on top of her, and smacked her head against the trunk of a downed tree. She blinked, dazed. A bright stab of pain lit up her left wrist, pinned under her in a position it shouldn't go. She knew what was happening, knew it was real, but her brain still couldn't wrap around it. There was a zombie on her—attacking her. Only the collar of her leather jacket had saved her from its bite.

The zombie gnawed on her upturned collar, but it wouldn't be enough. She was wedged alongside the downed tree, the gray and white lichens and splinters of decaying wood pinching against her cheek. Moans, snarls, and hisses filled the forest. Stumbling feet, bare and in rotting shoes, closed in on her. And the smell of death, thick and cloying, clogging her senses and lighting up her lizard brain with one message: run.

Delilah's snarls mingled with the zombie's grunts. Miranda could see the pit bull's front paws digging into the earth while she pulled on whatever part of the zombie she'd latched on to.

The zombie on her grunted, sounding impatient that it was making no progress through the leather of her jacket. She saw her knife—jarred from her hand, just out of reach. She scrabbled the fingers of her free hand in the decomposing leaf litter that blanketed the forest floor, writhing under the zombie's weight. If she could push up with the arm pinned beneath her, maybe she could get out from under it, but she couldn't. She stretched her arm, screaming out with the effort. The tip of the knife's blade was so close. The zombie's weight shifted, its knee digging into the back of her thigh. She screamed, but her throat was dry, making it sound like a croak. The reek of what on anything else would be its breath curled around her face.

A low-pitched *zing* cleaved the air, ending with a dull *thwack.* The zombie slumped, dead weight pressing her against the ground. Cold liquid reeking of death dripped on her head.

"Come on," Phineas said, dragging the zombie away. He grabbed Miranda by the arm, propelling her forward, onto her feet. Delilah raced ahead of them, jumping onto a zombie about to stumble into Alec.

"My arm is fucked," she gasped.

"Just a little farther."

Alec's knife flashed in one hand, his machete in the other. They had to keep up or they'd lose the wake he and Delilah were clearing through the encroaching horde.

"I see it!" Alec shouted.

A zombie reached from his left. He twirled, stabbing the knife into its open mouth with an upward thrust. Miranda cringed when his gloved hand scraped against its teeth. He raised his foot and freed his knife with a kick to the zombie's midsection.

Her injured wrist glanced off a tree as they ran. She cried out when the fiery pain shot through her fingertips. Phineas' grip on her arm tightened so much it hurt. Alec looked back.

She could see it now, the blast door to the bunker, only twenty yards away. Alec hacked and stabbed ahead of them. Phineas' labored breathing huffed in and out, along with her own. They half slid into the bowl-shaped depression leading to the ramp.

Alec jerked to a halt under the lintel that sheltered the blast door. Shouting into the intercom, he said, "Kendall! Let us in!"

Another jab of pain lanced her side as she and Phineas stumbled up the ramp, but it was just a side stitch.

"Kendall," she gasped, her breathing labored. "Please! Let us in."

The moans that they had briefly outdistanced grew louder. Phineas' pleas were frantic with fear. The zombies had started to stumble into the bowl. Some tripped over the zombies that littered the ground from the last time they'd entered, pursued then as now. Sweat stung Miranda's eyes. She looked up to the camera.

"Kendall," she said, so desperate that she'd agree to whatever he wanted. She didn't care—she'd do it. "Please! Open the—"

Everything else became a roar of background noise when the pneumatic hiss of the door's locking mechanism engaged. Slowly, so slowly, it hissed like a punctured tire slowly losing air, then was followed by a soft clunk. They crowded at the gap as the door swung inward. Alec shoved her forward, heedless of her cries when he grabbed her by her injured wrist. The door wasn't open quite wide enough, and the knobby bones of her upper back scraped against the wall. She tripped over Delilah as she fell into the entryway between the two blast doors. Phineas, then Alec, squeezed through. Phineas slammed on the red button that reversed the door's direction.

A desiccated, rotting hand shot through the gap as the door thudded shut. The hand sagged but didn't fall, still attached to the crushed arm—and zombie—on the other side. The gasps of their labored breathing echoed off the concrete walls.

"We made it," she said. The hiss of the second blast door sounded like a symphony.

"I'll take tigers any day," Phineas wheezed.

A minute later, running footsteps echoed from beyond the first switchback down into the bunker. Miranda wiped at her sweaty forehead, then looked at Alec. His face was flushed, with dirt and mud and splashes of black zombie gunk.

"I can't believe he let us in," Alec said.

Kendall burst into view at the switchback, barely missing a step when he saw them. Miranda climbed to her feet, the effort gargantuan. Kendall only slowed when he was almost to them. His eyes were wide as he looked them over. Then he looked at Miranda. She had never been happier to see that puzzled owl blink.

"Are you okay?" Kendall asked.

Tears began to pool in her eyes, then overspilled. Wonder and gratitude overwhelmed her.

"You saved us."

IT TOOK A SECOND TO REMEMBER WHERE SHE WAS. THE bunker, she thought, relief flooding her system. The lights in the living area of the dome were dimmed, and a blanket had been thrown over her. She heard Delilah wuffle in her sleep. When she looked to find her, she groaned and rubbed her neck with her right hand. She had a crick in her neck, right at the base of her skull, but after today it wasn't worth mentioning. Delilah wuffled again, and Miranda located her on the couch. The pit bull's paws twitched, carrying her as she ran in her dreams.

Miranda remembered sitting in the recliner earlier. The gel ice pack wrapped around her wrist—which was immobilized by a splint—was a mushy room temperature. She pressed the button to lower the footrest, grateful it wasn't something that required her injured arm. Her body felt heavy when she stood, the muscles depleted after all the running, but she didn't think she'd fall back asleep. After getting a decent stretch of sleep without nightmares, she wanted to quit while she was ahead.

She got a drink of water and took more of the anti-inflammatory meds that Kendall had supplied from Med/Surg, then decided she'd go the library to get a book. Even as she walked down the outer ring corridor, she knew she wasn't going there. Part of her shied away from talking to Kendall, but she knew she had to. Only when she bypassed the closest lounge leading to the center of the dome did she admit to herself she was seeking him out.

Palestrina, or something very like it, was playing. Not "Like as the Hart," she'd have recognized that, but an acapella choral piece with melodies and harmonies that swelled and receded, sometimes together, sometimes apart. The warm, moist air of the garden dome wrapped around her like a hug, but her heart still pounded in her chest. Her palms were suddenly tacky with sweat. She could hear Kendall's warm tenor singing along with the music and allowed herself a moment to enjoy it. This was the Kendall she liked most—the guy who grew vegetables and sang so beautifully it made her heart ache. The fact that he'd let them inside had to mean that this was who Kendall was fundamentally—didn't it?

She walked toward his voice, past the potting table and the music player in the center of the garden. He looked up as she approached, then went back to his work. He didn't stop singing, and she didn't interrupt him. She looked around and saw a five-gallon bucket with two inches of water at the bottom. She tipped the water out and turned the bucket upside-down so she could sit.

Kendall worked for another ten minutes, then fiddled in a pocket of the gardening smock he wore. The music faded low enough to become background music. He looked at her, though his face was tipped down, like a shy teenager might do.

"How are you feeling?"

"Okay. Alive, thanks to you."

Kendall looked away, dismissing her praise. "Now I know what to do with a dislocated wrist."

"You and Alec did a good job." She took a deep breath, working up her nerve. She wasn't good at this, but it was past time she started working on it. "I'm sorry for the way I acted before we left. I was so out of line. Rich dying wasn't your fault. How I felt about it is beside the point." She sighed. "You came through when it counted, and I owe you my life. We'd be dead if you hadn't let us in. I certainly didn't give you a reason to want to."

He looked at her again from the cover of his downcast face. Then he tipped another nearby five-gallon bucket upside down and sat down next to her, gnawing on his lip. "I don't know why I lied about how long the codes were good for except... This is all I have. I know it's a lot. Too much, really. You were right to be angry."

You idiot, she thought. How on Earth had she missed it? Of course Kendall was afraid to lose what he had—it was *all* he had. Of course he'd be ambivalent, and withhold, and be unsure about their motives. In retrospect, it was incredible that he'd been so generous. Or so starved for human interaction that he felt like he needed to buy their interest and attention. A wave of sadness crashed over her, that anyone would feel that desperate. She'd seen how much Kendall had, and taken his ambivalence for greed and selfishness, but she'd been wrong.

He'd been afraid, and why wouldn't he be? Alone all this time, and then they show up. And we do want his food, she thought.

And on top of all that, she'd been a bit of an asshole to him.

"I should have realized," she said softly. "I misjudged you, Kendall. I'm sorry for that. We do want something from you." She chuffed out a laugh. "Shit, we were planning to take it from you, if you wouldn't give it. You were right to be afraid, and to question our motives."

"Really?" Kendall said, surprise raising his eyebrows almost to his hairline.

"Yeah," she said. "We lost a lot of our crops when the zombies got inside our defenses, when San Jose attacked LO. Then we lost most of what was left to a blight. We don't have enough food, and we've got people coming for the vaccine that we can't turn away. Everything nearby has already been picked clean, so we have to send people out farther, for less, and it's really dangerous. And it still might not be enough."

Kendall said, "Huh." He owl blinked at her a few times. "I knew there was something, but I couldn't figure out what it was. But you were all so...nice. I wasn't sure what to think."

"Yeah," she said. "Us, neither. I mean, we'd want to help you even if we didn't need the food, but we didn't know you, so we couldn't just ask. If you said no, that would get awkward fast. And then—" She stopped. She could feel a hot blush creeping up her face. "And then you seemed to like me... I didn't want to lead you on, but we needed to see if you might just give us the food so I...kind of played along." Her voice trailed away, and she sighed. "Christ on a bike...it's all so..."

"Tawdry?"

She laughed, startled by his suggestion. "Yeah," she said, and was pleased to see that he smiled. "Tawdry."

She enjoyed the feeling of sitting together, the shared joke softening the edges of what had been difficult to admit.

"Are you still planning to just take the food?" Kendall asked her.

Miranda shrugged. "Do we need to?"

"No," he said.

The relief that washed over her didn't feel like a wave. It felt like tsunami. "That's good, because we don't know where it is."

Kendall owl blinked and actually grinned. "If you'd asked before, I probably would have said no. You weren't wrong."

Miranda sighed. "Why are words so damn hard? I've always sucked at this."

Kendall didn't reply at first, then said, "I don't think words are the problem, Miranda. It's taking a risk and being powerless to change the outcome."

Unbidden, she thought of Mario's smile, the one that softened his hard edges. The dark eyes that changed from severe to approachable as soon as the crow's feet that crinkled their corners appeared, the swell of his cheek as it morphed from chiseled to...she didn't know what to call it, but it was softer —sweeter.

"Can I ask you something?"

"Yes," she said, relieved to have her train of thought derailed.

"Did you ever feel...anything for me?"

She forced herself to look at him, because it would be easier to look at her feet. Kendall deserved more than that. "Beyond friendship, no."

"You're in love with Alec, aren't you?"

She was too stunned to speak for a moment. "You know about that?"

Kendall gave her a pained look. "I'm socially awkward, Miranda. I'm not blind."

"No," she said softly, with a rueful smile. "I guess you're

not. And no, I'm not in love with him. I like Alec a lot, but it's new. I'm not looking for anything serious."

Kendall's appraising stare seemed to go right through her. It surprised her, in part because she'd never seen this before. He was analyzing, calculating, evaluating, and a glimpse of the CEO he'd once been peeked out from across the years. "But there's someone."

"No," she said, shaking her head. "There's not."

He narrowed his eyes, and looked as if he were about to disagree, then nodded. "It'll be better this time, won't it? You being stuck here because of all the zombies outside."

"No lies? No ulterior motives? It'll be downright boring," she said. She fell silent, thinking about the disaster of getting halfway down Mount Hood, then needing to fall back. They'd only left the bunker twelve hours ago but it felt like a lifetime. "I don't know how we're going to get home. If we had a vehicle, we could do it, but on foot? It's not going to happen right now."

"I've got a couple vehicles."

"You do?" she said, a squeak of surprise in her voice.

"Of course I do," he said, the owl blink making him looked puzzled. "It's a secret doomsday bunker, Miranda. I'll show you everything tomorrow, okay? With Alec and Phineas."

"Okay," she said. It was a wish coming true—the food, a vehicle, this lightness between them. She ought to be able to manage something better, but she added, equally lamely, "That'll be great."

She stood, feeling a thousand pounds lighter than when she'd entered. Even her wrist didn't feel as sore, though she knew it would again, and soon.

She fell in step beside Kendall, thinking about how different this week was ending, compared to how it had begun. Grace undeserved and freely given—that was what Connor had said to her once—was what she was feeling now. She wondered how much food there was, and what Kendall was willing to give them. How they'd get it to LO safely with so many zombies roaming around, but she'd think about that tomorrow.

Unable to help herself, she craned her neck to look up at Kendall, feeling the crick in her neck. "I don't suppose you have a lot of trucks. Like a fleet of zombie-proof vehicles we can use to get the food home?"

The faintest trace of smile ghosted over Kendall's face. He looked like the cat that's eaten the cream.

"Don't worry about that," he said. "If we can find someone who can get it working, I have something much better."

***

"HOLY SHIT."

Phineas' voice was hoarse and filled with disbelief. Miranda nodded, even though she knew none of the others were looking at her. Above her, the lights clanked on by sections, from one end of the cavernous space to the other.

When she'd seen the food storeroom, she thought nothing else could surprise her. She'd severely underestimated Kendall's ability to boggle the mind.

They'd been right about there being more to the bunker, and access was through Kendall's quarters as they'd thought. The revelations began with his quarters, which hadn't started out that way. Originally, his double dome had been the armory, which accounted for the weird layout, and the utilitarian kitchen and bathroom. Kendall had moved all the weapons out, torn down shelves, added lighting and fixtures, and repurposed dividers to hang his art collection. This was after he realized the security guys who'd been his only company weren't coming back. He'd needed something to do, he'd told them, and something big, because he'd started cracking up. Everything he'd shown them so far had been gobsmackingly stunning. Stunning in the truest sense of the word—senses overwhelmed to the point of being dulled, astonishment that rooted you in place and left you dazed.

But this... This was like stepping into a James Bond movie at the part where the villain's secret lair is revealed. She stood in a hanger bay, with a ceiling so high it was lost in shadow. There were blast doors at the far end bigger than a house. A row of vehicles lined the walls at this end, but it was what sat near the blast doors that stole the show. She roused herself, following the others to the helicopter.

"This is military," Alec said as she joined them.

Kendall nodded. "It's a Sikorsky S-61R. The Air Force and Coast Guard used them. Grendall had a contract with the D.O.D to develop an alternative, renewable power source, so they wouldn't be reliant on fossil fuels. Across the board, I mean. This was the second prototype. When we went on to the third, well..." He shrugged. "I shouldn't have it, but you know how it is."

Miranda barked out a laugh. "I don't think we do. It's huge."

Kendall grinned at her. "It's seventy-three feet long and eighteen feet high. The rotor diameter is sixty-two feet." He jutted his chin at the blast doors beyond the helicopter. "We modeled the blast doors on Cheyenne Mountain."

"What's that?" Phineas asked.

"*How* old are you?" Kendall asked.

"Twenty," said Phineas.

"Never mind," Kendall said, shaking his head.

Miranda walked along the helicopter, the metal of its body cool under her hand. She turned back to Kendall. "How big is this room?"

Kendall pursed his lips and squinted his eyes, which looked up and to the left while he thought. "I don't remember," he finally said, shrugging his shoulders. "There's a pad outside that's big enough for taking off and landing."

Alec had climbed into the helicopter through the open side door. He turned around and said, "How the hell did you build this place?"

"It took a long time," Kendall said.

"I meant who did you pay off, to do it so close to a major metropolitan area?" When Kendall didn't say anything right away, Alec added, "Reporter. Remember?"

"You probably don't want to know," Kendall said, looking sheepish.

The sly smile stole across Alec's lips. "I probably do. Does it still work? Can you fly it?"

Kendall shrugged again. "I don't know if it will still work. I can't fly it, but the fuel cell we developed still works. I've maintained it... It gave me something to do. But the rest..." He waved vaguely at the helicopter. "I'm sure it needs maintenance, maybe some repairs, after sitting so long."

"All we need is a pilot!" Phineas called, excited. "This thing's dope!"

Miranda looked around, trying to see where Phineas had gone. Alec hopped down, out of the helicopter, and jutted his chin toward the cockpit. "He's in there."

When she stood on tiptoes, Miranda could see Phineas in the pilot's seat. He looked like a kid on a free toy shopping spree.

"Don't touch anything, Phineas!" she barked at him. "Christ," she said to Alec. "It's probably got missiles. How much you wanna bet he's pressing buttons?"

Phineas appeared in the open side door a moment later. "I heard that, Miranda, but now I'm wondering." He smiled hopefully, his dark eyes flashing. "If I learn how to fly this thing, will I get that date?"

Miranda laughed. "Sure. If you can fly it, you've got it."

Phineas' mouth fell open. "Really?"

"Of course not," she said, laughing harder.

"I'd go out with you, Phineas, if it meant you could fly it," Alec said. Then he added, "Where the hell are we going to find a pilot?"

Miranda looked from face to face, wishing one of them had an idea. They all seemed to be doing the same.

"There's got to be someone who can do it," Phineas said.

"There must," Kendall agreed.

Miranda glanced at Alec. The doubt in his eyes reflected her own.

"You can still use the trucks. To get home," Kendall said. "And as many as you need to get the food there."

Miranda straightened up. The helicopter was impressive, and if they could use it... Her mind raced with the possibilities. Then, reluctantly, she dismissed them for now. Spending time thinking about how to use this helicopter was like wasting the day planning how to spend your lottery millions.

"C'mon," she said. "Let's check out the trucks."

23

"THE BRIDGE IS JUST AHEAD," Phineas said. "Looks locked up tight."

"Good," Miranda said.

The rush of relief felt good, even though they weren't really home yet. They'd spent two days getting a truck in working order. Even though the truck they now drove needed the least amount of work, they'd still had to replace deteriorated hoses, drain and refill fluids, and replace rusted brake rotors. It had taken a while to track down the parts, since Kendall had moved things around when he moved the armory, but not kept track of where he'd put what. Traveling to Portland from the bunker hadn't been so bad with a vehicle. Portland east of the Willamette had been trickier, but manageable. They just needed to get through the rest of the city on the other side of the river, and they'd be golden.

"Sorry," Alec said, when he hit a pothole hard enough that it jarred the truck.

Miranda winced, her wrist flaring when Delilah jostled it. She looked over her shoulder as much as she could to check the bed. It was filled with crates of food, plus one or two of booze from the liquor store they'd discovered on the way to the bunker. They'd had to cool their jets for a few hours because there were so many zombies moving around, and hideouts might as well have booze.

"Nothing fell off," she said, nudging Alec with her elbow. "I guess you can stay."

He gave her the sharp edge of a grin, and the flash in his eye made her pulse speed up. Alec slowed the truck to a halt, then Miranda and Phineas and Delilah got out. She peered through the bars and mesh of the barricade. The barricade at the other end of the Ross Island Bridge was similarly intact. They were stopping because everyone had to pee. Unlike Delilah, the people were waiting to get inside the waypoint to do it.

"What do you think, Phineas?"

"Looks good to me," he said.

They opened the gate. Alec drove the truck through. As soon as the gate was closed again, Miranda squatted beside the truck to pee.

"That's better," she sighed, wiggling her foot out of the way. She didn't need boots that smelled like piss.

Alec rejoined her when he finished his business, looking similarly relieved, but Phineas stayed by the steel and concrete parapet overlooking the Willamette River. Delilah trotted from one spot to another, sniffing things.

"There's a boat on the river. Looks like they're mooring at the island," Phineas said.

Alec took Miranda's hand as they went to join Phineas. She felt a little self-conscious, even though she and Alec had been openly affectionate—a little bit—since they'd returned to the bunker. Phineas turned at their approaching footsteps.

"I can't believe you moved in on my girl," he said to Alec, amused long-suffering suffusing his voice.

"Believe it," Alec said, giving her hand a squeeze before releasing it.

Miranda looked down to Ross Island, a tear-shaped atoll in the middle of the river. It was where she, Doug, and Mario had moored their yacht when they arrived in Portland last year. She saw the boat, on the western side of island, and gasped. Her heart leaped out of her chest, pounding so hard the guys had to hear it.

"Miranda, what's wrong?" Alec asked, his voice laced with concern.

She gripped the parapet like it was the only thing holding her up, the concrete's nubbly surface biting into her fingers. It wasn't a boat on the river—it was a yacht. The bow pointed north, toward them, so she couldn't see its name, but the size and color were right. There was no canopy over the cockpit, but that didn't mean anything. It could have been taken down for any number of reasons.

Mario's back, she thought, a rush of emotion hitting her so hard she felt dizzy. Was he okay, and were Doug and Skye? What were they doing here? She was dying to see them—see him—with everything in her, which brought her up short. She was still...indifferently angry with him, if that was even possible, yet awash with anxiety, needing to know if he was all right. Coming back hadn't been the plan, so something was wrong. Something had—

"Is it them?" Phineas said.

Miranda nodded, then said breathlessly, "Yeah. I think so."

THE DINGY WAS THIRTY FEET FROM SHORE WHEN SHE realized it wasn't them. The anticipation and anxiety collapsed in on itself, pulling the glimmer of hopeful surprise with it.

"It's not them," she said.

They stood on the riverbank, a silent trio as the dingy rowed closer. When it was twenty feet out, one of the people opposite the person rowing called out, "Ahoy!"

She looked at the people in the dingy, people who were not Mario or Doug or Skye or Tessa. Since there were only three of them, that was maybe a good thing. Whoever they were, whatever their story was, the disappointment tasted bitter in her mouth.

Alec crouched down and grabbed the rope the people tossed. A minute later they had disembarked. The man, who'd been rowing, introduced himself as Hussein. He was middle-aged and slim, with dark eyes and dark hair. He introduced the two women with him. The older was Fatima, his mother. She looked to be in her seventies, which apart from the priests at SCU wasn't so common anymore. She and her son shared a strong resemblance, except that her black hair that peeked out from under her headscarf didn't have any gray. She had an accent that Miranda couldn't place, apart from Middle Eastern. The younger woman was about thirty and Hussein's daughter, Salma, who'd interrupted her father to say, "Call me Susie." Her face was rounder than her dad's, and her eyes were blue. Like her father, Susie's accent sounded as generic North American as they came.

"You've come from British Columbia?" Miranda said, repeating what Susie had just told her. "Vancouver?"

"I wish. Farther north, from Mackenzie." At their blank looks, she said, "Yeah, we'd never heard of it either until we ended up there. We were on vacation. Dad wanted to see the Canadian Rockies."

Hussein smiled as his head dipped in acknowledgement of his responsibility for ending up in small-town Canada.

Alec said, "Where are you headed?"

"Here," Susie said. "We heard about the vaccine in San Jose a couple years ago. We finally decided to go, but we met some people who told us San Jose was pretty awful, and we'd be better off coming to Portland."

"Beaverton," Fatima said, a note of correction in her voice.

"Yes, *nene*. Beaverton," Susie answered. She pointed to the bridge behind them. "That is the Ross Island Bridge, right? Doug said if—"

"Doug? Doug Michel?" Miranda interrupted, her heart leaping. She held her uninjured hand above her head. "Really tall and skinny?"

Susie's face lit up. "Yes! You know him!"

Then everyone talked at once, but eventually they learned that Susie, Hussein, and Fatima had crossed paths with their friends in Eureka, California.

"And they're okay?"

"Yes," Hussein said. "When we saw them. That was..." He looked to his daughter. "Six or seven weeks ago?"

"That long?" Miranda said. "Then they've made it to San Jose by now."

"I'm sure they did," Hussein said. "They stopped in Eureka because Tessa and Mario were unwell—"

"Mario was sick?" she asked, anxiety spiking through her. So many things could go wrong when traveling long distances. Or short ones, for that matter. What had been so serious that they'd had to interrupt their journey? "Sick with what?"

"Pneumonia," Susie said. "Dad checked them out. He's a doctor."

Hussein said, "They did everything right in terms of treatment: getting off the water for a while to get somewhere drier and warmer, antibiotics, but they didn't have the right ones." He shrugged, grinning. "We did. They were recovering nicely by the time we left."

Miranda nodded, biting on her lower lip as she fell silent. She had no reason to doubt anything they were saying. All they could relay was what they'd known weeks ago, not what had happened since.

Alec said, "But you just got here. It doesn't take six weeks to get here from Northern California on a rig like that." He waved in the direction of the river and the yacht.

Hussein nodded. He crossed his arms and gave his daughter a serious stink eye, his voice arch with reproach. "Unless someone insists on eating questionable sardines and gets so sick she almost dies." He looked back to Alec. "That set us back three weeks."

"She's learned her lesson," Fatima said, patting her son's shoulder.

Susie looked chastened. Her illness had clearly rattled her father and been as bad as he said.

"All's well that ends well," Alec said, smoothing over the awkwardness.

Within the half hour, Fatima and Hussein were sitting in the cab of the truck with Phineas. Miranda, Alec, and Susie sat in the back, the crates rearranged to accommodate them and the belongings of their new acquaintances. Delilah sat between Miranda's knees, since Fatima was nervous of dogs. Alec held on to Miranda's hand, and even though they both wore gloves, his thumb stroked over the back of it. He glanced at her often and, able to see that she was distracted, carried most of the conversation with Susie.

The roar of Miranda's thoughts was deafening, ricocheting until they circled back to their starting point, only to begin again. Just like her tongue had poked at the empty spot of a fallen out tooth when she was a girl, her mind kept poking at the news they'd just received. Mario, Doug and Skye, and Tessa had been on track six or seven weeks ago, which meant they must be back in San Jose for several weeks now. She'd managed to put their journey out of her mind after they left, except for when she had nightmares. It didn't pay to think too hard about where anyone who was traveling might be at any given time, given the danger it always entailed. Better to believe it had gone well.

But this time, arriving safely at their destination didn't mean the danger had passed. Mario's brother Dominic was the head of the City Council now. He'd ordered the attack on LO that had contributed to the possibility of starvation before Kendall's aid was secured. She didn't even know if the Jesuits still held SCU, since they'd been gearing up for a conflict with the Council when she'd left.

All of the anxiety of not knowing surfaced, jumping up and down in her head so hard that she couldn't ignore it. Mario was going after his brother. He'd needed to be ruthless during his years undercover, but it had been for survival—to execute his mission to steal the vaccine. He still felt guilty about the things he'd had to do, the people he'd had to stand by and watch die, and the ones he'd killed himself to keep his cover intact. Dominic was ruthless in a different way. It came naturally to him and was centered in self-interest. Dominic never lost a wink of sleep because of the things he'd done. Dominic might get a pang of sorrow about killing his brother, but it would be only a pang, and would be about what he'd lost, not what he'd done.

Maybe Rocco hadn't been wrong to let Victor work on the ham radio, not that she trusted Victor any more than she ever had. Maybe they'd heard something while she'd been away this time.

Even though she shied away from it, she needed to know what had happened to Mario, and if he was okay. It was over between them—for good—not like before. She didn't want another chance any more than she wanted something serious with Alec. But for the first time since he'd left, she wasn't thinking in terms of how Mario had wronged her, but of his welfare. However she spun it, she was worried.

IT HAD BEGUN TO RAIN ALMOST AS SOON AS THEY GOT ON the road after picking up Hussein, Fatima, and Susie, which shifted the weather from cold to creep-into-your-bones chilling. So Miranda wasn't surprised that the group waiting for them in LO's parking lot was small.

Immediately, Miranda picked out Rocco at the back of the group. He was talking to Mathilde. Miranda could barely move her limbs to climb out of the truck bed. Her body felt leaden and at the same time, filled with anxious energy. She could see Mathilde searching the group, trying to find Rich.

She hated this, fucking hated it—another wife widowed, more children left fatherless, a hole punched into the lives of so many people that would never be filled. She knew for a fact that Rocco had been talking to Rich about splitting up the responsibilities of commander between the two of them and River. In addition to losing a good friend, he was losing a partner in running LO and keeping everyone safe. Rich had been here almost from the start. He'd earned the community's trust. His absence would leave a void that couldn't be filled.

She took a deep breath and caught Rocco's eye. He blinked, and she saw recognition in his eyes almost immediately that something was wrong. Mathilde had stopped and stood shivering as she searched the group for Rich. She only wore a shirt, with a thin cardigan sweater over it that didn't look very warm. She must have dashed over from wherever she'd been without bothering with her coat. A confused hesitance had drawn her eyebrows together and pursed her lips. When she saw Miranda coming toward her, her china-blue eyes went blank, and her jaw slack.

"No," she whispered.

When her hand dropped to her abdomen, Miranda missed a step. Oh Jesus, she's pregnant, she thought, heart plummeting. Mathilde wasn't showing yet, but she knew instinctively what the gesture meant. Rich hadn't said anything... He probably hadn't known yet that he would be a father again, maybe a girl this time after two boys. Mathilde took another step back, her head shaking back and forth, as if she could change what was coming if she refused to believe it. The people around Mathilde had realized something was wrong. They rippled away, as if misfortune were contagious.

"I couldn't save him," Miranda said, now a few feet away. Behind Mathilde, Rocco put his hand on her shoulder. She didn't even notice.

"No. Miranda, no," Mathilde said, her voice imploring. Tears glittered in her eyes, balancing on the tangle of her eyelashes.

"I'm so sorry," Miranda said, feeling her own face screw up.

Mathilde crumpled, her raw sobs soft as a whisper. Rocco pulled Mathilde into his arms, dwarfing her petite frame. Miranda stood in the freezing rain, helpless to do anything but watch the devastation play out again.

THEY MADE IT BACK TO HER PLACE A FEW HOURS LATER. The townhouse looked so normal, as if nothing had changed, when it felt like everything had. It had taken a few hours to get Mathilde settled. Then they'd needed to update Rocco on the good—Kendall agreeing to help them with food and anything else he might have that he could spare, and the bad—how Rich had been killed, and that her repellant effect was gone, too. And they'd wanted to check in on Hussein, Fatima, and Susie, and make sure that they were settled. Now, she felt wrung out, but wired, too.

Alec pulled the door shut behind them. "D'you want a drink, lass?"

"Yeah," she said, giving him an almost weak smile. "Delilah will want her supper. There's dog food in the pantry, if you don't mind."

He shrugged out of his jacket and hung it on a hook by the door, giving her shoulder a squeeze as he walked past her to the kitchen. She peeled off her own coat and unlaced her combat boots enough to tug her feet free. Her socks were damp, so she pulled them off, too. She started to adjust her bra, which had gotten wet along with her shirt, after she took off her coat and wrapped it around Mathilde. It was still damp and had been driving her crazy. She wriggled it off from under her shirt, mostly successful at not jostling her wrist. She threw the bra at her boots; it snagged on one of the top clasps like a tatty flag. Alec returned and handed her a glass. She hadn't realized he'd brought a bottle of the Scotch with him, but the amber liquid at the bottom couldn't be anything else.

She said, "You're prepared for everything, aren't you?"

He smiled at her, a mixture of sad and gentle. Tiredness tugged at his eyes, giving them an almost glassy reflectiveness.

"That sucked," he said.

She laughed, but it was brittle, and without mirth. "Nothing like telling someone their husband is dead to take the shine off things."

She took another drink, a gulp this time. She'd known she had to break the news to Mathilde, but learning she was pregnant made it so much worse. The day's discovery about Mario and her friends felt like a low hum at the base of her skull. The only good thing about coming home—apart from being safe behind the palisade—had been telling Rocco that Kendall would help them. For a moment, Miranda thought he was going to cry.

She felt out of sorts after learning that the people they'd found had seen her friends, Mario most of all. It left her restless and agitated. Passing on the news, retelling Rich's final moments, had only increased her disquiet. She wanted to crawl out of her skin to get away from the curdled feeling of loss.

Alec took a step closer and tipped her chin up so that she looked into his hazel eyes. "Is there anything I can do?"

It was just a question, a sincere one. A query to see if he could comfort her in a way that would help. Her skin lit like a firecracker. Her breathing shallowed. She could almost feel her pupils dilate as a tidal wave of desire crashed over her.

"I want you to fuck me."

She saw the surprise in his eyes, but also the same hunger that gnawed her insides—the hunger to know he was still alive. And wanting to forget for a little while. He kissed her, not with gentleness, but force. She moaned into his mouth, filled with a need to connect, to overwhelm, to drown herself in him. His tongue raked across hers, his strong hands tangling in her hair. She pushed against him, nipples already hard when they pressed against his chest. He pulled her shirt over her head, ripped his own off just as quickly, and seized her soft breasts with hands made rough by an urgency that matched her own. When he ducked his head to suckle, lips hot and teeth sharp, she gasped at the electric current of pleasure that rushed through her body, straight to her center.

She pulled him up to her mouth again, rocking her hips against his. She felt his cock trapped between them, already hard. She fumbled one-handed to unfasten his belt. He finished the button fly, pushing his jeans and briefs down. He came free and she took him in her hand, fingers closing around his hardness and heat. He gasped, then groaned into the side of her neck. She bumped against the wall while he unfastened her jeans and shoved them down. When he pulled her to him, his tongue hard against hers, hands hot where they gripped her waist, she wanted to tell him everything...about Tadpole and Mario and how she'd burned them to the ground without understanding why. About fighting with Doug and how much hearing about them both today had stirred things up and whipped her about, until she felt disoriented and lost, at the mercy of feelings she couldn't name and hadn't known were there, buried deep under the anger.

But Alec whirled her around and pushed her against the wall, and the moment passed. Her arms slid up above her head, bending back at the elbows. She shuddered at the painful squeeze of her breasts against the textured plaster, at the unyielding grip of Alec's hand on the base of her skull as he kissed her shoulders, her neck, the shivers racing across her skin crackling like air charged before a storm.

She arched her low back, pushing her ass against him. He shoved into her soft wetness, his breath hot on her neck. A head rush of desire at this rough treatment electrified her, setting every nerve ending in her body on fire. It was exactly what she wanted, to be fucked rough and hard, to feel his desire and need churn into hers. She quaked at the rush of pleasure when his cock filled her, raking back and forth over her G-spot. She funneled her anger at every fucked-up thing that had happened into the movement of her body against his, letting it stoke her desire, feed off the lush pleasure of his body on hers.

A moan escaped her, low in her throat. The heat and ire, the frustration and loneliness, welled up inside her. Alec set their punishing rhythm as the tension built. His breath was ragged, the growl in his throat ringing in her ears. She whimpered, crying out, arching her back even more. She wanted to feel all of him—the sizzle of his chest against her shoulders, the sharp pull of his fingers tangled in her hair, his fingernails digging into the side of her waist, the slap of his pelvis against her ass as he thrust his cock inside her, trapping her between him and the wall.

The abyss rushed toward her, suspending her on its razor-thin edge. He groaned her name, and she knew he wouldn't last much longer. The thought sent her flying like sparks from a fire, the dizzying updraft almost making her come. Her engorged womb trembled, so, so close, a hair's breadth away. His cock raked over her G-spot again and she disappeared, engulfed by the orgasm that consumed her. Nothing—pain or loss, confusion or anger, hope or sorrow—could withstand the force of the white-hot pleasure rippling out from his cock's blunt incursion. He followed her moments later, driving deep inside her as he shuddered through his climax.

Miranda panted in uneven gulps. Sweat trickled down the swell of her compressed breasts. Alec's body lay heavy against her, pinning her in place, the heat of his ragged breath soft on her neck. Her wrist throbbed in time with her heart. They stood together, gasping and raw, until his grip on the back of her head grew slack. She turned in his arms, melting against him, as the first sob slipped out. Despite her relief over LO's deliverance, what had been lost and could never be salvaged overwhelmed it.

Alec's hand stroked her hair, just above her ear, the gesture so gentle it made her cry harder.

"It's all right, lass," he whispered. "It'll be all right."

WHEN SHE WAS ALMOST TO THE DOOR, SHE REALIZED THE banging wasn't on her door, but Noelle's. She tried without success to get Delilah to shut up. Her barking could raise the dead; on more than one occasion, it had. Concern for her neighbor flared in her chest, because nobody banged on a door like that unless something was wrong. She had only seen Noelle and Gemma for maybe an hour since getting back yesterday. She and Alec had stopped by Mathilde's in the morning—one of those short, shitty visits that you ended up being glad you made. Then Alec had made himself scarce, which she appreciated. She'd had her own stuff to do, helping Rocco figure out logistics for getting the food to LO, mostly. They'd be doing it by ground, what with helicopter pilots being in short supply.

She yanked the door open. Larry, the Comm Shack Operator, stood at Noelle's open door. He looked red-faced and was out of breath.

"Larry," she said. "What's going on?"

"Oh, Miranda. Good, I was going to get you, too."

"For what?"

A man's large frame filled the space of Noelle's front door, holding Gemma on his hip. Miranda's heart sank. Clearly, Noelle had paid no attention to anything she'd told her.

She said, with narrowed eyes and undisguised hostility, "Victor?" at the exact same time that Larry, his voice filled with relief, said, "Victor!"

"What is—" she began, but Larry cut her off.

"We need you at the Comm Shack," Larry said to Victor. "Your guy is on the ham radio, but he's being really squirrely. I'm not sure he'll even wait."

Victor nodded. "Let me get my boots on." As he turned back inside, Miranda heard him say to Gemma, "I gotta go to work, Gemmy. I'll have to come back..."

"What guy?" Miranda said to Larry.

"Victor found someone on the ham just outside San Jose. They've been trading information."

"Does Rocco know about this?"

"Yeah, yeah," Larry said, distracted. "You should come, too, Miranda. Rocco will meet us there."

Victor returned, and Delilah started barking again. Miranda looked at Larry, then at Victor, feeling severely out of the loop. Larry was in a state. She'd get more answers if she just went along.

"Let me get my coat."

They arrived at the Comm Shack a few minutes later. Phineas leaped out of the chair, handing off the handset to Victor. Rocco nodded a greeting as he stepped out of Victor's way.

Victor depressed the button, waited a few seconds, then said, "This is SEA-TAC for SJC. Are you watching the game this weekend? Over."

The radio crackled, then an anxious voice said, "SEA-TAC? Who are you rooting for, Stanford or Cal? Over."

It had to be a code to confirm identity, and perhaps if both parties could talk. Victor said, "Cal, of course. Over."

"Me too," SJC said, sounding relieved. "I know it's been a few weeks... I couldn't get away." Miranda's brow scrunched. Something about the voice sounded familiar. "Stanford won this time. Cal's not playing anymore. Over."

Victor's eyes darted quickly to Miranda, then away. "Did they sack the quarterback? Over."

"No," SJC said. "Not sure where he's practicing. Half the team is with him. The rest were cut. Over."

Victor frowned. "How long ago did this happen? Over."

"Three weeks ago." They waited for a long moment, then SJC added belatedly, "Sorry. Over."

The flat, midwestern consonants. The fussy, flustered anxiety at forgetting the radio etiquette. She knew that voice...

"You've got to be fucking kidding me," Miranda said.

Everyone looked at her. Rocco mouthed, 'What?' but she barely noticed because she was looking at Victor. He was shaking his head and chuckling softly, impressed confirmation in his eyes. Victor was talking to Harold, her go-to, get anything, lingerie-connection colleague from the Farm. Harold had gotten her the gear they'd needed to escape San Jose with the vaccine serum, but left out the part about selling them out to the Council. She reached out and caught Victor's hand that held the handset.

"Wait a second," she said. "Who is he talking about?"

Victor didn't miss a beat. "The Council—Stanford—has overrun your people at SCU; they're Cal. The QB is Father Walter, and I'm guessing cut means captured or executed."

"What?" Miranda gasped. The Council had attacked the Jesuits, and now held SCU? Half of them were in hiding, the others dead? Victor waited the stunned few moments she took to process what he was saying.

"SEA-TAC, are you still there? Over."

"Can I answer?" Victor said to her.

Miranda nodded, still reeling. This was new information, so it had only happened recently. What the hell was going on at home?

"SJC, please stand by. Over."

"What about our people there?" Rocco said. "Find out if they got caught up in this."

Miranda took a deep breath, then another. "That's Harold, from the Farm."

"Yeah," Victor said.

Then she realized what Rocco had said. "Are you talking about Mario and Doug?" she said, so horrified she hardly got the words out. Because of course they'd be at SCU. Skye and Tessa, too, and now the Council had finally managed to defeat them?

She rounded on Victor. "I knew it," she said softly. "I fucking knew we couldn't trust you. You sold them out."

Rocco said, "Tucci, what's going—"

Miranda lunged for Victor. There was no plan of attack, no strategy, no thought—just rage. Victor barely got his hands up before she collided with him.

"I haven't sold anyone out," he said, trying to fend her off.

Rocco's huge arm wrapped around Miranda's chest and shoulders. He yanked her away from Victor like she weighed no more than a doll. The tension filling the Comm Shack was sudden and thick, and so combustible it would only take a spark to blow off the roof.

"SEA-TAC?"

Not bothering to get permission this time, Victor snapped, "*Stand by.*"

"Tucci," Rocco said softly in Miranda's ear, his arm holding her tight. "What do you mean?"

She could barely hear Rocco over her own ragged breath. He turned her around to face him, his huge hands holding her by her shoulders.

"Tucci," Rocco said again. "What do you mean?"

"Harold...he's the one who betrayed us when we left San Jose for Santa Cruz. We were attacked, and then we found out later he'd been—that part doesn't matter. But if he—" She glared at Victor. "If he's working with Harold, he's already told the Council we're not dead. They've probably got another strike team on the way here!"

Rocco took a deep breath, scrunching his eyes shut. "Listen to me, Tucci," he said, his brown eyes steady and calm. "I need you to settle down. Can you do that for me?"

"Rocco—"

"Can you do that for me?" Rocco said again. His brows knitted together, and his brown eyes drilled through her. Even though his voice was soft, he looked like the intimidating, unfriendly guy she'd met last year. The guy who'd snap anyone giving him shit like a twig and never give it a second thought.

"Yes."

Again, the radio crackled. "SEA-TAC?"

Rocco pushed Miranda behind him and said to Victor, "Do we have a problem here?"

"No," Victor said, his voice firm. "I've been straight with you, Rocco. I," he hesitated, glancing at Miranda with something like trepidation. Then he continued in a softer voice. "I want to be here for Noelle and Gemma. I'm not going to fuck that up."

Rocco looked at Victor for an agonizingly long moment, then said, "Find out if our people were taken."

Miranda bit her tongue to keep from screaming, so hard she tasted blood. What was Rocco thinking, still letting Victor near that radio? How could he not see what she did, that Victor not only couldn't be trusted, but had probably already betrayed them?

Victor turned back to the radio unit. "Sorry about that, SJC. Some tailgaters were coming your way for the game. Should have arrived around the last time we talked. Can you tell me if anyone arrived before Stanford won? Over."

Harold's voice said, "I need a little more than that to go on."

Which meant names. Which meant...

"Why is Harold even cooperating with you?" Miranda demanded.

"I'll tell you when we're done here," Victor said to her.

"Rocco, we can't trust him."

"We don't have a choice," Rocco answered. "Who do we ask him about—Mario or Doug?"

It felt like the ground was crumbling under her feet. If Harold knew either Mario or Doug were back in San Jose and he was still working with the Council, as soon as this call ended, he'd tell them. They'd turn the Valley upside down until they found them. Unless they already had, and they were among those the Council had already killed... Her stomach heaved at the thought, the acid burn of bile hitting the back of her throat. A rush of light-headedness made her dizzy. If they were still alive and Victor and Harold were betraying them, whoever's name she gave would be a death sentence, perhaps for both of them.

"No," she said to Rocco, shaking her head.

"Tucci," he said, his voice brooking no argument. "Who is he more likely to have information about, Mario or Doug?"

Her head swam, and her stomach roiled. Her lover or her best friend? It was an impossible choice, whoever she chose, and she could never take it back.

"Doug," she said, barely able to hear her own voice. It sounded hollow and distorted, like it had traveled through a thousand gallons of water. But the click of the handset sounded as final as the crack of a judge's gavel.

"Doug Michel. Over."

No response, then a bark of surprise. "Doug Michel? Father Doug Michel? Are... Are you shitting me?" Harold's high, tinny laugh squeaked through the speakers. "No. He left almost a year ago and hasn't been back."

The silence that filled the Comm Shack felt leaden. Miranda felt dizzy...light-headed. There was no air, no oxygen, nothing to breathe. If Doug and the others had made it to San Jose, and the Council had attacked the Jesuits and won, someone like Harold—who traded information—should know.

Someone would have seen Doug during the fighting. That he'd go unnoticed under those circumstances beggared belief. Doug would defend SCU with his life, whether he was a priest or not.

But if he wasn't there, where was he? And what had happened to the others?

24

"WHY DID YOU CHOOSE DOUG?"

The voice was disembodied, coming from everywhere and nowhere. Miranda looked around. There was no one beside her on the bench, nor the other a few feet away. No one stood by the statue of Saint Clare. She stood, gravel crunching under her feet, the darkness complete. She walked to the statue, in case whoever it was stood behind it, but no one did. She was alone in Saint Clare's garden.

The scent of rosemary hung heavy in the air. There were no lights anywhere, none at all, not even the moon or stars overhead. She should be able to see a light somewhere, at one of the gates, or in one of the buildings, or the ambient glow of downtown San Jose a mile away, but there was nothing. But she cast a shadow. She could see its clear edges, the elongated silhouette of her body on the gravel path before it climbed up the side of the statue. That's not right, she thought. She looked again. Several hundred yards away, lights were on at The Hut, the dive bar near the original north border of SCU's campus.

"Are you going to tell me or not?"

Mario sat on the bench—their bench—where they used to sit and talk. The bench where he'd told her that he loved her and changed their lives forever. His face was in shadow, since the lights from The Hut were behind him.

She said, "Tell you what?"

"Why you didn't give my name."

Her head ached, unable to parse anything from the jumble that filled it. Then a heavy feeling of dread descended. The acrid scent of fear filled the air, overwhelming the earthy aroma of the rosemary.

"I don't know," she said, her voice small—helpless.

Mario stood up, his face still in shadow, and approached her. He held his arms close to his body. A mewling sound caught her ear, and at first she thought he was holding a kitten.

"Do you want it?" he said.

"Oh my God," she said, retreating a step. He was holding a baby, its wriggling form wrapped in a blanket. She knew it was dead. It was unnatural, that it should be dead but still wriggling, dead but still mewling as if it were hungry.

"No? Okay." The mewling stopped. The baby was gone. It was just Mario. His brown eyes were warm, but filled with a grief so profound it hurt to witness. When he spoke again, his voice was so gentle it felt like a caress. "Wouldn't you feel better if you just admitted it?"

"No," she said, a sob building in her chest. She threw the baby at him...she'd been holding it all this time. Her arms ached and throbbed. How long had she been holding it? Something wet rubbed her face. She flinched away—

Delilah whimpered beside her, sniffing and licking her cheek. The wet thing on her face...it was Delilah. She sat up, looking around her living room. The lights were on. Her jeans felt wet, and she realized she'd spilled her glass when she'd passed out.

She reached for the bottle of Scotch on the coffee table. As soon as she lifted it, she could tell by its weight it was empty. It had been almost two-thirds full when she'd started. She got up, barking her shin on the table's sharp corner. Tears filled her eyes, the flare of pain slow to fade as she got another bottle, cracking the seal while she climbed the steps to her bedroom. She slugged it back, straight from the bottle. Alec was right—it was pure savage to drink it like this, but she didn't care. She wasn't drinking for enjoyment.

She flipped the bathroom switch, squinting in the sudden glare. She set the bottle down with a bang on the back of the toilet, hard enough that she winced and expected to see a crack in the porcelain. When she opened the medicine cabinet, they were on the shelf where she'd left them. They gleamed, like the welcoming smile of a friend.

She didn't realize she was crying until she shut the cabinet door. The woman looking back at her in the mirror looked like hell...eyes red, face puffy. The razor was cool against her fingers. She sat on the toilet seat. A raw, angry sob shoved up from her chest.

"I gave them Doug's name... Oh, Jesus."

She pushed up her sleeve, already anticipating how it would feel. The bite of the blade, the warmth of the blood. The maelstrom inside her head would subside. She'd be able to quit crying, quit dreaming, quit hating herself, for a little while. She wiped her nose with the back of her hand, lay the back of her arm on her knee, exposing the scarred inner side of her arm. She could feel it scratching under her skin for release, urging her to hurry, hurry, hurry.

"And then what?"

She didn't realize she'd spoken at first. Her voice sounded

rough and tremulous, not like her own, but the question lingered in the still air. After she cut and bled, after she let the misery out in a burst so strong it felt like coming for the first time—then what? Do it again, when getting blind drunk wasn't enough? Do it again, until she ran out of razors and had to use a knife? Do it again, until she got so tired of feeling like this that she cut deep enough to never need to cut herself again?

She stared at the razor, gleaming up at her. Winking, like a star, like a flame... Like the teeth of a shark.

"I can't keep doing this," she whispered.

There was no one to hear, no reason to say it out loud, but she did. When she set the razor on the vanity, the metal clicking against the porcelain, she whimpered, sounding like she felt—adrift and unmoored.

She picked up the Scotch, meandering through the bedroom and down the stairs to the kitchen. She stood in the center of the room. Delilah whimpered in the hallway. She jumped at the knock on the front door, watching Delilah, compact and solid, barking as she ran to the door. When the door swung open, Rocco filled the doorway, illuminated from behind by the overhead porch light, just like Mario had been in her dream.

"Tucci?"

"Go away," she said.

"Jesus," he said. Ignoring her, he came inside. When he reached her, he grimaced. He took the bottle from her and said, "How fucked up are you?"

"Just...go away."

"I don't think that's a good idea."

She backed up until she bumped against the sink, then slid to the floor. "Why did you make me choose?"

Rocco shrugged out of his jacket and tossed it over a chair.

Then he sat down beside her, his hands resting on his bent knees.

"Why does it matter?"

"I screwed up," she said, beginning to weep. She was tired of holding it in, tired of its weight. "I screwed everything up. I pushed him away, and now he's gone." She took a shuddering breath. "I can never fix it. You made me choose, and I..."

The last tissue-thin shred of resistance dissolved. She'd fought it so hard. Raged and stoked her anger so diligently, and now it was gone, leaving nothing but ruin in its wake. She'd chosen Doug, not Mario, and she couldn't pretend that she didn't know why.

"I said so many terrible things to him, Rocco," her admission low in her throat, wanting to stay there. "Things you can't come back from."

"You mean Mario."

Her nod was punctuated by a fresh burst of tears.

"Tucci," Rocco said. "Mario loves you. I know he does. What could you have possibly said to change that?"

A fresh wave of misery washed over her, amplified because she was drunk. If she told Rocco what she'd said, and why she'd said it... If she told him what she'd done, he would hate her, too. She knew it; she knew he would. How could he not?

"Miranda."

She looked at Rocco, her attention thoroughly snared, because he never called her Miranda. His dark-brown eyes were filled with concern, overflowed with a well of compassion so deep that he reminded her of Father Walter. He pushed her hair out of her face, more gently than she would have thought possible for a man so big and gruff.

"You have to trust somebody, Miranda, because whatever's going on with you, it's eating you up inside. I can see it. River can see it. Phineas can see it. Anyone who knows you can see it... Alec can too. Whatever it was, whatever you did or said, telling me is not going kill you. And it's not going to change my opinion of you. Trust me on this."

Stay or go? She stood on a threshold, knowing she had to choose. Afraid to move forward, but not wanting to stay where she was. Not wanting to keep doing *this*.

"I, I," she said haltingly. "We— he asked me what I was thinking, when I went with Doug that night. When Jeremiah bit me. And when I said there was no way I could know what might happen, he said that was the point."

She stopped, taking a gasping breath. She had started; there was no going back. She couldn't stop now, and she wanted to. Even though Rocco had said whatever she told him wouldn't change his opinion of her, it would, and she'd lose him, too.

"I accused him of not being there, of leaving me. Of leaving us." Without realizing it, her hand slipped down to rest below her belly button. And he—" Her voice dropped to a whisper, so low that Rocco had to lean in to hear her. "He said if anyone left the baby behind, it was me."

She could barely see, her tears fell so fast and thick. She leaned over her knees, unable to speak through the garrote of pain twisting around her throat.

Rocco's hand rubbed her back up and down, slow and steady. "He shouldn't have said that, Miranda. It wasn't fa—"

"And I said..."

She moaned, her stomach roiling so hard she knew she was going to throw up. She looked up at Rocco, her breath coming in shallow gasps.

"I said what did he care? That he had three kids, he'd just abandoned ours faster."

"Aw, Miranda," Rocco said softly, his voice overflowing with gentleness. "You didn't mean that."

She put her elbows on her knees, her head in her hands,

knowing she couldn't go on. Knowing it would be so much easier to just lie down and die. Her stomach hurt from sobbing, her heart pulverized, as if Rocco had jumped up and down on it instead of sitting beside her, being kind.

"I didn't think. Doug even said something and I blew him off. I was still thinking I'd have an abortion... It didn't seem important. Then everything changed but it was too late. I just didn't know it." She wiped at her tear-stained face. "It's my fault that the baby died. It's all my fault. We both knew it, and I couldn't stand that he knew."

Rocco pulled her to him, rocking her while she sobbed into his chest, while she wailed like a forlorn child, while her body convulsed with the grief and shame of having made the wrong decision and blamed the wrong person. The storm of emotions rocked and battered and consumed, shook her in its powerful jaws. Eventually, she couldn't breathe, but she didn't want to raise her head. Didn't want to see the look on Rocco's face. She felt him twist around and saw his arm reach up to the sink above them from the corner of her eye.

"Here," he said, pushing a dish towel at her.

She took it, still crying, and blew her nose. Her sinuses felt filled with cement. She wrung the dish towel in her hands, tears leaking from her eyes like they had when she'd been pregnant and her hormones had run amok. She didn't want to hear what she expected him to say, to hear him agree with her, but she wanted to get it over with. Then she'd know where she stood.

"Do you—"

"Shh," Rocco said.

When she opened her mouth again, he said, "Just sit with this, okay? That was a lot to get off your chest."

Miranda slumped, defeated. Rocco's arm across her shoulders shifted, but he didn't pull away. Instead, it bent at the elbow, and very lightly he stroked the top of her head. It didn't escape her that he was petting her like a dog, but it felt comforting. Right now, she needed comfort, more than anything else in the world. They sat that way, in silence, letting everything settle while Rocco stroked her hair. Delilah had sidled up on her other side and lay her head and paws on one of Miranda's feet.

"Listen to me, Miranda," Rocco said softly after some time had passed. "I want you to listen to me very carefully, okay? Because what I'm going to tell you is real important."

She nodded.

"What happened to your baby wasn't your fault."

Miranda shook her head and opened her mouth, but Rocco pointed his finger at her.

"Nuh-uh," he said gently. "It's my turn to talk."

When she obeyed, he continued.

"You really fucked up," he said, but not unkindly. "You went outside that night because it's what you do. You didn't stop to think about how things might have changed for you, but that doesn't make what happened after your fault."

"But Doug—"

"Shh," Rocco said, the sound sharp, but the look in his eyes, the slight upward quirk at the corners of his mouth, betraying only compassion. "My turn, not yours."

When she nodded, chastened, he continued. "You're like me. When bad things happen, you act. Most people aren't like that. Most people...fear gets the better of them, even if they want to do the right thing. But they can't, they don't, not when it matters."

Miranda took a shaky breath.

"What matters now, one of the things, anyway, is what you do going forward. Because you got a hard lesson, Miranda. Real hard. Even though your instinct is to act, you gotta think, too. You gotta use that brain that God gave you, that I know is in there," he said, tapping her head lightly with a finger. "Take just a second to ask yourself, 'Should I be doing this?'"

"You didn't ask yourself that question," he said. "You made the mistake of not thinking it through. That's all. And yeah, you lost the baby because of that mistake, but that's all it was. That's all you did. The only thing *you* did was make a mistake. Jeremiah's the one who tried to escape. Jeremiah's the one who manipulated Courtney, who was just a dumb kid, and she died because of it. *Jeremiah* is the one who bit you. Maybe he didn't know he could get you sick and turn people into zombies. Maybe he did, and he was just saving it for a rainy day."

Rocco shrugged. "He's the reason you got sick, Miranda. He's the reason you went out there in the first place. He's the reason your baby's heart and legs and arms were deformed, and why he was going to die no matter what you did next. All of that is on him, not you."

Miranda whimpered, the ultrasound image of Tadpole's malformed limbs emblazoned in her brain, flashing at her like neon. But also the swell of his cheek, and the curve of his perfect little head.

"Can I talk now?" she asked miserably.

"Yeah," Rocco said, giving her shoulders a squeeze.

"He needed me so much, but it felt like he was pulling me under while he drowned. I could see how much he needed me but I couldn't do it. I couldn't...be kind, and he was so kind to me. Even though he knew it was my fault, he was kind, and it pissed me off so much. I was so angry that he wasn't angry with me. I felt like I was drowning in it, and if I didn't let it out, it was going to suck me under, too. I felt so awful, and alone, and he didn't seem to blame me, no matter what I did or what I said. So I blamed him for all of it. And now..."

Rocco squeezed her shoulders. "You don't know what Mario knew or what he thought unless you asked him, which you didn't. What he said during an argument doesn't count. You weren't in your right mind, Miranda. People grieve in different ways, at different paces. Even without all the extra stuff you had going on, they aren't always compatible." He paused, then said, "My twin sister died when we were fifteen."

Miranda looked at him, horrified. To lose a sibling was bad enough, but to lose your twin had to be so much worse. He'd never said anything about it.

"I'm so sorry."

"I'm sorry, too. Rosie was my best friend. After she died, it all fell apart. My parents split up. My mom got remarried too fast and guess what? It didn't work out. My dad had a falling out with his sisters over the goddamned headstone. It was all so stupid." He laughed without mirth, sounding incredulous, the look on his face like that of a child adrift and alone. "My family turned into a war zone. I went to live with my nana eventually, after my folks split up, 'cause I just couldn't take being in that house."

He sighed. "Years later, when I was in grad school, I was talking about it with a professor of mine. He told me something that helped a lot. He said, 'Your family was a wounded animal after your sister died, but none of you knew it. A wounded animal doesn't act rationally; it just tries to protect itself. No wonder your family imploded.'"

"It all made sense to me after that," Rocco said, his voice soft. "Maybe if we'd all been kinder to each other we might have made it through, but we were all wounded animals trying to survive. Your little family was too."

"Because of me."

"No," he countered. "Because of Jeremiah. Your mistake kicked it off, but the rest isn't on you. It's not."

She wanted to believe him so much it ached, but how could

he be right? And even if he was, what she'd said and done to Mario was unforgivable.

"I could see how hard it was for you to open up, Miranda. To let yourself want your baby. It would have been easier to get rid of it, and probably smarter, too, with the world we live in. But you took a chance on loving him, on opening yourself up to that, even though it scared the shit out of you. I was real proud of you."

She started weeping again. She hadn't realized that somehow, Rocco knew. He tousled her hair and pulled her close.

"If you hadn't made a mistake, you'd be sleep-deprived and changing diapers right now, and I'm real sorry that didn't happen." A note of teasing entered his voice. "I mean, you were gonna ask me to be his godfather, right?"

Despite herself, Miranda laughed. "No," she said, shaking her head. "We were going to ask Doug."

Rocco snorted. "That's typical," he grumbled, but she could tell he was teasing.

"I screwed things up with Mario so badly."

"You said some really dumb things. He did too."

She puffed out a breath. "We got a second chance, and I blew it. He'll never forgive me."

"Did you mean those things you said to him?"

Miranda shook her head. "No, of course not."

"Then what do you think the chances are that he didn't mean what he said to you?"

"I still feel responsible," she said, tears overflowing again. "I still feel like it's my fault."

"I know you do," Rocco said, gripping her knee in his enormous hand. "You might feel that way for a long time. You're punishing yourself for not being able to see the future, which nobody can do. You've gotta take this fucker of a lesson to heart. Take that second to ask yourself if you should be doing what you're doing. Otherwise, you're pissing on your baby's memory."

Miranda sighed and lay her head on Rocco's shoulder. She felt like a wrung-out rag, an old one that was frayed, with lots of holes and threadbare patches. Not being able to tell the future. She hadn't ever considered that she was crucifying herself for not being able to predict what would happen in a situation where no one had known what Jeremiah was capable of.

"You've never asked me what I did before this, Tucci," Rocco said.

He sounded amused, like he did when he was about to good-naturedly harass her. Miranda realized she never had.

"Guess I never thought about it," she said. "What did you do before?"

"I was a therapist."

Miranda stared at him for a second, then burst out laughing. Rocco grinned, looking really pleased with himself.

"I can spot someone who's avoided dealing with their shit a mile away, but you? Ten miles, easy."

"You've been picking my brain since you met me, haven't you?"

Rocco smiled. "No. I've been poking," he said, poking her side. "At those feelings you lock up. I swear to God... The toughest nuts to crack always think therapy is about the intellect, because you're all totally out of touch with your feelings."

She thought, suddenly, of Doug. Priest or not, she knew what he would say about the covert therapy Rocco had apparently been conducting; that God sends what you need whether you want it or not.

"That's probably why I have such a bad temper."

Rocco barked out a laugh. Then he kept on laughing, so hard he began to weep. It was so infectious that Miranda couldn't help but laugh, too, even though she didn't know what had struck him as so funny.

"No, that's not it," he finally said, wiping tears from his eyes. "It's because you're a bit of an asshole."

Miranda laughed harder, in on the joke this time. "I think it's why we get along so well."

Rocco climbed to his feet. She took the hand he offered and let him pull her up.

"Thanks. I feel... Awful, but better. You're a better friend than I deserve."

"Tell me something I don't already know." Then his expression became serious. "Seriously, though. You deserve good friends. You're a good person, Miranda. You're just kind of rampantly dysfunctional. But you're getting there."

Miranda rubbed her forehead with the heels of her hands. The insistent pounding behind her eyes felt worse. Not from crying, but from all the alcohol, though the crying hadn't helped. She also wanted to hide the new tears that prickled the corners of her eyes because of what Rocco had just said—that she was a good person. She'd made so many mistakes. That he believed that about her meant more than he knew.

"Drink a lot of water, and go to bed," Rocco continued. "You look exhausted."

He was right about that as well. She felt enervated, like she could barely manage to move her feet, let alone climb into her bed. The idea of sleeping there alone felt overwhelming, endless and awful and too much to face. For a split second she thought of tracking Alec down so she wouldn't have to, but it didn't feel right anymore.

"Will you stay?" she heard herself say. "I can't sleep in that bed by myself, not tonight."

Rocco looked at her, long-suffering plastered on his face, then rolled his eyes.

"Jesus, Mary, and Joseph... You're killing me, Tucci." He pulled her to him, wrapping his arm around her neck and shaking her a little, like an obnoxious big brother. He cemented it by rubbing his knuckles against her head. "I'll stay. But if you tell anybody how nice I'm being, you're dead to me."

25

SILAS.

Mario tried not to think. He'd convinced himself over the past few days that if he could just not think, then he also wouldn't feel. It wasn't working, but still, he tried. The trick might be to keep at it. He squinted up at the sky as they walked. It was well past its zenith but still unrelentingly hot, with not a scrap of shade. As was normal for early October, the weather was magnificent, with clear blue skies and warm to hot days full of sunshine. The leaves of the vines in the now wild vineyards were beginning to turn yellow and red. After several nights at the little winery, they were underway again. Once they reached the top of the ridge, the walk into the Napa Valley was downhill the entire way. On another day, the stroke of lucky topography would have been a topic of conversation—but not today.

Oh, Silas.

Violet held his hand and walked alongside him. She was a trooper when it came to walking. When she tired and began to lag, he carried her. The others offered to carry her, too, but

Mario always said no. He needed to keep her within reach. If the price of that was arms so tired they felt like cement, or his neck and shoulders cramped from her little hands holding on when she rode piggyback, so be it. The real reason, though, was it assuaged his panic that he'd fail her, too.

I slapped your little sister, Silas. And then she comforted me.

His shame felt bottomless, like it would never end. He didn't want it to, because he'd slapped a little girl who had just seen her brother die, horribly. He didn't know he was crying until he felt the tear drip from his jaw. He didn't bother to wipe them away, nor get his hanky from his pocket. Pop Pop Santorello, a man as gentle as his son had been violent, had used handkerchiefs. Pop Pop was who Mario picked up the habit from as a very small boy. He'd felt so special when Pop Pop gave him one of his hankies, freshly laundered and ironed smooth. He had a distinct memory of using that hanky in kindergarten. When zombies appeared, he still had it, threadbare and delicate, stowed safely in his sock drawer.

He only had one, now. He'd given Silas the other.

"Do you want to stop?" Doug asked.

Mario shook his head no. When Violet patted his hand, he looked down at her. She looked up at him, her brown eyes solemn, and leaned against him. He swiped at his face with his other hand, but didn't even try to pull himself together. He didn't have the energy.

"Thanks, Violittle."

Doug hovered, and a good thing, too. They'd stopped to take a leak near the top of the ridge, and Mario completely missed the zombie walking toward them. It approached from his side and was loud as hell once he was roused from his stupor, never mind the stink. But it wasn't until Doug walked over to kill it, before it started moaning, that he realized it was there. He was zoned out in a way he'd never been before. He couldn't concentrate or recognize threats, couldn't figure out simple things. And what he could felt overwhelming. Impossible. He was in shock, he knew this, but even that seemed like a distant, faraway concept. The only thing he seemed able to manage was putting one foot in front of the other and keeping Violet close.

Right now, he was dangerous—a hazard.

He wondered if this was what it felt like just before a dissociative state. Miranda had told him about them. How, sometimes, she hovered near the ceiling or the tops of trees. She would look down on herself, unable to feel whatever it was that Miranda below was mired in. He'd worried about her after she told him that. That had been before, when they were only friends. As with most difficult topics back then, and even now, she'd laughed and blown it off—and quit telling him. She didn't share anything like that again until much, much later, when they lay together in her bed, their bodies wrapped together in the warmth of making love. He had whispered how much he loved her, how it would be all right, while she sobbed for the latest person she'd lost like her heart would break —again.

Oh Miri, he thought, shying away even as the memories bubbled. He couldn't go there, couldn't allow himself another second thinking about her, because that managed to pierce the haze of his grief. It cut just as deep, and let all the horror of losing Silas pour out.

"Vehicle ahead," Skye said.

Mario looked down the long ribbon of road. A truck was approaching. He checked to make sure he still held Violet's hand, twisting his arm behind his body when she hid behind him. Doug planted himself ahead of Mario. Skye did, too. Tessa pulled Violet to her, and set Mister Bun Bun's carrier at Mario's feet. If he were the kind of man who looked for slights, Mario might have been insulted that he was entrusted to protect only a rabbit, but it was an accurate assessment just now.

The truck was a really old Japanese one, like he'd had in college. There had been an inverse relationship between how well the truck ran and how bad it looked. He'd called it his Mexican Gardener truck, and when his mother heard this and began to scold him, he'd told her, 'No, no, Ma. I've had three different Mexican gardeners offer to buy it. It doesn't have a lot of electronics, so if you know how to work on cars, they're really easy to keep running.' This had mollified his mother a little, but she still told him he shouldn't call it that.

As the truck began to slow, Mario could see that there were three people in its cab. A white man with a weather-beaten complexion, sandy hair that was going gray, and a friendly face, got out on the passenger side, followed by a black woman. Mario's whole body relaxed when she appeared. He noticed that everyone else's posture softened some, too. Then the driver got out, also a woman. Her face was shaded by a baseball cap, which made it difficult to see.

"Hello," the man said. "We saw you and thought you might like a ride, or a place for the night. It's a hot day to be walking."

"It is hot," Doug said. His hand went to his holster. Not as a threat, just to let them know that they weren't defenseless. "We've been walking a—"

"Mario?"

The woman in the baseball cap looked at him intently. She pulled the cap off and walked closer. Her dark eyes were wide-set under perfectly arched eyebrows that matched her raven-black hair. Her cheekbones were high, her nose straight and elegant. Even though he felt like he was looking at the world through layers of fog, Mario knew who she was immediately. He'd know that face anywhere.

"Maria-Elena."

She nodded, smiling. "Yeah. It's me."

MARIA-ELENA, WHO HAD LIVED UP THE STREET IN THE OLD neighborhood, lived in a castle.

Like, for real.

After introductions were made—the man's name was Bob, and the woman was Candy, Maria-Elena's wife—they climbed in the truck for the short drive to Castello Di Saraceno Winery.

Mario had been to Castello Di Saraceno so long ago that he'd almost forgotten about the place. When zombies came to town, this should have been the number one destination on his list. It had a moat and drawbridge, a lake, acres of still tended vineyards, and food crops, too. It had towers, ramparts, and courtyards. The chandeliers of the massive, vaulted wine cellars in the underground levels were now lit with oil lamps, but that didn't detract at all. If anything, the flickering lamps deepened the romance of rows upon rows of four-foot-high iron-banded barrels that lay stacked on their sides. The castle had terra-cotta tiles on the roof, stained glass and vaulted ceilings, and grand dining halls with gorgeous frescos painted on the walls. It had an armory, a chapel, and stables. It even had a dungeon. The only thing it didn't have were giant cauldrons on the ramparts from which boiling oil could be poured upon hostile forces. Mario kind of thought maybe, just maybe, they were lying around somewhere, but only pulled out when the situation warranted.

They'd arrived in time for the evening meal, so after they'd had a chance to clean up, Maria-Elena and Candy brought them to the Grand Hall.

"You can read the book they used to sell in the gift store," Candy said. "It's an authentic, medieval castle, or as close as they could get and still be up to code. It took almost ten years to build. The stone is from her—from California—but the furniture is from Europe. Everything's handmade."

Candy pushed the tall arched doors to the main dining room open. There was no denying the room was indeed gorgeous, with the long, polished tables that stretched the length of the room, wooden chairs the color of dark honey, and brilliant medieval-style frescos on the walls that featured jesters and friars, wimpled maidens, and knights on horseback.

Mario jerked to a stop just inside the doors, jerking Violet along with him. He was surrounded by the appetizing aroma of expertly cooked food, the friendly chatter of a hundred people, maybe more, and it was too much. He had to force himself to not bolt away.

When Maria-Elena noticed he wasn't with them, she looked around, then came back.

"Are you okay?"

"It's a little much, is all."

"Oh," she said, as if it hadn't occurred to her before. "We can go to one of the smaller dining rooms. Wait here. I'll get the others."

THREE HOURS LATER, THEY LINGERED OVER THE DINNER table, talking and drinking wine. Maria-Elena had steered them to a much smaller dining room called the King's Chamber. Mario's first impression of it, with the diamond patterned gold and red frescoed walls, was that it was a little busy. Beautiful, of course, with rough hewn timbers above them, but busy. The shutters on the windows that looked out on the vineyard grounds were opened wide. As the sky outside faded to an orange sunset, followed by a velvety, star-speckled sky, the busyness of the room began to feel cozy. Candlelight was the only illumination, which intensified the effect. All the wine he'd drunk probably hadn't hurt, either.

The King's Chamber only held twelve people, so it afforded a level of privacy that the Great Hall couldn't match. Bob stopped by after they finished their meal. He was one of the five people who ran things at the winery, having been the general manager years ago. He was the only one of them here at the moment; the others were visiting at other wineries, where other communities had also sprung up. It was he—in an official capacity—and Maria-Elena and Candy, to whom they told their tale, beginning with the Jesuit plot to liberate the people of Silicon Valley.

"There's a working vaccine up in Portland?" Bob said. "And it's really free? Wow."

"Almost killed the first few people it was given to," Doug said, squeezing Skye's hand under the table. She gave it a squeeze back, the reassuring sidelong glance she directed his way full of love. "But yeah. It works. Most of the worst of the side effects had been mitigated when we left... How long ago?"

"I have no idea," Tessa confessed.

Mario shrugged. He had no idea, either.

"Makes San Jose pretty irrelevant, once word gets out," Bob said thoughtfully.

"That was the idea," said Mario.

He took a sip of his wine, which was excellent, and stroked Violet's soft, curly hair. It was still on the short side, but growing in. She had fallen asleep and lay on the chair next to him, with her head in his lap.

Bob raised his glass. "That deserves a toast, because San Jose is a mess." He waited for the others to raise their glasses. "To cleaning house."

Glasses were clinked, wine was drunk, another bottle was

opened. Bob said good night, with a promise to arrange sleeping quarters for them. Not long after he did so, yawns began flying fast and fierce.

"I think they need to go to bed, honey," Carmen said to Maria-Elena.

Maria-Elena nodded, but put her hand on Mario's arm. "I need a little time to talk to Mario. Do you mind getting everyone settled?"

"Violet needs to be put to bed," Mario said, regretful, because he really wanted to talk with Maria-Elena.

"We'll take her," Doug said. "And we'll make sure you're near her," he added when Mario opened his mouth.

"All right then," Candy said, her tone brisk, like she meant business. "Let's see where Bob's put you. Probably back in some crevice where you'll get lost all the time. He never seems to realize that no one knows the castle as well as he does."

Violet murmured but never really woke up when Mario handed her off to Doug after kissing her forehead. Soon he and Maria-Elena were alone, seated together at one end of the table.

"It's so good to see you, Mario."

"I know," he said. "I still can't believe it."

"Of all the gin joints, right?" she said, laughing. "I knew it couldn't be true, what they said you'd done in San Jose with the vaccine. I just knew there had to be more to it."

Mario smiled, but it was tempered by sadness. "That's very loyal of you, Maria-Elena. It means a lot."

She shrugged the compliment away. "Oh, please. What kind of friend would I be if I believed it?"

"The kind who believes the evidence in front of her?"

She shook her head at him, dismissing his rebuttal.

"And you're married?"

"Yeah," he said. "My wife's name is Emily. We're still married, but we haven't been together for...a while. We got married for all the wrong reasons, though I can't regret it. We have three kids who are amazing, and Em is a wonderful mother." Mario shrugged. "She's a good person. She was just—" He searched for the word. "Damaged by it all, you know?"

Maria-Elena nodded, taking a sip of her wine. "You look lost, my friend."

He took a sip of his own wine to give himself another few seconds. "Violet's brother..."

When he didn't continue, she said, "Silas?"

"Yeah," he said, taking a shaky breath, tears suddenly filling his eyes. "We couldn't... I couldn't even spare him..."

She held his hand tight between hers. "I'm so sorry. You must have loved him very much."

Mario nodded, unable to speak, the tears falling fast and thick. He drained his wineglass and refilled it. When he felt more composed, he continued, even though he was ashamed. But if anyone would understand, could hold him accountable, it was Maria-Elena.

"I slapped Violet," he said, looking to his friend, then quickly away. "I couldn't... after Silas. Not being able to do anything but watch them." He took a shuddering breath, anguish pumping from his thumping heart. "The Tesla's batteries finally died. She was having a tantrum, and I couldn't get her to settle down. It was too loud. And then I was shouting at her to shut the fuck up, just like my dad, and I slapped her."

"Oh, Mario," Maria-Elena said.

"She just looked up at me, frightened. And I couldn't believe what I'd just done. I...lost it," he said, his voice breaking.

"Oh, Mario," she said, sounding like her own heart was breaking. "I am so sorry."

"I swore I'd never hit my children. All I ever wanted was to not be like my dad, but I abandoned my kids, and I couldn't save Silas, or Tadpole. I hit Violet, and—"

"Stop it, *mi amor*," Maria-Elena said gently. "You are not like your father. You're not. You would never beat anyone, especially a child, like he did your mother, and you and Dominic. I'm not saying you didn't mess up, but you're not your father, Mario. You're a better man than he ever was."

"But I hit her... I'm afraid I'll lose her, too," he whispered miserably.

Maria-Elena shook her head. "Violet loves you. I could see it. Whatever the harm, it's not irreparable."

Coming from her, the words had weight, held comfort, because she knew. She'd seen the bruises and split lips, the black eyes and stitches, after his father's drunken rampages. She'd heard the cutting remarks when his father was sober, the constant, determined campaign to undermine Mario's confidence, and his mother's and brother's as well. The door at the Suárez house had always been open to Mario and Dominic, and their mother, too. Without judgment or demands that their mother must find the courage to do something she wasn't capable of doing. His dad had finally gotten sober, become less toxic, after Mario left for college, but by then it was too late. He'd wanted nothing to do with him, and he made sure the son of a bitch knew it.

Mario took a deep breath, then blew it out in a rush of air. "You're a good friend, Maria-Elena."

She smiled. "So are you. And such a wonderful surprise, to see you again after all this time."

"It really is," he agreed, noticing the differences that had come with age: fine lines from laughter and tears, a few strands of gray in her raven hair, but the things that mattered hadn't changed one bit.

She took a sip of her wine, then said, "You mentioned Tadpole... The baby you lost?"

Mario nodded. "Yeah. Our nickname for him."

"And you and his mother... There's really no hope of working it out?"

"If there is, I can't see it," he said. "We let it divide us. I mean, she hated me when she thought I betrayed everyone, but that was..."

"Understandable?" Maria-Elena supplied with a grin.

"Yeah," he said, amused for a moment. "But this... She just put up this wall, and I pushed too hard and we fought. I said some really terrible things to her."

"You know what Mama would say? Where there's life, there's hope. You're both still alive, and we can't know what God's plan is for us, but He has one."

Mario leaned back in his chair. "I think God's plans are pretty shit, quite frankly, but it's so good to see you."

"I know," she said, the warmth in her voice making it seem like she had said much more. "You need to go to bed, my friend. You're worn out."

He grabbed the corner of the table when he stood, because the room felt more spinny than he'd anticipated.

"You are so drunk," she said, laughing.

"It's a good thing you're walking me to my room."

"It's not the first time I've gotten your drunk ass home. I pray it won't be the last."

Mario walked alongside Maria-Elena through the vineyard. Violet's hand in his felt comforting, and he was cheered when she skipped ahead a few times to peer under the vines to catch a glimpse of the wildlife that scampered through the vineyard, or to eat some grapes. She never left his side for long, though, as if she needed to reassure herself that he was still there. His and Maria-Elena's adult conversation was boring, as she had told them several times—loudly—so they had turned back, cutting their walk short.

"You look better than when you arrived," Maria-Elena said as they approached the castle.

They were let through the gate by the farmhouse into the large interior courtyard. A group of children filed in the farmhouse's front door under the watchful eye of an older woman.

"That's Evelyn," Maria-Elena said, giving the woman a wave. "She's the teacher for the school."

Mario waved, too. He'd tried to take Violet a few days ago, just so she could be with the other children. He'd even offered to stay with her, but she'd flat-out refused. She had even turned down Skye's offer to go with her, which was uncharacteristic. Usually she was amenable to anything Skye suggested. This was a good place, the kind of place where Violet should be, a place where she'd be safe.

"I want to see Mister Bun Bun," Violet said.

Mario looked down at her. "I'm hungry. I want to eat lunch."

Violet's face screwed into a frown. Then she said, "Mawree, Mister Bun Bun needs lunch, too. We should see him first."

"Okay," Mario said, knowing she had outmaneuvered him. He said to Maria-Elena, "If you can get us to the kitchen to get some greens for him, I think I can find the way back to our rooms."

"This way," she answered. Then she said to Violet, "We can't have a starving rabbit."

An hour later, Mister Bun Bun had been fed and Violet was crashed out and napping. She'd been napping a lot since Silas had died. So have I, Mario thought, thinking about how he'd spent his time over the past six days at the Castello. He knew grief was exhausting, but still, it surprised him just how much.

After three false starts, he finally managed to find the smaller courtyard. Usually, he had a good sense of direction, but the interior of the castle always seemed to turn him around. The courtyard had a loggia on three sides—a covered walkway with graceful arches and a sloping roof of terra-cotta tiles—that its residents called *The Loggia*. The chapel's edifice made the courtyard's fourth 'wall,' and was as peaceful a space as the name implied. Round cafe tables were arranged in the courtyard along the loggia and scattered across its center, with faded umbrellas to block the sun. It was just one of the many beautiful places where one could spend their time when not working. As guests, they were loafing most of the time—and they'd needed it. Even though it was wonderful to spend time with Maria-Elena, and make new connections with others, Mario was beginning to get antsy. They needed to get on the road again—to get home. If he'd no obligations, he could be tempted to stay. It was refreshing to again be somewhere where people cooperated so that everyone prospered. But even though the Council seemed hell-bent on making sure San Jose was an amoral cesspool of pain and inequity, it was still home.

A waving arm caught his attention. Skye and Doug were sitting at a table along the wall just ahead, the remains of their lunch in front of them. He caught a flash of blond hair leaving the courtyard on the far side—Tessa, with a guy she'd been spending a lot of time with. Mario's stomach rumbled, reminding him that he'd wanted to eat an hour ago. Instead, he'd supervised Mister Bun Bun's lunch and waited until Violet fell asleep. Remembering how delighted Violet had been to feed and pet him made him smile.

"Hey," Mario said, pulling over a chair from the empty table beside them. He pointed at the half of Doug's sandwich still on his plate. "Are you going to eat that? I'm starving."

Doug pushed his plate to Mario. "Have at it, it's great. I think Mary has decided to fatten me up. She always gives me too much food."

"I think she likes you," Skye teased, taking Doug's hand. "She gives you more food than me every time."

Doug looked at Skye, the affection in his soft smile lighting his face and reflecting hers. Loneliness swelled in Mario's chest. He was happy that Doug had found someone who made him so happy that he was willing to upend his life to be with her, and who was obviously crazy about him. But the way they looked at one another, the easy physical affection that they showered upon the other, made Mario lonelier than he thought it was possible to be. Miranda had looked at him like that once, with a softness that made her eyes glow. Now, it felt like a dream. She was gone from his life as completely as she'd once filled it.

He shook off the melancholy. The food, locally and organically grown, was delicious. Now such an emphasis was of necessity, rather than as a part of California's boutique food culture: back-to-the-land, slow food, sustainable, plant-based... take your pick. Maria-Elena had told him all about the lean early years as the small communities among several wineries in the area struggled to survive, but they had made it, even thrived.

"It saves me a trip to the kitchen," Mario said between bites of ham and cheese on soft, crusty bread. "She can try to fatten him up as much as she wants as far as I'm concerned."

"Where's your shadow?" Skye asked.

"Napping," Mario said.

"Ah," Skye said. "How's she doing?"

Mario shrugged. "Hard to know. As okay as she can be, considering."

Skye reached over and gave his hand a squeeze.

"So," Doug said. "What do you guys want to do? We'll need to talk again when Tessa's here, but how long do you want to stay?"

Mario was acutely aware that they were both looking at him. How long did he want to stay was the real question. He finished chewing the last bite of the sandwich.

"We should get going again in the next few days, I think." Just say it, he told to himself. His heartbeat sped up, and his hands felt clammy. He took a deep breath. "I'm going to leave Violet here, with Maria-Elena and Candy, until I can come back for her."

For a beat, no reaction from either of them, apart from blank stares.

"You're not serious," Doug said.

"Mario," Skye said softly. "That's...a terrible idea. We— you're—all she has. We can't just leave her, especially now."

"It's not 'just leaving' her," Mario said. "I'll come back for her once things are settled at home. It's just—"

He had rehearsed this conversation so many times, but now that it was happening, he felt tongue-tied and defensive.

"It's too dangerous," he finally said. "And here...it's not. It's a castle, for crying out loud. There could be a siege and they'd be okay with all the stores of food they have. They can keep her safe, and I—we—can't." He stopped, a sob threatening to push its way up his throat. His throat constricted, making it hard to get the words out. "I can't lose her, too."

Doug's brow furrowed. Gently, he said, "Do you really think it'll be good for her to be abandoned by the only people she knows and trusts? And loves, for that matter."

Anger flared in Mario's chest. "I'm not abandoning her," he

said, with more heat than he'd intended. "I'm not. I just...
There's a school here."

"That she won't set foot in," Doug said.

"She'll get over that," Mario countered. Doug laughed
softly, derisive and disbelieving, but Mario persisted. "People
get along here. They work together, unlike home."

"We got along just fine at SCU," Doug said.

Mario tried again. "I trust Maria-Elena to keep her safe and
happy and know that she's loved."

"Mario," Doug said, beginning to sound impatient.

Skye put her hand on Doug's arm, then said, "What's right
for you isn't the same as what's right for Violet. We know it's
dangerous to bring her with us, but she's just lost her brother,
and she's attached to you more than the rest of us. I know
you're devastated about Silas, we all are, but this is only going
to make things worse for Violet."

Mario flinched at Skye's words. He hadn't thought about it
that way, and of course Skye was right. He recognized that
immediately.

"I can't do it and bring Violet along," he said, feeling
weak when tears filled his eyes. "I can't. And I *have* to go
home to protect my family. I can't do it and maybe lose her,
too."

Mario averted his gaze, wiping the tears away. If he could
just not love her, then he could rationalize bringing Violet with
them, but he did. He loved that stubborn frown when she
didn't get her way, and her whole-body laugh, and those soft,
brown eyes. He loved the flash of her white teeth against her
mahogany skin, and how her curled hair was beginning to look
like a free-form halo as it grew in. He loved how her features
softened while she slept, when the resemblance to Silas was
strongest. He loved her as much as any of his other children.
He couldn't bear to lose her.

Skye said, "It's not going to be less dangerous if you come back for her later."

"Stay here," Doug said urgently. "Stay here with Violet, until you *are* ready. We'll go on ahead."

Mario raised his head, shaking it no. "But my kids—"

"Don't make this about choosing one kid over another," Doug said forcefully. "You said you wanted to raise Silas and Violet, make them part of your family. This kid needs you the most right now—that's all. We'll go on ahead and get the rest of them."

"I can't do that, Doug. You know I can't."

"I know you won't," Doug snapped, his patience finally hitting its breaking point. "If you want to leave Violet behind, *you* fucking tell her."

Doug stood up abruptly and stalked away. His anger took Mario aback. It was so unlike him. Mario hadn't expected the conversation to be easy, but he hadn't anticipated that Doug would react like this. He looked to Skye, whose troubled face looked pensive.

"I think this is a mistake, Mario," she said. "Just think about it, okay?"

"That's all I've done since we got here," he said.

Violet hadn't talked to him the past few days. When he came into the room, her little face became a thunderhead, daggers of lightning flashing from her eyes before she stomped away. Mario supposed he deserved it. His friends, even Maria-Elena, thought he was making a mistake, but he knew he was doing the right thing. He couldn't fail to protect one more child he'd come to love—he just couldn't—even if it meant leaving her behind for a little while.

It's for her own safety, he told himself for the millionth time. He repeated it like a mantra, over and over, because it was starting to not feel that way. He felt like he was dying inside, like he was abandoning her, even though he told himself that he wasn't. Because he would come back for her, he would. But right now he had to think of her safety.

He sighed, hoisting his pack onto his back. He felt depleted as he navigated the corridors down to the large courtyard, as if every molecule of energy had been sucked from his body. He was finally able to find his way around the Castello without getting lost more than once, and was sorry to leave. The Castello had been a safe harbor when he'd needed one, and seeing Maria-Elena again was like the old hymn promised: a balm, to heal the sin sick soul. Her laughter and friendship and love had helped blunt the sharpest edge of his grief enough that he could go on. But nothing would change the fact that they should be leaving with Silas and Violet, and were not.

At the pass-through that led from The Loggia to the larger courtyard, Doug, Skye, and Tessa were saying their farewells. Mario took a deep breath, then set out to join the others. Bob saw him first and greeted him with a smile.

"I'm sorry to see you go, Mario," Bob said, pumping his hand. "Safe travels."

"Me, too," Mario said. "But I'll be back for Violet as soon as I can."

"Of course," Bob said.

Maria-Elena cocked her head to the side and smiled at him. "It's been so wonderful to see you again."

She wrapped him in an embrace that felt fierce, which was how he thought of her. She had always loved fiercely, defended fiercely, had fun in a way that she caught between her teeth. Zombies hadn't changed that, even though she'd had her share of sorrow.

"Are you sure about this?" she whispered in his ear. He nodded, unable to speak. She let go of him and held him at arm's length. "I'll take good care of her. Hurry back."

"I will," he said, relieved to see only love, and not judgment, in her eyes. "Stay safe."

Mario dropped to a crouch. Violet hovered behind Maria-Elena, half-hidden by the first column of the loggia. Maria-Elena leaned over and whispered in Violet's ear. A moment later, Violet stepped out from behind her. She held her arms straight and stiff at her sides and frowned at Mario.

"Hey, Violittle," he said, his throat abruptly tight. "I know you're mad at me, and that's okay. I'll come back for you as soon as I can."

Violet's lower lip began to wobble, and Mario felt his own do the same. He swiped at his damp eyes.

"I love you, Violet," he said, trying, and failing, to smile.

Violet's battle with the lip wobble collapsed, and tears began to roll down her face. Heartrending cries of a child utterly bereft escaped her. She ran at Mario, almost knocking him over, and clutched him tightly around his neck.

"I'll be good," she sobbed. "I'll be a good girl. I'll listen, I promise."

"Oh, Violet," Mario said. "You are a good girl. You didn't do anything bad. That's not why you're staying. I can't keep you safe out there. That's why you're staying."

Her cries were inconsolable, ripping at his heart. "Please don't leave me, Mawree. *Please*. I'll be a good girl. Please."

"I'll be back for you, I promise," he said, his voice strangled. "Maria-Elena will take good care of you... You won't be alone."

Violet's shuddering gasps flayed his heart wide and roiled his gut. The impulse to give in, to heed her desperate pleas, was overwhelming. She clutched him tight, her breath hot against his neck, huffing in uneven gusts. He tried to unwrap her, but she clung to him tighter, howling like an animal caught in a trap. Over her shoulder he saw Maria-Elena approach and take Violet's little arms.

"Come, *mi pequeña niña*," she said. "Come to me."

Violet began to thrash, her sobs echoing off the stone walls of the courtyard. Her fingers scratched along Mario's cheek as she was dragged away. A flush tinged her dark skin and snot ran from her nose.

"No," she shrieked. "No!"

"Mario, go," Maria-Elena said, looking stricken herself as she bent over Violet's thrashing body. "She'll be okay. Go my friend, and be well."

Mario lurched to his feet, stunned. He hadn't expected this raw grief from Violet. He turned on his heel, stumbling as he walked away. Violet continued to scream and wail, the keening cries of nightmares. Doug fell in step beside him as they emerged into the large courtyard.

"She'll be okay," Doug said softly.

Mario didn't—couldn't—respond. He felt sick and dizzy, like the world was spinning too fast and he the axis upon which it spun. Tears coursed down his face that he didn't bother to wipe away. They slid down his neck before dampening the collar of his shirt. He looked ahead to the drawbridge, almost unseeing, walking across the courtyard like an automaton.

"No!" Violet shrieked, her cries echoing across the court-yard. "No! *Mawree!*"

Mario stumbled to a halt, swaying in place.

He'd heard people talk about their life flashing before their eyes, but he'd thought it was a metaphor. Now, he knew it wasn't, because he saw his mother, his grandparents, his brother. His first day of school, the year he got a bike for his birthday, the first time he'd fled to Maria-Elena's after a beating, the first girl he kissed. He saw his graduation from Cal. The day he'd met Emily, when she hammered on his car window, begging him to take her with him before the zombies caught up with them, and the first time he'd held Michael and Anthony and Maureen...all so tiny and pink and perfect. He saw Miranda, in a blur of beauty and heat and loss. He saw Silas, asking about the wild rabbit, eyes bright in his gentle face.

After he'd stolen the serum, there'd been no choice, no options, no solution for his predicament. Once his role in the Jesuits's plot was revealed, it would only have been a matter of time till the Council managed to kill him. Doug had told him that he hadn't abandoned his kids...that he just couldn't stay. Maybe it was true.

What's right for you isn't the same as doing what's right for Violet.

The vowels and consonants of Skye's words were as sharp and jagged as her voice had been soft and kind. He'd done this before. After Tadpole died, he'd wanted what *he* needed to be what Miranda needed, but he couldn't see it at the time. He'd felt abandoned, as if his grief and pain hadn't mattered to her, so he pressed when he should have backed off, clung tight when he should have let go. He decided she didn't care, instead of recognizing that she'd been hurting as much as him. And now they were where they were, heartsick and miserable.

But this time, he wasn't powerless. He wasn't at the mercy of Fate's whims, his options narrowed and his hand forced. He was more frightened than he'd ever been that he couldn't keep someone he loved safe, but he didn't have to do this. He didn't have to break the heart of his little girl, who'd already lost everyone else.

This time, he had a choice.

He heard Doug say, from what seemed a very far distance, "Are you okay?"

Mario shrugged out of his pack. The dull thud when it hit

the gray flagstones sounded a thousand miles away. At the mouth of the pass-through into the large courtyard, Maria-Elena knelt beside Violet. Sweet little Violet, who thought she was being left behind because of something she'd done. Who had just lost her brother. Who just needed him to love her, which was as natural as breathing because he loved her so much. He almost couldn't remember a time when Violet and Silas hadn't been part of his heart. In every way that mattered, they were his, even if Silas couldn't be with them. And he wanted all of his children—Michael and Anthony and Maureen and Violet—together.

He took one step, and another, and then he was running. Maria-Elena must have let go of Violet, because she rocketed toward him like a kite whipping into the sky after being held against the wind too long. He dropped to his knees, and Violet bowled into him. Her small arms wrapped around his neck once more. She cried into his shoulder, her small body shaking. He held her close, the rightness of his child in his arms overwhelming, his heart overfull with how much he loved this little girl he'd almost left behind—almost failed—because of his own fear.

"I'm sorry, Violet," he said, crying too. "I'm so sorry."

Violet whimpered in his ear. "Why did you do that?"

Mario half sobbed, half laughed. Her question—direct and demanding—reminded him so much of Miranda that it hurt.

Mario untangled from her enough to see her tear-streaked face, runny nose, and puffy eyes. He fished in his pocket for a hanky, then dried her face and held it to her nose.

"Blow," he said, and she did. He took a deep breath. "Because I'm scared. I'm scared I might lose you, like Silas," he said, his voice breaking. "I love you just as much, and I don't want anything bad to happen to you."

"I miss Silas," Violet said, fresh tears brimming in her brown eyes.

"I know," Mario said. "I do, too."

"I want to be with you," she whispered, looking down.

Mario put his finger under her chin and tipped her face up. "I want to be with you," he said softly. "A lot."

Violet's lip began to wobble, and the tears overspilled. "You won't leave me again?"

His lip wobbled, too. He wiped her tears with his thumb. "As long as it's up to me, I won't leave you behind again. I can't promise, Violet, because it's dangerous out there, but being with you will always be my first choice."

Violet exhaled. "Okay," she said softly.

"Okay." Relief rushed through him that she was willing to trust him. How that was possible he couldn't fathom, but he was so grateful. "I love you, Violittle."

Violet's smile was less tremulous this time. "That's not my name, Mawree."

"I know. But it's my special name for you."

Violet leaned against him, her head resting on his shoulder. "Are we going now?"

"No," Mario said. "Not today. All this crying has tired me out."

"I'm tired, too."

"We should probably take a nap, then."

He felt the nod of Violet's head on his shoulder. "Mister Bun Bun, too?"

Mario held Violet tight. Love for his little girl swelled in his heart. "Yeah," he said. "Mister Bun Bun, too."

26

WHEN MIRANDA WOKE the next morning, her hangover was bad enough that she felt ill. She stayed in bed all day. Finally, at four o'clock, she threw up. She still felt like shit, but it was a normal level of hangover. She managed to get a shower and pull on some of the stretchy, comfy clothes she'd brought back from the bunker. She finished sipping a mug of hot water sweetened with honey, and was waiting to see if she'd throw it up. She was hungry, but had decided against going over to the Boy's Home dining hall for dinner. Whether she could hold anything down wasn't clear yet, but one whiff of the wrong thing would make sure she didn't. And it would be loud at the dining hall, which her head couldn't take. She stayed on the couch, propped on a pillow, with a wet cloth over her eyes.

She winced at the soft tap on her door before it opened. She pulled the towel away as Delilah trotted in, tail wagging enthusiastically while she licked Miranda's hand. She rubbed her hand against the pit bull's strong jaw, working her way up to the top of her head. Gemma followed Delilah and rushed over to Miranda. Victor and Noelle hovered in the doorway.

"I brought Liley back," Gemma said, almost shouting.

"Gemma! Inside voice," Noelle said, hurrying to her daughter. "Miranda's not feeling well."

Gemma looked at Miranda, her mouth turned down. She patted Miranda's hand. "Sorry," she whispered.

"It's okay, kiddo," Miranda said, grimacing.

Noelle frowned at Miranda, maternal worry on her face. "We're going to dinner now. I'll bring you something, if you want."

"That's okay, but thanks," she said, levering herself up to a sitting position.

"Thanks for letting Gemma play with Delilah."

"Anytime."

Noelle took Gemma's hand and headed for the door. Miranda heard the low rumble of Victor's voice but couldn't make out what he said. Noelle murmured something about heading over now, and she and Gemma left. Victor stepped over the threshold.

"I know you're not feeling well, Miranda, but can I talk to you for a minute?"

She squinted at him and was just about to tell him to fuck off, but he wasn't wearing that superior smirk she associated with him. His mouth was downturned, but it betrayed an expectation of being refused, not dislike. His blue eyes looked uncertain. Despite wanting to die, since it would be preferable to how wretched she felt, and her general dislike of the mercenary, she was curious to know what could make him look like that. She held out her mug to him.

"Boil some water. Add honey."

Victor nodded and took the mug. A few minutes later he reappeared and handed it to her. It smelled sweet, and her stomach didn't so much as burble.

"You can sit," she said.

He shook his head. "No need." He paused. "You don't like me, and I get it. What I told you before, about Harold being on the outs with the Council and needing to get out of the City, is true. That's why I believe him. You worked with him. The guy can find anything, including information."

"Okay," she said, her tone neutral.

Rocco had confirmed that Victor had told Harold he was in the Seattle area, thus the SEA-TAC airport abbreviation. He'd also assured her that Victor never used the ham radio alone, and that it was guarded twenty-four seven. She took that with a grain of salt. Victor was a sleaze, but he was personable. She could see him getting buddy-buddy with a guard and working that person for as long as it took. She didn't think he was there yet, so she hadn't pressed it, but she planned to.

"I'd really like to start over here. You not being so hostile would help."

Miranda's brow wrinkled. Even that small movement hurt. "I don't know why you'd think that. I haven't even been here a year."

"But you're tight with Rocco. People respect him, so it extends to you. They're a little afraid of you, since you killed that guy with a pencil?" He raised his eyebrows, respect and a bit of nervous amusement almost curling the corners of his mouth up. "Your hostility makes them afraid of me." He swallowed, then added, "Well, more afraid, given what I did."

"That's a nice and tidy way to put it."

He fixed her with a hard stare. "I led an attack and killed people here. I know what I've done, believe me." He looked away; the flex of his clenched jaw reminded her of vicious dog. Then his blue eyes met hers. "I wasn't always who I am now, just like you. Rocco's given me a chance to try to find my way back and be something else. Someone better."

Miranda snorted, her contempt and derision plain. "Love of a good woman reformed you?"

Victor crossed his arms, like he was holding a secret close. "I would never have tried to get to know Noelle, but for Gemma. She reminds me—" Pain spasmed across his face, just for a second. Then he smoothed it away, the cool, blank mask reasserting itself. "She wouldn't give me the time of day after you told her who I was, but Gemma liked me. She didn't want to scare her by telling her to stay away."

Using a kid, she thought—contemptuously, automatically—but was brought up short. Normally, she'd believe the uncharitable thought. But that look on his face when he'd thought about his daughter or niece or some other little girl he'd cared about once, gave her pause.

"We're not together, like you think," he said, his wish that they were plain in his voice. "It could head in that direction. Maybe. Whatever happens, I care about them both. What you think matters to Noelle."

"It does?" she said, shocked.

Miranda liked Noelle. She'd made a point of getting to know her because Gemma liked Delilah so much. And because she'd been lonely, since Doug and Skye and Mario left. She'd been lonely before that, but would never have admitted it to anyone. Noelle had seemed lonely, too. Miranda had been surprised to find—once she loosened up—that they had a bit in common, but they were hardly bosom buddies.

"Yeah," Victor said. "It does. Less frost on your part would go a long way."

Miranda very blatantly looked Victor over, head to toe. She still didn't trust the guy as far as she could throw him. Rocco thought he was redeemable, despite what he'd done. Now that she knew Rocco was a therapist, she had a better idea of why they met every week. She trusted Rocco's assessment a bit more—he'd at least been trained to identify pathology. She still thought he was insane to do anything with the guy but lock him up, but Victor was a hard worker, like Rocco had said. Putting him to work at least meant LO got something out of him being here. For Victor's part, it would have been easier to split, rather than stay in a place where the cards were so stacked against him. She allowed that it counted for something.

"I'll think about it," she finally said.

He looked astonished. Her answer was clearly not what he'd expected. "That's great," he said. "Really. I, uh... I appreciate it." He grinned tentatively, with hope. The expression looked strange on his face, like it had been a long time since the muscles had accommodated the motion required. "I thought this would go..."

"Worse?" she supplied.

He nodded. "At least as hard as learning to fly a helo."

"Fly a what?" she said.

"A helo—a helicopter. I did search and rescue in the real Navy, and the Coast Guard, too, before all this."

She stared at him a moment, openmouthed. Then she stood up, pounding head be damned. Slowly, she said, "You were a helicopter pilot."

"Yeah. Sikorsky Sea King and S61s in the service. And civilian aircraft, too."

A rush of excitement hit her. It made her headache worse, but she didn't care. If they could get Kendall's helicopter airworthy, not only could they get the food to LO more safely than by ground, but maybe she could go home. A tiny flicker ignited in her chest, so fragile it could be blown out by the lightest puff of breeze. Maybe, she could find out what had happened to Mario and Doug and Skye, to Emily and the kids, Father Walter and the rest of the Jesuits, Tessa and Karen and everyone else. Could help, even, without the journey taking weeks of perilous travel.

Arriving in a helicopter wouldn't hurt, either. It wasn't even the guns and missiles, but the psychological advantage of an operational military helicopter. Her mind raced, almost unable to imagine how that would play out. Nobody had working helicopters anymore, because of the fuel, but Kendall's didn't need it. Showing up in San Jose in that helicopter would be a psy-ops coup even the Council couldn't withstand without some damage.

"Come on," she said. "We need to talk to Rocco."

As soon as she'd learned Victor could fly a helicopter, a whining electrical hum, like placing her hand on a speaker amp set on low, charged Miranda's body. Victor hadn't been sure that he'd be able to perform the repairs it might need, though Kendall's helicopter being one that he'd flown was helpful. He'd taken great pains to make sure they knew he wasn't a helicopter mechanic per se, but he was willing to give it a try. Sean was drafted, too, readily agreeing to help get a couple more trucks working. He'd even offered to help with the helicopter to the extent that he could.

Miranda helped Rocco brainstorm about who to take to the bunker. Phineas, Alec, Rocco, and herself, of course. River, too, because Kendall hadn't seen a doctor in years. They needed people who had strong backs, but also discretion, because they had to respect Kendall's desire to keep the bunker's location secret. Kendall knew they would need to bring more people in order to get the food loaded, especially since they'd probably be doing it by truck. She also knew he'd be nervous about it.

She'd also run around doing anything she could find to do the last few days because she was avoiding Alec. She'd begged off spending time together without telling him why the last few days. He was true to his word about keeping things easy and light. He wasn't making it into a big deal, which was a relief, but he knew something was up. She felt bad about not being straight with him. She lugged her pack down the stairs and set it in the entryway, then checked her watch. Dinner was in an hour, and they were leaving for the bunker in the morning. She knew she'd see Alec at dinner. She'd pull him aside and talk to him afterward.

She jumped and yelped at the knock on the door, a there and gone jolt of fight or flight instinct ripping through her from head to toe. This is totally ridiculous, she told herself while her racing heart settled. She reminded herself that they weren't even dating, for Pete's sake, and to get a grip. She pulled the door open and froze. Alec stood on the stoop, the sly smile slipping across his lips.

"Did ya see a ghost, Miranda?"

"What? No," she said. "I just— I was just here at the door. Your knock startled me."

"Sorry about that." Then he looked at her but didn't say more. She was just about to make an excuse that she needed to go meet Rocco, because she apparently was going to wimp out, when he said, "You've been avoiding me."

She opened her mouth to deny it, but one look at Alec's face told her that he would call bullshit if she tried. Besides, what did she think it was going to accomplish? She looked down at the ground, chewing on her bottom lip, before looking back to him.

"Yeah," she said, drawing the word out so that the wince didn't show only on her face. "I have."

Alec's grin filled with surprise. "I thought you'd deny it."

"I almost did, but you wouldn't buy it." They looked at one another, then she said, "I guess you better come in."

Alec stepped inside, following her to the kitchen, and shook his head no when she offered him a drink. She leaned against the counter, and he did the same, so close beside her that their arms and shoulders touched. He was as casually relaxed—and sexy—as ever. Like he always was. It made her relax, and wonder why she had bothered avoiding him in the first place.

"You know," she said, then stopped. She looked at the wall in front of her, unsure where to begin or how to explain.

When it became obvious that she didn't have more to say, he said, "I really don't. You're going to have to tell me."

She turned her head, giving him a half smile, because she would swear he was purring with the way his accent burred his Rs. It tickled her ear in the nicest way.

"You make everything so easy, Alec. Sometimes I wonder what the hell is wrong with me, and why I can't just run with it."

That smile of his, slow and sly, arced to his eyes, crinkling their corners. Amusement filled his voice. "You've never once in your life taken the easy way, Miranda."

A small laugh escaped her. She felt caught out, a mixture of embarrassment and bashfulness swirling within her, that he already knew her so well.

"I don't...I don't know what to tell you. I like you so much, Alec." She groaned. "God, that sounds lame."

She didn't want to say that she wanted to be friends. She did, of course, but it was so weak. And usually, when you weren't the one saying it, insulting. Besides, it wasn't accurate. It didn't come close to conveying what he meant to her, but she wasn't sure what would.

"But you've got unfinished business to attend to," he said softly.

And just like that, her eyes filled with tears. She looked down at her feet, hating that she was crying. Again.

She searched for the right words, making two false starts. "I don't— I didn't— It's always been...complicated, one way or the other. I wanted to be done with it—with him—so much...just *move on*. But he's there." She shrugged. "I don't even know what he wants anymore, but..."

Alec pulled her to him. His arms around her felt good and right. Her chest began to hitch, but she managed to avert a full-on sobfest by concentrating on how his body felt against hers. She let his warmth, the feel of him, ground her, pull her back into the moment, like he always did. He took her face in both his hands, wiping away a tear with his thumb. His smile was gentle and unguarded, as were his eyes.

"However it goes, you have to figure it out. You've become..." It was his turn to cast about for the right word. "So much more than a friend." He let go of her face, and the sly grin returned. "It's probably for the best anyway."

"Yeah?"

"I've been thinking of breaking my rule for you. Maybe see if I liked getting tangled up."

"Really?" she said, startled and flattered. A woman would be hard-pressed to do better than Alec.

"Aye," he said. "But if I'm going to do something like that, I should probably pick a lass who's actually interested."

She smiled, a flush of embarrassment coloring her face as she swiped at her eyes, because it wasn't that she couldn't be interested if things were different. He caught her hand in his. She looked at him, feeling shy, and almost wishing that things could be different.

"We'll take a step back, then," he said. "I could tell there'd been something recent, and that you weren't going to talk about it. And I'd said nothing serious. I wasn't going to break my word. Phineas filled me in."

"Fucking Phineas," she said. "There's no such thing as privacy anymore."

"Ah, he's a good lad. He was concerned, that's all, and I appreciated it." His eyes became wistful, and his smile faded, tinging his handsome face with a hint of sadness. He brushed her cheekbone lightly, like a wisp of fog. "I don't like feeling that I'm taking advantage of you."

"You're not," she said, because it was true. "My mess is...my mess. You've never taken advantage of me, Alec. Never."

"But I'm starting to feel that way, whether you agree or not. I won't do that to you."

She looked at him for a long moment, then said softly, "You're making this so much easier than anyone else would."

"I wouldn't be a very good friend if I made it hard."

He kissed her, pulling her close, his lips warm and familiar by now. His scent overwhelmed her, earthy and sweet. Gratitude flooded her heart, that she had stumbled into the warmth of the circle cast by Alec's generosity. His kiss told her he was open to more if that was where she landed, but also to letting her go. She was breathless when they broke apart. Her body cried out to have him touch her, to feel his skin against hers, and despite everything that she had so recently admitted to herself about how she felt, and who she loved, there was a part of her that wanted to feel how they moved together one last time.

His heathered hazel eyes were as beautiful as she'd ever seen them when he whispered, "If you end up with him, remember that you're my bonny lass."

She ran her thumb over his chin, committing to memory the sandpapery feel of his dark scruff. "I could never forget."

He took a step back, but not, somehow, away. "I'll see you at dinner with the rest of the gang?"

"You will," she said, knowing that it wouldn't be weird between them, but easy, like it always was. Like it was now.

She walked him to the door, and after he left, leaned against it. She'd never done anything like this, wanting to remain friends, to stay connected with a lover after saying good-bye. She had always moved on after scorching the earth behind her, never looking back because it hurt to remember the good. Instead, she'd always held close the bad. But there hadn't been any bad with Alec. Maybe that was the trick—to get out before there was.

Unfinished business... So much was unfinished, muddled up and dredged to the surface since encountering Hussein, Fatima, and Susie. She'd been so sure it was Mario, and the thrill of seeing him again had taken her by complete surprise. She hadn't anticipated the feeling any more than she'd antici-pated the event, and now... Now her stomach felt like a pit of anxiety and fear that she couldn't get out from under.

Which made what had just transpired between her and Alec all the more remarkable. He was an easy target—the perfect target. She could have directed all the uncomfortable feelings and confusion at him. Once, she would have, but she was tired of blowing things up. She was tired of needing to scorch the difficult things out of existence before she could move on, or turning the hurt on herself, with razors and alcohol and whatever else was at hand.

Perhaps Rocco was right. Perhaps she was—finally, fitfully—opening up, without the expectation that all the world would give her in return was heartache and sorrow. Perhaps she was beginning to let herself experience the good without holding herself back or apart, in anticipation of the moment it all came crashing down. Perhaps she could untangle the knots she had bound herself with, without needing to fasten new ones in their place. Perhaps she wasn't to blame for what had happened to her baby, and was wasting everyone's time by insisting that she was.

But that thought was too diaphanous to hold on to, slipping into and out of her grasp like a strand of silk plucked from a spider's web. She needed to know if Mario meant what he'd said—if he really believed she'd left their baby behind. Whatever his answer might be, for the first time she knew it wouldn't kill her if he blamed her. It would hurt, wound her deeply for a time—a long time. But whatever his answer, one way or the other, she thought—she hoped—that it might set her free.

THE BEST PART OF THE LAST SEVERAL DAYS, BY FAR, WAS Rocco's stunned, slack face, followed by a 'Jesus, Mary, and Joseph,' that wasn't exasperated and directed at her. The waiting since, however, more than offset it. Miranda was a hair's breadth away from going around the bend if this took much longer.

Pallets of food were in place in the hangar. Two more trucks were in running condition and would be used if they couldn't get the helicopter repaired. Victor had done nothing but work on it since they'd arrived. Once the trucks were ready, Sean joined him. If will and desperation were able to assist the repairs, Miranda was doing her part. Sean and Victor pulled bird nests from the engine exhaust, and wasp nests from pitot tubes, whatever they were. Kendall thought the birds might had gotten in through the ventilation system, as he'd seen them from time to time. She knew they'd been doing something with the rotors...greasing the blades, and something about a hub. She didn't know what any of it meant, except that they were maybe getting closer to getting the damn thing to fly.

She hovered by a pallet of food in the almost deserted hangar. It was just past seven in the morning. She'd been surprised to find Victor and Sean already at work, and was trying not to be too obvious about the fact that she was loitering.

Sean's feet appeared on the rear ramp, followed by the rest of him. He pushed his red hair off his face and raised his voice. "At least tell me you have coffee."

"Yes," she said, grabbing the thermos she'd brought with her. When she reached him, she said, "How's it going?"

"Nearly there, I think. Victor's testing the ignition sequence right now."

"Really?"

Sean nodded.

"Goddammit! Goddamn, asshole, motherfucking piece of shit," was followed by Victor stomping into view and jumping down from the helicopter's side door. Miranda almost felt the floor rumble under her feet.

"Guess that didn't go well," Sean said to Miranda.

"I give up," Victor said, sounding disgusted.

"The whatchamathingie?" Sean asked.

"What else?"

"What's the whatchamathingie?" Miranda asked.

Victor's frowning face was a thunderhead of frustration. "Electrical."

"Electrical how?" she asked, trying to think of who might be able to help. Tessa was gone, but there had to be someone else at LO who could help. Or the guy at P-Land, but first they'd have to ask Kendall if it would be okay to bring him here.

"Just electrical," Victor growled, his glower almost daring her to push her luck by asking again. He reminded her of a toddler who had missed his nap and was a hair's breadth away from a meltdown. There were bags under his blue eyes, and fatigue made his movements sluggish.

"Oh," she said, as if he'd cleared everything up.

"I'm gonna get some sleep," he continued, rubbing on his eyes with the heels of his hands. "I've been up a while."

"Almost twenty hours," Sean said helpfully.

Victor grunted, then walked away. Based on his uneven gait, it looked to Miranda like he was nodding off as he walked.

Sean said, "He was still here when I arrived an hour ago. I don't know how the guy does it. If we don't get this puppy flying, it won't be for lack of trying."

"Do you have any idea how much longer it'll be?"

Sean shrugged. "None, but the closer we get, the crankier he is when he can't get something to work. Cars are my speciality, so I'm just a glorified assistant." He yawned, then drank more coffee as he stood. "You up for some breakfast? I'm starving."

Miranda nodded. "Maybe Rocco will join us."

Sean's eyes flicked quickly to her when he nodded, and she saw a flash of pleasure in them. Huh, she thought. She barely knew Sean, but the glimmer in his eye did not look platonic. She smiled to herself. God knew she needed a distraction, and mentally playing matchmaker wasn't a bad way to do it. She'd have to find out more about what kind of people Sean liked to get busy with.

She was going to lose her mind if Victor didn't make a decision on the helicopter soon. She'd been itching to leave for San Jose almost as soon as she'd learned Victor could fly it, even though she hadn't discussed the idea with anyone. With the fuel cell Kendall's company had developed, the helicopter's range—which was normally twelve hundred miles—increased by another five hundred before it needed to be recharged. Or whatever it was that it needed to stay powered; Miranda was still a little fuzzy on that. But first they had to get it flying, and ferry food to LO.

She paused in the door to the stairwell, glancing back across the hangar. The helicopter looked like a squat, prickly sentinel. Or maybe a reluctant hero, waiting to be pressed into service. She needed a hero right about now, to carry her home as quick as they could. Home wasn't a place, but the people she loved.

"Please," she whispered as she followed Sean into the corridor. "Please God, let this work."

She heard Kendall and Rocco's voices as she entered the garden dome.

"I know diddly about this stuff," Rocco said. "Hydroponics are a whole other thing."

Kendall's voice was lower, his reply a murmur that Miranda's ear couldn't catch. Rocco and Kendall had their heads together by one of the hydroponic units—the one growing beautiful heads of butter lettuce. A pang of longing twisted her insides. She'd taken over the day-to-day of farming at LO since she'd decided to stay behind and hadn't really missed the Farm. Seeing their heads together while Kendall explained the system to Rocco filled her with longing. She didn't miss the bullshit and the politics and the constant scheming required to keep the Council at bay, but the Farm had been her idea, her baby. Instead of returning home to it with the others, she'd let it go without much thought.

"Hey guys," she said.

They looked up at the same time, Rocco's relaxed, blunt features a contrast to Kendall's finer, more anxious ones. Even so, she was pretty sure Kendall was comfortable around Rocco, which she got. You knew where you stood with him, whether you wanted to or not. Rocco had also softened his usual bull in a china shop approach.

"Can you believe this? You barely mentioned what this guy can do with PVC pipes and gravel."

"I know how to do this stuff, too, Rocco," Miranda said. "It's more than pipes and gravel."

"Miranda is very knowledgeable about hydroponic systems," Kendall agreed.

"Yeah, well, I guess hearing about it and seeing are different," Rocco said. "How's it going with the repairs?"

"I don't know," she said, her discouragement showing. "They've been saying they're close for the last two days now."

"I'm actually quite impressed with their progress," said Kendall. "Apart from the fuel cell, that helicopter hasn't been properly maintained for a decade."

"I know," she said. "It's just, it'll be safer to take the food there than drive." She bit her lip, reluctant to admit why she really wanted the damn thing to work.

Rocco glanced at Kendall. "She wants to take your helicopter to San Jose."

"Rocco!" she cried.

She stole a look at Kendall, afraid to see a look of feeling used on his face. Instead, he said,

"Given the recent events there, that makes sense."

"I wanted to talk to you about it first," she said to Kendall, shooting Rocco a filthy look. "I'm not assuming anything, Kendall. It's your helicopter, and I'm not a nine-year-old who's too afraid to ask."

She glared at Rocco again. He looked unrepentant.

"Of course you can use it," Kendall said. "But first we'd need to be sure it's good for a long distance."

Relief hit her in waves. She hadn't realized she was so nervous about his answer.

"And Victor will have to agree," Rocco added.

The wave of relief transformed into a cold shock of icy water. She hadn't thought about that part—at all.

"Won't he just do what you tell him?"

Rocco smirked. "I thought you weren't a nine-year-old too afraid to ask."

"I'm not," she answered, too quickly. "I just..." She glanced to Kendall. "We don't really get along."

Rocco's laughter boomed and echoed off the walls the dome. "That's the understatement of the century. And it's you who doesn't get along. He wants to, but you... Jesus, Mary, and Joseph, you're stubborn."

"Will you ask him for me?" she said, a cringe in her voice that grated on her ear.

Rocco gave her a baleful stare. "You're the one who needs a pilot, and I'm not the one who's treated him like pond scum the last few months. Clean up your own mess, Tucci."

She'd known he'd refuse, but she couldn't help being a little annoyed.

Kendall said, "I could ask—"

"No!" Rocco and Miranda said simultaneously.

Kendall actually took a step back, looking startled.

"I'm sorry," she said quickly.

"Me too, Kendall," Rocco said.

Kendall nodded, the owl blink going ninety miles per hour, still looking taken aback by their vociferous agreement. Much as she hated to admit it, Rocco was right. She still felt perfectly justified in her loathing for Victor up to the point of him asking her to not hate him so publicly. His being a helicopter pilot had gone a fair way toward, if not changing her mind, at least changing her opinion of his usefulness. Not just for herself, but for LO. She'd asked around a little. Some people seemed to be coming around to him, more were reserving judgment. When she'd said something neutral about him to Noelle, she had looked so hopeful it actually hurt. Even Miranda wasn't vindictive enough to want to squash Noelle's hope for a chance at a future she wanted. Victor did seem to treat her like a queen, much as it killed Miranda to admit it. Failing an actionable offense on Victor's part that proved his treachery, she was going to have to adjust her attitude. She just hadn't gotten as far as actually doing it.

"Thank you, Kendall," she said again. "I really appreciate the offer, but if you ask, Rocco will never let me live it down."

"Damn right," Rocco said.

Kendall looked apologetic when he said, "He has to get it running first."

"Yeah," Miranda said, as she tried, and failed, to temper the hope that fluttered in her chest.

She'd run a few miles along the dome's outer corridor, followed by a solid hour of weights in the gym. When that hadn't been enough to help her shake off the anxious energy that wrapped around her like a soupy fog, she decided to drink. It was only lunchtime, but what the hell. That had never stopped her before.

Even though she was day drinking now, she'd been drinking less—a lot less—since she'd told Rocco everything and he'd treated her not with the condemnation she'd expected, but compassion. She'd been sleeping better, too, better than she had in months. Admitting to herself how she felt about losing Tadpole, how she felt about Mario and how horribly their relationship had ended, seemed to be what the dreams had wanted.

She still woke up anxious sometimes, with her heart pounding, but she rarely remembered what those dreams were about.

She topped up her glass, then set the bottle on the coffee table. The living area of their dome felt huge and empty, which only made her anxious impatience worse. If Victor and Sean couldn't get the helicopter flying, she was going to have a nervous breakdown.

"Want company?"

Miranda looked up. Alec's bedroom door was open. He was walking toward her while he toweled off his head, wearing jeans slung low on his hips and nothing else. His muscled abs, and chest and shoulders—she was a sucker for a good set of shoulders—were still glistening in spots his towel had missed. It wasn't like she was going to sleep with him again, but he could at least take pity on her and put on a shirt.

"Sure. I'm one step short of drinking alone in the dark. Even I know that's bad."

Alec chuckled, then went to get a glass. A minute later he was settled on the couch beside her, smacking his lips.

"Rich people really lived in a different world," he said. "I never drank wine like this before zombies."

"You're not kidding. Secret bunkers and helicopters...my family didn't come close."

"You did all right, lass," Alec said. "You're still here."

He was right about the wine—a chewy, heavy red that slid over her tongue like silk. "If they don't get that helicopter flying soon, I'm going to lose my mind."

"So you're definitely going home?"

"If Victor will do it."

The tension in her shoulders ratcheted up a notch. She was dying to get home. If they couldn't fly and get there quickly, she was still going, but she knew in her gut it would be too late.

"So tell me about your man," Alec said.

"My man?" At Alec's 'come on' expression, a sudden self-consciousness made her stomach tight. "Oh. You mean Mario?"

Alec nodded. "Anyone who's got you tied up in this many knots is either brilliant or an arsehole."

Miranda laughed, which caused wine to go up her nose. "Don't do that," she sputtered, looking down at her wine-stained shirt.

Alec merely grinned his sly grin.

She said, "Well...okay. He's—"

Heavy footsteps pounded outside the door to their dome. Sean tumbled through the door a moment later, his face flushed and his eyes sparkling with a manic glee.

"He did it," Sean said. "Victor got the helicopter started."

Then he disappeared as if he'd never been there. Miranda stared at where he'd been for a moment, then said to Alec, "Did he just say—?"

"Yeah," Alec said. He took her hand and gave it a tug. "Come on."

27

"YOU'RE NOT GOING, TUCCI," Rocco said, shouting to be heard.

She'd thought the hangar was spacious before, but with the blast doors open and flooded with weak October sunlight, it felt massive. On the ledge outside the open hangar doors, the rotors of the helicopter were a spinning, semi-translucent blur. Victor sat in the pilot's seat; between the white helmet and his mirrored sunglasses, his expression was unreadable.

Rocco's hand thumped on her shoulder and twirled her around.

"You've been drinking, for Christ's sake!"

Despite the truth of his statement, it had been one glass of wine. She knew she'd be fine. She shouted over the roar of the rotors. "Do you trust him to come back? Because I don't."

Rocco's exasperation was plain. He leaned closer to her ear. "Exactly what do you think you can do? If he wants to fly off, you can't stop him!"

She looked into Rocco's brown eyes. She'd never noticed how warm they were—how caring—until the night she'd broken down and told him everything. Now she didn't know how she'd missed it.

"See you later."

Phineas waved as she walked through the blast doors. Alec waited on the helipad. He gave her the sharp edge of a grin when he leaned in close.

"Good luck."

She nodded, glad that he was here to see her off. Now that she was doing it, she was nervous. She took the few steps to the cockpit, pausing before stepping inside. You've got this, she told herself.

Victor looked up and pointed to the helmet on her seat. She picked it up, surprised at the weight, and slipped it on as she sat down. She adjusted the chin strap. It was still a little big. Then Victor's voice buzzed in her ears.

"You don't need to do this," Victor said, his voice tinny through the headset. "I'm not gonna fly off and leave you guys."

"That's what Rocco thinks," she replied.

Victor's mouth twisted to the side, then he shook his head. "Fasten your harness. And be quiet. It's been a while... I need to concentrate."

Miranda gave him a thumbs-up, then looked forward. Her heart thumped in her chest. She'd never flown in a helicopter before, and despite her bravado, was kind of freaked out. This thing had been mothballed for a decade, and now she was going to fly off in it with a guy she wouldn't trust to tell her sunshine was warm. Rocco was right that she wouldn't be able to do anything if Victor decided to fly off to only God knew where. She could pull her gun on him, but she couldn't shoot him unless she wanted to die in a crash. Even she didn't have that much of a death wish.

The vibration of the helicopter penetrated her bones, and even with the noise-canceling headsets, was noisy as hell. The vibration intensified, the whine and roar of the rotors growing louder. And then...a feeling of weightlessness, as if her seat had been welded tight to the Earth and then broke free. They rose into the air with a light rocking motion that was unlike flying in a plane, rising above the forest ceiling and into the gray sky above. Below her, the vista of trees and mountain, of buildings in the distance too far away to look neglected, opened wide. She inhaled sharply, overwhelmed by the vantage point, by a view that had once been commonplace from aircraft and ski lifts and skyscrapers. They soared through the air, gravity's hold loosened by human ingenuity.

They banked left with a swoop, and Miranda's stomach lurched. "Oh no."

"You okay?"

She looked at Victor. He looked straight ahead, glancing at the seemingly endless dials on the dashboard. "It's a little swoopy."

He glanced at her. "You don't get motion sick, do you?"

"Kinda," she said, a sinking feeling that the helicopter played no part of hitting her in the stomach.

Victor's large arm pointed across her. "Airsick bags." He paused, then said, "I have to put this thing through its paces. You might get sick."

She whimpered, the sound lost in the drone of the rotors. People make their own hell, she thought, and she was no exception.

She tried to distract herself with the view as they flew north. She'd assumed they would fly west, over Portland, but they hugged the spine of the Cascade Range. Victor barely spoke, and when he did, it was to himself as the helicopter swooped right and left, up and down. He even turned it three hundred sixty degrees in place. He checked dials and readouts and at one point, tapped on the glass over one of them, which sent a jolt of anxiety through her. She thought they only did that kind of thing in movies.

Victor's voice crackled through the headset. "That's Mount Saint Helens to the northeast."

She followed the line of his pointing finger, hoping her quick compliance would return his hand back to flying the helicopter. The flattened, almost horizontal summit of Mount Saint Helens stood in contrast to the pointed peak of Mount Hood, a reminder of the violent eruption that had blown off the top of the volcano. She looked straight ahead again. It wasn't quite as bad as looking sideways, which caused an unpleasant constriction in the back of her throat.

A few minutes later, a break in the clouds to her left revealed the blunted peak of Mount Rainier. Its white shroud of snow melted into the dark blues and greens of the forest on its lower slopes. Miranda had seen it countless times since she used to visit Portland as a child, but never from this vantage point. Even on a day like this, when the gray of late autumn dampened the light, it filled her with awe.

"It's beautiful," she said.

"Sure is," Victor said.

She hadn't realized she'd spoken aloud, and didn't say anything in reply. They flew north for about ten minutes more, then the helicopter banked east—but not sharply.

"Are we going back?"

"Yeah. Got what I needed."

When he didn't say more, she said, "So it's working okay?"

"It'll do."

Her spirits soared, like the non-nauseous birds of prey she had tried to picture herself as. "Is it good for long distances?"

"Should be."

"And we're going back to the bunker now, right?"

"Just like I said." He glanced at her, grinning, then his gaze stayed on her. She couldn't see his eyes, but his lips compressed into a frown. "Are you okay?"

She was so relieved, giddy even, that the helicopter was working—and that he seemed to be keeping his word. She was also immersed in the struggle to not throw up, so for a moment his question didn't register.

"Pretty green," she said, seeing no point in lying.

"Sorry about that. I had to make sure—"

"It's fine," she said, cutting him off. Needing to concentrate on his voice made the nausea worse. Ahead of them to the south, the colors of Mount Hood seemed smudged by the veil of clouds that had drifted across it.

Victor said, "No more fancy stuff. You'll be on the ground before you know it."

"Thank God."

He laughed. She struggled to tease out the tone of his voice and was startled when she realized it was sympathy. Even more surprising, it made her dislike him a tiny bit less, which made her uncomfortable. She knew she had to adjust her attitude about him, but she hadn't considered that she might actually be wrong. Maybe he really did want to make a fresh start. Maybe he hadn't always been a creep. Or maybe this generous impulse on her part was due to the lack of swooping and dipping.

The ground beneath them sped past, and soon they were following the line of the Columbia River. Even though conifer trees were more predominant in Oregon, there were a lot of deciduous trees, too. Miranda admired the yellows and reds of their turning leaves. Mount Hood grew larger, and she tried to figure out how far up the mountain the bunker was.

"How are you going to find the helipad again?" she asked, suddenly alarmed. She had no idea where it was, or how one navigated in a helicopter.

He must have heard the concern in her voice, for he said,

"Don't worry. I've got the coord—" He stopped talking, then said, "On the ground ahead, your one o'clock. Doesn't look good."

Where Victor had indicated, the land nudged the river into a northward bend. The bend was over a mile long before the river wound south again, with a ragged-edged sandy beach between the water and the forest. The beach was deep, a quarter mile in some places, the trees held in abeyance by the inhospitable sand. Hundreds of zombies spilled out from the trees, tumbling onto the beach, already halfway to the river. A group of people—twenty, maybe more—huddled on the sandy riverbank.

The helicopter began to descend.

"What are you doing?"

"Landing," Victor said, as if it were self-evident. "We have to get them."

On the beach, some of the trapped people had formed a fan-shaped perimeter around the rest of their group, the fighters, the strongest of them, attempting to defend the rest in a doomed last stand.

She knew they had to help, but she could see it playing out in her mind's eye like a movie—too many people rushing them, climbing on board, weighing them down. Zombies latching on to the skids as they tried to lift off, the added weight tipping them sideways. Rotors chopping into the sand before smashing, jagged pieces of the blades hurtling across the beach. The moans and snarls and hisses as the undead overwhelmed them. If the helicopter didn't crash, they might get away. They might reach the river and swim to safety, like the people down there should be doing. But they might not, and then she'd never get home. She'd never see Mario again, never make things right. Never know what happened to Father Walter and Doug and the rest of her friends. Never coax Kendall out of his bunker and into the world. Never know if the Portland vaccine would end the ruthless reign of the Council.

"We can't risk the helicopter," she said.

"There are people down there," Victor said, sounding aghast at her unstated suggestion that they leave the people stranded below to their fate.

"What if there's too many and we can't lift off?"

"You do what I say when we land," Victor said. Even through the mild distortion of the headset, his tone brooked no argument. "Now shut up."

She bit her lip to keep from saying something stupid. She knew he was right, and she knew that if he listened to her, she'd hate herself for it. But the idea of it ending here, with all the damage she'd done never healed, was almost too much to bear. She was ashamed of how much she wanted to keep going, to turn away rather than risk it.

The people on the beach had noticed them. Those near the water's edge jumped up and down, waving their arms frantically. Some of those on the firing line did, too, but more stayed facing the horde. They flew low over the river now, and Miranda thought Victor would go straight for the people. Instead, they dropped even lower and flew to the zombies.

Zombies didn't have good balance at the best of times. But now, with the rotor wash pounding down, they toppled like pieces of straw. They banked left, making another pass. As they flew by, she saw some of the people on the beach had been knocked down, too. They made a final pass, but this time they didn't overshoot the huddled group waiting for them. Slowly, the helicopter descended. Even though most of them were struggling on the ground to get back to their feet, Miranda's breath caught in her throat when she saw how close the leading edge of the horde was. She could distinguish faces as the zombies crawled and lurched to their feet.

When the skids hit the ground, Victor started flipping switches. Then he leaped from his seat, shouting for her to follow. She scrambled after him, not taking her helmet off since Victor hadn't taken off his. He stood at the side door just behind the cockpit. He had opened a box near the top of the mounted gun in the door and was feeding a bandolier of .50 caliber shells into it. He pointed at the tail of the helicopter.

"We can't open the ramp because of the rear gun." She nodded. The gun in the center at the back of the helicopter was huge. He pointed at the door almost directly across from them. "Open that door and get them inside."

He slammed the lid on the gun shut and got behind it. It erupted in a staccato barrage of gunfire. The bullets blew off legs, vaporized heads, cut down swaths of the coming horde, many with enough damage that they couldn't get up. They still dragged or rolled, writhing toward the noise of the helicopter. And still, behind them, the endless waves of zombies spilled out from the trees, but now the horde's attention was on the roar of the helicopter. A primal jolt of fear ripped through Miranda's core as they turned and adjusted course, almost as one organism.

She tore herself away and opened the door, struggling with the handle for what felt like a year. She shoved the door open, thinking she was ready for the rotor wash as she jumped out, but it pushed her hard against the body of the helicopter. She bent her knees, steadying herself. Sand and grit pinged off her helmet and visor. The people were already running toward the helicopter, dragging others along. Their hair swirled wildly, eyes squinted almost shut.

"Jesus," she gasped.

The ones who'd been behind the line of defenders were mostly children. The older children ran alongside the adults. She didn't need to encourage anyone inside, though she boosted many of them up. She took children from the adults carrying them and shoved them through the door while the adults ran back to help others. She scanned the beach but the last person, a dirty, bedraggled woman, was beside her.

"Is that everyone?" she shouted, wanting to make sure.

The woman nodded. Miranda motioned for her to climb inside, giving her a nudge. When she was inside herself, she pulled the door shut behind her, making sure it was locked.

Miranda patted Victor's shoulder. "Everyone's inside."

Zombies still surged from under the tall pines. Closer, the beach was a mass of blown-apart bodies. Black blood stained the sand, made trails behind the zombies that crawled and dragged themselves forward, like the unnatural slime of toxic snails.

Immediately, the gunfire ceased. Miranda turned back to their passengers, who huddled on the seats along the walls and around the rear gun, which took up much of the cargo area.

"Sit down," she told the few people still standing. "Hold on to something."

When she reached the cockpit, Victor already had his hand on the stick. She pulled her harness into place. By the time she felt the buckle snap, the skids had broken gravity's grip. The zombies behind the charnel of the first wave stumbled and tripped. Those that fell got up, like they always did.

An alarmed cry filled the cargo hold when they banked left abruptly. Miranda tried to twist in her seat to see if anyone had been hurt, but she didn't have a clear line of sight. It would have to wait until they got somewhere safe.

Victor's voice filled her ears when he said, "Good job."

She looked at him, but he was absorbed in the task of flying the helicopter.

"You too," she said.

THERE WAS JUST ENOUGH ROOM TO LAND THE HELICOPTER in the gap between the trench and LO's palisade. Their arrival had created quite a stir, and an initial welcome of pointed gun barrels and wary faces, until those inside recognized Miranda and Victor.

For a while, Miranda would have sworn that every single person at LO was in the kidney-shaped parking lot. Larry, the Comm Shack operator and designated 'In Charge' person while Rocco was away, had quickly taken charge of the chaotic scene and getting the new arrivals to quarantine. Most of the gawkers had dispersed, but an undercurrent of excited energy made the air hum. The people they'd rescued had been making their way to Portland—they'd heard about the vaccine—when their boat hit something in the river and rapidly sank. Of the forty-two people on board, fourteen adults and eighteen children had made it to the beach. A scouting party of four people left to find a safe place. One returned, along with the horde that had been in the trees. It had been coincidence, luck, that Miranda and Victor had arrived when they did. Even five minutes later—

Miranda shuddered. She didn't want to think about what would have happened if they'd arrived later, or if Victor had listened to her. Every grateful thank-you from the shell-shocked survivors had shamed her, until she'd retreated to the main gate's watchtower. She stood on the catwalk, even though it reminded her of the terrible night when she, Doug, and Rocco had struggled to get the drawbridge up to save the community from a different horde. Victor had been part of why that night had happened, been part of the attack that almost wiped out LO. Miranda found she couldn't dredge up the usual bitterness.

Larry and Victor came into view around the last turn of the narrow road from the parking lot. Miranda sighed, happy that they'd be leaving for the bunker. They'd been gone almost two hours. Everyone there must be frantic. Larry was smiling at Victor; a genuine smile, not the guarded one she'd seen on his face before when Victor was around. She was just about to call out to them when a woman darted into view behind them. It was Noelle, looking pale and anxious.

"Victor!"

Victor turned back, then said, sounding distracted, "Give me a minute."

"That was some entrance, Miranda," Larry said when he reached her at the gate; she'd come down to meet him. He ran his hand over his comb-over, looking a bit awestruck.

"I guess it was."

She wasn't close enough that she could hear their conversation, but Noelle's face glowed with relief, quickly followed by concern. She didn't know where Victor had gone or what he was doing, and then he showed up in a helicopter, so it was understandable. Her eyes were moist and bright. Victor's tender smile, and the gentleness with which he cupped his hand alongside Noelle's cheek, made no secret of how he felt about her.

"If they don't hit the sheets when he gets back, one of them is gay," Miranda said under her breath.

Larry laughed. "I'm starting to think he might be all right." His voice became thoughtful. "He got really uncomfortable when he heard me telling people what he did to save those people, like he didn't deserve any credit. He said he hadn't been sure about it because you guys might get mobbed."

"That's not what happened," Miranda said. "He—" She snapped her mouth shut. She'd almost said that Victor never hesitated, that she'd been the one who hadn't wanted to stop, but she couldn't admit that, not yet. At Larry's quizzical expression, she said, "Doesn't matter."

"Maybe he really is trying to turn over a new leaf."

Part of her didn't want to agree with Larry, but after the day's events, she couldn't come up with a counter-argument. She still didn't trust Victor, but perhaps what he'd said about wanting to get back to the person he'd been before all this had been true. She sucked at trusting people—she might not be the best judge. Softly, she said, "I think he is."

When they were out of the gate, Miranda said, "What did you tell Noelle about the helicopter?"

Victor glanced at her, his brows knitted low. 'Are you kidding me?' was written all over his face. "Nothing. Just that I'd be back when I could."

"You did a good thing today, Victor. I may have misjudged you."

He stopped midstep, his blue eyes wide with a surprise that he quickly covered. "It really wasn't a big deal."

"Tell that to the people who were on the beach."

His mouth settled into a frown. He looked at her, but he wasn't seeing her. After a long moment, he said, "I don't deserve any pats on the back. I have a lot to make up for."

She knew how that felt. "You were right. I'm glad you didn't listen to me."

Victor's mouth opened, then closed. After another moment's hesitation, he said, "That's not your style. I don't know you well, but I know that."

She'd never wanted the earth to open up and swallow her whole more than she did right now. Of all the people she never wanted to admit something like this to, Victor was at the top of the list. She looked at her feet, unable to meet his eyes, then steeled herself to peek up at him.

"I was afraid if... If we lost the helicopter, then I wouldn't be able to use it to get home."

"You're going to need a pilot to do that."

"Yeah," she said, so uncomfortable she wanted to crawl out of her skin. "I was going to ask you. You have no reason to do it, I get that. I haven't been very...nice...to you."

One corner of his mouth quirked up, and a glint of amusement flickered in his eyes. "Seeing you the day after we heard about SCU, I figured you'd want to go home. Looked like you went on a hell of a bender."

"Something like that," she muttered, remembering how drunk she'd been when she'd finally confessed everything she'd been holding inside to Rocco.

Victor turned away, and her heart sank. He wasn't going to help her. It was what she'd expected, but the disappointment tasted bitter in her mouth.

"Get a move on," he said over his shoulder. "The sooner we get the food here, the sooner we can go."

"Are you sure you won't come? Just for a little while?"

Miranda and Kendall stood in the bunker's hangar. The others were already in the helicopter with the last of the food they were taking to LO for now. Kendall's hands fidgeted, his thumb worrying the broken section of another of his fingernails. He smiled, but it didn't reach his eyes.

"I'm not ready for that."

Miranda sighed, hope draining down into her toes.

"I don't know what's going to happen when we get to San Jose. There's a chance I may never come back."

Kendall nodded, the owl blink kicking into high gear. "I know."

The corners of her eyes began to prickle, promising tears. Kendall hadn't set foot outside the bunker since Rich died. It didn't seem likely he would anytime soon, and it was her fault. Even though she knew Rocco had every intention of coming out regularly to check on Kendall, and Kendall had even said he might be open to people coming out to live here once he had time to get used to the idea, she hated him being stuck here. She felt responsible. She'd accused him of being the reason Rich died, and all the progress he'd made fizzled. He was still trapped in his gilded cage.

She almost couldn't bear it, but she'd have to. Shame welled up into her throat, making it tight.

"Don't cry," Kendall said, sounding alarmed.

She dashed the unwelcome tears away and bit down on her tongue to get them under control. When she thought she could speak without sounding too emotional, she said, "Will you promise to at least try?"

Kendall smiled, a tentative one. "I'll try. I promise."

She wrapped her arms around him, holding him tight. He returned the hug with just as much emotion

. "Thank you," she said softly.

When the hug ended, she took a step back, glancing over to the helicopter.

"Good luck," Kendall said. "I hope this guy knows what he has in you."

That made her grin. If he knew what she'd put Mario through, he might revise that assessment. She took Kendall in one last time...the dark eyes and hair, the slender frame, the owl blink. He did look stronger, more sure of himself than when she'd first met him. Maybe someday he'd find it in himself to leave this place.

"See you when I see you," she said.

She turned and walked quickly to the helicopter. She didn't look back, afraid of how much it would hurt to watch him stay behind. Phineas gave her a thumbs-up from the cockpit as she approached, his face split by a grin below the helmet he wore. Phineas was so excited to be sitting in the cockpit that she was surprised he wasn't levitating. Rocco gave her a hand up. She strapped herself into one of the jump seats along the cargo hold wall, between River and Alec. Clicks and beeps began in the cockpit, followed by the hum of the engine and the slow vibration of the rotors beginning to turn.

As the helicopter lifted off, Alec gave her knee a quick squeeze, and said, "He'll be all right."

She nodded but felt distracted. A tight ball of anxiety twisted her stomach. It radiated out to the tips of her toes and fingers and the crown of her head, as if her stomach were the sun and the rest of her body the solar system. At least now she knew to take something for motion sickness so she wasn't queasy. She forced herself to breathe, in and out, steady and slow, because the closer they got to LO, the more anxious she became. She was one step closer to going home. They were leaving tomorrow at first light. She was getting exactly what she wanted: to go home, to see if she could find and help the people she loved. If they were even there, even alive. If she never got the chance to—

Stop it, she said to herself, trying to push her fear away, lest she somehow make it come true.

"They're okay," she muttered to herself.

They had to be okay. Mario would be there, and she'd tell him she hadn't meant the horrible things she'd said. She'd tell him how sorry she was, and that she still loved him, and beg him to give her another chance.

She prayed it would be enough.

28

LIKE A THIEF IN THE NIGHT, Doug thought as he crept up the road.

For you yourselves are fully aware that the day of the Lord will come like a thief in the night... First Thessalonians. He'd always felt that the Apostle Paul had gotten a bad rap for that bit in First Corinthians about women being silent—

"Christ Almighty...focus," he muttered to himself.

They'd left the Castello a week after that first, disastrous attempt to leave without Violet. Doug's relief that Mario had changed his mind hadn't been as profound as when Skye pulled through her illness after testing the vaccine, but it had been in the ballpark. He knew Mario would regret his actions and torture himself over it forever, never mind the trauma it would have caused poor Violet. Almost leaving had freaked the poor kid out as it was, but her anxiety was lessening every day. And blessedly, she didn't get seasick. Their trip down the Napa River to the southern part of San Francisco Bay had been nerve-racking. The whole trip had taken several days since they were trying to keep a low profile and the bay offered little cover. But at least it had been a puke-free, if nerve-racking, journey.

The closer they got to San Jose, the more Doug found himself thinking about Biblical texts, and his years as a priest, and his life now that he was leaving. It was almost Halloween... Samhaim, and then All Soul's Day. Everything converged during this time when the boundary between the worlds of the living and the dead became blurred. Doug felt himself dwelling in this liminal space, at once in both and neither. He had dreams where Walter had told him too bad, he was stuck being a priest whether he wanted to be or not. In other dreams, he never bothered to leave the priesthood, instead carrying on a furtive relationship with Skye. And while that flavor of dream resulted in seriously hot, forbidden dream sex, the rest of it was so stressful that on balance, the hot dream sex didn't outweigh the anxiety that lingered after he woke.

As a special not bonus, he'd begun to have dreams about Brother Rupert. When they'd left for Santa Cruz last year, Brother Rupert had been in charge of the safe house they were headed to now. He'd disagreed—often and loud—with Walter's decision to cut short Doug's formation as a priest. Jesuits had the longest formation of any Roman Catholic order—anywhere from eight to eighteen years. Doug's had been four. He could take any form of abuse if it meant being with Skye, including the withering 'I told you so's' that Rupert would dish out, but he wanted to tell Walter first.

Walter would be disappointed, but he'd understand. Rupert would just be an asshole.

"Eyes on the prize," Doug whispered to himself.

He slowed as he approached the cul-de-sac where the safe house was located. There were two two-story houses on Wentworth Place; the safe house was in one of them. Doug scanned the area for any signs of disturbance—for any signs of zombies—

but it was hard to see on this almost moonless night. They had no idea what they were coming home to, which was why they'd decided to make landfall on the east side of the South Bay, in Fremont. There had been lots of zombies to avoid, and to kill, to get here from where they made landfall.

After a last glance around the cul-de-sac, Doug stepped off the curb and crossed it. When he reached the sidewalk outside the safe house, he heard a soft snick. He froze. That would be the sentry's gun, which had probably been trained on him for a good minute or two. Two figures moved around the side of the house, visible only because his eyes somehow tracked the movement. A red light flicked on and shone in Doug's face. The red glow wouldn't be as visible if anyone was looking, and it didn't mess up night vision. He'd still squinted, startled, since he hadn't been expecting it.

"Doug?" The man's incredulous voice was familiar, but Doug couldn't place it.

"Yeah, it's me."

"When did you get here?"

"This morning," he said. "I've got others with me."

He felt more than saw the man's posture stiffen. "How many? Where are they?"

"Three adults—a man and two women—and a child. And a rabbit. They're a block away."

"Go tell Rupert that Doug is here," the man said to his companion.

Doug still couldn't place him. Just as he was about to ask, the man said, "A rabbit? Well, it's good to see you in one piece, Father Doug. Let's get your friends and get inside."

Half an hour later, Violet was in bed; Doug, Skye, Mario, and Tessa had been fed, and Brother Rupert had finished his evening prayers and joined them.

"It's good to see you, brother," Rupert said, clapping Doug on the back as he gave him a hug.

"Likewise," Doug said.

Rupert's shoulders filled the doorway of the kitchen. He was as tall as Doug and in his late fifties, but where Doug was wiry to the point of thinness, Rupert was broad and brawny. He claimed it was from growing up on a dairy farm in Minnesota. Doug believed it, but he also thought, given Rupert's pale skin, white-blond hair, and light-blue eyes, that it was also due to his Norwegian ancestors being Vikings. Given Rupert's tendency to be a bit of a hard-ass, Doug figured they'd been on the take no prisoners, rape and pillage everything in their path kind of Vikings.

"Mario," Rupert said warmly, extending his hand. "It's good to see you. Doug tells me you've done it again."

"Good to see you, too, Rupert," Mario answered. "I had a lot of help. It wasn't just me."

Rupert smiled. "It never is. The little one's in bed?" At Mario's nod, he added, "Then I'll meet her tomorrow."

"This is Tessa," Doug said, and Tessa stepped forward.

Rupert's large hand engulfed hers. "Pleased to meet you, Tessa. Any friend of Doug's and Mario's is a friend of mine."

"Likewise," Tessa said, looking as tired as she was dirty. "Just happy to have made it in one piece."

Rupert turned to Skye.

"I'm Rupert Vargen, pleased to meet you."

"Skye Swanson," Skye said, shaking his hand and giving him a winning smile.

"We're happy to have you with us," Rupert said.

"Um...actually," Doug said.

He stopped when all eyes in the room swiveled to him. An amused grin skittered over Mario's lips before he could hide it. Tessa watched with keen interest. She and Mario had a bet riding on how this would go. Being unacquainted with Rupert, she suffered from the delusion that because he was a priest, he'd fall on the compassionate end of the spectrum. Skye just looked nervous. Doug stepped behind Skye and put his hand on her shoulder, steeling himself. His mouth felt dusty when he said, "Actually, Skye's my girlfriend."

Rupert and Adam, whose voice Doug hadn't been able to place outside, looked at him blankly. Adam looked to Rupert, unsure what to make of Doug's declaration. A second later, Rupert's booming laugh filled the kitchen.

"Ha! That's a good one! Of course she is!" Still chuckling, Rupert said to Skye, "I thought Doug's formation was too short. Well, it was too short, but never mind. He never misses a chance to pull my leg. A real joker, this one."

Doug stared at Rupert, stunned. Of all the reactions he'd envisioned, this had not been one of them.

"No, no, Rupert," Doug said. He chanced a quick glance at Skye. "She really is my girlfriend. I'm leaving the priesthood."

Rupert looked at Doug, then Skye. He opened his mouth, then closed it. Then he said, sounding annoyed, "Well, of course she is. I told Walter your formation was too short, but did he listen to me?"

Skye squinted up at Rupert. "I hope you won't hold it against me."

"What?" Rupert said, sounding genuinely surprised. "You seem perfectly lovely, my dear." He flapped his hand at Doug. "I always knew this one wasn't going to last."

Doug felt a little light-headed. Not from relief, but because he'd been holding his breath without realizing it. He exhaled heavily and took a shallow breath. He saw Tessa lean in to Mario and say softly, "Pay up."

"That went better than I thought it would," Doug said. "You kind of freaked me out by laughing, Rupert. I figured you'd flip out, not think it was a joke."

Rupert almost cracked a smile. "It's too late, and I'm too old to get worked up over the state of your vows. That's between you and God, and thank God for it! Like I have the time or energy to deal with your..." He waved his hand at them in a vague sort of way without bothering to finish his sentence.

"I told you," Skye said, giving Doug a smile, and goddamn if she wasn't prettier than ever.

"There are more important things going on," Rupert said. If Doug hadn't known better, he'd have said Rupert's tone was testy, and given that it was Rupert, that would be an entirely reasonable assumption. But it was more than that. Rupert looked anxious, as if he wasn't happy to the bearer of the news he had for them.

Rupert pulled out the free chair at the table and sat, motioning for Doug to do the same. He leaned in, his eyes serious.

"Has Adam told you the situation here?"

"No," Doug said.

"We know Dominic ended up on top with the Council, but that's all," Mario added.

"I'm sorry to be the one to tell you," Rupert said, clearly distressed. "But SCU has fallen." He paused at the gasps, and Doug's cry of 'What?' before continuing. "The City attacked the night you left, but we repelled them. They tried again two months later, and we repelled them then, too, but the third time..." He shrugged. "They sent us packing. Killed sixteen priests. The rest are in hiding like we are, or locked up."

"What?" Doug said, horrified. He could feel the blood

draining from his face. The Jesuit community wasn't that big to begin with. Sixteen dead? "Who?" he asked, then added, feeling as if the floor was opening up below him, "Was Walter one of them?"

"No, no," Rupert said. "Walter went into hiding, but they caught up with him last month. There's a trial happening now, a real dog and pony show. We've been trying to come up with a plan to get him out because there will only be one verdict —guilty."

"Jesus," Mario said. "How long do we have to get him?"

"A week, at most," Rupert answered. "We're finalizing the details of a rescue now."

"Who's in charge of it?" Doug demanded, fear thrumming through his body like a storm on high seas. "Where are they holding him?"

"I'm running the rescue op," Adam said. "Walter is at the Westin hotel."

"They're not using the county jail anymore?" Doug asked.

Adam shook his head. "All the 'high value prisoners' are at the Westin or the city jail. There was a problem at the county jail a few months back. Zombies got in and..." He shrugged. "It was a bit of a shit show, from what I hear. Besides, down-town they can walk him to the plaza, make a real production of it."

"Zombies got into a jail?" Tessa asked, sounding incredulous.

"The county jail is outside the walls," Doug answered. "To keep people from trying to escape."

"Jesus," Tessa whispered, looking horrified.

Skye looked at him in frank disbelief. "I believed you when you said things were bad here, but..." She shivered as her voice trailed away.

"What about my family?" Mario asked. "Where are they?"

Rupert looked to Mario, his mouth twisting into a pained frown. Doug watched the color drain from Mario's face.

"Your family's okay, Mario," Rupert said. "But your brother took them back to Palo Alto and moved into your house with them. His husband is with them, too. Emily's under lock and key, the children a little less so, from what we can tell."

Mario's head dropped into his hands. "I knew it," he said softly, venomously. He looked up, his eyes blazing with murderous anger. "I knew he'd do something."

"We'll get them out," Doug said, willing Mario to believe him. "You can't run off and do something stupid, Mario. We'll get them out, but we've got to be smart about this. All of it."

"Of course we will," Skye said. She reached over and took Mario's hand in her own. "Your brother didn't succeed at home. He won't here, either."

Mario didn't say more, but Doug didn't care for the look in his eye. He hadn't really believed it when Mario had threatened to kill his brother before, but looking at him now, he wasn't so sure.

Turning to Rupert, Doug said, "Tell us everything."

MARIO CLIMBED THE STAIRS TO THE BEDROOM WHERE Violet slept, a plan already taking form. He looked at his watch: almost two in the morning. What he wanted to do was crawl into bed and sleep, but that wasn't an option anymore. He knew Doug would be pissed when he discovered what Mario planned to do, but he had to do it, and do it now. Waiting wasn't an option he could live with.

But there was one thing he needed to do first.

He walked down the dark hallway to the room where Violet slept and eased the door open. The nightlight by her bed cast distorted shadows that ended almost where they began along the edge of the small circle of light. Violet lay on her stomach, thumb in her mouth. She'd started the thumb sucking after he'd tried to leave her behind at the Castello. Mario didn't care about the thumb sucking, but what it signified—regression from him almost leaving her behind. With a little luck and lot of consistency, he'd do his best to help her feel more secure.

He sat on the edge of the bed and took a moment. Long dark lashes dusted the edge of her closed eyes like a fringed fan. Lightly, he set his hand on her shoulder, felt the warmth of her sleeping form, but didn't lean over her.

"Violet," he said, his voice low. "Violet, wake up."

Violet opened her eyes, then bolted upright. He'd found out the hard way, with the crack of her head against his cheek or forehead, that most of the time she woke up completely, immediately, and ready to flee.

"It's okay, sweetheart. Everything's okay," he said. She looked at him and yawned. Mario took her small hand in his. "I have to go out for a little while. I probably won't be back until late tomorrow night. Maybe even after you've gone to bed, but I don't want you to worry."

She cocked her head to the side, looking worried anyway. "Where are you going?"

"I have to go see my other kids, your brothers and sisters. The ones you haven't met yet."

She frowned. "They can't come here?"

Mario shook his head. "Not right now. That's why I have to go to where they are. Doug and Skye will take care of you until I get back." Violet's eyes began to fill with apprehension. Mario squeezed her hand. "I'm not leaving you behind, sweetheart. That's why I woke you up to tell you."

She didn't say anything for a few moments, then said, hope and fear mixed together, "Are you really coming back?"

Mario sighed, the leaden feeling of failure blooming inside his chest. He'd made his share of parenting mistakes, but never as badly as he'd screwed up with Violet. He gave her the only answer he could, along with a silent prayer that it would be the truth.

"I'm really coming back." He almost said I promise. It was on the tip of his tongue, pounding against the inside of his teeth, but he couldn't do that to her. He added, "And if for some reason I don't, it's not because I didn't try, or because I don't want to, but because I can't."

She looked up at him, her face pensive.

"What is it?"

"You'd rather be with your own little girl."

He shook his head. "No. I want to be with both of my little girls," he said, tapping the tip of her nose on 'both.' "I want all of you together right now, but that's gonna take a little longer. I love you as much as I love Michael and Anthony and Maureen. As much as I loved Silas. You're all my kids."

"Really?" Violet whispered.

The tentative hope he saw in her eyes and heard in her voice, that she was as loved as he said, made Mario's heart ache.

"Really." He forced himself to smile, hoping it would reassure her. "You need to go back to sleep now." Violet lay back against the pillow. Mario pulled the sheet and blanket up, and retucked her into bed. "I'll wait until you fall asleep," he said. "And if you're sleeping when I get back, I'll wake you up so you know I'm here."

"Okay," she said. "Will you say the good night again?"

The good night Violet wanted had evolved over the years. Some of it was from he and Emily, some from the kids. He didn't remember which one of them had added the last bit, probably Michael, the musician. It didn't matter who had added what. What made it special was that it was theirs. And now it was Violet's, too. He leaned over and kissed the top of her head. Softly, he recited the words in her ear.

"Good night, sleep tight, don't let the bed bugs bite. Peace, I love you, and all that jazz."

FIFTEEN MINUTES LATER, MARIO LEANED THE BIKE against the garage wall and pulled the person-sized door that opened to the side yard shut. He'd lost it when he first saw the bikes in the garage, for Silas had wanted one so much. But time and necessity were cruel taskmasters, forcing him to shove it aside and save the sadness for later. Tonight, he had a task to do.

"You know this is a bad idea, right?"

Mario took a deep breath, trying to tamp down his body's fight or flight response, for the voice had startled him. Doug stood in the shadows.

"I have to make sure they're all right."

"You're going to get caught, Mario." The urgency in Doug's voice implored him to reconsider. "You're smarter than this."

"They're my kids and their mother. I have to see if they're okay."

"You won't even get close."

"Doug, I have to try."

Silence fell between them.

After half a minute, Doug said, "What am I supposed to tell Violet?"

"I just told her."

Doug's breath came out in a long, peevish sigh. "Well. You've thought of everything." He gripped Mario's shoulder. "Good luck, idiot. Don't get caught or eaten. Or shot."

With a bravado he didn't feel, he said, "I'll do my best."

Two hours later, the long expanse of the Dumbarton Bridge was behind him. Mario had heard it was tricky in the daytime; it was a damn sight trickier at night. The bike's gears ticked as he navigated across the Bayshore Freeway onto University Avenue. He could hear the moans of zombies in the distance. The white lights along the top of the outer north wall of New Palo Alto looked like the edge of an elevated landing strip. He knew the no man's land between the inner and outer walls would be as bright as day. Lighting along the outside of the outer wall was enough to see if zombies approached, but would expose him as well.

He slowed when he crossed the intersection at Cowper Street. His house was almost two miles down Cowper. If he could ride the bike straight there, it wouldn't even take ten minutes. He pedaled through the ruins of Palo Alto's old commercial strip, passing restaurants and clothing stores, cell phone vendors and the Apple Store. God, he'd hated the Apple Store...always so busy that it felt like a circle of hell.

He ditched the bike at the intersection with Bryant Street. If he managed to pull this off, it would be waiting for him when he returned. He walked down the dark road, toward the concrete wall with its bright strip of lights. He pulled a baseball cap from his back pocket and slipped it on. It wasn't much, but it would shield his face a little.

When it came to security, Mario had to admit that New Palo Alto mostly had its shit together, but that didn't mean there weren't chinks. The settlement's walls took the path of least resistance, built along streets and freeways, but there were two places where only a single wall had been built. The stretch along the Bayshore Freeway was a single wall because of the wetlands on the other side.

The other place where there was a single wall was because of a unique feature: the emergency evacuation exit. That exit was a tunnel large enough for a semi to drive through at the north end of Alma Street, built under the wall. Nothing could get through its blast doors, so Mario wouldn't go near it. The single wall started three blocks northeast of the exit, along Emerson Street. A regular, vehicle-sized emergency exit had been built into that section of the single wall and was sheltered from view where the inner and outer walls merged. The idea was someone could get outside quickly in case the blast door controls had to be operated manually from the outside. Why it was three blocks away, Mario didn't know. He'd never gotten a straight answer to that, and figured someone had fucked up and then decided to pretend it had been the plan all along. It was blocked by a bunch of shrubs on the inside 'to keep it low profile,' which would render it difficult to use at best, but whatever—it had been built before his time there.

The chink wasn't this second, secret emergency exit as much as who knew about it. Only Security and Council members living in New Palo Alto were supposed to know of its existence, but human nature being predictable, spouses and other romantic partners knew about it, too. Mario had told Emily immediately after learning of its existence, and insisted she learn how to monitor it. It had freaked her out at first, but there was no way he was going to keep an escape route from her.

Security hadn't wanted any civilians knowing about this smaller emergency exit, but members of the Council were used to getting their way. The ensuing half-assed solution that left everyone unhappy had been to make the alarms on that door so sensitive that they sent false breach warnings all the time. Mario had been the only Council member who really paid attention to it in addition to the three dedicated security guys.

They did their job well but considered the door glitchy. Glitchy didn't instill a sense of urgency in anyone, just annoyance, which Mario knew firsthand. The whole thing was stupid, an accident waiting to happen, but wasn't that the story of every impenetrable fortress until it fell?

Mario had put a back door in the access code system for this door, one only he and Emily knew about. He figured his chances were fifty-fifty that anyone had found it. Assuming no one saw him, if he did set off any alarms, it would be put down to glitching.

Two blocks away he stopped, hiding behind the corner of the ruin that had been Whole Foods Market. The zombie moans seemed louder, but he wasn't sure if it was real, or if he was just amped on adrenaline. Blood pounded in his ears as he watched and waited. Figures moved along the line of lights at the top. He checked his watch and settled in. After half and hour, they hadn't deviated from walking by every five minutes. They'd shortened the patrol interval since he'd left, probably because of all the recent fighting with SCU. He sidled along the building, staying in the shadows. The block after this one had been razed, so once he reached the corner of the building he either ran for the wall or fell back. He figured he had two minutes, maybe, to get inside before the next patrol might see him.

His breath rasped in and out of his lungs as he watched the next set of head and shoulders walk along the top of the wall. As soon as they vanished from sight, he

sprinted for the door. Almost immediately, he heard a shout. Fuck, he thought, but kept running. Then the ground around him seemed to erupt, tiny puffs of earth exploding around his feet. He ran, not allowing himself to think about the bullets whizzing around him. A few seconds later, he slammed into the wall. The bullets stopped, the shallow angle of the junction of the outer and inner walls offering a sliver of shadow. Mario sidled over to the keypad, knowing in his heart that it was over. He tapped in the code and pressed enter, expecting nothing to happen.

The door began to slide open. He squeezed through almost before there was enough room and lunged for the red button that would stop the door opening all the way. Then he pushed it again, and the door closed.

Already he could hear voices getting closer, and the pounding of boots. Maybe they'd changed the protocol for how many people responded to the alarm. He sprinted down the dark street ahead of him, hard breaths scraping in and out of his lungs. Halfway down the block, he pushed his way through a high boxwood hedge. He gripped the top of the fence behind it and jumped. Pain ripped through his right calf. He grunted, hoisting himself up, and grabbed the limb of an overhanging tree.

He was just about to drop down into the yard behind the fence when more voices approached. He climbed higher into the tree, his arms beginning to feel rubbery. He should have listened to Doug, should have been smarter. Once they caught him, his brother would know he wasn't dead and—

Footsteps, coming at a jog, jolted him from his panic attack. He hugged himself closer to the tree's main trunk.

"It's that stupid alarm is all. It goes off all the time."

"He said he saw a person running from the door."

The first voice snorted as two shadowy figures approached.

Everyone knows Joey smokes too much weed. He probably sees little green men, too."

The men didn't stop. Mario watched them turn the corner. He squinted back at the wall. Lights were on by the door, and three men searched the area.

His calf throbbed, and he could feel blood seeping into his boot.

"Got myself shot in the fucking bargain," he muttered.

He didn't reach down to feel his calf to try and assess the damage. He stayed still, hoping the tree's leaves and branches, and his stillness, would hide him. Eventually, the lights at the door were turned off. No one else passed by his perch. Mario stayed put for what felt like an eternity. He checked his watch, shielding the backlight with his jacket. It had only been forty minutes and was now 4:13 a.m. He had to get into place before dawn broke, or he might as well walk to his house and turn himself in.

Carefully, he lowered himself down and dropped from the tree onto the fence, then to the ground. He walked its length behind the hedge, then emerged into the street. He stuck to shadows when they were available, keeping his pace steady but not too fast, topping out at a fast limp. He continued on Emerson for a few more blocks on well-maintained sidewalks, passing dark houses tucked in snug for the night. This had felt normal before he left the Valley; now it felt like another planet. He slowed at the intersection with Seale Street, where he would turn right. His house, his family, was three blocks in the other direction.

It felt like being in the gravity well of a planet, the pull of an irresistible force so strong, so overwhelming, that for a brief, insane moment, he almost gave in to it. An irresistible force was something you couldn't fight. You couldn't beat it. It was foolish to even try. He looked down the shadowy street, the longing a physical ache that pushed away the pain in his calf. Home, where his children and Emily slept in their beds, so close he could almost touch it.

He turned away, hobbling in the other direction. When he reached Alma, he crossed the street. The strip of land between

Alma and the Caltrain tracks was planted with hedges, so it provided good cover most of the way as Mario made his way south. The sky above him shifted to predawn gray.

He saw the first cat, then several more that scurried away, alarmed at his approach. The astringent smell of cat piss filled his nostrils. He picked up the pace, energized by finally reaching his goal: the Oregon Expressway.

As the sky lightened, the concrete gully of the expressway came into focus. Alma Street continued on its course above the expressway, via an overpass, but a section of the next overpass had collapsed and dangled down as if on a hinge, forming a crude, steep ramp.

The smell of cat piss grew stronger, along with the mews, as Mario moved farther into the feral cat colony. Lithe shapes slunk close to the ground as they scurried out of sight, away from the lumbering human among them.

A stab of pain lanced through his calf. "Goddamn, that hurts," he said, to the cats he guessed, as he climbed over the guardrails that divided the road.

He ducked under the section of Alma Street that had collapsed and sat down. Angry hisses preceded the scurry of feet over crumbling concrete. More faintly were plaintive cries, squeaky and high-pitched. Relief crashed through him at the confirmation that there were kittens here. He stretched and twisted his leg to inspect his calf in the watery light. It was still bleeding. He skimmed his calf with his fingertips until he found a painful, hard lump, so tender he had to bite his lip to stop himself from crying out. The bullet was lodged in his calf.

"Fuck, fuck, fuck," he said.

He pulled his knife from its sheath. He took a couple quick breaths, psyching himself up, and wriggled the knife into the wound. Tears streamed down his face. When he caught the bullet with the knife's tip, he pressed against it from the outside of his calf with his thumb. He continued this way, wriggling the knife and pushing on his damaged muscle, until the bullet was out. He was trembling and sweaty by the time he was done, and thought he might puke.

"Oh my God," he gasped, resting his head in his hands.

When he finally thought he wouldn't upchuck the contents of his stomach, he reached into his jacket and pulled out the hankies he had tucked inside. Gently but firmly, he wrapped them around his calf. When he had finished, he moved a little farther under the section of the collapsed overpass. He could hear the stealthy scurrying of mama cats returning to their kittens.

It had sounded like the children weren't under lock and key like their mother. They were just kids, after all, and how could they escape a fortress like New Palo Alto? If this was actually the case, then Anthony would come. Even if it wasn't, Anthony would come. He searched for litters of kittens every single day before school, whether it was kitten season or not. Mario leaned against the wall, closed his eyes as he tipped his head back to rest, and waited for his son.

29

MARIO JERKED AWAKE, panic flooding his body. Bright morning sunshine had replaced the early dawn's pink-tinted gray. He hadn't meant to fall asleep, but by the time he settled into his hiding place he'd been up for almost twenty hours. Then he realized what had woke him. Singing—a child's voice, high and piping. Anthony's voice; his bet had paid off. The desire to rush out to meet him flooded his nervous system, its power intoxicating, but Mario stayed still in the shadows. If anyone was with his son, he couldn't risk approaching him.

Anthony walked into view, the bright sunlight limning him in gold. He had grown a couple inches, and his dark-brown hair was longer. It reminded Mario of the haircuts sported by The Beatles when they first hit the American charts, on their way to becoming the biggest band in the world. Anthony carried a large cat carrier. It was too big for him to manage well, so he moved awkwardly, like Silas had when he'd insisted on carrying Mister Bun Bun. A wave of grief crashed over Mario, despite his joy at seeing Anthony. He'd already thought of the boys as brothers, but it would never happen now.

He heard Anthony's footsteps but couldn't see him, so he crept toward the edge of the fallen overpass, staying well back in the shadows. When Anthony reappeared on the other side, he reached over the center divider between the four lanes. Carefully, he set the carrier down on the other side of the divider, then scrambled over it. He walked to a sheltered corner near the on-ramp, thirty feet from where Mario was hiding. An old concrete barrier had been placed at a diagonal to it. Pipes overgrown with weeds that had withered during the dry summer ran up the side of the concrete. Anthony squeezed through a gap at the end of the barrier. A puffed up black and white cat bolted from behind it.

"I'm sorry, Mama Cat," Anthony said.

He crouched down, only the top of his head visible. Mario heard the rattle of the carrier door being opened. Anthony's voice never stopped—he was talking to the kittens he was collecting—but all Mario could hear was a soothing murmur. The top of his son's head ducked out of sight, then popped back up. Mario turned to look the way Anthony had come. There was no one in sight. He walked to the edge of the overhang so that when Anthony turned around, he'd be visible.

Anthony stood up. The expression on his face was satisfied, but also a little sad. "I'm sorry, Mama Cat," he said again, his voice raised. "I'll take good care of your kittens. Only nice people will adopt them." He paused, then added, "Maybe I'll catch you soon, and then you won't have to keep having them."

Mario said, "Anthony."

Anthony looked up, curious, then seemed to slump. His face went slack and blank. His mouth fell open. When Mario held his finger up to his lips, indicating that he should be quiet, it broke the spell. Anthony rocketed to him, kittens forgotten, and hit Mario so hard that he knocked him down. Anthony didn't say anything. He sobbed, his cries heartrending. Mario held his son close, rocking him like he'd done when Anthony was a baby.

"It's all right," he managed to choke out, almost sobbing himself. "It's all right, Anthony."

He felt Anthony's head nod. He looked up at Mario, his face tear-streaked, confused. "Is it really you, Daddy?"

The overwhelming relief of seeing his son alive and whole and still collecting kittens, of being able to hold him in his arms and wipe away his tears, was too much to take in. "Yeah," he whispered, looking into those serious brown eyes. "It's me."

They sat on the ground, the reek of cat piss blown away by the gentle breeze from the east, and he held his son. Eventually, he said, "Are you okay?"

Anthony straightened up and looked at Mario. "Yeah. I'm okay."

"What about Mommy and Michael and Maureen?"

"They're okay, too." His voice became hopeful. "Are you coming home?"

Was there anything worse than watching the hope in the eyes of your child die? Mario was pretty sure there wasn't. He wanted so much to spare Anthony that pain, that disappointment, but he couldn't.

"Not yet," he said. "I'm sorry, but not yet. I want to but—"

"Uncle Dom."

Mario nodded. "Yeah. And because I stole the serum for the vaccine."

Anthony almost smiled. "Mommy told us. Uncle Dom was so mad...like, scary mad. We didn't get to stay with the priests very long before he brought us back home."

"I know," Mario said. "That's why I came. To see you, and do something about Uncle Dom." Anthony nodded, but didn't say more, so Mario continued. "I need you to do me a favor, but you can't tell anyone. And I mean nobody. Nobody can know."

"Okay," Anthony said, his voice sounding small. He was nine, but suddenly seemed so much younger. Mario hated having to pull him into this.

"Tell Mommy I'm here, and that I'm coming to see her tonight."

Anthony shook his head. "You won't be able to, Dad. They watch her too much."

Mario had figured as much, but he still had to try. "Your mom is really smart. She'll figure something out. What time does Uncle Dom get home, or does he work from the house?"

Anthony shook his head. "He goes to work. He gets home near bedtime."

"Still nine o'clock?"

"Yeah."

Mario ruffled Anthony's hair. "Tell her I'll be along the back fence, at eight. If she comes out and I'm not there, then I couldn't make it. She shouldn't wait for me. Can you remember that?"

"Yes." Anthony looked like he wanted to say more but didn't.

"What is it?" Mario asked.

"She's scared all the time, Dad. She says she's not, but I can tell. But she's mad, too. And Uncle Alan makes her crazy."

Mario laughed softly, "Uncle Alan makes everyone crazy. He's an idiot."

Anthony grinned. "That's what Mom says."

"Are there a lot of guards at the house?"

"Yes. There are fifteen now."

Mario smiled at the precision, but precise was how Anthony had always been. Even as a toddler he had wanted his toys in particular places, arranged in a particular way, and noticed everything.

"None of the ones when you were at home. They're different. They act nice but they're not our friends." Anthony's mouth twisted with disgust, then his eyes filled with devilment. "They can't figure out how I sneak out to get the kittens and it's driving them crazy. I don't go on the same days, or the same time." He snorted, the condescension for stupid adults only a child can possess coming through loud and clear. "There are, like, four ways to do it. They're too stupid to find them."

"Remind me never to get on your bad side, kiddo."

Mario checked his watch. His stomach lurched. He and Anthony had spent half an hour together. If he didn't get home soon, the guards might notice he was missing and come looking for him.

"You need to go now, Anthony. Before anyone comes looking for you." He held his son's face in his hands. "I love you so much, Anthony."

"I love you, too, Dad."

Anthony's eyes filled with tears, just like Mario's were doing.

"I know it's hard," he said, wishing he had something to tell Anthony that didn't feel—wasn't—so inadequate. "I'll be home as soon as I can."

Anthony nodded, and Mario pulled him close, knowing it could very well be the last time. The last time he smelled Anthony's skin, felt his soft hair against his cheek. He drank it all in like a man dying of thirst, the sight and smell and feel of his son, so that he would always remember. The boy in his arms, the rest of his family only blocks away, were the fuel for what he had to do to end all this.

"Go on, now," he said, untangling himself from Anthony. It hurt so much to let go of him, like he was ripping off a limb. "Remember, don't—"

"Tell anyone," Anthony said, interrupting him.

"That's right. You're going to want to, but you cannot tell

Michael or Maureen, okay?" He waited until Anthony nodded. "I love you so much, Anthony."

"I love you too, Dad."

Mario's eyes filled with tears again. He watched as Anthony began to walk carefully through the scattered concrete and rocks beneath the fallen overpass. Then he remembered.

"Anthony!" he said. Anthony spun back to face him. "The kittens."

Anthony's face filled with surprise. "The kittens!"

He ran past his father without stopping, to the carrier still out on the road beside the center divider. He crouched down on hands and knees, then turned around, smiling, and gave a thumbs-up. Mario wanted to go over and help him get the carrier over the center divider, but he couldn't risk being spotted. Anthony set the carrier across the gap between the back-to-back steel guardrails, then climbed over. He picked up the carrier of kittens and looked back to Mario. His brown eyes were bright, face hopeful.

Mario's love for his children, deep and boundless, fierce and unstoppable, filled him. He would get them away from his brother, get them all in the same place. He would make things right.

He walked to other side of the overpass when Anthony walked out of sight. When he reappeared, he looked over his shoulder, squinting a little, so Mario took one more step toward the opening. Anthony smiled. Mario blew him a kiss. Anthony smiled more broadly, with a touch of 'I'm too old for that; on his face, but pleased nonetheless. Then he turned away and ran out of sight.

Mario watched him go. Then he crept back, closer to the fallen edge of the overpass, where the cover was better, to sleep.

But before he drifted into dreamless oblivion, he wept.

MARIO WAS AT THE CORNER OF THE FIRST BLOCK INTO THE neighborhood when he realized something was off. Almost every house had its porch light on. Some people always turned on their porch lights, but just as many didn't. He dropped back into the shadow of the giant sycamore tree near the corner. He pushed up the bill of his baseball cap. Lots of people were out, going from house to house in groups. Then he saw them...children on the well-lit stoop a third of the way up the block, dressed as witches and firemen, ballerinas and pirates. Shit, he thought, just as they chimed, "Trick or treat!"

Halloween...it's fucking Halloween.

Mario checked his watch again: 7:55 p.m. He cursed himself for instructing Anthony to tell Emily not to wait if he was late. He didn't want her putting herself in danger by waiting for him, but this was going to slow him down.

The other side of the street had a couple porch lights that weren't on. He pulled the cap down low and crossed the street. The throb in his calf flared into a sharp jab with every step, worse when he tried not to limp. He walked as quickly as he could, but not so much that it would look like he was in a hurry.

"Happy Halloween," a woman said as she walked by. The group of children she was minding had run ahead in a pack, shrieking and laughing.

"You too," he replied, nodding.

His heart felt like it might thump out of his chest. What time did trick-or-treating usually end? Eight thirty? Nine? Not soon enough, he thought, stepping to the grass parking strip alongside the sidewalk for a group of firemen and fairies to hurry by.

"Great weather for this, isn't it?" a man with another group of children said to him.

"Sure is," Mario said, sweat drenching his back and armpits while he smiled and dipped his head low. By the time he got to the neighbor's property on Waverly Street, which backed onto his, he was so rattled he just walked down the driveway like he belonged there. He'd planned to walk by, give it a good look and make sure the coast was clear, but now he just wanted to get off the street.

He slowed as he got to the garage, staying in shadow. There were lights on in the front of the house; someone was probably giving out candy. The kitchen at the back of the house, facing the yard, was also lit up. He could see the glow of the lights of his house on the other side of the high hedge that ran along the wrought iron fence along his backyard. He crept to the back patio, trying to stay out of areas where the kitchen's light spilled out, and looked for the best place to wait. The pool house wasn't far from the fence, but he had to cross the patio, which was illuminated by the kitchen light and small accent lights. Better than motion sensors, but still not ideal. He checked the house again, then darted across the patio and slipped around corner of the pool house. He checked his watch. He was seven minutes late.

"Fuck," he muttered.

The neighborhood seemed to be quieting down. Normally this would be good, indicating nothing was out of the ordinary was going on, but every second he spent leaning against the pool house made his body hum with anxiety and dread. He checked his watch—a minute had passed. The watch beckoned him to check again. He resisted, but when he finally gave in, only two more minutes had passed. If he was on time, Dominic would be getting home in about forty minutes.

I'll give it five more minutes, he thought. After that, it would be cutting it too close to when Dom would arrive home.

A branch snapped. An electric charge thrummed through Mario's body. He tensed, preparing to flee.

"Mario?"

Relief felt like a ten-ton weight lifting from his shoulders.

"Over here," he said.

A few moments later, Emily wriggled into the space between the tall boxwood hedge and the wrought iron fence.

"Oh my God!" she said, reaching for him through the bars. "What are you doing here?"

"Are you okay?" he asked, taking her face in his hands.

Her skin felt warm and soft and smooth, and a faint waft of perfume—Coco, by Chanel—clung to her. A dark baseball cap covered her bright blond hair.

"I'm fine, we're all fine, but you shouldn't be here," she said, her face pinched with anxiety.

"I had to make sure you were okay."

A deep sorrow over the failure of their marriage blossomed inside him. He and Emily had gotten married too quickly, for the wrong reasons. Even if that hadn't been the case, marriages fell apart all the time. But his upbringing—the good and the bad—was always there, buried deep and disapproving, especially because he carried most of the blame for what had happened to theirs. You stayed with your wife and took care of your family. You stayed with your husband, even if he beat you, like his mother had. It was old-fashioned and outdated and sometimes unhealthy, but a sliver still persisted, woven into his DNA.

"We're fine," she said. "Is Connor with you?"

"Oh, Em," Mario said, pulled up short. Of course she couldn't know, and somehow, he'd never thought about it. "He's...no, he's not. He's— He was infected, Em. He's gone."

Emily whimpered, then slumped, her head resting against the bars of the fence. She took shallow, shuddering breaths as her shoulders shook. Mario patted one, feeling completely inadequate to the task—and terrible for wanting to hurry her up—because they couldn't be here long. She looked up at him, but her face was twisted with anger.

"I'm going to kill him, I swear to God," she hissed. "Your fucking brother... I'll fucking kill him."

Mario's eyes widened in surprise. The grief and sorrow he'd expected, but not anger.

"I'm sorry," she said, shaking it off as she wiped her eyes. It was hard to tell in the weak moonlight, but Mario thought he saw a steely determination in their depths. "They're going to execute Father Walter tomorrow."

"What?"

"You have to let them know," she said. "They have to get him out of there now."

"Okay," Mario said, his brain spinning like a top.

Brother Rupert and the others thought they had maybe a week, but they didn't. Their plan to rescue Walter in three days would be too late.

"Are you sure you're all okay?" Mario asked again. When she nodded, he said. "I'm coming back for you, all of you. I will get you out of here. And I'll deal with Dominic."

Emily smiled, and her face softened. "You think I don't already know that? It never crossed my mind that you wouldn't come for us if you knew what was going on. Though you could have picked a better night than Halloween."

"Tell me about it... I didn't realize."

"How's—" She paused, then said, sounding unsure, "You and Miri...you're together again?"

Words failed him. What could he say in this moment, when every second he spent with Emily put her in danger? How could he answer her question and have it make any sense when he barely understood what had happened to them himself?

She must have taken his hesitation as reluctance to say something that might hurt her, for she added, "I'm happy for you, Mario. For both of you."

He could tell she meant it, and it hurt—more than he could have ever imagined.

"We aren't right for each other, Mar. I needed you at first, and I did fall in love with you. It didn't start out that way and it didn't last, but for a while..." She sighed. "Being with you made me think I couldn't cope, that I was helpless, but I'm not. I realize that now, because I haven't been allowed to be helpless since you left. I've had to get on with it, and I found out that I can."

The lump in Mario's throat made it hard to speak. "I can see that now, Em, how strong you are. I'm sorry for how it all happened, with me and Miranda. I never meant to hurt you, but I did."

"There's a lot to be sorry for, for both of us. I'm—" She stopped, and he could see the nervous energy in the tilt of her head, how she shifted her weight back and forth, the suddenly higher pitch of her voice. She bit her lip as she looked at him without seeing him, as if she was searching for the right word. "Ashamed, for using the boys the way I did."

"What are you talking about?" He was genuinely confused, because Emily was a wonderful mother. She always had been.

Her mouth fell open. Haltingly, she said, "When I... took them out... Beyond the walls. When you said you were leaving me. I thought— Oh Jesus, Mario, I thought you figured it out. I didn't want you to leave, and I knew we'd be spotted right away, and that you'd be there. I knew there weren't any zombies near-by." Her voice dropped to a whisper. "When I think of how I could have been wrong..."

For a moment, her words didn't make sense.

"Doug was right," he said, so softly she didn't hear him.

She hadn't lost it or been pushed too far, not in the way he'd thought, anyway. She hadn't cracked up or been out of her mind when she took the boys outside SCU's walls all those years ago. It had been a thought-out, calculated decision. She had manipulated him, and he had fallen for it, hook, line, and sinker.

She reached out and touched his cheek, but hesitantly, like he might shove her away.

"I'm so sorry."

Mario had known Emily for eleven years, been married to her for most of them. Hell, he still was. He'd seen her at her best and her worst, made love to her with passion and tenderness, and sometimes, bitterness. Had a family with her, built a life together, yet he felt like he was seeing her—really seeing her for who she was, not the wounded person he'd thought of her as—for the very first time. He covered her hand with his own, a different kind of love for her swelling in his heart. One grounded in respect instead of rescue, in recognition instead of projection.

"Em, it doesn't matter now."

They looked at one another, an ending hovering between them that held the other with compassion.

"I should go," Mario said, wiping away the tears that had sprung to his eyes. "Anthony said Dom gets back around nine. You've been here too long already."

Emily laughed softly. "They haven't even noticed I'm gone yet, trust me. I started a grease fire in the kitchen."

"What?"

She began to laugh harder, yet still stayed quiet. "It's okay, Mario. Really. The kids set up a tent in the yard. They're in there stuffing their faces with candy. The fire wasn't that bad, even if I did manage to accidentally spill flaming grease across the floor. I pretended to freak out and ran away screaming to look for the kids."

"Oh my God," Mario said, alarm giving way to amazement. "Who are you, and what have you done with my wife?"

Emily's smile mirrored his own. She took his hands and gave them a squeeze. "I'll keep the kids safe. Be careful, okay?"

"I will."

He leaned toward her between the bars of the fence, then hesitated, but Emily met him halfway. Her lips on his were soft and familiar, but the kiss they shared was entirely new. It said all the things that he didn't know how to put into words. That he wished he'd met this Emily first. That he was sorry for the pain he'd caused her, and grateful that she didn't begrudge him the happiness he had found—however fleeting—with Miranda. That he'd loved her once, too, for a time...inconsistently, badly, in a way that had stunted her, though he'd never meant for that to happen. That he'd forgive any and everything she might have done, because that was what a man who had once loved and still respected his wife did. Not because he had to, but because it felt right, because she was the mother of his children and they would always share that bond. That he was grateful they'd reached this place of understanding, of compassion and care, for one another.

The kiss said goodbye to the life they had shared, imperfect as it was, but not to the family they would always be, even as their paths diverged. Mario was breathless, and a little dizzy, when the kiss ended, and surprised by the heat it sparked between them. They stood, foreheads touching.

"Be careful," Emily whispered.

"Always," he said. "Kiss the kids for me."

She kissed him again, and he responded, wishing the fence wasn't between them. He ached to hold her in his arms, feel the warmth of her body's familiar contours against his own. They were both breathless when she disappeared through the hedge. Mario stood for a moment, the endings and beginnings of his life seeming to surround and hold him close, all of them at once. He let them swaddle him tight for a bittersweet moment, before they dissipated into the warm night air, and set him free.

———

HE MANAGED TO NOT LIMP TOO MUCH, KEEPING HIS PACE steady. The trick-or-treating was over, thank God, but there was still the occasional person out. He'd already passed a woman on a run, and an older man walking a fluffy little dog at a brisk pace. Mario had adjusted his baseball cap as they passed one another, as if doffing his cap, while he shielded his face with his upraised arm.

He followed Waverly north as far as Kingsley. The wall was three blocks straight ahead, and the gate three blocks west. He turned the corner, his proximity to the wall so close it felt like a magnet pulling on him. Music blared from the house on the corner, laughing people in costumes visible in the brightly lit windows. Mario picked up the pace, anxious to reach the next block.

He crossed the street and could see the mouth of an alley halfway down the block. Then bright lights flared on his left. The squeal of tires, and the shrill squeak of brakes hit too hard shattered the quiet night. He was slammed from behind, his feet scooped out from under him. He tumbled over the warm hood of a car, then backflipped off it on the passenger side. His shoulder cracked against the pavement. Bright sparks he was pretty sure weren't really there lit up his vision. Mario rolled onto his side, moaning. Pain flared in his lower back, where his Sig dug into his spine. Pain from his injured calf radiated through his toes and into his thigh. He pushed himself to sitting, trying to orient himself. The world seemed to be spinning around him.

A car door opened. "Are you okay?"

Mario barely heard the voice—a man's voice. He had to get away, had to run. He couldn't let the driver help him. Mario staggered to his feet and slowly, painfully, he started to walk away. He'd have run if he could.

"Wait up!"

Mario stumbled, but righted himself. His pulse pounded in his ears. He could hear the man's footsteps behind him. He was going to be caught. After everything, he was going to be caught, and if that happened, he was dead.

He stumbled again. The dark alley was just ahead.

"Hey! Wait!"

Mario waved him off, "I'm okay," he said, but his words sounded slurry.

A hand closed on his bicep. He tried to keep going but the man's grip was strong.

"I didn't see you. Your clothes are so dark."

This close, the voice sounded familiar. The man got in front of him, still holding on to Mario's arm. He was a little taller than Mario, with a heavier build, well dressed, and reeked of gin. Mario squinted at him, and shock cut through the muddle of his concussed brain. In an instant the world around him came into focus, the shadows sharply exaggerated.

It was Dominic.

Dominic's face went slack, mouth falling open. Color drained from his face like he'd just seen a ghost. "Mario?"

Mario shoved, driving his shoulder into Dominic's solar plexus, knocking him into the dark alley. Dominic staggered, pinwheeling his arms to keep his balance. Mario charged, fist leading the way for a Superman punch. He connected squarely with Dominic's chin. Dominic teetered for a split second, then fell backward with an *oof*.

"You fucking piece of shit."

Mario pulled the Sig from the waistband of his pants. Wrath flowed through his veins. His injured body felt numb, the pain distant. He approached his brother's prone form like an avenging angel.

"Mario, thank God!" Dominic said, pulling himself to sitting.

Mario kicked him. The crack of ribs against his boot felt good. Dominic groaned, clutching his side.

"I know, you motherfucker. I know what you did."

"Mar!" Dominic's voice was high—panicked. "I don't what you're—"

Mario kicked him again, harder than before. He pressed the barrel of the gun against Dominic's head, and he quit writhing. The only sound was the wheeze of his breath and the faint dinging from the car.

"You tried to kill Miranda."

"What are you talking about?"

"She was pregnant. Did you know that? She was pregnant when you hatched your little scheme."

"A baby?" He could hear the fear in Dominic's voice, smell it pouring from his alcohol-soaked pores. "That's great, Mar. Congratulations."

Mario cocked the hammer of his gun. "If one more lie comes out of your mouth, I'll blow your fucking head off."

Dominic whimpered. It was a pathetic sound, like a scared puppy might make. From the street behind them, Mario heard voices. He looked up. People from the party were coming to see what had happened.

"I know everything. If it was just me," he said. "But it wasn't. You had to go after Miranda, too."

His finger trembled on the trigger, itching to squeeze it.

"Is everything okay there?"

Mario glanced down the alley. A woman dressed as Cleopatra stood in the street, the gold cape affixed to the shoulders of her dress falling behind her and fluttering around her ankles. She squinted, her eyes bright against the heavy, black kohl encircling them. A guy dressed like a Viking was a few steps behind her. She'd asked if everything was okay, so she obviously couldn't see them well enough to know Mario was holding a gun to Dominic's head.

"Just trying to get this guy up," Mario said. "He's drunk." Cleopatra took a step forward. "A little combative, though."

She hesitated. "We heard the brakes, and I saw someone getting up from the ground."

"That was me, but I'm fine. I fell getting out of the way. He came to see if I was okay, but started puking," Mario said, trying to make it sound like it wasn't a big deal. "We've all had a few too many. No harm, no foul."

The Viking arrived. "What's going on?"

"He says the guy's drunk," she said to him. "But that he didn't hit him like we thought."

The Viking squinted down the alley at them. "Do you need help?"

"Thanks, but no. He just needs to sleep this off. I've already called security to drive him home."

"Are you sure?" Cleopatra asked, her voice anxious.

"My dad was a drunk. I've been dealing with guys like this all my life."

"Well," she said uncertainly. "If you're sure."

"I'll wait with you," the Viking said.

"That's so kind, but you really don't need to," Mario said, a calm in his voice that he did not feel infusing warmth into his words. "Your party's been interrupted enough... I'm so sorry."

"Well, if you're sure," he said.

"I'm sure. Security will get the car. They're so on top of stuff like that."

The Viking nodded, and Mario thought his shoulders relaxed. Only people who belonged here knew how efficient security was when it came to cleaning up messes.

"Let's go, honey," the Viking said. "If he's already called security..."

Cleopatra hesitated for several seconds. "Well, okay. Come over for a drink, if you want. My name's—"

"Cleopatra, Queen of the Nile," Mario said, a smile in his voice.

She laughed. "Yeah. Have a good night."

She turned away, taking the Viking's hand, and they walked back to the house. For a few seconds, Mario thought they might change their minds and come back, but they didn't.

Dominic must have been watching them, too. When he spoke, the pretense of surprise and concern was gone. "Just do it," he said. "Just get it over with."

Mario looked down at the dark form of his brother. He could feel Dominic trembling through the barrel of the gun pressed against his temple. His little brother, who had sided with the Council from the start, and used the worst calamity in human history to enrich himself. Dominic joked about shooting migrants, and toyed with the Dosers working as dishwashers at restaurants if he got a dirty knife, insisting the offender be brought to the dining room so they could grovel for his forgiveness. He was also the boy Mario had taught to ride a bike, who imitated the old German priest in their parish so well that Mario had laughed until he cried. Mario had taken beatings from their father to keep his little brother safe, and he'd repaid him, all these years later, by trying to kill the woman Mario loved.

His arm trembled as he curled his finger around the trigger. Just squeeze, he told himself... He tried to kill Miranda. Just do it.

Anger howled inside him like a cyclone, bludgeoning the inside of his skull, shoving and pushing, but not enough. The tension in his arm slackened, because he couldn't do it. He couldn't shoot his little brother.

"Get up."

"What?"

"Get. Up."

Dominic scrambled to his feet. He swayed a little, but given how he smelled, Mario was surprised he could stand upright. Mario gripped his brother's arm with one hand and shoved the Sig into his side.

"We're walking back to your car. You'll get in the passenger seat. I'll drive."

"Where are we going?"

Mario gave him a shove. "Shut up."

Mario's mind raced as they walked down the alley, spinning out scenarios. The safest thing to do would be to kidnap Dominic, take his car, and leave, but that wasn't what he was going to do.

He was going home, to get his family.

30

THE TWIN BEACONS of the sports car's headlights cut into the dark mouth of the alley, door flung wide and chime ringing. Mario pressed the barrel of the Sig into Dominic's ribs. When he shied away, he stumbled. Mario jerked him close, realizing that Dominic was far more drunk than he'd realized.

"You aren't really—"

"Shut up," Mario growled. "When we get to the car, you're going to open the passenger door and get in. I don't want to shoot you, Dom," he said, his voice getting tight. "But if comes down to you or me, I will."

He saw Dominic's Adam's apple bob in his throat. They reached the car, and Dominic reached for the handle. Mario kept the Sig against Dominic's body, standing clear enough that his brother couldn't shove him off using the door. Dominic's feet tangled, and he practically fell into the car.

"Mario," his brother began.

Mario leaned in close, cocked his arm back at the elbow, and pistol-whipped Dominic on the temple. He collapsed against the seat with a groan. Mario jabbed him, to make sure he wasn't just dazed. He glanced around the car's interior but didn't see anything he could tie his hands with. He'd have to chance it.

He straightened up, shut the door, and walked around the car to get inside. He turned the ignition and the engine roared to life. He shifted into first, and the car leaped forward, the powerful engine catching Mario by surprise. He sped down the block, turning right onto Bryant, then looping back around it until he reached Webster. Then he worked his way to home, turning at almost every block to avoid taking a direct path.

Halfway down Santa Rita, before the intersection with Cowper, he pulled to the side of the road and turned it off. He checked Dominic—still out. He pulled the keys from the ignition and hurried to the trunk, hoping Dominic had some spare clothes there. He needed to bullshit his way past security at the gate, and it would be a lot easier if he didn't look like he'd spent the night in his clothes and been hit by a car. He sighed with relief when the trunk opened, revealing a dark suit and white shirt. He snatched them from the trunk and slammed it shut, then hurriedly changed into the suit and jacket. No tie, but he couldn't worry about that now. He wished he had an earpiece, but he couldn't do anything about that, either.

At the corner he turned left onto Cowper. He could see the lights of the entrance gates to his home ahead. Nothing that would be considered garish, but enough to signify that there was something important about the address. Mario took a few deep breaths, checking his face in the visor mirror again and smoothing back his hair with shaking hands. His back was beginning to throb, and his shoulder ached. He moved the visor to the top of his car door window and flipped it down. He hoped the position wouldn't seem too weird at night, but he needed to shield his face. He offered up a silent prayer as the sports car glided to a halt at the security booth.

The guard looked up, then opened the window.

"Mr. Santorello?"

Mario didn't lean forward, trying to make the most of the lowered visor.

"Nah, he's out cold. I'm surprised you can't smell the gin."

The guard squinted, lowering his head to look past Mario. Because of the partially lowered visor, the man had to hunch down lower than he'd normally need to. Sweat popped out on Mario's forehead, the slight breeze cooling his brow, but he was so anxious he felt as hot as a blast furnace.

"He's been hitting it pretty hard lately, hasn't he?"

Mario chuckled, as if this was not news to him. "You're not kidding."

He shifted his weight, so he was leaning a little more toward Dominic. He looked at him and saw his eyelids flutter. He looked back at the guard, and realized the guard was out here on his own.

The guard said, "I don't recognize you. What's your name?"

"Why's it just you out here?" Mario asked, ignoring the guard's question, in a tone that implied the man was falling down on the job. "There should be at least two people here."

"There was a fire in the kitchen," the guard said, his voice slightly defensive.

"A fire?"

"The lady of the house... Turned out to be nothing, but Jones and Allemany had to go up."

The guard's tone implied he didn't think much of Emily. It was all Mario could do to not whimper at this new piece of information. He didn't know how many guards were in the house, but he knew there were two more than normal. Not realizing he'd get an opportunity to come back tonight, he hadn't thought to ask Emily.

Then he realized he was taking just a bit too long to answer, so he said, "Fucking hell... A pyro on top of being a head case?"

The guard chuckled. Dominic groaned again.

"Come on, man, he's waking up," Mario said. "He's obnoxious when he's loaded. You know he made a pass at Allemany the last time."

"Really?" The guard sounded surprised, and like this was the best gossip he had heard in quite a while. "He never said... but I guess he wouldn't. I can't wait to yank his chain."

Mario gave a thumbs-up, a surge of relief rushing through his body when the gate opened. He eased the car through and wound up the drive. Ahead, the house was partially lit, but looked quiet enough. Mario approached the garage, wondering if the car had an RFID chip that would open it automatically. A second later, both garage doors began to open—question answered. The third spot was empty. He pulled in. Dominic was groaning again, but still not awake.

He parked the car and climbed out, snugging the Sig more securely in his waistband. The faint whiff of biodiesel exhaust filled his nose. Quickly, he walked to the storage locker at the back of the garage and opened the nearest one. Inside were gardening supplies and tools—and a bag of pins and a clothesline. Mario grabbed the thin coil, its surface smooth from regular use. He tried the driver's door of the Mercedes sedan parked in the middle spot, breathing a sigh of relief when it opened. He reached inside and popped the trunk. He opened the passenger door of the sports car; Dominic groaned and stirred. Quickly, he bound Dominic's hands, then pulled his feet out and turned him.

"Oooh," Dominic groaned.

"Come on, Dom," Mario said. "On your feet." He caught Dominic under his armpits and dragged him upright. "Christ, you're heavy," he grunted.

Mario wasn't small at six feet, and was in good shape, but Dom had been bigger and stronger since they were teenagers. Dominic took a few stumbling steps while Mario pulled and dragged. When they got to the Mercedes, he pushed Dominic into the open trunk.

"Hey," he protested, but it was feeble at best. Mario shoved his legs and feet inside.

He loosened and stripped Dominic's tie, then stuffed it in his mouth. He looked for something to tie it in place. He didn't have anything to cut the clothesline and he didn't want to waste time looking for something to use. He stuck his hand in the suit coat pocket, and it closed around a bundle of silky material, a tie wound around itself.

He fastened the second tie around Dominic's mouth, then eased the trunk shut. He checked his watch—10:02 p.m. He took a moment to think. The Mercedes was electric, so fuel wasn't an issue, and it was big enough that everyone would fit. He had to find Emily, collect the kids, and evade an unknown number of guards. He ran back through his and Emily's conversation and realized she hadn't said what time Father Walter's execution was. They'd been in such a hurry that he hadn't asked.

He reached for the Sig as he walked to the mudroom door. The backs of his thighs were throbbing from where the car had hit him. His breathing felt a little constricted between his shoulder blades. The mudroom's door was in a direct line with the kitchen door, which was made of a single pane of glass framed by a wood sash. If he opened the mudroom door at the wrong time, he'd have a few seconds at most of being mistaken for Dominic.

Mario took a deep breath, grasped the doorknob in his sweaty hand, and twisted it. He eased the door open a few inches and peeked through. Even with the door shut, the acrid smell of burned grease hit him like his face had been shoved into a charcoal grill. The kitchen ceiling was covered in greasy, black soot. The stovetop was along the wall, covered in white powder from the fire extinguishers. The combination of the two covered the front of the oven, trailing across the floor almost to the mudroom door.

A tall fire extinguisher sat on the island behind Emily, who was cleaning the stove. Two burly men were in the kitchen with her. One stood at the island, his back to Mario while he wiped a counter. The other was on Emily's far side, the long handle of a broom sticking up from his bent form. Mario eased into the mudroom. Emily looked up. Their eyes locked, hers going so wide she reminded Mario of an owl. Before Mario could do anything, she turned around, picked up the fire extinguisher in both hands, and swung. It connected with the head of the guard standing at the island with a sickening crack. The fire extinguisher hit the tile floor with a metallic clang, along with the muffled thump of the man she'd just brained.

The other guard dropped the broom as he bolted up, his speed incongruous with his size.

"What are you doing?" he yelled.

Emily stood by the island, chest heaving, as the other man rushed past her, half-knocking her over the countertop. Mario yanked the kitchen door open at the exact moment the guard saw him. The guard charged, reaching for his firearm.

Mario backed up into the mudroom. Before he could squeeze the trigger, the guard lurched forward and tripped. Mario jumped back to avoid being dragged down by the falling man. Behind him was Emily, her arms extended in front of her. Mario kicked the man, then slammed the Sig against the back of his head. The guard slumped, unmoving.

"What are you doing here?" Emily said, breathless.

Mario looked at her flushed face and wide eyes. She'd

shoved the guy at his feet to the ground after cracking another guy in the head, hard enough that he might be dead. He was not acquainted with this Emily—at all.

"I'll tell you later," he said. "We're leaving. Where are the kids? How many guards are here in the house?"

"The boys are still in the yard in their tent. Maureen got scared and she's up in her room. There are three or four more guards around the house?" she said, her answer a question.

"What is it—three or four?"

"I don't know, it's always changing. Alan's here too. He and Dominic are using the guest room on the same hall as Maureen's room. I thought I heard Dominic's car—"

"Get the boys," Mario said, interrupting her. "I'll get Maureen. You don't need to worry about Dominic."

Emily opened her mouth to speak, a question in her eyes, then thought better of it. She turned away, running to the French doors that opened onto the veranda. She flung them wide and disappeared.

Mario hurried through the kitchen, then skulked down the short hall, stopping short of the junction with the foyer. He crouched low, hoping to avoid attracting attention at eye level, and looked around the corner. The foyer was two stories, open to the second floor's balcony hallway directly above him. Mario crept out. When he didn't see anyone above, he darted across the foyer to the foot of the curved staircase. He looked up, and seeing no one, took the steps two at a time.

At the top of the stairs, he looked to make sure the hallway to the south side of the house was clear. Then he went the other direction, scanning for shadows and listening for footsteps on the hardwood floors. He crept past the guest suite that Dominic shared with Alan to the room beyond. He eased the door open and slipped inside, closing it softly behind him. The nightlight cast a cozy glow at Maureen's bedside. His daughter was sprawled across the bed crosswise, blankets tangled around her legs. Her blond hair was in a braid, the tip of her thumb in the corner of her mouth.

She'd grown so much in the past nine months. She didn't have the babyish look of the three-year-old he left behind. She was four now, and the transformation from toddler to young child was complete. He'd missed it entirely. Her legs were thin and longer, not chubby and short. Her face had traded the softness of toddler pudge for the less pronounced softness of a very young girl. Tears prickled the corners of Mario's eyes. His daughter was more beautiful, more precious, than he'd remembered.

He knelt beside her bed, set the Sig on the nightstand, and shook her gently. Not even an eyelid flutter. Once Maureen really fell asleep, it was hard to wake her, which would be helpful right now. Nine months was a long time for a kid Maureen's age. She might not recognize him.

"It's Daddy, Maureen," he said anyway. "I've come for you and Mom and the boys."

She mumbled something, but it was in her sleep. Mario lifted her up and hoisted her onto his hip. She was heavier than he remembered, but the soft, warm breath on his neck, the sunshiny smell of her hair, was the same. He picked up the Sig again, crossed the room, and eased the door open. The hallway was still clear. Mario crept past the closed doors and emerged on the balcony. Emily waited at the bottom of the staircase, relief flooding her face when she saw him. She met him halfway.

"Let me take her," she said.

As she reached for Maureen, a voice behind him said, "Dominic?"

Mario froze. The high-pitched, nasal voice grated on his ear. It was Alan, Dominic's husband.

"Keep moving," Mario said, finishing the transfer to Emily. They started down the stairs.

"Emily! Dominic!" Alan demanded. "What's going on?"

Mario heard Alan on the stairs behind them. Emily reached the foot of the staircase and ran for the kitchen.

"Dominic!" Alan cried.

When Mario turned at the foot of the staircase to cross the foyer, he heard Alan gasp.

"What are you doing here?" he demanded. "Where's Dominic?"

Finally, Mario looked back at his brother-in-law. Alan's tall, thin form rushed forward. His dark eyes flashed, and his Adam's apple jiggled up and down so quickly it looked like a fishing bobber.

"I'm leaving with my family, Alan. Don't get in my way."

"Dominic!" Alan yelled. "Guards! Security! Help!"

Mario sprinted for the kitchen. He entered in time to see a hulk of a man dragging Emily back through the door from the garage into the mudroom.

"Let go!" Emily shouted.

Beyond her, Mario could hear Maureen crying and Michael and Anthony shouting. A hand closed around Mario's wrist. He tried to shake it off but was turned back by the strong grip.

"Where's Dominic?" Alan shouted, his beady brown eyes seeming to bore through Mario's skull. "What have you done with him?"

Mario wrenched free of Alan's grip and ran for Emily, now fully overpowered by the man.

"Let go of me!" Emily screamed, struggling against the guard's firm hold around her waist. "Kids, get back in the car!"

Maureen started to wail. Mario charged, hitting the huge guard in the back. He barely seemed to notice, apart from whipping his free arm back and landing a glancing blow on Mario's cheek. Mario staggered back, colliding with Alan.

"Where's Dominic!" Alan screeched.

"Holy shit," the guard said, taking in who Mario was. He touched his ear and began to speak. "Need immediate ba—"

Mario didn't think—he didn't have time to. He had to stop the guard before he said anything more. He didn't register his wife, struggling in the man's arms, or the tear-streaked faces of his children in the doorway beyond them, or the screeching demands of his brother-in-law behind him. His focus narrowed, everything beyond the threat of the guard with his hand to his ear graying out. He raised the Sig and fired. The gunshot sounded like a thunderclap as the man's face exploded into a spray of red and pink.

The guard sagged and fell, almost pulling Emily down with him. Mario rushed to her, his ears ringing, suddenly aware that if he'd missed, he might have killed Emily. His knees felt weak at the thought. He caught Emily's elbow as she twisted free of her dead captor.

"You okay?" he gasped, almost unable to catch his breath. When Emily nodded, he said, "Let's go."

Emily ran out the door ahead of him, scooping up Maureen. A cold ring of steel pressed against the back of Mario's head. He froze, trying to figure out what the fuck was happening.

"Where's Dominic?"

Alan...right, he thought. How the hell had he forgotten about Alan?

"I don't know, and I don't care," he said. "I just want my family."

"You're lying," Alan snarled, jabbing the gun harder against Mario's head. "You couldn't do this without getting him out of the way! What have you done with him?"

He heard the car start, saw the glow of the taillights beyond the SUV that blocked his view of the Mercedes. He heard the safety of the gun that Alan held click, and realized that this might be it. He might not get out of this one. If that happened, where could his family go? Emily didn't know about the safe house in Fremont; he hadn't told her. Where could they go to ground long enough to reach safety?

"Drop your gun and kick it away," Alan said, his voice angrier than Mario had ever heard before.

Slowly, Mario set the gun on the counter and pushed it away. "Dom's in the Mercedes," he said. Alan gasped. "We'll let him go if you let us go."

The pressure of the barrel against his head lightened for a split second. Mario almost tried to twist away but thought better of it.

"Go," Alan shouted, shoving Mario's shoulder.

Mario walked across the kitchen tiles, the grit of the fire suppressant from the extinguisher crunching into the layer of grease beneath it. They walked through the mudroom, then the garage, to the Mercedes. Michael's face, pale and pinched, his gray eyes filled with terror, looked out at Mario from the back passenger seat.

"Where is he?" Alan said.

"The trunk."

Alan made a sound like a smothered sob, but it was angry, not hopeless. "Open it!"

"I don't have the keys," Mario said, sweat trickling down the back of his neck. From his peripheral vision, he could see someone walking up the long drive—a guard. They were going to be caught, and then they'd all be dead.

Alan shoved Mario around the end of the car. Emily looked back at them, eyes fearful.

"Let us go, Alan!" she cried.

Alan said, "Turn off the car and open the trunk, Emily, or I swear I'll shoot him!"

"Okay," Emily said, "I'm turning it off."

Alan grabbed Mario's shoulder again. Anthony and Maureen stared at them through the backseat window, wide-eyed. The trunk release clicked audibly, almost echoing in the silence. The lid flipped up, and Alan, gun still pressed against Mario's head, stepped behind the Mercedes.

"Dom," he cried. "Oh no, Dom!"

Dom's muffled voice was cut short when the car lurched backward. Mario stared, not understanding. The rear bumper hit Alan with a dull thud, then he disappeared from sight, the car thumping over him. Dominic's muffled screams competed with the squealing tires. Mario's feet were rooted to the spot. His brother-in-law had been run over. What had just happened?

"Shut the trunk! Get in!"

Emily's voice snapped Mario from his frozen shock. Dominic was struggling to get out of the trunk, screams lost in his gag. Mario punched him twice, short, savage blows, and shoved him back inside. He slammed the trunk shut, then ran around the car, yanking the passenger side door open and diving inside.

"Are you okay?" Emily asked, her voice terse.

The car jerked as Emily finished backing up. He winced at the thumps that could only be Alan.

"Yeah, I'm fine," he said. He looked to the children, crying and huddled in the back seat. "Are you okay?"

"Daddy!" one, or maybe all of them, wailed.

"It's okay," Mario said, anger and worry intertwined as he looked into the traumatized faces of his children. "You have to buckle up. Now!"

When they didn't comply, Mario hoisted himself through

the seats. The car jerked forward, and he almost face-planted into Maureen's lap. Reaching for her seat belt set Anthony and Michael into action. By the time Mario twisted into his seat, the guard he'd seen walking up the drive was behind them. The gate ahead was opening—they streaked through, tires squealing as Emily turned south. She yanked the steering wheel to turn the skidding car east on the Oregon Expressway.

"I thought you turned the car off," he said.

"Electric, remember? It's silent, and Alan was too distracted trying to kill you. Where are we going?"

"Fremont," Mario answered as the dark streets of New Palo Alto streaked by. "I came on the Dunbarton Bridge, but—"

"We can't take that," Emily said, eyes on the road. "We can try the Charleston Street Gate."

"Okay," Mario said, struggling to gather his thoughts. "But you can't drive us through."

Emily frowned. "You're right. We should switch. You can try to pass for Dominic. You look enough alike."

"Where are we going, Mom?" Michael asked, his voice tight with anxiety.

Emily cast a sidelong glance at Mario. He turned to the children in the back seat.

"Somewhere safe, Michael," he said, reaching out to squeeze Michael's knee.

Emily pulled the car to the side of the road and opened her door. Mario had already pulled the handle and was turning away to do the same when he heard Maureen whisper to Anthony.

"Is that Daddy?"

"Yeah, honey," he said. "It's me. It's Daddy."

"It's Daddy," Anthony said.

At Anthony's confirmation, Maureen's brow smoothed a little. "I wasn't sure."

Mario forced a quick smile at the children, then got out of the car. Emily waited at his door. "Are we going to get out of here, Mar?"

"I don't know."

He hurried around the car and got back inside, then sped down the street. Tension filled the air, pressing against Mario like a yoke. The children had fallen silent in the back seat. Emily twisted her necklace nervously. Then a muffled thump began in the back of the car.

"Quit kicking, Michael," Emily said.

"I'm not!"

Emily twisted in her seat toward him. "Then what is... Oh shit."

It was Dominic, in the trunk.

"Should we stop?" Emily asked.

Mario's mind raced as he turned the corner and gunned the engine. They were almost to the gate. He'd have to knock Dominic out to get him quiet again, but what if it didn't work? What if Dominic got away?

"We'll have to chance it," Mario said.

"What if he pulls the emergency release?" Emily said.

Mario had forgotten about that. "I don't know, Em."

"Are we going to be okay?" Anthony asked, his voice tremulous.

"Just hang tight, Anthony," Mario said, glancing at the pinched, frightened faces of his children in the rearview mirror. "We need you kids to be quiet—" Mario stopped the car. "No."

"No?" Michael squeaked.

"Kids, listen to me," Mario said. "When we get to the gate up there, I need you to cry. Start fighting with each other."

"I'm scared," Anthony said, on the verge of tears.

"I know you are," Emily said, and Mario realized she was crying. "I'm scared too, but just do what Daddy says, okay?"

As soon as the children realized Emily was crying, the switch flipped. Anthony started to cry—for real. A moment later, so did Maureen and Michael. Mario turned the last corner, his nerves thrumming like a high voltage wire. The border wall was three blocks ahead of them, brightly lit, and growing larger and more imposing every second. Mario couldn't remember being this scared, ever. He'd been in danger before, on his own and with others, but never with his family— not like this.

He'd always feared for their safety, feared what the Council might do to them, especially when he first defected so he could try to get the vaccine back. He'd barely been able to think straight, he'd been so afraid for them. But this...those other times didn't come close.

Mario flicked down the visor along the top of his window and pulled his hair into his eyes as he turned left onto Loma Verde Avenue. The tall concrete border wall was straight ahead. This was the only other entry point into New Palo Alto where there wasn't a double wall, because of the wetlands on the other side of the Bayshore Freeway. Instead, there was an interior holding area made of chain-link fence attached to a steel frame. The lights were daytime-bright, and the sight of so many guards slicked Mario's body with sweat.

The kids were all-out wailing as he stopped the car at the guard booth outside the holding area. Mario hit the button to open the window once, the buzz of the motor that controlled the window lost in the din. The guard shot out of the booth and hurried to the car. Mario glanced out the window quickly, then looked straight ahead.

"Mister Santorello," the guard said, surprise evident in his voice, as well as relief. "You're okay! Security hasn't been able to locate you since... After the..." His voice trailed, an acceptable characterization of what had happened back at the house clearly escaping him. He peered into the back seat. "Is everyone all right?"

"No thanks to you," Mario snapped. "Open the goddamn gate."

"Uh...we were told to seal the exits, sir. After what happened to Mister Reynolds."

So, Alan was dead, as he'd feared.

"By the same people who failed to protect him?"

"Well, um..." the guard stammered.

Mario turned his head, just catching the man's eye while trying to keep his face inside the window and out of the bright light.

"We need to get somewhere safe, since none of you can do your job," he said, the danger of their predicament fueling the fury in his voice.

Emily was still crying, trying to console the children, to no effect. Her maternal instinct to soothe them couldn't be circumvented, Mario knew, because it was all he wanted to do, too, even though they needed the distraction their distress provided.

"Sir, I don't know—"

The guard wasn't cooperating, and he knew he couldn't play it safe. If he did, they were never getting out of here. Mario leaned out the window. He pushed some of the hair in his face aside and looked directly into the guard's watery blue eyes. The guard recoiled, taking an involuntary step backward, as the color drained from his face. He gulped so loudly that even over his hysterical children, Mario could hear it.

"My husband was just murdered," he said, a deadly promise in his voice. "I need to get my sister-in-law and her children somewhere safe, and that's not here. Open the fucking gate before I get out of the car and break your neck."

The guard nodded, his Adam's apple bobbing. He took another step backward. Then he raised his arm, making a circling motion with his hand before he turned and almost ran to guard's booth. Immediately, an obnoxiously loud buzzer sounded. Yellow lights along the top of the holding booth flashed in time with the buzzer, and the inner gate began to slide open to the side, like a single elevator door.

Despite every instinct in his body telling him to rush, to flee, Mario drove the Mercedes into the holding booth at a snail's pace. The gate behind them rattled shut. Emily looked at Mario, eyes bright with fear, her hand pressed to her mouth. After a torturous age, which in reality was only thirty seconds, the outer gate began to lift, pulled up inside the massive concrete wall.

As soon as there was enough clearance, Mario floored it. The Mercedes catapulted forward, streaking into the night like a rocket.

TEN MINUTES LATER, THEY SPED SOUTH ON THE Expressway. Mario checked his mirrors and scanned the road ahead with a compulsive alertness. He kept expecting the black SUVs of Council Security to appear his rearview mirror, as implacable and relentless as Mad Max, until they ran them down. Emily had mostly quieted the children. Her own lack of tears had helped, but Mario couldn't blame her for any loss of composure. They were in danger; if he hadn't needed to bluster their way through the gate, he would have cried, too. Dom had quit banging in the trunk, which Mario hoped was a good sign. He knew they needed to stop and make sure he was secure, but that would have to wait. They had to get away first.

A clunk jarred Mario from his thoughts. "What was— Shit!"

The lid of the trunk sprang into the rearview mirror. Mario

jammed on the brakes, so hard the tires squealed. In the back seat the kids cried out in fright.

"Mario, what's—?"

Emily's question was lost as Mario jammed the car into PARK and scrambled out. "Stay in the car," he barked.

A good ways behind them, Dominic was struggling to his feet. Mario wasn't sure how fast he'd been going, but he'd never have tried jumping out of a car at the speed they'd been traveling. Dom was lucky he wasn't dead.

Mario sprinted for his brother. He wasn't sure where on the Expressway they were, since the walls blocked the view. The only area with a lot of tall buildings was downtown San Jose, and they hadn't gone that far. Dominic had regained his footing and was running, faster than Mario would have credited. His head start on Mario grew. Dom had always been a swift runner. Whatever he'd hit leaping from the car, it hadn't been his legs. Mario raised his hand, shading his eyes from the lights ahead, and saw a walled-off exit ramp.

Mario pushed himself harder, lungs burning with effort, cursing himself for jumping out of the car and making chase on foot. He hadn't expected Dominic to be able to flee. *I'm not going to catch up*, he thought, even as he dug deep, calling on reserves of energy his muscles screamed they didn't have. But Mario knew better. He knew he could push, could hurt, could keep going. It was just that Dom knew it too, and was too far ahead of him, still that eighth of a mile.

Without stopping, Mario pulled the Sig from his waistband at the small of his back. He pointed the gun in Dom's direction and fired—a warning shot, no need to sight up. Dominic was out of range, and Mario knew it, but maybe it would be enough to stop him.

Dominic slowed, about fifty feet from the first concrete wall, and looked over his shoulder. Mario kept up his flat-out run. He could see that Dom's hands were still tied in front of him, his face a pale oval under a dark mop of hair. He looked at Mario for a long moment, then turned away and ran at the wall. Mario watched in wonder as Dominic jumped, his arms upraised, and managed to catch the top. It had to be ten and a half feet, and Dominic got his hands on it.

Still Mario ran as Dom struggled to climb the wall. Despite the poor purchase his dress shoes would give, he managed to swing a leg up and get his foot over. Mario stopped. Gasping for air, he raised the Sig. He might get lucky—if you could call getting a clean shot on your only brother lucky. Despite everything that his brother had done, this wasn't what Mario wanted, it wasn't how he wanted it to end, but he couldn't let Dominic get away. Not just because he would raise the alarm that Mario was back in San Jose if he got through the zombie-infested territory around them. Not just because if he got away, it would make their goal of overthrowing the Council more difficult. He had to get him because of everything else. His brother had imprisoned his family, and Mario knew he would have killed them—even the kids—if he thought it would work to his advantage. He'd been behind the attack on LO, and people Dominic had never even heard of—good, kind people whose only crime was wanting to live and help others—had died. He'd embraced the self-serving depravity of the Council, actively participated in the subjugation of the people of Silicon Valley, persecuted the weakest and most vulnerable, so that he could become powerful and rich. His brother had tried to kill him, and Doug, all so he could keep what he had. He didn't care about the cost, because it would always be other people who paid it. And he'd tried to kill Miranda. If the attack had been successful, if she hadn't lost the baby, he might have killed their child, too.

Mario sighted up and took a deep breath. Dominic got his leg the whole way over the wall and sat upright astride it. Mario exhaled and squeezed the trigger. Dominic jerked, then fell from sight, but he couldn't be sure he'd gotten him. The jerk could have been overcorrecting his balance. Maybe he hit him, but even if he had, he doubted it was fatal.

Mario stood for another few seconds, catching his breath, staring at the wall at the top of the ramp. Below the roar of blood in his ears he could hear zombies moaning, the gunshots having attracted the attention of the wretched, undead souls wandering in the Expressway's shadow.

He turned away. Emily stood by the car in a puddle of light from the open door. The pale faces of his children peeked out the back window, shining like a beacon, beckoning him closer. He cast one last glance over his shoulder, then ended his pursuit of the man who had once been his brother.

31

TENSION RICOCHETED inside Doug's body, his frustration with Mario and his fool's errand having nowhere to go. It had taken everything he had to not punch him, hopefully hard enough to knock him out.

"Going to get himself fucking killed," he muttered angrily. "And I'll be the one who has to tell Miranda."

He turned and walked back through the garage door, then into the kitchen. Skye and Tessa were sitting at the table, yawning widely.

"Where's Mario?" Skye asked him.

Doug shook his head. "Don't ask."

Her eyebrows raised, probably because of his preemptory tone. "Now I have to."

In the next room, Doug heard Rupert and Adams' voices, discussing where everyone would sleep. Doug collapsed into the chair next to Skye.

"He went to check on his family, who just happen to be in one of the most fortified places in the Valley. Because that makes sense," he added, sarcasm heavy in his voice.

"Oh," Tessa said, surprised. "What is he—"

"He's not thinking clearly," Skye said.

"No shit."

As Rupert and Adam entered the kitchen, Doug reached for the glass of water he'd left on the table when he'd seen Mario skulking into the garage. He started to glug the water down.

Rupert said, "Tessa, you'll be in the guest room off the family room. Through there," he said, pointing. "You look exhausted."

"I am," she said, yawning again.

Skye looked at Rupert expectantly. "Where are Doug and I sleeping?"

Doug choked on his drink, water spraying across the table. He started to cough and shot Skye a bug-eyed look of *What the fuck?* Realization dawned in her eyes.

"Not together," Doug sputtered, coughing.

Mortification coursed through his veins. Rupert and Adam weren't idiots. They knew he and Skye were together in every sense of the word, but Christ Almighty... It was times like this that he really wished Skye was Catholic.

"Of course, right," Skye said, her face flushing crimson. Apologetically, she said to Rupert, "I'm sorry. I wasn't thinking."

Rupert shook his head at her, then chuckled. "It's quite all right, my dear."

But they did end up together, making love on the floor of Skye's room like teenagers. That hadn't been Doug's plan. He'd genuinely meant to just say good night. But when she kissed him, her lips warm and soft and yielding, her supple body pressed lightly against his, it was like being sucked into a vortex of desire as strong and irresistible as the event horizon of a black hole. The next thing he knew they were on the floor, half their clothes discarded while they moved together, fiery and silent. The tiny squeak Skye made when she came had made him laugh... She'd sounded just like a mouse. He had to hand it to her, though; she'd been quiet.

He'd slept fitfully, alone in his bed, his dreams filled with pursuit and capture. The entire day had been an exercise in torture. He couldn't stop checking his watch, only to find half an hour had passed, tops, while he worried about Mario. Had he been captured, killed, or something even worse? Tessa and Skye kept Violet occupied most of the day, though Doug had played Candyland with her for a while. Gumdrop Mountains and Peppermint Stick Forests and Molasses Swamps—Violet had loved them all. Her little face lit up at the brightly colored board filled with treats she'd never had. Twice she'd asked him when Mawree would be back, and all he could tell her was, "Soon."

Doug walked down the dark hallway beyond the blackout drape, the interminable waiting of the day now an endless night. He and Skye had said good night downstairs. It wasn't that he'd have minded ending up on the floor with her again, but they shouldn't push their luck. He tapped lightly on the door to the master bedroom, where Adam kept watch, then opened the door just far enough that he could pop his head through.

"Mind if I join you?"

Adam waved him over to where he sat by the window, on a stool high enough that he could see over the small balcony beyond the sliding glass doors. The other windows in the room were also covered with blackout fabric—only the sliding glass doors were uncovered. Anyone looking in from the outside would be hard-pressed to see anything.

Before Doug could ask, Adam said, "Nothing yet."

"I figured as much." After a moment's silence, he said, "How long have you been out here?"

"In this house? Only since the Council drove the Jesuits out."

"You aren't a Jesuit."

"No," Adam said, and Doug thought he could hear a smile in the man's voice. "Almost, back in the day, but I met a girl before I got very far."

"Simpler that way than mine," Doug said ruefully.

"Yes," Adam agreed. "Though quitting is a lot less complicated now than it was before. No waiting for it to go through Rome."

"I hadn't thought about that," Doug said. He thought he knew the answer to the next question but asked anyway. "And the girl?"

"Didn't last," Adam said. Again, a smile in his voice. "But the next girl was the one. Got married three months after we met. She died a year before all this happened—breast cancer. Never thought I'd be thankful for it, but I am."

"I'm sorry," Doug said.

He understood what Adam meant. He wouldn't wish this world on anyone, but he couldn't imagine ever being thankful that Skye wasn't with him. He knew what Adam said could be true, but it didn't compute when applied to Skye.

"We've got movement," Adam said, his voice softer than before. He opened the sliding glass door a few inches and raised the rifle that had been resting on his knees to his shoulder. "I think it's your friend, but he's got people with him—a woman and two...no, three children."

"What? He got Emily and the kids?"

"There's a rifle with a scope in the corner behind you. Get it and take a look."

Doug turned around and carefully felt along the wall until his fingertips brushed cool steel. His hand slipped around the rifle's smooth wood stock. He stepped back to the window and peered through the scope.

"They're at my two o'clock," Adam said.

Doug adjusted to Adam's two, neon greens and black filling the scope. Mario stumbled as he entered the cul-de-sac, swaying slightly as he righted himself. He held a small child, had to be Maureen, in his arms. Emily walked beside him, dropping the hand of the child between them to put a steadying hand on Mario's shoulder. A taller child was on Emily's left.

"Holy shit," Doug whispered. He pushed the door open so that he could step onto the balcony, but Adam stayed him.

"Could still be a trap," Adam said. He stepped onto the balcony and said, his voice raised enough to carry across the cul-de-sac, but no further, "Are you okay?"

Doug saw Mario close his eyes and say something to Emily that looked a lot like fuck. He was having trouble remembering the pass phrase that Rupert and Adam had shared with them.

After a long moment, he said, "I've got a splitting headache."

"We've got aspirin," Adam said, in response to Mario's correct answer.

"I'm going down to meet them," Doug said.

"Take the rifle, just in case."

Doug held on to the rifle, walking as quickly as was safe through the dark house. He slipped out the back door and a moment later was through the side gate. Mario, Emily, and the children had reached the sidewalk that ran alongside the house.

"It's good to see you, man," Doug said, clasping Mario's shoulder.

"It's good to be seen."

Doug turned to Emily, whom he pulled into a hug. She sagged against him, as if she were a wrung-out rag, and he felt a lump in his throat.

"I didn't expect to see you," he said. "My God, Em." He reached over and squeezed Michael's shoulder; the sense of amazement flooding through his body felt sharp and bright. "All of you."

The gate opened behind them. "Come out of the street," Brother Rupert's voice said.

"Can you take her, Em?"

Maureen murmured in her sleep as they passed her between them, but didn't wake. Doug held out his hand to usher Emily and boys through, then followed Mario, pulling the gate shut behind him. By the time he finished securing the lock, Emily and the children had already rounded the corner of the house with Rupert.

"I was getting worried," he said to Mario. "How—"

"Inside," Mario said. "I need to talk to Rupert. The Council might know I'm back."

"What happened?" Doug asked, a million questions popping into his head.

"That's not the worst part. We need to get Walter now. His execution is in the morning."

"What?"

"Give me a couple minutes," Mario said, as if he hadn't just dropped a bomb of earth-shattering proportions into the conversation. "I promised Violet I'd tell her when I got back."

"She's asleep," Doug said, his urgency to know what was going on mushrooming with every second that Mario put it off.

"She won't mind if I wake her."

MOST PEOPLE DIDN'T REALIZE HOW WELL DEVELOPED THE Jesuits' spy network was. Everyone assumed that the Jesuits and the Council spied on one another, but the Jesuits had managed to infiltrate almost every aspect of city administration under the Council's control. It had been disrupted when the Jesuits were driven out of SCU, just how severely laid bare by the bad intel they had on Walter. No one at the safe house had the slightest inkling that his execution was scheduled for tomorrow.

Because they had to scramble, all of Adam's special operators—apart from an imposing brute of man named Jonathan—weren't here yet. They were slated to arrive midday tomorrow, but they couldn't afford to wait, especially since they didn't have an exact time for when Walter's execution was supposed to take place.

A shiver started at the base of Doug's spine, causing his whole body to quiver. If Mario had listened to him, Walter would have been killed before they could do anything. Doug was still filled with a low-level buzz of amazement. Not only had Mario gotten in and out of one of the most fortified communities in the area, he'd managed to bring Emily and the children with him. He had the devil's own luck, or maybe not, Doug thought, thinking of Miranda and Tadpole, not to mention his brother.

Doug brought up the rear of the rescue party, waiting at the top of the ramp across from Skye, while Adam and Jonathan skulked to the service entrance into the Westin hotel. It occupied the entire block within the walled city of San Jose. Doug glanced over his shoulder as Jonathan and Adam approached the double doors of the maintenance entrance, then looked back to the street. The darkened storefronts of restaurants and bars seemed to hold no surprises. Nothing was moving at this hour, the bars having closed a couple hours earlier. Bars still closed at two in the morning; why, Doug had no idea.

"All clear," Adam's voice buzzed in Doug's ear. Jonathan waited at the door as they approached, opened far enough for them to slip through one by one. Doug squinted in the low light of the dingy hallway. It stretched away from them, as far as the length of the building it seemed.

"Everyone clear on the plan?" Adam asked.

Adam was short and compactly built, with small piggy eyes. His taciturn manner was matter-of-fact. He'd accepted the change in circumstances without so much as a blink of an eye. Doug had been impressed by how quickly he adjusted their strategy, since the players were different, and he'd never worked with him and Skye before. Jonathan, who was tall with broad shoulders looked like he spent every spare moment at the gym. He'd been in the service, but had been evasive about which branch, shrugging off Doug's interest. That was okay. It probably meant he'd done and seen a lot that regular people hadn't thought much about before zombies, except for in movies and television shows. He and Adam had been working together for years. If Adam thought he was the right guy for their hastily assembled plan, Doug had confidence he was.

The ruse of posing as members of hotel staff had been discarded in favor of a straightforward smash and grab. They would get in, get Walter, and get out. In case they were unsuccessful, a sniper was getting into position on the roof of the Knight Ridder building, which had a clear view of the Plaza de Cesar Chavez. Mario was with them. He'd insisted on doing something, despite being banged up from being hit by a car. Doug shook his head...he was tough as fucking nails and stubborn as an ox. A gallows had been erected over the plaza's fountain during Dominic's Stalin-like purge after he'd consolidated power.

Just to make sure everyone was clear, Adam outlined the plan again.

"The stairs are kitty-corner to one another. The north stairs, which me and Jonathan will take, are on this side, and come out directly down the hallway from where they're holding Walter in room 942. His room is midpoint down the hallway. Doug and Skye, you're taking the south stairs on the other side of the building. Last intel says there are two guards outside each staircase, and three outside the room. You two need to take out the guards—quietly—then create a distraction to pull at least one of the guards on Walter's room away. Then we move on the room, get Walter, and get out."

"The elevators are inoperative, right?" Jonathan asked.

Adam nodded. "The doors are welded shut, so don't get any bright ideas about trying to open them to pitch someone down the shaft. If things go pear-shaped, get the hell out. The sniper team will take it from there. Questions?"

When no one spoke, he nodded. "Let's get to work."

DOUG AND SKYE TURNED THE CORNER AFTER CHECKING TO make sure the coast was clear. Jonathan and Adam had already disappeared into the north stairwell. Doug could see a brightly lit red EXIT sign halfway down the corridor. A maid's cart was parked against the wall. As they passed it, Doug heard an indignant female voice.

"So then he said, 'Why is this all on me?'"

"What?" a second woman's voice said, sounding scandalized.

"Yeah. How exactly is him not keeping it in his pants anything but all on him?"

The voices were coming closer. Doug and Skye scrambled

around the corner of the cart and crouched low. Doug peeked around it, his head almost at floor level. Two women, an older white lady and a younger Hispanic one, walked toward them.

"I hate to say it, Rosie," the older lady said, their footsteps drawing near.

Rosie groaned. "I know, I know. You told me he was a deadbeat."

"He has three kids with three different women, and two of them born within months of each other."

Doug pulled his head behind the cart. He made a punching motion, tipping his head at the women. Skye nodded. The women's footsteps stopped on the other side of the cart. The cart shifted toward him and Skye about six inches.

A reluctant note of not wanting to admit defeat in her voice, Rosie said, "It's just he's—"

"A deadbeat."

Rosie sighed. "I know you're—dammit. I left my smokes in the break room."

"I'll get them and meet you," the other said. "You're going to twelve?"

"I'll come with you," Rosie said. "Most of those rooms are already clean. I don't know why he insists on us going through clean rooms."

Their footsteps and voices faded while the women chattered about their unreasonable boss and Rosie's bad boyfriend. Doug peeked around the corner of the cart again. The women turned into a room near the end of the corridor. The door he and Skye needed was just beyond it, on the other side to the hall.

"Let's go," he said, getting up. "We can clock them up if we need to, but we can't waste more time."

Skye grabbed a gray smock and some towels from the cart before following him. Doug didn't ask—she could explain later.

The women's voices grew louder as they drew near the open break room door. Skye walked right past it like she belonged there, despite her dark clothes and the fact that she was bristling with weapons. Doug followed. Ten seconds later they were in the stairwell.

"That was close," Doug said as they started up the stairs.

Skye tucked the smock and towels under her left arm, then pulled her handgun from its holster as Doug did likewise with his Glock. "I wouldn't have minded hearing more about Rosie's deadbeat boyfriend."

"What's with the towels?"

She shrugged. "They might come in handy."

They climbed the stairs in silence, always checking above. The only sound was the shallow echoes of their boots. They slowed on the landing before the top floor. Doug peered up, but didn't see anyone through the door's small inset window.

"Can't see anything," he said softly. He looked at Skye. She had slipped the smock over her tactical vest. "Planning to tap on the door, since you're a beautiful, nonthreatening woman?"

"Something like that."

When they reached the top landing, which put them kitty-corner from where Adam and Jonathan waited at the top of the stairs on the other side of the building, Doug scurried into the corner along the wall on the same side as the door and crouched low. Skye tapped on the glass.

"Can you help me?" she asked.

"What are you doing here?" a voice barked a beat later. "What's your authorization? Where's your ident card?"

"My card? Rosie sent me up with some towels for room 942." She lifted the towels so the man could see. "She didn't say anything about needing a card." Skye sounded perplexed as she threw the unsuspecting Rosie under the bus.

"Rosie?"

"Yeah. Rosie from housekeeping?"

A different voice said, "Rosie doesn't have authorization for that."

"All I know is Rosie sent me up here," Skye said, sounding helpless. She smiled tentatively and bit her lip. "It's my first day... I don't want to cause trouble."

A dull murmur of voices followed. Skye dipped her head, then gave another tentative smile.

"Hold on a second," the first voice said, then the hooked door handle turned down.

"Oh, thank you so much," Skye said, her voice breathy with relief. Then she added, sounding dingy as hell, "Oh gosh! My card is in my pocket."

Doug had to hand it to her, she was laying on the dumb blond routine with startling authenticity.

The door opened, and a large man stepped into the doorway, his tone softening. "Give me the towels. I'll deliver them."

If he'd been paying attention to anything other than Skye, he should have seen Doug by now, but he wasn't.

Skye shoved the towels at him. Her hand whipped up, the gun's hand grip smashing against the underside of his chin. His jaw snapped shut so hard that Doug heard his teeth click. Then she gripped the lapels of his jacket and pulled, flattening herself against the open door. He staggered sideways, stunned, and tumbled down the stairs. Doug launched himself from the corner. Skye had dropped low and darted through the open door. Doug heard the surprised *oof* and thump of impact. By the time he reached the door, the other guard was unconscious at Skye's feet.

Quickly, he checked the guard sprawled on the landing below. The guy was out cold. Blood seeped from the behind his head on the concrete landing. Maybe just a cut, maybe a skull fracture. Either way, he wasn't waking up anytime soon. Doug grasped him under the arms pulled him into the corner. He wanted a clear path, just in case they needed to get back down this staircase fast. When he reached the hallway, Skye was emerging from a darkened doorway. The hallway was clear.

"Vending area," she said, gesturing behind her. "He's out."

Doug drank in the sight of her for a brief moment, her arresting blue-gold eyes, the pale hair, and rosebud-pink lips. Her cheeks were flushed. She'd taken out both guards before he even had a chance to assist. There wasn't a woman on the planet who'd ever be hotter than Skye.

Skye tipped her head the direction they needed to go and said, "Quit gawking."

They crept down the long hallway. Even though he knew no one else was on this floor, Doug couldn't help feeling that someone would open one of the guest room doors. Tension and excitement fizzed in his guts. Maybe Skye was right about him never settling down behind the safety of SCU's walls.

"Wait here," Doug said, just above a whisper, when they reached the corner. He took a peek. The hallway was clear, except for the two men guarding the stairwell door at the far end. He pulled back and tapped his earpiece.

"We're in position. Distraction as soon as you confirm."

Adam's voice sounded soft in Doug's ear. "Confirmed. Good luck."

Doug nodded to Skye, then stepped into the hallway, just like they'd agreed.

"Hey, guys," he said.

The heads of the men guarding the north stairwell door snapped to him.

"Who the hell are you?" the bigger of the two said. He started forward, reaching for his firearm. His partner took a step forward, but stayed by the door.

Doug held his hands up. "Dude, no need to be so aggro."

Before the man could say another word, the door behind his partner opened. Adam took one quick step and grabbed the man's head. Doug darted back to Skye.

"Stop!"

They fell back. A torrent of gunfire erupted from the other side of the building. Their pursuer wasn't distracted. He fired at them as he rounded the corner of the hallway,

Skye ducked into the vending room. A bullet whizzed past Doug's ear. He flung himself against the opposite wall, adrenaline making the colors bright and edges sharp. He pressed flat against a closed door to a guest room, tried the door—locked. The guy didn't let up, the report of his weapon getting louder. Skye fired from the doorway of vending area, hitting him center mass before his head jerked back, erupting in a spray of red.

"Are you okay?" she asked, running to Doug.

Now there was shouting at Adam and Jonathan's position, but the comm was garbled. The gunfire hadn't let up. A strangled cry came from around the corner.

"I'm good," Doug said. "Let's—"

He heard a clunk from the stairwell they had emerged from minutes ago. He grabbed Skye's hand. "They're behind us!"

They sprinted down the hallway.

"Stop!" a voice shouted.

They didn't. Instead, they raced around the corner, Doug praying not into a hail of bullets. The hallway was clear of hostiles and gunfire, but not bodies. An opponent was still on the floor a few feet from them, a pool of blood staining the light-tan carpet. There were more bodies by the door to the stairwell ahead of them.

"Go," Doug said. "I'll be right behind you."

He peeked around the corner from the direction they'd come. The drywall exploded inches from his face. He shot off two rounds blind, then bolted after Skye, leaping over the dead man. They were pulled up short at the end, just across from the stairwell door. The guard Adam had killed lay crumpled ahead of them. Jonathan was beside him. Bloody foam coated his lips, but it wasn't growing or moving—he wasn't breathing—and his vacant eyes stared at the ceiling, seeing nothing. Heavy gunfire continued around the corner, along the hall where Walter's room was located. The glass of the mediocre hotel art exploded.

Doug fired behind them, hoping to stall their pursuers. More gunfire erupted from the direction of Walter's room. Adam fell back to the door; his dark piggy eyes widened when he saw them. Then he was punched against the wall, bullets riddling his body.

"Jesus," Skye said. She peeked around the corner, then jerked back.

The door to the stairwell by the bodies of Jonathan, Adam, and the dead guard's body opened.

"Hold your fire," the person opening it shouted.

The door opened, and Skye leaped, screaming like a wild beast. She hit the man full on, shoving him backwards. Two shots, then she whirled around to cover Doug. An explosion of sparks glittered by her head, making her flinch away. Their pursuer had caught up with them. The bullet had practically shaved her head before hitting the steel door.

"Go!" Doug shouted. "Get out of here!"

Doug threw away the Glock and fell to his stomach, hands on his head, unsure that it would be enough to not get shot. For an agonizing second, his eyes locked with Skye's. He saw the life he wanted with her flash in front of him, vivid as the moment in *The Wizard of Oz* when the film changed from black and white to color. The adventures they would have had while taking the vaccine to pockets of survivors once the Council was overthrown. Lazy days spent in bed, talking and reading and making love. Children with her silvery-blond hair and tinkling, fairy-dust laugh.

He saw everything...how it could have been, how happy he could have made her, and she him, for capture now could only mean his death. The anguish clouding the kaleidoscope of her blue-gold eyes told him that she saw it, too, and knew it was slipping away, before she disappeared into the stairwell.

32

MARIO STRETCHED HIS NECK, tilting his ear toward his shoulder. The pull of his tight muscles ached, but in a good way, as he let gravity take hold. He could feel the stretch from behind his ear to halfway up his head. He shifted his weight, the worn-out passenger seat of the beater van more uncomfortable by the second. It stunk of old cooking grease from the cheap biodiesel conversion. If he wasn't able to catch the occasional whiff of fresh air from the two inches of open window, he'd probably have puked after sitting here for the last hour.

"We should have heard something by now," he said, his voice hushed.

"Yeah," said Barbie, cracking her gum.

Barbie was a sniper, and from what Mario had seen of the smooth, practiced movements when she disassembled and then reassembled her rifle before they left, she knew what she was doing.

"If nothing happens in the next five minutes, we have to assume the others were blown and move into position," said Barbie. She raised her voice and said, "You awake, Christos?"

There was a groan from behind them in the cargo area of the van, then a heavily accented man's voice said, sounding groggy, "I'm up."

Mario heard Christos mutter something about regretting ever leaving Crete as he rustled behind them. They lapsed into silence again. Mario checked his watch for the millionth time, but it was still only going on five a.m. If the others didn't get here soon, it would complicate getting out of the city. He checked the side mirror again. His pulse sped up. A figure—a woman—had turned the corner and walked up the block. She hugged the buildings, walking briskly, the only person on the street.

"Somebody's coming up the block," Mario said, squinting. "It's Skye, and she's alone. Shit, shit, shit."

A moment later Skye was scrambling into the van by the sliding side door.

"Where are the others?" Christos asked when the door was shut.

The sky was beginning to lighten behind Mario and Barbie. He could see Skye's huge eyes. Her face crumpled as she spoke.

"They captured Doug, I think," she said. "And Jonathan and Adam are dead. We never even got to Father Walter. Oh, my God," she said, looking at Mario. "They'll kill him."

Skye told them what happened, how they had been discovered and outmaneuvered before Doug had given her enough time to flee. Mario had never seen her so distraught.

"I barely got out of the building. They had people everywhere. I ran almost a mile and hid before trying to get back. I couldn't get here sooner..."

Her voice trailed. She started crying again, wiping at her face. Mario tried to absorb the news. Jonathan and Adam were dead and they had Doug? Mario pulled a handkerchief from his pocket and handed it to Skye. He'd never seen her this shaken up, not even after the zombie grabbed her by the hair when they'd lost Silas.

"That's why we're here. Let's look lively," Barbie said, her voice all business. She looked at Skye. "Can you pull it together? We might need you."

Skye nodded, pressing the handkerchief to her eyes, before returning Barbie's steady gaze. "Yeah, I'll be fine."

Barbie nodded. She turned forward and started the van.

Still looking backward, Mario clasped Skye's hand. "We'll get him back."

Skye nodded, but on autopilot. Mario turned back around in his seat as the van left the curb, more worried than ever that Dominic and the Council would win and kill his friends. If that happened, nothing would change. The pain and suffering would continue. And the years he had sacrificed, when he could have been with Miranda, would be for nothing.

MIRANDA WIPED HER SWEATY HANDS ON HER THIGHS FOR what seemed the zillionth time. She'd tied a bandana over her head to try to help with the helmet's fit. It didn't seem to be doing any good.

Below, California sped by—parched and brown—except for the occasional green patch where late autumnal rains had fallen. The rumble of the helicopter's powerful engines had become a low hum in her bones, one that was not unpleasant. After the first hour, conversation had petered out. In addition to her and Victor, Sean and Phineas had come with them. Alec had volunteered, which she appreciated, but it had too much potential to get weird. Delta Force they were not, but they'd have to do.

They'd flown over San Francisco twenty minutes ago and

had just passed San Francisco International Airport. She'd been surprised at the emotional wallop of seeing her hometown. The Golden Gate Bridge was mottled with rust. The Presidio, a former naval base that had always been a forested patch of green, didn't look all that different. She hadn't been able to pick out her street as they swung east over the city, but still found Nob Hill's Grace Cathedral with ease, could still identify the cable car lines, Union Square, Coit Tower, and Saints Peter & Paul Church in North Beach, where she had been baptized.

She felt twitchy and anxious as she fidgeted in the co-pilot's seat of the cockpit. She wasn't any help to Victor with flying, but being able to see where they were going, along with a whole lot of motion sickness medicine, kept the nausea down to the level of unreliable suitor.

Victor's voice came through the headset. "The San Jose airport is about a klick dead ahead. If there aren't too many zombies, we'll land. Otherwise, we'll have to figure out an alternate spot."

She nodded, before remembering Phineas and Sean in the cargo hold. Busy flying the helicopter, Victor wouldn't see her nodding, either. "Sounds good. Sean, Phineas, you ready?"

"I'm always ready for you to order me around," Phineas said.

She rolled her eyes, but also smiled. His answer had the effect she thought he was probably going for: helping her settle the fuck down.

"Ready to go," said Sean.

"Roger that," Victor said. "Looks clear so far. We'll circle the airfield to be sure, but we should touch down in three—"

Miranda heard a boom and turned her head to look. "What the fuck was that?"

It only took twenty minutes to get Barbie and Christos in position on the roof of the Knight Ridder building. Barbie set up her rifle with practiced ease while Christos, acting as spotter, adjusted his scopes and settled in beside her. Mario and Skye sat next to the two RPG cases they'd lugged up from the van—weapons of last resort. Mario grew more antsy, and Skye more distraught. Barbie cracked her gum about once a minute. It grated on Mario's ear, and nerves. Skye had pulled it together, as she'd promised Barbie she would, but Mario could see the grief in her eyes. She thought Doug was dead, or soon would be. Mario couldn't talk himself into any scenario where she was wrong. Council Security SUVs lined the streets below along the Plaza de Cesar Chavez. The large crowd assembled in front of the gallows that had been erected over the fountain kept growing in size. Among the crowd were people on their side, including a medic, ready to take advantage of the chaos Barbie's sniping would cause to save Walter and Doug. They'd also try to kidnap members of the Council, but that was just gravy. Mario wasn't too optimistic about that part of the plan, but it would be been stupid to pass up any opportunity to destabilize the Council.

Mario had taken the kids to the Place de Cesar Chavez when they'd visited him at City Hall. He could still see their excited faces as they ran through the ground-level fountain on hot summer days, and hear the burble of water that spurted up from the dark, stone squares.

They murdered people there now.

"Got something," Christos said, his voice just loud enough for Mario and Skye to hear.

Mario raised the pair of small field binoculars that Barbie had given him. Several SUVs pulled up by the fountain gallows. Burly men, in dark suits with watchful faces that screamed bodyguard, got out. They scanned the area, then opened the rear doors. Mario held his breath, waiting. Dominic climbed out of the third SUV. He limped, his arm in a sling. Mario exhaled, part of him relieved that his brother was alive, despite everything he'd done.

"My brother's alive," he said to Skye. He passed the binoculars to her. "The one with his arm in a sling."

Skye held the binoculars for a moment, like she didn't know what they were for. Face pale, she raised them to her eyes. "He looks just like you," she said.

They fell silent, waiting, the tension as thick as treacle.

Skye made a strangled sound, then said, "I see them."

Mario squinted, trying to see what Skye had. A second later he spotted Doug and Walter walking around from behind the gallows, two guards before and behind them. Walter's posture was ramrod straight, as was Doug's, as they were led through the gap between the gallows and the crowd. Their hands were tied in front of them.

Skye shoved the binoculars into Mario's hands. Tears slicked her face again. Barbie and Christos were speaking to one another, but Mario couldn't make out their words over the sudden rush of blood in his ears. Skye's breathing became shallow, to the point she was almost panting. Mario wanted to reassure her, but what could he say? They had to trust that Barbie and Christos were up to the job.

Mario swept the binoculars across the gallows until he found Dominic. Discolored splotches covered his face. Bruising, no doubt, from when he leaped from the car. His lips were pinched tight. He stood stiff, like he was in pain, but his eyes glowed in triumph.

"Goddamn you," Mario whispered.

Walter and Doug were moved into place near the waiting

ropes. Barbie cracked her gum. The gallows began to jump, and Mario realized his hands were shaking.

"What are they waiting for?" Skye asked, her voice a moan of pain.

Then Barbie said, "I have Target A, two mils crotch to head."

Christos answered, "Roger, two mils crotch to head." Then he added, "Two point three mil up."

"Roger, two point three mil up," Barbie said.

"Wind full value right to left seven miles per hour. Hold half mil right." Barbie repeated it back, and then Christos said, "Send it."

The crack of the rifle shattered the sky. Mario whipped up the binoculars. The rifle cracked again, and again. He was vaguely aware of Skye's hand gripping his shoulder and his heart thundering in his chest. Screams filled the air as the assembled crowd scattered. A melee of panic had engulfed the gallows. Two men were down, blood spilling across the dusty plywood of the gallows platform. A tangle of arms and legs and bodies swarmed and ran, thwarting the efforts of others who were trying to scramble to safety.

"I don't see them!" Skye cried. "Where are they?"

The rifle cracked again and again in quick succession. Mario sucked in his breath when the man hurrying Dominic to the stairs jerked against his brother's shoulder, his head snapping sharply to the side, as if an invisible hand was pulling him aloft by his hair. A mist of red filled the air around them. The force of the bullet sent the bodyguard spinning away as he fell to the ground.

Another crack, and another. But the next one sounded different. Mario spun around. The door that opened onto the roof was splintering down the middle.

"Behind us!" he shouted.

He grabbed Skye's hand, pulling her with him to take cover behind the HVAC units. The door to the roof flew open. Skye popped up from behind the HVAC unit and started firing, the report of her weapon echoing off the buildings around them. Mario looked for Barbie and Christos. They had scrambled to cover, taking Barbie's rifle with them, but he could see a blood trail. One of them had been hit.

Mario fired nonstop, trying to keep the intruders at bay. In the break from the sniper fire, men were dragging Walter and Doug back to the waiting nooses. Then Skye screamed.

"No!"

She broke cover, diving for the cases with the RPGs. She hefted one onto her shoulder. Mario knew she wouldn't shoot the gallows and risk killing Doug. She'd try to disrupt it. Distracted by her, Mario stopped firing.

A figure darted from the shelter of the doorway, raising his gun to shoot Skye. He was so focused on her that he wasn't paying attention to his footing, and didn't see the six-inch step where one section of the roof met the other. He stumbled, then sprawled onto the pebbled rooftop. His gun flew out of his hand.

Gunfire came from the doorway, sending Mario diving for cover. He saw the man after Skye get back to his feet. Just as Mario heard the *whoosh* of the rocket propelled grenade beginning to fire, the man slammed into Skye from behind. His arms wrapped around her midsection, jostling her, sending the rocket wild.

Mario popped up from behind the HVAC. The other intruder was reloading, but hadn't backed up enough. Mario sighted up and fired, never letting up. The man looked like he was dancing before he toppled backwards down the stairs.

An explosion—the RPG—boomed below them.

"What the fuck is what?" Phineas said, sounding alarmed.

To the southeast, a plume of black smoke billowed into the sky.

"An explosion maybe?" Miranda asked.

"What!" Phineas barked into the comm, at the same time Sean said, "Are we crashing?"

"We're fine," Victor said, cutting across their chatter. The helicopter changed direction, toward the plume of smoke. "I want to check that out, just in case it's something we need to know about. We're coming in blind as it is."

"Okay," she said, feeling tense and light-headed. She was sure that whatever had happened, it was bad.

The size of the smoke plume grew, deepening to a darker inky black. It could be anything, but the most likely she could think of was that a building had caught fire. They followed the path of the Highway 87 section of the Secured Expressway toward the plume.

They veered east, away from the line of the freeway toward downtown San Jose. They flew over the Cathedral Basilica of Saint Joseph flashed by as they approached a long ellipse of mostly green park, its rounded ends lined with palm trees and blocks-long, straight sides hemmed in by downtown streets. Something down there had gone very wrong.

"That's the plaza," Miranda said.

The center of the park was an open square of gravel and stone. One pie-shaped section of it had been a ground-level fountain built of gray and black squares of paving stones. The fountain had operated intermittently over the years, but now there was a structure on it: long and low and black. It hulked over the rest of the open area, its lines and angles those of ruthless practicality. It looked like a stage, but something about it wasn't right. The plume of smoke billowed up from a crater ten meters from the structure. A few cars that had been parked alongside the park were turned on their sides, wheels turning lazily in the air. The whole place churned with bodies, some running blindly, others being hustled into cars and SUVs.

"Are they zombies?" Miranda gasped, horrified.

"People. They're running away from that impact crater," Victor said tersely.

Victor cut the airspeed, and Miranda saw glimpses of faces, contorted in pain or fear, as the people who must have been assembled just minutes ago fled the explosion.

"What's going on out there?" Sean's disembodied voice asked.

"Some kind of public gathering," Miranda said. "Something exploded."

She squinted at the structure. It looked like people were being dragged against their will.

"Are those ropes?" Victor asked.

Miranda squinted as they flew by, her line of sight obstructed by the smoke. "I can't tell."

"What's going on out there?" Sean asked.

There was a break in the smoke. There were ropes hanging down, but they weren't just ropes...

"It's a gallows!" Miranda cried. Then she spied a tall, spindly figure with a shock of sandy hair blowing in all directions from the rotor wash. Doug, and he was being dragged toward the nooses.

"It's Doug!" she cried. "They're going to hang him! Land! Land now!"

THE GRAVEL ON THE ROOF SPIT FROM UNDER MARIO'S feet. He sprinted to the edifice—to the other RPG. A faint *wub, wub, wub*—the sound of his hammering heart—filled the air around him. He scooped up the second RPG from its case. The *wub, wub, wub* of his heart grew louder. He could see that Skye's shot had gone wide, exploding on the side of the plaza nearer to them, not the gallows. Black smoke billowed into the sky from the smoking crater the RPG had made.

Even though the shot had gone wide, it helped. There were fewer men trying to slip nooses around Doug's and Walter's heads, but Mario could hear gunfire. Even though his hands were still tied, Mario saw Doug fighting. He jerked himself forward, smacking his forehead into the head of his attacker. The man staggered back, stunned.

Mario hoisted the RPG to his shoulder, the *wub, wub, wub* of his heart louder than ever. Skye was stomping on the head of the downed man in front of her. The *wub, wub, wub* was almost deafening—almost on top of them.

"Holy shit," Mario said, his mouth feeling as if it had been filled with dust as he put it together.

A second later, a helicopter streaked overhead. He hadn't seen a helicopter in the sky in years, and now the Council had one?

"Shoot it down," Skye shouted.

The helicopter zoomed over and past them. Military grade, and it looked like a flying tank. Gunfire erupted from the helicopter as the wind beat down on them, causing him and Skye to crouch, almost curling up into balls on the hot roof. By the time Mario was back on his feet, strafing fire from the helicopter was bisecting the plaza.

"Mario! Shoot it down!"

He couldn't see what was happening on the gallows; the helicopter filled the RPG's sights. The targeting indicated ready. His finger curled around the trigger. But who were they? Air support didn't make sense. The City didn't have helicopters. Things hadn't changed that much while he'd been away. Skye's screams, urging him to fire, filled his ears. Debris flew up around the helicopter, people on the ground crouching and falling flat in the wash of its rotors. He could see the matchstick-sized figures in the helicopter's open doors, preparing to exit when they touched down.

He hesitated. What if the people on that helicopter weren't on the side of the Council? What if they were here to help? Rooted to the spot, unable to decide, he watched the helicopter's struts ease against the ground, dust swirling around it.

BELOW THEM, MOST PEOPLE ON THE GROUND AND gallows huddled, or fell as if they'd been sucker punched off their feet. Some crawled, unable to get up against the fierce barrage of the helicopter's rotor wash hammering down on them. It felt like hours, but was probably only ten seconds before Miranda felt the skids settle lightly on the ground.

She unbuckled her safety harness, then scrambled from her seat. Sean and Phineas were already on their feet by the time she reached the cargo hold door.

"You're with me," she said to them, unholstering her gun. "They're trying to hang Doug on that gallows!"

She wrenched the door open and jumped down, adrenaline pumping into her bloodstream. It was a storm of noise outside the helicopter, with alarms and shouts and the cries of the injured—and gunfire. It occurred to her that she was charging in with no idea how badly they might be outgunned, but it didn't matter. She had to save Doug.

Dirt and pebbles pinged off her helmet, stinging and biting

against her exposed chin. She crouched as she ran around the helicopter and out from under the slowing orbit of the rotors. The gallows was seven or eight feet from the ground, too high for her to climb.

She jammed her gun into her holster. "Boost me up," she said to Phineas, not wanting to waste time trying to find the stairs.

He laced his hands and she stepped into them, then almost face-planted when she landed above from how hard he pushed her. She got to her feet and looked around. Doug was crouched low and had gotten his shoulder under the legs of another man, whom they'd started to hang. Horror overwhelmed her when she realized the purpling face was Father Walter's.

She sprinted forward, knife in hand. Sean held Father Walter by the waist, loosening the tension while Miranda cut the rope. Miranda tugged at the noose as Sean lowered him to the floor. She pulled off her helmet to screaming, car alarms, crackling fire, and choking smoke. Volleys of gunfire were to their left, but sounded a block or two away. It could have been six inches away—Miranda wasn't leaving Father Walter.

A woman ran over and trained her gun on Miranda. "Freeze! Let him go!" Miranda glanced up at the woman as if she was nothing more than an annoying fly. The woman's eyes drew together, and she blinked in surprise in rapid succession, as if she didn't believe what she was seeing. "Miranda?"

Miranda turned back to Father Walter.

"Father Walter," she said desperately, turning to his slight form. She leaned down to start mouth to mouth, but Father Walter gasped and coughed in her face. "Father Walter," she cried again.

His hazel eyes focused on her, his face already pinkening to a healthier shade. His croaking voice was barely audible.

"Miranda?"

"It's me," she said, leaning over him again. "You're going to be okay."

The woman who'd pulled her gun on Miranda stood beside them, keeping a watch on the rest of gallows, for chaos had engulfed it. Smoke from the explosion whipped around them. Shouts and screams seemed to come from every direction. The guards and executioners were running away, unnerved by the appearance of the helicopter, and probably thinking there were more than four people on it. Some of them had been tackled to the ground by people in civilian clothes who restrained them.

Miranda said to Sean, "See if you can find a medic or something."

"We had someone near that end of the gallows. Look there," the woman guarding them said. As Sean left, Miranda suddenly realized the woman was one of the bartenders from The Hut.

Sean nodded and disappeared. Before Miranda could turn her attention back to Father Walter, someone dropped beside her and pulled her into a hug.

"Miri...my God. Where the hell did you come from?"

She returned the hug, recognizing Doug from the hundreds that had preceded this one before her brain caught up. His incredulous voice felt like a caress against her ear.

"Are you okay?" she said, breaking away to look at him.

Blood dripped through an eyebrow and down his face from a nasty gash on his forehead. She pulled off her bandana and pressed it against his forehead. He flinched and grimaced, but then smiled as he raised his hand to hold the bandana in place.

"Better than okay," he said, but he cast an anxious glance at Walter.

"He's breathing," she said.

Doug slumped against her. "Thank God."

She took Father Walter's hand, warm and gentle, in hers.

When he opened his mouth, she said, "I don't think you should talk until someone looks at you."

He nodded weakly and smiled at her. She squeezed his hand again. Phineas skidded into view.

"He's with us," Miranda said before their sentry bartender shot him. She had lost track of Phineas, only now realizing it. He cradled an assault rifle in his arms that he must have picked up here, because they hadn't brought it with them.

"I just saw Sean with a lady who said she's a nurse. They'll be here in a sec," Phineas said. "The helicopter really freaked people out, just like you thought it would. They're all running off." Then he said, sounding disappointed, "They're not very tough bad guys."

"What are you doing here?" Doug said to him, sounding stunned.

Phineas' teeth flashed white against the sharp edge of a relieved grin that mirrored Miranda's own. "I couldn't let my best girl do this without backup," he said, winking.

Doug reached over and ruffled Miranda's hair, pulling some free of the pins holding it tight against her head. "I can't believe I'm saying this, Coppertop, but you're like an angel, swooping in here at the last minute to save us."

Miranda laughed. Happiness, relief, joy...the swirl of emotions swelled inside her until she felt they might overflow. Doug's glacier-blue eyes flashed with relief and amazement. Father Walter's hand was warm against hers, his gentle, plain face overflowing with love. Phineas hovered over them, his eagerness to help shining through the chaos and noise. The love she felt for them welled up inside her, sharp and true. She'd missed them so much, more than she'd known—her friend, her mentor...her family.

In the plaza below, the blades of the helicopter were slowing to a lazy orbit around the aircraft. The guards and executioners and council members in attendance were all running for cover. They seemed more intent on getting away than mounting much of a defense. Bodies lay still, and a running gunfight was taking place between a group of Council Security and people in plain clothes a few blocks from the plaza. Walter lay on the gallows, the people from the helicopter crouching around him. The man who'd cut the rope took off his white helmet, a bright-blue bandana tied tight over his head. He dropped to his knees and leaned over Walter, blocking Mario's view. Then he straightened up, and the tense posture of those surrounding him and Walter relaxed.

"Skye!" Mario shouted. "I see Doug. He's alive!"

Mario picked up the discarded binoculars and looked through them. Blood gushed down Doug's face from a cut on his forehead, but his hands were now free. He dropped to his knees beside the man in the blue bandana and pulled him into an embrace. They parted a few seconds later, and the guy pulled the bandana from his head and pressed it against Doug's forehead.

Mario's knees buckled.

He felt them giving out, his stomach plummeting down to meet them while it also tried to vomit itself out of his mouth. Then his knees kicked back in, bearing his weight. He looked at the RPG at his feet, feeling dizzy and sick, then back to gallows through the binoculars. It took him a minute to find them again, between the smoke from the explosion, and all the people streaming away. City Council SUVs raced away from the park, and bodies—some in the dark suits of Council Security, others in civilian clothes—lay inert on the ground. Then Doug came into focus, his hand on the *woman's* shoulders. Her fiery-red hair was wound tight against her head. The happiness on her face had an almost unnatural incandescence. Her profile was clear as crystal, like a deep lake so still and transparent you can see all the way to the bottom without realizing its depth.

The pointy chin and high forehead. The straight nose and freckles. The dimple in her cheek. He knew them instantly, could have identified them in the dark vacuum of space. His whole body ached with longing to touch the familiar contours of Miranda's beaming face.

33

SEVENTEEN FLOORS TO THE GROUND. Mario skidded around another landing, taking the stairs three and four at a time, Skye following so close behind him that it felt like she was going to trip over his heels. His brain kept shouting at him to slow down before he fell and broke his neck. He'd already wiped out once and been damn lucky it hadn't been worse. His banged-up frame screeched, *Don't you know you got hit by a car last night, dipshit?* But he couldn't slow down... Couldn't stop the hammering of his heart, the harsh rasp of breath, the urgency propelling him forward, insisting he not stop, not slow down, and *get there*. He felt trapped by the echoing beige walls, by the endless stairs that had sucked him into a horror show where his destination moved farther and farther away no matter how hard and fast he ran.

When he finally saw sunlight brightening the landing below, he caught the bannister post, slingshotting himself one hundred eighty degrees. Dread gripped him in its icy fist. He'd had the RPG on his shoulder, the helicopter in his sights, the targeting software urging him to take the shot, and he'd almost done it. He'd almost killed the woman he loved.

Mario burst through the doors and into the pedestrian walkway. He sprinted through the double circle of palm trees in front of the building, smoke from the RPG detonation burning his throat. He hit Market Street at a full run, then crashed to a halt.

"Watch it!"

Mario caught a blur of a man's angry face, and a woman's, drawn and pale and bloodied, as he pushed away from the human obstacle in his path. The crush of dazed, fleeing onlookers pushed him backward. Car alarms blared from the far side of the park, adding to the chaotic mix of fear and danger. He shoved and pushed, fighting for every inch of ground.

He stumbled along the edge of the crowd, through a thinning veil of smoke. The ground slipped out from beneath his feet and he teetered for a long moment. Then gravel bit his hands, the impact with the ground happening before he realized he was falling. He'd fallen over the lip of the still smoldering crater, a jagged edge of concrete slicing into his knee. The brutish hulk of the helicopter loomed ahead, a dragon made of steel and glass.

Skye darted ahead of him. He followed her around the front of the helicopter. He glanced at the pilot, but it was impossible to see who it was because of the helmet and mirrored sunglasses.

"Doug!" Skye cried, desperation filling her voice.

Mario saw her change direction and almost knock Doug over when she reached him, colliding into his embrace. Mario searched the gallows, where he'd last seen Miranda, but there were so many people up there, and bodies, too. He hurried up the steps he'd seen Doug and Walter march up not ten minutes ago. If she was anywhere, she'd be with Walter. Mario hoped he wasn't badly injured and that he hadn't been moved, taking Miranda with him.

At the top of the steps, Mario searched the platform, his anxiety growing with every second. A lone noose swung in the dying gusts of the helicopter's rotors. Beside it hung a cut rope. A group of Council and City officials sat in the center of the gallows platform, hands tied, looking like they couldn't believe the reversal in their fortunes. Mario thought he caught a glimpse of Phineas...what the hell was he doing here?

He looked back toward the park, and there she was.

She knelt beside Walter, who looked gray and old and frail. She held his hand, nodding at him, and Mario stood, transfixed. She looked just like he remembered, and not. She leaned toward Walter, putting her fingers on his lips. He recognized the expression on her face. She was laying down the law, telling Walter what was what for his own good, but the naked vulnerability on her face was new. The armored facade she usually wore was absent. He could see the difference even in the small movements of her hands, mixed with anxiety as she admonished him not to speak. Worry carved into the lines at the edges of her smile, pinched the crinkles at the corners of her eyes, even as her love for the priest who had become like a father to her radiated from her. He caught a flash of cornflower blue, and the last time he'd seen her rushed back, when she'd looked at him across the bustling parking lot before he left LO. Then, her face had been a study of puzzlement, like she didn't understand what he was, or how he'd once fit into her life, before she turned away.

A woman with a small red medical kit knelt beside Walter across from Miranda. Miranda's face lit up with recognition, and she reached out to grab the woman's hand. They spoke for a moment, before the medic motioned for Miranda to get out of the way. She leaned over Walter, kissed him on the forehead, then scooted back and stood up.

She looked around, then her eyes met his. Mario watched them go wide with shock. Blood drained from her face. Suddenly, she looked on the verge of tears. She rubbed her hands on her shirt, took a tentative step in his direction, and he realized she was scared. Her mouth had fallen open a little, and the world around him began to look watery. Her chest rose and fell rapidly enough that he could see it. His feet felt rooted to the spot. He wanted to go to her, touch her, make sure she was real, but he couldn't get his body to cooperate. What if she still felt the same as when he'd last seen her?

She took another step toward him, then another. Mario felt like he was going to pass out when a warm flutter stirred in his chest. Tiny and soft, like a puff of breeze on a still day, or the tentative beginning of a gentle spring rain. It nudged him, whispering softly in his ear. He took another step, letting the strange, insistent feeling guide him, and realized it was hope.

THE WORLD AROUND HER SPUN. MARIO STOOD THIRTY feet away.

He was alive.

A sob filled her throat. The relief that rushed through her body made her feel as if she would float away, up through the clouds, and never touch down. He was battered and bruised and so beautiful it hurt to look at him. His face was thinner, clothes torn, cuts on his palms seeping blood. His dark hair was longer than she remembered, and her fingers twitched, wanting to feel it under her fingertips.

She wiped them on her shirt to stop the twitching desire. She needed to tell him what happened to them had been her fault. That she regretted all of it, would take it back if she could. That she loved him so much, and seeing him made her ache. She'd rehearsed it so many times in her head, but she couldn't move. Fear flooded her body, a sucking swamp of terror threatening to pull her under its murky surface.

He looked like he was caught in a spider's web, but the look on his face was unfamiliar. She knew her mouth was open but she couldn't seem to close it. Her heart beat so hard that if she didn't know better, she'd have thought she was having a heart attack. She took a step forward, drawn to him like a moth following a beam of moonlight. The world at the edges of her vision spun faster. Her feet moved of their own volition, then faltered when he took a step.

She was so relieved he was alive, choking on fear that rose up from her stomach in waves, but she had to tell him. Even if he didn't love her anymore, even if he couldn't forgive her, she had to tell him the truth. She jerked to a halt, so close she could touch him if she had the nerve to reach out her hand. He was so close she could see that he hadn't shaved, and blood smudged his cheek, but the space between them felt like a chasm. When he spoke, it sounded like a gasp.

"Miri."

She opened her mouth to say something, anything, but the words lodged in her throat. She felt her face crumple. Tears blurred her vision as she started to cry. Her longing overwhelmed everything else. She didn't know where to start or what to say. Didn't know what he needed to hear that would make him believe her. She just stood, staring at him, while tears ran down her face, the soft, small animal of her body aching to curl around the soft, small animal of his. She had no defenses, no lies she still believed. She clung to the only thing she had left—the truth.

"I'm sorry," she said. "I'm so, so sorry."

The swirl of emotion on his face blossomed into something gentle and strong. He closed the last step between them, cradling her face in his hands. They felt tacky against her skin from the bleeding cuts, but their warmth felt like sunshine, just like she remembered. The dark depths of his eyes were tender, anticipation and relief twirling in them like dancers. He took a shuddering breath, then pulled her close.

His breath was soft against her ear when he said, his voice choked, "I'm sorry too."

THE NEXT FEW HOURS PASSED IN A BLUR. SHE DIDN'T remember how they'd gotten back to SCU, but rounding up the flunkies the Council had installed there hadn't been as hard as Miranda feared. The residents of SCU had only needed a spark to flare into open rebellion. The dramatic arrival of Miranda and her friends on the helicopter, and their rescue of Father Walter and Doug, had been more than enough. SCU residents had already rounded up some of the Council's functionaries by the time Miranda and her friends got there.

The one constant as each moment blurred into the next was Mario. He was always nearby, catching her eye with a look that said he had so much to tell, and wanted to hear what she had to tell him. When he took her hand throughout the day, his fingers brushing the inside of her wrist, or hers feeling the familiar contours of his arm, she was hit by a rush of longing for all the casual touches they used to share. She hungered, ravenous, for every small moment they had missed, and the time she'd squandered. When Doc told them that Father Walter would be all right, and it finally seemed there was nothing else to do, she looked around for him, but he wasn't there.

"Settle down, Coppertop," Doug said as he walked into the living room of the Jesuit Residence holding Skye's hand. They flopped on the couch opposite her. "I think he went to find a place for you two to spend the night."

"Right, of course," she said, sinking to the closest couch and trying to tamp down her sudden panic that maybe he'd changed his mind and didn't really want to be around her after all. She was too tired, too frazzled, to drive home and unlock her house, too overwhelmed by the day's events. She hadn't even thought about it till now, but Mario had. She wished Delilah was here, even though she was glad the pit bull was being spoiled by River back in Portland. She could use the snuggly weight of the too-big-to-be-a-lapdog pittie in her lap, which always cheered and calmed her. She realized she hadn't really thought through the decision to leave her behind. She'd have to go back to LO to get her.

"How's the head?" she asked.

Doug reached up and gingerly felt the inch-long line of stitches on his forehead. "Okay, I guess. A little sore. Skye said it makes me even sexier."

"I did not; that's not funny," Skye said, sounding distressed, her eyes glistening with tears. Miranda could see how exhausted she was, and after hearing about the last twenty-four hours, had a fair idea of how she must have been feeling. "I thought you were dead, and when I finally found you alive, you looked like you'd been stabbed."

Doug's face softened. He pulled Skye to him. "I'm sorry, sweetheart."

Doug caught Miranda's eye. She mouthed without speaking aloud, "Too soon, idiot."

Skye adjusted herself to snuggle into Doug's side, wiping at her eyes.

"Is City Hall still burning?" Miranda asked.

Doug shrugged, then said through a yawn, "Last I heard, but the fire brigade was fighting it." He yawned again. "Brother Rupert and a couple others went downtown to make sure people didn't start summary executions. We hammered out plans for a tribunal a few years back, for when the Council finally bit the dust. Thought it would be a good idea to have some sort of plan. It's chaotic enough without starting from zero."

"I always pictured you in the thick of all that," Miranda said.

Behind Doug and Skye, she saw Mario walking down the hall toward her. Doug saw her distraction and looked over his shoulder. He nodded to Mario, then said to Miranda, "I've got the same plans as you, Miri. I'm going to bed with my girlfriend and sleeping for a week."

Butterflies churned in Miranda's stomach. More than butterflies...something along the lines of an anxious herd of rhinos. Mario had already showered. He looked a little less beat up in the clean clothes, and without dirt and blood smudged on his face and neck, though still tired. His eyes lit up when he saw her.

"I found a place for us for tonight," he said. "Ready?"

Miranda nodded as she stood, her tentative smile fading to what felt like a grimace. She wanted to be alone with him but was so nervous. She felt like a bride in an arranged marriage on her way to the bridal suite, with a groom she'd only just met.

"See you later," she said to Doug and Skye.

Doug caught her hand as she passed him and said softly, "Don't look so tragic. It'll be all right."

Mario had secured a small guest apartment in Nobili Hall. He'd sent her off for a shower with a smile so gentle, tears had rushed to her eyes. She stood under the hot water, eyes closed, the thick lather of soap sluicing from her body to circle around her feet before disappearing into the drain. She was eager to be alone with him, and nervous, too. When she finally stepped out from under the water, she wrapped a robe that hung on the back of the door around her dripping body, the soft, thin flannel sticking to her like a hug. She gripped the doorknob, offering up a silent prayer that it would be all right. That she would find the right words to make him understand.

She blew out a breath and pulled the door open. He was fussing with the blanket on the bed, wearing only a pair of sweatpants that hung low on his hips. He smiled as he turned to her, the muscles of his torso rippling as he moved, and the swooning sensation it caused made her light-headed. He looked tentative, and she could see that he was nervous, too.

"Feel better?" he asked.

She nodded, cat firmly in possession of her tongue, because he was here with her. Against all odds, he was here. They looked at one another for a few moments, then she finally said, "I don't know where to start."

"How about here?"

He opened his arms. She melted into his embrace...the warmth of his arms around her, his body against hers, a balm. Then his lips found hers, pushing everything else away. Heat radiated from her center as desire consumed her. She gasped when he kissed her neck, her head falling back as the feel of his lips on her skin overwhelmed her. The robe puddled at her feet. She pulled him to the bed, the need to feel their bodies meld together too strong to delay.

He kicked off the sweats, following her as she slid higher up the bed. He hovered over her for a moment, lips slightly parted and breathing hard. The naked vulnerability, the hunger for her that she saw in his eyes filled hers with tears. They spilled over, pooling beneath her eyelashes before sliding down her temples, for it mirrored her own. She had never felt so open, so present, so exposed, but for the first time, she wasn't afraid to be. She wasn't afraid to let him see the part of herself she'd always kept hidden and locked away, even from him. The part that used razors and alcohol to cope, to numb, to keep her from feeling all the things that had been too painful to feel. The things she'd been sure would kill her if she did.

She hadn't understood how precious the love they shared was, and how close she'd come to destroying it, until she finally let him see all of her.

They moved together, joined by more than their bodies, desire fueled by discovery old and new, by the need to know that the love they shared was still there. She could feel it spooling between them, binding them fast, unfurling inside her as Mario held her close, whispering her name, telling her how much he loved her—had ached for and needed her—always. It still burned in his eyes and coursed through the heart she felt pounding in his chest. It still captured her soul, overwhelming her senses with its heady perfume. It beckoned her closer, stormy waves of sweet oblivion catching her in an undertow that she let pull her out, into the deep, where she knew he would be waiting.

LATER, THEY LAY SIDE BY SIDE, FOREHEADS ALMOST touching. Moonlight spilled through the window, its glow illuminating the otherwise dark room.

"It was my fault," she whispered. She felt her face screw up and a sharp pressure push against her sternum. "If I hadn't gone outside that night, hadn't done what I always do. You knew what I'd done, and I couldn't stand it."

"Miri, I—"

"Rocco says not stopping to think, not thinking it through, that's the part that's my fault, not what happened after. I want to believe him, but... I should have known what might happen next."

"That's not true," he said, brushing her hair back from her face. "I've never thought—"

She felt his body tense, even though they barely touched. His words had banged against her denial for months, growing more and more insistent, until they broke through her misdirected anger, demanding to be recognized. She could tell by his sudden stillness that he'd remembered, too.

But it's not me that's dead because you put yourself in harm's way, is it? And it's not you, either. If one of us left the baby behind, it sure as shit wasn't me.

"It *was* my fault. I left him behind, just like you said, and then I let myself *want* him. After he was gone, I couldn't...I couldn't stand you being good to me."

She felt, rather than saw, his eyes lock with hers, for his face was almost hidden in shadow. But she could see enough to recognize that it was a study of regret. Not just for Tadpole, but everything—the dreams their world had crushed, the heartache and betrayal and horror and fear. His bewilderment at how his choices had snowballed, one leading to the next, accumulating the weight of a lifetime. The family he'd made with Emily, that he loved and needed. The little boy Silas, who he'd told her about in these few, stolen hours, who he'd loved so much, only to have him ripped away in the cruelest way imaginable. His inability to help her when she needed him most, no matter that she'd done everything she could to drive him away. And their own little Tadpole, who they never even met.

"I didn't mean it," he said, his shaking voice filled with more pain than four words could hold. "It *wasn't* your fault, Miranda. It was never your fault. I swear on my children that I didn't mean it. I was hurt, and angry, and I forgot that you were hurting, too."

She felt the pressure building behind the dam she had built, the bricks of pain she had hoarded stacked one upon the other. Tears welled in her eyes. Her chest started to hitch. She felt it deep in her belly, where she had cradled Tadpole once. Felt it claw through her chest, squeeze through her throat. It slipped out of her mouth, and the dam broke with it. Mario pulled her into his arms as she sobbed. For Tadpole. For him. For herself. For their tiny little family that never was. For the small, soft, foolish dream she'd let herself have, let herself want, only to have this world destroy it like it had all the others.

"I'm sorry, Miri. I'm so, so sorry," Mario whispered over and over. He held her tight to his chest, crooning in her ear. "I didn't mean it."

"He's gone," she whispered. "We'll never get him back."

She clung to him, and he to her, as they wept for Tadpole —together.

Eventually, the sobs subsided. Her temples pounded, the pain of grief suppressed too long lingering in the thin muscles of her scalp. Her sinuses were stuffed, nose runny. Mario reached over her, hanging off the side of the bed for a moment, then came back up with the sweatpants he'd been wearing before. He switched the lamp on the bedside table on, its low light making the old dorm room feel cozy. From the pocket of the sweatpants he pulled out a handkerchief. He had another for himself, because of course he did. Of course he had two hankies a decade after the end of the world.

She sat up, pulling on a tee shirt he handed her when she said she was cold, then leaned against the wall at the head of the bed. After a good blow, she almost felt like she could breathe again. Mario sat beside her, holding her hand, their fingers interlaced. The crow's feet at the corners of his eyes had deepened. He looked remorseful, but she saw a spark in his eyes, tiny and fragile, that hadn't been there when last she'd seen him at LO.

She took a deep breath. "I didn't mean what I said, either. That you abandoned us. That you didn't love Tadpole as much."

Mario squeezed her hand. "I know you didn't. I forgave that a long time ago." He paused, then said, his voice so tender that her eyes welled up again, "Rocco's right. You should believe him. The only thing you did wrong that night was not think it through. What happened wasn't your fault. There was no way for you to know."

She nodded, not wanting to speak because she'd start crying again.

Mario said, "I want you to promise me that you'll try to believe it."

"Okay," she whispered, unable to fathom how she ever could. But he'd asked her to try, so she would. "I promise."

He smiled at her, looking careworn, but happy.

"Do you think—" She swallowed, feeling nervous again. "Do you think we could start over?"

His bark of laughter echoed off the walls. "I thought we already had." He pushed her hair behind her ear, looking at her like she was something precious, which made her feel shy.

Then, seeming to realize that she needed to hear him say it, he said, "I would like that very much."

She let go of the breath suspended in her lungs. It flooded back again, how much she loved him, like it had so many times today, filling her body with a lightness that made her feel like she would float away.

"I'm sor—"

"Shhh," he said, putting two fingers on her lips. He wiped the tears that would not quit from below her eyes with his thumb. "There's nothing to be sorry about. Not anymore."

She felt bashful, and relieved, and so fucking tired. It felt like she had carried the guilt and shame of blaming herself forever.

"I love you," she said. "Even when I convinced myself it was gone, it was always there."

She pressed her lips to his. Their supple strength and tender yield, his hunger for her that she could feel, made her whimper with relief. When they parted, she saw how much he loved her in his dark, serious eyes, burning clear and steady and true. They were alight with joy. And underneath, a sadness, for everything they'd lost and never properly begun to grieve until now.

"I've missed you," he said softly. "Maybe we'll get it right this time. You know, three times a charm?"

"Thanks for not giving up on me."

Mario's delighted laughter rumbled in his chest as he gathered her into his arms. "Oh, Miranda... Only a fool would give up on you."

34

EMILY SAID, "You look better today, Miri."

Miranda smiled, glancing over to her friend. "I feel better. It feels like I've done nothing but sleep the past ten days."

Through the windows, the voices of the children rose and fell as they ran around the backyard of Emily and Mario's Palo Alto home. They were playing hide and seek. Violet and Maureen burst from behind a Jacaranda tree, shrieking like banshees. Anthony pursued, hot on their heels, his arm outstretched. Violet dragged Maureen with her, but Maureen's legs were too short to keep up. Anthony lunged, tumbling to the ground, but managed to tag Maureen on her ankle. Michael's head popped out from behind a bush, took a look at the littler kids, and disappeared again. Anthony and Violet conferred. Then Violet began to count, despite Maureen having been tagged. Anthony took Maureen's hand and they streaked away to hide.

Miranda and Mario were staying in the guesthouse at Mario and Emily's house in Palo Alto. Violet too, some nights. The residents of the walled community had traded the members of the Council living among them to the tribunal convening in San Jose in exchange for being left alone—for now. There had been grumbling about this, but the Jesuits had made the case for dealing with one thing at a time. They'd also made it clear that everyone complicit with the Council had to be held accountable eventually. Miranda found the response of Palo Alto's residents to the looming tribunals, and the Truth and Reconciliation plan that would follow, amusing. They ranged from serious ass-kissing of the Jesuits to those who tried to flee. So far, those who opted for flight had ended up in the city jail in San Jose. All of it was a startling reversal of fortune for those who'd thought themselves removed from the nastier side of what had made their lives seem so idyllic.

Miranda and Mario were also here because Palo Alto still had some of the best security in the Valley. In the many town hall meetings and forums since the Council was deposed, Father Walter had told the people of the Valley that Mario had been on their side all along. That he'd gone undercover at Father Walter's request, and was responsible for not only getting the vaccine back, but developing another in Portland. Despite his efforts, there was a growing faction that wanted him tried for war crimes. With all the comings and goings at SCU as the citizens of the Valley worked together with the Jesuits to establish a real form of governance, SCU's security was too porous. Father Walter was afraid that Mario wouldn't be safe there, and Miranda agreed.

Turning away from watching the children through the window, Miranda said, "Violet fits like she's always been here."

"She does," Emily agreed. She pulled plates from the cupboard and set them on the counter. "I thought it would take longer for them to bond like this. I'm sure they'll make up for it when they're teenagers. Bets on which of us gets 'You're not my mom' first?"

Miranda almost forced a laugh, but couldn't manage it. She bit her lip, then said, "Are you sure this isn't too weird, us being here?"

Emily reached out and gave her arm a squeeze. "It's not. I really am happy for you two."

Emily's voice was steady, her manner confident and self-assured. Miranda hadn't seen her like this since before zombies. She'd almost forgotten this Emily had ever existed.

"I'm not happy you had to run for your lives, or for the way Mario left," Emily continued. "But I'm better than I've been in a long time. I don't think—no, I know that would never have happened if Mario and I were still together."

Something had happened between Mario and Emily. They might still be married on paper, but they'd come to a resolution; their marriage was over. They both seemed relieved, yet closer than ever. It made Miranda feel unsure—of herself, of Mario, and Emily, too, and how they fit together.

Voices carried in from the foyer, followed by the soft click of the front door being closed. Moments later Mario, Tessa, Father Walter, Karen, and Doug and Skye trooped into the kitchen. Karen rushed across the room to them.

"Is she wearing heels?" Miranda asked Emily under her breath.

"Oh yeah," Emily said.

Then Karen was in front of her. Miranda gave her friend a hug, and let the shoes slide.

CANDLES LIT THE TABLE, WHICH WAS LITTERED WITH napkins and half-full wine and water glasses. Whatever unease Miranda had felt before was gone, sloughed away by the food and wine, and the comfort of being with the people who'd been with her since the beginning. Tessa and Skye weren't those people, technically, but it felt like they were. The old, familiar rhythms of conversation had settled in like they'd never been interrupted. It was a welcome break from the simmering tension of the last week.

Emily sat at one end of the table, Father Walter the other. Doug and Emily were on the same corner and had talked a mile a minute through the entire meal. Karen was dating another jerk who, unsurprisingly, had bailed instead of coming with her tonight like he'd promised.

Miranda also sat at one of the table's corners, by Father Walter. She leaned toward him, taking his hand.

"It's been great craic tonight," she said.

"Great craic altogether," Father Walter agreed. "I wasn't sure if I'd ever see you again. Having you here is a miracle."

"Oh, please," Miranda said, scoffing good-naturedly. "I've never been a miracle. Now that," she said, tipping her head ever so slightly toward Doug and Skye. "That's a miracle."

Father Walter snorted softly. When he spoke, his voice was amused. "He thinks I'm angry with him."

"Are you?"

"Ah no, of course not. God's plan for him changed. Vocations aren't for everyone." His voice lowered confidentially. "If I'd met Skye when I was younger, the priesthood might not have been for me, either."

Miranda laughed. "It's good to be home."

Father Walter's smile faded. His hazel eyes, which reminded her of Alec—except that Walter's were even more startlingly beautiful—became serious. "Miranda, you know we need to talk to him again."

"I know," she said softly. "He doesn't want to hear it."

Mario's hand slid over hers. "What are you two talking about?"

Miranda looked at him. "Nothing really."

Mario said, teasing, "I don't believe that for a minute."

Father Walter jumped in and said, "We're just talking about what's going on right now. We can talk about it later."

The other conversations around the table were winding down, and almost everyone else looked their way. Miranda felt Mario's hand tense around hers before he pulled it away. His face seemed to shutter in on itself. A little too loudly, he said, "You mean you wanting us to leave."

"Let's talk about it later," Miranda said, acutely aware of everyone's eyes on them.

Mario shook his head. Testily he said, "Why don't we talk about it now?"

She could see he thought they were ganging up on him, and this wasn't the place to have this discussion. But if he wanted to do it here, fine.

"It's not just Father Walter who thinks we need to leave. I think so, too. So does Doug," Miranda said.

Doug nodded. Karen's lips screwed into an unhappy frown.

"She's right, Mario," Father Walter said gently. "We shouldn't need to have this conversation, but it's not a small faction anymore and it's growing. If you stay, you're going to end up before the tribunal."

"I'm not leaving my family behind," Mario said, as if his word was final.

"It's your family you should be thinking of," Father Walter said.

"This whole thing is bullshit," Emily said. "He was undercover for you, Father Walter. He got the vaccine back and made another one. You've told everyone the truth! What is it going to take to convince people Mario isn't the bad guy here?"

Silence filled the room, oppressive and hard.

Doug said, "It's not fair, Emily, but people want justice."

"They want vengeance," she countered.

"Yeah, that too," Doug conceded.

Walter said, "That's what the tribunal is for. So that it's justice, not a lynching."

"Can we please just stop talking about this?" Mario said. "I'm not going anywhere. I'm not leaving my kids again."

"You're the one who wanted to talk about it now in the first place," Miranda said, both incredulous and annoyed that he was being so stubborn. "But as soon as people don't tell you what you want to hear, you don't want to anymore?"

Mario shot her a filthy look, the intensity of his anger so hot that Miranda almost flinched.

"Even I think you should go," said Karen, sounding dispirited. "I don't want to lose you all again, but staying here? It's just not an option."

Mario leaned back in his seat and crossed his arms, the line of his mouth hard. Miranda knew that look, that stance. He was digging in.

"Why don't we all go?" Emily said. "What do you think? Me and the kids...we could all go."

"Really?" Miranda squeaked. It had never occurred to her to ask, but now that Emily had said it, she couldn't believe she hadn't thought of it before.

"I can't ask you to do that," Mario said.

"You're not asking me," Emily said. "If leaving the kids is the problem, I'll come, too. You and the kids are the only family I've got. If it's safe in Portland, why not?"

Mario's head shook from side to side. "I'm not uprooting all of you because of something I did. It's dangerous, even in a helicopter. I already lost—" He stopped, then continued, his voice tight. "I'm not losing anyone else. If I have to deal with the consequences of my part in all this, then so be it."

"So be it?" Miranda said, her temper flaring. She heard

Father Walter say something, no doubt meant to defuse her anger, but she ignored him. "After all we've been through, after what you went through to get here, you'll just march up to that gallows like it's *A Tale of Two Cities*? What about the rest of us?"

Mario took an impatient breath. "You know that's not what I meant."

"Then what do you mean?"

They were on the verge of an argument—one that wouldn't be pretty. She needed to reel herself in, not give in to her anger. She almost wanted to, because they finally had their chance. Emily had thrown them a lifeline. His stubbornness made absolutely no sense.

There's something else going on here, she thought, realizing that if she could take a step back and not lose her temper, he'd tell her. She knew he would. She put her hand on Mario's arm. His muscles tensed under her fingers.

"Let's talk about this later," she said more gently.

From the corner of her eye, she saw Doug's mouth fall open in shock. Mario's eyebrows knitted together. He looked at her like she was a bomb that might still explode, then nodded.

The table was silent. Miranda took a sip of her wine. "You don't want to come to LO anyway, Karen," she said, trying to jump-start the conversation. "Nobody's wearing heels there."

Karen said something sassy, and the others joined in. Doug looked at her like she'd been swapped out for a pod person, then burst out laughing when she scratched at her cheek with a raised middle finger. She had parent manners when she wanted to, and she saw no reason to scandalize Father Walter into his grave.

After a few minutes, Mario slipped his hand into hers. Their eyes met, and she saw a cautious openness that had been absent just moments ago. She'd figure out what was going on, and then make him see sense. They hadn't come this far to blow it now.

SHE LEANED AGAINST THE WALL IN THE DARK HALLWAY, looking into the bedroom. Soft light puddled around the side table between two twin beds. Violet and Anthony were crammed into one bed; Mario sat near their feet. Violet's arms were stretched above her head, her fingertips walking up and down the headboard.

"Violet's really good with the kittens," Anthony said. "They were still too small to take last week, but they might be ready now. We're getting up early to go see."

"We're bringing them home," Violet said, her eyes sparkling with excitement.

"Maybe," said Anthony.

Violet nodded, as if Anthony's caveat was a minor detail.

"You two better get to sleep, then," Mario said, ruffling each child's hair with a hand. He hooked a thumb to the other bed. "One of you in there. There's no room for you both unless someone falls on the floor."

Violet yawned, with so much effort she reminded Miranda of a baby. Anthony got into the other bed.

"What about our story?" Violet said.

"We spent all our time talking about kittens," Mario answered.

"Daddy can tell us stories tomorrow," Anthony said through a yawn.

Violet's mouth twisted into a frown, then she said, "Okay. But let's say the good night."

They did, all three of them, running through the lines of the Santorello bedtime fare-thee-well. Miranda smiled, listening to them, and wondering how many more years they'd want to do it. A lot, she hoped. Mario's face was soft when he looked at the children, his love for them in every quirk of his lips or wrinkle of his nose. He turned off the light, then joined her in the hallway.

They walked to the living room in silence. It wasn't an easy silence, but it also wasn't charged by an inevitable and looming argument.

"Michael and Maureen stayed in the house?" Miranda asked him. She handed Mario a glass of wine, then got her own, before settling down next to him on the couch.

"Michael didn't want to be with the babies, and you saw Maureen. She was out before dessert."

"Where were Phineas, Sean, and Victor? They were invited, right?"

"They were," she assured him. "I don't know what Sean and Victor decided to do, but Phineas met a girl at SCU, so..."

They lapsed into silence again as Miranda leaned against him. Eventually, Mario said, "I'm sorry about before, at dinner. I didn't mean to be so..."

"It's all right." She turned her head and rested her chin on his shoulder. "Are you going to tell me what's wrong?"

Another long silence. She sipped her wine some more. Now that they might talk about it, the suspense was killing her.

"I— It's just— The trip is so dangerous. One mechanical problem and we're screwed, dropped right in the middle of it." He sighed, frustration creasing his forehead and curling his mouth down in a frown. "It's Anthony's kittens, and the girl Michael likes, and you and Emily being forced to leave because of me."

"Nobody's forcing me to do anything, and living here in Palo Alto wasn't always the easiest time for Emily. Maybe she could do with a fresh start."

He sighed. "I just keep thinking there's got to be a way to make it work. I know you want to be here. I want to be here."

There was something else. He wasn't twisted into knots about the kids being uprooted. The family being together was what was most important to him, not where it happened.

Then the penny dropped, and she couldn't believe she hadn't figured it out sooner.

"This is about your brother, isn't it?"

Another long sigh, then a reluctant, "Yeah."

She turned fully sideways on the couch to better see him.

"He wants to see me," Mario said. "I got the message earlier today."

Careful to keep her tone neutral, she said, "What do you want to do?"

"He's my brother, Miri. I feel like I have to."

She shook her head. "This isn't about obligation."

Mario looked away, but not before she saw the pain in his eyes. Goddamn you, Dominic, she thought. He'd drag Mario into his messes to the bitter end.

Mario gave her a wry look. "I was going to kill him when I got here. So much for that plan."

"Michael Corleone you are not," she said. "I'm glad you couldn't do it."

"I don't know what to do."

Mario looked at her like she knew the answer. He was desperate enough to do what she advised, if it meant taking responsibility for the decision off his shoulders. Miranda knew that Dominic was at the city jail. She wished that they were still using the county jail, and that he was there. Even though it was in zombie territory, it was outside the city walls. The idea of Mario going into San Jose, where there were people who wanted to haul him in front of the tribunal, made her sick, never mind him actually going to the jail itself.

"I think it's stupid and dangerous to go see him, but I can't make this decision for you."

Mario closed his eyes for a long moment. When he opened them, he said, "I have to go."

She'd known he would go as soon as he'd told her, because she knew how they'd grown up. Mario had been his brother's protector his entire life. For good or for ill, by visiting Dominic, he would play that role one last time.

She set her wineglass down. Gently, with infinite care, she smoothed his hair back. She studied the contours of his face—the intense dark eyes and Roman nose, the strong, square chin and just right lips. She thought of Alec, of how good he'd been to her, and how much she'd liked being with him. Sitting here with Mario, her time with Alec seemed like a wisp of a half-forgotten dream. Everything she wanted was here, with this man. He'd seen her at her best and her absolute worst, and he was still here. He was cool where she was fiery, measured where she was rash, kinder to her than she sometimes was to him. He was always there, always true, as constant and faithful as the North Star. He wasn't perfect by a long shot; neither was she. But together they were more than the sum of their parts. Together, they worked.

"Then you should go tomorrow."

She leaned into him, breathing deep, the scent of his skin musky and sweet. His lips brushed hers, soft and warm, as heat between them blazed. When she lay below him moments later, shirt thrown on the floor, shivering at the touch of his lips on the swell of her breasts, the clink of his unbuckling belt tinkling against her ear, a vague part of her mind knew they should go to the bedroom because of the kids, but her body didn't care.

Tomorrow he would go see his brother, but right now, he was hers.

35

WALTER'S ANXIOUS VOICE ASKED, "Are you set on this, Mario? I think this is a bad idea after what I heard this morning."

"He's my brother. I have to try."

Walter didn't agree. Mario could tell from the thin line of his lips, and the flash of anger in his hazel eyes, but he didn't say more. From where he sat between Walter and Rupert in the back seat of a massive, old Suburban SUV, Mario resumed looking out the windshield.

"Don't worry, Father," Victor said. Mario saw him glance in the rearview mirror. "Nobody's getting their hands on him. That's why Doug is here."

Doug, in the front passenger seat, said, "To get him out of trouble or take his place?"

"The former would be better, but the latter will do, if all else fails," Victor said, grinning.

How he could joke right now, Mario had no idea. The tension filling the vehicle felt like a bomb with a glitchy trigger device. Victor turned the old Suburban around the corner, then hit the brakes hard. The shoulder strap of Mario's seat belt engaged, holding him in place. A large crowd—at least five hundred—was assembled in the street and down the block outside the city jail. Signs dotted the crowd, a lot of them with slogans along the lines of "Both Santorellos Must Go," and "He made a vaccine. He's still a war criminal."

Without saying a word, Victor turned in his seat, arm across its back, and backed up fast. When they were a hundred yards past the corner they had just turned, he U-turned and drove them in the opposite direction. The Suburban was a boat of a vehicle, and the street narrow. Mario wasn't sure how he managed it. A minute later, they had circled around into an alley at the far end of the block behind the jail.

"New plan," Victor said, taking the next turn and pulling to the curb. He turned to speak over the seat. "Father Walter, I need you to go in. Ask for Julio Fontalva, tell him I sent you and that you want to see Dominic. He owes me a favor. After he takes you down, I need him to come get us at the employee entrance, get us down to where you'll be visiting with Dominic, and then get us out."

"How do you know all this?" Mario asked.

"Not relevant," Victor said.

"Why didn't you do this in the first place?" Walter asked, incredulous.

"Because I didn't want to call in a favor unless we really needed it."

Victor radiated authority and calm, dismissing Walter's question as done and dusted in a way Mario had seen few people do. More surprising was that Walter accepted his explanation without another word.

"If Doug, Mario, and I go inside, and that's a big if," he said, giving Mario a hard look. "Rupert, you'll stay with the vehicle. If that crowd approaches and you think they're going to cause problems, if somebody looks at you wrong, leave. Will you do that?"

"Yes," Rupert said.

"I need to see my brother, not run away if people look at us funny," Mario said, feeling that the situation was spinning out of his control.

"No," Victor said. "We need to make sure you're not grabbed by anyone who might want to make an example of you. Seeing your brother is a bonus."

"But—"

"You're either letting me run this, or you're not," Victor said, cutting him off. "If you aren't, we're leaving right now."

Mario looked to Doug, who sat in the passenger seat, for support. Doug shook his head.

"He's right, Mario. We do it his way, or we're done here."

He stared at Doug, gobsmacked. Victor didn't give a shit if he saw his brother or not, and apparently, neither did Doug.

"What happens when we do it your way, get back here, and Rupert's gone? Then what?"

"Walter doesn't need protection. He can leave separately if necessary. You, Doug, and I will run two blocks south, to the trashed red Lexus I parked there last night. And if that one doesn't work, we keep going to the next one."

Anger rushed through Mario's body, making his muscles hum. He wanted to punch Victor, puncture his calm and collected authority, just to get a reaction. He hadn't realized when they put Victor in charge their goals were different, and that the former mercenary wasn't invested in what Mario wanted, but making sure that he wasn't detained.

"Okay," he said, knowing he had to agree. "But next time, tell me what your objectives really are so I don't waste my time."

Victor said, "I did. You just weren't listening. Father Walter, do you mind?"

Walter nodded, fumbling for the handle, and exited the Suburban. Mario watched him walk up the alley that ran along the building until he reached the corner at the front of the jail and turned out of sight. The next fifteen minutes passed in tense silence, until a door of the jail building along the alley opened. A short, slim man stepped out from the door and scanned the area.

"Okay," Victor said. "That's Julio. Let's go."

Rupert got behind the wheel as Victor, Mario, and Doug walked quickly to the door. They followed Julio inside, then paused when the door closed behind them.

"What the hell are you doing back in town, man? And what are you doing with these guys?" Julio said to Victor, his tone warm, but the expression on his thin face incredulous.

"Long story," Victor said.

Julio looked increasingly unhappy while Victor explained what they needed: a way in for Mario to see Dominic, and if it came to it, help getting him out. He ran a hand across his face, then over his short black hair.

"I owe you, brother, but *¡Santa Madre de Dios!*" Julio said. "I'll do my best. He's got five minutes in there, tops. If I say we need to go, we go."

"That's all we need," Victor said.

Julio scowled. "I should have known you'd call in your favor for something like this. Damn, Victor." He added, to everyone, "Keep your weapons holstered, just so we aren't escalating anything unnecessarily. C'mon."

He led them down the long institutional-gray corridor. They passed a stairwell door on the right, then Julio motioned for them to stay back as he approached the corner. On Julio's left, a door marked LOCKER ROOM opened. Julio blocked the door.

"Give me five minutes, man."

Whoever was inside the locker room door said, "What?"

"Give me five minutes and later on, you can honestly say you had no idea."

A pause, then the voice said, "Okay, Julio."

The door closed, and Julio motioned them by. They entered the next stairwell and started down, footsteps echoing against the concrete walls. At the next landing, Julio turned to them.

"Wait here. If I'm not back in five minutes, go out the way you came."

Mario's pulse skyrocketed. He wanted to scream with frustration at Julio's instructions and Victor's nod. He wasn't doing this to not see Dominic. He was also questioning why the hell he was doing this. Why was he risking his safety for the man who'd tried to kill him? All he could come up with was a lifetime of obligation and habit that left him unable to turn away. They'd been through too much growing up, and however much he didn't want to admit it, he still loved his little brother.

Julio returned, now holding a ring of keys. Mario shoved his frustration and doubts aside, angry that he was in this situation, and knowing he had only himself to blame.

"Let's go," Julio said.

They followed him down the corridor, toward the front of the building, and took the first right. Julio almost walked into a tall, beefy guard. The air became charged, the line between calm and violence only a hair's breadth. Mario flicked the snap on his holster, curling his hand around the grip of his Sig.

"What the fuck, man?" Julio said.

The man glanced past Julio to Mario and his companions. His eyebrows seemed to levitate to his hairline.

"I had to come back for—"

"Just get the fuck out of here," Julio snapped. "You didn't see no one, got it?"

Despite the fact that the man towered over Julio, he beat a hasty retreat, the steel doors behind them clunking open and shut. Two bulletproof glass and steel security doors formed a checkpoint into the lockup.

Julio turned the lock on the first door, then the second, and motioned them through. He tossed a wooden wedge to Victor, then started to work a key off the ring.

"Prop this door, Victor, but not enough that it'll look open from down the hall, and stand inside the checkpoint. I'll be out here. He's near the end, where the priest is," Julio said, motioning with a jut of his chin. He handed Victor the key. "This opens the doors at the far end of the cell block. When I tell you to go, go that way. Take the stairs up one flight to the hallway you entered into the building. Only difference is you'll be closer to the exit." He checked his watch. "Five minutes."

"Why didn't we just come in by that door?" Doug said.

"Only opens from this side," Julio then said to Victor. "Punch me."

Victor said, "Really?"

Julio glared at him. Victor threw the punch so fast that Mario didn't see it, just Julio staggering back against the counter. He stood for a moment, dazed.

"Doug, cover our exit," Victor said, tossing him the key.

"God damn," Julio muttered, his eyes watering as he held his face and waved them through.

Doug fell in step beside Mario. They walked down the long corridor, Doug and the concrete wall on his right, cells on his left. They were all empty, with the doors open and lights off, thin foam mats rolled up on the cots. It looked just as grim as

Mario had imagined. Walter met them at the cell before Dominic's. He patted Mario's shoulder.

"Wait with me, Walter," Doug said.

Lights were on in the next cell. Mario could see his brother at the bars, looking at him. Doug and Walter continued on, to stand by the exit.

As Mario drew near, Dominic said, "I knew you'd come."

Dominic's hair was washed, and while he looked haggard, it was clear he wasn't being maltreated. The priests would have insisted on that. As soon as he laid eyes on Mario, confidence blossomed across his brother's face.

Mario stared at him for a moment, realizing that his reasons for coming here couldn't be more different than Dominic's reasons for asking him to come. Somehow, he was only figuring that out now, and it felt like a punch to gut.

"What do you want?" he said, the words scraping against his gritted teeth, already regretting his decision to come here. What on Earth had made him think that this was worth the risk of never being with Miranda and his family again?

"I want you to get me out of here." When Mario didn't say anything, Dominic added hastily, "I know I fucked up. I should never have gone after you like I did, and I'm—"

"Gone after me?" Mario said, his voice rising in disbelief.

Dominic flinched, his brown eyes betraying the telltale desire to shift the blame for his actions somewhere else. "You don't understand," he said, but his voice trailed under Mario's withering glare.

"I *understand* that you tried to kill me. I *understand* that if Miranda hadn't lost the baby, you would have killed our child."

Dominic blanched. "I couldn't have known, Mario. I didn't—"

"What about Walter and Doug? Did you know then?" he

demanded. "I saw you on that gallows while the ropes were put around their necks!"

"Mario, listen to—"

"You've let thousands of people turn, Dominic—*thousands* —so that you could be powerful and important, and now you want me to get you out of here?"

"Do you think you're any better?" Dominic countered, the venom in his voice like ice.

The accusation felt like a blow. Not because it wasn't true, but because of the man making it. Mario could feel his heart shrinking, becoming so small it would fit on the head of a pin. Dominic hadn't asked to see him because they shared the kind of bond only siblings can—because they were brothers. Mario could see, for the first time, that Dominic didn't understand why Mario had provoked their father so that he'd get the beating. He didn't get why Mario got him out of childhood scrapes or gave him a job when he couldn't settle down to the realities of being an adult.

He'd protected his brother because that's what big brothers do, because he loved him, but Dominic didn't get it. He didn't get any of it. He saw Mario as a means to an end. Dominic needed something, and he thought Mario could get it for him, and that was all.

Mario took a shuddering breath. It felt like there was no air in the room. His throat closed, as if it didn't want him to say the words. "I tried to protect you and Mom from Dad. I tried to protect you from everything, I really did. You're my brother, Dominic, and I love you, but I can't protect you from this."

He turned away, blinking back the tears in his eyes. Dominic reached through the bars and grabbed his arm. Mario could see that it had never occurred to him that Mario couldn't, or wouldn't, help him.

"You can get me out of here; I know you can! Walter

forgave me. Why can't you?" His grip on Mario's arm tightened, and his voice got mean. "You *owe* me!"

From the checkpoint, Mario heard Julio say, "You need to go! Now!"

Victor's pounding footsteps approached them. Mario heard the metallic slide of the key, then the snick of the lock on the door Doug was opening. A calm came over him, smooth and cold, pushing the heat of the pain away. He wrenched his arm from Dominic's grip.

"I don't owe you this, Dom," he said softly. "I don't owe you anything."

"Mario!" Dominic screamed, his face purple with rage.

Mario was already turning away. Figures gathered outside the checkpoint at the other end of the lockup, shouting at Julio. He stood in the way, arms gesticulating wildly, doing his best to block the narrow confines of the checkpoint.

Victor's large hand shoved against Mario's back, hurrying him. Doug slammed the door behind them shut, the tumblers of the locks falling into place. Doug snapped the key off in the lock, a manic grin on his face. They dashed up the stairwell, muffled but furious shouts and pounding on the door below following them.

Mario and Doug each grabbed one of Walter's arms, hurrying him along.

"I can keep up," Walter snapped, but his raspy voice betrayed his injuries from almost being hanged, and his breathing was labored.

They exploded into the corridor they'd traveled not ten minutes before. Voices and heavy footfalls were coming from the T junction of the hallway where it met the locker room. As Doug pushed the door to the alleyway open, a voice behind them shouted, "It's him! It's Santorello!"

They tumbled into the alleyway.

The Suburban wasn't there.

"This way," Victor said, pointing south as he strong-armed Mario forward.

"I can't keep up," Walter said. "Go without me."

He smiled, that nervous, tentative smile that betrayed his shyness. At least he didn't have to worry about his safety. That's what he said, anyway. Mario hoped to God it was true, because the mob definitely wanted him, and Walter had just been seen helping him flee.

He ran hard, boots striking the pavement. He almost kept pace with Doug, who had always been faster. As they reached the end of the alleyway, Mario heard the door behind them slam open. But in those two seconds, they were already around the corner. Victor pulled alongside him, eyes flashing with determination, and Mario ran—like his life depended on it.

DOUG PEEKED OVER MIRANDA'S SHOULDER TO WHERE Mario sat in the front row of the Mission Church with Emily and the kids, except for Violet. "Are you sure he's up for this? He looked pretty shaken up."

"All he has to do is be a guest. If anything's bothering him, it's that now this is a rush job."

Doug frowned, not sure he agreed with her assessment of Mario's state of mind. It had taken them two hours to get back to campus, playing a deadly game of cat and mouse with the mob baying for Mario's blood. Miranda was right, though; it was happening now, ninety minutes after their return.

A nervous thrill zipped through him, making his stomach flutter. He looked at the rows of carved chairs of dark wood that were used in place of pews in the Mission Church. Every time he stole a look into the sanctuary from the sacristy, there were more people. Doug stepped back, and Miranda closed the door.

"There were supposed to be like, ten people, in secret, but it's almost full," Doug said. "How did that happen?"

Miranda grinned at him. "How did you think that Father Doug Michel getting married was going to stay a secret?"

Doug shrugged and gnawed on his fingernail. "I didn't really think about it."

Miranda pulled his hand away from his mouth and took it in hers. Her hair was pulled back from her face in a low barrette, and she was wearing makeup. Just a little eyeliner, blush, and lip gloss, but it made her even prettier. She wore a green, flowy dress, with long sleeves and simple lines, and a pair of silvery flats. The outfit suited her.

"You look really nice, Miri."

She looked up at him. "You know Karen did this all this. You look amazing. I'm glad she got a blue suit. It brings out your eyes."

He twitched his hair out of his eyes. "Karen's in her element with this stuff."

"I had to draw the line at wearing heels. You should have seen the death traps she wanted me to wear." Her grin grew wider. "Wait till you see Skye."

The butterflies flared up again. His body felt like it did when he was climbing a mountain or fighting zombies—totally amped and ready to do something—but the only thing he could do was wait.

"Is it time yet? Shouldn't Walter be here by now?"

"He'll come in from the arbor; go see. You're fidgeting like crazy."

"I'm nervous as hell," he admitted.

"It'll be fine," she said. "Now scoot."

In seconds he was tugging at the door that opened near the

long wisteria arbor that ran parallel to the church. It's too bad it's the wrong time of year, he thought. It would have been nice for Skye to see the wisteria in bloom and smell the heavy perfume of the clumps of trailing purple flowers that hung from the gnarled vines. Walter was hurrying his way, talking to Brother Rupert.

"For fuck's sake, Rupert," Walter snapped, color high in his cheeks as they approached. The breeze riffled his thinning hair. "Who am I supposed to write to in Rome? I released him from his vows, and now I'm going to say the Mass and marry him."

Both men saw him and froze. Rupert glared at Doug as he skirted by and entered the church by the door Doug had just exited.

"I'm sorry you had to hear that," Walter said. "You know how Rupert is."

When they reached sacristy door, Doug said, "Hold on a sec."

Walter looked up at him, a question in his eyes.

"I'm sorry that I'm leaving all of this to you, Walter. I never meant to leave you stuck or anything. It's just...there was Skye, and before I knew it, she was all there was."

Walter smiled at him, affection brightening his eyes and smile. "Our lives change. Who we are changes. You've been by my side for seven years. You've been devoted and loyal, and you've loved God as much as anyone. You kind of fell down on keeping your vows at the end," he said, sounding rueful. "But that's between you and Him."

"Your theology is more forgiving than Rupert's."

"He means well. He's just a know-it-all," Walter said. "Now. I have a wedding to perform, unless you want to keep the bride waiting."

Doug gulped. "I don't."

Five minutes later they were assembled at the altar,

Miranda by Doug's side as his best woman. Pillar candles on tall stands were lit along the first ten pews, as were the giant candelabras above the altar, making the large church feel cozy and intimate. The seats were packed—there were even people standing in the back. A detached part of Doug's brain thought this would be the perfect time to attack SCU. Thank God the mob after Mario wasn't that big.

The doors opened, the twilight beyond them offered the barest of silhouettes. A moment later, Violet—the maid of honor—appeared. Her eyes were huge as she took in the people. Doug wiggled his fingers at her and she smiled. She walked to them with purpose, hesitating at the end of the aisle, looking unsure of where she should go. She searched the faces of the Portlanders and her new family in the first row until she found her dad. Mario grinned and pointed to Walter, which got her back on track.

The massive doors at the front of the church closed. The last of the sunset's reflection on the hills to the east vanished.

In its place was Skye.

A lump formed in Doug's throat as she drew near. They'd done something with her hair to make it wispy, pulled off to the side in a swoop across her forehead. Karen had applied a little makeup that made her blue-gold eyes shimmer, and mascara that made them more prominent. The fabric of her dress looked like it was woven from a glittering spider's web, the style so simple it almost looked like a floor-length slip. It draped close to her, the shine of the fabric moving and rippling with the motion of her body. He felt mesmerized, her graceful movements casting a spell, for she looked like her laugh—shimmering and magical.

Skye grinned at him, the loose bouquet of the last of the campus roses an explosion of color and scent. He grinned back, still not able to figure out what he'd done to deserve her. Miranda nudged his elbow.

"Quit staring and take her hand," she whispered.

Startled, he held his hand out to her. "You look beautiful."

"You look pretty snazzy yourself."

Walter beamed at his former brother-priest, then at Skye. "We're only delighted that you're joining our family, Skye."

"Me too," she said. She glanced sidelong at Doug and said, "There's still time, if you want to back out."

He must have made a face, for she laughed. It only strengthened the illusion that she was made of starlight and moonbeams. Doug's heart swelled, full to bursting.

"Not a chance."

Walter cleared his throat. He said, almost severely, "If you two can pipe down..."

His stern countenance gave all of them—Violet, Miranda, and he and Skye—the giggles. When they showed no signs of subsiding, Skye said to Walter, "Maybe you should just start? We'll stop...I think."

Walter shook his head, looking happily exasperated. Doug took a deep breath, trying to get hold of himself, wanting to remember everything—the softness of Skye's hand, its warmth and strength, and how right it felt in his. Her smile as it arced to her blue-gold eyes, their kaleidoscope of colors shining with love. The silvery-blond hair framing her face like fine, spun silk, and how it brushed her neck while she tried to stifle her giggles. And the way she had moved coming down the aisle, soft as a breeze, and so beautiful his heart ached.

He made the sign of the cross by rote as the Mass began. Walter said, "The grace of our Lord Jesus Christ, the love of God, and the communion of the Holy Spirit, be with you all."

But all Doug saw and heard was the sparkling, fairy-dust woman beside him, and the tinkling sound of her laughter.

Miranda slid her hand through the crook of Father Walter's arm. Everyone else was on the helicopter. Miranda shivered, chilled by more than the cold evening, for it was time to go.

They halted twenty feet from the helicopter. Victor was in the cockpit, helmet on, his hands moving over dials and clicking levers. Through the side door she saw a flash of blond hair, Emily or Skye helping the kids get strapped in.

"I wish you could come with us," she said.

"You don't need an old man like me," Walter said, affection filling his voice.

She turned to face him. "More like an old man like you is needed here, to make sure things are done right this time."

Father Walter gave her a wry smile. "They'd get along just fine without me."

"That's bullshit and you know it."

"Ach, Miranda... d'you have to swear all the time?"

"Sorry."

She looked at him, committing to memory the shape of his face, the sweetness of his shy smile, the well of compassion and kindness behind the sparkle in his hazel eyes. He'd been her father for so many years. He always would be.

"I'm going to miss you," she said, her eyes welling with sudden tears. "Maybe in a couple years we'll get sound defenses everywhere, and you can come visit us at LO."

She didn't want to leave him behind. It felt as if she was crossing a personal Rubicon that once forded, she could never retreat across again. She'd gone back to college all those years ago, not knowing she was going nowhere else. Not knowing it would become her home, and the people who survived, her family. There'd been so many things she hadn't known then, and she learned most of them the hard way. Father Walter had been the one constant, a fixed point in time and space. He still will be, she told herself, but leaving this time wasn't the same. This time, it felt final.

"That would be grand altogether. Now don't cry, there's a good girl," Walter said, not taking his own advice. He jutted his chin to the helicopter. "Let Mario look after you. And could you both try to not bollocks it up this time?"

Her bark of laughter was almost a sob. He pulled her close, rocking her as he held her tight. "I love you, Miranda *ágra*."

"I love you, too," she whispered.

He gave her a final squeeze, then held her at arm's length. "Go on now," he said, his voice filled with emotion. Tears slipped down his cheeks, but his smile was warm. "Give Delilah a tummy rub from me."

"I will," she said, forcing herself to smile through her tears. If this was the last time she saw Father Walter, she wanted him to remember her being able to smile.

A quick peck on his cheek, another whispered 'I love you,' then she climbed into the helicopter. Father Walter stood on the tarmac, a slight, slim man, his graying hair blowing away from his face. His hands were jammed deep in his pockets, but he raised one over his head in farewell. Miranda kissed her hand, then blew it away, and was rewarded with one last smile.

She found the empty jump seat between Tessa and Mario and slid into it, grateful she didn't have to hold herself upright. She wasn't sure she'd be able to.

"Ready?" Tessa said.

Miranda nodded, but she didn't feel ready to leave her home for good.

"You okay?" Mario asked her. His hand closed around hers like a warm coat.

She started to answer, then paused. Maureen sat on Mario's

other side, watching her with a worried expression. Beside
Maureen sat Violet, who leaned to look under her seat at the
pet carrier strapped beneath it. Sean, who sat next to Violet,
creased his brow at her antics. Then Violet sat upright and said,
"Mister Bun Bun says it's okay, Miranda."

"Is that right?"

Violet nodded.

Sean laughed, and said something to Violet that Miranda
didn't catch. Emily, Michael, and Anthony sat across from
them on the other side of the helicopter. Beside them, Doug
and Skye radiated a newlywed glow. Another pet carrier was
strapped beneath Anthony's seat for three kittens he hadn't
been able to find homes for on purpose. Michael's guitar case
took up the space beneath his and his mother's seat. Emily
flashed Miranda a smile. She looked nervous, but excited, too.

Phineas appeared in the opening to the cockpit, his dark
skin and white grin all that was visible below his helmet's visor.
"Victor's going to fire her up. Is everybody ready?"

He looked them all over and nodded, apparently liking
what he saw. He was almost in the cockpit when he turned
back. "Don't be moving in on my girl, Mario."

Miranda heard Mario's chuckle. She shook her head, a tiny
smile lifting the corners of her mouth as she watched Phineas
disappear back to the cockpit.

She said to Mario, affection in her voice, "That fucking
kid."

"Hey," he said. He traced the back of his index finger along
her jaw. A high whine sounded over their heads as the helicopter's ignition sequence began. "Are you okay?"

Mario's eyes were gentle, the love undergirding his voice
and gaze steady and strong. She would miss Father Walter, and
Karen, the community at SCU, even San Jose, as imperfect and
unjust as it had been while she'd lived there. She hadn't even

bothered to track down Harold and kick his ass for selling them out when they'd fled to Santa Cruz with the vaccine, she realized. Contentment was making her soft. Harold hadn't been conspiring with the Council while talking to Victor on the ham radio, but hadn't come back inside the city walls yet. She hoped it was because he was afraid of her.

She looked at the others, the moment sharp and clear, every color ultra-bright as reality seemed to shift and rearrange itself. All of it beautiful in its way, and she open to it: the struggle and the work, the happiness and the pain, the beauty and the ugliness. Each played its part in life; they were all of a piece. Armoring herself against the pain had kept her from truly experiencing the joy. She'd sold herself short for so long, but not anymore.

Every single one of them, from Victor, who she'd once thought irredeemable, down to Violet's rabbit and Anthony's kittens, were starting anew. She knew there would be more hard times and pain, but also new joys and triumphs—more life.

She smiled at Mario, the bitter and the sweet of the moment holding her in a gentle embrace, and said, "Yeah. I think I am."

EPILOGUE

MIRANDA SQUINTED HER EYES, shading them with her hand. They'd removed the Jeep's canvas top last week to enjoy the sun, now that it had finally arrived. The brakes squeaked gently, then they came to a stop.

"This road gets worse every time," Mario said.

As soon as he cut the ignition, the birdsong and the rustling trees above them filled the air. Miranda pushed the door open and levered herself out. She placed her hands on her lower back, groaning as she arched it. Delilah leaped from the back seat, like she wasn't ten years old, and ran off to pee.

"Liley, wait," Violet said, scrambling out from the Jeep's back seat. She ran after the pit pull, all arms and legs and bright eyes, a little clumsy from the latest growing spurt that had added four inches to her height.

Delilah dashed away from Violet, beginning a game of chase. Mario walked around the Jeep, watching her, his delight at the antics of his little girl plain.

"We really need to get people out here to work on the road," Miranda said.

"That's what you said six months ago."

She arched her eyebrow, pairing it with a withering stare, "Six months ago I didn't have a boulder on my bladder."

His grin faded, and he looked appropriately chastened. She reached into the back seat as Mario followed after Violet. Gently, she shook the small form sleeping in the back seat.

"Walter," she said softly. "Walter, wake up."

The boy whimpered, screwing up his face. His brown eyes glared at her through squinted lids. He scowled, not fully awake.

"We're here?"

Miranda smothered a giggle. Walter didn't like when you laughed at him for being grumpy. He was a funny little person, her son, a mixture of her spontaneity and Mario's measured caution and patience. He assessed new situations until he was sure of them, where Miranda had thrown herself into anything new with abandon as a child. The fact that he was hers, and was so beautiful, always filled her with awe.

"Yep, we're here. Come on."

She took his small hand in hers. He jumped down from the Jeep's open door, then beamed up at her, proud of his accomplishment, his sunny disposition already supplanting the grumpy wake-me-ups. Mario and Violet rejoined them.

Mario pulled the day bag from the back seat, then said to Violet, "Did you remember your swimsuit?"

Violet nodded. "Uh-huh."

She skipped ahead, familiar with the path. Mario took Walter's other hand. Delilah followed them, but a little haphazardly while she sniffed the interesting places.

"Where is it, Mama?"

"It's just at the end of the path."

They walked, twigs snapping under their feet, Walter's face upturned.

"These are the tall trees, remember?" Mario said.

"I thought…" Walter's voice trailed. "I thought they were bigger than our woods."

"They are," Mario said. "They're just different kinds of trees."

The path wound down, and Walter pulled his hands away to run ahead. Delilah trotted after him.

"Be careful," Miranda said, out of habit more than need.

Mario called, "Watch your brother, Violet." She turned back and waited for Walter.

"She's so patient with Walter and Maureen," Miranda said, feeling grateful. "I'm too freaking big to chase after them."

Mario slipped his arm around her, pulling her close. He set his other hand on her rounded belly. "Two more months. Then you can go back to being lithe and dangerous."

"You know it," she said.

Violet, Walter, and Liley followed the curve of the path out of sight. They caught up to find them standing in the middle of the trail. Walter regarded the blast door warily.

"That's the bunker," Violet said. "We'll go swimming."

They walked up the long ramp, memories of Phineas and the tiger on the day they stumbled across the bunker flashing through Miranda's mind. They stopped at the blast door, under the straight, horizontal lintel that had given the bunker away all those years ago. Miranda looked up to the video monitor, still making its lazy back and forth sweep.

"Kendall," she said. "We're here."

They waited a few minutes, long enough that Walter was getting fidgety, when Kendall's voice came through the speakers.

"Hi, guys!" His voice was bright and animated. "Be right there."

"What's that?" Walter said, looking around when the door unlocked with a pneumatic hiss, followed by a deep clunk.

"That's the door," said Miranda. She held out her hand to him. "Come on."

Delilah streaked ahead of them, but was with Kendall when they met halfway down the ramp. He looked the same as ever: dark hair slightly unkempt, his lean frame clothed in jeans and a tee shirt. The owl blink was rare these days, and a smile danced in his dark-brown eyes.

"Uncle Kendall," Violet squealed, running to meet him.

Kendall scooped her up in a hug. "You're almost as tall as me! What are they feeding you, kiddo?"

Violet shrugged. "Nothing very good like here," she said.

"I might have some chocolate for you," he whispered.

Violet squealed again, clapping her hands.

"You're early," Kendall said, giving Miranda a hug.

"Walter woke up from his nap early." She looked him up and down when their embrace ended. "You look good."

"You look enormous," he said.

"Never heard that before."

Kendall turned to Mario, greeting him warmly with a hug and a handshake. Then he squatted so he was eye level with Walter, who had retreated behind Miranda's legs.

"Hi, Walter," Kendall said. "Remember me?"

Walter regarded him solemnly.

"It's Uncle Kendall," Miranda said.

Kendall looked up at Miranda and grinned. "Six months is a long time for a four-year-old. C'mon, I've got lunch ready."

The biggest difference in the bunker these days was how alive it felt. There was wear and tear on the furniture, and children's paintings taped to the walls. The bunker felt like a home, not a mausoleum for an extinct way of life. Almost sixty people lived here now, and many stopped by while they ate to say a quick hello. A group of teenagers ran by, shrieking with laughter, before their noise echoed up the ramp to the surface. The inner airlock was usually left open now. Only the blast doors were kept closed all the time.

"God, they're loud," Miranda said. "How is that possible?"

Kendall snorted. "Being oblivious helps. They're having a party, probably snuck out some booze."

"None of yours, I hope," Mario said.

"That's under lock and key," Kendall said. "I can only imagine them watering down the liquor."

Walter's reticence faded, and he wandered a little, exploring the activity rooms.

"Can we go swimming, Dad?" Violet said.

"Okay," he said. "Let's clear the plates first." He looked to Miranda. "See you in a bit."

"Don't let them drown," she said.

Mario gave her peck on the cheek. "I'll keep them alive. I promise."

After they left, Miranda and Kendall went to the garden dome. The humid air, smelling of earth and plants, felt like an old friend.

"They look good," Miranda said, after making a circuit to inspect the plants. "But they always do."

"They're better than the last crop," Kendall said. He walked to the electronic equipment by the potting table. A moment later, "Like as the Hart" filled the air.

"I love this one," Miranda sighed.

"I know."

He sat beside her on a bench. They lapsed into silence for a while, just listening. Miranda remembered the first time she'd heard this song, how it had stopped her in her tracks, and gave her that first glimpse of who Kendall really was.

"Have you been sick a lot this time?" he asked her.

"The first few months. Now I just want this kid out."

"Is Mario having an easier time?"

"Yes, thank God. I'd have shown up on your doorstep a long time ago if I had to go through that again."

She'd never forget the color draining from Mario's face when she'd told him she was pregnant with Walter. Then the denial... She couldn't be, she shouldn't be, he wasn't willing to risk losing her again. He'd been a nervous wreck the whole time. Any disagreement, anything even approaching a spat, had seemed to him like a harbinger of the end.

"If it wasn't for Doug and Alec, I think I would've killed him. They kept him busy, let him talk. He's a completely different guy this time."

"It was traumatic for him, too," Kendall said.

She'd fled to the bunker for a few weeks to get a break from Mario's hysteria when she was pregnant with Walter. She'd told Kendall all of it: Jeremiah and losing that first pregnancy, and everything falling apart. Relief spread through her that it was better this time.

"Any chance you'll come with us today?" Miranda said. "Just for a visit?"

Kendall gave her a lopsided grin, but the owl blink betrayed him. He shook his head. "No. But I stood in the open door."

For a second, she couldn't even speak.

"The blast door?" she finally said. He nodded. She could only look at him, stunned. This was a new development since her last visit, one she'd almost despaired of. "That's amazing, Kendall."

He shrugged. "I thought about what you said. How the sound defenses are almost to the Rockies. How there haven't been any zombies here for almost two years. I'm not sure the mountains will ever be secure...that'll take decades." He pursed his lips, eyes narrowing as he thought. "But zombies aren't much for hard climbing. Apart from the interstate, there probably aren't that many, considering the square acreage."

Miranda tried to absorb what he'd told her. He'd stood in the open door. He'd actually done it. She almost couldn't believe it, but Kendall didn't lie.

Quietly, he said, "I'm trying. I'm just not ready yet."

Her throat felt tight, and her eyes prickled with tears she couldn't set free, not in front of him. Guilt churned inside her, making her lunch feel like a rock in her stomach. Her nana's voice echoed in her head: never stop a child singing. Five years...five fucking years, but he'd stood in the open blast door. She smiled at him sidelong, hope that he'd get there springing to life.

She slipped her hand in his. "You will be."

THE DRIVE HOME WAS UNEVENTFUL. WALTER AND VIOLET fell asleep, which meant they'd be up well past bedtime. Conversation with Mario petered out as they enjoyed the weather and tired of having to shout to be heard over the wind. The buzz of the Jeep's tires on the drawbridge pulled Miranda from her reverie of everything and nothing. She checked her watch.

"Oh, wow," she said, stretching her arms over her head. "It's almost dinnertime."

As they eased to a halt in the parking lot, Alec waved to them.

"Uncle Alec, wait!" Violet shouted, jumping from the back seat. "Has Misty had her kittens?"

"Violet!" Miranda and Mario both said, but she landed true and ran across the parking lot.

"I'm going to tie her into the damn seat," Mario said,

looking rattled. "She's going to jump out before we stop next time."

"I'll bring her to dinner," Alec called to them, Violet's hand in his. "See you in a few."

Miranda shook off the momentary heart attack Violet had almost given her. "You're the one who suggested she start climbing with Skye. Now she's fearless."

"Do you know why he's walking around with that shit-eating grin?" Mario asked her. "He's been grinning like an idiot the last week."

"Oh!" Miranda said, excitement hitting her anew. "Emily's expecting, she told me this morning. I meant to tell you, but I forgot with getting ready to go see Kendall."

"Yeah?" Mario said, his eyebrows rising.

"Yeah."

"That's great," he said. "I know they've been trying for a while. Must be something in the water. Everywhere I look lately there's another pregnant woman."

"Yeah, no," Miranda said, climbing out of the Jeep. "It's not the water, honey."

Mario carried Walter as they walked through the Big Woods to the housing plan. There were so many people these days, enough that some she knew only to see them. They stopped at the townhouse so Walter could use the potty, and her too, then walked through the spit of trees to the grounds of the Boy's Home. Delilah didn't race ahead, but trotted beside them. Just like when she'd been expecting Walter, Delilah kept her human close. The first stars appeared as the sky morphed from dark pink to shades of purple. People approached the dining hall from all directions.

"Doug knows to save us a space, right?" Mario said.

"He will. Or the kids will."

Mario looked at her sidelong. "I'm glad you and Violet

made up from your spat last week about her wanting to wear makeup."

"Even though I'm not her real mom."

Mario chuckled. "She's gonna be a handful in a few years."

Miranda grimaced. She didn't even want to think of the mischief Violet would get up to as a teenager; Anthony and Michael were bad enough. The idea of adding a rebellious Violet into the mix made her a little nauseous. Violet and Maureen were still little girls; she'd almost be happy if they stayed that way forever.

Ahead, Alec and Emily walked hand in hand, Violet and Anthony trailing them. Mario said, "Mind if I go ahead to congratulate them?"

"Of course not."

He picked up his pace enough that even with Walter in his arms, he caught them as they reached the door. The dining hall windows were beginning to glow as twilight deepened. Amidst kisses, hugs, and handshakes, Mario followed Alec and Emily inside, walking with them to the table they all shared. He put Walter in a chair beside Skye, who was nursing the baby. Matthew raced around the end of the table, his silvery-blond hair flashing, before Doug scooped him up.

When she saw Noelle, who was going into the building by the side door with Victor and Gemma, she waved.

That kid's gonna weigh ten pounds... She's bigger than me and I'm due first, Miranda thought.

She stopped on the path, watching them all. Her eyebrows knitted together when she didn't see him, but then Father Walter approached their table from the direction of the bathrooms. A warmth spread through her, the feeling light and joyful. The West Coast was safe enough that Father Walter had come to visit. She remembered them talking about it, the day they'd left San Jose. She'd thought it just one of those things you said to get through painful farewells, not something that might come true, but it had.

The dining hall doors opened, and Mario walked up the path to meet her. "You coming, sweetheart?" he said.

"I was just watching you all through the window."

He cocked his head to the side. "Are you okay? You've been quiet since we went to visit Kendall."

"I'm fine," she said on a sigh. "It's just...my life feels so big, with you and the kids and everyone else. Father Walter is *visiting*, for Pete's sake. Kendall's life is still so small. He's not alone anymore, but he's stuck."

She didn't bother to say she still felt responsible. Mario would only tell her to quit beating up on herself because it wouldn't change anything. That all she could do was support and encourage Kendall. And he was right, but the last time Kendall had gone outside was the day Rich was killed. She'd blamed him for it, told him it was his fault. Maybe it was Rich being killed that had done the real damage, but it didn't feel that way.

Mario nodded, sympathy in his eyes. "He stood in the open door. That's a big deal." He brushed her hair behind her ear, his touch matching the softness in his voice. "You've never given up on him. He'll get there."

The rush of affection for him that hit her like a wave nearly knocked her over. "We all need someone who never gives up on us."

"It's like I said... Only a fool would give up on you." Mario pulled her to him, his arms around her strong and familiar. His lips brushed hers, the lightest caress of a kiss. His dark eyes were serious. "I love you, if that helps."

"It does," she said, warming under the glow that was all for her. The easy affection they shared always made her heart swell. "I love you, too. You know that, right?"

"I do."

"Tucci! Mario!" Rocco's voice shouted. He stood in the open door of the dining hall, glaring at them. "For the love of all that's holy, will you get a move on? I wanna introduce Father Walter!" Then he disappeared back through the door.

Miranda groaned. "He's making an announcement? Father Walter will hate that."

"Yeah, well... You know how Rocco is," Mario said. His voice became high and animated. "The priest has come to dinner! It's a big deal for the family!"

"Oh my God," she said, covering her mouth as a laugh chuffed in her throat. "That's so true."

Another voice from the dining hall doors called out to them, but this one sounded desperate.

"Can you please come inside?" Sean ran his hand through his red hair. "Rocco is going to have a heart attack if he can't introduce Father Walter soon, and I won't be able to live with him if he keeps carrying on like this. Murdering your spouse isn't great for a marriage, but I'm thinking about it."

"Okay, we'll be right there," Miranda said.

"Rocco is a nut," Mario said. Then he added, a glint of mischief sparkling in his eyes, "But we should join the others. I'm perished with the hunger."

She smiled, as she always did, when Mario borrowed the sayings that only Father Walter used. As she laced her fingers with his, a deep wellspring of hope filled her heart—for Mario, and the family they had knitted together to include more people than she'd ever have imagined. For the friends and community they were part of, and her hope that Kendall would feel safe enough to leave the bunker someday soon. For this world, which she had once thought so hostile and cruel. It almost puzzled her that for so long she hadn't been able to see that while those things could be true, it was also filled with wonder.

She held the feeling close, its warmth expanding in her chest. Mario pulled the door open, and the noisy bustle and wonderful aroma of dinnertime spilled out around them. She caught the door in her hand, but he didn't let go.

"I'm pregnant, not feeble. I can hold a door."

"You're the boss," Mario said, but the sparkle in his eye told her that he'd held the door on purpose, just to get her goat. He patted her round belly. "Brace yourself, kid."

"Brat," she said, swatting at him, but he ducked just out of reach and grinned at her, unrepentant.

Miranda paused on the threshold, eyes narrowed and lips pursed, before she gave up the ghost and laughed. She held the door long enough for Delilah to scoot by, and followed him inside.

Be an ARC Reader for my new series, Steel City Apocalypse. You can find the first book, Undead Menagerie, on Story Origin.

Sign up for my newsletter and be the first to get the latest news and special treats.

Please leave a review at your preferred retailer if you enjoyed this book. They don't need to be long, and I appreciate every single one. Thank you!

SOCIAL MEDIA

- Visit Anne's website: http://ww.amgeever.com
- Sign up for my newsletter: http://bit.ly/amgeevnews
- Like my Facebook page: http://bit.ly/amgeeverfb
- Follow me on Instagram: http://bit.ly/amgeeverinsta
- Follow me on Goodreads: http://bit.ly/amgbb
- Follow me on Bookbub: http://bit.ly/amgbb
- Join me in A.M. Geever's Zombie Apocalypse Bunker on Facebook: http://bit.ly/zabunker

ACKNOWLEDGMENTS

Huge and humble thanks, and deepest gratitude, to my readers. I'm still amazed that people read my books. When I hear someone say they loved the book, it seriously blows my mind (it's also way better than the people who give them one star, lol). My readers, and getting to know them through the emails they send and interactions we have on social media, is what makes me want to keep telling stories and get them out into the world.

Thanks to my family, whose support and love means *everything*, especially during this pandemic year.

Beta Readers:

Sarah Lyons Fleming, **Lauren Millar**, **Rachel Bouwkamp Meyers**, **Rhonna Woodie**, **& Roseann Powell**, for pointing out all the gaps, inconsistencies, and opportunities I didn't see that made the story better. You gals make me look good.

Editing:

Arianne "Tex" Thompson, **Developmental Editor Extraordinaire**. I could gush forever, but suffice to say, this trilogy would have sucked without you, Tex. Thank you!

Kimberly at Kimberly Dawn Editing, who fixed all the crap to make the story shine.

Creatives:

Molly Phipps of **We Got You Covered Book Design** for the kick ass covers.

Anti-Flag, for being so generous with the use of your lyrics in *The Undead Age*. See you in Vegas in September—live music again, finally!

Very Special Thanks:

My super cool cousin, **Kenny Koda,** whose can-do, *Semper Fi* spirit helped the gang get through California alive (mostly) and your advice about which wineries might just survive the zombie apocalypse. And for that wine you sent... such good wine!

Amy Karavlan, for sharing her expertise and methods for helping kids deal with anxiety.

Clay Morgan, who answered my post in a Facebook helicopter group. Clay ran me through the ins and outs so I could write about fixing and piloting a helicopter, and then he sent me sketches, diagrams, pictures, and gently suggested that I didn't need the helicopter that can pull a destroyer (not making that up, those Sea Dragons...wow!). Luckily, he knew which helicopter I needed from his time flying in the United States Coast Guard. Thank you so much, Clay!!! And thanks for keeping people safe from pirates.

Arthur Crivella, for your generous loan of Na-Wak-Wa Lodge, not just for the re-writing, but for the next phase of *The Undead Age!*

Mel Walker & Sylvester Barzey, for your much needed and valued advice.

Lindsey Pogue, thank you for talking me off the ledge. I owe you, girl. Whew!

And as always, my **Three Favorite Pieces**. *My dad Eamon*, who lifts my heart out of my shoes (he's part pookie, which helps!). *My husband Drew*, who I'm still married to as we begin to emerge from this COVID-19 pandemic year (and counting), which I'm pretty freaking proud of...we even still like each other! *And Justin*, who wears many hats: rocker, activist, animal sucker, seasoned artist who shows this newbie artist how it's done, and (in my humble opinion) the most important hat of all: coolest little brother in the world.

— May 19, 2021

ABOUT THE AUTHOR

A.M. Geever lives in her hometown of Pittsburgh, Pennsylvania. An avid reader of science fiction and fantasy from an early age, the only job she ever wanted—besides being a writer—was to be a Star Fleet Officer.

The idea of becoming a zombie because her car runs out of gas gets her to the gas station when she would rather not bother, and when not dreaming up disaster survival tales, she spends most of her time with her family and fur babies, and loves to travel to exotic locales.

For more information, check out her website, www.amgeever.com

www.ingramcontent.com/pod-product-compliance
Lightning Source LLC
Chambersburg PA
CBHW020224110726
47898CB00004B/1137